ARRIVAL

After seven years of flight, after traveling a billion miles from Earth, the human spacecraft *Cassini* reached Saturn . . .

A fat pie-dish shape, ten feet across, clung to the side of the *Cassini* stack. It was a combined aeroshell and heat shield for a separate spacecraft, called *Huygens*, which was designed to land on Saturn's largest moon, Titan.

Pyrotechnic bolts fired, silently, releasing puffs of vapor that immediately crystallized and dispersed. Three springs pushed *Huygens* away from *Cassini*, and a curved track and roller made the released probe spin, at seven revolutions per minute.

The probe began to fall faster, into the deep ocean of air . . . Diaphragms slid back. A series of small portals opened in the protective shell of the craft, and sensors peered out.

At last, the probe crashed into the slush. Slowed by Titan's low surface gravity and the density of the lower air—half again as dense as Earth's—the impact was slow, as gentle as an apple falling from a tree.

The probe continued its battery of experiments. . . . Just six minutes after landing, the probe's internal batteries were exhausted.

Melted slush frosted over the buried portals of the inert, cooling lander. And a thin rain of light brown organic material began to settle on the upper casing. The chatter of telemetry to *Cassini* fell silent. The orbiter passed beneath the horizon and then turne dits high gain antenna away from Titan, toward Earth. Patiently, *Cassini* downloaded everything the lander had observed.

Some of the results were unexpected.

Acclaim for Stephen Baxter's
Previous Novel

VOYAGE

BOOKS BY STEPHEN BAXTER

Raft
Timelike Infinity
Anti-Ice *
Flux *
Ring *
The Time Ships *
Voyage *
Titan *
Moonseed *

*Published by HarperPrism

Stephen Baxter

TITAN

HarperPrism
A Division of HarperCollinsPublishers

HarperPrism
A Division of HarperCollins*Publishers*
10 East 53rd Street, New York, NY 10022-5299

This is a work of fiction. The characters, incidents, and
dialogues are products of the author's imagination and are not to
be construed as real. Any resemblance to actual events or
persons, living or dead, is entirely coincidental.

An earlier version of one chapter of this novel appeared in
a very different form in *Interzone* magazine, No. 105, 1996.

ISBN 0-06-105713-4

HarperCollins®, 🏭®, and HarperPrism®
are trademarks of HarperCollins Publishers, Inc.

Cover photographs © 1997 by SUPERSTOCK
Photo composit by Carl D. Galian

A hardcover edition of this book was published
in 1997 by HarperPrism.

First paperback printing: November 1998

Printed in the United States of America

Visit HarperPrism on the World Wide Web at
http://www.harperprism.com

❖ 10 9 8 7 6 5 4 3 2 1

For Tony, Christine, and Catherine

Acknowledgments

I am grateful to the following for assistance with research, suggestions, and comments:

- Jardine Barrington-Cook and his colleagues of the Space Division, Logica U.K. Ltd., who developed the guidance software for the *Huygens* Titan landing probe.

- Mitchell Clapp of Pioneer Rocketplanes, author of the *Black Horse* spaceplane proposal.

- Martyn Fogg, author of *Terraforming: Engineering Planetary Environments*, the standard text on the subject.

- Dr. J. F. Zarnecki of the Space Sciences Unit, Kent University, U.K., who developed the surface science package for the *Huygens* probe.

and to the following for reading versions of the manuscript:

- Simon Bradshaw

- Eric Brown

- Kent Joosten of the Solar System Exploration Division, Johnson Space Center, NASA.

Prologue

After seven years of flight, after traveling a billion miles from Earth, the human spacecraft *Cassini* reached Saturn.

Cassini was about the size of a school bus. Thick, multilayer insulation blankets covered most of the craft's structure and radiation-hardened equipment. The blankets' outermost layer was translucent amber-colored Kevlar, with shiny aluminum beneath; the two layers together made it look as if the spacecraft had been sewn into gold.

But *Cassini* looked its age.

The blankets were yellowed, and showed pits and scars from micrometeorite impacts. The brave red, white and blue flags and logos of the U.S., NASA, ESA and the contributing European countries, fixed as decals on the insulation, had faded badly in the years since launch. *Cassini*'s close approach to the sun, with the intense heat and solar wind there, had done most of the damage.

A fat pie-dish shape, ten feet across, clung to the side of the *Cassini* stack, so that the craft looked like a robot warrior going to battle, clutching a shield. In fact, the shield was a combined aeroshell and heat shield for a separate spacecraft, called *Huygens*, which was designed to land on Saturn's largest moon, Titan. The results *Huygens* gathered would serve as "ground truth," confirmation and calibration for the more extensive orbital surveys *Cassini* would perform of the moon.

Now *Cassini* reached a point in space almost four million miles from Saturn's cloud tops.

From here, the planet looked the size of a quarter-inch ball bearing held at arm's length. Spinning in just ten hours, the planet was visibly flattened. A telescope might have shown its yellowish cloud tops, with their streaky shading and complex, anti-cyclonally rotating cloud systems. The sun was off to the right, with its close cluster of inner planets, so Saturn, seen from the probe, was half in shadow. The ring system, tight around the planet, was almost edge-on to the spacecraft, all but invisible, and it cast sharp shadows on the cloud tops.

Titan—the largest of the moons, orbiting twenty Saturn radii from its parent—was a reddish-orange pinprick, well outside the ring system.

Titan appeared to lie directly ahead of the spacecraft.

It was time.

Pyrotechnic bolts fired, silently, releasing puffs of vapor that immediately crystallized and dispersed. Three springs pushed *Huygens* away from *Cassini*, and a curved track and roller made the released probe spin, at seven revolutions per minute.

The path of *Huygens* and its parent probe diverged, at half a mile per hour.

Two days after the release, with the two craft about thirty miles apart—each clearly visible from the other, as a bright, complex star—*Cassini* fired its main engine once more, to deflect its orbit. Now *Cassini* and *Huygens* parted more rapidly.

Cassini's nominal mission was a four-year orbital tour of the Saturn system. Its objectives were to study Saturn's atmosphere, the atmosphere and surface of Titan, the smaller icy satellites, the rings, and the structure and physical dynamics of the magnetosphere.

And while *Cassini* flew on, *Huygens*—dormant, unpowered, a mere ten feet across, spinning slowly for stability—fell directly towards the burnt-orange face of Titan.

It was November 6, 2004.

. . . It would be a second-generation star.

It formed from a spinning cloud, of primordial hydrogen and helium, polluted by silicon, carbon and oxygen: rock and snow, manufactured by the first stars, the oldest in the Universe.

The cloud was a hundred times the width of the Solar System, to which it would give birth.

The cloud collapsed, and spun faster. It heated up. At last, the cloud became unstable, and broke up into successively smaller fragments.

It shrank. The cloud became opaque, and the heat it generated as it collapsed could no longer escape.

The core imploded suddenly.

The collapse made the core, a protostar, shine brilliantly, ten thousand times as bright as the sun that would shine on mankind.

Eventually the core was so hot that hydrogen nuclei began to fuse to helium. The thermonuclear energy generated balanced the inward gravitational force. The protostar stopped contracting.

It was a star. The sun.

The remaining nebula cloud condensed into dust particles and snowflakes. The orbiting particles collided with each other, and— because of the stickiness of the ice, and the organic tars coating the dust—they formed a flat disc of swarming planetesimals, objects ranging in size from a few yards across to several miles.

The planetesimals collided; some grew in size, forming planets, and others fragmented.

Most of the nebula's mass was lost in the process.

Earth formed in a million years. Earth was dominated by rock, its snow boiled away by the young sun's heat, its surface pounded by planetesimals.

Further out, it was different.

Further out, everything was moving more slowly, and the nebula was less dense. It was cold enough for water, carbon dioxide, ammonia and methane to condense into ice. So while the inner planets were dominated by rock, the accreting planetesimals at Jupiter's orbit and beyond swept up dirty snow.

Hundreds of millions of years after Earth, Saturn formed, gigantic, gaseous. It radiated heat as it collapsed, warming the orbiting fragments of nebula gas and dust.

Around Saturn, an accretion disc formed. Moons coalesced, from a mixture of water ice, silicates, ammonia, methane and other trace elements.

One of them was massive.

It was half rock, half ice. It heated as it collapsed, because of its huge mass; the primordial ices melted and vaporized. The rock settled to the center, because of its greater density. At last, at the core of the moon, a ball of silicate formed, overlaid by a shell of ice, six hundred miles thick.

An ocean gathered. It was a mixture of ammonia and methane. A dense atmosphere was raised over it. The new world was a cauldron, with pressures hundreds of times that of Earth's sea level in human times, and temperatures measured in hundreds of degrees.

The high pressure and temperature were sustained, for millions of years. And in the organic soup of the ammonia-water ocean, complex chemistry seethed.

But the new ocean and atmosphere were not stable. Ultraviolet flux from the young sun beat down; planetesimals continued to fall, blasting away swathes of the air; the atmospheric gases dissolved in the ocean.

The atmosphere cooled and thinned. The pressure dropped.

The ocean froze over.

New methane lakes formed, which converted slowly to ethane. Sunlight broke up atmospheric ammonia, to release a new atmosphere of nitrogen.

The moon settled into its long freeze.

But it was not inert. Ultraviolet photons from the sun and charged particles trapped in Saturn's magnetic field beat down on the thick layer of air. Chemistry continued in the new atmosphere, and complex organic deposits rained down on the frozen surface . . .

Thus, for billions of years, Titan waited.

An object looking a little like a comet streaked across the sky of Titan, battering atmospheric gases to a plasma twice as hot as the surface of the sun itself.

Cooling, it fell towards the surface slush.

A parachute blossomed above it.

Huygens was built like a shellfish, with a tough outer cover shielding a softer kernel, with its fragile load of instrumentation. When its job was done, the outer aeroshell broke open, like the two halves of a clam shell, and the main chute unfolded.

So, after being carried across a billion miles, the aeroshell was discarded. It had absorbed nearly a third of the probe's entire mass.

The descent module, exposed, was built around a disc-shaped platform of thick aluminum. Experiments and probe systems were bolted to the platform. The equipment was shrouded by a shell of aluminum, with a spherical cap for a nose and a truncated cone for a tail. It looked something like an inverted clam. Now cutouts in the shell opened, and booms unfolded from the main body. Instruments peered through the cutouts, or were held mounted on the booms, away from the main body.

Tentatively, the lander sought contact with the orbiter.

Fifteen minutes after its unpackaging, the main chute was cut away, and a smaller stabilizer chute opened.

The probe began to fall faster, into the deep ocean of air. Vanes around its rim made it rotate in the thickening air.

Diaphragms slid back. A series of small portals opened in the protective shell of the craft, and sensors peered out.

At the base of Titan's stratosphere, some thirty miles above the surface, the temperature began to rise a little. Gradually, the surface became visible. Downward-pointing imagers peered, in visible and infrared light, and as the probe slowly rotated, mosaic panoramas were built up.

At last, the probe crashed into the slush. Slowed by Titan's low surface gravity, and the density of the lower air—half again as dense as Earth's—the impact was slow, as gentle as an apple falling from a tree.

The probe continued its battery of experiments, pumping telemetry up to the orbiter, which sailed onward towards Saturn.

Huygens was primarily an atmospheric probe. It had not been certain that the probe would survive the impact. And the probe had actually been designed to float if need be, for none of its mission planners had been sure whether oceans or lakes existed here, or if they did how extensive they were, or whether the chosen landing site would be covered by liquid or not.

Just six minutes after landing, the probe's internal batteries were exhausted.

Melted slush frosted over the buried portals of the inert, cooling lander. And a thin rain of light brown organic material began to settle on the upper casing.

The chatter of telemetry to *Cassini* fell silent. The orbiter passed beneath the horizon, and then turned its high gain antenna away from Titan, to Earth. Patiently, *Cassini* began to download everything the lander had observed.

Some of the results were unexpected.

Paula Benacerraf worked through her EVA suit checklist.

She connected her Snoopy hat comms carrier to the suit's umbilical. She set the sliding oxygen control on her chest pack to PRESS. She put on her gloves and snapped home the connecting rings. Then she lifted her helmet over her head. The suit built up to an overpressure, and she tested it for leaks.

The ritual of checks was oddly comforting. It took her mind off what she was about to do.

Tom Lamb rapped on her backpack.

Paula Benacerraf turned awkwardly. Foot restraints held them both in standing positions, packed in head-to-toe. In her EMU—her suit, her EVA mobility unit—she felt ludicrously bulky, awkward in the confines of *Columbia*'s airlock, which was just a cramped, cylindrical chamber in the orbiter's mid deck.

"That's it, Paula. I think we're go."

She said, "Already?"

"Already." Lamb grinned out of his helmet at her, and she could see silvery stubble in the creases of his leathery cheeks. "You're an independent spacecraft now."

Her heart was hammering under the tough surface of her HUT, her hard upper torso unit. "Spaceship Paula. It feels good."

Tom Lamb had once been the youngest Moonwalker. Now, at sixty-two, he was one of the oldest humans to have flown in space.

And Benacerraf, forty-five, a grandmother, was one of the oldest rookies.

Benacerraf disconnected her suit from the wall mount.

Lamb said, "Houston, we've got the hatch closed and we're waiting for a go for depress on time." His native Iowan twang was overlaid with a Texan drawl acquired over long years at Houston.

"Affirmative, EV1; you have a go for depress."

Lamb turned to the control panel and turned the depress switch to position 5. Then, with the pressure down to five psi, Lamb turned the switch to its second position. "Depress valve to zero."

Benacerraf heard a distant hiss. She moved the oxygen control on her chest pack to its EVA position.

"Pressure down to point two," Lamb said now. "Let's motor." He kicked his feet out of their restraints. With a confident motion he twisted the handle of the outer airlock hatch. Benacerraf thought the hinges and handle looked old, like bits of a school bus, with the polish of long use.

Lamb pushed the hatch outward, and Paula Benacerraf gazed into space.

She was looking along the length of the orbiter's payload bay. The big bay doors were gaping open, the silvered Teflon surfaces of their radiator panels gleaming, and the bay itself was a complex trench, crammed with equipment, stretching sixty feet ahead of her. There was no direct sunlight; the bay was in the shadow of a wing, and the light in the bay was like a diffuse daylight.

Tom Lamb moved out through the airlock's round hatchway, and drifted over to the left payload bay door hinge. There was a handrail and two slide wires that ran the length of the big hinge, and Lamb tethered himself to the wires. She could see his bright EV1 armbands.

He turned and waited for her.

"Houston, the hatch is open and EV1 is out."

"We see you, Tom."

"EV2 is halfway out, getting ready."

Benacerraf, with her hands on the doorway, felt as if she was frozen in place, as if she really couldn't step out there.

Lamb lifted up his big gold visor, so she could see his face. "Just stay with it, kid. One step at a time."

She grunted. "Some kid," she said.

Somehow, though, Lamb's gravelly words punctured her tension.

She kept her eyes down on the floor of the payload bay and drifted through the hatch, just as she had done a hundred times in training, in the big swimming pool in the Sonny Center Facility at Ellington Field. She fixed her own tether in place. Now, at least, she wouldn't go drifting off into space.

For the first time she looked up.

Columbia was flying with her instrument-laden payload bay pointing at Earth, so that the planet was a ceiling of light above Benacerraf, a belly of ocean strewn with white, shadowed clouds.

Earth flooded the orbiter with light.

When he saw she was tethered, Lamb pulled himself along the length of the payload bay with practiced ease. He reached the far end, and, diminished, he performed a simple pirouette, his tether flailing around him slowly.

"Hey, Paula," Lamb said now. "Look at your hands."

She lifted up a gloved hand before her face. There was

grease on the glove, from the payload bay door hinge.

When she'd first joined the astronaut corps six years ago Benacerraf had been in complete awe of Tom Lamb.

He was the last Apollo veteran still working in the program, all of thirty-two years since the last Lunar Module had lifted off that remote surface. Tom Lamb still called himself an aviator, Navy style. She knew he had some kind of antique aeronautics degree from some technology institute in Georgia. But as far as he was concerned, Lamb was primarily a graduate of the Naval Pilot Test School at Patuxent River, in Maryland. She knew he had been known as a superb stick-and-rudder man, and his specialism had been night carrier landings, the hairiest flying in the Navy.

And as a young teenager Paula Benacerraf had watched Lamb and his commander Marcus White bounce like sun-drenched beach balls over the rubble-strewn floor of Copernicus.

How could you meet, how could you *work with*, a man like that?

But the awe had soon worn off, for Benacerraf.

Benacerraf was an engineering specialist—her discipline was orbital construction techniques—and she'd come into NASA with a hatful of qualifications, awards and degrees. She'd worked as a ground-based contractor on a number of Space Station construction missions. It was only when, because of Shuttle launch wave-offs and Russian construction delays, the Station assembly sequence had started to fall drastically behind its timeline that the need had been identified to draft the right experience directly into the program.

So—against the advice of her daughter Jackie, against the resistance of her employers—Benacerraf had given up her fancy consultant's salary and her nice apartment in Seattle, and moved down to the humid stink of Houston, on Government pay.

At first she'd worked as a specialist in the backrooms behind the Mission Control rooms, in Building 30 of JSC, the Johnson

Space Center. Then she'd been promoted to work as a Mission Controller, in the FCR—the Flight Control Room—itself.

But it still wasn't enough. It was pretty obvious that this construction project—if it was ever going to get back on schedule—needed foremen in space.

Benacerraf had been a space nut since watching Lamb and his buddies on the Moon, all those years ago. But the thought of actually going up there herself, in a dinged-up old Space Shuttle, pretty much appalled her.

Tom Lamb himself had been deputed to talk her round. He'd used all the grizzled charm at his disposal.

. . . But I've got two grandchildren, Tom.

Hell, so have I. And if I can still cut it, a couple of years off my pension, why not you?

She was given promises of cooperation, special provisions, fast-tracks through the training. Even bonuses, to compensate her for her dropped salary. *You'll be treated with respect,* drawled Tom Lamb. *We need you, kid.*

The training maybe hadn't been quite as smooth as she'd been led to believe—too much resistance from the Spaceflight Training Division for that, who had insisted she had to work her way through their hierarchy of trainers and simulators, fast-track or no fast-track. But the pumped-up pay had come in as promised.

She just hadn't bargained for the *respect.*

As an ascan, an astronaut candidate, she was royalty—at the rank of princess, at any rate, until she flew. People around the JSC campus were truthfully in awe of her, and the deference with which she was suddenly treated embarrassed her deeply.

But if she was a princess, Tom Lamb was a king among kings. And he loved it. She would watch him stroll through the Public Affairs Office or the clinic or the Crew Systems Lab, and people come running to serve him. And Lamb just lapped it up. It was as if Lamb had spent the whole of his adult life preparing for this role. Which, in a sense, he had.

Her opinion about Tom Lamb had evolved rapidly.

☆   ☆   ☆

She pulled herself tentatively along the slide wire.

The orbiter was like a splayed-open aircraft. Before her she could see the big delta wings, spreading out to either side of the payload bay. Straight ahead, at the far end of the bay, was the bulky, rounded propulsion system housing, with its tanks and the engine bells for the main engines and the orbital maneuvering system. Behind her was the flat rear bulkhead of the cabin section, like the wall of a big roomy shack, which contained the rest of the crew.

The curve of the wings was elegant. But for her, the design was spoiled by the softscreen mission sponsors' logos displayed there: the US Alliance, Boeing, Lockheed, Disney-Coke. She knew that stuff brought in a lot of money to NASA, but for her it was a step too far.

At the back of the bay she could see the EDO wafer, the extended-duration pallet with its supplement of lox and liquid hydrogen for the orbiter's fuel cells, which would allow *Columbia* to stretch out this mission to sixteen days. One objective of this flight had been to test the new EDO wafer in extremes of temperature, so the orbiter had been aligned to keep the payload bay in shadow for hours at a time, longer periods than on most flights.

Tom Lamb approached her, along the starboard fuselage longerons. "You ready for the MMU?"

"Sure."

"Houston, EV2 preparing to deploy MMU."

"Copy that, Tom."

Benacerraf made her way to the MMU station. The Manned Maneuvering Unit was a big backpack shaped like the back and arms of an armchair. Since launch it had been stored in its station in the payload bay against the rear cabin bulkhead, on the starboard side.

Lamb had got there first, and he ran a quick check of the MMU's systems.

"You ready?"

"Let's do it."

Lamb held her arms. He turned her around, and she backed into the MMU. She felt latches clasp her suit's backpack.

"Houston, EV2," she said. "EMU latches closed."

"Copy that."

She pulled the MMU's arms out around her. She closed her gloved hands around the controllers, which were simple hand-controllers on the end of the arms. A fiber-optic data cable plugged into her suit from the MMU.

Lamb released the tethers which still clipped her to the pay-load bay slide wires, and reached around her. "Captive latches released."

"Copy."

He shoved her gently in the back, and she floated away from the bulkhead. "Don't even think about it," he said calmly. "It's just like the sims."

. . . Suddenly she didn't have hold of anything, and she was *falling*.

"Oh, shit."

"We didn't copy that, EV2," the capcom said humorlessly.

Lamb ignored him. "Come on, Paula. Turn around."

She had two big nitrogen-filled fuel tanks on her back now, and there were twenty-four small reaction control system noz-zles. She grasped her right-hand controller, and pushed it left. There was a soft tone in her helmet as the thruster worked; she saw a faint sparkle of nitrogen crystals, to her right. In response to the thrust, she tipped a little to the left.

The controller was intuitive; moving it up or down made her pitch, her feet tipping up; left or right gave her a yaw, a sideways tilt. She twisted the handle, and made herself roll about an axis through her head to her feet.

The payload bay rotated around her.

"It's heavy," she said. "I can feel the unit's inertia as I roll."

"You mass more than seven hundred pounds, suit and all, Paula."

She blipped the RCS thrusters again, and slowed her roll. She finished up facing Lamb, where he clung to the aft cabin bulkhead. She pushed her left-hand controller, which drove her forward and back. There was a gentle shove, and her drifting slowed.

The MMU seemed to be working well, but its scuffs and scorch marks showed its age. And things most definitely did not feel the same, up here, as in the tethered sims on the ground. When she started moving, she just kept on going, until she stopped herself. She was in a frictionless, three-dimensional environment, like a huge ice-rink, where Newton's laws held sway in their bare simplicity.

No wonder the Station assembly had proceeded so slowly, she thought. We just aren't evolved for this environment.

"Okay, Paula," Lamb called. "You ready for your one small step?"

No, she thought.

"Let's do it."

"Houston, EV2 is preparing to leave the payload bay."

"We copy, Tom."

Benacerraf tipped herself up so she was facing Earth, with the orbiter behind her.

Earth, before her, was immense, overwhelming. The overall impression was of blue sea and white clouds, the white of an intensity that hurt her eyes. When she looked towards the horizon she could see the atmosphere, a thin blue shell around the planet.

She gave herself a single, firm thrust with the RCS. She felt a small, definite shove in the small of her back.

She rose out of the bay towards the face of Earth; she saw the big silvered doors to either side of her recede.

A tone sounded softly in her helmet, startling her.

"Oh-two alarm, EV2," the capcom reported.

An oxygen leak. Holed fabric, maybe. "Houston, EV2. Should I come back? I— "

"Belay that, EV2," Lamb said. "Paula, just take a couple of deep breaths. Relax. You're safe and snug in there."

She became aware of her breathing, which was shallow and rapid. Her suit monitors had misinterpreted her high oxygen consumption as a leak.

Deliberately, she slowed her breathing; she tried to unclench her muscles, to relax in the warm cocoon of the suit.

"Just look at the view, kid."

She looked at the view.

She was flying up towards Africa. The clouds piled over the equator seemed to reach down towards her, clearly three-dimensional and casting long shadows. She could see the Nile, and the ribbon development along it, surrounded by the baked-hard surface of the desert; the dependence of the people on the Nile's water was clear.

She was extraordinarily comfortable. The suit was quiet, warm, safe. She could hear the whir of her backpack's twenty-thousand rpm fan—it sounded like a pc fan. She heard squeaks and pops on the radio, as she drifted over UHF stations on the ground. In her bubble helmet she had a hundred and eighty degree vision, and she had a great sense of freedom. She knew that when she returned to the cabin, after the EVA, it would seem constricting, absurdly confining.

As she gazed at Earth—at all of humanity, save for the six on orbit with her on *Columbia* and a handful on Station—she felt some of the tension drain out of her, as if it was being drawn up to the planet. She felt lifted out of the web of concerns that dominated her life: the difficulties of her career, the frustrating pace of the space program, her unsatisfactory relationship with Jackie, her daughter, the blizzard of hassles that made up every day, mail and balky technology and her car and her apartment and accounts she had to pay and . . .

No wonder people get hooked on this, she thought.

"Okay, EV2, Houston. Coming up to your three hundred feet limit."

"Copy that." Three hundred feet was as far as she could allow herself to travel. Moving away from *Columbia*, Benacerraf was actually entering a slightly different orbit. If she went much further, return to the orbiter would become a full-scale rendezvous, a matter of complex course correction maneuvers.

She passed out of the shadow of the wing, and into sunlight; her EMU seemed to glow.

"I see your light, Paula," Lamb called.

"I'm pleased to hear it, Tom."

"EV2, Houston. Confirming your ground-to-MMU direct link is operational."

"Thank you."

"And your transponder beacon is functioning."

"Copy that."

"EV2, Houston. You have a lot of green-eyed people watching you; looks like you're having a lot of fun."

"Sure. This is working very nicely. Ah, I'm glad I've got old Brer Rabbit out here with me, out in the briar patch where he belongs."

She heard Lamb chuckle at that, back in the payload bay. She was aping the first words he'd spoken on the Moon.

Most astronauts got off the active list after four or five flights. They moved out into industry, or up into some kind of program management position within NASA. What kind of man was it who would keep on subjecting himself—and his family—to the grind of training, two years for every Shuttle mission, the enormous dangers of the missions themselves, flight after flight, year after year, logging up the spaceflight hours well into his sixties, endlessly defying the survival odds?

She'd even formulated the thought that maybe Lamb wasn't actually good for anything else. To stay in the office you had to resist promotion, after all. You had to demonstrate sustained mediocrity. John Young, the other great surviving Moonwalker, had been taken off the active roster when he'd been so vocal in criticizing NASA safety procedures after *Challenger.*

Besides, all that ancient astronaut-as-Cold Warrior garbage from the 1960s, which still clung around NASA, just did not cut any ice with Benacerraf. It had nothing to do with the future of space travel as she saw it, which could only be about a steady, logical and gradual expansion of the space frontier, beyond Earth. Or even with the actions required of NASA, the space agency, to survive in a future of decreasing funding, increasing irrationality, a growing sense of military threat from China and elsewhere which was causing the ancient Cold Warriors to come rearing from their bunkers once more . . .

It might take all of her career to build the Space Station; she might never get to see another human being walk on the Moon. Well, that was fine by her. Space was a damn difficult place to work.

But as long as Lamb, and one or two others, still hung around, you still had the hero-centered distortion of the whole organization. As if everything that had happened after 1972 had been a long, dull coda. Even the Mission Controllers and their backroom staff were mostly aviation people of some kind, she was finding; and a startling number of the controllers—who were supposed to be there as specialist engineers or scientists— would apply to join the astronaut office at every recruitment round, regular as clockwork.

. . . But all that was before she'd begun to train with Lamb for this flight, STS-143. Before she'd sat with him through hours of sims, observed his prowess at the antique complexities of the Shuttle system, seen him demonstrate his calm control in the abort options. Tom Lamb could *handle* things, she'd come to realize. His old-fashioned jock bull hid a central, deep-rooted competence.

As she'd been strapped into *Columbia*'s flight deck for her first launch, she'd been grateful for Lamb's calm voice, responding to the ground. If anyone could get her home alive, it would be Tom Lamb.

And anyhow, now she was up here, she started to see his point of view.

She swung herself around, and faced back down into the payload bay. She blipped her left-hand controller to slow her rotation.

Columbia's cabin was above her head, the tail section below her feet. The starboard wing was in the shadow of the sun; the big Stars and Stripes on the port wing was obscured by the open bay doors. Her eyes were dark-adapted to Earthlight, so she could see no stars beyond the orbiter. *Columbia* was like a complex toy, brilliant white and silver, set against complete blackness.

At first glance *Columbia* looked faintly ridiculous: that fat, boxy body, the patchy coloration of the thermal protection system, the snub nose, those thick wings and that huge tail: *Columbia* was like an airliner stranded in space, its aerodynamic surfaces useless in vacuum. *Columbia*, the first of the five Shuttle orbiters built—and so the most primitive—weighed all of a hundred and eighty thousand pounds dry. You had to haul all that mass up into orbit, and back down again, every flight, to deliver just fifty thousand pounds of payload to orbit.

And after thirty flights *Columbia* was showing her age. She could see how the white-painted hull was scarred and battered, the slight discolorations between the tiles, the scuffs on the windows that sparkled in the sunlight, the stains on the thermal fabric lining the payload bay.

But all of that seemed to fade from her awareness, as she saw the orbiter drifting serenely against the blackness of space. Bizarrely, *Columbia* looked as if she belonged up here.

The Shuttle system was the technology of the 1970s, still flying in the '00s, with the hard wisdom of the intervening years built into it. And, realistically, no replacement system in sight. *Columbia* was fresh paint over rusty, obsolescent technology. But somehow, up here, she was able to make out the 1960s von Braun dream of spaceplanes which the orbiter embodied.

Her throat hurt. Damn it, she felt as if she was going to cry.

The light around her changed. The shadow of the starboard wing was growing longer. *Columbia* was passing into another forty-five minute night.

". . . Hey, Paula," Tom Lamb said now. "Scuttlebutt from home. Some double-dome from JPL is saying he's found life on Titan."

"Really?"

"So they say. Nice place to hear about it, huh."

"Yes," she said.

. . . She turned again, to face Earth.

At the rim of the planet she could see the airglow layer, a bright layer of oxygen radiating at the top of the atmosphere, like a false horizon. The lights of cities, strung along the coasts of the land, looked like streetlights scattered along a road. There was a thunderstorm over central Africa, and she could see lightning sparking constantly, over cloud systems spanning thousands of miles. The lightning propagated through the clouds like a living thing, growing and spreading; its glow shone from beneath the layer of cloud, and she could see three-dimensional structure within the cloud, edges and swirls of purple.

The leading edges of *Columbia* glowed, a faint orange, in an aura a few inches thick. The glow came from a thin hail of atoms of atomic oxygen, interacting with the orbiter's surfaces.

Even here, she thought, they were not truly free of Earth.

She thought about the news from Titan, wondering vaguely what it might mean for her.

The low-level arc floodlights in the payload bay glowed like a captive constellation.

The suit technician removed the protective cover from Jiang Ling's helmet. Jiang sat down on the lip of the hatch and hauled herself into the orbital module, head first. Another technician pulled off her outer boots, and she swung her legs inside the module.

She was alone, here in this orbital compartment, this elongated sphere within which she would spend a week in low Earth orbit. The compartment was like a miniature space station, crammed with storage lockers, provisions, scientific equipment and literature. Everything was gleaming white, new and shiny.

The technicians were framed in the hatchway. They were both Han Chinese: military officers, with their brown uniforms visible under their white coats. They grinned at her. But, she thought, their eyes were hard.

One of them passed her a small brass bell. She took it in her gloved hand. It was inscribed with the face of Mao Zedong, in comfortable, corpulent middle age.

The technician grinned at her. "Maybe *ta laorenjia* will bring you luck."

She raised her hand in thanks.

The technicians stepped back into the white room beyond the doorway, and hauled the hatch closed. It shut with finality. Even the quality of the sound changed. She was aware of a sense of enclosure, almost of claustrophobia.

Clutching the brass bell, she put such thoughts aside as irrelevant.

Beneath her was an inner hatch. She twisted around and lowered herself through this. Now she was entering the second of her craft's three modules, called the command compartment, which she would ride to orbit—and home to Earth again, to her planned soft landing in the Gobi Desert.

Below her, inaccessible now, was the third part of her craft: an equipment module, containing fuel tanks, oxygen, water supplies, life support, and the mass of equipment that ran the on-board systems. The equipment module would be used to maneuver the craft in orbit, and when Jiang finally returned to

Earth this stage would be used as a retro-rocket, before being jettisoned along with the orbital module.

She settled into her couch. The command compartment was a compact half-sphere, its walls curving up before her. There were bulky compartments and packs all around her, strapped to the walls and floor, most of them containing equipment that would be needed for the return to Earth: parachutes, flotation gear, emergency rations, blankets and thick clothes. The spacecraft's main controls were set out before her: an artificial horizon, handsets for attitude controls, communications and monitoring gear.

She was hemmed in, embedded in this solid mass of equipment like a wrapped-up porcelain doll.

The astronaut trainees, morbidly, called the command compartment the *xiaohao*, after the small isolation cells which were still operated within Qincheng Prison in Beijing. But her brief feeling of confinement had passed, for the capsule was already alive: the cabin floodlights glowed cheerfully, complex graphics scrolled through the softscreens embedded in the walls, and green lights shone all over the instrument panels.

There were two small circular windows, one to either side of her. Now there was only darkness within them, because the spacecraft—perched here a hundred and seventy feet above the ground at the tip of the Long March booster—was enclosed within its protective fairing. But there was a small periscope, its eyepiece set in the center of the instrument panel before her, whose extension poked out beyond the fairing.

Seen through the periscope, the sky was a vast blue dome, devoid of moisture.

This was Inner Mongolia, the northeast of China. The desert was a vast, tan brown expanse, as flat as a table-top, stretching to the horizon in every direction. Beijing was hundreds of miles east of here. To the north, beyond the shadow of the Great Wall, camel trains still worked across the Mongolian Gobi.

The Jiuquan launch center itself was modest. There were just three launch pads set in a rough triangle a few hundred yards apart. The pads were concrete tables, a hundred feet across, with minimal equipment at each; there was a single gantry almost as tall as the Long March booster itself, which was moved on rails between the pads. She could see the railway spurs which brought booster stages here. There was no surrounding industrial complex, as at Cape Canaveral or Tyuratam. There was only an igloo-like blockhouse close to each pad, buried partly underground, containing the firing rooms; further away there were gleaming tanks and snaking pipelines for propellant storage and delivery, and a small power station.

The launch complex, in fact, was dwarfed by the thousand-mile hugeness of the Gobi.

To Jiang, the elemental simplicity of this facility was its power. Here in the mouth of the desert it was as if her booster had barely any connection with the Earth it was soon to shake off. To Jiang, Jiuquan was the reality of spaceflight, reduced to its core . . .

The flight was still to come, of course. But already, she sensed, the worst of her mission was over: the public tours, the attention from TV and net correspondents, the speeches to thousands of Party cadres in Tiananmen Square, even the meeting with the Great Helmsman himself. Of course there would be many more such chores after the flight, but that was far from her mind.

For now she was alone in here, contained within the *xiao-hao*—in this environment she had come to know so well. Here, she was in command, and she was ready to confront destiny: to become the first Chinese, in five thousand years of history, to break the bonds of Earth itself.

A voice crackled in the small speakers on her headset. "*Lei Feng* Number One from the firing room. Are you ready to begin your checklist?"

She was still clutching the brass bell. She reached up, and

fixed it to the handle of the hatch above her with a twist of wire. She touched Mao's face with a spacesuited finger. The bell rang gently. She smiled. Now, *ta laorenjia* could protect her as he did millions of Chinese; Mao Zedong, three decades after his death, had become the most popular household folk god.

She settled back in her couch. "This is Jiang Ling in *Lei Feng* Number One. Yes, I can confirm I am ready to proceed with the checklist. Today is a good day to fly!"

The work seemed to come in waves, with clusters of switches to throw and settings to check in a short time. In addition she had to record measurements in her log book. And she had to work to reduce the condensation inside the cramped compartment. In orbit this would be done automatically, but on the ground the light pumps were overwhelmed by Earth's gravity, and she had to open and close valves at set times, and she had a little hand-pump she used to move condensate from one part of the cabin to another.

There were several long holds in the countdown, when malfunctions were encountered. During these periods she had literally nothing to do, and she found them difficult times.

She was aware of continual movement and noise. She could feel the rocket *swaying* as the thin desert wind hit its flanks; and there was a succession of thumps, bangs and shudders, as ancillary equipment was moved to and from the booster. She was very aware that she was suspended at the top of a thin, fragile steel tower housing thousands of tons of highly explosive propellant.

There were cameras all over the cabin, focused on her face behind its open visor, their black lenses glinting in the floods. She tried to keep her expression clear, her movements calm and assured.

She felt a deep nervousness gnaw at her, more worrying even than the prospect that some catastrophe might claim her life, today. If something went wrong, if the mission was aborted, was it possible that she would somehow be blamed?

Jiang was not Han Chinese. She was a Turkic Uighur, a Muslim minority which emanated from the westernmost province of Xinjiang. Jiang's family came from the desert capital Urumqi; her family had moved to Beijing when she was a child when Jiang's father, a mid-ranking Party cadre, was posted to the Minorities Institute in the capital in the 1970s. Since her father was both an official and a Uighur, the family had been treated with a special deference reserved for select representatives of minority groups who served as symbols for the Party's efforts to build "socialist solidarity" between central China and the non-Han regions. In Beijing, Jiang had attended a special "experimental" school reserved for the children of the Party élite.

Among the Han astronaut trainees there had been some resentment at her promotion—sometimes suppressed, sometimes not. And there had been genuine surprise when she had been selected for the honor of this first flight, ahead of the Han candidates.

Jiang believed that it was on the basis of her superior abilities. Perhaps that was true. But she knew that she could not help but accrue rivals and enemies, now, as she moved into national, even international prominence.

Meanwhile the *xiaodao xiaoxi*—the back-alley scuttlebutt—was that the Chinese space program, in its thirty-year history, had already killed five hundred people. Even worse, it was said, one astronaut had already lost his—or her—life, in a clandestine suborbital test of the *Lei Feng*-Long March system.

Jiang Ling believed some of this, but not all. She would be a fool to try to deny that she was exposing herself to enormous risks, here in the *Lei Feng*. Perhaps more risks than any other astronaut from East or West since the first pioneers themselves.

But for Jiang it was worth it. And not for the glory for being what the *People's Daily* called a *jianghu haojie*, a modern-day knight errant—and certainly not for the "iron rice bowl" which her status afforded her. To Jiang, it was simply this moment, the hours and days to come: to be thrust into orbit, to look down on the Earth like a glowing carpet below. To Jiang, that was worth any risk.

As she'd come to the pad, a technician had told her the Americans were claiming to have found life on Titan, moon of Saturn.

Lying here now, Jiang tried to absorb the news. What could it mean? Could it be true?

In the end she dismissed the speculation. What value was a mission to Saturn? What use was life on Titan, even if it existed? Perhaps the stars were for America, but Earth was for China.

And now the holds started to clear up, and her mood lifted.

Jackie Benacerraf didn't know what to expect of JPL. She certainly didn't rely on the descriptions from her mother, the famous spacewoman.

She drove her hired car out along the Glendale Freeway, out of downtown LA, along tree-lined roads. She drove through swank suburbs, following the softscreen map in the car, and was surprised when she rounded a turn, and came upon JPL.

At first glance JPL could have been any reasonably modern corporate or college site, maybe a hospital: it was spread over two hundred acres, nestling in the eroded, green-clad shoulders of the San Gabriel Mountains, the blocky office buildings interspersed with Southern California palms. She caught glimpses of some kind of campus inside the security fences, fountains and trees.

But the roads here were called Mariner Road, and Surveyor Road, and Ranger Road. For the Jet Propulsion Laboratory had built and run spacecraft which had reached every planet in the Solar System, save only Pluto. And, right now, the scientists here were gathering information from the moons of Saturn.

She parked her car. Isaac Rosenberg was there to meet her at the visitors' reception. "Jackie. Thanks for coming in."

"Isaac, it's good to meet you again."

He pushed his John Lennon spectacles a little further back up his nose. "Rosenberg. Everybody calls me Rosenberg."

"Rosenberg, then."

He was somewhere in his mid-twenties, she figured, maybe a couple of years older than she was. He didn't look as if he lived too well; his face was pale and badly shaved, and his prematurely thinning black hair, none too clean, was tied back in a pony tail.

But none of that mattered, compared to the look in his brown eyes.

He said, "Thanks for coming out. Listen, you want me to get you a coffee? A doughnut, maybe?"

"No, thanks, Rosenberg. I want you to tell me about your results. At the party the other night, you were so——"

"Out of it."

"Were you serious? Are the press reports true? How come the official spokesmen won't answer questions on it?"

"Come see the results for yourself."

He led her through the reception area and across the campus, to a long, low building he called the SFOF, for Space Flight Operations Facility. He took her up to the second floor, to a big windowless loft of a room, painted gray, with gray carpeting. It was divided up into rows of cubicles, within which worked—Rosenberg said—the engineers and scientists who controlled *Cassini*'s systems. So this is a spacecraft control center, she thought. It was about as lively as a bank's back office.

They crossed the engineering room, and then passed through a hall to a science area, and entered a new warren of cubicles, the science back room. Rosenberg took her to his own cubicle, which was cluttered up with papers and rolled-up softscreens and an old-fashioned hard-key calculator. There were reproductions of the covers of antique science fiction magazines taped to the cubicle walls, she saw: *By Spaceship to Saturn*, and *Raiders of Saturn's Rings*, and *Missing Men of Saturn*.

He showed her a Packard Bell softscreen, stuck to one wall, which was cycling through displays of what turned out to be a thermal profile through Titan's atmosphere, as sampled by the descending *Huygens* lander. Grabbing a mouse, he cleared down the screen and pulled up data from a fresh database.

She'd met him a few days before at a party at her old sorority at Caltech, where he was getting steadily drunk on ice beer and talking too much, loud and fast and humorlessly, about his work here at JPL on the *Cassini/Huygens* mission. He'd attracted a rotating audience of student types, some intrigued, some argumentative; as the group cycled, Rosenberg would happily launch into his obsessive monologue again, as far as Jackie could tell pretty much from the beginning.

He was talking about biochemistry—the chemistry of life—on Saturn's moon, Titan.

Jackie was intrigued. Here was a classic loser magnet, but with a story of such compelling intensity that it was attracting a crowd, if a transient one. And she got even more interested, when the sensational claims about life on Titan had started appearing in the press and the net.

She was in the middle of a new effort to revive her once-promising career in journalism, which had been pretty much dormant since her second kid was born. If she was going to progress, she knew, she was going to have to develop a nose for a story, her own story, something dramatic and compelling—but out of the way, far from the attention span of the big boys.

And maybe—she'd thought, listening to this skinny mono-maniac mouthing off to a bunch of strangers about weird chemistry results from Titan, and with his eyes shining—maybe, she'd found it.

Before the end of that party she'd buttonholed Rosenberg and arranged to meet him here, at JPL. She'd figured it was a better than evens chance that he would have forgotten all about her, in which case she would have driven all this way out here to the arroyo for nothing. But when she'd arrived at the security gate, she found he'd left a media pass for her to collect.

Soon the softscreen was covered by chemical notation and complex molecular structure charts.

He said, "How much biochemistry do you know?"

Actually, she'd picked up a little in her graduate days. But she said, "Nothing."

"All right. I'm working in the group responsible for the GCMS results."

"GCMS?"

"Gas chromatograph and mass spectrometer. In-situ measurements of the chemical composition of gases and aerosols in Titan's atmosphere, and at the end of *Huygens*'s descent, a direct sample of the surface. The lead scientist is a guy at Goddard. On the lander, a slug sample was drawn in through filters and into an oven furnace, which——"

"Enough. Tell me what *you* do."

"I'm working on high atomic number results. Complex molecules. Look—— what do you know about conditions on the surface of Titan?"

"Only what I've seen in the pop press the last few weeks."

"All right. Titan is an ice moon, with a thick layer of atmosphere. The only moon with a significant layer of air, anywhere. In a lot of ways, Titan right now is like primeval Earth—say, four and a half billion years ago. Its chemistry is mostly based around carbon, hydrogen and nitrogen. And chemistry like that produces a lot of the key molecules of prebiotic chemistry."

"Prebiotic?"

"The components of life. But there's a crucial difference. Titan has no liquid water. It's too cold for that. The importance of water on primitive Earth is that it was a solvent. It allowed the polymerization of volatile reactive organics and the hydrolysis of prebiotic oligomers into biomolecules . . . I'm sorry. Look, you need water as a solution medium, so that the components, the building blocks, can assemble themselves into proteins and nucleic acids, the main macromolecules of our form of life."

Our form of life. That phrase made her shiver. "But maybe there are other solvents."

"Correct. Maybe there are other solvents. In particular, ammonia. And we knew before *Huygens* that there is ammonia on Titan. Now. Look here. Look what the *Huygens* GCMS found." He pointed to a diagram of a molecule shaped like a figure eight on its side, with some of its edges highlighted in blue for double covalent bonds.

"What is it?"

"Ammono-guanine. That is, guanine with the water chemistry systematically replaced by ammonia." He looked up at her, the multicolored diagram reflected in his glasses. "Do you get it? Exactly what we'd have expected to have found, if some ammonia-based analogue of terrestrial life processes was going on down there. Look at these ratios." He pulled up another image. "See that? Here, close to the surface, you have a depletion of methane and gaseous nitrogen, and a surplus of ammonia and cyanogen, compared to the atmosphere's average. The analogy is clear. Methane and nitrogen are being used in place of monose sugars and oxygen, and you have ammonia and cyanogen instead of water and carbon dioxide—"

"What are you saying, Rosenberg?"

"Respiration," he said. "Don't you get it? Something down there has been breathing nitrogen, and exhaling ammonia."

"So, could it mean life?"

He looked puzzled by the question. "Yes. That's the point. Of course it could."

She frowned, staring at the molecular imagery. It was exciting, yes, but it was hardly the electric thrill she'd been hoping for. Even those blurred images of the microfossils in that meteorite from Mars had had more sex appeal than this obscure stuff.

"What do you think we should do about this?"

"Send another probe, of course," he said, staring into the screen. "It ought to be a sample-return. We've just got to follow this up. *Look* at this."

He studied his results, and Jackie studied him.

Right now, her own mother was on orbit, in *Columbia*.

In the long months of her mother's work absences, Jackie had often wondered why it was always people with no life of their own on this planet—Rosenberg, her own mother after her lawyer husband walked out with his secretary—who became obsessive about finding life on others.

Anyhow it was academic. The funding just wasn't there. Maybe not for the rest of your working life, Rosenberg, she thought sadly. This data, here, might be all you'll ever see.

Rosenberg flexed his fingers, as if itching to thrust them into the ammonia-soaked slush of Titan.

"*Lei Feng* Number One, there are five minutes to go. Please close the mask of your helmet."

Jiang obeyed, locking the heavy visor in place with a click of aluminum. "My helmet is shut. I am in the preparation regime."

"Four minutes and thirty seconds to go."

As her helmet enclosed her she was aware of a change in the ambient sound; she was shut in with the sound of her own voice, the soft words of the launch controllers in the firing room, the hiss of oxygen and the scratch of her own breathing.

Impatience overwhelmed her. Let the count proceed, let her fly to orbit, or die in the attempt!

Still the holds kept off: still she waited for the final, devastating malfunction which might abort the flight completely.

But the holds did not come; the counting continued.

The voices of the firing room controllers fell silent. There was a moment of stillness.

Jiang lay in the warm, ticking comfort of her *xiaohao*, the little Mao bell motionless above her, the couch a comfortable pressure beneath her, no sound but the soft hiss of static in the speakers pressed against her ear.

She closed her eyes.

And so the countdown reached its climax, as it had for Gagarin, Glenn and Armstrong before her.

Book One
LANDING

As the pilots prepared for the landing, *Columbia*'s flight deck took on the air of a little cave, Benacerraf thought, a cave glowing with the light of the crew's fluorescent glareshields, and of Earth. Despite promises of upgrades, this wasn't like a modern airliner, with its "glass" cockpit of computer displays. The battleship-gray walls were encrusted with switches and instruments that shone white and yellow with internal light, though the surfaces in which they were embedded were battered and scuffed with age. There was even an eight-ball attitude indicator, right in front of Tom Lamb, like something out of World War Two; and he had controls the Wright brothers would have recognized: pedals at his feet, a joystick between his legs.

There was a constant, high-pitched whir, of environment control pumps and fans.

Lamb, sitting in *Columbia*'s left-hand commander's seat, punched the deorbit coast mode program into the keyboard to his right. Benacerraf, sitting behind the pilots in the Flight Engineer's jump seat, followed his keystrokes. OPS 301 PRO. Right. Now he began to check the burn target parameters.

Bill Angel, *Columbia*'s pilot, was sitting on the right-hand side of the flight deck. "I hate snapping switches," he said. "Here we are in a new millennium and we still have to snap switches." He grinned, a little tightly. It was his first flight, and now he was coming up to his first landing. And, she thought, it showed.

Lamb smiled, without turning his head. "Give me a break," he said evenly. "I'm still trying to get used to fly by wire."

"Still missing that old prop wash, huh, Tom?"

"You got it."

Amid the bull, the two of them began to prepare the OMS

orbital maneuvering engines for their deorbit thrusting. Lamb and Angel worked through their checklist competently and calmly: Lamb with his dark, almost Italian looks, flecked now with gray, and Angel the classic WASP military type, with a round, blond head, shaven at the neck, eyes as blue as windows.

Benacerraf was kitted out for the landing, in her altitude protection suit with its oxygen equipment, parachutes, life-raft and survival equipment. She was strapped to her seat, a frame of metal and canvas. Her helmet visor was closed.

She had felt safe on orbit, cocooned by the Shuttle's humming systems and whirring fans. Even the energies of launch had become a remote memory. But now it was time to come home. Now, rocket engines had to burn to knock *Columbia* out of orbit, and then the orbiter would become a simple glider, shedding its huge orbital energy in a fall through the atmosphere thousands of miles long, relying on its power units to work its aerosurfaces.

They would get one try only. *Columbia* had no fuel for a second attempt.

Benacerraf folded her hands in her lap and watched the pilots, following her own copy of the checklist, boredom competing with apprehension. It was, she thought, like going over the lip of the world's biggest roller-coaster.

On the morning of *Columbia*'s landing at Edwards, Jake Hadamard flew into LAX.

An Agency limousine was waiting for him, and he was driven out through the rectangular-grid suburbs of LA, across the San Gabriel Mountains, and into the Mojave. His driver—a college kid from UCLA earning her way through an aeronautics degree— seemed excited to have NASA's Administrator in the back of her car, and she wanted to talk, find out how he felt about the landing today, the latest Station delays, the future of humans in space.

Hadamard was able to shut her down within a few minutes, and get on with the paperwork in his briefcase.

He was fifty-two. And he knew that with his brushed-back

silver-blond hair, his high forehead and his cold blue eyes—augmented by the steel-rimmed spectacles he favoured—he could look chilling, a whiplash-thin power from the inner circles of government. Which was how he thought of himself.

The paperwork—contained in a softscreen which he unfolded over his knees—was all about next year's budget submission for the Agency. What else? Hadamard had been Administrator for three years now, and every one of those years, almost all his energy had been devoted to preparing the budget submission: trying to coax some kind of reasonable data and projections out of the temperamental assholes who ran NASA's centers, then forcing it through the White House, and through its submission to Congress, and all the complex negotiations that followed, before the final cuts were agreed.

And that was always the nature of it, of course: cuts.

Hadamard understood that.

Jake Hadamard, NASA Administrator, wasn't any kind of engineer, or aerospace nut. He'd risen to the board of a multinational supplier of commodity staples—basic foodstuffs, bathroom paper, soap and shampoo. High-volume, low differentiation; you made your profit by driving down costs, and keeping your prices the lowest in the marketplace. Hadamard had achieved just that by a process of ruthless vertical integration and horizontal acquisition. He hadn't made himself popular with the unions and the welfare groups. But he sure was popular with the shareholders.

After that he'd taken on Microsoft, after that company had fallen on hard times, and Bill Gates was finally deposed and sent off to dream his Disneyland dreams. By cost-cutting, rationalization and excising a lot of Gates's dumber, more expensive fantasies—and by ruthlessly using Microsoft's widespread presence to exclude the competition, so smartly and subtly that the antitrust suits never had a chance to keep up—Hadamard had taken Microsoft back to massive profit within a couple of years.

With a profile like that, Hadamard was a natural for NASA Administrator, in these opening years of the third millennium.

And even in his first month he'd won a lot of praise from the White House for the way he'd beat up on the United Space Alliance, the Boeing-Lockheed consortium that ran Shuttle launches, and then on Loral, the company which had bought out IBM's space software support division.

Hadamard planned to do this job for a couple more years, then move up to something more senior, probably within the White House. The long-term plan for NASA, of course, was to subsume it within the Department of Agriculture, but Hadamard didn't intend to be around that long. Let somebody else take whatever political fallout there was from that final dismantling, when all the wrinkly old Moonwalker guys like Tom Lamb and Marcus White got on the TV again, with their premature osteoporosis and their heart problems, and started bleating about the heroic days.

Hadamard was under no illusion about his own position. He wasn't here to deliver some kind of terrific new Apollo program. He was here to administer a declining budget, as gracefully as he could, not to bring home Moonrocks.

There had been no big new spacecraft project since the *Cassini* thing to Saturn that was launched in 1997, and even half of that was paid for by the Europeans. There sure as hell wasn't going to be any new generation of Space Shuttle —not in his time, not as long as a couple of decades' more mileage could be wrung out of the four beat-up old birds they had flying up there. The aerospace companies—Boeing North America, Lockheed Martin—did a lot of crying about the lack of seed-corn money from NASA, the stretching-out of the X-33 Shuttle replacement program. But if the companies were so dumb, so politically naïve, as not to be able to see that NASA wasn't actually *supposed* to make access to space easy and routine, then the hell with them.

The car turned onto Rosamond Boulevard, passed a checkpoint, and then arrived at the main gate of Edwards Air Force Base. The driver showed her pass, and the limo was waved through.

He folded up his softscreen and put it in his breast pocket.

They arrived at the center of the base, the Dryden Flight Research Center. The parking lot was maybe half full, and there was a mass of network trucks and relay equipment outside the cafeteria.

He shivered when he got out of the car; the November sun still hadn't driven off the chill of the desert night. The dry lake beds stretched off into the distance, and he could see sage brush and Joshua trees peppered over the dirt, diminishing to the eroded mountains at the horizon. Hadamard looked for his reception.

Barbara Fahy settled into her position in the FCR—pronounced "Ficker," for Flight Control Room. She was the lead Flight Director with overall responsibility for STS-143, and the Flight Director of the team of controllers for the upcoming entry phase.

Right now, *Columbia* was still half a planet away from the Edwards Air Force Base landing site at California; the primary landing site, at Kennedy, had waved off because of a storm there. Now Fahy checked weather conditions at Edwards. The data came in from a meteorology group here at JSC. Cloud cover under ten thou was less than five percent. Visibility was eight miles. Crosswinds were under ten knots. There were no thunderstorms or rain showers for forty miles. It was all well within the mission rules for landing.

Everything, right now, looked nominal.

She glanced around the FCR. There was an air of quiet expectancy as her crew took over their stations and settled in, preparing for this mission's final, crucial—and dangerous—phase.

This FCR was the newest of the three control rooms here

in JSC's Building 30; the oldest, on the third floor, dated back to the days of Gemini and Apollo, and had been flash-frozen as a monument to those brave old days. Fahy still preferred the older rooms, with their blocky rows of benches, the workstations with bolted-in terminals and crude CRTs and keyboards, all hard-wired, so limited the controllers would bring in fold-up softscreens to do the heavy number-crunching. Damn it, she'd liked the old Gemini mission patches on the walls, and the framed retirement plaques, and the big old US flag at front right, beside the plot screens; she even liked the ceiling tiles and the dingy yellow gloom, and the comforting litter of yellow stickies and styrofoam coffee cups and the ring binders full of mission rules . . .

But this room was more modern. The controllers' DEC Alpha workstations were huge, black and sleek, with UNIX-controlled touch screens. The display/control system, the big projection screens at the front of the FCR, showed a mix of plots, timing data and images of an empty runway at Edwards. The decor was already dated—very nineties, done out in blue and gray, with a row of absurd pot-plants at the back of the room, which everyone ritually tried to poison with coffee dregs and soda. It was soulless. Nothing heroic had happened here. Of course, Fahy hoped nothing would, today.

Fahy began to monitor the flow of operations, through her console and the quiet voices of her controllers on their loops: *Helium isolation switches closed, all four. Tank isolation switches open, all eight. Crossfeed switches closed. Checking aft RCS. Helium press switches open . . .*

Fahy went around the horn, checking readiness for the deorbit burn.

"Got the comms locked in there, Inco?"

"Nice strong signal, Flight."

"How about you, Fido?"

"Coming down the center of the runway, Flight, no problem."

"Guidance, you happy?"

"Go, Flight."

"DPS?"

"All four general purpose computers and the backup are up, Flight; all four GPCs loaded with OPS 3 and linked as redundant set. OMS data checked out."

"Surgeon?"

"Everyone's healthy, Flight."

"Prop?"

"OMS and RCS consumables nominal, Flight."

"GNC?"

"Guidance and control systems all nominal."

"MMACS?"

"Thrust vector control gimbals are go. Vent door closed."

"EGIL?"

"EGIL" was responsible for electrical systems, including the fuel cells. "Rog, Flight. Single APU start . . ."

And so it went. Mission Control was jargon-ridden, seemingly complex and full of acronyms, but the processes at its heart were simple enough. The three key functions were TT&C: telemetry, tracking and command. Telemetry flowed down from the spacecraft into Fahy's control center, for analysis, decision-making and control, and commands and ranging information were uploaded back to the craft.

It was simple. Fahy knew her job thoroughly, and was in control. She felt a thrill of adrenaline pumping through her veins, and she laid her hands on the cool surface of her workstation.

She'd come a long way to get to this position.

She'd started as a USAF officer, working as a launch crew commander on a Minuteman ICBM, and as a launch director for operational test launches out on the Air Force's western test range. She'd come here to JSC to work on a couple of DoD Shuttle missions. After that she had resigned from the USAF to continue with NASA as a Flight Director.

As a kid, she'd longed to be an astronaut: more than that, a *pilot*, of a Shuttle. But as soon as she spent some time in Mission Control she realized that Shuttle was a ground show. Shuttle could fly itself to orbit and back to a smooth landing without any humans aboard at all. But it wouldn't get off the ground without its Mission Controllers. This was the true bridge of what was still the world's most advanced spacecraft.

She'd been involved with this mission, STS-143, for more than a year now, all the way back to the cargo integration review. In the endless integrated sims she'd pulled the crew and her team—called Black Gold Flight, after the Dallas oil-fields close to her home—into a tight unit.

And she'd been down to KSC several times before the launch, just so she could sit in OV-102—*Columbia*—and crawl around every inch of space she could get to. As far as she was concerned the orbiter was her machine, five million pounds of living, breathing aluminum, kapton and wires. She liked to know the orbiter as well as she knew the mission commander, and every one of the four orbiters had its own personality, like custom cars.

Columbia, especially, was like a dear old friend, the first spacegoing orbiter to be built, a spacecraft which had traveled as far as from Earth to the sun.

And now Barbara Fahy was going to bring *Columbia* home.

"Capcom, tell the crew we have a go for deorbit burn."

Lamb acknowledged the capcom. "Rog. Go for deorbit."

The capcom said, "We want to report *Columbia* is in super shape. Almost no write-ups. We want her back in the hangar."

"Okay, Joe. We know it. This old lady's flying like a champ."

"We're watching," the capcom, Joe Shaw, said. "Tom, you can start to maneuver to burn attitude whenever convenient."

"You got it."

Lamb and Angel started throwing switches in a tight chore-ography, working their way down their spiral-bound checklists. Benacerraf shadowed them. She watched the backs of their heads as they worked. The two military-shaved necks moved in synchronization, like components of some greater machine.

Lamb grasped his flight controller, a big chunky joystick, in his right hand. "Hold onto your lunch, Paula."

"Don't worry about me."

Lamb blipped the reaction control jets.

Columbia's nose began to pitch up. Benacerraf watched through the flight deck's airliner-cockpit windows as Earth wheeled. The huge, wrinkled-blue belly of the Indian Ocean dominated the planet, with the spiral of a big swirling anticy-clone painted across it.

Now *Columbia* flew tail-first and upside down.

"Houston, *Columbia*. Maneuver to burn attitude complete."

"Copy that, Tom. *Columbia*, everything looks good to us. You are still go for the deorbit burn."

Lamb replied, "That's the best news we've had in sixteen days."

Angel said, "The Earth is real beautiful up here, pal. I wish you could see how beautiful it was . . ."

"Okay, let's go for APU start," Lamb said. "Number one APU fuel tank valve to open."

"Number one APU control switch to start. Hydraulic pump switches to off."

"Confirm I got a green light on the hydraulic pressure indi-cator. Houston, *Columbia*. We have single APU start, over."

"Copy that . . ."

The APUs were big hydrazine-burning auxiliary power units. They powered the orbiter's hydraulics system. During the launch, they had swiveled the big main engines, and now they would be used to adjust *Columbia*'s aerosurfaces during the descent. During its glide down the orbiter would be reliant on the APUs; without them, and without engines to provide power, it would have no control over its fall to Earth. The power units were clustered in the orbiter's tail, beneath the pods of the OMS—rhyming with "domes," the smaller orbital maneuvering system engines which would slow *Columbia* out of its orbit.

"Okay, let's arm those babies," Lamb said. "Digital pilot to auto mode."

"Left and right OMS pressure isolation switches to GPC. Engine switches to arm/press."

"Gotcha. Houston, OMS engines are armed, over."

"Roger, you are go for burn countdown."

Lamb scratched the silvery stubble on his cheek. He looked sideways at Angel. "What do you say? Shall we fire these old engines, or take another couple of swings around the bay?"

"Aw, I'm done sightseeing."

Lamb pressed the EXEC button on his computer keyboard. "Five. Four. Three. Two."

There was a jolt, and a remote rumble, and then a steady push at Benacerraf's back.

The CRT displays cycled between a complex display of the orbiter's horizontal position, and a burn status screen.

". . . Hey." Angel shifted; something about his body language changed. He was looking at a panel in front of him. "I got a warning on prop tank pressure, in the right OMS engine pod."

"High or low?"

"High. Two eighty-five psi."

Lamb grunted. "Well, the relief valve should blow at two eighty-six. Anyhow, we only need another few minutes."

The burn continued.

Fahy's controllers saw the excess pressure immediately.

"Flight, Prop."

"Go."

"I've got some anomalies in the right-hand OMS engine

pod. The relief valve has just blown and resealed, the way Tom said. That brought us down to the operating range. But now I'm seeing a pressure rise again."

"Will we get through the burn?"

"Uncertain, Flight. The trend is unsteady."

"All right. Anyone else got anything in that OMS engine pod? EECOM, how about you?"

"Flight, EECOM. The temperature in there looks okay. I guess the heaters have been functioning."

"You *guess*?"

"Flight, the data looks a little flat to me . . ."

That meant the environment control people thought they might be seeing some kind of instrumentation fault with the wraparound heaters which kept the fuel lines from freezing up.

Fahy wasn't too worried by the anomaly, obscure as it was. At the back of the orbiter, in the OMS engine pods, was a complex, interconnected system of engines and fuel and oxidizer tanks. For safety the tanks were situated in the two separate OMS engine pods, on either side of the orbiter. But they could feed, through isolation valves and crossfeed lines, both the big orbital maneuvering engines and the smaller reaction control engines in either pod.

Even if there were a real tank defect of some kind in the *right* pod, it was highly unlikely that it could affect the *left* pod. The left pod's tanks could then keep feeding both left and right OMS engines through the pod crossfeed lines. If the defect were severe enough to kill the right OMS engine itself, the left engine could keep firing to complete the burn. And even if both OMS engines were lost, the smaller reaction control engines maneuvering jets could fire and maintain the burn, using up the excess OMS propellant.

There was a *lot* of redundancy in Shuttle.

It was a nagging worry, though.

She knew that those OMS engine pods, and their contents, were rated for a hundred flights; the pods flying today had completed eight and nine flights respectively. But the refurbishment schedule had been cut down in the last couple of years, by the United Space Alliance, the private consortium to which Shuttle ground operations had been outsourced.

She made a mental note to recommend the strip-down of that right OMS engine pod, maybe the left as well.

There were only a couple of minutes left in the burn anyhow. She watched the big mission clock on the display/control screen at the front of the FCR, counting down to the end of the burn.

That was when the master alarm sounded.

The flight deck was filled with a loud, oscillating tone. Four big red push-button alarm lights lit up on the instrument panels around the cabin.

Lamb pushed a glowing button on a central panel, above a CRT; the lights and the tone died. "Now what the hell?"

Benacerraf heard her breath scratch in the confines of her helmet.

A master alarm. *Shit.*

. . . But, she realized, the tone hadn't been a siren, which would have been set off by the smoke detection system, or a klaxon, which would have meant loss of cabin pressure.

Whatever was coming down, it couldn't be as bad as that, at least.

She tried to steady her breathing. She was supposed to be here to help, after all.

At the center of the cockpit consoles there was a forty-light caution/warning display. A small panel marked "right OMS" glowed red. The engine, then.

Angel said. "I think——"

There was a jarring bang, sharp and abrupt.

The orbiter shuddered; Benacerraf felt the rattle through her canvas seat, and she heard the creak of stressed metal. Long-wavelength vibrations washed along the structure of the orbiter, powerful, energy-dense.

She could feel it. The thrust of both OMS engines had died, halfway through the burn.

The master alarm sounded again. Now both left and right OMS lights on the caution/warning light array glowed red.

Lamb killed the noise with a stab at a red button. "Goddamn squawks."

Angel seemed to have frozen; he turned to Lamb, his mouth open. "That bang was like a howitzer in the back yard. What was it, some kind of hard light?"

Lamb was pressing at an overhead panel. "Losing OMS pressure," he barked. "Losing OMS propellant."

Angel seemed to come to himself. "Okay. Uh, Houston, we seem to——"

"Houston, *Columbia*," Lamb broke in. "We have a situation up here. We lost OMS."

The master alarm sounded again; Lamb killed it again.

It was like the worst simulation in the world, Benacerraf thought.

Tell me this isn't happening, Fahy thought. She stared at the numbers on her screen, at the flickering alarm indicators, unable, for the moment, to act—unable, in fact, to believe her eyes.

The capcom said, "Can you confirm that, *Columbia*?"

"We lost both OMS, halfway through the burn."

"Copy that."

The capcom—a balding trainee astronaut called Joe Shaw—turned and looked to her for guidance, for instructions on what to say next.

Fahy tried to think.

"EECOM, tell me what you got."

"I see a sealed can, Flight."

EECOM was telling her that the spacecraft was intact; the crew still had a life-sustaining environment. That was always the first priority, in any situation like this. It gave her time to react.

"DPS, how about you?"

"We think there's maybe a telemetry problem with a wrap-around heater."

"Where?"

"On one of the right OMS engine pod propellant lines."

"EECOM, you got a comment on that? It's your heater."

"It's possible, Flight. That heater might be down. We don't have the data."

In which case that fuel line could be frozen. Or melting, depending on the situation.

"All right. Prop, talk to me."

"Prop" was the propulsion engineer. "I've lost nitrogen tet and hydrazine pressure in the OMS tanks," Prop said miserably. Nitrogen tetroxide was the oxidizer, monomethyl hydrazine the fuel for the OMS engines. "If my telemetry's right."

"Which tanks?"

"Both."

"What? Both pods? But they're on opposite sides of the bird." And besides, the OMS engines—because of their importance—were among the simplest systems in the orbiter. They were hypergolic; fuel and oxidizer ignited on contact, without the need for any kind of ignition system, unlike the big main engines. There was hardly anything that *could* go wrong. "How the hell is that possible?"

"We're working on that, Flight."

"How much of a loss are you seeing?"

"I'm down to zero. It's as if the tanks don't exist any more. There has to be some telemetry screw-up here."

But we have that report from Lamb, she thought. We know the OMS have shut down. This is something real, physical, not just telemetry.

Another call came in. "Flight, Egil. I got me an unhappy power unit. Number two is in trouble."

"What's the cause?"

"We can't tell you that yet, Flight."

"Can you keep it on line?"

"For now. Can't tell how long. Anyhow, performance should still be nominal with two out of three APUs."

"Could that be linked to this OMS issue?"

"Can't say yet, Flight."

Christ, she thought.

"Flight, Capcom." Joe Shaw, at the workstation to her right, was still looking across at her. "What do I tell the crew?"

For a moment she listened to her controllers, on the open loops. Every one of them seemed to be reporting problems, and batting them back and forth to their backrooms. Fido and Guidance were worried how the orbiter was diverging from its trajectory. EECOM was concerned about excessive temperatures in the main engine compartment at the rear of the orbiter. He was shouting at DPS, worrying about the quality of the rest of his telemetry following the heater defect. And Egil, in addition to his worries about the power units, thought the warning systems, pumping out their multiple alarms, were giving false readings.

Thus, most of the controllers seemed to think some kind of instrumentation problem or flaky telemetry was screwing their data. They couldn't recognize the system signature they were getting. In such situations controllers had a bad habit of retreating into their specialisms, thinking in tight little boxes, blaming the data.

Except there had also been a crew report. Something real had happened to her ship up there.

Behind her, the FCR's viewing gallery was starting to fill up. Bad news traveled fast, around JSC.

STS-143 was falling apart, and on her watch.

Another call: "Flight, Prop. I'm reading RCS crossfeed. It's Tom Lamb, Flight. I think he's going to burn his reaction thrusters."

He's trying to complete the burn, Fahy thought.

☆   ☆   ☆

Lamb thumbed through a checklist quickly. "All right, Bill, I'm going to feed the RCS with my left pod OMS tank. I'm assuming I've still got some pressure in there, despite what these readouts say . . . Here we go. Aft left tank isolation switches one, two, three, four, five A, three, four, five B to close, left and right . . ."

Lamb was, Benacerraf realized, intending to burn the reaction control engines, without waiting either for the okay from Houston or even for burn targets. He was just, in his can-do 1960s kind of way, going ahead and doing it.

Angel was watching Lamb. He was working switches on an overhead panel. His gestures were hurried, careless, Benacerraf thought. His blue eyes were shining; he grinned, and his face was flushed. He was enjoying this, she realized, enjoying being stuck in the middle of a deorbit burn with two failed engines. Relishing a chance to show off his competence.

She felt a deep and growing unease.

Lamb grasped his flight control handle. "Initiating burn." He pushed the handle forward, keeping his eye on his displays. "Houston, *Columbia*. RCS burn started."

"Copy that."

"Please upload burn targets for me."

"We're working, Tom. Hang in there."

Benacerraf said, "Are we committed to the deorbit yet? Maybe we could just abort the burn and stay up a little longer."

Tom Lamb glanced back at her, still holding down the flight stick. "The rear RCS bells are back in the OMS engine pods, remember. If something big has taken out the OMS, we don't know how long we'll have the RCS."

My God, she thought. He's right. We have to use the reaction control system while we have it, use those smaller thrusters to try to complete the burn. Because it's all we have, to get us home.

Her perspective changed. It was, she realized, perfectly possible that she wasn't going to make it through; that suddenly so quickly it had become her day to die.

For the first time since the events of this incident had started to blizzard past her, she felt real fear.

And, she thought, Lamb figured all of that out, in the first couple of seconds, in the middle of this roller-coaster ride. And made the right choice, took the appropriate action.

"Okay, *Columbia*, Houston."

"Reading you, Joe," Lamb said.

"We want to confirm you're doing the right thing. We're figuring those burn parameters now. Uh, I have the targets. They're being uplinked now. And I'll voice up the parameters to you, Tom."

Lamb nodded at Angel, who fumbled for a scratch pad, and copied down the timings the capcom read up.

The residual burn lasted a full seven minutes.

"Okay, *Columbia*, Houston. Counting you down out of the burn."

"Good. My arm's getting kind of stiff, Joe," Lamb said.

"Ten. Five. Three, two, one."

Lamb released the flight control stick. He checked the orbiter's attitude, altitude and velocity using his analogue instruments, and compared them to the CRT. "Hey, we got a good burn. How about that."

"Copy that, *Columbia*. Residuals are three-tenths. You're a little off U.S. One, a little delayed, but we figure you can recover on the way in."

Benacerraf found she was gripping her checklist so hard her fingers hurt.

Is that it? Is it over?

The master alarm sounded, jarring.

More lights appeared on the caution/warning array, and on another display to Angel's right hand. Lamb killed the alarm.

"Uh oh," said Angel. "There goes power unit two."

The capcom said, "Copy that, *Columbia*. We confirm, APU two down."

Lamb said evenly, "Well, we still have two out of three APUs up and running, so we're still nominal." But Benacerraf thought she could see something in the set of his shoulders.

The auxiliary power units sat in back of the orbiter, close to the OMS engine pods. And they already knew something serious had happened in that part of the ship. Lamb, she sensed, was starting to fear that the problem back there, whatever it was, might be spreading.

The cabin darkened; *Columbia* had flown for the last time into the shadow of Earth.

Hadamard took his seat on the podium for NASA officers, astronauts and guests, at the end of the press line. The PA was intoning the usual incomprehensible timeline technicalities, mixed in with the crackle of air-to-ground loops. A bunch of Morton Thiokol executives came to sit with Hadamard; they were clutching their blank commemorative stamp covers, that they could get stamped at the Base post office later. Everybody loved spaceships and astronaut pilot heroes, even these crusty aerospace types. Hadamard felt sour.

A plane, sleek and white, flew low over the landing site. Hadamard recognized it; it was a Shuttle Training Aircraft, a modified Grumman Gulfstream executive jet with a computer on board that modified the plane's handling characteristics so that the astronauts could train for the orbiter's unique landing approach. There used to be two STAs; Hadamard had cut one, soon after he got his job. It was a waste of money. There just wasn't the demand for that many new Shuttle pilots.

He looked out over the landing site.

The lake bed was a plain of dried-out, cracked mud, stretching all the way to the mountains that shouldered over the horizon. The runway was just painted on the surface, as simple as that. It was fifteen thousand feet long, twice as long and wide as most commercial runways, with a five-mile overrun stretching off into the lake bed. Hadamard could see a team working its way along the runway on foot, looking out for foreign objects that might have settled there. Where the desert mud had been scuffed by feet and tires, it had turned to a fine powder that blew in the soft breeze across the press stands; Hadamard could see it settling on his patent leather shoes.

Beyond the runway Hadamard recognized the big blocky gantry of the mate-demate device, that would lift the orbiter onto its transport aircraft for the trip back to the Cape. It looked like some huge car-wash. A recovery convoy had gathered in a parking area, within sight of the runway. There was a big white-painted fire-tender in the middle of it all, and towing tractors, and a vapor dispersal truck with its big blowers, and there were the ground power and purging vehicles with their long, dangling umbilical hoses. There was a feeling of business, of competence, out there in the desert heat.

To Hadamard, a city boy whose haunt was Washington, D.C., this was a bleak alien place, inhabited by incomprehensible machines; he might as well have been transported to Mars.

There was a stir in the crowd around him.

He looked around, seeking its source. Some of the grizzled old veteran-type astronauts were looking up at the PA stands, shielding their eyes against the low sun. The air-to-ground loop sounded a lot tenser than before, with a lot of chatter about orbiter components called APUs.

Something, evidently, was going wrong.

Despite the gathering warmth of the sun, he started to feel cold.

He sure as hell didn't want any major malfunctions showing up during this landing, or any other. It was a thought he hauled around with him constantly, during every one of these damn missions. As illogical as it might be, he knew he'd carry the can for any new *Challenger*-type débâcle.

Not that he'd hesitate to take several others down with him.

A couple of small, slim needle-nose jets went screaming overhead, heading up into the blue dome of the sky. They were

T-38s. Hadamard knew that sending up chase planes like that wasn't routine.

He looked around for someone to explain to him what was happening.

"What the hell happened to APU two, Egil?"

"I can't tell yet, Flight."

"Are the other power units stable?"

"I'm still looking at high temperatures back there."

"What does that mean?"

"Maybe a fire, Flight. I can't tell yet."

A fire, Fahy knew, would mean the orbiter could lose all three of its power units. Loss of power units at this point of the entry would put *Columbia* right in the middle of a non-survivable window in the mission profile: without the power units, without hydraulics, *Columbia* couldn't work its aerosurfaces, and control its glide. Without the power units, *Columbia* would tumble and burn up.

A fire would mean they would lose the orbiter.

Jesus, she thought.

Prop was coming up with a diagnosis of the OMS flame-out.

"We've been studying the temperature rise in the fuel feeds, just before OMS loss. We figure we must have had a slug of hydrazine, frozen in there."

"How could that happen?"

"Maybe during the EDO thermal tests . . . if we had a failed wraparound heater—"

"Copy that." During the long hours in orbit, when the payload bay had been held in shadow—to test the extended-operations pallet's tolerance to cold—maybe a little hydrazine had actually frozen in a fuel line, wrapped in a faulty heater, with no telemetry to indicate anything was wrong.

"Then, when the burn came, and that slug heated up . . . The data's chancy. The line might have exploded, Flight."

"What would that do?"

"It would have gone off like a small grenade. It would have made a hell of a mess of the OMS engine pod. If the lines were ruptured, you'd have fuel and oxidizer sprayed all over that pod."

"But what about the second pod?"

"Flight, there's a crossfeed to take propellant from one pod to the other. We figure that's how the fire crossed over. Maybe the slug was even in the crossfeed. There's also a crossfeed to the RCS, from the OMS propellant tanks. We're lucky we didn't lose the RCS as well, before the burn was completed."

"Thank you."

"Flight, Egil. APU one and three temperatures still rising . . ."

On it went. And now the surgeon started talking about the stress levels manifesting themselves in the biotelemetry from the orbiter. There wasn't much Fahy could do about that, any more than she could manage down her own stress levels. And behind her, she could hear the MOD manager talking quietly into his microphone. The mission operations directorate manager was a link from the FCR to NASA and JSC senior management.

It all continued to unravel.

Fahy tried to get a handle on all of this, to make some decisions.

None of her training, her experience, her orderly approach to contingency management, seemed to be helping her think her way through this. The problems here weren't to do with her control, or with her team, but with the crummy technology which was falling apart in front of her. Even so, she was aware that she wasn't handling this well, that Tom Lamb, with his fast decision to go for the reaction control burn, had actually achieved a lot more in this crisis than she had. With that action he might have saved the mission, in fact.

Multiple failures would always get you; it was impossible to plan for every contingency.

But maybe, she thought sourly, if the orbiter mission preparation process hadn't been cut back to the bone, somebody might have caught this problem, before it blew up in their faces.

The master alarm sounded again.

Marcus White, Tom Lamb's commander from his Apollo mission, was at JSC that day, for a Gemini fortieth anniversary dinner. When he heard what was going down over in Building 30, he came over fast. Now, he stood in the viewing gallery at the back of the FCR and watched as Barbara Fahy and her team of kids struggled to understand what was happening.

Unlike Lamb, Marcus White had long since retired from NASA. After his Moon landing he was passed over for the Skylab missions and ASTP. He went into training for the Shuttle flights. But when the development delays started to hit, and the first flights were pushed back past the end of the 1970s, he got a little pissed off at kicking his heels around JSC.

So he retired from NASA. At least his wife was pleased about that. He joined McDonnell Douglas out at Long Beach, and watched from outside as NASA and Rockwell between them royally screwed up the Space Shuttle program.

If *Columbia* failed today, it would be a horror, but not a surprise, to Marcus White. He hated Shuttle; he always had. Its flaws went all the way back to the compromises that were involved in its design in the first place, back in the '70s. You put solid rocket boosters on a manned ship, you're going to get a *Challenger*. You turn your spacecraft into an unpowered glider for the entry, you'll have this, a *Columbia*. His only regret was that now, in its final failure, *Columbia* might take Tom with it.

Angel pushed the red button again. "APU temperature this time."

"There's nothing we can do about that," Lamb said briskly. "Let's position for entry." He grasped his control stick again, and pushed.

Under the control of her RCS jets the orbiter somersaulted gracefully forward, briefly as graceful as a *2001* space clipper. Earth wheeled, the cabin light shifting, until the planet showed before the front windows.

Columbia was facing forward now, her nose pitched up at an angle of about thirty degrees. Earth was spread out below the cockpit, a glowing blue carpet, subtly curved. The orbiter was the right way up, and descending.

Suddenly, it started to feel like a landing to Benacerraf.

"Houston, *Columbia*. We are in entry attitude."

"Copy that, *Columbia*. Looking good at this time. Are you ready for your entry switch checklist?"

Lamb grinned at Angel. "Just like the other five times I've done this, Joe."

"I'm glad it's you up there, Tom, if we've got to have a bad day."

"Wish you were here too, Joe. Okay, Bill. Cabin relief A and B enabled. Antiskid on. Nose wheel steering off. Entry roll mode off. Throttles full forward . . ."

"Okay," Lamb said. "Loading the entry software." Confidently, as Benacerraf watched, he punched in OPS 304 PRO. Angel said, "Throttle to auto. Pitch, roll, yaw auto. Body flap to manual."

"*Columbia*, Houston. Rog. Moving right along, Tom. Nice and easy does it. We're all riding with you."

"Roger that . . . Paula. Don't miss the view."

Benacerraf leaned forward and peered through the picture windows. She could see no stars, and Earth was a carpet of city lights below the prow of the craft.

She saw flashes of color, red and green.

Angel grinned. "The lights of the reaction engines, reflected from the upper atmosphere. Pretty."

"Yes."

Lamb said, "Houston, *Columbia*. Entry interface."

Four hundred thousand feet, Benacerraf thought. The informal gateway to the atmosphere.

Home again.

The burn had knocked *Columbia* out of its orbit. But they were still more than five thousand miles from Edwards, still moving with a near-orbital velocity of Mach 25, and from now on without engines. After all they'd been through already— with a disabled engine system, and power units and RCS motors in an unknown condition—the key entry steps had still to come; the orbiter still had to shed most of its kinetic energy, and glide on home.

Now *Columbia*, with a rattle of reaction control solenoids, leveled its wings, and tipped up to a new angle of attack.

"*Columbia*, Houston. Ready for loss of signal."

"Yeah. See you at Mach 12, Joe."

A pinkish glow gathered beneath the windows, diffuse and pure, then deepening to orange. The orbiter was colliding with the thicker layers of air. The orange glow brightened, and turned white. In the corners of the windows, Benacerraf could see some kind of turbulent flow, swirls of superheated plasma. It looked like drops of rain on a car window.

Now, for the first time in sixteen days, Benacerraf felt a feather-touch of gravity, a soft pressure pulling her down into her seat.

The altimeter was steadily clicking off.

The telemetry on the controllers' consoles turned briefly to garbage, then blanked out. A static hiss filled the air-to-ground loop.

All around the room, Fahy saw the posture of her controllers shift, subtly. They sat back from their terminals, from the suddenly empty screens, and stared at the big TV images of Edwards Air Force Base at the front of the room.

The plasma shield building up around the orbiter would soon block all transmissions, voice and telemetry, between the orbiter and the ground. The blackout would last twelve minutes, on a nominal entry anyhow. During that time the ground would have no way of influencing events on the damaged spacecraft.

And it was during the blackout that *Columbia* would become reliant on her aerosurfaces. It was entirely possible, Fahy thought, that if the power units failed now, *Columbia* wouldn't emerge from her blackout at all.

It was going to be a long twelve minutes. Fahy felt past and future hinge around her.

It just shouldn't be like this, Marcus White thought. We should never have built the Shuttle for the money they allowed us. We should have just refused.

When McDonnell's DC-X experimental rocket project came along—a step towards a new generation of launch systems—White had just grabbed onto it.

He liked working with the McDonnell boys again. It was a relief after NASA. McDonnell had built both Mercury and Gemini, and it was on Gemini that White had cut his teeth. And with the DC-X, just like with Gemini, the guys at McDonnell had rolled up their sleeves and got on with it. They built their prototype for just sixty million bucks: less than the cost of two replacement microgravity toilets on Shuttle, for Christ's sake. White liked to say that the DC-X's liftoff weight was less than that of the paperwork required for each Shuttle launch. And so on.

But that had all changed, when the original McDonnell project ran out of money in 1993, and the DC-X was moved into the suffocating embrace of NASA. McDonnell had been forced to take the bird back to the factory at Huntington Beach, and bolt in all kinds of fancy modifications, like a new graphite epoxy hydrogen tank, a lox tank made from some kind of goddamn Russian aluminum-lithium alloy, and an oxygen-hydrogen reaction control system that used excess fuel from the main tanks.

It was all typical NASA. Not one of these "innovations" had

upgraded the bird's performance, as far as White could tell; but they had all increased costs, reduced reliability, and sent the testing schedules spiraling off to eternity.

White wasn't surprised when, at the end of a test flight in 1996, they let the damn thing fall over and blow up.

White just couldn't understand it. To him, things were simple. You built ships, and you flew them. And you took the risks that went with it. That was all. He couldn't see why the hell things should be any different.

The truth was—in White's view—the U.S. government was scared of developing cheap launch systems.

An SSTO, a single-stage-to-orbit new-generation bird, would come up against a lot of vested interests. It took an empire of nine thousand people to launch the Shuttle, and a lot of money went flowing out of NASA to the contractors. That was a lot of turf to be defended.

What if it *was* possible to demonstrate that you really only needed a launch and maintenance effort of a few percent of NASA's huge investment? What if it was demonstrated that every country in the world could afford its own SSTO launcher, flying out of existing airports?

The optimists said there would be an explosive expansion into space. Huge industrial efforts up there, new multinational stations, a fast return to the Moon. Blah blah. The military analysts said that von Braun visionary stuff was for the birds. What would be the military consequence of every tinpot country in the world having access to space? How about another Saddam Hussein?

Private launch contractors weren't pushing too hard either. One or two SSTOs could mop up the whole of the world's launch capacity, and force all the existing commercial operators out of business.

Nobody wanted SSTO. And that was why—as far as White could see—it was NASA's job to kill programs like the DC-X: to kill it with bureaucracy, with study groups and change review boards and new, ineffective technologies.

NASA's purpose, consistent over three decades, was to block access to space, not to build for it. Which was why Marcus White's good buddy Tom Lamb was up there now, hanging out his hide trying to save a thirty-year-old piece of shit called *Columbia*, risking his life for a monumental lie.

It wasn't good enough, for Marcus White.

As angry as he'd felt in years, White made a decision.

He marched out of the viewing area, and round into the FCR, and went straight up to Barbara Fahy. He'd been all the way to the Moon with Tom Lamb, he said, and now he was going to capcom Tom all the way home.

Benacerraf was forced deeper into her seat as the orbiter shed velocity.

Under the control of its guidance software, the orbiter tipped itself up, to change its angle of attack, and then banked slightly, to increase its sink rate into the atmosphere. Right now, the orbiter was flying blind, its external sensors overwhelmed by the plasma. Lights flickered over a panel ahead of Lamb, showing how the orbiter's software was working the RCS jets.

The idea of the antique, crippled spacecraft doing its level best to survive, to bring home its human cargo, was somehow touching, to Benacerraf.

"I got ten psi," Lamb said now. "Roll thrusters off. Here we go, twenty psi. Pressure climbing fast. Pitch thrusters off. Elevon control. Three hundred thousand feet."

"Maximum heating," Angel said. "Our leading edges are up to three thousand degrees."

Columbia was already too deep in the atmosphere, now, to maneuver like a spacecraft with its reaction thrusters. From now on the orbiter had to fly like an aircraft: elevons, flaps in the trailing edge of the wings, would now control the craft's pitch and roll. If the hydraulics worked.

The sky was a rich, deep royal blue. Looking out, she could see the curve of Earth, and the closed curvature of the horizon.

She could make out the whole of the western seaboard of the USA, it seemed, from San Francisco to Mexico.

Columbia broke into sunrise, abruptly. Earth was still dark below, and the plasma glow was fading back to orange. Against the black landscape, she could still see the plasma glow, but where the sun was rising, there was a blue stripe on the horizon before her. For a second she was looking *through* the atmosphere at the sun, and shadows of clouds fled across the ocean towards her. But then the cabin was flooded with light, forcing Benacerraf to shield her eyes.

. . . She'd felt like this once before. She rummaged through her memories.

1969. A wonderful family holiday, up in the woods of British Columbia; she was ten years old, the perfect age to be a child. She hadn't wanted to come home, to climb back down.

She had the grim feeling that she would never, quite, get over the memory of all this wonderful light, and lightness.

The Gs continued to mount, impossibly heavy. The deceleration pulled her down into her chair, and she felt as if she couldn't keep her neck straight, as if her head was a huge, heavy box filled with concrete.

The master alarm clamored again.

Lamb punched it off. "What now?"

Angel checked. "We're losing hydraulic pressure, Tom. Shit."

And suddenly the orbiter dropped like a stone.

"Flight, Egil. I got you a diagnosis on the APU situation."

"Go."

"We think we got a fire back there, Flight. In fact the system signature is looking a little like STS-9."

STS-9 had been John Young's last flight. During the final landing approach on that flight, the power units had caught fire; all but one had failed on the way to the ground.

Egil said, "Probably we have a hydrazine leak from one of

the APUs. If that's the case, we'll have volatile hydrazine spraying over the hot surfaces in there."

"STS-9 was survivable," Fahy said. "The crew got down safely and walked away." That was true; the power unit fire—even a subsequent explosion—hadn't been detected until the orbiter was back on the ground.

"But on STS-9 the leak occurred just before touchdown. Here, the leak came a lot earlier, during entry . . ."

"Flight, Prop. If we have had some kind of rupture of the OMS fuel lines, maybe that's linked to these APU problems. The position of the APU tanks, in the tail section—"

"Save it for the board of inquiry. Egil, Flight. What's the worst case?"

"That we'll be looking at an APU loss scenario. We'll have to recommend a ditch, Flight."

Fahy remembered, now, that the orbiter on STS-9 had been *Columbia*.

For long seconds, it was like a roller-coaster ride—what the controllers called a phugoid mode—as the control system tried to stabilize the trajectory. When the ocillations stopped, the orbiter was still deep in blackout.

Lamb flexed his gloved fingers, and closed his hand carefully around his hand controller. "Let's see how this mother flies."

Benacerraf knew it was time for the first big maneuver in the atmosphere, a wide, banking S-turn. On a nominal descent, the automatic systems were generally allowed to fly the orbiter most of the way home. Today, it looked as if Tom Lamb wasn't going to trust the automatics any more than he had to. Looking at the broad back of Lamb's gloved hand wrapped around the control stick, Benacerraf felt obscurely reassured.

"ADI rate switch to high. Roll/yaw switch to the control stick . . ." Lamb clenched his hand. He pulled the stick to the left.

The orbiter banked to port. The Pacific tipped up, a glittering blue skin in the morning light. Shadows shifted across the cabin, sending complex highlights from the instrument surfaces.

The master alarm sounded. Angel killed it. "We lost another APU, number three. Number one still online."

Lamb leaned into his control, and the orbiter pitched over further.

"I'm only showing seventy degrees bank," Lamb said. "It's all I can get."

"You figure the elevons are screwed?"

"It's that low hydraulic pressure. Or maybe the last APU is going down. God damn this. I'm at the edge of the envelope, here."

Now, at Mach 18, *Columbia* rolled to the right. Below the prow, Benacerraf could see the coast of California, a brown line coalescing along the misty horizon, tipping up as the orbiter rolled.

"—Houston. *Columbia*, Houston. Can you hear me, Tom?"

The blackout was over. Benacerraf felt a surge of relief, illogical, profound.

Lamb said, "*Columbia*, copy. Holy shit, Marcus, is that you? How do you read?"

"*Columbia*, Houston. We read you fine. Tom, we read you low on energy, and off the ground track."

"Tell me about it. I went phugoid back there and came out low energy. Houston, we're down to one APU up here, and I think we may be losing hydraulic press. The elevons aren't responding too well. Going into the second S-turn." Lamb leaned to the left, dragging the control stick.

"Copy that. We see you rolling left. We have you at a hundred and fifty thousand feet, Mach 9. Looking good. Just like barnstorming old Copernicus, huh."

"Like hell," Lamb said dourly. He pulled back on the speed brake handle. That opened flaps on the vertical stabilizer at the back of the orbiter; Benacerraf could feel the increased drag. "Brake indicator shows a hundred percent. Initiating third roll." He pulled the stick across to the right, and the orbiter tipped again.

The coastline of America fled beneath the prow of the orbiter, impossibly quickly.

Bill Angel said, "What a way to visit California."

Voices crackled on the air-to-ground loops of the PA.

There was a ragged cheer from the press stand. The blackout had seemed to last for ever, but here was physical proof that the orbiter was back in the atmosphere, at least.

Now four big rescue helicopters went flapping over the press stand. They were like metal buzzards, Hadamard thought.

A couple of people had climbed out of the press stand and had tried to get over closer to the runway. A NASA car was patrolling back and forth, keeping them back.

Hadamard began to calculate what the fallout would be, depending on how this damn thing worked out.

There were a number of scenarios: the crew could survive, or not; the orbiter could survive, or not.

If everything came through more or less intact there would be a lot of bullshit in the press about NASA's incompetence, and Hadamard would be able to come down hard on whichever contractor had screwed up this time, and the whole thing would be forgotten in a couple of days.

At the other end of the scale—if he was looking at another *Challenger*, here—Hadamard expected to be facing some kind of shutdown. There would be inquiries, both internal and external, forced on NASA by the White House and Congress. And Hadamard himself would be thoroughly fucked over in the process, he knew.

But in between those extremes there were a whole range of other contingencies. If the crew walked away from this, then you were looking at an *Apollo 13*, not a *Challenger*. And that could give him a lot of leverage. Hadamard had always thought NASA threw away the bonus of *Apollo 13*'s world attention and PR, a real gift from the political gods if ever there was one.

Hadamard wouldn't waste a similar opportunity, if it was presented to him. He began to calculate, figuring which of his personal goals he might be able to advance on the back of the events here today.

Someone pointed up towards the zenith.

Squinting, Hadamard could make out a tiny white spark, trailing contrails. Chase planes closed in on it, streaking across the sky.

"Flight, Egil. Number one APU is still online. But I can't give you a prediction of how long for."

"All right. What else? Fido?"

"We're in good shape for a contingency landing, Flight. We're well off the runway, but we're flying down into a lake bed, after all . . ."

"Inco?"

"No problems, Flight."

Fahy allowed a seed of hope to germinate. Maybe she could get through this after all, without losing her ship.

"Fido, Flight. You got a recommendation?"

The Flight Dynamics Officer—FDO, Fido—had the role of recommending intact abort options. The controller—fat, young, sweating—turned to face Fahy across the FCR. "We ought to egress, Flight. As soon as possible; the orbiter has to hold steady during the egress maneuver, and if that last APU goes down that won't be possible."

Egress. He meant, abandon the orbiter.

Fahy suddenly felt faint, and her senses seemed to be fading out; she grabbed onto the edge of her workstation, as if holding onto reality.

Egress. The crux of history. On this moment, on her decision now, she sensed, pivoted her own life, the destiny of the mission, maybe the future of the space program.

"You're sure about that, Fido?"

"Flight, get them out of there."

At bottom, Fahy did not want to become the first Flight Director to lose an orbiter since 51-L, *Challenger*. But she knew Fido was right.

Hope died.

"Marcus. You may instruct the crew."

Emerging from the blindness of the blackout, *Columbia* was now able to use external sensors to confirm its state vector, its map of its position and trajectory.

To Benacerraf, now that the alarms had stopped sounding off, Lamb and Angel seemed tense but calm. Suddenly, it was like the sims once more.

. . . But now the capcom was saying: "*Columbia*, Houston. We, ah, we recommend you prepare for egress. Emergency egress."

Angel stared at Lamb.

"Say again, Marcus."

"Recommend you prepare for egress. The status of your APUs—"

Lamb said, "We're bringing this bird home yet, Marcus."

"Tom, I'm instructed to remind you that an orbiter ditching is not survivable."

"And landing on the Moon without a fucking radar is not survivable either, and we did that," Lamb said. "Ninety thousand feet. Speed brake back to sixty-five percent."

"Copy," Angel said.

"Tom," the capcom said, "you must make a decision at sixty thousand. A decision on the egress. We've little confidence in that last power unit holding out through the landing. Tom? Do you copy that?"

The deceleration mounted; Benacerraf was forced forward, against the straps of her harness.

"God damn it," Lamb growled. "Yeah, I copy, Marcus. But we ain't at sixty thou yet. Fourth roll reversal."

For the last time, *Columbia* banked over. When the orbiter straightened up, Benacerraf could see *Columbia* was flying over the town of Bakersfield, the bleak landmark at the fringe of the Mojave.

Almost home, Benacerraf thought. They were flying through the atmosphere of Earth. Egress—abandoning the orbiter now—seemed absurd.

But the ground was approaching awfully quickly. And they were miles off track.

Lamb checked his altitude. "Sixty thousand feet. God damn it all to hell. Bill, Paula, get down to the mid deck."

"Tom—"

"Move it, Bill! You've got ninety seconds. I'll configure the computer mode for egress, then follow you out. Do it, guys."

Angel stared at Lamb for maybe five seconds. Then he unclipped his harness and stood up, shakily.

Benacerraf, her heart pounding, unfastened her lap belt. She had to lift her harness back over her head, and disconnect her oxygen tube from her thigh, and unhook the hose bringing her cooling water. She stood up, cautiously. She started to hunt for the egress cue card.

Now the decision was made—now that Lamb, up there in the hot seat, had actually concurred—Fahy began to feel a little calmer.

On the open loop, she said, "All right, everybody. Let's keep things nice and tight, now. This is STS-143, not 51-L. And we're still Black Gold Flight, remember. In a couple of minutes we should have our crew out of there. Let's follow the book, and bring those guys home. Capcom, you want to start Tom on his checklist?"

White said, "Rog, Flight."

"Guidance, DPS, let's get that bail-out software mode loaded and running in the GPCs."

"Affirm, Flight."

"Fido, get a good hack on the trajectory. I want no mistakes during the egress . . ."

As *Columbia* went subsonic, it hit Mach buffeting. The orbiter shuddered, like a car going over a gravel road, as the airflow over its wings adjusted.

Leading the way, Benacerraf clambered through the narrow interdeck opening on the left of the cabin. Her legs felt shaky, microgravity-attenuated, but they held her up, despite the rattling of the orbiter.

She scrambled down the ladder to the mid deck area. The four mission specialists—Chandran, de Wilde, Gamble and Reeve—were sitting in their orange pressure suits, strapped into their fold-away metal and canvas seats. They looked at her through their big bubble visors. There was only fear in their faces, none of the forced banter she'd endured on the flight deck.

Phil Gamble—an orbiter systems specialist, tall, slim, bald—had thrown up, Benacerraf saw; the vomit had splashed against the lower half of his visor, and was pooled inside his helmet, at his neck.

The mid deck—brightly lit by fluorescent floods behind translucent ceiling panels—had been roomy living quarters during the flight. Now, with the return of gravity, it seemed cramped, awkward, crowded out by the airlock and the big avionics bays at the back, full of metal angles and places to bang her knees. She felt an odd stab of nostalgia, for the days she had spent safely cocooned here, in orbit.

"Egress," she said briskly. "Chandran, you're the jump master."

Sanjai Chandran was sitting in the leftmost forward seat, in front of the big bulge of the airlock. He was around fifty but looked older; his lined face and gray moustache peered out at her, full of concern. He tried to smile. "Yeah. But I didn't sign up for this."

"Who the hell did? Come on, Sanjai——"

Chandran released his restraints. He reached down to the floor, lifted a cover and pulled a T-handle. Benacerraf heard a sharp pyrotechnic crack; a valve had blown to equalize air pressure. Then Chandran hauled on another T-handle set in the floor. More pyros exploded around the hinge of the big circular wall hatch. The noise was violent, startling, and for an instant the mid deck was filled with dense smoke. But then three small thrusters blew, pushing the severed hatch out and away from the orbiter.

The hatchway became a hole, through which Benacerraf could see the sky. Wind noise forced its way into the crew compartment, drowning any other sound. The opened hatchway was like a wound, cut into the side of the cozy den of the mid deck.

Suddenly, Benacerraf's heart was racing. It was as if, cocooned in the warm, gentle comfort of the orbiter, she'd not accepted the reality of the obscure technical failures which had plagued the landing. But that hole in the wall was a violation, a rip in the universe.

Chandran reached down, stiffly. He pulled a pin and worked a ratchet handle.

A telescopic escape pole sprouted out of the ceiling over the hatch opening, forced out by spring tension. The steel pole snaked out of the hatch and bent backward like a reed, forced back by the wind beyond the hull.

Chandran pulled a lanyard assembly out of a magazine close to the hatch. This was a hook suspended from a Kevlar strap. Chandran wrapped the strap around the pole, and fixed the hook to his pressure suit.

Holding the Kevlar strap in his right hand, he stepped up to the hatchway.

At the last second he turned. His mouth was half-open, a spray of spittle over the inside of his visor.

With awful slowness, he turned again. Clinging with both

hands to the Kevlar strap, he stood on the rim of the hatchway. Then, ponderously, he let himself fall out.

Benacerraf could see Chandran sliding down the bent pole. He was twisting in the sudden gale, his orange pressure suit flapping against his flesh. Thread stitching on the Kevlar strap tore, absorbing some of Chandran's momentum. He slid off the end of the pole, and started to fall away from the hull. Benacerraf could see his parachute opening, like a slowly blossoming flower.

For a moment, the egress seemed to have worked.

But then a gust picked up Chandran, and he soared in the air, his limbs loose as a doll's.

He caromed into the black leading edge of the orbiter's big port wing, against the toughest heatshield surface the orbiter carried. He fell over the wing's upper surface, his parachute limp and trailing, and smashed into the big OMS engine pod at the rear of the orbiter.

After that he fell out of Benacerraf's sight.

Sanjai Chandran—astrophysicist, father of two—was gone. It had taken just a second.

Benacerraf felt her stomach turn over, and saliva pooled at the back of her throat.

As the crew tried to bail out—tried to work through that dumb-ass tacked-on Shuttle egress system—Marcus White tried to focus on the job he'd volunteered for.

. . . *He remembered coming down to the surface of the Moon, with Tom Lamb at his side:*

He leaned forward in his spacesuit, against the restraints that held him standing in his place, trying to see. The LM went through its pitchover maneuver, and suddenly there was the Moon below him, a black and white panorama, as battered as a B-52 bombing range, the shadows long in the lunar morning. There was too much detail, almost a crowd of craters. Really, it was nothing like the sims, with their little cameras flying over plaster-of-paris mocked-up landscapes.

But there was his target, the little collection of eroded craters they'd dubbed the Parking Lot, almost lost in that black and white sea of craters. "Hey, there it is," he'd said. "Son of a gun, Tom. Right down the middle of the road . . ."

The Moon's surface had plummeted up to meet them; they were coming in like a bullet, and he'd tipped the LM back to slow it, and the eight-ball had tilted sharply . . .

Shit, shit. Focus, you old asshole.

It was Benacerraf's turn.

She took a fresh lanyard assembly from the magazine, hooked into her suit, and slid it over the pole. Then she stepped up to the rim of the hatch. She clung to a handhold there, facing the air, framed by metal.

She could sense the wind, just inches away from her. The hull of the orbiter was still hot from the frictional heating of the entry, and she could feel its warmth, seeping through her boots. To her left, the wing and tail assembly were huge, blocky, black and white shapes.

And, far below, astonishingly far, she could see the Mojave. It was a brown plain, gently curving like a shallow dome, crisscrossed by pale road surfaces, and the dry salt lakes shone like glass.

Bill Angel grabbed her shoulder. "I know it's hard," he shouted. "But Sanjai knew the rules. You got to play the hand you've been dealt, Paula. Godspeed."

She turned and looked at him. His eyes were shining. This was, she realized, Bill's apotheosis, what he lived for.

She thought of Chandran, and felt disgust at such bullshit.

She loosened her grip on the handhold—

—she would never have the guts to do this, to follow Sanjai—

—she leaned over the lip of the hatch, feeling the pole taking some of her weight—

—and she pushed herself out of the hatch, kicking against its sill as hard as she could.

She skimmed down the pole. She felt the brisk rip of the breakaway stitching. The hook, sliding roughly over the pole, made a noise like a roar. In a second she reached the pole's end, and she fell away into the air.

It was like slamming into a wall. The breath was knocked out of her. And there was nothing beneath her feet for four miles. There were sharp tugs at her back as her pilot and drogue chutes opened automatically. She felt herself being hauled sideways and upward.

She looked up.

She was already dropping away from the orbiter. She'd fallen under the port wing, and the orbiter was a delta shape, hanging in the sky only a few yards above her, the big silica tiles on its underside scarred and scorched. Black smoke trailed from the fat OMS engine pods on the tail.

Then it was gone, falling away into the huge air around her, trailing contrails. The white felt of its upper heatshield seemed to shine in the low morning sunlight.

Her main chute opened above her, and she fell into her harness with an impact that jarred the wind out of her.

She was no longer falling. She was just dangling here, and when she looked at her feet, she could see the thinly scattered towns of the Mojave rim, still miles below, obscured by mist. And there was the orbiter, a white delta shape, dropping like a stone, already beneath her. Skimming above the mist, it was the most vivid object in the world, receding rapidly.

She looked up. She could see four more chutes, opening out in the air.

Of Sanjai Chandran, of course, there was no sign.

She felt a sudden warmth between her legs, as her bladder released.

Gently, Lamb worked his pedals, and the control stick. He felt the crippled orbiter respond to his touch. He'd flown big aircraft, 747s and KC-135s. In them there was always a certain lag. But the orbiter was much more responsive, given its size more like a fighter than a liner; he could feel he was flying a big craft, but the responses to the controls were positive and crisp.

Today, though, *Columbia* was sluggish.

It was time for his own egress . . .

Things were calming down, though.

The master alarm hadn't sounded for, oh, three or four minutes. And when he scanned his instruments, when he put it together, the data from his eight-ball and his CRT and his alpha-mach indicators told him that things weren't too bad. He still had, in fact, enough energy and altitude for a feasible landing profile. Miles from the runway, maybe, but feasible, out on a dry lake somewhere.

He felt as if he'd spent half his life in front of these displays. Maybe he had, he thought. He felt at home here, in this busy, competent, glowing little cockpit.

Just a day at the office.

Lamb didn't want to throw his life away. On the other hand, if *Columbia* was lost, that was the end of the space program, for sure.

Maybe it was time to rewrite the rule books, one last time.

He thought his way ahead, through the uncertainties of the next few minutes. He would have to manage his energy. He actually had to accelerate, to get to the ground with enough airspeed; by the time he got down to ten thousand feet he needed to have picked up two hundred and ninety knots, plus or minus a few percent.

He pitched *Columbia*'s nose down. His airspeed rose sharply.

"Flight, Surgeon. I got six bail-outs. We lost one."

". . . Six? Capcom—"

White said, "*Columbia*, Houston. What's going on? You're dropping out of fifteen thousand. Tom, you asshole, are you still on the flight deck?"

Fahy climbed away from her workstation and crossed to the

capcom's station. She plugged her headset into White's loop. "Tom, this is Fahy. Get your ass out of there."

"You're breaking up, Barbara. Anyway, since when has a Flight Director spoken direct on air-to-ground?"

There was a stir among the controllers.

A picture of the orbiter had come up on the big screen at the front of the FCR. It was hazy with distance and magnification. White contrails looped back from the wings' trailing edges. And black smoke poured from the OMS engine pods.

Thirteen thousand feet.

Lamb looked down at the baked desert surface. It was flat, semi-infinite, like one huge runway. It was why Edwards had been sited out here in the first place.

Columbia flew over the straight black line of U.S. 58.

This would make a hell of a tale to tell the boys over a couple of Baltics at Juanita's, like the old days.

Fahy was still talking.

Patiently, he said, "If you're going to be the capcom, give me my heading."

"Tom—"

"Give me a heading, damn it."

"Uh, surface wind two zero zero. Seven knots. Set one zero niner niner. Tom—"

Now he was down to ten thousand feet, and that dip had earned him around three hundred knots extra velocity. Not so bad; he ought to be able to land within six or seven miles if he worked at it . . .

He got another master alarm. Main bus undervolt. That last power unit was giving out on him. But it wasn't dead yet.

He punched the red button to kill the clamor.

There was no sound at the press stand, save the barking crackle of the PA's air-to-ground loop.

The recovery convoy was racing off across the desert surface, towards the orbiter's projected touchdown position, miles from the runway. They raised a dust cloud a thousand feet tall.

The orbiter was huge as it came in, impossibly ungainly. It was gliding down a steep entry path, as smooth as if it were mounted on invisible rails.

You could tell the bird was sick. Even Hadamard could see that, at a glance. There was some kind of black smoke billowing out of the fat engine pods at the orbiter's tail. The pods themselves were badly charred and buckled. And there were yellow flames, actual flames, licking along the leading edge of that big tail fin. The public affairs officer said that was hydrazine, leaking out of ruptured power units over the orbiter's hot surfaces.

But it wasn't a disaster yet. In the distance Hadamard could see five billowing white parachutes, like thistledown, drifting down through the air.

Hadamard tried to think ahead. He was going to have trouble with that arrogant old asshole Tom Lamb, when he emerged from this, covered in fresh glory. He'd have to be kicked upstairs to somewhere he and his old Apollo-era buddies could be kept quiet, once the first PR burst was over . . .

Arrogant old asshole. Suddenly he pictured Tom Lamb sitting on the flight deck of that battered old orbiter, alone, struggling to bring his spacecraft home.

His calculation receded. Hadamard found he was holding his breath.

To increase his rate of descent, he pushed forward on his stick. The back end of the bird came up a little, and the attitude change increased his sink rate.

It was a steep descent: at seventeen degrees, five times as steep as the normal airliner approach, dropping three feet in every fifteen flown. He was pretty much hanging in the straps now, falling fast. He tried to keep his speed constant, by opening and closing the speed-brake with the throttle lever. He could feel the brake take hold, dragging at the air.

Way to his right, he could see where the runway had been painted on the bare desert surface, remote, useless. Beyond it was a group of drab, dun buildings: it was the Wherry housing area, where he'd once lived, when he'd flown F-104 chasers for the X-15s. But that had been in the middle of a different century, a hundred lifetimes ago.

Two thousand feet.

"Beginning preflare." Using his hand controller and his speed-brake, he started to shallow his glideslope to two degrees.

Columbia responded, sluggishly, to the maneuver. But his speed was about right.

It was still possible. Even if the landing gear collapsed, even if the orbiter slid across half the Mojave on its belly. As long as he held her steady, through this final couple of thousand feet.

The baked desert surface fled beneath the prow of the orbiter, already shimmering with heat haze.

At a hundred and thirty-five feet, the orbiter bottomed out of its dip. He lifted the cover of the landing gear arming switch, and pressed it. At ninety feet, he pushed the switch.

He heard a clump beneath him, as the heavy gear dropped and locked into place.

"*Columbia*, Houston. Gear down. We can see it, Tom."

"Gear down, rog. I'm going to take this damn thing right into the hangar, Marcus."

"Maybe we'll dust it off a little first."

Just a few more feet. Damn it, he could jump down from here and walk into Eddy.

"Coming in a little steep, Tom."

"Yeah. Could do with a little prop wash right here."

"Hell," said White, "stop complaining. You never had to nurse a sick jet home to a carrier, in pitch darkness, in the middle of forty-foot Atlantic swells. Even a black-shoe surface Navy guy like you can handle this . . ."

Now for the final maneuver, a nose-up flare, to shed a little more velocity.

But now the master alarm sounded again. He didn't have time to kill it.

According to the warning array, the last power unit had failed.

He jammed on the speed-brake, and shoved at his stick. If he could pitch her forward, get her nose flat—maybe there would be just a little hydraulic pressure left—

But the stick was loose in his hand, the throttle lever unresponsive.

The orbiter tipped back.

He heard an immense bang from the rear of the craft, as the tail section struck Earth.

Columbia was still traveling at more than two hundred knots.

The orbiter bounced forward, tipping down as its aerosurfaces fluttered. He could feel the bounce, the longitudinal shudder of the airframe. And then came the stall. The orbiter had lost too much of its airspeed in that tail-end scrape to sustain lift.

The nose pointed to the ground.

Now—with the master alarm still crying in his ear, and the caution/warning array a constellation of red lights—the Mojave came up to meet him, exploding in unwelcome detail, more hostile than the surface of the Moon.

Barbara Fahy watched every freeze-framed step in the destruction of STS-143.

The second impact broke the orbiter's spine. The big delta wings crumpled, sending thermal protection tiles spinning into the air. The crew compartment, the nose of the craft, emerged from the impact apparently undamaged, trailing umbilical wires torn from the payload bay. Then it toppled over and drove itself nose-first into the desert. It broke apart, into shapeless, unrecognizable fragments. The tail section cracked open—perhaps that was the rupture of the helium pressurization tanks—and Fahy could see the hulks of the three big main engines come bouncing out of the expanding cloud of debris, still attached to their load-bearing structures and trailing feed pipes and cables.

The black smoke billowing from the tail section was suddenly brightened by reddish-orange flames, as the residual RCS fuel there burned.

The orbiter's drag chute billowed out of its container in the tail. Briefly it flared to its full expanse, a half-globe of red, white and blue; then it crumpled, and fell to the dust, irrelevant.

White thought of Tom Lamb. It was like a vision, blinding him.

. . . *Tom came loping out of a shallow crater, towards White. Tom looked like a human-shaped beach ball, his suit brilliant white against the black sky, bouncing happily over the sandy surface of the Moon. Tom had one glove up over his chest, obscuring the tubes which connected his backpack to his oxygen and water inlets. His white oversuit was covered in dust splashes. His gold sun visor was up, and inside his white helmet White could see Tom's face, with its four-day growth of beard . . .*

Damn, damn. It was as if it was yesterday. That was how he was going to remember his friend, he knew; as he was during those three sun-drenched days they'd had together on the Moon, both of them feeling light as feathers: the most vivid moments of his life, three days that had shaped his whole damn existence.

He turned away from the FCR screens.

The morning California sunlight was bright. It illuminated the expanding cloud of dust and smoke, turning it into a kind of three-dimensional, kinetic sculpture of light, set against the remote hills surrounding the dry lake beds.

Hadamard, beyond calculation, knew he would spend the rest of his life with this brief sequence of images, watching them over and again.

☆   ☆   ☆

Jiang gazed at the glistening curvature of Earth: the wrinkled oceans, the shadow-casting clouds stacked tall over the equator. Outside the cabin, all the way to infinity, there was no air; just silence. She felt small, fragile, barely protected by the thin skin of the *xiaohao*.

Where she passed, she relayed revolutionary messages, reading from a book she had carried in a pocket of her pressure suit. "Warm greetings from space," she said. "Everything that is good in me I owe to our Communist Party and the Helmsman of the Country. This date is one on which mankind's most cherished dreams come true, and also marks the triumph of Chinese science and technology . . ."

The words were so familiar to her, homilies from classes in politics, as to be almost meaningless. And yet, here, alone in the blackness of space, with the blue light of Earth illuminating the pages of the book, she felt filled with a deep, unfocused nostalgia. She felt growing within her an abiding attachment for her huge country, for the billion-strong horde of her countrymen: the brash entrepreneurial class in the bustling coastal cities, the peasants still scratching at their fields as they had done for five millennia. She was of them, and so of the Party which, after seven decades, still ruled; she would, she knew, never be anything more or less than that.

But now the ground controllers were telling her, in clipped sentences, of some disaster involving the American Space Shuttle. They sounded jubilant, she thought. They had her intone words of sympathy, of fellowship, broadcast from orbit.

The truth was she felt little concern, for whatever might have befallen the American astronauts. This was her moment; nothing could diminish that.

Though she knew she would be under pressure to become an ambassador for the space program, for the Party, and for China, Jiang intended to battle to stay within the unfolding program itself. The Helmsman had stated that a Chinese astronaut would walk on the surface of the Moon before 2019: the seventieth anniversary of Mao's proclamation of the People's Republic. Jiang felt her grin tighten as she thought about that. It would be a remarkable achievement, an affirmation that China would, after all, awake from her centuries-long slumber and become the dominant world power in the new millennium.

And it was only fifteen years away.

Jiang would still be less than fifty. Americans and Russians had flown at much greater ages than that . . .

And so she read the simple words of soldier and Party leaders, as she sailed over the skin of Earth.

Paula Benacerraf, suspended, could hear sounds, drifting up to her from the huge, empty ground below. Her own breathing was loud in her ears.

This was the end of the U.S. space program, and the end of her own career.

Earth was claiming her. For the rest of her life.

She could see her future, mapped out. Her destiny was no more than to be a survivor of *Columbia*, and somebody's mother, somebody's grandmother, for the rest of her life.

She'd never get back to space again. She'd never again drift in all that light, never see the lights of her spacecraft as it drifted in its own orbit beneath her.

Like hell, she thought. There has to be an option.

She tucked up her legs, keeping away from the Earth as long as she could. But the impact in the dirt, when it came, was hard.

Book Two
LOW EARTH ORBIT

A.D. 2004–A.D. 2008

W hat did you think you were doing, Rosenberg?"

Marcia Delbruck, Rosenberg's project boss, was pacing around her office, formidable in her Berkeley sweatshirt and frizzed-up hair; she had a copy of Jackie Benacerraf's life-on-Titan article loaded on her big wall-mounted softscreen. "You've made a joke of us all, of the whole project."

"That's ridiculous, Marcia."

"You let this woman Jackie Benacerraf get to you. You just can't handle women, can you, Rosenberg?"

Actually, he thought, no. But he wasn't going to sit here and take this. "All I did was speculate a little."

"About life on Titan? Jesus Christ. Do you know how much damage that kind of crap can do?"

"No. No, I don't really see what damage that kind of crap can do. I know it's bad science to go shooting my mouth off about tentative hypotheses before——"

"It's not the science. It's the PR. Don't you understand any of this?" She sat down behind her desk. "Isaac, you have to look at the situation we're in. Think back to the past. Look at 1964, when the first Mariner reached Mars. It was run out of JPL, right here——"

"What has some forty-year-old probe got to do with anything?"

"Lessons of history, Rosenberg. Back then, NASA was already thinking about how to follow on from Apollo. Mars would have been the next logical step, right? Move onward and outward, human expansion into the Solar System.

"But Mariner found craters, like the Moon's. They'd directed the craft over an area where they were expecting canals, for God's sake.

"All of a sudden, there was no point going to Mars after all, because there was nothing there except another sterile, irradiated ball of rock. You could say that handful of pictures, from that first Mariner, turned the history of space exploration. If Mars had been worth going to, we'd be there by now. Instead, NASA was just wound down."

"I know about the disappointment," he said icily. "I read Bradbury, and Clarke, and Heinlein. I can imagine how it was."

"NASA learned its corporate lesson, slowly and painfully." She thumped the desk with her closed fist to emphasize her words. "Look how carefully they handled the story of the organic materials they found in the Martian meteorite . . ."

"Careful, yeah. But so what? They still haven't flown a Mars sample-return mission to confirm—"

"It's not the point, Rosenberg," she snapped. "You don't promise what you don't deliver. You don't yap to the media about finding life on Titan."

"All I talked about was the preliminary results, and what they might mean. You can hear the same stuff in the canteen here any day of the week."

She tapped the clipping on her screen. "This isn't the JPL canteen, Rosenberg."

"Anyway, what does NASA have to do with it? JPL's an arm of Caltech; it's organizationally independent—"

"Don't be smart, Rosenberg. Who the hell do you think you are? Maybe it's escaped your notice, but you're just one of a team here."

The team lecture, he thought with dread. "I know." Rosenberg pushed the heels of his hands into his eye sockets. "I know about the line, and the matrix management structure, and my office, division, section, group and subgroup. I know about the organization charts and documentation trees." It was true. He did know all about that; he'd had to learn. An education in JPL's peculiar politics was like a return to grade school biology, learning about kingdoms and phyla and classes.

"Then," she snapped, "you know that you occupy one space

in that organization, one little bitty square, and that's where you should damn well stay. Leave the press to the PR people; they know how to handle it right . . . Look, Rosenberg, you have to come to some kind of accommodation with me. I'm telling you there's no other way to run a major project like a deep space mission except with a tight, lean organization like ours. And it works. As long as we all work within it."

"Come on, Marcia. We shouldn't be talking about organizational forms, for God's sake. At the very least we've got evidence of a new kind of biochemistry, something completely new, out on the surface of that moon. We should be talking about the data, the results. About going back, a sample-return mission—"

"Going back?" She laughed. "Don't you follow the news, Rosenberg? The Space Shuttle just crashed. Nobody knows what the hell the future is for NASA. If it has one at all."

"But we have to go back to Titan."

"Why?"

He couldn't see why she would even pose the question. "Because there's so much more to learn."

"Let me give you some advice, Rosenberg," she said. "We aren't going back to Titan. Not in my lifetime, or yours. No matter what *Huygens* has found. Just as we aren't going back to Venus, or Mercury, or Neptune. We'll be lucky to shoot off a few more probes to Mars. Get used to the fact. And the way to do that is to get a life. I understand you, Rosenberg. Better than you think I do. Probably better than you understand yourself. Titan is always going to be out there. What's the rush? What you're talking about is yourself. What you mean is that you want to discover it all, before you die. That's what motivates you. You can't bear the thought of the universe going on without you, its events unfolding without your invaluable brain still being around to process them. Right?"

This sudden descent into personal analysis startled him; he had no idea what to say.

She sat back. "Look. I know you're a good worker; I know we need people like you, who can think out of the box. But I don't need you shooting your mouth off to the press. It's not three months since *Columbia* came down. We're trying to preserve *Cassini*, the last of the great JPL probes; you must know we haven't secured funding for the extended mission yet. If you attract enough hostility, you could get us shut down, future projects killed . . ."

Slowly, he realized that she meant it. She was expressing a genuine fear: that if space scientists attracted too much attention—if they sounded as if they weren't being "responsible," as if they were shooting for the Moon again—then they'd be closed down.

In the first decade of a new millennium, a sense of wonder was dangerous.

Discreetly he checked his watch. He was meeting Paula Benacerraf later today. Maybe he could find some new way forward, with her. And . . .

But Delbruck was still talking at him. "Have you got it, Rosenberg? Have you?"

Rosenberg came to pick Benacerraf up, in person, from LAX. She shook Rosenberg's offered hand, and climbed into the car.

Rosenberg swung through Glendale and then turned north on Linda Vista to go past the Rose Bowl. For a few miles they drove in silence, except for the rattling of the car, which was a clunker.

Rosenberg, half Benacerraf's age, seemed almost shy.

Rosenberg's driving was erratic—he took it at speed, with not much room for error—and he was a little wild-eyed, as if he'd been missing out on sleep. Probably he had; he seemed the type.

JPL wasn't NASA, strictly speaking. She'd never been out here before, but she'd heard from insiders that JPL's spirit of independence and its campus-like atmosphere were important to it, and notorious in the rest of the Agency.

So maybe she shouldn't have been surprised to have been summoned out here like this, by Isaac Rosenberg, a skinny guy in his mid-twenties with glasses, bad skin, and thinning hair tied back in a fashion that had died out, to her knowledge, thirty years ago.

"This seems a way to go," she remarked after a while. "We're a long way out of Pasadena."

"Yeah," Rosenberg said. "Well, they used to test rockets here. Hence 'Jet Propulsion Laboratory' . . ." He kept talking; it seemed to make him feel more comfortable. "The history's kind of interesting. It all started with a low-budget bunch of guys working out of Caltech, flying their rockets out of the Arroyo Seco, before the Second World War. They had huts of frame and corrugated metal, unheated and drafty, so crammed with rocket plumbing there was no room for a desk . . . And then a sprawling, expensive suburb got built all around them.

"After the war the lab became an eyesore, and the residents in Flintridge and Altadena and La Canada started to complain about the static motor tests, and the flashing red lights at night."

"Red lights?"

He grinned. "It was missile test crews heading off for White Sands. But the rumors were that the lights were ambulances taking out bodies of workers killed in rocket tests."

She smiled. "Are you sure they were just test crews? Or——"

"Or maybe there's been a cover-up." He whistled a snatch of the classic *X-Files* theme, and they both laughed. "I used to love that show," he said. "But I never got over the ice-dance version."

He entered La Canada, an upper-middle-class suburb, lawns and children and ranch-style, white-painted houses, and turned a corner, and there was JPL. The lab was hemmed into a cramped and smoggy site, roughly triangular, bounded by the San Gabriel Mountains, the Arroyo Seco, and the neat homes of La Canada.

Rosenberg swung the car off the road.

There was a guard at the campus entrance; he waved them into a lot.

Rosenberg walked her through visitor control, and offered to show her around the campus.

They walked slowly down a central mall that was adorned with a fountain. The mall stretched from the gate into the main working area of the laboratory. Office buildings filled the Arroyo; some of them were drab, military-standard boxy structures, but there was also a tower of steel and glass, on the north side of the mall, and an auditorium on the south.

Crammed in here, it was evident that the only way JPL had been able to build was up.

Rosenberg said, "That's the von Karman auditorium. A lot of great news conferences and public events took place in there: the first pictures from Mars, the *Voyager* pictures of Jupiter and Saturn—"

"What about the glass tower?"

"Building 180, for the administrators. Can't you tell? Nine storys of marble and glass sheathing." He pointed. "Executive suites on the top floor. I expect you'll be up there later to meet the Director."

The current JPL Director was a retired Air Force general. "Maybe," said Benacerraf. "It's not on my schedule." And besides, she'd had enough Air Force in her face recently. "I wasn't expecting quite so much landscaping."

"Yeah, but it's limited to the public areas. I always think the place looks like a junior college that ran out of money halfway through a building program. When the trees and flower pots appeared, the old-timers say, they knew it was all over for the organization. Landscaping is a sure sign of institutional decadence. You come to JPL to do the final far-out things, not for pot plants . . ."

She watched him. "You love the place, don't you?"

He looked briefly embarrassed; it was clear he'd rather be

talking at her than be analyzed. "Hell, I don't know. I like what's been achieved here, I guess. Ms. Benacerraf—"

"Paula."

He looked confused, comically. "Call me Rosenberg. But things are changing now. It seems to me I'm living through the long, drawn-out consequences of massive policy mistakes made long before I was born. And that makes me angry."

"Is that why you asked me to come out here?"

"Kind of."

He guided her into one of the buildings. He led her through corridors littered with computer terminals, storage media and printouts; there were close-up *Ranger* photographs of the Moon's surface, casually framed and stuck on the walls.

But those Moon photographs were all of forty years old: just historic curios, as meaningless now as a Victorian naturalist's collection of dead, pinned insects. There was an air of age, of decay about the place, she thought; the narrow corridors with their ceiling tiles were redolent of the corporate buildings of the middle of the last century.

JPL was showing its age. It had become a place of the past, not the future.

How sad.

He led her out back of the campus buildings, to a dusty area compressed against the Arroyo and the mountain. Here, the rough-hewn character of the original 1940s laboratory remained: a huddle of two- and three-story Army base buildings—now more than sixty years old—in standard-issue military paintwork.

Rosenberg pointed. "Even by the end of the war there were still only about a hundred workers here. Just lashed-up structures of corrugated metal, redwood tie and stone. See over there? They had a string of test pits dug into the side of the hill, lined with railroad ties. They called it the gulch. You had to drive to the site over a bumpy road that washed out in the rainy season . . . It was as crude as hell. And yet, the exploration of the Solar System started right here."

"Why are you showing me all this, Rosenberg?"

He took off his glasses and polished them on a corner of his T-shirt. "Because it's all over for JPL," he said. "For decades, as far back as Apollo, NASA has starved JPL and space science to pay for Man-In-Space. And now, hell, I presume you've heard the scuttlebutt. They're even going to close down the Deep Space Network. They're already talking about mothballing the Hubble. And Goldstone will be turned over to the USAF for some kind of navel-searching reconnaissance work."

"It's all politics, Rosenberg," Benacerraf said gently. "You have to understand. The White House has to respond to pressure from the likes of Congressman Maclachlan. They have to appear in control of their space budgets. So if they are throwing money at new launch vehicles to replace Shuttle, they have to cut somewhere else . . ."

"But when we all calm down from our fright about the Chinese, they'll just cut the launcher budgets anyhow, and we'll be left with nothing. Paula, when it's gone, it's gone. The signals coming in from the last probes—the Voyagers, *Galileo*, *Cassini*—will fall on a deaf world. Think about that. And as for JPL, those sharks in the USAF have been waiting for something like *Columbia*, waiting for NASA to weaken. It's as if they're taking revenge. They're going to turn us into a DoD-dedicated laboratory. The NASA links will be severed, and we'll lose the space work, and all of our research will be classified, for good and all. The Pentagon calls it weaponization."

"Rosenberg—"

He looked into the sky. "Paula, in another decade, the planets are going to be no more than what they were, before 1960: just lights in the sky. The space program is over at last, killed by NASA and the USAF and the aerospace companies . . ."

No, she thought automatically. It's more complex than that. It always was. The space program is a major national investment. It's been shaped from the beginning by political, economic, technical factors, beyond anyone's control . . .

And yet, she thought, standing here in the arroyo dust, she had the instinctive sense that Rosenberg was right. We've blown it. We could have done a hell of a lot more. We could have sent robot probes everywhere, multiplied our understanding a hundredfold.

Lights in the sky. That phrase snagged at her. She thought of the forty-year-old Moon photographs. At the LAX bookstalls she'd found rows of astrology books, on the science shelves. Was that the future she wanted to bequeath her grandchildren?

The sense of claustrophobia, of enclosure, she'd felt since returning to Earth increased.

"Rosenberg, what is it you want?"

He put on his glasses and looked at her. "I want you people to start paying back."

"I'm listening."

He guided her back towards the main campus. "If you had a free choice, which planet would you choose to go to? The Moon is dead, Venus is an inferno, and Mars is an ice ball, with a few fossils we might dig out of the deep rocks if we sent a team of geologists up there for a century."

"Then where?"

"Titan," he said. *"Titan . . ."*

He led her to his cubicle in the science back room. It was piled deep with papers, journals, printout; the walls were coated with softscreens.

He sat down. He cleared a softscreen and dug out a *Cassini* image; it showed the shadowed limb of a smooth, orange-brown globe, billiard-ball featureless. "The *Cassini-Huygens* results have already taught us a hell of a lot about Titan," Rosenberg said. "It's a moon of Saturn. But it's as big as Mercury; hell, it's a world in its own right. If it wasn't in orbit around Saturn, if it had its own solar orbit, maybe we would have justified a mission to Titan for its own sake by now . . ."

Rosenberg brought up a low-altitude image, taken by the

Huygens probe a few hundred yards above the surface. The quality was good, though the illumination was low. It was a landscape, she realized suddenly, and Rosenberg expanded on what she saw.

    . . . A reddish color dominated everything, although swathes of darker, older material streaked the landscape. Towards the horizon, beyond the slushy plain below, there were rolling hills with peaks stained dark red and yellow, with slashes of ochre on their flanks. But they were mountains of ice, not rock. An ethane lake had eroded the base of the hills, and there were visible scars in the hills' profiles.

    Clouds, red and orange, swirled above the hills and flooded the craters . . .

It was extraordinarily beautiful. Benacerraf felt she was being drawn into the screen, and she wanted to step through and float down through the thick air, her boots crunching into that slushy surface.

Rosenberg said, "Titan is the only moon in the Solar System with air, an atmosphere double the mass of Earth's, mostly nitrogen, with some methane and hydrogen. The sunlight breaks down the methane into tholins—a mixture of hydrocarbons, nitriles and other polymers. That's the orange-brown smog you can see here. Titan is an ice moon, pocked with craters, which are flooded with ethane. Crater lakes, Paula. The tholins rain out on the surface all the time; *Huygens* landed in a tholin slush, and we figure there is probably a layer, in some places a hundred yards thick, laid down over the dry land. Titan is an organic chemistry paradise . . ."

Benacerraf felt faintly bored. "I know about the science, Rosenberg."

"Paula, I want you to start thinking of Titan in a different way: not as a site of some vague scientific interest, but as a resource."

"Resource?"

He began to snap out his words, precise, rehearsed. "Think about what we have here. Titan is an organic-synthesis machine, way off in the outer Solar System, which we can tune to serve Earthly life. It could become a factory, churning out fibers, food, any organic-chemistry product you like. Such as CHON food."

"Huh?"

"Food manufactured from carbon, hydrogen, oxygen, nitrogen. Paula, we know how to do this. Generally the comets have been suggested as an off-Earth resource for such raw materials. Titan's a hell of a lot closer than most comets, and has vastly more mass besides." She could not help but see how his mind was working, so clear were his speculations, so transparent his body language.

"So a colony could survive there," she said.

"More than that. You could export foodstuffs to other colonies, to the inner planets, to Earth itself."

She nodded. "Maybe. There must be cheaper ways to boost the food supply, though . . . What about a shorter term payoff?"

"Oh, that's easy. Helium-3, from Saturn."

"Huh?"

He said patiently, "We mine helium-3 from Saturn's outer atmosphere, by scooping it off, and export it to Earth, to power fusion reactors. Helium-3 is a better fuel than deuterium. And you know the Earth-Moon system is almost barren of it."

She nodded slowly.

He said, "And further out in time, on a bigger scale, you could start exporting Titan's volatiles, to inner planets lacking them."

"What volatiles?"

"Nitrogen," he said. "An Earth-like biosphere needs nitrogen. Mars has none; Titan has plenty." He looked at her closely. "Paula, are you following me? *Titan nitrogen could be used to terraform Mars.*" He started talking more rapidly. "That's why Titan is vital. We may have only one shot at this, with the technology we have available now. If we could establish some kind of beachhead on Titan, we could use it as a base, long-term, for the colonization of the rest of the System. If we don't—hell, it might be centuries before we could assemble the resources for another shot. If ever. I've thought this through. I have an integrated plan, on how a colony on Titan could be used as a springboard to open up the outer System, over short, medium and long scales . . . I'll give you a copy."

"Yeah." She was starting to feel bewildered. My God, she thought. We can't even fly our handful of thirty-year-old spaceplanes. We've sent one cut-price bucket of bolts down into Titan's atmosphere. And here is this guy, this hairy JPL wacko, talking about interplanetary commerce, terraforming the bodies of the Solar System.

Future and past were seriously mixed up here, at JPL.

"Rosenberg, don't you think we ought to take this one step at a time? If we're going to fly to other worlds, wouldn't it be smarter to go somewhere closer to home? The Moon, even Mars?"

"The old Tsiolkovsky plan," he said dismissively. "The von Braun scheme. Expand in an orderly way, one step at a time. But hasn't the history of the last half-century taught us that it just won't be like that? Paula, the Solar System is a big, empty, hostile place. You can't envisage an orderly, progressive expansion out there; it will be more like the colonization of Polynesia—fragile ships, limping across the ocean to remote islands. And when you find somewhere friendly, you stop, colonize, and use it as a base to move on. Titan is about the friendliest island we can see; it's resource-rich, with a shallow gravity well, and it's a hell of a long way out from the sun. And that's not all."

"What else?"

"Paula, we think we've found life down there."

"I know. I read the *World Weekly News*."

He looked offended. "It wasn't *World Weekly News*. And it was your daughter's report . . . Anyhow, this changes everything. Don't you see? *Titan is the future*: not just for us, the space program, but for life itself in the Solar System."

She looked, sideways, at his thin face, the orange light of Titan reflecting from his glasses. He didn't look as if anybody had held him, close, maybe since his early teenage years. And here he was, trying to reach out across a billion miles, to putative beings in some murky puddle on another world.

She'd seen people like this before, on the fringes of the space program. Mostly lonely men. Rosenberg was dreaming of an impossible future. She wondered what it was inside of him he was trying to heal by doing this.

She felt sorry for him.

"Let me get this straight," she said. "You want me to back a proposal to send another mission to Titan. Is that right? More probes—maybe some kind of sample return?"

He was shaking his head. She sensed that this situation was about to get worse.

"No. You haven't been listening. Not another probe. *People*," he said. "We have to send a crewed mission to Titan. We have to send people there." He turned in his seat and faced her, deadly serious.

"Rosenberg, if I'd known you were going to propose something like this—"

"I know." He grinned, and suddenly his looks were boyish. "You wouldn't have flown out. That's why I didn't tell you. But I'm not crazy, and I don't want to waste your time. Just listen."

"We don't have the technology," she said. "We probably never will."

"But we do have the technology. What the hell else are you going to do with your grounded Shuttle fleet?"

"You want to use *Shuttle hardware* to reach Titan? Rosenberg, it's crazy even to think of going to Saturn with chemical rockets. It would take years—"

"Actually, getting there is easy. So is surviving on the surface. The hard part is coming home . . ."

At a console, Rosenberg started showing her the prelimi-

nary delta-vee and propellant mass calculations he'd made; he
was talking too quickly, and she tried to pay attention, following his argument.

She listened.

It was, of course, crazy.

But . . .

She found herself grinning. Sending people to Titan, huh?

Well, working on a proposal like this, if it could be made to
hang together at all, would be a hell of a lot more fun than
trawling around the crash inquiries and consultancy circuit forever. It would put bugs up a lot of asses. Including, she thought
wickedly, Jackie's.

In a satisfying way, in fact, her own involvement in this craziness was all Jackie's fault.

And, what if it all resulted in something tangible? A Titan
adventure would be a peg for a lot of young imaginations, in a
future which was looking enclosing and bleak. JPL might be
finished. So might the Shuttle program, all of America's first
space efforts. But maybe, out of their ashes, some kind of
marker to a better future could be drawn.

Or maybe she just wanted to get back at Jackie.

She had a couple of hours before the flight back to Houston.
She could afford to indulge Rosenberg a little more.

It would be a thought experiment. It might make a neat little paper for the *Journal of Spacecraft and Rockets*. Or maybe one
of the sci-fi magazines.

She sat down and started to go through Rosenberg's back-
of-the-envelope numbers more carefully, trying to find the
mistake that had to be in there, the hole that would make the
whole thing fall apart, the reason why it was impossible to send
people to Titan.

Nicola Mott did not want to go home.

She and Siobhan Libet, her sole crewmate on Station, had spent the last day packing the Soyuz reentry module as best they could with results from their work—biological and medical samples, data cassettes and diskettes, film cartridges, notebooks and softscreens. Then Libet dimmed the floods in the Service Module, the Station's main component, and pulled out her sleeping bag.

But Mott didn't want to sleep. She wanted to spin out these last few hours as much as she could.

So, alone, she made her way through the open hatch and down to the end of the FGB module, the Russian-built energy block docked on the end of the Service Module.

She stared out the window at the shining, wrinkled surface of the Pacific.

The shadows of the light, high clouds on the water grew longer, and the Station passed abruptly into night. She huddled by the window, curling up into a fetal ball. She could see the lights of a ship, crawling across the skin of the darkened ocean.

She—Nicola Mott, English-born astronaut—might be the last Westerner ever to see such sights, she thought.

She was too young to remember Apollo, barely old enough to remember Skylab and ASTP. She'd been eleven, in the middle of an English spring, when *Columbia* made her maiden flight, and it had been a hell of a thrill. But after a while she started to wonder why these beautiful spaceships kept on flying up to orbit and coming back down without ever *going* anywhere.

And when she'd come to understand that, she started to realize that she'd been born at the wrong time: born too late to witness, still less participate in, Apollo; born too early, probably, to witness whatever came next.

Still, she'd decided to make her own way. She'd moved to America and worked through a short career at McDonnell Douglas, where she'd worked on the design and construction

of a component of Station called the Integrated Truss Segment
S0, a piece that now looked as if it would never be shipped out
of the McDonnell plant at Huntington Beach. She'd enjoyed
her time at Huntington, looking back; the Balsa Avenue assembly area had the air of an ordinary industrial plant, no fancy
NASA-style airlocks or clean rooms . . .

Anyhow, then she'd transferred to NASA. She'd worked as a
payload controller in Mission Control, and then, at her third
attempt, made it into the Astronaut Office. She'd paid her dues
as an ascan, and finally been attached to a Shuttle flight—STS-
141, *Atlantis*—and come flying up here, to Station, for a six-
month vigil.

It turned out to be a question of just surviving in this shack
of a Service Module, boring a hole in the sky for month after
month. Russian and American crews, brought up by Shuttle,
had been rotating up here on six-month shifts, struggling to do
some real research in these primitive conditions, their main
purpose to keep this rump of the Station alive with basic maintenance and housekeeping.

Even so, at first she'd been thrilled just to be in space, all
these years after those Illinois dreams. And as her relationship
with Siobhan Libet had matured, the experience had come to
seem magical.

Then, after a few weeks of circling the Earth, she'd got
oddly frustrated. She got bored with the stodgy Russian food
and with the daily regime of exercise and dull maintenance.
The Station blocks were so small compared to the huge spaces
out there; it seemed absurd to be so confined, to huddle up
against the warm skin of Earth like this.

Damn it, she wanted to go somewhere. Such as Titan, where
those hairies at JPL thought they'd found life signs . . . But
nobody was offering a ride.

It wasn't really the great tragic downfall in human destiny
that was bothering her, she admitted. It was her own screwed-
up career.

Mott was thirty-four years old, and she wasn't given to morbid late-night thoughts like these. She started to feel cold, and, suddenly, terribly lonely. Staying up all night no longer seemed such a great idea.

She pulled herself back through to the Service Module.

The interior of Station was cramped and crowded. The walls were lined with instrument panels, wall mounts for air-scrubbing lithium chlorate canisters, other equipment. These two modules had been serving alone as the core of the Space Station for too many years now, and as parts had worn out replacements had been flown up and crudely bolted in place, and new experiments had been brought up here and fixed to whatever wall space was available. As a result the clutter was prodigious; cables and pipes and lagged ducts trailed everywhere, and there was a sour smell, the stink of people locked up in a small space for too long.

She pressurized the water tank, and fired the spigot. A globe of water came shimmering through the air towards her face, the lights of the module sharply reflected in its meniscus. She opened her mouth and let the water drift in; when she closed her mouth around the globule it was as if the water exploded over her palate, crisp and cold.

If she couldn't get back into space, she'd never in her life be able to take a drink like that again, she thought. Returning to Earth was going to be like a little death.

Her sleeping compartment was a space like a broom cupboard, with its own window, cluttered with bits of gear and clothing. Her sleeping bag was fixed straight up and down against the wall of the module, and she had to crane her neck to see out of her window, at the slice of Earth which drifted past there. With the Earthlight, and the subdued floods of the compartment, the Service Module was pretty bright, and the pumps and ventilation fans kept up a continual rattle. It was like being in the guts of some huge machine.

She pulled herself deeper into her sleeping bag, which soon became warm enough for her to be able to forget the endless vacuum a few inches away from her face, beyond the module's cladded hull.

After an unmeasured time, she felt a hand stroking her back. She turned in her bag. Siobhan, naked, her hair floating around her face in a big burst of color, was silhouetted against the cabin lights.

Mott smiled and reached out. She brushed Libet's hair back, revealing her fine, high brow. "You look like Barbarella," she said.

"In your dreams. Are you going to let me in?"

The sleeping bags were too small for two people. But they'd found a way of zipping their two bags together. It was cold, the opening at the top liable to let in draughts, but their bodies would soon build up a layer of warm air around them.

"Anyhow," Mott said, "I thought you wanted to sleep."

"I did. I do. But I guess I can spend the rest of my life asleep. Down there, at the bottom of the gravity well. This seems too good an opportunity to pass up. The last time anyone will be having sex in space, for a long, long time . . ."

Mott clung to Libet.

Libet stroked her back. "Who was the first, do you think? The first orgasm in space."

Mott snorted. "Yuri Gagarin, probably. Or one of those Mercury assholes fulfilling a bet. Maybe even old Al Shepard managed it."

"Oh, come on. He only had fifteen minutes. Even Big Al couldn't have done it in that time. Anyway, those Mercury suits were hard to open up."

"Fifteen minutes. Well, we haven't got much longer."

Libet's hand, warm now, moved over Mott's stomach. "From first to last."

"From first to last," Mott said, and she closed her eyes.

☆   ☆   ☆

She was woken by a buzzer alarm, at 4 a.m. It felt as if she hadn't slept at all.

They prepared a hasty meal: tinned fish and potatoes, tubes of soft cheese, and a vegetable puree that had to be reconstituted with hot water. The rations were Russian standard, and, as usual, tasted salty and heavy with butter and cream to Mott. She drank sweet coffee from a plastic bag with a roll-out spout. She tried not to drink too much; she was going to be in her pressure suit for a long time.

Libet went down to the Soyuz to run a final check, and Mott got herself dressed in her stiff Russian-design pressure suit.

Libet suited up in her turn, and they pressurized each other's suits, making sure they were airtight. Then Mott tested her pressure-release valve, a large knob on the suit's chest panel.

She pocketed some souvenirs: her Swiss army knife, photographs.

By six A.M. they were both ready to leave.

A TV camera was mounted in one corner of the Service Module, all but concealed amid the equipment lockers and cables there. The camera was mute, no red light showing. It looked as if nobody wanted to record these last acts of the American manned space program, two unhappy astronauts clambering into Russian pressure suits.

Mott led the way for the last time out of the Service Module and through the FGB towards Soyuz. Behind her, Libet killed the lights in the Service Module.

The waiting Soyuz was stuck on the side of the FGB, nose-first.

She could see through blister windows in the FGB that the body of the ship was a light blue-green, an oddly beautiful, Earthlike color. The Soyuz looked something like a pepperpot, a bug-like shape nine feet across. Two matte-black solar panels jutted from its rounded flanks, like unfolded wings, and a parabolic antenna was held away from the ship, on a light gantry. Soyuz was basically a Gemini-era craft, still flying in this first decade of a new millennium. And today, Mott and Libet were going to have to ride Soyuz home.

The Soyuz was strictly an assured crew return vehicle, in the nomenclature of the Station project, a simple mechanism for the crew to make it back to Earth in case the Shuttle, the primary crew ferry, couldn't make it in some emergency. The Mission Controllers, down in Houston and Kalinin, had decided that the *Columbia* incident and subsequent Shuttle grounding constituted just such an emergency.

The Soyuz's Orbital Module was a ball stuck to the craft's front end, lined with lockers, just big enough for one person to stretch out. It would be discarded to burn up during the reentry, so Mott and Libet had packed it full of garbage. Now Mott had to struggle through discarded food containers and clothing and equipment wrappers, many of them floating around, to get through to the Descent Module. It was like struggling through a surreal blizzard.

The Descent Module, the headlight-shaped compartment in which they would make their return to Earth, was laid out superficially like an Apollo Command Module, with three lumpy-looking molded couches set out in a fan formation, their lower halves touching. There were two circular windows, facing out beside the two outer seats. Big electronics racks filled up the space beneath the couches, and a large molded compartment on one wall contained the main parachute. Mott slid herself in, feet-first, wriggling until she could feel the contours of the right-hand seat under her. The seat was too short for her, and compressed her at her shoulders and calves.

There was a small, circular pane of glass at Mott's right elbow. She peered out of this now, trying to lose herself in the view of blue Earth.

After a few minutes, Libet floated headfirst into the compartment. She pushed the last of the garbage back into the Orbital Module, and dogged the hatch closed. Then she somersaulted neatly and slid into the center couch, compressing

Mott against the wall; their lower legs were in contact, and there was no space for her to move away.

The two of them began to work through a pre-entry checklist.

At a little after 9.00 A.M., it was time for the undocking. The clamps that held the craft together were released. A spring connector pushed at the Soyuz; there was a gentle thump, and the Soyuz drifted gently away from Station.

For an hour, Libet used the Soyuz's crude hand controller to fly the ferry around Station. Mott was supposed to take a final set of photographs of the abandoned Station before the descent. She had to sit up out of her couch and wedge herself in the small porthole to get the shots.

Mott could see the whole assembly, floating against a curving horizon, with the meniscus of clouds masking the ground below. In the light of Earth, Station was brightly illuminated, a T-shaped mélange of grays, greens, whites. It looked quite delicate and beautiful.

The unfinished Station looked pretty much like *Mir* had, in an early stage of its construction, she supposed. The two main blocks, both orbited by Russian Protons, were the Service Module, a three-crew habitat based closely on the *Mir*'s base block, and the FGB, based on the *Mir*'s *Kvant* supply module. The two modules were squat cylinders, docked end-to-end, punctuated with small round portholes, and coated with thermal insulation, a powdery cloth that was peppered by fist-sized meteorite scars. Small solar panels stretched out to either side of each module, like battered wings, with big charcoal-black cells and fat wires fixed in place with crude blobs of solder. A Progress unmanned ferry, another Soyuz variant, was docked to the Service Module's aft port, on the other side from the FGB.

On the forward port of the FGB was docked the main American contribution to date, a small module called Resource Node 1, which had provided storage space for supplies and equipment, berthing ports, a Shuttle docking port, and attachment points for more modules and the Station's large truss: a gantry that would have stretched all of three hundred and sixty feet long, with the huge photovoltaic arrays stretching out to either side.

But the assembly hadn't got that far. Only the first piece of the truss, a small complex element called Z1, had been hauled up by *Endeavour* and fitted to the top of Node 1. Future flights would have brought up more truss segments, the comparatively luxurious U.S. habitation module, and the multinational lab modules, sleek, modern-looking cylinders the size of railway carriages which would have clustered closely around the Resource Nodes.

In fact, the completed Station would have looked, she thought, like a collision between the twenty-first century and the twentieth—the modern American design, components and concepts inherited from the billions invested in abortive Space Station studies since 1984, forced together with a second-generation Russian *Mir*.

It was all such a waste.

If they'd flown up one more mission, STS-94, at least they'd have had a serious science facility up here. STS-94 would have been the fifth U.S. assembly flight; it would have delivered the first U.S. lab module, complete with thirteen racks of science equipment, life support, maintenance and control gear. And they would have been able to do some real work up here, instead of the small-scale make-work experiments they'd had to run: monitoring herself for drug metabolism by taking saliva samples, checking for radiation health with miniature dosimeters strapped to her body, checking her respiration during exercises on the treadmill, investigating the relationship between bone density and venous pressure by wearing dumb little tourniquets around her ankle . . .

STS-94 had been scheduled for early 1999. Delays, funding cuts and problems with the early Station modules and operations had pushed back its launch five years. And now, it would never fly, and Station would never be completed.

Soyuz was passing over South America. Mott could see the pale fresh water of the Amazon, the current so strong it had still failed to mingle, hundreds of miles off shore, with the dark salt ocean.

The retro rockets fired with a solid thump. For the first time in four months a sensation of weight returned to Mott, and she was pressed into her seat.

When the burn was done, the feeling of weight disappeared. But now the Soyuz was no longer in a free orbit but was falling rapidly towards Earth.

There was something wrong with her eyes. She lifted up her hand, and found salt water, big thick drops of it, welling over her cheeks.

She was crying. Damn it.

"Dabro pazhalavat," Siobhan Libet said softly. "Welcome home."

Through her window now she could see nothing but blackness.

Jake Hadamard called Benacerraf. She was in her room in the Astronaut Office at JSC, poring over a technical reconstruction of the multiple failures that had destroyed *Columbia*'s APUs.

"Hi. I'm here at JSC. Look, I need to talk to you. Can you get away?"

When she heard the Administrator's dry voice, she felt pressure piling up on top of her, a force as tangible as the deceleration which had dragged her down into her canvas seat, during that last reentry from space. What now? "Do you want me to come over?"

"No. Let's get out of here, for a couple of hours. Meet me at the Public Affairs Office parking lot . . ."

It was a bizarre request, but Benacerraf sure as hell needed a break. She pulled on a light white sweatshirt and a broad-brimmed hat, and went out to the elevator.

It was three P.M. on a hot July afternoon.

She emerged into a Mediterranean flat heat—after the dry, cold air-conditioning it was like walking into a wall of dampness—and she was immersed in the steady chirp of crickets. She walked across the courtyard of the JSC campus towards Second Street, which led to the main gate.

The blocky black and white buildings of JSC were scattered over the landscaped lawns like children's blocks, with big black nursery-style identifying numbers on their sides. Between the buildings were Chinese tallow trees and tough, thick-bladed, glowing green Texas grass; sprinklers seemed to work all the time, hissing peacefully, a sound that always reminded her of a Joni Mitchell album she'd gotten too fond of in her teenage years.

But JSC was showing its age. Most of the buildings were more than forty years old; despite the boldness of the chunky 1960s style the buildings themselves were visibly aging, and after decades of budget cutbacks looked shabby: the concrete stained, the paint peeling. On her first visits here she'd been struck by the narrow corridors and gloomy ceiling tiles of many of the older buildings; it was more like some beat-up welfare agency than the core of a space program.

As he'd promised, Jake Hadamard was waiting for her at the car park close to the PAO. The lot was pretty full: old hands said wearily that there hadn't been so much press interest in NASA since *Challenger*.

They piled into Hadamard's car. It was a small '00 Dodge. He drove out through the security barrier, down Second Street, and towards NASA Road One, the public highway. Hadamard grinned. "I have a limousine here I can use, with a driver," he said. "But my job is kind of diffuse. I like to be able to do things personally from time to time."

Benacerraf said, "So, you drive for release."

"I guess."

To the right of Second Street, which ran through the heart of JSC, was the Center's rocket garden. There was a Little Joe—a test rocket for Apollo—and a Mercury-Redstone, looking absurdly small and delicate. The black-and-white-striped Redstone booster was just a simple tube, so slim the Mercury capsule's heat shield overhung it. The Redstone was upright but braced against wind damage with wires; it looked, Benacerraf thought, as if it had been tied to the Earth, Gulliver-style. And, just before the big stone LYNDON B. JOHNSON SPACE CENTER entry sign at NASA One, they passed, on the right, the Big S itself: a Saturn V moon rocket, complete with Apollo, broken into pieces and lying on its side.

A small group of tourists, evidently bussed over from the visitors' center, Space Center Houston, hung about in front of the Redstone. They wore shorts and baseball caps, and their bare skin was coated with image-tattoos, and they looked up at the Redstone with baffled incomprehension.

But then, Benacerraf thought, it was already more than four decades since Alan Shepard's first sub-orbital lob in a tin can like this. Two generations. No wonder these young bedecked visitors looked on these crude Cold War relics with bemusement.

Hadamard pulled out onto NASA Road One, and headed west. As he drove he sat upright, his gray-blond hair close-cropped, his hands resting confidently on the wheel as the car's internal processor took them smoothly through the traffic.

They cut south down West NASA Boulevard, and pulled off the road and into a park. Hadamard drove into a parking area. The lot was empty save for a big yellow school bus.

"Let's walk," Hadamard said.

They got out of the car.

The park was wide, flat, tree-lined, green. The air was still, silent, save for the sharp-edged rustle of crickets, and the distant voices of a bunch of children, presumably decanted from the bus. Benacerraf could see the kids in the middle distance, running back and forth, some kind of sports day.

Hadamard, wearing neat dark sunglasses and a NASA baseball cap, led the way across the field.

Benacerraf took a big breath of air, and swung her arms around in the empty space.

Hadamard grinned at her, and his shades cast dazzling highlights. "Feels like coming home, huh."

"You bet." She thought about it. "You know, I don't think I've walked on grass, except for taking short cuts across the JSC campus, since I got back from orbit."

"You should get out more." He scuffed at the grass with his patent leather shoes. "This is where we belong, after all. Here, on Earth, where we've spent four billion years adapting to the weather."

"So you don't think we ought to be traveling in space."

He shrugged, and patted at his belly. "Not in this kind of design. A big heavy bag of water. Spacecraft are mostly plumbing, after all . . . Humans don't belong up there."

"Oh, come on."

"Well, they don't. You should hear what the scientists say to me. Every time someone sneezes on Station, a microgravity protein growth experiment is wrecked."

Benacerraf said, "You're repeating the criticisms that are coming out in the Commission hearings. You know, it's like 1967 over again, after the Apollo fire."

"Yes, but back then they managed to restrict the inquiries afterward to a NASA internal investigation. And that meant they could keep most of the recommendations technical rather than managerial."

Benacerraf grunted. "Neat trick."

Hadamard laughed. "Well, the Administrator back then was a wily old fox who knew how to play those guys up on the Hill.

But I'm no Jim Webb. After *Challenger* we had a Presidential Commission, just like the one that we're facing now."

They reached the woods, and the seagull-like cries of the children receded.

Eventually they came to a glade. A monument stood on a little square of bark-covered ground, enclosed by the trees, and the dappled sunlight reflected from its upper surface. It was boxlike, waist high, and constructed of some kind of black granite.

It was peaceful here. She wondered what the hell Hadamard wanted.

Jake Hadamard took a deep breath, pulled off his sunglasses, and looked at Benacerraf. "Paula, do you know where you are? When I first came to work at NASA, I was struck by the——" he hesitated "——the invisibility of the *Challenger* incident. I mean, there are plenty of monuments around JSC to the great triumphs of the past, like *Apollo 11*. Pictures on the walls, the flight directors' retirement plaques, Mission Control in Building 30 restored 1960s style as a national monument, for God's sake.

"But *Challenger* might never have happened.

"It's the same if you go around the Visitors' Center. You have your Lego exhibits and your Station displays and your pig-iron toy Shuttles in the playground, and that inspirational music playing on a tape loop all the time. But again, *Challenger* might never have happened.

"*Outside* NASA, it's different. For the rest of us, *Challenger* was one of the defining moments of the 1980s. The moment when a dream died."

He said *us*. Benacerraf found the word startling; she studied Hadamard with new interest.

He said, "Look around Houston and Clear Lake. You have *Challenger* malls and car lots and drug stores . . . And look at this monument."

Benacerraf bent to see. The monument's white lettering

had weathered badly, but she could still make out the Harris County shield inset on the front, and, on the top, the mission patch for *Challenger*'s final flight: against a Stars-and-Stripes background, the doomed orbiter flying around Earth, with those seven too-familiar names around the rim: McNair, Onizuka, Resnik, Scobee, Smith, Jarvis, McAuliffe.

"We're in the *Challenger Seven* Memorial Park," Hadamard said. "You see, what's interesting to me is that this little monument wasn't raised by NASA, but by the local people."

"I don't see what you're getting at, Jake."

"I'm trying to understand how, over two decades, these NASA people have come to terms with the *Challenger* thing. Because I need to learn how to size up the recommendations I'm getting from you for the way forward after *Columbia*."

Benacerraf said, "You want to know if you can trust us."

He didn't smile.

"NASA people didn't launch that Chinese girl into orbit," she said. "And that's the source of the pressure on you to come up with some way to keep flying."

"Is it?"

Benacerraf decided to probe. "You know, now that I'm getting to know you, you aren't what I expected."

He smiled. "Not just a bean counter, a politico on the make? Paula, I am both of those things. I'm not going to deny it, and I'm not ashamed of either of them. We need politicos and bean counters to make our world go round. But—"

"What?"

"I wasn't born an accountant. I was seventeen when *Apollo 11* landed. I painted my room black with stars, and had a big Moon map on the ceiling—"

"You?"

"Sure."

"And you're the NASA Administrator."

He shrugged. "I'm the Administrator who was on watch when *Columbia* turned into a footprint on that salt lake.

"I'm going through hell, frankly, facing that White House Commission. Phil Gamble is getting the whipping in the media, but the Commission are just beating up on me. And then there's the pressure from the Air Force. You know, over the years the Air Force has made some big mistakes chasing manned spaceflight. They wasted a lot of money on projects that didn't come to fruition: the X-20 spaceplane, the Manned Orbiting Laboratory . . . In the 1970s they were pushed into relying on the Shuttle as their sole launch vehicle. That single space policy mistake cost them twenty billion dollars, they tell me, in today's money. And now we got *Columbia*, and the fleet is grounded again. You can bet that if Shuttle never flies again, there will be plenty in USAF who won't shed a tear.

"Now, facing lobbies like that, with institutional rivalries going back a half century, I sure as hell am not prepared to go to bat for any kind of shit-headed NASA insider stuff about how everything is fine and dandy, just another technical glitch we can get over with a little work. Did you know that the NASA management recommended just continuing with the Shuttle launch schedule in the immediate wake of *Challenger*? They had to be *forced* to take a hiatus while they figured out and fixed the problems. You will not find this Administrator making the same mistake."

"I'll tell you how we can minimize risk," Benacerraf said hotly. "We just won't fly. Jake, we're flying experimental aircraft, here. You just can't expect the public to see it this way. We're the professionals. We understand the risks, and we accept them. That's why there are no *Challenger* tombstones and memorials and plaques all over JSC. Jake, you have to have a little taste. You can't keep looking back at some disaster, all the time. We have to move on. We're looking at the future of humanity here, the expansion of the human race into——"

Hadamard waved her silent. "Let's save the speeches, Paula. Besides, I think you are too smart to believe it. The truth is we are never going to move out into deep space. There's nowhere to go.

The Moon's dead, Venus is an inferno, Mars is almost as dead as the Moon. And even if there was a worthwhile destination the journey would kill us. We're not going anywhere, not in our lifetimes, probably not ever. It was always just a dream. People understand that, instinctively, in a way they never did in the 1960s, during Apollo. That's why, I fear, they're sick of spaceflight—Shuttle, the Station—and sick of the people who promote it."

His words, though mildly expressed, seemed brutally hard. Benacerraf shivered, suddenly, despite the continuing warmth of the day. My God, she thought. He's going to let it go. Is that what he's brought me here to tell me?

Here in this nondescript wood, beside this slightly tacky memorial, she could be witnessing the death of the U.S. manned space program.

They turned and began to walk out of the wood, back towards the car.

"Why did you ask to see me, today? What do you want of me?"

"We're going to be hit hard by Congress and the White House and the DoD over *Columbia*, Paula. Whatever I decide, I might not survive myself. And even if I do I'm going to have to shake up many levels of the management hierarchy, in all the centers. I'm trying to think ahead.

"I know I'm going to need someone to take over the Shuttle program. A fresh face. A management outsider, Paula, someone who's untainted by all the NASA crap."

She frowned. "You mean me?"

"You've the right qualifications, the right experience. I've watched how you've handled yourself in the fall-out from *Columbia*, and I've been impressed. And you have the right air of distance from the real insiders."

She said, "My God. You're asking me to oversee the dismantling of the Shuttle program."

"Mothballing, Paula. That's the language we'll use. Look, it's an important job."

"To you?"

He grinned. "Hell, yes, to me. What did you think I meant?"

"But what about all the other programs? The stuff you started after Chinese-Sputnik panic, the RLV initiatives . . ."

"Frankly," Hadamard said, "I don't much care. If some damn Shuttle II ever flies, it will be long after I'm out of the hot seat. And if it ever does fly you know Maclachlan will just shut it down, when he takes the White House. All that matters to me is how to use up the Shuttle technology. That project, unlike RLV, will come to fruition during my term."

Benacerraf got it. It could be that a judicious, sensitively handled wind-down of Shuttle would be the criterion on which Hadamard would be judged: on which the rest of his career might depend.

"Sure. So what about the components? What do we do with the three remaining orbiters?"

"You've heard some of the suggestions. You'll hear more. The dreamers at Marshall want to respond to the Chinese, to go to the Moon. As ever. The USAF want nuclear space battle stations, or to practice sub-orbital bomb runs over Moscow. The Navy want to use the birds as target practice. And so on."

"Do you have a preference?"

"Only that whatever you come up with fits the mood." He smiled sadly. "Anyhow, JSC could use a new lawn ornament. The one we have now is getting a little rusty."

"I understand," she said sourly.

Lawn ornaments. Jesus.

She did understand. Hadamard wanted her to guide what was left of the Shuttle program through the current panic about the Chinese, all the way to the usual run-down and cancellations that would follow.

But, she thought, maybe it didn't have to be like that.

If she took this job, she would move into a position where she could make things happen.

And there are, she thought, other possibilities than turning spaceships into lawn ornaments. Even if doing anything constructive would mean battling past the opposition of a lot of interests, not least the USAF. And even if it would all, it seemed, have to be a race against time, ensuring that whatever was set up was in place before Congressman Xavier Maclachlan became President and had a chance to shoot it in the head . . .

It was a hell of a challenge. But suddenly dreams like Rosenberg's didn't seem so remote. Suddenly she was in a position to move proposals like that out of the realms of thought experiments, even make them happen.

They emerged into the bright sunlight of the field beyond the wood. In the distance, the children continued to play, their calls rising to the sky.

For the first time since hitting the dirt at Edwards, she felt her pulse pick up a beat of excitement.

She said to Hadamard, "I'll do the job." But, she thought, maybe not the way you expect me to.

On Monday morning she moved into her new office at JSC. She called in her secretary and asked him to set up a series of meetings. George, a somber but competent young man with his hair woven into tight plaits, took notes and began his work.

She needed a team. So she made a list for George: Marcus White, the stranded Moonwalker; Barbara Fahy, the woman who had tried to bring *Columbia* home; the young Station astronauts Mott and Libet; Bill Angel, the nearest thing to a competent pilot she knew. And Isaac Rosenberg, the dreamer, the crazy man who wanted to go to Titan.

George went off to set up meetings.

After a few minutes, she called him back in.

"Look, George, things are going to start popping around

here," she said. "I can't tell you what it is right now, but I want you to keep a log of the people I talk to. And keep it in a secure directory."

After all, she reflected, they could be making history here, in the next few weeks and months. Maybe historians of the future would care enough to understand how this decision had come about.

Or, she thought in her gloomier moments, not.

George seemed intrigued, but complied without questioning.

She got to work.

Rosenberg called Paula from Hobby Airport, ten miles southeast of downtown Houston. His plane, from Pasadena, had landed a half-hour late, after four in the afternoon.

"Get a cab to JSC," she told him. "I'll pick you up in my car at security."

Rosenberg hadn't been out this way before. He stood waiting by the security gate on NASA Road One, staring with undisguised curiosity at the aging black-and-white buildings.

From JSC she drove east with the home-bound rush-hour traffic, further out from Houston, heading for Clear Lake.

Benacerraf said, "You ought to do the tourist bit, while you're here. Space Center Houston. They've got a terrific Mars-walk immersive VR. I'm told."

"I prefer RL."

"RL?"

"You don't get online much, do you?"

The road paralleled the north coast of Clear Lake, which was an inlet of Galveston Bay. They passed the glittering tower of the Nassau Bay Hilton, its glass walls coated with softscreen animated posters.

Rosenberg said, "We could be anywhere. Any coast area, anywhere. You wouldn't think—"

"I know." She stared at the shabby roadside buildings, the tough, scrub grass. "Erosion runs fast here," she said. "And now that the space effort is receding—" and the wilder rumors now were that most of the NASA centers, JSC included, were to be mothballed "—all that erosion is going to have a field day. A hundred years from now, JSC will just be a cow pasture again."

"But a cow pasture with immersive VR facilities."

Benacerraf lived on Shorewood Drive, a small road that curved parallel to the shore of Taylor Lake, itself an inlet of Clear Lake. This was the smart residential community called El Lago. Rosenberg stared out the window, without commenting.

She tried to see the little community through his eyes. Home town America, circa 1961: garages and air-conditioners and bicycles and shining lawns, the houses neat and dark with hints of ranch style, or mock Tudor flourishes, or discreet Spanish designs. Uniformly ersatz. Even the trees were all the same age, she realized now.

Give it up, Benacerraf. He's probably thinking how much he needs to pee. El Lago is a dormitory for the Space Age, planned and artificial, no more, no less.

They reached her home. There were four other cars already parked in a ragged row along the side of the road: her other guests, arrived ahead of her, the rest of her team.

She observed Rosenberg sizing up the house.

It was a ranch house, an individually styled bungalow, wood framed with stone cladding. The trees, pine and fern, looked manicured. The lawn was luminous green in the last light of the sun, its little sprinkler heads glittering. At the back of the house was a small private jetty, with space for a couple of boats.

"Nice," Rosenberg said neutrally.

She searched for her key. "Astronaut country, 1960s style. Nice if you come from Illinois. Or if you like the water."

"And you don't?"

She shrugged. "I prefer Seattle. And I don't sail. Anyhow this is rental only."

"Smart."

"Yes. Property prices have been falling like crazy around here, ever since *Columbia*."

She fired the key's infrared beam at the door, and it swung open with a soft hiss of hydraulics.

Benacerraf's housekeeper, Kevin, had let the rest of her guests in. When Benacerraf and Rosenberg arrived, the house-keeper served them drinks and began to lay out dinner.

The guests were gathered in the gazebo. It was a new kind of conservatory, connected to the house by a flexible joint, and mounted on a platform. It rotated to follow the sun, flowerlike.

Rosenberg seemed to love it. "Bradbury," he said.

"What?"

"Never mind. It's just very appropriate."

Everyone had turned up, Benacerraf noted with satisfaction: seven of them—Benacerraf herself with Rosenberg, Marcus White, Bill Angel, Barbara Fahy, and the two younger astro-nauts Benacerraf didn't know so well, Siobhan Libet and Nicola Mott.

Marcus White grinned at Benacerraf. He was working through seven and sevens, and he looked oiled already. He grinned at Rosenberg, around a mouthful of peanuts, and the room's candlelight caught the silvery stubble on his creased cheeks.

"So, Rosenberg. You're the asshole who wants to go to Titan. Why the hell?"

Rosenberg didn't seem awed; he looked back levelly, holding his drink up before him. "Suppose," he said, "you tell me why *you* want to go."

White snorted.

"He has a point, Marcus." Benacerraf had already outlined

the purpose of the dinner party. "Rosenberg thinks Titan is El Dorado, a treasure house of exotic chemicals, even life. But what about you? You wouldn't be here if you weren't interested yourself."

White looked fleetingly embarrassed. To cover, he shoveled more peanuts into his mouth. "What the hell," he said, his lips shiny with grease. "If this comes off, it's the first human flight beyond low Earth orbit since *Apollo 17*. And probably the last. Who wouldn't want to go?"

"Then there's your reason," Bill Angel said. "Titan as Everest. We should go because it's there. Why the hell not?" Benacerraf watched him drain his glass again, his hand like a claw on the frosted surface.

She didn't need to ask why Angel was here. He had no choice. He would find it easier to climb Everest, to go to Titan, than to face himself, alone in a room, with no goals left. She'd seen it before, a dozen times, in the Astronaut Office. The blight of the co-pilot. At least Marcus had the wisdom to know himself. The stories were Angel had been doing a lot of drinking since the *Columbia* incident.

But, she thought, he was competent.

The younger astronauts, Libet and Mott, seemed embarrassed; they dropped their eyes and worked steadily on their drinks.

Barbara Fahy cleared her throat. "The way I figure nobody is going the hell anywhere, let alone Titan." She looked around, at a circle of glum faces. "I mean it. It's just unworkable."

Benacerraf said mildly, "How so?"

Fahy said, "I've done some back-of-the-envelope figuring. How do you fly to Saturn? Saturn is ten times as far from the sun as Earth, remember. A Hohmann orbit, a minimum-energy transfer—which is all we could manage with chemical technology, which is all we got—would be a long, skinny ellipse touching Earth's orbit at one extreme, and Saturn's at the other. It would take six years to get there. Then you'd have to wait out a year at Saturn, until the planets got back into their correct alignment, and ride out the other half of the ellipse, back home. Total mission time thirteen years. Now, what size crew are you talking about? Five, six? How the hell are you going to supply and sustain a crew for a thirteen-year mission—all of it isolated from Earth? Christ, the longest missions we've run in Earth orbit without resupply are only a couple of months—"

"ISRU," said Siobhan Libet.

Fahy looked at her. "Huh?"

Rosenberg said, "She's right. In-situ resource utilization. You wouldn't carry food for the Titan stopover. We're landing, remember? There's carbon, hydrogen, oxygen, nitrogen down there. All sorts of organic and carbohydrate compounds."

"So that gets you through the year stopover. Maybe you could even resupply for the journey home," Fahy said. "But the main point still stands. You'd need to carry fuel to slow into Titan orbit. And all that fuel has to be hauled up and launched, in its turn, from an initial low Earth orbit. The numbers just multiply.

"I figure you're looking at millions of pounds of fuel to be hauled up to low Earth orbit. And the cargo capacity of the Shuttle to LEO is only sixty-five thousand pounds. Are you seriously proposing thirty, forty Shuttle missions?"

"But you'd use gravity assists," Nicola Mott said. "Wouldn't you? Like *Cassini*. You wouldn't follow a simple Hohmann trajectory. You'd play the usual interplanetary pool: bounce off Earth, Venus, Jupiter maybe, and each time steal a little of their energy of rotation around the sun."

"Fine," said Angel thickly, "but if you're talking about going in to Venus you'd have to carry sun-shields, and—"

"Details," Marcus White said. "Fucking details. You always were a windy bastard, Angel."

Angel grinned. He said, "Okay. But even if you cut your initial mass in LEO by, say, fifty percent, you're still looking at dozens of Shuttle launches. And there's no way Hadamard would back such a mission."

Barbara Fahy sighed. "He's right, I'm afraid."

"No, he isn't," Isaac Rosenberg said. "You're making the wrong assumptions."

Angel said, "Huh?"

Rosenberg said mildly, "What if you don't come home?"

There was a long silence.

Kevin, the housekeeper, called them to eat.

The meal was set up in small china dishes on candle-heated plate-warmers, all arranged on a big rotating serving platform on top of Benacerraf's favorite piece of furniture, her walnut dining table. There was hot and sour soup, spare ribs, chicken in ginger, corn with spring onions, Szechuan prawns, and a variety of rice and noodle plates; there was water, beer and wine on the table.

Angel drained his glass again. "That kid of yours fixes a good drink," he said.

"Yes. He's a good cook, too."

White said, "What is he, working his way through college?"

". . . Something like that." She left it there. She doubted that White, who'd spent his adult life in the monkish confines of the space program, would understand much more.

Kevin, from Galveston, was a pleasant, plump boy, twenty-three years old, already a college graduate. Actually he was earning his keep while he paid off his college debt, and pursued his art.

Benacerraf had given him a garage, to use as a studio. Once, Kevin had shown Benacerraf his work. It was sculpture. The main piece was a large block of rendered animal-fat, made into a half-scale self-portrait of Kevin. The statue showed Kevin lowering his shorts and stroking his own genitals. The statue hadn't been carved; Kevin had gnawed it, crudely, with his teeth. The marks of the teeth were clearly visible, especially where Kevin had used his chipped left incisor. Kevin explained that this was only a sketch; the final version would be made of human fat liposuctioned from his own body. Or maybe his feces.

Benacerraf didn't go back into the garage after that.

The thing of it was, Kevin didn't have any other skills. He was a college graduate; his degree had been in recursive and self-referential art, with special studies of the greats of the 1990s: Janine Antoni, Sean Landers, Gregory Green, Charles Long.

Demographic projections for Kevin's age-group—with modern medical care, preventative programs, reduced-calorie dieting and prosthetics—predicted a full century of active life ahead of him. That, thought Benacerraf, provided time for a lot of shit-gnawing.

At that, gnawing shit was better than creating nothing at all, which was to be the fate, as far as Benacerraf could see, of most of Kevin's generation, as they lay in their VR-beds and pushed increasingly stale, second-hand information around the net.

Kevin, anyhow, was a satisfactory housekeeper. Benacerraf paid his wages, and tried not to think about his future. She didn't see what else she could do for him, or the millions like him, unemployed and unemployable . . .

The seven of them gathered around the table and began to spoon food into their small bowls. Everyone but Marcus White opted to use chopsticks.

Benacerraf, looking around at the ring of relaxed, candlelit faces, felt pleased. There was a warm, friendly, domestic atmosphere here; they were seven humans, rooted to the Earth, enjoying a shared ritual that dated back to the emergence of humanity.

Her purpose, tonight, was to try to build this group into a team, who would have to work together to achieve something no other humans had attempted and, if, impossibly, this proposal came to fruition, some of whom might soon depart the Earth forever.

She still hadn't decided whether to put her weight behind

this dumb-ass Titan proposal. Up to now, it had just been a hobby, something to take her mind off the hierarchy of Flight Readiness Review records from STS-143. The reaction of the group, tonight, could decide that.

They started talking about Titan again.

Nicola Mott said, "Let me go through this again. From the top. You're seriously suggesting that we send a manned mission. That we travel one way, to colonize Titan."

"Why not?" Rosenberg said. "Maybe we're done with dipping our toes in the water and running."

"Like with Apollo," Marcus White said heavily.

"Like with Apollo."

Rosenberg said, "Look, the whole point of this proposal is that we're going to prove that a colony on Titan would be viable. More than that: it would soon become an actual economic asset to the United States, to Earth. How are we going to do that, if we aren't prepared to put ourselves on the line, give up a few home comforts?" He sounded irritated, frustrated at his inability to communicate, their inability to *see*. "We go out there to stay for years, build a home, survive until a retrieval capability is put together. We cannibalize the ship that carries us, turn it into surface shelters. We use ISRU, as Siobhan says. We make Titan such an attractive place that resupply and retrieval missions have to follow."

Marcus White said, " 'We,' Rosenberg?"

"Yes." He looked uncomfortable, the candlelight shining from his glasses. "If there's a ship going to Titan, I want to be on it. I'm best qualified. Isn't that what this is all about?"

White grinned. "Hell, yes. I'd go myself."

In the silence that followed, the others stared at him.

"When I walked on that lava plain south of Copernicus, with Tom Lamb, I sure as hell never figured I'd only get the one shot at it. There would have been an extended-Apollo program, with lunar orbital missions, and long-stay shelters hauled up by dual-launched Saturn Vs, and all the rest. And then more: flyby flights to Venus and Mars, the space station, permanent colonies on the Moon, eventually landing flights to Mars itself . . .

"But the whole damn thing shut down, even before Armstrong stepped out at Tranquillity." He put down his drink, and the fingers of his big hands knitted together, restless. "I must have talked about my Moon trip a thousand times. Ten thousand. And the one thing I've never managed to put over is how it feels *not to be able to get back*. Ever." He grinned at Benacerraf, embarrassed, uneasy. "They should shoot us poor fucking Moonwalkers in the head. Anyhow, it won't be me. I realize that. Christ, I'm seventy-four years old, already. I'm a grandpa three times over. But I'll tell you, I'd just like to see one more guy lift off out of the gravity well and *go* someplace—plant Old Glory on one more moon—before the last of us sad old Apollo geezers dies of old age."

"And," Mott pressed, "if we don't succeed? —if Earth doesn't jump for the bait? If we set out, and they just let the space facilities rust? What then?"

Marcus White leaned towards Mott over the table. "The question for you is, having heard that—would you go?"

Mott thought for a moment. She opened her mouth.

But, Benacerraf noted, she didn't immediately say no.

White leaned back. "You know, they used to ask us a question like that, during our interviews for the Astronaut Office. *Marcus, would you submit to a two-year journey to Mars? Suppose I tell you that the chances of surviving the trip are one in two. Do you go?* Absolutely not, said I. Nine in ten, maybe." He looked at Mott. "I got it right. The point was partly to see how dumb I was, how foolhardy. But also to find out if I had it in me."

"What?"

"Wanderlust."

Rosenberg said, "Being an astronaut on this mission won't be just another job, a line on your résumé. This will be about going somewhere, where nobody else has ever been. Making a difference. What the job used to be about."

White laughed. "That," he said, "and glory, and fast cars, and the women."

"I get it," Siobhan Libet said. "This isn't Apollo. It's a *Mayflower* option."

"Maybe," Barbara Fahy murmured. "The *Mayflower* colonists went because they had to. They did it because they couldn't find a place to fit, at home."

Marcus White grunted. "There sure as hell has been little enough room on Earth for astronauts, since 1972."

Rosenberg said, "The costs don't have to defeat us. We don't need any massive technical development. We use chemical propulsion, existing technology wherever possible. For instance, the Space Station hab module for the journey shelter."

Benacerraf nodded confirmation of that. "The thing's been sitting in a hangar at Boeing, intact, since 1999. It wouldn't take much modification . . ."

Rosenberg said, "You'd wrap a cut-down Shuttle orbiter around it. With the hab module in the cargo bay, you'd use the orbiter's OMS and RCS for course corrections, and the main engines for the interplanetary injections."

Angel and White exchanged glances.

White said, "A Shuttle orbiter to Saturn? Well, why the hell not? It's the nearest thing to a spaceship we got." He turned to Rosenberg, grinning. "You know, I *love* the way you think."

Angel said, "How are you going to get a Space Station hab module down to the surface of Titan?"

"Easy," Rosenberg said, chewing. "Titan has a thick atmosphere, and a low gravity. You'd *glide* the hab module down, inside your Shuttle orbiter. Which is why you'd take the orbiter. The aerosurfaces would need some modification, but—"

"Holy shit," Libet said. "You've worked this out. You're serious, aren't you, kid?"

Angel said, "Okay, so this is just a mind game, right? A bull session. Maybe you're right, Rosenberg. Maybe you could do that quickly and cheaply. But not if you wanted a man-rated system."

Siobhan Libet said, "But we aren't talking about the kind of assured safety we have in the current program, Bill. We know this whole thing would be risky as hell."

Bill Angel said curtly, "I'm talking about some kind of entry profile that would actually be survivable."

"It wouldn't have to be," Rosenberg said.

Marcus White groaned and helped himself to some more wine. "Oh, shit," he said. "He has another idea."

"Send the orbiter down to Titan unmanned," Rosenberg said. "Then it can land as hard as you like."

"And what about the crew?" Angel said.

"All you need is a couple of simple man-rated entry capsules," Rosenberg said. "Remember, we aren't talking about any kind of ascent-to-orbit capability; it's a one-way trip." He grinned. "You still aren't thinking big enough, Bill."

"And you," Angel snapped back, "are talking out of your ass. An entry capsule like that is still a billion-dollar development. We just don't have that kind of resource."

Rosenberg looked flustered, and Benacerraf realized that for the first time he didn't have an answer.

She felt an immense sadness descend on her. Is it possible that this is the hole that destroys the proposal? That, after all, it ends here?

How sad. It was a beautiful dream, while it lasted.

They argued for a while, about requirements and likely costs. It started to get heated, with gestures illustrated by pointed chopsticks. Barbara Fahy held her hands up, palms outward. "Hold it," she said. "I hate to say it, but I think I have a solution."

Benacerraf frowned. "Tell me."

Fahy looked around the table. "We use the most advanced entry capsules we ever built. Apollo Command Modules."

Marcus White was laughing. "Oh, man. That is outrageous. Just fucking outrageous. It's beautiful. Man, I love it."

Fahy said, "All you'd have to do is refurbish the interior, maybe fix up the heatshield, reconfigure for a Titan entry profile."

Benacerraf said, "Marcus, where's the old Apollo hardware now?"

White was trying to be serious, but grins kept busting out over his face. "There were three series of Command Modules: boilerplates, Block Is and Block IIs. The Block IIs flew all the manned missions; they contained most of the post-fire modifications. The Block IIs are what you'd want to use." He closed his eyes. "As I recall, Rockwell built twenty-five Block II CMs in all. Okay. Of those twenty-five ships, eleven flew on the Apollo Moon program. Three more flew manned Skylab missions, and one flew on ASTP. Fifteen, right?"

"Where are they?" Benacerraf asked. "Museums? Could we refurbish an Apollo that's already been flown?"

Angel frowned. "I don't see how. Those things were pretty much beat up by the time they were recovered. You got the ablation of the heatshield, thermal stresses throughout the structure, salt-water damage from the ocean recovery. The heatshield alone would be a hell of a reconstruction job."

Benacerraf said, "Marcus, what happened to the ten spares? Do you remember?"

"I sure do," he said ruefully. "Since they symbolized my career, as it went down the toilet, I followed the fate of those Moon ships with close interest." He closed his eyes. "They used four for various tests: thermal vacuum and pogo, acoustic, pad checkout. And another three for Skylab tests. They pretty much took those babies apart, for the purposes of the tests."

"That leaves three," Angel said evenly.

"Yeah. First you got a Skylab backup. It sat on the pad on top of a Saturn IB as a rescue capability, through the whole Skylab program. And then there were two Moon-trip Apollos, never flown. 'Requirement deleted.' Three man-rated spacecraft, never flown, just mothballed."

Benacerraf felt herself smile. "Maybe we're about to undelete those requirements."

There was another moment of silence.

Then they started to talk at once. "Where are those CMs?" "All in storage at JSC, or Downey." "Three CMs. Two flight birds and one test vehicle, for verifying the redesign and refurbishment." "The electronics should be easy. Those old clunky guidance computers they had took up so much damned room. All that core rope and shit . . ."

Benacerraf let it run on.

It's coming together, she thought. She felt a core of excitement gather in her gut.

Angel, still drinking hard, was doodling spacecraft configurations and shapes on a smoothed-out paper napkin. "Okay," he said. "If we're going to do this one-way shot, we ought to get away with a fuel load, in Earth orbit, of one and a half million pounds. And of that, around two hundred thousand pounds would be hauled out to Saturn for braking there."

"That," said Benacerraf, "is less than a single Shuttle External Tank."

"Yeah," White growled. "But you're still looking at a couple of dozen Shuttle flights to put it up there."

Siobhan Libet said, "But you wouldn't need to use the full Shuttle system. You're not carrying crew, except on one final flight to orbit."

Benacerraf prompted, "So what do we do instead?"

"Shuttle-C," said Libet promptly. "A stripped-down cargo-carrying variant of the Shuttle system. The payload capacity would be raised to a hundred and seventy thousand pounds."

Mott nodded. "But the Shuttle-C is an expendable variant. Essentially you'd be using up the orbiter fleet."

"But that doesn't matter," Libet said.

"She's right," White said. "Nicola, we're working to different rules now. The damn things wouldn't fly again anyhow. It's a choice of putting them to work one last time, or stick 'em out in the rain as monuments."

"Okay. But even so this is only a partial solution," Angel said. "We have three orbiters left: *Endeavour*, *Atlantis*, *Discovery*. You'd want to retain one for the final crew launch, so you're left with two Shuttle-C launches. That would only account for a quarter, maybe, of the total mass in LEO for Titan."

Libet said, "There were two more pre-flight orbiters."

"Yes," said Benacerraf. "*Enterprise* and *Pathfinder*. Now, what the hell happened to them?" She went to a bookcase, and searched through her yellowing Shuttle training materials. "Here we go. 'Shuttle Orbiter *Enterprise*: Orbiter Vehicle-101. *Enterprise*, the first Space Shuttle orbiter, was originally to be named *Constitution*, for the Bicentennial. However, *Star Trek* viewers started a write-in campaign urging the White House to rename the vehicle to *Enterprise* . . . blah blah . . . OV-101 was rolled out of Rockwell's Air Force Plant 42, Site—'"

White shrugged. "They used *Enterprise* for the approach and landing tests. Then they decided it would cost too much to upgrade *Enterprise* for spaceflight. Tough on all those propellerhead *Star Trek* fans. So they stripped her. She's a museum piece now."

Libet asked, "What about *Pathfinder*?"

Benacerraf dug through her documents. "'The *Pathfinder* Shuttle Test Article . . . *Pathfinder* is a seventy-five ton orbiter simulator that was created to work out the procedures for moving and handling the Shuttle. It was a steel structure roughly the size, weight and shape of an orbiter . . . *Pathfinder* was returned to Marshall and now is on permanent display at the Alabama Space and Rocket Center in Huntsville—'"

Libet said, "I imagine *Pathfinder* would be a lot more problematic to adapt for Shuttle-C than *Enterprise*, or the flight orbiters. But if we can do it—"

"Then," Barbara Fahy said, "you'd have four Shuttle-Cs. But they still aren't enough."

"No." Angel scratched numbers quickly on his napkin. "We still need twice the carrying capacity. What else?"

"The Energiya," Rosenberg said. "The old Soviet heavy-lift booster. How about that? What was its lifting capacity?"

"Three hundred thousand pounds to LEO," Angel said.

"So," Rosenberg said, "two or three Energiya launches—"

"I don't think it would work," Siobhan Libet said. "I'm sorry." Benacerraf could see she was genuinely regretful. "I was shown around the Energiya facilities at Tyuratam when I was training for Soyuz Station return. Actually the Energiya facility was built on the site of their old N–1 launch facility, the Soviets' attempt at a lunar-mission heavy-lift booster. The Russians have killed it. The integration hall is—spectral. Full of moth-balled strap-on boosters, tanks, engines, other Energiya components, pretty much deteriorated; I don't think it could be refurbished."

"Damn waste of time and money," White said. "I once saw one of their Shuttle flight models. They've set it up in Gorky Park, for kids to play at being astronauts."

Angel blew out his cheeks. "So we're stuck again. What else?"

"We could go to the Air Force," Siobhan Libet said. "Use their heavy-lift boosters, the new Delta IVs."

Benacerraf shook her head. "We could try an approach, but they wouldn't buy it. Believe me, I've seen enough politics since *Columbia*. The USAF will hinder us, not cooperate. Anyhow, Delta can't lift more than forty thousand pounds to LEO. The number of launches required would be prohibitive."

"Then we're screwed," Angel said. He threw his pen down on the table, and crumpled up his napkin.

But Marcus White was grinning. He scratched his cheek; the stubble made a rasping noise against his fingernails. "Lawn ornaments," he said.

Angel, his arms folded, looked at him. "What?"

"You know, there are NASA centers with Moon rockets lying around on their driveways, for dumb fucking kids to gawp at. JSC, Kennedy, Michoud, Marshall. Now, what if—"

"You're kidding," Angel said.

"I'm only talking about refurbishing the existing flight hardware, and a few test engines, not reviving the whole damn production line. All you'd have to do is bring the things in from the rain, scrape off the moss, give them a fresh lick of paint . . . I know they have some engines in bonded storage, down at Michoud. And I'll bet there are still a few of those old bastards around who worked on the original development in the 1960s."

Barbara Fahy frowned. "I guess it could be done. The old launch complexes at the Cape, 39-A and 39-B, are still operational. They were adapted for Shuttle."

"Then they can be unadapted," White snapped back.

Angel was figuring. "So to complement our four Shuttle-C launches, and allowing a margin for boiloff, assembly equipment—we'd need four launches."

"And four birds," White said, "is what we got, lying around." He counted on his fingers. "There are two operational articles—AS-514 and -515, from the deleted Moon flights—at JSC and Michoud. Then you have two test articles, AS-500D and -500T, at Marshall and Kennedy. I guess bringing them up to specification would be more of a challenge, but I bet it could be done." White looked triumphant, somehow vindicated, Benacerraf thought. "I'd love to see those birds fired off at last, after all these years. The idea of those spaceships just lying around in the rain has always bugged me . . ."

"And if we can do that," Angel said, 'then it's feasible. We have enough heavy-lift capability." He looked at Rosenberg and laughed. "Good grief, Rosenberg. I think we've done it; we've found a way to close the design."

Libet looked confused, as this talk swirled around her. "What are you talking about?"

Mott took her hand and squeezed it gently. "Saturn Vs," she said. "They're talking about flying Saturn Vs again . . ."

"Oh," said Libet. "Oh, my God."

They talked on, debating details and approaches, as the candles burned steadily down.

The one topic they never approached—as if skirting around it—was the risk.

If the risk of not returning from an Apollo flight had been something like one in ten—and most engineers agreed the risk on Shuttle was around one in a hundred—and given the distances and the extent of this venture outside of the experience base and the difficulty of maintaining political will behind a project spanning so many years—what was the risk of not returning from Titan?

A lot worse than fifty-fifty, Benacerraf thought. Each of them, here, was signing up for Russian roulette, with the barrels loaded against them. And each of them had to know that.

But they were prepared to go anyhow. They all had to be crazy, by any conventional definition.

They were a motley crew, Benacerraf thought: Rosenberg the dreamer, Fahy the tough, wounded engineer, Angel the burned-up, goal-oriented drinker, White the stranded Moonwalker, Libet and Mott younger, enigmatic, but still, she sensed, touched with the wanderlust. And herself: determined to do something with the rest of her life other than just survive *Columbia*.

Flawed people, all of them. And not one of them had anything to live for that was more meaningful than dreams of a jaunt to Titan.

Maybe that was necessary; maybe it had always been true. Who else would go on such a mission? Nobody happy with her life, that was for sure.

And who would come up with such a vision, she thought, but a misfit like Rosenberg? Rosenberg, with his sense of his place in the cosmos—a sense of depth, change, flux—that sense that he doesn't belong here, that he's a mere conduit of celestial matters and forces . . .

Yeah. A better sense of the Universe than of what's going on in the heads of his fellow human beings.

Maybe NASA had been wise, all these years, to neglect the psychology of its space travelers. Maybe that was the only possible approach. In this room alone there was probably enough material for a three-day shrinks' conference.

But what the hell. All that mattered was—she had her team.

And it was some dream. With a colony on Titan—even one scraping a precarious living from the slush—it just wouldn't be possible for the folks here at home to slump back into some kind of flat-Earth mentality. The Universe would always be alive, with humans living on an island up in the sky.

Maybe, she thought, Rosenberg is single-handedly saving the future.

Now, she thought wryly, all they had to do was convince NASA, the Government, and the rest of the goddamn human race to let them do this. The real work started here.

Kevin, the housekeeper, came in to clear up the dishes and deliver coffee and more drinks. Benacerraf watched him as he worked, the heady talk of Titan and Shuttle-Cs and Apollos flowing around him. Kevin's smooth, moonlike face was blank, incurious; Benacerraf doubted he heard a word that was said.

He had a new image-tattoo on his forehead, Benacerraf saw. The lozenge-shaped patch of glowing photochemicals cycled through images of smoky star-clusters, evidently downloaded from one of the Hubble picture libraries.

She found she'd made her decision.

Here, in this room, she thought, it starts. And it won't end until we land on Titan.

As he left, Marcus White winked at Benacerraf. "Everest, El Dorado, *Mayflower*. I don't know whether we're going to Titan or not, or why the hell. But you sure do throw one great party, kid."

The first task was to flesh out the mission profile.

Benacerraf set Barbara Fahy working on the feasibility of adapting mission control software and techniques to handle the Saturn and Shuttle-C launches, and the extended mission profile after that.

She quickly came back to Benacerraf with a schedule and costing. Fahy had shown how STS mission control techniques could be adapted with a little effort to run Shuttle-C and revived Saturn programs. Then, looking ahead for a feasible way to run a manned mission to Saturn, Fahy argued that you didn't want to have a full team of controllers employed for all six or eight or ten years. Fahy's projection showed how a scaled-down Mission Control operation would suffice to run the flight itself after the initial interplanetary injection sequence; hands-off techniques developed to run extended Earth-orbit operations aboard Station could be adapted. It would be necessary to rehire staff or attach contract workers during the later crucial mission phases, like a Jupiter encounter. But it could all be done for a containable cost.

Benacerraf was working to a timetable she hadn't yet shared with many people. And to her, the setup schedule even for this ground-based aspect of the mission looked tight. But then, *everything* would be tight, pushing against the clock, until the last Shuttle lifted off the pad . . .

Benacerraf worked through Fahy's case carefully.

Barbara Fahy was almost pathetically eager to work on this proposal, to find some way of redeeming her self-respect after being lead Flight on *Columbia*. It seemed to do no good to point out that Fahy was not responsible for the hardware and testing flaws that had led to the orbiter's destruction, that no blame had been attached to her—that, in fact, her career had been done no perceptible damage at all.

As far as Fahy was concerned, it had been her mission. And she'd lost it.

Still, her judgment was unimpaired; her work on this issue looked good.

Benacerraf accepted the recommendation, but a seed of doubt lodged in her mind. A scaled down Mission Control would be fine, but if some kind of *Apollo 13* situation blew up, halfway to Jupiter, the crew would need fast backup by experts on the ground: revised procedures, survival techniques, simulator proving . . . there mightn't be time to hire up and train the people needed.

Anyhow, with that basic framework in hand, Barbara Fahy called in the senior members of her control team, and, with Benacerraf, talked them through the proposed flight.

They listened in silence—stunned, frightened silence, Benacerraf thought.

If NASA sent a spacecraft to Saturn, it would be these young, smart people or their peers who would have the responsibility for seeing that all the burns happened at the right times, for the right durations, with the spacecraft in the right attitudes; they would have to oversee navigation all the way to Titan, and prepare abort contingency plans.

There was a lot of skepticism. Even hostility. "How do you think we're gonna do this?" "We can't possibly. All our systems are designed for low Earth orbit missions." "How can you think—"

Fahy knew her people, however, and she let them run down. "Just chew it over for a few days," she told them. "You don't have to come up with all the answers at once. And talk to people. Talk to the Apollo old-timers, about the problems of deep space manned missions. Talk to the guys at JPL, about interplanetary navigation techniques. I know it's one hell of a challenge, guys, the biggest since Apollo—"

"But," said one languid young man—introduced by Fahy as Gary Munn— "those 1960s guys could look forward to some kind of career within NASA. More than one mission, a future. Not just a one-off stunt like this."

Fahy glared at him. "We're talking about going to Saturn, for God's sake. The greatest adventure in human history. A journey that will be talked about as long as mankind survives. An exploration that even eclipses Armstrong's. Don't you *care* about being a part of that?"

But Munn just stared back, his expression unreadable to Benacerraf.

I really don't understand this new generation, she thought.

After a couple of days, Benacerraf had Fahy and her planners host a wider meeting at which the details of the mission were explored. Big, powerful suites of trajectory-mapping software— primed with precise predictions of the planets' positions for decades to come—were deployed by the planners, running through option after option, with mission duration and initial mass in Earth orbit numbers scrolling over spread-out soft-screens.

The programs soon converged on an optimal trajectory. It was essentially similar to the complex path taken by *Cassini* to make the same trip, with the early part of the trajectory wrapped around the inner planets, slingshots off Earth and Venus, before unwinding towards the outer Solar System, and a final gravity assist from Jupiter. The meeting argued around the details and parameters, before settling on a recommendation:

To launch in January, 2008.

It would be, Benacerraf realized, one hell of a tight development schedule. Maybe even unachievable.

But it fit her internal timetable. It would be a whole year before Maclachlan was scheduled to take office and ground everything, and only a year for the bad guys in the USAF and beyond to find a way to close down NASA, and maybe not so far in the future that all of the current post-Chinese push back into space had worn off.

There really was no choice. The window of opportunity was closing quickly. If Americans were going to travel beyond the Moon, it would have to be in 2008. Or *never*.

Benacerraf studied the smooth trajectory curves scrolling across the softscreens. "We understand this stuff so well," she said to Fahy. "It's astonishing how quickly we can produce material like this."

"Oh, yes," Barbara Fahy said sourly. "Our civilization has become expert at interplanetary navigation. It's just that we've chosen to abandon the capability to *do* any of it."

"Actually," Gary Munn said brightly, "we can run the projections forward and back. Even as far back as the 1960s there were proposals to slingshot off Venus and fly to Mars, and so forth, in the near future of the time; it's interesting to move the planets back to their configurations, in 1982 or 1986, and see how accurately those old guys got their predictions." He worked his keypad briskly, and Benacerraf watched trajectory curves wrap around the sun, depicting the paths of spacecraft that never were, traveling to Mars in 1982 and 1986 and 1992.

To Benacerraf, this precise, beautiful, useless rendering of all those lost missions was painful, almost physically.

Munn whistled as he worked the programs.

Benacerraf called in Mal Beardsley, her assistant program manager responsible for flight safety.

Mal was a bluff old-timer who had come in from solid-booster supplier Morton Thiokol after the *Challenger* accident, and he thought she was crazy. They spent a half-hour Benacerraf couldn't really afford debating the pros and cons of the mission.

Beardsley left the room, grinning and tapping his graying temple. It was a reaction that Benacerraf figured she was going to have to get used to, and she forced a smile.

Still, Beardsley had a report in her softscreen within two days.

Beardsley had tried to devise abort options for the Titan mission.

A key objective in NASA mission planning had always been to provide abort options. And that philosophy had borne a lot of fruit. Even the use of the Lunar Module as a lifeboat, after the *Apollo 13* Service Module was crippled, had been practiced on an earlier flight. After *Challenger*, many more abort possibilities were built into the Shuttle mission profile, particularly the ascent phase. It all increased the survivability of the flights, on paper and in practice.

The flight to Earth orbit would be no real problem; standard Shuttle abort modes would be sufficient. And after the Titan ship left orbit, firing up its Shuttle main engines, abort options were still available: for instance, if the main engines malfunctioned, they could be shut down and the smaller OMS and RCS engines used to bring the craft around a huge U-turn and back to Earth. That would work up to a point, anyhow. Once the main engines had burned for long enough to apply more delta-vee than the OMS and RCS could compensate for, the crew would be committed to an interplanetary flight of some kind. But even here, aborts were possible. The craft could modify its trajectory and slingshot around Venus, back to an early rendezvous with Earth. Even a slingshot back home around Jupiter would be possible.

Of course the problems of reentry from such an interplanetary jaunt would be formidable. Beardsley figured that the Apollo Command Modules, which had been built to withstand a direct entry into Earth's atmosphere from the Moon, would be the most survivable possibility for the crew, and he recommended strongly against weakening the Apollos' heatshields.

It would be one hell of an abort, however, Benacerraf reflected: the round trip to Venus or Jupiter would take months, even years, during which time the crew would presumably be struggling to survive in a crippled ship.

Past Jupiter, even Beardsley could find no meaningful aborts.

☆   ☆   ☆

She started to make contacts with other senior NASA managers.

One of the first was with the JSC director, a tough, cost-conscious woman in her sixties called Millie Rimini. Benacerraf walked up two flights of stairs to Rimini's office, and took in Barbara Fahy to give her pitch more technical plausibility.

Rimini's job, as Benacerraf understood it, was—post-*Columbia*—to manage the rundown of JSC, to complete a part of Hadamard's greater mission. So Benacerraf pitched the Titan mission as part makework, part cosmetic. Maybe the mission would actually save some jobs, at JSC. At worst, it would create a buzz of enthusiasm and raise morale; being able to work on a new program would sweeten the pill, for many, of the transfers and early retirements and layoffs that were to come. And so on. And the same applied to all the NASA centers.

Benacerraf had run big-budget engineering projects before; she knew how these things worked. People weren't usually self-less; people sought to achieve their own personal goals, and treated projects as an arena in which to achieve those goals. In successful projects, the goals of the key players were in line with those of the project. Thus, managers like Rimini had to see benefits for themselves in the proposal, ways they could use it to achieve their own objectives, even as the Shuttles lifted off for Saturn. It was up to Benacerraf to figure out those benefits and present them.

It took a morning to convince Rimini that they should work seriously on this.

After that, Rimini encouraged Benacerraf to take the proposal to a wider group of NASA managers. Rimini set up a meeting at Marshall Spaceflight Center, in Alabama, of senior officials from Houston, the Cape, and Marshall, and from relevant NASA internal divisions. Rimini chaired the meeting.

Benacerraf was surprised to meet some opposition from the hard-line space buffs in some of the centers. The Cape managers, primed by a sweet-talk approach by Marcus White, could see no showstopper obstacles to refurbishing a Saturn launch complex, given the time and money. And the Shuttle-C flights would just be variants on STS launch procedures they'd already run a hundred and forty-three times—simplified variants, at that. But the old guys from Marshall, with their tough, conservative, confrontational approach to engineering that dated all the way back to Wernher von Braun, were more resistant. This stuff is only one chart deep, she was told. This is all way outside the experience base. Going to Saturn with chemical technology is a spectacularly dumb thing to do. What we have to do is revive the NERVA fission rocket program, and launch a set of nuclear stages into orbit in Shuttle orbiters, and, and . . .

It wasn't hard to point out that nobody was going to endorse putting a nuclear rocket through the dangers of a Shuttle launch. Or, come to that, any near-future successor to the Shuttle. And besides, a program like NERVA, shut down in 1970, would cost billions to revive, if you were going to do it cleanly.

It was true. Going to Saturn with chemical was a dumb thing to do, dumb almost to the point of infeasibility. Like exploring Antarctica in a skiff. But it was the only boat leaving port, for the foreseeable future.

Slowly the Marshall people came round.

They all agreed to work on the proposal some more; it wasn't yet time, they concurred, to take this to Jake Hadamard.

The work went on, sometimes around the clock. Benacerraf asked Millie Rimini to chair a critical review of the proposal, at JSC. It took two days of intensive briefings. Benacerraf had steeled herself to play devil's advocate if she had to, to make sure all the tough questions were asked and answered. She found it wasn't necessary; there was more than enough skepticism in the air, and the two days were long and hard.

Even so, the conclusion was that there was no technical obstacle to the Saturn flight.

Still Benacerraf wasn't satisfied.

She had Beardsley run another safety review of the proposal, and she held a further briefing with senior Shuttle program executives and representatives of the principal contractors. Later, Rimini hosted a NASA management meeting at NASA Headquarters in Washington, to go over everything one more time. Then Benacerraf held a series of smaller, informal meetings with her key players, rehearsing and rehashing the arguments . . .

And on, and on.

Through all this, Benacerraf planned and replanned her campaign. It was going to take eighteen months, of figuring and investigating and re-evaluating. And all the time she was consciously building momentum, the Big Mo, behind her plan, working to persuade people that, yes, they could do this thing—that they *should* do this thing. If NASA could send *Apollo 8* around the Moon on the first manned Saturn V, then surely, after five decades of spaceflight, it could assemble the will for this one last effort . . .

On the whole, the response was good. But then, she hadn't yet attempted to take the proposal outside NASA's inner circles. And—aging and stale as they might be—most people who worked for NASA, even now, were pretty much space nuts.

NASA insiders were just the type to love crazy ideas like going to Titan. And NASA's overenthusiasm had, she knew, caused a kind of collective lapse in good political judgment many times before. NASA insiders had a vision that the rest of the world, she told herself brutally, generally didn't share.

And, she thought, nor did Jake Hadamard, which was why he had been appointed.

She knew that Hadamard would perceive grave risks, for the Agency and himself, in taking such an extravagant option. Giving the Shuttle orbiters to the Navy for gunnery practice was cheaper, and would cost no lives. And if failure were to come, she knew that the reaction would be that anyone should have known better than to undertake such a hubristic mission.

It would be Hadamard who would have to answer such charges. Working out her approach to Hadamard was the key part of Benacerraf's planning.

She moved a camp bed into her office at JSC. Sometimes, she didn't go home to Clear Lake for days on end.

From the air, Jiang Ling thought the Houston area looked like the surface of another planet, occupied and systematically bombed, perhaps, by malevolent aliens. The coastline was riddled with bays, canals, lakes, bayous and lagoons, all filled with oily water. A perceptible smog hovered over the glittering refineries around Galveston Bay.

Her NASA host pointed out Galveston Island, where she could make out a long, clear yellow slice of coastline: evidently a fine sandy beach, with what looked like a bulky oil rig, out to sea. The NASA person told her that the rig was there to dredge up sea-bottom sand, and pump it to the shore. The beach used to be stony, and the sand was only about eleven years old! Jiang was startled by the note of pride in the woman's voice at this comical monument.

The plane—an aging Cathay 747—began its descent.

She was bustled off the plane and processed briskly through customs. The terminal building felt cool—chill, in fact. Jiang wore only a light jacket and trousers; she wished briefly she had brought something heavier. But when she emerged from the terminal building into the full strength of the July noontime

Houston sun, the heat and humidity hit her as if she'd walked into a wall. The air was tangibly moist, the light intense, great polarized sheets of it bouncing into her eyes from the soft-looking asphalt surface, and the glinting metal carapaces of the cars which clustered here.

Waiting for her was a limousine, jet black, with a big softscreen panel, bearing a message which scrolled across the doors and wing. WELCOME JIANG LING, CHINA'S NUMBER ONE SPACEWOMAN. The message was repeated in Spanish, Chinese, and English.

She clambered into the back of the limousine. It was like climbing through a long, padded corridor. There was a little drinks table, molded into the upholstery, with champagne glasses and a decanter, and there were tiny TVs and softscreens. Waiting for her was a Chinese: Xu Shiyou, a senior Party official attached to the Embassy here, who would chaperon her. He was a fat man—American-diet fat, she thought—and his bald head was a round, sleek globe. Jiang was used to such meticulous planning and control; she was prepared to accept that she was a valued asset of the Party now, who required careful management.

It was a price she would pay, as she worked her way through these ceremonial duties, en route to space once more, some time in the imagined future.

The door was closed behind her, cocooning her in a little bubble of glass and new-smelling leather upholstery. The driver was sealed off by a partition; Jiang could only make out the back of the woman's head.

The limousine pulled away. The windows of the car were clear, but Jiang became aware of a faint rippling effect, as the landscape slid past. The glass was thick, no doubt bullet-proof. She shivered, not just from the cold. Though she had circled the Earth in the *Lei Feng* Number One, she had never before traveled outside China. Now she wondered how she, as her country's first space traveler, was going to be welcomed here in the home of Glenn and Armstrong.

The airport was on the northern outskirts of the Houston conurbation, and Jiang's limousine, at the heart of a little cluster of cars, swept down the freeway towards downtown. The traffic was heavy, the smog thick in the air.

The land was hot, flat, the conurbation sprawling. The infrastructure—the layout of the roads—was clean and functional. And yet she had an impression—not of newness—but of middle age. Much of Houston's growth, she knew, dated back to the space program growth period of the 1960s, and the oil boom of the 1970s. But those times were decades gone, and Houston was starting to age, to slump back into the plain.

Much of the time her view was obstructed by the roadside ads—huge, colorful, many of them animated—which battered at her senses, exploiting their slivers of competitive advantage. Most of the signs and ads were in Spanish.

There were water towers on the horizon, rusted, dominating. The land was greener than she had expected, but parklike, with orderly trees and thick-bladed grass; there seemed to be water sprinklers buried everywhere, many of them in full operation even now at high noon, when much of the water would be wasted. Jiang looked at those glittering fountains, the shining green lawns, imagining the tons of water vapor being lost to the air each second, all over this baking city.

She remarked on this to Xu Shiyou. The contrast with the water shortages suffered in her own country was marked, she said severely. And it was a global problem: the growth in the population and the demands of the industrializing nations—including China—was poised to outstrip the planetary supply of fresh water which fell from the sky . . .

Xu smiled. "That is of course true," he said. "But until we can build pipelines to link the aquifers of Texas with the parched gardens of Beijing, there is little we can achieve by complaining about it."

Jiang had the disquieting sense that Xu was mocking her.

"You are nevertheless right in your perception," said Xu

Shiyou, comfortingly. He waved a hand at Houston, beyond the car window. "America is a crass, empty-headed culture. And— look at that!—in the middle of this shower of advertising, you have their God, great neon crosses and beaming preachers, sold with the same methods as hamburgers."

She looked out of the window anew. Xu was right, she saw; the ads for hair products and soft drinks and face implants were punctuated with immense crucifixes, images of Jesus.

"Americans are free," Xu Shiyou murmured. "No intelligent person would deny that. But freedom is the minimum. I have lived and worked here for three years, and it is obvious to me that the Americans don't understand the world beyond their borders—that they fear it, in fact." He looked through the window; animated electronic light glimmered in his eyes.

She stared out of the car as he lectured her. The office blocks of downtown Houston thrust out of the plain like a collection of launch gantries, gray in the mist and smog.

The Big S, JSC's trophy Saturn V, was cordoned off from the public tours today and encased in scaffolding. Under Benacerraf's instruction the bird was being surveyed, to see if it could indeed be made operational once more. But Marcus White had been asked to host the Chinese space girl, Jiang Ling, on her brief tour of JSC, and he couldn't think of a better item to show her. So he got hold of a couple of hard hats and escorted Jiang inside the fenced-off rectangle that contained the booster.

Besides, he wanted to see the Big S for himself. He figured he may as well combine this makeweight ex-astronaut public relations chore with a little useful work.

The two of them walked along the three hundred and sixty feet of the fallen white-and-black-painted rocket, from its escape tower and Apollo capsule—both dummies—past the widening cylinders of the third and second stages, all the way to the gaping mouths of the five big F-1 engines of the huge first stage. The Saturn V—AS-514, built and ready to fly a late J-series Apollo mission to the Moon—was lying on its side, its stages and components separated. This was so the engines and other details of the mid-stages could be viewed, but it looked, White thought, as if the booster had shattered into cylindrical fragments on hitting the ground.

After three decades on the grass, the aging of the Saturn was obvious. He could make out corrosion, cobwebs laced across the big wheeled A-frames which pinned the booster to the ground. The Stars and Stripes painted on the side of the second stage, the hydrogen-oxygen S-II, was washed out, with big red stripes of paint running down over the white hull. There was even lichen, growing on the fabric parts of the rocket engines.

They are not looking after this old lady well, he thought.

They weren't alone in here; workers from JSC's Plant Engineering Division were moving around the rocket, laboring through their detailed survey. One of them, attached to ropes like a mountaineer, was walking along the top of the big S-IC first stage, taking samples of the skin up there.

Jiang stood, slim and composed, looking up at the pressurization tanks of the second stage's five J-2 engines, big silver spheres which glowed in the diffuse Houston sunlight. She said, "It is beautiful." She smiled.

"Yeah," White growled. "But the damn space program was more than a series of photo-calls."

"Was it?" Jiang looked sad. "But this creature, General White, is a dream of the 1950s. So crude!—a painted monster of rivets and bolts and gloss paint—"

"To me," White said, "it's not rivets and bolts and paint. This baby was designed to fly to the Moon. But it's having a tough time fulfilling the mission we finally gave it: lying for four decades horizontally, in the Houston climate."

There was an access hatch open near the top of the second stage, the S-II. Jiang and White took turns peering in.

"You know," White said, "when they first opened this up for

the first time in fifteen years they found little skeletons, mice and small birds, a foot deep. And the base of the stage was coated in guano, from pigeons and owls, islands of it in lakes of moisture trapped in there. After all, the drainage of this damn thing was designed to be end to end, not side to side."

"They made no effort to protect it from such erosion?"

"Oh, sure," White said. "All the openings large enough to allow in birds were covered with screens; there were ventilation openings knocked in the hull . . . but none of that is going to work, if you neglect the upkeep for long enough. They did try coating the second stage with polyurethane foam for insulation. But the sunlight takes its toll. All the uv we get these days. There are whole chunks of the insulation missing, great big pock marks . . . If you went up to the top of the S-II, you'd think you were walking on the surface of the Moon. Even the paint work isn't authentic. They use big decals, as if it was a Revell kit, to fake up the lettering and the flags. How about that. It's like spray-painting the Sistine Chapel. This poor old lady is going to require one hell of a refurbishment project."

Jiang looked at him sharply. "Refurbishment?"

White knew he shouldn't say any more. But there was no point in living seven decades and flying to the Moon and back if you couldn't shoot your mouth off to a young girl once in a while. So he said, "Sure. You know, manufacturing has come a long way since the Saturns were put together. CAD/CAM techniques, total quality programs, composites and aluminum-lithium alloys that are a lot lighter and stronger than this old aluminum shit . . . If we were to rebuild this bird, we could upgrade her performance a hell of a way."

Jiang laughed, but not unkindly. "Perhaps. It is a fine dream. Certainly I sense how angry you are at this, the condition of your 'big S.'"

"I guess the bad guys did a pretty good job of killing off this old lady after all. All they had to do was let her lie here and rust. And they got to show her off as their capture."

Jiang grimaced. "Like a trophy from a hunt. Yes; humans are rarely logical, even within a space program. But it could have been worse. At least the remaining Saturn hardware is honored as a relic of a great triumph."

White ran his hand along the corroded hull of AS-514. "A relic," he repeated.

This kid seemed to understand. She'd picked the right word. *Relic.* Maybe. But not for much longer.

His anger dissipated as he thought about that. The technicians crawling over the rocket were busy, competent, bustling. They nodded to White, smiled at the girl.

Okay, there had been some savage mistakes in the past, and this poor broken bird was a symbol of them. And maybe NASA was never going to be the same again; maybe it even deserved to be busted up and subsumed into Agriculture or whatever. But he had the feeling that the old days were coming back, just once more, as it had been working on Apollo, when everyone worked a hundred and ten percent and the color of your carpet didn't matter so much as what you knew and what you could do. For just a short time, maybe NASA was going to pull together again, to achieve the Titan mission, to achieve one more moment of greatness.

If it came off, it would be a hell of a thing.

The Houston Coliseum was a huge underground arena that reminded Jake Hadamard of nothing so much as a gigantic, hollowed-out car park. Today, the roof was hung with cute little models of the *Lei Feng* Number One spaceship. The air-conditioning, he thought, was typically Texan, which is to say the whole place was so chilly you could have stored corpses in here. As they waited for the Chinese party, everybody seemed to be standing up, and Hadamard found himself shivering in his suit jacket.

There were hundreds of people here, standing in rows: bands, police and firemen and National Guard in neat ranks, politicians and industrialists in open-topped convertibles. And Hadamard himself had brought a little party of senior NASA people: Marcus White, Paula Benacerraf and her family, some of the managers from JSC.

On a stage at one end of the arena stood Xavier T. Maclachlan, the ambitious Texas Congressman who had engineered the event. He was a thin, jug-eared man of about fifty. Now he whooped noisily into a microphone, and waved his big ten-gallon hat in the air, and gladhanded his guests.

Hadamard, bored and cold, checked his watch; there were still some minutes to endure before the Chinese spacewoman arrived.

Al Hartle came bearing down on him, resplendent in his Brigadier General's uniform. He was clutching a full tumbler of bourbon. Hartle was a power in the USAF Space Command; Hadamard had encountered him in briefings for the Cabinet. "This is some display," Hartle said. "Some fucking display."

Hadamard was amused; Hartle was upright and rigid, his head like a steel cylinder jutting up from his great box of a body. But he was clearly a little drunk, and anger seemed to be seething inside him, hot and deliquescent, like a pupa within its rigid chrysalis.

He prompted, "You think so?"

"In 1961 we sent John Glenn on a fucking world tour. Now we're on the receiving end of the tours, and we have to kowtow to some damn Red Chinese."

"Well, they have made it to orbit, Al."

"For the same reasons we did," Hartle growled. "Geopolitics. Just to prove their balls are as big as ours."

"Space as the symbolic arena. Well, I guess you're right. But they hardly need symbols, Al. China's GDP passed ours years ago."

"I know. That, and this woman in orbit, and this damn Shuttle crash, have sent us all into a fucking panic. I tell you, it's like Sputnik all over again. And look what came out of the

dumb decisions that were made when Sputnik went up. Apollo.
Holy shit. A disaster that has reverberated for fifty years." He
eyed Hadamard. "So you still throwing money down the john
for another Shuttle?"

Hadamard laughed. "I'll tell you all about it when you tell
me about your Black Horse program, Al."

Hartle grunted, and took a deep slug of his bourbon. "And
your space cadets haven't responded to our L5 proposal yet."

The L5 proposal was the Air Force's official recommendation
on what to do with the left-over Shuttle and Station technology.
The Station should be completed, and converted to a surveillance station—maybe even some kind of weapons-bearing
battle station—and towed out to L5, the stable Lagrangian point
two hundred and forty thousand miles from Earth, at the third
corner of a triangle including Earth and Moon.

Hartle stabbed a finger at Hadamard's chest. "You heard the
case. It's the new heartland of space. Circumterrestrial space
encapsulates Earth to an altitude of fifty thousand miles. Who
rules circumterrestrial space commands Earth; who rules the
Moon commands circumterrestrial space; who rules L4 and L5
commands the Earth-Moon system."

Hadamard sipped his drink. "Maybe you're right, Al. But—"

"The Red Chinese," Hartle hissed. "*The Red Chinese*. Those
bastards think this is going to be their century. They're making
expansionist noises all over, impacting ten countries, from
Taiwan to Russian East Asia to the Spratly Islands in the South
China Sea . . . Christ, even the Australians are worried."

Hadamard murmured, "Is it really so bad? Our weaponry is
still so far ahead of theirs that we can contain them for a long
time to come. And—"

But Hartle wasn't listening. "If we don't take Lagrange
soon, we'll find the damn Red Chinese up there waiting for us.
And then we'll have lost, Hadamard. We'll be paying tribute to
the bastards for the rest of time. Just like the days of the Qing
Dynasty. Read your history, boy." He approached Hadamard,

and thrust forward his hawklike face, weathered by altitude and desert sun, and that inner anger burst to the surface. "Listen to me," he said, his voice a thick rasp. "I know some of those assholes in the NASA centers are putting forward dumb-ass schemes about leveraging this Chinese-in-space stuff into some big new Flash Gordon adventure in space. They want to start the whole damn thing over again. But that's bullshit. You hear me? You try to fly any such damn thing and we will shoot you down, boy."

He backed off, fixing Hadamard with a final glare, and stalked off into the crowd.

Good grief, Hadamard thought. He found himself trembling. He took a slug of his own drink, to regain his composure.

What anger. But we're not at war, he thought, cowed by Hartle's intensity. For all his political antennae, he couldn't tell if Hartle's anger was representative of the thinking inside the closed doors of the military, or if Hartle was some kind of aging maverick, frustrated because he was unable to get his case accepted.

In fact Hadamard still had to make his decision, about disposing of the Shuttle assets.

Nobody wanted to go back to a regular flight schedule with the three remaining orbiters—the cumulative risk was just unacceptable—but some kind of one-off mission was still plausible, politically. And besides, he was still waiting for Benacerraf's recommendation.

Anyhow, Hartle was threatening the wrong guy. Hadamard was no space buff. He was interested, he told himself, solely in managing budgets; if NASA never flew more than another July 4 skyrocket he could care less.

. . . But, oddly, against his expectations, he found himself leaning more towards proposals like the ones coming out of Marshall, about fantastic jaunts to the Moon or Mars or Venus, rather than building some monstrous Buck Rogers space battle station in the sky.

He couldn't get the image of the crashing orbiter out of his head, the idea of the grizzled old Moonwalker at the controls to the last.

He found Paula Benacerraf, who was here with her daughter, and a kid: a boy, who looked bored and restless. Maybe he needed a pee, Hadamard thought sourly. On the daughter's cheek was an image-tattoo that was tuned to black; on her colorless dress she wore a simple, old-fashioned button-badge that said, mysteriously, NED.

Hadamard grunted. "I've seen a few of those blacked-out tattoos. I thought it was some kind of comms problem—"

Jackie Benacerraf shook her head. "It's a mute protest."

"At what?"

"At shutting down the net."

"Oh. Right." Oh, Christ, he thought. She was talking about the Communications Decency Act, which had been extended during the winter. With a flurry of publicity about pedophiles and neo-Nazis and bomb-makers, the police had shut down and prosecuted any net service provider who could be shown to have passed on any of the material that fell outside the provisions of the Act. And that was almost all of them.

"I was never much of a net user," Hadamard admitted.

"Just to get you up to date," Jackie Benacerraf said sourly, "we now have one licensed service provider, which is Disney-Coke, and all net access software has built-in censorship filters. We're just like China now, where everything goes through the official news agency, Xinhua; that poor space kid must feel right at home."

Benacerraf raised an eyebrow at him. "She's a journalist. Jackie takes these things seriously."

Jackie scowled. "Wouldn't you, if your career had just been fucked over?"

Hadamard shrugged; he didn't have strong opinions.

The comprehensive net shutdown had been necessary

because the tech-heads who loved all that stuff had proven too damn smart at getting around any reasonable restriction put in place. Like putting encoded messages of race-hate and smut into graphics files, for instance: that had meant banning all graphics and sound files, and the World Wide Web had just withered. He knew there had been some squealing among genuine discussion groups on the net, and academics and researchers who suddenly found their access to online libraries shut down, and businesses who were no longer allowed to send secure encrypted messages, and . . . But screw it. To Hadamard, the net had been just a big conduit of bullshit; everyone was better off without it.

Jackie was still droning on, in the sanctimonious way that might have been patented by serious young people. "This is the greatest reverse in free access to information since Gutenberg. The net was never meant to be sanitized and controlled. The shutdown will hit technological development, education, jobs . . ."

Hadamard was quickly bored. His glance was caught again by Jackie's button-badge which sat, he couldn't help notice, over her breast, which was small and firm. Her little boy clung to her leg.

"NED. Who's that, a rock star?"

"New Luddites," Paula Benacerraf said.

"Oh. I heard of them."

"Believe me, Jake, you don't want to get into that either."

Maybe I do, Hadamard thought.

He knew Xavier Maclachlan had picked up on some of what the Luddites were arguing for. The Luddites had attracted a broad band of the younger generations who responded to a core anti-science message with, it seemed to Hadamard, their guts, not their heads. And that gut response was what Maclachlan was tapping into.

In his heart, Hadamard was uncomfortable with Maclachlan: his protectionism, his fundamentalist Christianity. But Hadamard had to concede that Maclachlan was hitting popular nerves among the electorate. It was, he thought, entirely possible that Maclachlan would indeed become the next President, just as the polls said. And if that happened, Jake Hadamard would be going to him for a new job.

Maybe I do need to figure out what's going on inside the head of the likes of Jackie Benacerraf, he thought.

Benacerraf said, "Speaking of Luddites, I hear we lost the Mars sample-return mission."

"Yeah." Now, there was a pisser, even for a space cynic like Hadamard. "You know how they stopped it in the end? We had to apply to register the returned Mars samples with the Department of Agriculture in the state we planned to land. Just in case there was life aboard, like in that meteorite a few years ago. But you could crashland anywhere, so we were forced to apply in every state in the Union. And then we had to start applying for similar permits abroad. All that damn paperwork, the legal tangles. And when the first refusal came in, that was pretty much it."

Benacerraf shook her head. "So we lost another fine mission, and any chance of confirming the biological stuff from the mete-orite. Damn, damn. Once, we sent spacecraft to Jupiter, the rings of Saturn, out of the Solar System altogether. Now, we're too scared to bring home a handful of Martian dust . . . You know, our attitudes don't seem to be shaped by the rational any more."

Hadamard shrugged. "It was predictable. The slightest sug-gestion of bugs from Mars was always going to raise a panic. It's the times we live in."

But now Jackie started in again, arguing with her mother.

Hadamard tuned out. He was still bored and cold, and he was getting no closer to Maclachlan like this. He made his excuses and moved on, abandoning Benacerraf to her dysfunc-tional family.

Up on the stage, Maclachlan started making a short, crass speech of welcome; evidently the Chinese party was on its way.

It seemed to Hadamard that Maclachlan was working his audience here almost greedily, as he stared into the camera lights. It was ironic that Maclachlan, the great protectionist and anti-space campaigner, was here to welcome a spacegirl from China. But it was politics. Maclachlan was turning this event, like everything else he touched, into just another part of his populist build-up towards what everyone expected would be a winning bid for the Republican nomination for the White House in 2008.

Hadamard glanced around the crowd, sizing up who was here, figuring how he could get to maximize his own contact time with Maclachlan.

There were ragged cheers. Hadamard turned. The Chinese party was arriving in their hard-top limos, rolling smoothly down the ramp from the overground. Led by Maclachlan, the waiting hundreds broke into noisy applause.

The limos did a brief turn around the Coliseum floor. Before stopping at Maclachlan's feet the cars came close to Hadamard; he found himself looking into the pretty, oval face of Jiang Ling, from no more than ten feet. She looked young, he thought, and scared. As she had every right to be.

When she got out of the car, accompanied by some fat Chinese official, she turned out to be slim, about thirty-five, delicate-looking in what looked like a peach-colored Chairman Mao jumpsuit with a neat little jacket over the top. She climbed the few steps up to meet Maclachlan, who grabbed her possessively and stuck his ten-gallon on her head.

Hadamard tried to imagine this fragile girl being launched into space, in the mouth of one of those huge, unreliable, 1950s-style Chinese boosters. Not for the first time the idea of spaceflight seemed monstrous to him: like a human sacrifice, to serve geopolitical ends.

But, he thought ruefully, as the head of the Agency which had just crashed a Space Shuttle he had no grounds for complacency.

Maclachlan, holding onto Jiang, finished up with a Chinese phrase, clumsily delivered. *"Ni chifanie meiyou?"* Jiang looked disconcerted; Maclachlan laughed and hugged her anew. "I said to her, 'Have you eaten yet?' Exactly what I'd be asked if I visited your home. Right, Ji-ang?" The slim Chinese girl smiled nervously. "Well, you sure as hell will eat fine here in our home—Texas-style! Enjoy, folks!" He whooped, the amplified noise ear-splitting.

And now the covers were taken off ten big barbecue pits, set up in the middle of the arena, and suddenly the air was full of the rich, cloying stink of burned cattle flesh. There was an eruption of applause. The girl astronaut looked utterly bewildered.

Maclachlan, holding tight onto his human Sputnik, clambered down off the platform and began to work his way through the crowd. Hadamard stepped forward, discreetly, towards the platform.

A year after the crash, Benacerraf's daughter, Jackie, came to stay for a couple of days. She brought her two children, Ben and Fred, four and five respectively. The boys seemed to fill Benacerraf's ranch house at Clear Lake with light and noise, and she spent as much time as she could with them. She got into a routine of working through the day at JSC, spending the early evenings with the children, and staying up nights to work on drafts of her recommendation to Hadamard.

One night, Jackie disturbed her. She came padding barefoot across the kitchen floor to where Benacerraf sat with her softscreen spread out over the big walnut dining table, at the center of a pool of scattered notes and documents.

"Mom, you must be crazy," Jackie said gently. She went to the refrigerator, and returned with glasses of apple juice. "Do you know what time it is? Three A.M."

"So it is," Benacerraf said. "I don't know where the time goes." She rubbed her face; the balls of her eyes felt gritty, the muscles aching and sore.

Jackie sat at the table. "So how long has this been going on?"

"Oh. Ten, eleven months or so."

"Ten months? My God, Mother."

"It isn't so bad. I travel a lot; I catnap on flights or in the car. And there's an end in sight. I'm working on a project. When it's done I'll be able to rest."

"Mom, you're not as young as you were."

Benacerraf sighed. "I guess it's a daughter's job to say things like that. Well, neither are you."

"But I know it. And you won't catch me working like that." Jackie smiled, vaguely. "Life's too short, Mom. After all, what job is worth wrecking your health for? Seriously, you shouldn't let them push you so hard."

Benacerraf reached behind to rub the muscles at the back of her neck. "There is no 'them.' Or I'm part of 'them.' I'm a senior official in the national space program. I have to try to make things happen. Besides, what doesn't seem to occur to you is that maybe this work makes me happy."

"If that's so, why are you so prickly?"

"I'm not prickly, damn it—" Benacerraf subsided, and Jackie grinned at her.

It was a familiar argument to Benacerraf. *What is it with you young people? What in hell happened to the work ethic? Don't you take anything seriously? . . .*

It was a long time since Jackie had tried to push ahead with her journalism. At times Benacerraf felt she couldn't stand to see Jackie drift through her life like this, like so many of her age group, floating from one career option to another, passing through relationships that coalesced briefly—sometimes leaving behind kids, as had Jackie's brief marriage—and on to the next vague destination.

It wasn't the structure of Jackie's life that bugged her, but her casualness, her lack of seriousness. There seemed no need to struggle, to take responsibility—no attempt to *build* things.

She suppressed the impulse to snap. Now, of all times, wasn't the moment to pick a fight with her daughter.

Anyhow, she thought, maybe Jackie and her generation are right. Look at me, slaving here in the small hours, over this huge Titan boondoggle. Maybe my day is done. Maybe this project is the last spasm of whatever drove us, in the last century, to our great, ambitious endeavors. Perhaps when this is over—when my generation has gone, the last great rocket ships fired off—the world will sink back, lapse into a kind of high-tech pastoralism.

Jackie got up and walked to Benacerraf's back, and took over rubbing her neck muscles for her.

"That feels good," Benacerraf said.

"Just like when I was a little girl, huh?"

"Even then you always had good hands."

"All that tennis I played."

"You could have been a surgeon. A physiotherapist—"

Jackie laughed. "A carpenter, like Jesus. Come on, Mom; you're sounding like a cliché again."

"Sorry."

Jackie pointed to the softscreen, which Benacerraf had folded over. "You going to tell me what you're working on?"

I'm not supposed to, Benacerraf thought. But you deserve to know.

"Here." She unfolded the softscreen and smoothed out its creases.

Jackie sat down again, pulled the softscreen to her, and ran her finger over its smooth fabric surface, a reading habit she'd developed as a child.

 . . . *The purpose of this memorandum is to obtain your approval to use Space Shuttle and ancillary technology to fly an open-ended manned mission to Saturn's moon, Titan, in the short-term timeframe, with a resupply and retrieval strategy in the medium-term based on new-generation Reusable Launch Vehicle technology.*

My recommendation is based on an exhaustive review of pertinent technical and operational factors and also careful consideration of the impact that either a success or a failure in this mission will have on the future of the Agency.

My objective has been to bring into meaningful perspective the trade-offs between total program risk and gain. As you know, this assessment process is inherently judgmental in nature. Many factors have been considered during a comprehensive series of reviews, conducted over the past several months, to examine in detail all facets of the considerations involved in planning for and providing a capability to fly a crew of five or six on a Titan landing mission. A key benefit for the Agency is the motivation such a mission provides for maintaining funding and commitment for the upcoming RLV program.

In conclusion, but with the proviso that all open work against the open-ended Titan mission is completed and certified, I request your approval to proceed with the implementation plan required to support an early launch readiness date.

Turning to details of the—

Jackie pushed the softscreen back across the table to her mother. "You can't be serious," she said.

Benacerraf sipped her apple juice. "Never more so."

"Is this to do with all that JPL shit? My God, the arrogance. You can't even fly to orbit and back without crashing all over the place. How do you imagine you can send people to Saturn?"

Benacerraf shrugged. "Do you really care? You'll learn all about it when it gets made public, if you're interested." As, she thought sourly, you probably won't be.

But Jackie was staring at her. "*Oh.* Hold up. Hold it right there. I think I'm just starting to figure this out."

"Jackie, I—"

"*You want to go.* Don't you? To Titan, on this ridiculous one-way jaunt." She slammed the table. "Mother, you are *not* going to Saturn."

Benacerraf was taken aback by her anger. "Jackie—"

"Don't you know what it's like for me, when you fly in space, in that ludicrous old technology? Every moment you were off the ground in *Columbia*, I could think of nothing but the danger. And when *Columbia* went through the crash, I was convinced I wouldn't see you again. Right now the kids are too young to understand, but soon . . . And now you talk about this, about leaving the Earth altogether?"

"It isn't like that. There's a retrieval strategy, based on——"

"You don't understand, do you?" Jackie's eyes were dry, her expression hard. "Listen to me. Flying into space is meaningless. It always was. The technology is antiquated and unsafe, and there's nowhere to go, and all your language of risk reduction is just a play with words. And for what? The whole thing is just a selfish stunt."

Benacerraf felt her own anger building in response. "I won't be called selfish by you. I'm more than just your mother, damn it. I've raised you, as best I could. And now you're grown, my life is my own——"

Jackie snapped, "Why don't you put that in your report?" She walked out of the kitchen.

Benacerraf sat for long minutes.

Then she pulled the softscreen towards her.

Hadamard hauled on the thermal meteoroid garment. It was a heavy, floppy, deflated balloon made of tough white Beta-cloth. There were sockets over the front, where he plugged in his backpack umbilicals for oxygen, water and telecommunications.

Alongside him, Buzz Aldrin—thirty-nine years old, bald as a coot, and eager as a virgin—was climbing into his own suit.

The Moon suit, authentically rendered, was unbelievably primitive, Hadamard reflected. To think you actually had to assemble it, here on the lunar surface. It was incredible none of the Moonwalkers had been killed, betrayed by leaky plumbing.

When his suit was closed Hadamard flicked a switch, and the pumps and fans in his backpack started. He heard the hum of machinery, and oxygen whooshed across his face.

The veracity of the experience was extraordinary, right down to the sensation of increasing pressure in his ears.

He gave Aldrin a thumbs-up, and through his shining bubble helmet, Aldrin grinned back at him.

The first line in the script was Hadamard's.

"Houston, this is Tranquillity. We're standing by for a go for cabin depress, over."

Tranquillity Base, this is Houston. You are go for cabin depressurize, over.

Aldrin opened the valve that would vent *Eagle*'s oxygen to space. The pressure crept downward, much more slowly than Hadamard had expected, despite his detailed knowledge of the timeline. It took all of three minutes to get down to four-tenths of a pound.

"Everything is go here," Hadamard said. "We're just waiting for the cabin pressure to bleed, to blow enough pressure to open the hatch . . ." Hadamard could hear a stiffness in his own tone, as he pronounced the scripted words.

The events of the Moonwalk—at any rate the few minutes surrounding the first footstep itself—had become utterly familiar, through a thousand reproductions and adaptations and digitizations and dramatizations; it was thought that a copy of this script resided in every home with online access, which meant most of mainland U.S. The rest of Apollo—the later flights, even the rest of the *Apollo 11* mission—had been largely forgotten now. But, Hadamard thought, the story of these few minutes of the first footstep was probably as familiar, in the public mind, as the story of the Nativity.

It was one hell of a legacy to manage.

"Let me see if it will open now," Aldrin said. Clumsily, he

reached down for the hatch handle. He tugged on the thin metal door, but it stayed firmly shut. Aldrin pulled vigorously, and Hadamard feared he might rip the thin metal shell of the Lunar Module. Finally Aldrin peeled back one corner of the door to break the seal.

The next part of the litany was Hadamard's. "The hatch is coming open," he said, and he heard, spontaneously, excitement creep into his voice.

As if it were all real.

A flurry of ice particles gushed out into the lunar vacuum beyond the hatch, the last of the LM's atmosphere.

Aldrin held the hatch open, and Hadamard sank to his knees and carefully moved his suited bulk backward through the opening. It was awkward, confining, more like struggling to escape from the neck of a sack than leaving an aircraft.

The Aldrin simulation gave him running guidance. "Jake, you're lined up nicely. Towards me a little bit. Okay, down. Roll to the left. Put your left foot to the right a little bit. You're doing fine . . ."

Hadamard crawled out onto a large platform called the porch, which bridged the gap between the hatch and the ladder to the surface. He groped backward with his boots, and found the top rung. He got hold of the porch's handrails and raised himself upright, cautiously.

"Okay, Houston, I'm on the porch."

Before him was the blocky, shadowed bulk of the LM. Beyond that, reaching all the way to the close horizon, was a pocked, rock-strewn, tan brown surface. There were craters everywhere, of all sizes, right down to the little micrometeorite pits on the sides of the rocks that the astronauts had called zap pits. On some of the rocks he saw an exotic sparkle, like a glaze. The colors, though, depended on which way he looked, on the angle to the sun, as if he was looking through a polarizing filter.

He knew this representation had been beefed up from the original photographs with fractal technology. Those zap pits weren't real, for instance. But it looked pretty convincing to Hadamard. He could well believe this place had been gardened, pulverized by meteorite strikes, for billions of years.

The land, he saw, actually curved, gently but noticeably, all the way to the horizon, and in every direction from him. He was standing on a rocky sphere, no more and no less. This was a small world indeed. The sky was utterly dark, save for the blue Earth, which was almost directly overhead, visible only if he tilted back his head . . .

"What do you think of it?"

He turned. An astronaut had come bounding around the far side of the LM, her suit glowing white.

"Paula?"

"Hi, Jake."

He felt an odd reluctance to come out of the illusion. "Disney-Coke has done a good job."

"Yes," she said. "Maybe this was what it was all about in the first place, do you think? Circus stunts, entertainment? And maybe in a few more years these visitors' centers will be all that's left . . ."

"Oh, how symbolic. And that's why you've dragged me here today, Paula. Correct?"

"Did you read my recommendation?"

"Not past the management summary. No."

"Then," she said coolly, "you're going to have to. Like it or not that recommendation is the result of eighteen months' study, and it comes with a lot of management weight behind it."

"Paula, I just couldn't believe what I read. I don't see how I'm going to be able to justify the costs, even of defining the proposal fully. It's ridiculous. You're talking about a manned mission to Saturn, for God's sake. Who's going to take that seriously?"

"There are costs associated with everything we do," she said. "Just mothballing the orbiters is going to cost. Probably we'll even make a loss out of scrapping the launch complexes, turning the VAB into a jungle gym . . . Jake, this is your job. But I know you've retained unexpended funding from the shut-down manned space program, from the last couple of fiscal years. Funding that's still at your discretion; funding above and beyond what you disclosed to me when I took on this job."

"You're aware of that, huh."

"It's not so hard to trace. We can cover this financially. It's just a question of whether you want to do this, or not. Whether you'll back it . . . You're getting behind your timeline."

"Oh, yeah." A prompter scrolled discreetly across the base of his visor, with his next few lines. The next part of the sequence was to pull a D-ring on the side of the *Eagle*. "I'm going to pull the camera out now." An equipment storage tray lowered on its hinges, bearing a small TV camera. "Houston, the MESA came down all right."

Hadamard could hear the capcom, Bruce McCandless, exclaim: *Houston, roger, we copy and we're standing by for your TV. Man, we're getting a picture on the TV!*

"That's a little gruff," Benacerraf observed. "McCandless was just a rookie astronaut in 1969. That sounded a lot older."

"Disney-Coke brought the real McCandless out of retire-ment, and got him to overdub his contributions. So I guess you have a clash of authenticity measures," Hadamard said drily. "Of course, McCandless went on to fly Shuttle. He was actually more expensive to get than Buzz Aldrin."

There's a great deal of contrast in it and currently it's upside down on our monitor, but we can make out a fair amount of detail . . . Okay, Jake, we can see you coming down the ladder now.

Hadamard began to descend the ladder, one rung at a time. His primitive suit, inflated like a big white balloon around him, was so stiff he had trouble bending his legs, and he found he had to just let go and drop from rung to rung.

When he got to the bottom rung he was still more than three feet off the ground. He could see the big dish of the foil-covered footpad beneath him. He dangled one foot, trying to build up the courage to take this final step. Then he pushed himself away from the ladder, gently.

He went into a slow-motion fall. It took maybe a second to drop to the footpad, but on Earth it would have taken less than half that. The difference was pleasingly noticeable. He couldn't feel the invisible harness supporting him at all.

He was in deep shadow here.

"I've also been receiving more proposals from the USAF for disposing of the Shuttle fleet," he said to Benacerraf.

"Proposals that went straight to you, over my head," she said mildly.

"I guess so. Well, that's the way it works, Paula. Those guys play for keeps."

"The USAF proposals are entirely destructive."

"I don't think that's entirely fair," he said. The USAF had given up on their grandiose L5 schemes. Now they proposed to use the remaining orbiters as unmanned testbeds, on suborbital flights inside and outside the atmosphere, probing hypersonic, high-altitude flight regimes which were still only partially understood. "We could get some good data out of there."

"For what purpose? The data, such as it would be, would sit locked away in big USAF databases. And for that dubious benefit they would destroy the orbiters, a national treasure."

But it would get Al Hartle off my back, he thought. "Give me a single good reason why I should recommend we go to Titan," he said.

"Because it represents the true high ground," she replied immediately. She turned, and started to Moonwalk; she drifted across the glowing lunar ground, dreamlike.

"That's a worn old phrase."

"But in this case, I think it applies," she said. "Titan is the key to the rest of the Solar System. You've seen Rosenberg's detailed plan—"

"Yes."

"It's almost like a business plan," she said. "On the surface it seems fantastic. But in fact it's orderly, logical."

"It's a dream," he said. "You're talking to an accountant, remember. It's not a business plan at all."

"Jake, we're overdue for a breakthrough in booster technology. That's been obvious for a couple of decades. The Shuttle system uses technology that goes back to Goddard in the 1920s. The Shuttle is just a V-2 with air conditioning. Somebody's going to make the breakthrough, sooner or later, to routine, cheap access to space. And once that happens, there will be an explosion off-world. You'll see factories, farms, power stations in LEO . . . and the next words spoken on the surface of the Moon will be Chinese. Or Korean, or Vietnamese. Soon after that, those guys will make it to Mars, the asteroids. We aren't investing in the right stuff, the core technologies. Any Americans who want to go will have to book passage.

"We're about to lose out on an historic opportunity, Jake. We've already lost the inner Solar System. Despite the panic, the rush to invest in space since the crash, I don't see any way to avoid that. We've spent too long looking inward, retrenching, cutting back, to change now."

Actually he agreed. Decadent, he thought. That's what we are now. We deserve to be overtaken, by younger, more vigorous economies.

She said, "But, right at this moment, *we have the ability to get to Titan*. And if we do that, we'll have control of a world of resources that are scarce in the rest of the System. Do you get it, Jake? We'll have just that one little island in the sky, but it will represent the high ground. As a nation we will still be in the game, in the medium and far future."

He grunted, unimpressed. "Is that all you have? This visionary crap?"

"No. I have a lot more visionary crap."

"Such as?"

"Jake, here you are on the surface of the Moon. Or as near as damn it. I've brought you here for a reason."

He laughed. "To sway me with flashy Disney-Coke virtuals."

"No. Well, maybe. Look, Jake, there are whole generations out there much too young to remember Apollo. If we don't give them this, they'll be left with nothing more than the memory of a Shuttle crash. We'll deserve to sink back into all the anti-rational garbage that's threatening to drown us. But if we act, now . . . You could be a hero, Jake."

Her voice, over his VHF loop, was thin, persistent, scratchy.

A hero. In fact, that had already occurred to him.

He wasn't about to tell Benacerraf this, but he hadn't in fact dismissed the Titan proposal out of hand, when it first came across his desk. On reflection, he'd calculated, it was possible that a lot of constituencies could be brought to unite behind this bizarre proposal: for instance there would be plenty of work, at least in the short term, for the NASA centers, which were engaged in their usual turf wars over the latest set of cutbacks. This last project could help in the management of the final decline and shutdown much of NASA faced.

The USAF would be more problematic. But even they—or most of their internal warring factions anyhow—could be brought into line, Hadamard thought, if it was pointed out that this exercise would at least destroy the Shuttle fleet, just as surely as using the orbiters for destructive tests or advanced-weapons target practice.

And meanwhile, inside the White House, there was—he had perceived—some pressure to keep NASA flying. Unusually, this Administration was trying to think ahead, beyond its own expected political death in 2008. They feared for the future of the country if—when—Xavier Maclachlan came to power, a future in which it seemed America was likely to lapse into fundamentalism, and isolationism, and a kind of high-tech Middle Ages.

A huge technological program already underway when

Maclachlan took office—an immense deep space mission lasting years, perhaps even spanning beyond Maclachlan's term— might be a way to keep the spark of rationalism alive. Surely even Maclachlan wouldn't be able to justify closing down the new launcher program if it meant stranding astronauts among the moons of Saturn.

And, Hadamard reflected, he himself could indeed become some kind of popular hero. When this was over—even if the mission failed in space, even if it failed to get off the ground altogether—he could present himself as more than a cost-cutter, a man who could combine the fiscal targets of his employers, even the final run-down of NASA, with a genuine sense of vision.

He could move from NASA, afterward, to his pick of jobs.

Benacerraf's proposal, all this crap about the higher ground, was just a ridiculous power fantasy to him, one in a long line of such dreams to emanate from the centers of NASA. But maybe he ought to back it, even so; maybe it could even be made to serve his own personal objectives.

And maybe it would even work. Maybe it would turn a few young heads back towards engineering, instead of aromatherapy or goddamn homeopathy.

And by the time it all failed, as it surely must, he would be long gone.

A part of his mind wondered if Benacerraf knew what he was thinking, if she wasn't as naive as she seemed. Maybe she was manipulating him on some level he didn't recognize. If so it didn't matter; all that counted, when it came to his decision, was the coincidence of this proposal with his own interests.

And, he sensed, the decision was shaping inside him, as the various factors slotted into place in his subconscious.

Perhaps Benacerraf would never know how. But, he suspected, she had won her argument today.

He, Jake Hadamard, was going to send astronauts to Saturn.

Good God. He'd come a long way since he took this job.

A soft chime sounded in his ears, reminding him that he was holding up the VR immersion. For a moment he forgot his lines; then the prompter scrolled across the bottom of his visor. "Uh, I'm at the foot of the ladder now. The LM footpads are only depressed in the surface about one or two inches. Although the surface appears to be very fine, fine grained, when you get close to it, it's almost like a powder. Down there it's very fine . . ."

Eagle looked like a gaunt spider, looming above him in the glaring sunlight, a filmy construct of gold leaf and aluminum, standing on this broad, level plain. He found it hard to concentrate, with Benacerraf standing there, tilted slightly forward under the weight of her backpack, watching him. A grandmother on the Moon was definitely not a part of Armstrong's original experience, he thought.

He got hold of the ladder with a gloved hand, and turned to his left and leaned outward. "I'm going to step off the LM now." Carefully, he raised his left boot over the lip of the footpad, and lowered his blue overshoe to the dust. He felt his heartbeat rise, and he felt foolish, knowing he was being monitored by invisible techs just a few feet away.

He felt as if he had stepped onto snow; the surface seemed to crunch as it took his weight. But then, a fraction of an inch in, he reached firm footing.

There he was, one foot on this angular machine from Earth, the other on the Moon itself.

It was time for the line.

"That's one small step for a man . . ."

Christ, he thought. He had a lump in his throat.

If only it hadn't been Armstrong, he thought. If only it had been someone less thoughtful, a bullshitter like Pete Conrad, who would have cracked a joke and whooped as he somersaulted down the ladder of the LM. Then we could all have dismissed the whole thing for what it was, a stunt, and got on with the rest of our lives.

Damn Neil Armstrong.

The lunar surface dissolved. The blocky walls of the immersive VR tank—the centerpiece of the visitors' center here at Kennedy—coalesced around him, breaking through the dark lunar sky. The harness suspending him relaxed, and his full weight descended on his shoulders once more, heavy and eternal. That feeling of buoyant lightness dissipated, and he was trapped on Earth.

So, he thought, it had all been a dream.

He felt a deep, sharp stab of regret, of loss.

Benacerraf called them all to a meeting at JPL. Rosenberg wanted to review landing sites. In the end, such were their commitments to the accelerating refurbishment and training programs, only Mott and Benacerraf could make it.

To Benacerraf, Rosenberg seemed more isolated than ever from his JPL. She'd expected some kind of excitement here at the heart of planetary exploration, now that Hadamard had announced the Titan program formally. But as they made their way through JPL's corridors, lined with pictures of Mars, hardly anyone acknowledged Rosenberg—though some of the natives, aging hairies, stared curiously at Benacerraf herself, the most media-friendly survivor of *Columbia*.

No wonder Rosenberg wants to leave so badly, Benacerraf thought. There is nothing here for him, even at JPL, his spiritual home.

Rosenberg had booked them a meeting room, a plain box with a big wooden table, over which he'd spread out a gigantic softscreen. A multicolored map filled the softscreen. It was a Mercator projection, of the surface of a world, pock-marked by craters.

It might have been a map of the Moon—or Mercury, or the

southern hemisphere of Mars, or any of the small bodies of the Solar System. *But this was Titan.* Much of the map was coarse-grained, and it featured long white strips where no terrain was shown at all, particularly towards the poles.

Rosenberg said, "This map was assembled from radar images returned by *Cassini*. *Cassini* is using Titan's gravity well to provide assists to climb on to other targets, but on each approach the radar sends back a noodle—a strip of the map, as it surveys a swathe of surface—and each time *Cassini* is occulted we study its radio signals, squeezing out a little more data about the nature and structure of the atmosphere . . ."

Mott said, "Why the radar? Why can't we see the ground?"

"Because of the smog," Rosenberg said. "Titan has virtually no magnetic field of its own—unlike Earth—so the solar wind and the magnetospheric plasma from Saturn can get at the upper atmosphere directly. Beams of electrons, plus ultraviolet light from the sun, fall on the upper air of Titan, and drive a lot of chemistry.

"The uv destroys upper-atmosphere methane, which then combines with nitrogen to form complex molecules like ethane, benzene, hydrogen cyanide, other nitriles. The hydrogen cyanide combines in big multimolecular groups to form adenine, a constituent of nucleic acids. The uv manufactures the simplest hydrocarbons, electrons, the rest . . .

"The hydrocarbons cluster in complex organic solids called tholins. The tholins make up the smog in the upper atmosphere, and they rain steadily down onto the land. And they've been doing it for four billion years . . . Now, Titan's deep cold has a number of subtle effects. To begin with, once molecules are synthesized down there, they are going to stick around: the higher the temperature, the faster molecules fall to pieces. On Titan, even the oldest molecules might still be there, in the deepest slush layers. Like deep-frozen primeval soup."

The map was color-coded for relief; one whole hemisphere was, Benacerraf saw, significantly brighter than the other.

"Here's the dominant surface feature on Titan," Rosenberg said. "It's a plateau, the size of Australia, sprawled across one whole hemisphere. Two and a half thousand miles across. A continent of ice. The mapmakers at the U.S. Geological Survey called it Cronos." He looked at them for response and got none. "Mythology. The leader of the Titans. Now, Titan is tidally locked to Saturn; as it completes its sixteen-day orbit of Saturn, just like the Moon around the Earth, it keeps the same face turned to its parent all the time. And this Australia-sized lump, Cronos, is on the leading edge, as Titan pushes around its orbit."

Benacerraf studied the map more closely. The whole surface of the moon was covered with craters, up to a couple of hundred miles across. Some of the crater floors were filled in with a pale blue color, up to a certain contour. And some had central peaks, which protruded from the washes of blue. The continent, Cronos, had less filled-in craters than the other, trailing hemisphere.

Rosenberg said, "The cratering is a record of Titan's history. Cronos appears to have an older surface, with a peak crater size of about ten miles—maybe a thousand of those—but also a handful of craters up to two hundred miles wide—big, old, eroded walled plains, their ice walls subsiding back into the landscape. The mapmakers call them palimpsests. Shadow craters. On the lowlands the cratering density is much less, and there is a peak size of crater of around forty miles diameter. That's consistent with a young surface-renewed by ammonia-water vulcanism—with the larger, older craters, and the smaller ones, pretty much wiped out by the geology . . ."

The meaning of the craters' blue coloration was obvious.

Benacerraf pointed. "Filled-in craters. Right?"

"Right. Titan is what you'd get if you flooded the Moon with paraffin: circular seas and lakes filled with liquid hydrocarbons.

"The nature of this hidden surface was the biggest mystery before *Cassini* got there. You see, the air should be depleted of methane in ten million years, by the photochemical processes that destroy it in the upper atmosphere. Titan's a lot older than that, and it has methane. So the methane must be replenished."

Mott asked, "Are the oceans made of methane?"

"No. It's too hot. But there should be a lot of liquid ethane down there. The oceans are liquid hydrocarbon—seas of paraffin—with methane dissolved in them. That is the source of the methane. But there's still a problem.

"The orbit of Titan isn't a perfect circle. It's elliptical. So, even though Titan rotates to keep the same face to Saturn, any surface liquid is going to slosh back and forth: *tides*. Which means a dissipation of energy by tidal friction, which means the circularization of the orbit. Like the Moon around the Earth. So you need an ocean to get the methane; but with a big ocean, you should have a circular orbit. It was a paradox. Oceans, or no oceans? Because of that mystery the planners didn't know what they were sending *Huygens* into. They designed that little probe to float, or sink in a less dense ocean, or to land in slush . . ."

"But now we know the answer," Benacerraf prompted.

"Now we know the answer." Rosenberg twisted to look at his map. "Those crater seas are big enough to serve as methane reservoirs, with maybe twenty percent of the fluid bulk provided by the methane. But in bodies of fluid that size the tidal friction should be negligible.

"Besides, it now looks as if Titan may have a partially liquid interior. That ought to dissipate the orbital energy even more quickly than the surface reservoirs, so the whole question of the tidal constraint is still open. Anyhow, so there you have the solution to the puzzle. The answer was obvious all along; we just weren't thinking Titan . . ."

As she stared at the map, Mott tried to smile. "And this smoggy bombsite," she said, "will be home."

Benacerraf touched her shoulder. "Hell, if you've lived in Houston long enough, a little smog is nothing."

Mott said, "What's it going to be like for us down there, Rosenberg?"

"Different," Rosenberg said bluntly. "Titan is an ice moon, like Pluto, Triton, Ganymede. The difference is, it's overlaid by that fat atmosphere. At the core is a ball of silicate, overlaid by a shell of ice, six hundred miles thick. And on the surface, over a water-ice crust, lies that slush of complex organic compounds.

"You have to understand that *Titan is not like Earth*. Its 'bedrock' is water ice, with a little silicate. We may see plate tectonics, for instance, and even volcanoes. But if so they are driven by ammonia-water vulcanism, deep in the icy mantle. We call it cryovulcanism. We're going to see a lot of unfamiliar processes . . . And the weather is shit," he said. "Cold. And overcast. Smoggy, as you can see."

"How cold?"

"Co—o—old. At the surface, we'll find a temperature of about ninety-four K—nearly two hundred degrees below the freezing point of water. And that's with a boost from a greenhouse effect; it could actually be worse. But the deep cold is the reason such a small world has been able to cling onto its air. And, under the smog, it's *dark*. We should pack flashlights, Paula."

Mott said, "Can we see Saturn?"

"From the surface? No. Sorry."

"Jesus."

"So, landing sites," said Benacerraf. "We have to choose an equatorial landing site, because that's all we can reach."

Rosenberg said, "Correct. But wherever we land it's going to look superficially the same. The atmosphere is so thick that the temperature scarcely varies, from pole to pole. What we need to find—for the science, and so we can supply our own needs—is an interface between geologic units. An area where several different types of terrain come together."

"You have a suggestion?"

"Yeah." He stabbed a finger at the map, near the center, close to the "coastline" of the continent, Cronos. "There's a mountain range here, sprawling right across the equator. And a few degrees to the south of the equator, just here, is the highest mountain on Titan. The Survey called it Mount Othrys."

Mott asked, "More mythology?"

"Yeah . . ."

Benacerraf said, "Why do we need to be near a mountain?"

"I told you everything is covered in slush, in tholins. We're going to need water ice, however. But there is rain. Ethane and methane rain," he said. "The rain evaporates before it reaches ground level. But it should wash the tholins off the elevated ground. So the peak of Othrys will be exposed bedrock."

"Bedrock," Mott said, not following.

"Think Titan," Rosenberg said.

"Oh. I get it. Exposed water ice."

"All right," Benacerraf said. "So we come down somewhere near this mountain." Just to the north of the mountain, she saw, there was a large crater, maybe twenty miles wide, filled with a cashew-nut shaped lake. "How about here?"

Mott studied the map. "The crater has no name."

Rosenberg shrugged. "The USGS didn't name anything much below a hundred miles across . . ."

"Then we'll have to," Benacerraf said decisively. "Niki, you got any suggestions? This is going to be home, after all."

Mott smiled. "A dingy stretch of fluid, overlaid by twenty-four-hour smog, and stinking of petrochemicals? Paula, as you say, it's just like Houston. We'll call it Clear Lake."

"Clear Lake it is."

They fell silent, then, and looked at each other, here in the muggy Californian warmth, the bright light of the meeting room.

Clear Lake.

Benacerraf thought, What the hell are we doing?

She tried to imagine how it would be down there, on the

surface of Titan. In the pitch dark, laboring through freezing, sticky slush. Completely alone, without resource, save for the companions she took with her and whatever they could land.

Possibly, probably, for the rest of her life.

It would be a cold version of hell.

But her heart was beating, fast, and she smiled.

Jackie's right, she thought. She was being selfish. Who could turn down an adventure like this?

The moment broke. The three of them pored over the map, picking out more features, assigning tentative names, on the world that awaited them.

Gareth Deeke, Air Force officer, drove steadily north on Colorado Highway 115. He drove with the windows down and his sun-roof open, despite the crisp chill of the autumn air. The sun, high and small, beat down on his scalp from the immense blue sky; but his eyes were shielded by his mirrored glasses, and visibility was good—in fact he could see for miles, as if the air was glass.

Deeke loved the mountains: the emptiness, the huge sweep of the landscape, the sense of scale and frozen geological drama opening out all around him. He relished the feeling that he was embedded like a fly in amber, in this flashbulb moment of time.

He reached the right turn for Cheyenne Mountain with regret.

He could see the car park. It was the tabletop of a plateau, which jutted out massively from the side of the mountain. The steel bodies of cars glittered on its surface, in their neat rows, like ranks of insects.

The plateau was artificial. It had been constructed by piling up the granite which Air Force engineers had scooped out of the heart of the mountain.

He really didn't want to descend into some hole in the ground, not on a day like this.

But he had his duty.

He was pretty sure the reason he'd been summoned here today was to do with the new NASA announcement, the incredible news that they were planning to send astronauts to Saturn.

Deeke, like many within the USAF, was no fan of NASA.

He was of the same vintage as the early astronauts, but his own career had run orthogonally to the Moonwalkers'. He was an old lifting-body man: after Patuxent, he'd flown the X-15, the youngest pilot to do so. When Shuttle came along, his X-15 experience paid off. The X-15 was an unpowered glider, when it landed. Just like Shuttle.

A still-young Air Force officer, Deeke had taken the first test orbiter, *Enterprise*, on captive flights—where it had been strapped to the back of a 747—and later on its first free landing tests. Then he'd flown on the third orbital flight, one of the system's shakedown cruises.

Later, when STS had become operational, Deeke had flown exclusively Department of Defense missions on Shuttle.

Deeke and his buddies had launched reconnaissance satellites, and tried out some techniques for orbital manned reconnaissance; they'd even tried out core technology for some of the more exotic anti-satellite weaponry system proposals, like lasers and particle beams, which had come out of SDI.

Nobody outside the military knew exactly what he'd got up to on those missions. But Shuttle was, after all, a military vehicle.

But after *Challenger*, the military missions had dried up, and it looked as if Deeke wasn't going to get to fly again.

Since then he'd assumed responsibility for advanced projects, in the USAF and outside. For instance he was an observer on NASA's RLV program. It was interesting, varied, senior work.

But it wasn't like flying. And as the years wore on, even as he got older and slowed up, he got steadily more frustrated.

But now NASA was launching this ludicrous jaunt to the outer Solar System, and he'd had the call to come here to Cheyenne from his old commander, Al Hartle, and his instincts were telling him something pretty exciting was coming down.

So here he was.

A neat little electric vehicle like a golf buggy took Deeke along the glowing length of the central tunnel, deep into the heart of the mountain. Then there was a left turn, through big blast doors—each of them steel plates three feet thick, like battleship hull—and into the heart of the command post itself.

He worked through the elaborate security clearances. He even had to pass through a series of chambers, like airlocks; at the heart of the mountain the incoming air was stringently filtered against chemical, biological and radioactive agents.

He'd been prepared for the delays; he sat patiently in the echoing, blue-painted, boxy rooms.

This complex, dug out of the granite core of the mountain, covered more than four acres. The rooms were all steel shells, supported on big metal springs which would act as shock absorbers, in the event of the nuclear attack which had never come. From this base, any aerospace battle over the U.S. would have been coordinated, and there were hot line links to the Pentagon and the White House. The place was designed to survive. It was hardened against EMP. Blast and heat from any explosion would have been channeled through that big entrance tunnel and vented on the other side of the mountain . . .

There was no reading matter in the waiting rooms, but there was public net access. He logged onto *Time*, and found himself staring at an image of the thin, serious face of Jake Hadamard, the NASA Administrator. The accompanying article lauded Hadamard and his team; the proposed Titan project was striking a chord, right now, with the public—although there was opposition, from the Luddites and various religious groups—and the project was turning out to be a "fitting capstone" to the U.S. manned space program. Far better to remember a final great triumph to conclude forty years of endeavor, than the sour memory of the *Columbia* fiasco. And so on.

Hadamard was clearly using the Titan proposal to propel himself from the relative obscurity of his previous accounting background to the front rank of national figures. Once the Titan mission was launched, and NASA's final affairs wound up and devolved, Hadamard would have his pick of jobs, in industry or politics. Hadamard, the article said, had every chance of becoming man of the year.

Deeke had to grin at that. Hadamard was one shrewd guy if he could turn a Shuttle crash into a good career move.

Somehow it was typical NASA. All bullshit.

At last an aide—a young MP—collected him, and walked him to the office of Brigadier General Albert Hartle.

Hartle came out from behind his desk, and shook Deeke's hand vigorously. "Gareth. It's good of you to come out here."

The MP brought Deeke a coffee. It was good quality, potent and rich. Then the MP left, closing the door behind him.

Hartle smiled thinly. "I'd offer you a drink. Baltics, that's what you Edwards boys used to drink, right?"

"I understand, sir. Not here."

"No. Not here."

Deeke sized up his surroundings. The office was just a box, like all the chambers in the complex. Hartle had left the walls unpainted; the bare steel shone in the harsh fluorescent strips. The biggest item of furniture was Hartle's desk, a severe battleship-gray affair that looked like it had been welded together out of gun metal. Its surface bore a blotter, a fountain pen, and a small old-fashioned computer terminal.

The only item of adornment on the walls was a North American Air Defense Command crest, behind Hartle; the

NORAD badge was a shield, with a sword and eagle wings upraised before the North American continent, sheltering it from the lightning strikes above.

Hartle was approaching sixty. The Brigadier General was small, trim and upright in his decorated uniform, his strong hands folded up before him.

He looked, Deeke thought, like part of the room, an extension of its severity.

This was Hartle's habitat. As far as Deeke knew Hartle had no family: nothing in his life but the Air Force, and what he saw as his mission. It was hard to imagine the old Cold Warrior anywhere else but here.

They'll probably have to bury him here, Deeke thought.

Hartle was studying him, his blue eyes predatory.

"I think you'd better tell me why I'm here, sir."

"Gareth, I want you to indulge me. I want to go over a little history with you. Because if we don't learn from the past, we're condemned to repeat it. Right? And by the end of the story, I think you'll agree with me that we need to take action now. A single, affirmative, decisive action. There are others who will support us . . ."

"Action, sir?"

"Bear with me."

Hartle started to tell Deeke how he had gotten involved in America's space activities as far back as the 1970s, after Apollo.

"Of course you know the truth about Apollo. McNamara— the Defense Secretary—supported the lunar thing to President Kennedy. Why the hell should the DoD support a big civilian man-in-space boondoggle? But in retrospect it's clear. McNamara had wider goals. With a big new program like Apollo, outside the reach of the USAF, McNamara could please the aerospace lobby and Congress, taking the pressure off himself, so that he could get on with budget-paring defense programs. Our programs.

"You must understand this point clearly, Gareth. The civilian space program, and its Agency, were actually used as bureaucratic weapons against the USAF. And hence, of course, against the national interest."

So, Deeke thought, our interpretation of history is that the U.S. went to the Moon in order to beat up on the USAF. Deeke suspected it wasn't as simple as that; he knew the USAF's space programs had been riven by infighting within the Air Force from the beginning. But it wasn't a bad theory.

Maybe old Al Hartle has been down this damn hole in the ground too long.

. . . But Deeke found he wanted to hear more. It all fit in, he realized, with his own instincts.

It had been years since Deeke's last visit to the complex.

Deeke was surprised by the subdued atmosphere. He remembered a buzz about the place, a sense of purpose and vigor. If the Big One had ever come, this might have been one of the last outposts of civilization, as the bright young people here monitored the launching of nuclear-tipped missiles across the planet. They could have survived down here for weeks, months even; there were big steel reservoirs, for instance, storing six million gallons of cool, uncontaminated Colorado Springs water.

The sense of mission, of power, had been palpable. Deeke missed it all, damn it.

But now it was different, right across the country, even the world; now, in hardened Minuteman silos that had cost millions to develop, farmers were being allowed to store grain.

Sometimes, Deeke thought, he just couldn't recognize the world, this odd, fragmented future into which he was slowly sliding, helplessly. None of the old certainties seemed to hold any more.

He could understand how Hartle felt, with his recitation of forty-year-old history, of historic crimes for which retribution was coming.

"Go on, sir."

☆   ☆   ☆

"We had to accept the Moon, but at least we were able to stop those assholes flying to fucking Mars . . .

"I worked on the study group that came up with the Shuttle recommendation. We forced NASA to accept a delta-winged orbiter, to give the bird a low angle of attack atmosphere entry—more heating, but greater cross-range abilities. And that big cargo bay was built for anti-sat work. The Shuttle was a military vehicle, no doubt about it. Then we started work on the Vandenberg launch site. We even essayed an orbital bombing run, over Moscow. But we were faced with nothing but delays and overruns. And then came fucking *Challenger*.

"Think how far back we've slipped, since the X-15 you flew. A fucking museum piece, but still the fastest aircraft in the world. Do you remember what we planned? The X-20, the B-70—a Mach 3 bomber—and the F-108—a Mach 3 fighter—all canceled by 1968. My God, they even canceled the Supersonic Transport because of the fucking environmentalists who said the human race would become extinct if it ever took to the air. Right now the USAF does not have a plane to catch the Russians' Foxbat . . .

"Gareth, NASA has been a thorn in our flesh ever since it was founded, by Eisenhower. Even when it hasn't been used as a positive weapon against us, it's acted to disrupt our programs and limit our capabilities. My God, if I had my way there would be NASA managers hauled into the courts to answer charges of treason, such is the damage they've inflicted.

"But it's been a long game. NASA has been weakening since 1969. It's been a slow decline but it's been steady. And now, at last, we're in a position to kill it."

"*Kill* it, sir?"

"Listen to me now. This damn Titan stunt is one last throw of the dice by those NASA assholes. If it succeeds, they're figuring, maybe they'll get back in the public eye, start clawing back some of the power and prestige and funding they've blown. We can't let that happen, Gareth.

"Look, we're working at many levels to stop this. We're pulling strings in the Pentagon and up on Capitol Hill. I'm calling in every favor I can. And, frankly, we can count on Xavier Maclachlan's support. If we can just delay the damn thing until Maclachlan gets into the White House in '08 we'll have won . . .

"But anyhow, this is an historic moment, and we must have the courage to act, to shape the future. Otherwise, we might have no future to shape. *The Red Chinese*, Gareth. Asia is stirring from its thousand-year sleep. Red China will soon be on the march. Think about that."

"You talked about action, sir."

Hartle came forward, and rested his thin hand on Deeke's uniformed shoulder. His face was a mask, the wrinkles in his cheeks pulled straight by his severe frown, and his shock of crewcut white hair was like a metal helmet. "I think we *can* stop this before they get to a launch. But we have to plan for the worst. You're going to be my linebacker. My last line of defense. I want you there in that hole, if that runner tries to break through . . ."

Deeke thought, Hartle has gone rogue. But he has backers. And a vision.

He felt adrenaline spurt in his system, as if he were once more in the cockpit of a rocket plane, readying for ignition.

Holy God, he thought. I'm going to get to fly again.

Hartle looked into Deeke's face, and nodded, as if satisfied.

Marcus White wanted to fly himself straight into Edwards for the F-1 test fire. But he couldn't get hold of a T-38. Like a lot of other NASA resources, the little needle-nosed supersonic trainers, used by the astronauts like sports cars and taxis, were being quietly withdrawn from service.

It was deeply shitty, White thought; there was a stench of decay about the whole enterprise. The sooner we get this damn Titan mission assembled and away the better.

Anyhow he had to get a commercial flight into LAX; from there he hired a car and drove north out of the city. The car was a late-model Chevy with a lot of smartass electronic features he couldn't switch off; it just seemed to go where it wanted to go, like a dumb old mule.

The F-1 was the big main engine that powered the S-IC, the Saturn V first stage. White knew the F-1 refurbishment program was going badly, and—as Benacerraf had told him when he'd gone along to bitch at her about the T-38s—his presence up there at Edwards would be a morale boost for the guys.

Not that he could do anything constructive, of course. He was an aviator, not a rocket scientist. He was just a kind of symbol, a presence, who still meant something to the guys working on this unlikely project. Maybe. But this was the last of it. After Titan was gone, his usefulness would be done.

He figured he'd have himself stuffed and mounted and stuck in the Smithsonian. Hang me up there with the Wright Flyer, boys.

The evening was coming on. The sky was cloudless, but the horizon was ringed with the sulphur-orange glow of Los Angeles, masking the stars.

At last he reached the desert. He could see it all around him as a flat, pale white crust in the starlight: the salt flats, like an immense runway, where they used to test the X-15.

He spent the night in the bar with Don Baylor, the old-time Rocketdyne engineer who had invited him to Edwards.

He woke up with a banging head. You ain't got the tanker capacity you used to have, boy.

But he pulled on his shorts and went for a run around the base.

The sun was barely above the horizon, and the cold of the desert night was lingering, making the air sharp as a blade as it cut into his lungs. He used to run until his heart was pumping, burning all the alcohol and toxins out of his system. But today he tired quickly.

He had to walk back to his room, the world graying around him, limping and wheezing like the old geezer he had become.

The test stand viewing bunker was just a couple of rows of seats behind a big picture window, with telemetry on the engine fed into little softscreens. When he arrived the bunker was already half-full, of managers and senior technicians; White knew that this was just a viewing point for the senior staff—managers and VIP types like White himself—and the real work would be done by technicians controlling the test from elsewhere.

It was mostly men in the bunker, mostly in rumpled suits. They were uniformly fat and aged. Many of these guys had been pulled out of retirement, to work on Saturn technology once more. White hair and bald scalps glowed in the low desert sunlight.

We all let ourselves get so damn old, White thought gloomily.

A countdown was proceeding, delivered by a smooth woman's voice. It sounded like the announcements in an airport departure lounge.

Donny Baylor was sitting in the front row of the stand, pale as a ghost, with his face half-covered by the biggest, thickest pair of sunshades White had ever seen.

White laughed and clapped Baylor on the back; Baylor blanched further.

"Asshole," Baylor said.

"Not as young as you used to be, Donny."

"Neither are you."

White settled into a seat beside Baylor. "I'll tell you the best damn hangover cure I ever knew. You'd take up your bird after a night of throwing them back, with all that alcohol still slosh-ing around your system. All you'd have to do was pull a few Gs and suck in oxygen to flush all that crap away . . ."

Baylor was a short, stocky man, and his face was a round, wizened button. He rubbed his forehead and scratched at the grizzled frosting that was all the years had left of his hair. "Things have changed, Marcus. When you think about it, it was pretty much you and me on our own last night."

"Too damn true," White said. In fact, he had a theory you could correlate the nation's decline with the growing adversity of these younger generations to a few cold ones.

Baylor checked his watch. "Ten minutes to the firing."

White looked out of the picture window. The sun was low and in his eyes, but the glass was polarized somehow. There was a small pair of binoculars in front of his seat, not much bigger than opera glasses. But when he lifted them to his eyes some kind of electronics in the optics started to work, and the test stand leapt into his view, as detailed as if he was standing next to it, the image as steady as a rock, the glasses somehow com-pensating for the shake of his hands.

The test stand itself was just a big square block of scaffold-ing, sitting on concrete trestles over a flame pit, anchored deep in the desert. The stand was maybe forty feet tall, and it was topped off by the two big silvery spheres which held oxidizer and propellant, RP-1 kerosene, for the test fires. There was frost, sparkling over the shell of the liquid oxygen tank.

The single F-1 engine under test today—a complex tangle of feed lines, electronics and gimbal bearings—was pretty much hidden by the test stand structure. But he could see the nozzle, protruding out beneath the scaffolding, and he could see the fat kerosene pipes wrapped around the bell; the fuel passed around the combustion chamber and engine bell, to cool them, before it was fed into the combustion chamber.

That single nozzle was all of twelve feet across. And a Saturn first stage would have no less than five of those mothers, in a neat cluster, all burning at once, every one of them five times as powerful as the Atlas rocket that had thrust John Glenn to orbit.

Even the test stand itself had had to be refurbished for this program, he knew. Most of the Saturn test facilities around the country had long been deactivated or converted to other uses. The Rocketdyne engine stands at Canoga Park had been converted for tests of the Atlas and Delta expendable boosters, for instance, and the stands here at Edwards had been used for Shuttle solid rocket motor tests. The Marshall facilities had been turned over to Shuttle main engine tests. And so on.

Well, to make the schedule, this reverse refurbishment had been brisk, he could see now. The desert sand around the test stand had been churned up, and left in great untidy heaps.

Beyond the stand, a line of worn, rocky hills shouldered over the horizon; the sky was high and blue, with a few wisps of cloud in layers. There was a great sense of emptiness, of bigness; White knew there wasn't a human being within a mile of that stand.

"So, Donny," White said. "That damn thing going to light on schedule?"

White was expecting the usual confident good-guy bull back from Baylor, and he was surprised when Baylor didn't respond in kind. Instead Baylor glanced at him, evidently troubled, despite that big mask of his sunglasses. "I'll tell you the truth, Marcus," he said. "We got ourselves one hell of a beast out there."

"You don't sound too confident."

"I'm not. Christ, Marcus, it's been like archaeology. We had to tear down one of the old flight spares for the component evaluation, and to get some experience of assembly and checkout. We had to buy fresh tooling and checkout equipment, and activate the old turbopump checkout facility. We had to adapt the thrust chamber assembly equipment we use for Shuttle main engine production. Only about half of the old suppliers are still in business, so we had to find new approved suppliers, for the heat exchanger duct assembly, the lox mating ring, the fuel pump housing, the pump housing machining . . . A dozen things. Some of the tools we needed we had to make. We had to redraw the tooling drawings, rework all the process and material specifications; they weren't compatible with the man-ufacturing processes we use now . . .

"I'll tell you what's really screwing us, though. Instability in the combustion chamber. See, the pumps bring the lox and kerosene to the injector plate. That's a metal slab, a disc a yard across and four inches thick. The point is to get a nice smooth flame front, where the propellants burn at a uniform tempera-ture, right across the face of the injector plate, all three feet of it . . ." Baylor started going into a lot of detail about how the lox and kerosene were brought into the chamber as fans, which impinged on each other. Pre-burners ignited the propellants at those points of impingement. Baylor mimed the little fans of lox and kerosene with his engineer's hands, his gnarly fingers splayed out, as brown and hard as wood carvings.

"And if you don't get a smooth flame front," Baylor said now, "you're fucked. Suppose one side of the plate has a slightly higher oxygen content than the other. Then that area will get hotter, and produce higher pressures on that side. Then, in an engine the size of the F-1, you get a racetrack, where you have a high-pressure wave rushing around the perimeter of the combustion chamber. Then—it only takes milliseconds—the heat flows inside the chamber get disrupted and start bouncing back and forth. You get positive feedback, and before you know it your combustion process is out of control. That's combus-tion instability, Marcus."

"So why are you telling me about it?"

"Because it's killing us. The slightest thing seems to trigger it: cavitation in the pumps, thermal shocks as the engines heat up, acoustical shocks at the moment of ignition."

"But that kind of instability can't have been a new problem, even in 1961," White said.

"Hell, no. The Germans had instability problems all the way back to the goddamn V-2. Each generation of rocket required new fixes. But all of the fixes were pretty much ad-hoc, Marcus; nobody really had a handle on it. And with the F-1 you had this immense size of engine to compound the problem. Maybe," he mused, "if we'd left well enough alone, and not fucked about with the configuration . . . but we didn't. We're trying to upgrade, to reach eighteen hundred K thrust, up from fifteen hundred. So we've made a whole stack of modifications: we increased the oxidizer inducer diameter, strengthened the gimbal seat and the cross block, strengthened the high pressure ducts and the thrust chambers, beefed up the turbine exhaust manifold, improved the heat exchanger, increased the power of the turbine . . . All of that screwed the stability of the flight configuration, basically. And we've had to try to fix it."

"Come on, Don. Those old guys in the 1960s, from Rocketdyne and Marshall, got the instability problem licked in the end. I mean, with due respect, I'm looking at one of those old bastards right now."

Baylor looked mournful. "That's just it, Marcus. I arrived too late. I came into propulsion engineering at Marshall in 1965, just about in time for the Saturn flight testing. I missed all the fun, from the early days, when the core team—the Combustion Devices Team—was working to solve the instability problem."

"Don't we have any members of that team left?"

Baylor looked grim. "Marcus, they even sent me around the old people's homes. Most of those guys are dead, and the rest are eating baby food and complaining about their catheters. Hell, you're talking about a project that's nearly fifty years gone. I was just a junior member of the team—and I joined late—and now I'm the most senior guy we have here." He shook his head. "If only we'd thought to do this twenty years ago—even ten . . ."

The count reached its final seconds. Baylor turned to the test stand, and picked up his binoculars.

In the last moments, tons of water cascaded down, into the

flame deflector pit at the base of the stand. White could hear the roar of that miniature Niagara even from here, even through the glass.

Baylor didn't seem aware White was here any more; his eyes, behind their big shades, were focused on that test stand.

White could picture what was happening inside the F-1.

The combustion chamber, the tough heart of the engine, was a barrel a yard wide and a little less long. Right now, a few seconds before ignition, in four small pre-burners inside that chamber pilot lights had lit up, providing a flame at the points where the sprays of lox and kerosene from the injector plate hit each other. The burning of exhaust gases from the turbines produced a thick orange smoke, which burst out of the nozzle and bounced off the flame deflector under the launcher, busting out to either side. The pumps were running up to speed, the valves were opening, and now the propellant poured in: a ton of kerosene, two tons of lox, in the first second alone, and in every second thereafter.

The gases produced by their ignition shouldered out through the nozzle throat at the bottom of the chamber. In these few seconds, as the engine built up to full power, the interior of the combustion chamber went from room temperature to as hot as the surface of the sun; pressure went from zero to a thousand pounds per square inch.

The flame directly under the engine turned to an incandescent white, and the orange smoke billowed outward and upward, enveloping the base of the nozzle. A pillar of pure white light exploded into life under the engine bell.

It was the brightest thing in White's view, brighter than the sun. His binoculars dimmed themselves down, compensating for that surge of brilliance, obscuring the rest of the test stand structure and dimming the bright blue sky to a muddy gray. The water gushing into the flame pit flashed to steam, and great clouds of it billowed out around the stand, unable to dim the brilliance of that light.

The noise reached them now, a great crackling explosion of nonlinear wave fronts that burst across the desert. The picture window rattled, visibly bowing, and in the depths of his gut White could feel a bass rumble.

White felt his lips pull back into a feral grin, and he whooped. He just let all that pure rocket light wash over his face. This was the way a rocket was supposed to be, he thought: pure liquid fire, none of that dirty yellow-orange shit that came spewing out of the solid-propellant firecrackers they strapped to the side of the Shuttle.

But then the torrent of fire sputtered, as if the engine was being throttled back, or was stalling. White thought he could see the whole test stand shudder.

The nozzle softened and deformed.

It happened in an instant: thick, high-strength steel plate burning through in a quarter of a second, guttering like candle wax. The metal just gushed down into the flame pit, swept away by the energy of the torrent of fire. And then that torrent, without the shaping of the nozzle, turned from a controlled explosion into an uncontrolled one.

Light gushed out of the test stand in a ball, flaring; steam billowed furiously. He thought he could feel the heat of the bang on his face, even across a mile of desert, even through the toughened glass. It was like a nova, White thought, a star exploding on the Earth.

The explosion lasted no more than a second. Then the test stand shut itself down, cutting off the flow of kerosene and oxidant to the failed engine.

The light faded, leaving the test stand exposed, huge clouds of steam still billowing up out of the flame deflector.

Baylor lifted his glasses and rubbed his face; White could see that his eyes were red-rimmed and rheumy, glossy with water. The eyes of an old man.

"Fuck," said Baylor. "See what I'm saying about the instability."

All around them, in the viewing bunker, the technicians and managers were moving out, with much gloomy talk and shaking of heads.

Now's the time for a bit of inspiration, Marcus. This is why you're here. Sprinkle a little of the old Moondust on them, and get them all fired up to go out there and take that motor to pieces, and go over it again and again until they get it right.

Like they used to in the old days.

But right now, damn his soul to hell, he couldn't think of a thing to say.

Outside, around the ruined test stand, the steam clouds continued to billow out of the flame deflector. Mojave sand was scattered around the test stand in rays: dead straight and maybe thirty feet long, reminding him of the raying on the lunar surface, around his LM descent stage, after the landing.

This wasn't like preparing for any other flight, Siobhan Libet found. This wasn't just routine, just another element in the assembly-line of Shuttle missions.

It wasn't just that it was the last. With this flight, she was entering realms of mythology. People *looked* at her differently.

And everywhere she went she faced the classic, unanswerable question. *What's it like to fly in space?*

She went up to Boeing's Shuttle orbiter assembly facility, at Palmdale, California.

Libet tried to remain inconspicuous as Billy Ray Jardine of Boeing conducted his tour. That wasn't too difficult at first; the little ten-strong group, of astronauts, NASA Shuttle and Titan program managers—including Libet and Barbara Fahy—were anonymously clad in bunny suits, long, crisp-white coats and hygiene-conscious caps. They looked, Libet thought wryly, like a group of food hygiene inspectors descending on a McDonald's.

The Palmdale assembly facility was huge, cavernous, a place of light and rectangles. The floor was a layer of some blue-gray resin, utterly flat, threaded with yellow demarcation lines and scarred with rubber skid marks from the little electric carts that rolled everywhere. The walls were painted with corporate red, white and blue stripes and huge Stars-and-Stripes. Around the edge of the floor were big, cuboid offices, like independent buildings spawned inside the gut of this monster, and the floor was littered with massive, anonymous machinery.

Billy Ray Jardine was the President of Boeing's space transportation division. Jardine looked every bit the corporate senior executive, with his gray suit jacket stretching over his ample, comfortable belly. He would have fit in just about any era since the Second World War, Libet thought; his type had been running the country for much longer than she had been alive. Only the full-color images cycling across the surface of his softscreen tie—of old successes in space, Rockwell's Saturn V second stage, Apollo, Shuttle itself, not to mention Boeing's own Saturn V first stage—gave any concession to modernity.

The facility was clean, bright, every metal surface shining and unscuffed. The assembly and manufacturing equipment around her looked state of the art. Here—by Rockwell, before the Boeing buyout—all five of the billion-dollar spacecraft of the Shuttle fleet had been assembled, from *Columbia* to the *Challenger* replacement *Endeavour*, which had first flown in 1992. And Boeing had evidently maintained this facility to the highest standard. Any time NASA had asked for a revival of the Shuttle construction program, Boeing would have been able to respond, ready to accept all those fat billion-buck NASA contracts once more.

But Libet felt depressed by all this sparkling readiness. Because this facility was never going to be used to build an orbiter again.

In fact, Boeing had adapted its facility to tear spacecraft apart.

The party was taken to a metal balcony which overlooked a sectioned-off part of the assembly area floor. Here, the Shuttle orbiter *Atlantis* had been brought for its hasty modification. The orbiter's boattail—the aft fuselage assembly—was facing Libet, with the nozzles of the three big main engines thrusting out of the scaffolding. The rest of the orbiter, foreshortened by perspective, was encased in scaffolding and protective sheeting. A little swarm of white-coated workers was busy all over the spacecraft; the air filled with the whine of drills and the ozone stink of oxy-acetylene burners. *Atlantis* looked, Libet thought, as if it was being deliberately crippled.

At first glance, the orbiter itself still looked much as it had done before. But, slowly, Libet made out differences.

For instance, the crew cabin—the nose of the orbiter—had been dismantled. Now, a simple aerodynamic cone fairing was being fixed to the orbiter's frame. And *Atlantis*'s payload bay had been lengthened, into the space vacated by the crew compartment, to more than eighty feet: a third more than the baseline design of the Shuttle system. The boattail, with the main engine assembly, was being left almost unmodified. But the smaller engines of the orbiter's orbital maneuvering system had been removed. Those engines brought the ship out of orbit at the end of its mission. And there was no need for a system to bring *Atlantis* home again.

And *Atlantis* had no wings.

Atlantis no longer needed wings, or a tailplane, or retro engines. *Atlantis* was no longer an orbiter. She had been reduced to a Shuttle-C Cargo Element, a so-called SCE, consisting of little more than a payload carrier bay and an aft fuselage, with engines. And SCEs were expendable. *Atlantis* would never again carry a crew. No effort would be made to return *Atlantis* to Earth after her final flight; its cargo delivered to orbit, *Atlantis* would be slowed by its reaction control thrusters, and allowed to burn up over the Pacific.

Libet could see the big delta-shaped wings, their leading edges battered by their multiple reentries, taken away from the orbiter hulk and stacked against a wall of the facility. Looking at the severed joint of each wing she could see their internal structure; the wings were just a skin of stiffened aluminum alloy over a framework of internal ribs and stringers. Detached from the orbiter, the wings looked crude, primitive. Something Howard Hughes might have recognized. The wings had been manufactured by Grumman, at their Bethpage plant in New York. Grumman had been the people who had manufactured the Lunar Module for Apollo. She wondered what the old-timers there thought of this day's work.

". . . Of course," Billy Ray Jardine was saying, "what you have here is an extension of the original Shuttle-C concept, which would have relied on the manufacture of wholly new SCEs—Shuttle-C Cargo Elements—rather than their adaptation from existing orbiters. Not that the manufacture of new SCEs would have presented in any way a challenge. But you have to understand that we have to pretty much take apart each orbiter to adapt it to serve as a Shuttle-C SCE. Naturally the modification of the old test articles is generally somewhat simpler than the flight articles.

"We have to make required modifications to the shroud and stringback, a new aluminum skin, and enhanced stringer and ringframe construction. We will deliver a fifteen feet by eighty-two feet usable payload space, of which fifteen by sixty is capable of changeout on the pad. Avionics and guidance, navigation and control systems are adapted from those on the orbiter; systems relating to manned life support, long duration orbit, descent, and landing are deleted . . ."

Jardine's accent was Texan, his voice brisk, clipped and competent; it depressed Libet even more to think that this man could show equal professional enthusiasm about taking apart his orbiters as assembling them.

Barbara Fahy was standing beside Libet. "That smooth corporate bull does have a way of putting you to sleep, doesn't it?" Fahy pushed back her hat and scratched her forehead. "Damn this thing."

"You don't look too happy," Libet said.

Fahy fixed her hat back in place. "Should I be? I looked up the original proposal for Shuttle-C, from the 1980s. They were asking for five years to complete the development, including six months for proposal evaluation and contract award, four years of design, fabrication and assembly, a comprehensive test program, and a couple of test flights before going operational. For better or worse Boeing is rushing through the modifications in half that time. And we'll be going straight to operational, without a chance for a single test flight. The same is true of the Saturn refurbishment program. I'm a big supporter of this program, Siobhan, this vision of Paula's to get us to Titan. But we just aren't giving this damn thing enough *time*."

"We don't have much choice. The bad guys are closing in, remember. In fact, Boeing is already behind schedule." It was true; it was the reason for their visit today.

"I know, I know. But all we need is one of these flights to fail, just one, and we won't have the lift capacity we need. And I might be the person who has to deliver one of those flights. And carry the can when it blows apart."

They were taken to the floor of the facility now, and walked underneath the still-graceful chin of the orbiter. The smooth, shaped surface of *Atlantis*'s belly loomed over Libet, dark and sheer, and she could see the complex mottling of the tiles and blankets of the thermal protection system.

Those tiles, all thirty thousand of them, had absorbed thousands of man-hours of development and testing. And then every one of them, shaped for a particular location on the orbiter's complex surface, had had to be fitted individually, by hand. It was a monumental, medieval labor.

But now, teams of technicians were again working on the belly of *Atlantis*. They were on movable platforms, and they reached up and scoured and painted and dug; each of them looked like Michelangelo working in the Sistine, she thought vaguely. But what they were doing was far from creative: they were detaching those painfully-applied tiles, one by one. All in the interests of saving weight; on her last mission, *Atlantis* didn't even need her thermal protection any more.

Discarded tiles lay around on the floor of the facility, some of them streaked and discolored by *Atlantis*'s final atmospheric entry.

The tiles on the underside of the craft were coated with a black, reflective glass patina. The shaped surface returned complex highlights from the bright working lights of the Boeing facility. The effect of the ceiling of tiles above her, with its subtle contours, was quite beautiful, she thought; it was like the roof of some modern church.

Libet shook her head. "My God. It's an act of vandalism. We're taking fully operational spacecraft, all this mature technology—national treasures, for God's sake—and stripping them down to serve as garbage scows."

Fahy smiled at Libet. "We've been through this. The only alternative to Shuttle-C is to turn the damn things into café bars, like the Russians did to *Buran*. You can't tell me you'd prefer that."

"Hell," Libet grumbled. "It's just—"

"What?"

"It's just, being an astronaut is all I ever wanted to do. Flying in space, traveling to new worlds. To Nimbar, or Vulcan, or Bajor, or through that damn wormhole . . . But here in the real universe I got nowhere to go, except Titan, and that's a lethal ice-ball, and we're having to burn up everything to get there. I keep on feeling I was born in the wrong universe."

Fahy laughed. "But you're lucky, Siobhan. At least you are heading out. And there ain't nobody who's going to follow you, not in my lifetime, or a long time afterward."

The party moved on.

They were taken to a balcony overlooking another area of the assembly facility floor. Here—Libet hadn't been expecting this—Boeing employees, maybe a couple of hundred of them, had gathered. They were standing in their white coats and plastic overshoes, looking up at their visitors.

Jardine started giving them a pep talk. ". . . We're scheduled to begin power-on systems testing in a couple more months," he said. He beamed out at his workers from under the brim of his white hat. "And that puts us significantly under budget and only a month behind schedule, which we *will* recover. I attribute that to a mature Shuttle program expertise, careful planning and foresight by Boeing and NASA, and, most importantly, the hard work of thousands of people. I mean you people, right here, and I have never worked with a better bunch of quality workers in all my years in this business . . ."

He got a ripple of applause for that.

Then, to Libet's horror, Jardine said something about how they were honored to have with them one of the people who this program was all about, the latest chapter in Boeing's long and proud space tradition . . . And Libet found herself being pushed forward, until she reached a discreet black microphone on a stand in front of her.

She looked back at Fahy, appealing. Fahy shrugged, apologetically, and held her palms out flat. Take it easy.

Libet looked out over the little pool of faces. Like so many in the space industry, the workers here weren't young, on average; there were plenty of gray hairs pushing out from under those gleaming white hats. This last effort probably meant the end of their careers, she realized. And they were all looking up at her from the assembly facility floor.

Their faces were—empty. Shining.

I fascinate them, she realized.

Holy shit, she thought. Astronauts nowadays weren't prepared for this stuff. All her PR training had been about playing down the wonder stuff. Being an astronaut was just a job, right?

But this was different. It was as if she was John Glenn, ready to go off to the high frontier. Maybe to die. Evidently Paula had been right in her hunch that this Titan mission would, one last time, grab the imagination of the people.

But, Libet thought, what in hell do I say?

Then the question came, called up from the floor. *What's it like to fly in space?*

There was a ripple of nervous laughter.

She held the microphone and tried to reply. ". . . It's like nothing you can imagine. The photos, the IMAX films, the VRs, nothing captures it. I feel like a child. I feel like I've been to a secret place. And now you guys are sending me back . . ."

They were watching her, expectant, silent.

She remembered stories of early astronauts as they'd toured similar facilities, fifty years ago. And she remembered what Grissom, or Cooper or Glenn or Shepard, had said in one such place, at Convair or McDonnell Douglas or Boeing.

She leaned forward to the microphone, and said: "Do good work."

There was a long silence.

Then applause started rippling around the assembly area floor, vigorous, laced by a couple of whistles.

Billy Ray Jardine's heavy hand clapped her back.

Deeply embarrassed, she retreated.

Barbara Fahy approached her, grinning. "Welcome to the space program," she said.

Marcus White kept track of the modifications Don Baylor and his team tried, to lick the instability problem in that balky old F-1 engine.

They put baffles into the combustion chamber, copper plates that extended down from the injector plate, that would interrupt those rebounding instability waves. But the baffles just bent over like blades of grass in a breeze. So they put in massive dams, slabs of two-inch-thick copper, cooled by a kerosene flow. That helped some, but the worst instabilities still overcame the damping effect of the baffles.

Eventually, sparked off by obscure test results from the old documentation, Baylor tried another approach. He changed the impingement angle of the propellant streams coming through the holes in the injector plate. That way the fans of lox and kerosene were formed further down inside the chamber. There was a cost to this, because the engine efficiency was reduced; the further down the streams met, the less completely they burned before being expelled from the chamber. But with that new angle of impingement, Baylor and his team managed, at last, to reduce substantially the occurrence of instability.

So they went to work on that basic design, fine-tuning it, shaving thin slices off the engine orifice, until at last they weren't getting the instability at all.

"Fucking A," White told him. "You ought to take your guys out and get oiled up and—"

"Marcus, you don't understand. For us there's no splash-down party. We never know for sure that we've won. Look, it's not as if we wrote out equations and ran computer models to show that we've removed the instability. All we've done is mod-ify the design until it went away. And we don't for sure know how. That instability is lurking in there, you can be sure about it. All I can do now is hope that it doesn't find some way to strike before we finish firing off those four birds."

"You're a pessimist, Baylor," White snapped. "Look, in the Apollo program they fired thirteen flights, sixty-five F-1 engines, and never a failure. So there, you got yourself a hun-dred percent reliable engine."

Baylor had laughed. "The logic doesn't work like that, Marcus. History is a poor indicator of reliability. Read Feynman."

"Who?"

"Never mind. You know, we ransacked the documentation they left behind from the 1960s but there's no real clue about how *they* mastered this in the end. There's a rumor they just got a bunch of craftsmen at Canoga Park to drill holes at random in the damn plate, until they found something that worked. Maybe it wasn't just a sea story . . ."

Baylor just wouldn't lighten up, to the end.

Anyhow, the F-1 refurbishment was done, for better or worse. And now it was time to launch.

Marcus White packed his bags for the Cape.

It was going to be the first Saturn V launch since 1973. And Barbara Fahy was going to get to direct it.

She followed the components of booster AS-514 through their refurbishment and assembly. The third stage, the S-IVB, was delivered to KSC from McDonnell by a "Super Guppy," a fat transport aircraft, one of the few of its type still flying. The two other stages arrived by barge, the S-II second stage from Boeing's facility at Seal Beach in California, and the S-IC from NASA's Michoud facility in Louisiana.

Fahy watched the S-IC arrive on a barge called *Neptune*, at the refurbished Saturn unloading facilities on the Banana River. The stage, a prone cylinder a hundred and forty feet long, was wrapped up in plastic like some bizarre piece of modern art. Teams of technicians descended on the stage, checking to make sure that the various wrappings and protective devices had not been damaged during the long transit. The techs were youngsters supervised by a handful of grizzled old heads who remembered this stuff from the last time they'd done it, in the 1970s.

The S-IC alone was gargantuan. Most of its cylindrical length was taken up by its fuel and oxidant tanks. The five F-1s, gleaming as if new, were fixed to a massive thrust structure, twenty-four tons of it. And beyond them the stage's fins flared above the technicians, spanning sixty feet.

Actually this S-IC had benefited from considerable rebuilding; much of the intertank, engine fairings and the fins had been replaced with new composite materials and lightweight aluminum-lithium alloys. The other two stages had been similarly reworked.

The S-IC was taken to the Low Bay of the Vehicle Assembly Building, where it was checked over prone for the final time. Then it was taken to the High Bay, where lines were attached from the crane overhead, and the S-IC lifted upright and settled gently into place aboard the mobile launch platform.

The second stage, the S-II—itself all of ninety feet long— was hauled three hundred feet into the air and set delicately atop the S-IC. It was like watching a skyscraper being assembled, in giant prefabricated chunks.

Back in the 1960s, the guys who ran the VAB cranes would boast that they could rest the hooks of their gigantic machines so delicately that they could touch an egg without breaking it. But those days were gone; now the cranes were fully automated and controlled to within fractions of an inch by sonar and infrared systems. The job of humans now was to watch the machines perform more precisely and reliably than they ever could.

When the two stages were aligned, technicians moved in to join them. Three big twelve-inch pins were set at equal spacings around the cylindrical geometry of the join, and over two hundred one-and-a-half-inch fasteners were fixed at six-inch intervals. It took three days to stitch the stages together. The guys in the '60s could do it in eight hours, the old timers said.

Next the S-IVB was lifted over the second stage and joined up similarly. And finally the payload—a cylindrical tank, swathed in insulation, that would hold a hundred and eighty thousand pounds of propellant for the Titan mission—was mated to the S-IVB.

Walking around the base of the assembled Saturn, Fahy peered at its upper stages, so remote they seemed lost in the misty air above. AS-514 was the operational Saturn which had for three decades sat on the lawn outside JSC in Houston, after its requirement as a lunar mission launcher was deleted. There was hope that this bird, which had at least been of operational standard back in the 1970s, would give them all fewer problems than the two upgraded test articles they would have to fly later.

Maybe. Fahy was expecting trouble.

This would be her first flight since *Columbia*. She wasn't the lead director for the mission, but she had been entrusted with the ascent phase, the most dangerous and complex phase of any flight.

She'd gone through the events of that final, fatal landing so many times that she could recite the mission logs. STS-143 had grown in her mind, until it was as if the particular circumstances of that mission were the only way any Shuttle mission could ever have been flown, as if the whole thing had been fixed and unalterable, its deadly script written into history even before *Columbia* had lifted off the pad.

But then, along had come Paula Benacerraf, with her bizarre and wonderful visions of a mission to Titan . . .

When she'd been offered the chance to work on this flight, Fahy had jumped at it.

It was just what she needed, she figured. Maybe she could prove to herself that she could act, make decisions, influence the unfolding of events—prove that she wasn't just a victim of some blind predetermined fate.

Then, perhaps, she could get on with the rest of her life.

And anyway, she reflected more cynically, a good performance here could be a way of restarting her damaged career, within the shrunken, emasculated NASA that was going to emerge from this mess.

. . . But the Saturn V overwhelmed personal considerations like that. The Saturn was so damned *big*.

Fahy had grown up with Shuttle. But the Saturn V was just

about twice as tall as the Shuttle stack. And those balky F-1s, which had given the guys at Marshall so much trouble, could each develop the power of *four* Shuttle main engines.

The Saturn, assembled, was like some dinosaur, returned to stalk the Earth. She began to feel intimidated by the booster, as if it would be impossible for her, a mere human, to control it.

Testing and check-out went on. There were hundreds of tests of the completed booster's electrical networks, fire detection, telemetry, tracking, gyroscopes, computers, pumps, transducers, valves, cables, plugs, hydraulics. That took four months alone. Then there was a further set of integrated tests of the booster with its payload and the ground support equipment. There were tests of contingency procedures in case of a malfunction at launch—for instance, if an umbilical swing arm failed to disconnect. There were integration tests to check the hundreds of wire and cable pathways connecting the stages and payload, tests of each of the hundreds of pins in the umbilicals' electrical interfaces with the vehicle.

Slowly, painfully, Fahy could see progress being made; verification seals and sign-offs started to accumulate, immersing the vehicle in a kind of invisible scaffolding of paperwork.

And, eventually, the booster was rolled out to Launch Complex 39-A.

At the pad, the technicians began more layers of tests: a plugs-in test of all the system's components, a flight readiness test, a full simulated launch and mission, and a Countdown Demonstration Test, a crucial checkout for the bird's preparation for launch. In the days of Apollo, CDTs would take maybe four days—sixty hours of testing, and thirty-six hours of planned holds. Fahy hoped they'd get away with not much more than that—say, six or seven days.

The test took seventeen days.

None of the equipment—either the stuff modified from Shuttle operations, or old Saturn gear dug out of storage and refurbished—seemed to work the way it was supposed to. The regulators which controlled the flow of propellants into the Saturn's stages kept throwing up problems; they simply weren't designed for such heavy flows. The Saturn V's own Instrument Unit—the brains of the bird, stuffed full of antique 1960s electronics which nobody dared tear out and replace—couldn't keep the electronics boxes as cool as they needed to be. Cable connections on the S-II shorted out, in the humidity and moisture around the pad; when they were checked they were proved to be corroded, damage missed by the refurbishment teams.

Everything took much longer than planned.

Even when propellant loading began, the process took hours, as more than a hundred truck-loads of kerosene, lox and liquid hydrogen were pumped into the Saturn's three stages. And every time the countdown test hit a problem and had to be stopped, the propellants guys had to stay in the Firing Room and detank, a process even more tedious than tanking.

The various teams became exhausted as the test dragged on. Eventually the managers ordered a two-day break.

But still the test limped on, eroding through its checklist. The team got through to the twenty-six-minute mark, the completion of the test of power transfer. Then they began the process of prechilling the thrust chambers in the second and third stages.

Then, amazingly, they reached the start of the automatic count sequence, at minus three minutes and seven seconds. Fahy watched as the final automatic procedures cycled through, controlled by 1960s software re-engineered to run on computer hardware vintage 2007 . . .

The clock stopped, as planned, at minus fourteen seconds.

Now, forty years late, AS-514 was at last a fueled, checked-out, fully operational vehicle, and the team had done everything it would do on the launch day except light the igniters.

There was a burst of ragged applause.

Good God almighty, she thought. We're really going to do this.

☆   ☆   ☆

On the last day, Fahy walked among the crowds at the KSC visitors' center. She heard grandparents pointing out the needle-slim Saturn on its pad. They tried to tell their grandchildren about how they'd watched the launch of *Apollo 11*—or *12*, or *13*, or *14*—when they were little kids themselves.

The kids looked on, bemused, asking questions—*they're really going to throw all of that away? how much junk did they leave on the Moon? is the Moon really as messed up as they say?*

Fahy rode up the gantry elevator to the payload check-out room at the top of the stack. The elevator was an open metal cage, and it rose with bumpy rattles and clangs; she climbed past steel beams, cables, work platforms.

When the elevator stopped, she stepped through the gate onto a railed catwalk. It spanned the gap between the elevator and the curving flank of the booster, with its open access panels. She looked down the complex, curved flank of the Saturn to the huge steel platforms far below, the flaring skirts over the big F-1 engines, diminished by perspective.

An ocean breeze picked up, and there was a ponderous creak of metal. The catwalk seemed to tilt, and she had to grab a handrail for support. This huge mountain of steel was *swaying*.

When she looked away from the booster, she had a panoramic view of the Atlantic coast. It was early evening, and the coastal towns strung out along the edge of the land sparkled like jewels. But the land itself looked flat, muddy, primeval, barely poking above the water, and the water of the ocean and marshes and canals shone like beaten metal. It was like, she imagined, the place where the first amphibian had crawled painfully, the air like fire in its new lungs, its belly and tail working at the sand, striving to get back to the water . . .

In a few years, she reflected—when the pads and gantries

were torn down and hauled away at last—maybe the sea, the ancient swamp, would swallow up this place once more.

Marcus White got to the Launch Control Center of KSC in the predawn, a couple of hours before the launch.

The Firing Room was a big hall, a third the size of a football field, with eight rows of consoles. White took his place in a glassed-in viewing area set off at an angle at the back of the Firing Room, and looked out through the big picture windows over the pads.

AS-514 was bathed in a cone of light, set up by big search-light beams that met at the tip of the stack, and the lights of its gantry gleamed like a ship's lamps.

The daylight started to come up. From the Firing Room, White was looking east, into the gathering dawn; soon Launch Complex 39-A was silhouetted against the sky. The breeze was blowing debris around the pad, and the wind meter at the top of the tower was spinning around. But the forecast said the windspeed would be within weather rules at launch time.

The paintwork of the refurbished Saturn gleamed, and the booster, slim beside the blocky orange tower, looked oddly feminine, delicate. White felt a lump, unwelcome and painful, gathering in his throat. To hell with Titan. It was all worth it, he thought, just to see that old lady fixed up and with the lichen and moss and streaked paint scraped off, raised up to where she belonged.

He followed the slow evolution of the count, under the control of the KSC Firing Room staff. Events were accelerating, as the tanks in the various stages went through their cycles of pre-cool, fill and replenish. It seemed inconceivable that AS-514 was going to lift on time. But there were no holds today. He sensed the buildup of the indefinable momentum that gathered about a mission, as it prepared for a crucial new phase.

At ten minutes before the launch, the thrust chambers in the second and third stages, both powered by lox and liquid hydrogen, went into chilldown. Pyro devices were armed. Some of the gantry access arms were withdrawn.

Still there were no holds.

At T minus three minutes and seven seconds the firing command was given, and the tanks in all three stages breathed in the helium they needed to force their propellants into the pumps. At minus fifty seconds, the Saturn's internal power took over; the bird was detaching itself from its dependence on the ground. With half a minute to go, the big turbine that drove the five engines of the first stage powered up.

At minus nine seconds, an electrical signal was sent to the igniters, and four small flames lit within the combustion chamber of each of Don Baylor's F-1s.

In the Firing Room, the spectators in Management Row swiveled around and lifted binoculars to their eyes, and peered through the row of windows at the back of the Launch Control Center. White knew they could close protective louvers over the windows if the booster blew up. If it did, the explosion would be equivalent to a three- or four-megaton nuclear bomb. But he figured that if that happened, the guys in here would just keep watching anyhow.

The familiar F-1 ignition process cut in. That rich flood of thick orange smoke burst out of the nozzle and bounced off the flame deflector under the launcher.

Then the main fuel valves opened.

The flame directly under the engines turned to an incandescent white, and the orange smoke billowed outward and upward, enveloping the base of the booster.

The thrust of the engines reached ninety percent of maximum. Still AS-514 hadn't moved.

To White, the spectacle was unfolding in an eerie silence; the noise of the burn had yet to cross the miles to the Firing Room.

The booster shuddered. An ice shower fell steadily, sheets and flakes of ice pouring away from the walls of the stages' cryogenic tanks, vaporizing as they hit the smoke and flames billowing below.

The booster lifted off the pad, its huge weight barely sustained by the thrust. It seemed impossible for anything so huge to move anywhere; it was like a building taking leave of the ground.

Now five umbilical swing arms had to get out of the way. First the outermost section of each arm retracted, and the arms themselves began to swing, to get away from the flanks of the booster. It was a complex and unlikely mechanical ballet.

The sound reached out across the marsh, and rammed into the windows of the viewing area: a series of staccato crackles, profound, physical, powerful. The glass shuddered in its frame, violently. Plaster dust from the roof showered down over him.

It was a sound White hadn't heard in thirty-five years, a noise he'd half-forgotten.

The booster climbed, but the trail of flames just continued to lengthen, all the way down to the pad. It wasn't until the booster was several hundreds of feet above the ground that the huge plume of flame lifted from the launch platform.

He felt as if his rationality was softening, guttering; the understanding he thought he'd developed of the forces shaping his age fell away from him.

How could we build a monument like this, and then turn our backs on it, let it rust on the lawn? Damn, damn. It made no sense. Maybe it never did.

The booster hauled after it a spear of fire eight hundred feet long. Shock waves danced along the flanks of the rocket, blurring its outline in White's binocular view. A mist of ionized gas expanded above the engines, a broad plume of flame in the thinning atmosphere.

When the S-IC died, it was as if the sky dimmed.

White could see the burst of light from the first stage's retro-rockets, and then the flare as the second stage ignited. The Saturn seemed to recede quickly now, heading east, diminishing to a star.

It was visible, he knew, for five hundred miles around.

White turned to follow the trajectory of the discarded first stage on the Firing Room's big display screens.

Tumbling, battering against the air, the S-IC quickly lost most of its forward momentum, and fell back to crash into the Atlantic, still carrying all of Don Baylor's beautifully restored engines, its story finally concluded after four decades.

White grinned. It was just, he thought, fucking unbelievable. Now, all we got to do is survive five more launches, and we can all retire for good . . .

Rosenberg's training for the mission began in earnest a year before the launch.

He had to move to Houston. He had to become an astronaut, in fact, an employee of NASA, and hence of the government.

Benacerraf put him up for a while in her house at Clear Lake, but they didn't get on too well, and Rosenberg started to look for an apartment.

But he gave that up, and moved into a room at the Nassau Bay Hilton. It was going to cost, and after a couple of months he began to run up a debt, but what the hell. He figured his money wasn't going to be much use any more anyhow. He squared it with the hotel management that they would be paid out of the government salary he would collect, in the years of his flight.

At the start of his training, Bill Angel took him to a regular Monday morning meeting in the Astronaut Office at JSC. This was a plain-looking room populated by hard blue chairs, and with Shuttle mission plaques, more than a hundred of them, crowding the walls.

There were more than a hundred astronauts in the corps, he

learned. But only a couple of dozen showed up today. Nobody would speak to him. Or Angel, come to that.

The thing of it was, nobody was going to get to fly again except for a couple of dull missions delivering components of the Titan mission to orbit—save for the Titan five themselves. And of those, one was a Brit—British-born, anyhow—and another was Rosenberg, a pony-tailed double-dome, who wasn't even in the fucking corps.

The resentment in that room was tangible, a living thing.

The training was split between Houston and the Cape. The crew, working together, progressed through hierarchies of trainers, all the way to the full-scale simulators. At first Rosenberg enjoyed the sims—the crew zipped into their orange pressure suits and their white helmets inside the simulators themselves, the controllers in the FCR, and the competing team of simulation supervisors, throwing at them every combination of defect, training them all to cope. It was fun. Like a computer game.

But the novelty soon palled, as they went over the same routine, over and again, toiling through jargon-laden checklists, jammed inside their stuffy suits.

They flew to the Cape in T-38s, the neat little needle-nose two-man trainers the astronauts used. Pilots, like Libet and Angel, were expected to put in at least four hours a week of flight experience. Piloted by Angel or Libet, Rosenberg was whisked back and forth between JSC and Cape—over eight hundred miles, an hour and a half each way—three or four times a week, encased in a flight suit and with a parachute on his back, as if he was a jock hero astronaut himself, for God's sake.

He got his first view of the Cape from the air, in fact, from the cockpit of a NASA T-38. It was a place of shining water, spits and isthmuses of low, dredged-up marshy land, concrete splashes of pads and crawlerways, the whole remarkably primitive, like the slow recovery from an immense bombing raid.

He was taken to see Shuttle orbiters in the Orbiter Processing Facility—PEOPLE MAKING DREAMS A REALITY, read the motto on the door—and in the Vehicle Assembly Building, and on the pad. He was stunned by the VAB, sitting in its car park like some immense department store, fifty storeys high. It was big enough to have assembled four Moon rockets at once, and it had doors tall enough to accommodate the Statue of Liberty. Inside was an industrial complex of riggings and girders and cranes, whole floors suspended like drawers in some immense piece of furniture, capable of being rolled forward and back as needed. And, suspended in the smoky, dim-lit air amid all this clunky scaffolding, he could see the shape of a Shuttle orbiter, unexpectedly graceful in this volume of right angles and pipes and tubes, upended and pinned like some huge white moth.

He was stunned by the scale of it all, his first gut under-standing, perhaps, of the huge energies and efforts that would be assembled under him to hurl his own fragile body into space.

The staff who worked here, preparing spacecraft for launch, were a type of human being he hadn't encountered before, either in the circles of scientists with whom he'd spent his working life, or among the closeted NASA engineers at the other centers, or even among the astronauts. These were peo-ple used to heavy work: dealing with millions of gallons of high-explosive fuel, with the slow controlled explosions of Shuttle launches, and doing it every few weeks, year in and year out. They must have a lot in common with oil-workers, he thought, or deep miners: hard-working, confident, muscled people.

All the crew went through an abbreviated program of train-ing on Apollo systems, at JSC and Kennedy. A basic curriculum was rapidly developed for them, based on 1960s material dug out of the archives. The simulations they were offered, working through key mission phases with teams of flight controllers in the FCR, were thorough, but they were fixed-based. The cost of adapting the motion-based simulators—which, with their six degrees of movement, afforded some of the sensations of spacecraft motion—was, it was said, too high. Rosenberg heard, however, that the real reason was that the motion-based sims were tagged to be a key attraction at the JSC visitors' center, bringing in revenue long after the Titan mission was history.

They were given briefings on the science aspects of the mission: the studies of the Sun, Venus and Jupiter they were expected to perform en route, what was being learned from *Cassini* and *Huygens* about the Saturn system, Titan itself.

Carl Sagan came out of retirement to give them a pep talk about the studies he'd made, as far back as the 1980s, on synthesizing the organic haze on Titan. And he talked to them about cosmology: how the Solar System had formed, the planets coalescing from concentric rings of rock and ice, how the sun would blossom into a red giant at the end of its life, shedding warmth—briefly—over the chill worlds of the outer System. Sagan was in his seventies, and he was a little bent, that famous voice even more gravel-filled, and his hair white as snow; but he was still as handsome as all hell. The science was baby stuff, of course, for Rosenberg. But Sagan's talk, brief as it was, turned out to be one of the highlights of the whole training program for him.

Then there was all the surgeon stuff.

A key objective for this mission, as far as the ground-based experts were concerned, was to find out once and for all how the human body adapted to long-duration spaceflight. Or not.

Of course the experienced astronauts might already have suffered much of the harm to which they were susceptible; some studies of past astronauts suggested that the major damage to many of the body's major systems happened in the first few hours of a spaceflight . . .

Anyhow, to achieve a sound study the surgeons had to have some kind of baseline, an understanding of what condition their various bodies had been in before being subjected to the rigors of the flight. So the crew were put through a comprehensive medical study. They had to submit, every two or three days, to electrocardiograms, seismocardiograms and measurements of their breathing rates and volume; and once a week they had to spend a whole day on a much more thorough check-out, which included sampling of body fluids, measurements of the phases of cardiac contraction, heartbeat volume, venous pressure, vascular tone in different parts of the body, blood circulation in the head, and lung ventilation.

After a few weeks of this Rosenberg figured that by the time he was launched there would be more of his body mass in test tubes in the labs around the country than aboard that Shuttle on the pad. And all the checkups meant a whole day lost out of every week, time which Rosenberg had no choice but to give up, but which he had to drag out of his continuing research, and other commitments . . .

In all, eighty percent of his training time was taken up with Shuttle emergency procedures: mostly to do with problems during launch, or a forced landing.

Apparently as part of NASA's post-*Challenger* adjustment, the crew families were encouraged to come in and observe the emergency stuff, so they could understand what was happening, if and when it all unraveled. So here were Nicola's aging parents from England, the mother with her prion-ruined face, and Paula's grandchildren, two boys who watched with baffled incomprehension as their grandmother clambered out of windows and hatchways and shimmied down ropes and slid down wires to the little green car that would whisk her away in case the Shuttle blew up on the pad.

There was nobody to come see Rosenberg, and he was more than glad of that.

Some of the preparation was chilling, then. But some was mundane, almost comical, and yet delivered with the usual NASA cheerful high-tech gloss. The crew was taken to the Food Systems Engineering Facility, for instance, where they were given samples of Shuttle food packs to try out, so they could select their own preferences. No salmon, Angel insisted. The stink of fish, in the enclosed places of a Shuttle, was just unacceptable. And then there was the john: the Waste Management Compartment trainer, where Rosenberg was trained, in all earnestness, how to go to the bathroom. It was an affair of rubber gloves he had to use to clean himself, and little plastic scraper tools, and fans that whirred noisily. There was even a little camera situated in the bowl, peering up at his ass, so he could tell if he was positioning his orifice correctly . . .

But in the midst of all that, the stuff that was so easily mocked, he came across signs and symbols that showed him where he was: here, at the heart of NASA, the Agency that had put men on the Moon. Bits of 1960s technology, capsules and rockets, that looked so primitive they might have come from the 1930s. Pictures he hadn't seen before, of Americans bounding across the surface of the Moon, working and joshing as if it was a field hike in Arizona.

And the astronauts: the hard core of them, the big-boned, blue-eyed WASPs of the earliest recruitment rounds, many of them graying now, few of them still active, but still fit and tanned and with faces like craggy lunar rock. Before these men—who had, after all, been the first—Rosenberg felt intimidated, weak and insignificant. But every time one of them walked past there was a powerful stink of male deodorant which wafted after him down the narrow corridors, all human scents suppressed, his surface somehow shining and impenetrable, as if he was already half-way to orbit just standing there, as if his purpose, the purpose of his race, had been to guide humanity to the stars.

Of his own crew, it was clearly Angel who aspired to membership of this élite group—which was, of course, impossible, for the role of hero astronaut had vanished long before Angel had joined NASA. But, anyhow, Angel walked through the space centers, mean-looking and tall, his muscles honed and hard, his language full of the dread-reducing jargon of contingencies and aborts. He even looked like them, with his blond-WASP hair and blue eyes, and he was almost schizoid, it seemed to Rosenberg, in his lack of reaction to the peril of his *Columbia* flight—and yet, despite that, there was a certain desperation in his empty eyes.

On it went, and Rosenberg became steadily more enmeshed in the procedures and practices and jargon of this huge organization. And yet, he thought, if you looked at it sideways, the whole Titan program was a remarkable event: here was a bureaucracy, dry and sane, devoting itself to the surreal: a gigantic adventure which everyone was committed to, but whose purpose and logic and meaning nobody could agree upon.

The hulking form of the B-52 sat on its runway in a puddle of light cast by a circle of big portable floods. Trailers and carts were clustered around the bomber. A fog of crisp liquid oxygen vapor shrouded the contours of the big plane, and people moved through the mist, speaking to each other calmly, working on the aircraft.

The X-15 itself hung from bomb shackles under the wing of the B-52, black and sleek, dark even in the glare of the floods, as if it actually absorbed the light.

There was a pungent stink of ammonia, which reached Gareth Deeke even across a hundred yards.

The smell, suffusing this gray January dawn, triggered his memories sharply, and he felt the years fall away from him; it was as if he was back at Edwards, preparing to burn off another vodka hangover in the exhilaration and terror of a high-altitude flight.

But as he walked towards the B-52, the ground crew parted

before him and avoided his eyes; there was none of the good-natured bull which he recalled from his days at Edwards. As if we are all doing something different now, he thought. Something wrong.

Here at Canaveral Air Force Base, he was only ten miles or so to the south of Kennedy Space Center, where *Endeavour* was being prepared for the last Shuttle launch of all. He peered into the north. Maybe he'd be able to pick out the illuminated pad: on clear nights the visibility of the pad's lights, looming on the horizon, was a symbol of the failure by Hartle and his contacts to impede or even slow the preparations for the final Titan launch, to stem the tide of public support which still seemed to be flowing, generally, in favor of the mission. Certainly, on launch day, this whole damn area would be flooded with rocket light. But today the mist was lingering in the cold January dawn, and to the north there was only darkness.

He reached the bomber.

X-15 looked more like a missile than a plane. Big frosted pipes lay on the surface of the runway, feeding liquids and gases into the rocket plane. But the black lines of the X-15 were spoiled by the attachment of a slim white cylinder, round-nosed and finned, under the center line of the forward fuse-lage.

It was an ASAT.

Gareth Deeke, heart pumping, walked around his bird. X-15, restored from the museum where it had waited out the decades, looked ready to fly, but today was not its day; this morning, under cover of darkness, the ground crew were rehearsing the procedures they would use to mount and fly the bird.

If it came to that.

The rocket plane was just a big propellant tank, made of a tough heat-resistant nickel-steel alloy, with a cockpit on the front and rocket engine on the back end. The tanks were nested cylinders, with a long, skinny pipe containing high pressure helium pressurization gas embedded within the big liquid oxygen tanks towards the front of the aircraft. The fuel tank, containing anhydrous ammonia, made up the rear section of the airplane.

Deeke walked past the frosted-up walls of the lox tank. He didn't get too close; the tank seemed to suck the warmth out of the air around him, cold as it was already. You could always tell how much lox was left in the tank by the level of frost on that outer skin. He could make out the three main fittings holding the rocket plane in place, and the quick-disconnect lines snaking out of the B-52 which topped up X-15 with nitrogen and liquid oxygen. Reaction control jet nozzles gaped in the hull around the nose, two on top, two on the bottom, and two to either side. Beside the nozzles there was a stenciled notice saying BEWARE OF BLAST.

He reached the cockpit, an aluminum box which would be pressurized with nitrogen to thirty-five thousand feet equivalent, and suspended inside the hull of the aircraft itself, isolated to keep it cool. Behind the cockpit was a big pressurized bay containing over a thousand pounds of instrumentation, to measure airspeed, altitude, pitch, yaw and roll rates, control surface positions, bending loads, temperatures . . . He had been assured that the handling characteristics and controls of the plane would be just as they had been back in 1961, though he didn't know how the hell they had got all that antique electronics to function again after forty years. Maybe they had cannibalized X-15A-2, the other surviving X-15, which was mothballed at the USAF museum at Wright-Patterson AFB.

He reached the engine compartment at the back of the plane. The XLR-99 rocket nozzle gaped at the back of the aircraft, two feet long. The rocket, which hadn't been fired in anger for forty years, looked as fresh as if it had come out of the Thiokol factory yesterday.

He allowed himself a stab of anger. He'd long lost count of the number of press releases he'd read which said the Shuttle's

main engine was the world's first truly throttleable engine. The
XLR–99 engine was a throttleable, restartable, reusable rocket
engine, with almost as much thrust as the throwaway Redstone
booster which had thrown Shepard and Grissom up on their
first Mercury suborbital lobs. The USAF had been happily flying the thing ten years before the Apollo Lunar Module's
much-vaunted throttleable rockets had carried men to the
Moon, and twenty years before Shuttle had first launched, years
before NASA had started pronouncing you couldn't build such
a thing.

We threw all this away, he thought, all the possibilities
summed up in the sleek black hide of this thing, because of
stupidity and greed, and fear of the Russians, and damn
bureaucratic infighting, a millennial madness reaching its final
flowering over on Pad 39-B even now.

In its flight days the X-15 had borne USAF decals on its
wings and fuselage, and big NASA strip decals on its tail. But
today, the hull was a bare black, unmarked save for information
and warning stencils, and its serial number, AF 5-6670.

And that, Deeke reflected sourly, was entirely appropriate.

The mist cleared a little. There were stars in the sky. One of
them, bright and clear, passed smoothly through the constellations, directly above him. That was the Shuttle orbiter *Discovery*,
its wings reshaped for Titan's thick air, already in orbit with its
cluster of fuel tanks and equipment, waiting for its crew.

It had to be stopped.

Determination surged in him. He put aside the doubts and
qualms of the ground techs. He had no doubts.

On the day, if the call came, he would be ready to fly.

At last, the schedule for STS-147 was firmed up.

STS-147 would be the last Shuttle launch: the last flight of

Endeavour, the mission that would take the crew—including Paula Benacerraf—up to Earth orbit.

When the launch date was finalized, Benacerraf found herself staring at it, on her softscreen, for minutes at a time. It was like the date of her own execution. She would not see the dawn of the following day—and, perhaps, no dawn on Earth ever after.

As that epochal day approached, the tempo of Benacerraf's life accelerated. She was doing three jobs now. As head of the Shuttle program she had responsibilities to discharge beyond the Titan mission, such as the disposal of the program's assets around the country after the final flights—including thousands of staff. Then, too, she retained a lot of responsibility for the Station hab module conversion, and she spent long hours at Marshall and Seattle working on that.

Finally she was an astronaut, trying to prepare for the mission itself.

And, in the midst of this crescendo of activity, Paula Benacerraf—human, grandmother—prepared to leave Earth.

After all, the Titan expedition was going to be an open-ended mission. So she figured she ought to shut down her life, here on Earth, as if she was indeed going to die.

She spent a lot of hours scanning images—photographs, movies and videos of Jackie and the grandchildren, a couple of pictures from the walls of her home—onto high-capacity, radiation-toughened discs. She sold everything she owned of value—her apartment, her car, her furniture, her books, her clothes—and what she couldn't sell she was going to give away to friends, or to charities. She wanted Jackie to have first choice. All she saved for herself was the few pounds of personal items she was going to be able to take to Titan. She had some bits of jewelery, and even a couple of precious paper books, sealed in baggies and wrapped up in her fireproof Beta-cloth Personal Preference Kit.

Benacerraf made out a will. But she tore up the draft.

Instead she had her bank draw up authorization for Jackie to become a joint holder of Benacerraf's accounts.

But she would need to meet Jackie, one last time, to finalize the transfer. And Jackie had refused even to take her calls, for more than a year.

Benacerraf kept trying.

Jackie would only agree to meet her in Green Town, a net Island.

Benacerraf hated the net and she resisted this. It was just another way of Jackie expressing her disapproval. But she had little choice.

Benacerraf had always refused to have any kind of net interface equipment in her home, beyond simple e-mail and browser. But there were plenty of public net cafés in downtown Houston; she found one in the Galleria which—though expensive—had a good variety of up-to-date equipment, and private booths you could lock yourself into.

Inside her booth, she wrapped the sensor mask across her face, and the gloves over the palms of her hands. She stood on the treadmill-like motion simulator, and—fumbling a little with the switch—dimmed the lights.

The mask on her face was soft and damp like flayed skin, she thought and, in the first few seconds of the immersion, quite dark. Then the moist contact pads on the surface of her eyes filled with light, blurred shapes of silver, black and green. She forced her vision muscles to relax; the images were set at virtual-infinity, and it did her no good to try to focus on the covers on her eyes.

The image resolved.

She was standing on a lawn of green grass.

Her arms held out for balance, Benacerraf stepped cautiously forward, over the glowing grass. It felt cool and damp under her feet; it was fresh cut, and she could smell the rich domestic scent of the crushed blades. A sprinkler was turning, droplets of water dancing in the sunlight.

She looked up, taking care not to move her head too quickly. Even so there was a characteristic delay between the motion of her head and the change in virtual scene in response; they said you got used to that with time, your sensorium accommodating the built-in delay. Benacerraf wasn't adapted and sure as hell didn't want to be, and the delay just made her feel motion-sick.

The lawn she was standing on was a little square, bordered by empty roads. The town was green and still. She could see houses of red brick and white-painted wood, with little white picket fences around their lawns. There were maples, elms and horse chestnut trees, their branches softly rustling in the breeze. There was even a church steeple, with a bell hanging silently. There was some kind of ornament on the lawn, a sculpture; it might have been an iron deer.

The sky was tall and blue, scattered with fluffy clouds. It felt like morning, and the sun was low, its light on her face flat and warm . . .

The sky wasn't all that impressive, actually. The color looked pretty-pretty fake and too uniform, and those clouds were lumpy, a fairly obvious application of fractal technology. That lawn sprinkler was actually the most ambitious part of this whole scene, she thought. The motion of the droplets had been modeled realistically, with the effect of the gentle breeze on the shape of the droplet cloud captured well. And when she looked more closely she could see how each droplet splashed and broke up when it hit the grass, and scattered in dewlike beads over the blades.

She could see nothing that looked as if it post-dated, say, 1940. But there was nothing to pin down the time and place here specifically, one way or the other. This was Green Town, probably Illinois, and as far as she was concerned it was just an anal-retentive fantasy, a dream of a middle America that had never existed anyhow, modeled with gigamips of processing power and the most up-to-date VR technology.

Decadent as all hell.

One of the houses seemed to stand out from the rest, its colors and outline a little more vivid. So that was probably where she was supposed to go. It was a tall brown Victorian design, the low sunlight making it look like something out of a Norman Rockwell painting. It was elaborately adorned, covered with rococo and scrolls, and its windows were stained, blue and pink, made of diamond-form leaded glass. There was a broad porch at the front, with a swing that rocked gently back and forth in the breeze, creaking.

She walked towards the house. She stumbled once, but recovered easily. The little iron deer was in her way, but she didn't bother to step around it; she walked right through the deer, and it disappeared in a burst of pixels.

She tramped heavily up the wooden stairs of the house, and onto its porch. The front door was open. She walked in, through a bead curtain. Wind chimes tinkled as she passed.

She entered a parlor. The furniture was old, covered in a maroon fabric, worn with use and obviously comfortable. There was a piano—an acoustic one—its legs covered up Victorian style. There was a piece of sheet music on the stand. *Beautiful Dreamer.*

Jackie emerged from a door at the back of the room. She was wearing a trim long dress of gingham, that pretty much covered her from neck to toe. Her hair was brushed back, and her face was recognizably her own—though, Benacerraf thought sourly, rather smoothed-over and more symmetrical than the real thing.

"Hi," Jackie said neutrally. She was carrying a glass pitcher of iced lemonade, which moved in viscous waves as she walked. "You want some lemonade?"

"Hell, no. I mean, no thanks." Eating or drinking in here meant letting the mask push its way into her mouth and throat.

They sat on overstuffed Morris chairs, beside a fireplace, under a framed painting.

Jackie poured herself a glass, and sipped it deliberately, watching her mother. Benacerraf thought she wore the same stubborn look she'd had since she'd learned to be defiant, at the age of five.

"Are the kids here?"

"They'll be over later," Jackie said. "It's a school day. So they're over on Nintendo Island right now. You have any trouble getting here?"

Benacerraf didn't much feel like playing this game; she didn't reply.

Jackie lit up a cigarette. The smoke curled into the air, blue and white, its form another complex application, Benacerraf thought, of fluid-mechanical modeling. And all utterly pointless.

"You know, you're honored," Jackie said. "Your fame must have spread. The great Saturn explorer." Her tone was contemptuous. "They don't normally let you land in the square; there's a port on a neighboring island, and you have to get a boat over here, then walk from the coast."

"So many rules," Benacerraf said.

Jackie shrugged. "It's a world in here, Paula. Of course you have to have rules. They underpin the world. Like the physical laws that govern us in RL—"

"Oh, come on," Benacerraf snapped. "This is virtual reality, for God's sake. Why the hell shouldn't I fly like Superman if I want to?"

"You think this is all too cute," Jackie said sourly. "Well, maybe. It's pretty much all we're allowed since the government opened up the net again. You know, police monitoring engines consume twice as many mips as the VR software itself."

Benacerraf waved a hand deliberately quickly, so fast the processing couldn't keep up, and she left a trail of pixels, ghostly shadows of her fingers. "But so what? None of this is real. None of it is even unpredictable, challenging. You bind yourselves up in these endless rules, and—"

"And by contrast," Jackie said coldly, "you and your little band are going off to break ground on the high frontier."

"Isn't that true? Isn't that more worthwhile, more *real* than this?"

Jackie said bleakly, "There's nothing out there but a collection of dead rocks and ice balls. Even the Earth is falling apart."

"So where else to go but inward, retreating into your own head? Right?"

Jackie sighed. "Is this why you've come here, Paula? To attack me again? Because if it is—"

Benacerraf held her hands up. "Time out, kid. Whenever we get together, we fall into the same old rut."

Jackie shrugged and didn't respond.

Showing she didn't care about their flawed relationship was, Benacerraf thought, the most hurtful response she could have made.

"So," Jackie said at length. "What do you want to talk about?"

"I need you to sign some documents."

Benacerraf explained her plan.

"Virtually all my assets are in the accounts, and my salary will continue to be paid into it, as long as I'm alive. I think you ought to have immediate access to those funds. But you have to sign authorization papers; we can do that here, electronically, in Green Town. I also tried to have my pension contributions made over in your favor, but they couldn't do it. Administrative reasons." It was ironic, thought Benacerraf; here was NASA busting all the technical and political barriers in the way of a ten-astronomical-unit mission to Titan, but the bean counters couldn't find any way around their own rule books . . .

Jackie listened to all this, her virtual face expressionless and unreadable. Benacerraf realized, belatedly, that she didn't even know where her daughter was.

In the end, Jackie wouldn't agree to Benacerraf's proposals.

"Look, Mother, you don't really care about me, or the kids.

If you did you wouldn't be indulging yourself in this ludicrous jaunt to Saturn."

"I'm trying to make you a gift, of all my property, for God's sake—"

"No," Jackie said, with a harshness not matched by the china-doll prettiness of her virtual face. "You're just trying to ease your damn conscience. Well, I don't see why I should make it so easy for you. I won't sign anything; I won't have any part of this."

They started to argue again.

It was like resuming a conversation, even though they hadn't spoken for so long.

Benacerraf struggled to understand.

Perhaps, she thought gloomily, this is more than some kind of generation gap. Perhaps the species has reached a bifurcation. One branch reaching for other worlds, the other receding into an online sea, swimming in great mindless shoals, twitching and turning in unison. Beautiful, but empty.

In another century, we may not recognize each other.

Or maybe, she thought gloomily, I'm just getting old.

Maybe it's just as well I'm getting the hell out, of a world I don't understand any more.

She tried, one last time, to marshal her thoughts.

"Jackie, your life is your own—as is mine, to do with as I please. And I think it's better to do this, to go to Titan—or die in the attempt—than to stay around here, getting steadily older, becoming a cliché for you. I'm sorry if it hurts. But I don't owe you anything."

"And what about the kids? What will I tell them when I have to explain they can't see grandma any more?"

"Oh, come on," Benacerraf said sadly. "In a few years they wouldn't be interested anyhow. And besides, there will be telecasts from the mission—"

Jackie stood up. "Don't you get it? Nobody will watch the telecasts. Nobody has cared for years. Only you, you old people. Nobody will give a damn, as you drift off into the darkness. If you go, I'll tell the boys you're dead," she said evenly. "That's the truth, isn't it? What is this, but an elaborate suicide?"

On and on.

They parted without affection. Jackie came forward to hug her, but Benacerraf couldn't bear to submit to such an electronic embrace.

Benacerraf walked out of the house, and back down the steps to the lawn where she'd first arrived. So, at the end of it all, they were reduced to this, a mother and daughter able to face each other only by locking themselves away in darkened rooms, hundreds of miles apart, with their faces buried inside electronic masks.

She tramped over the grass, fumbling at the mask which covered her face.

When she emerged into the booth in the Galleria, she got out as quickly as she could. She half-ran out of the mall, and when she got outside, under a murky sky, she sucked in great lungfuls of hot, smoggy Houston air.

As the launch itself approached, the intensity of the training slackened, and it seemed to Rosenberg that they started to enter a realm of tradition, and superstition, and magic.

A couple of weeks before the liftoff, for example, they all went down to the Outpost Tavern. This was a wooden shack outside the gates of KSC, and the tradition was that every astronaut had to drink in there. Its walls were encrusted with signed photos of grinning spacemen, and Rosenberg learned— it was incredible—that the Outpost had originally been situated at Ellington, near Houston, and moved out here plank by wooden, beer-stained plank.

He didn't dare question any of this stuff. It was understandable when you remembered that space travel was almost fifty years old now, and like any other human activity it was bound to accrete its own traditions. If these NASA people, under their WASP technocratic hides, believed some kind of white magic was necessary to get their birds off the ground, Rosenberg wasn't going to start arguing now.

And then, a week before the launch, they were moved into the quarantine facilities at Houston, and then the crew quarters at the Cape, and now nobody from the outside world was allowed in—not even families—unless they passed a strict medical. That made sense to Rosenberg; he had no wish to take infection into space.

But, incredibly, a couple of days before leaving, they were allowed to greet their families one last time, face to face in the open air, on a grassy sward close to the crew quarters, separated only by a fifteen-foot ditch. Rosenberg couldn't believe it. He recognized Jackie Benacerraf, Paula's daughter, over there with her boys, and, standing there in cold January sunshine, they had a short, shouted, embarrassed conversation about life on Titan.

He observed how tough it was for the others—particularly Paula—to say good-bye, this one last time, without even being able to touch their family members. As a quarantine procedure it was dubious. And as a piece of psychology, he thought, it was truly, spectacularly dumb.

And then there were two days to go.

And then one.

And then, a subtle knock by a WASP fist on the door of his room, and he was awake on Earth for the last time, for it was the morning of the launch.

He even had a personal checklist:

9:00 P.M. Wake up

9:30 P.M. Breakfast

2:58 A.M. Lunch and crew photo
3:28 A.M. Weather briefing
3:38 A.M. Don launch and entry suits
3:50 A.M. Crew suiting photo
4:08 A.M. Depart for pad 39-B . . .

Rosenberg went through the routines he'd practiced so often in a daze; he let the various techs just manage him through.

It took him a full hour to be loaded into his pressure suit, for instance. The rubber sleeves and neck were tight, and he had to squeeze in there, like putting on a tight-fitting sweater. The suits were actually a post-*Challenger* modification designed to close a few more non-survivability windows in case of malfunction. Nobody had been prepared to tell Rosenberg, for all his pressing and all the training time they'd spent on disaster recovery, whether in the pinch the suits would be any use at all.

There was a lot of tension, forced humor, in that suiting room. The US Alliance technicians were bland, smiling and competent, like well-trained nurses preparing him for an operation.

Angel was in his element. At one point he slapped Rosenberg on the back. "How do you feel, buddy? Just like being in the locker room before a basketball game at high school. Right?"

Wrong, thought Rosenberg. Dead wrong.

There were more rituals, as they headed out of the building towards the bus that would take them to the pad. There was a card game called Possum's Fargo that they had to play, for instance, with a couple of the techs. Rosenberg couldn't believe his eyes. Here they were, the five of them, like huge insects in their glaring orange pressure suits, standing around a table to play what seemed like, to him, a kid's version of poker. But— rigid tradition had it—they couldn't leave, until the commander, Angel, in this case, had lost a hand.

It took six hands.

☆   ☆   ☆

They emerged into the chill pre-dawn.

The five of them clambered, bulky and clumsy, into a bus. The bus was cramped, depressingly ordinary. Rosenberg, short of sleep, felt compressed by mundanity, the gritty ordinariness of things; he felt irritable, as if his imagination had been switched off.

He suspected much of the news of the day was being kept from them, but he'd heard a little scuttlebutt over breakfast. The launch, possibly the last spectacular space event at KSC, was attracting crowds, to the bayous and motels of Florida. But the forces which had opposed the Titan program were gathering too. USAF spokesmen were steadily denouncing NASA. There were demonstrations at the security gates, and there was talk of a group calling themselves Nullists who had got as far as the pad itself, and lain down their bodies in the flame bucket. Even within NASA, there wasn't a unanimity of support: Rosenberg had heard of resignations from Barbara Fahy's team of controllers at JSC, problems with suppliers here at the Cape . . .

It was all falling apart at last, he thought. But it just had to hang together a few more hours, long enough to release him from Earth.

The road stretched ahead, straight-infinite, glowing in the headlights of the bus. And on the horizon, at the end of the road, he could see the pad itself, the glowing Shuttle waiting for him in a pyramid of searchlights.

At the pad, three hours before launch time, they were taken up the gantry elevator to the White Room, all of two hundred feet above the Earth. And now, at the far end of the room, Rosenberg found himself facing the spacecraft at last, a slab of *Endeavour*'s powder-white tiled skin, the tight round scuffed-metal hatch embedded in it.

He took a breath. Salt. It seemed entirely appropriate, he

thought, that his last lungful of Earth air should smell of the sea.

He had to crawl into the orbiter through the tight hatch, as if being born in reverse. A white-suited tech was there to peel off his rubber overshoes, and to place him in his metal-frame seat, tipped up so he lay on his back, gently placing his helmet and parachute pack.

The tech had the US ALLIANCE logo on his back; he wasn't a NASA employee, Rosenberg reflected, but a worker for the lowest bidder in a contracted-out operation. Comforting.

". . . Okay, real good. Put your other arm through there and I'll hold it for you. Okay. Now your comms check. Talk to the OTC on that button."

Rosenberg pressed the button. "OTC, this is MS-1."

"Loud and clear. Good morning."

The tech said, "Now put your visor down on the right."

"It's down."

"Tighten your helmet a little bit at the back. Make sure it's snug but not too tight. Push this button right here and tell the LTD comm check."

"LTD, MS-1. Comm check."

"Loud and clear."

"Now raise your visor with a little push with your right hand. Right hand there. That's good. Now we'll put this little air pack where it feels most comfortable to you, about here, beside your seat. Feel it there? Okay? You're ready. Doing good. Watch your arm there, Isaac. Now, while I hook up Nicola you're going to lose comms for a while . . ."

And thus Rosenberg, already toilet-trained, was fussed over as if by a parent loading a toddler into a push-chair, as he was strapped into this couch, upended between two gigantic rocket boosters, while a mountain of liquid fuel was pumped in below his spine.

The Shuttle was launched from the Cape, and, in the course of its routine operation, was supposed to come back down to the Cape, to America. After landing a version of the White Room was clamped onto the hatchway of the Shuttle, clean and enclosed and populated by more smiling, hand-shaking technicians, and the shaky astronauts were helped down, and delivered to their families once more, as if they'd never left, as if Shuttle was just a huge elevator system, he thought, lifting Americans in hygienic enclosure to the stars and back again, with all the mystery washed out by routine.

Except today, he thought, this old elevator is going up to the sky, and ain't never coming back down again.

The long count continued. And as supercooled fuel was pumped into the stack, the metal walls creaked and moaned.

At Canaveral Air Force Base, Gareth Deeke was woken by a phone call. A one-word command.

He closed his fist. He was going to get his flight.

He climbed out of bed and marched to the shower. On the wall, a softscreen TV, activated by his movement, filled up with pictures of a glowing Shuttle.

"*Endeavour*, resume countdown on my mark. Three, two, one. Mark. Ground launch sequencer auto sequence started."

Bill Angel was lying on his back in the left-hand commander's seat. Benacerraf was behind him once more, in the flight engineer's position. Siobhan Libet, for this last flight, was pilot.

With the orbiter in its vertical takeoff position, the cabin was upended. To Benacerraf, in her flight engineer's seat, Angel and Libet were precariously suspended above her, like pupae in their orange partial-pressure suits. The rest of *Endeavour*'s final crew—Mott and Rosenberg—were in the mid deck area behind Benacerraf.

Angel reached over and pressed a button on a center instrument panel. "Event timer switched to start," he called. "Operations recorders confirmed on."

"Copy, Bill. Have a good trip, you guys."

"We'll send *Endeavour* back home to the Smithsonian in a week, safe and sound . . ."

Now, the software controlling launch events had started its operation; the event timer, a clock on the flight deck's instrument panel, started counting down.

So, it started. Barring malfunctions, there would be no more holds. To Benacerraf this moment was like falling off a cliff; now she was falling through time, all the way towards the launch, with the inevitability of aging.

Endeavour's windows, pointing upward, were open to the sky. Benacerraf could see a slab of gray, forbidding cloud. The flight deck was warm and comfortable, the calm voices of the pilots over the whir of pumps steady and reassuring.

But she had already cut her ties with Earth.

The complex prelaunch ritual continued.

Inside the suit van, Deeke stripped down to his long johns. Here—refurbished and restored, just like X-15 itself—was his pressure suit.

The suit was of reinforced rubber, fitted with hoses, knobs and a big metal neck ring. It was tight and uncomfortable, like a full-body girdle. The damn thing had always been a chore to put on, even when he was a lot younger and more lithe than he was now.

When the inner garment was zipped up, the techs helped him into a silver-colored coverall of a tough artificial fabric, designed to protect the pressure garment in case he had to eject. Next came boots, gloves and helmet. He made sure his mirrored glasses were firmly set in place before the helmet was lifted over his head. When he was a kid, he hadn't needed any optical correction, of course. Those days were long ago.

A lengthy check-out followed. The suit techs pressurized his garments and checked every joint of the forty-year-old gear for leakage and mobility. Deeke stood there in the van, enduring the prodding and fingering of the techs.

These guys were all pretty young; even the senior officer here in the van looked no more than thirty-five. They avoided his gaze. Their expressions were blank, busy, competent. They seemed to typify, to him, the newer generation of military people: calm, assured, expecting to be cocooned and protected and fed information by the high technology systems in which they were immersed. Different from the old days: different from Deeke's generation, and those who'd gone before, those who'd fought in Vietnam and Korea and the Pacific, who built birds with their bare hands, who'd been prepared to fly to Moscow loaded with nukes.

He wondered what those old guys would think of him and his mission, when they heard.

Now there was a call for pilot entry. Equipment specialists formed up to either side of him, carrying a portable liquid oxygen breathing and cooling unit, hooked up to his suit.

Deeke stepped out of the van. Outside, light was starting to leak into the sky.

Deeke walked across the tarmac to the X-15. Inside the pressure suit it took some effort just to move his legs forward, and by the time he got to the bird he could feel his lungs dragging at the oxygen fed to him by the suit.

He climbed the ladder to the access platform over the open cockpit. The roomy cockpit was dominated by the big ejection seat. He could see the seat's folded-up fins and booms, designed to bloom out after ejection, and the big beefy handles pivoted around the arm rests that would lock his arms and upper body in place in case he had to eject. He'd always found the massive seat terrifying; he'd never had to trust himself to its crushing, over-complicated embrace, and hoped he wouldn't have to today.

He slid on in. Suit techs began to strap Deeke in, pulling harnesses around him and hooking him up to his bailout kit, the aircraft's breathing oxygen supply, and the suit pressurization and cooling gas.

The seat wasn't adjustable. He had to have pads for the seat, back and armrests.

As he looked around the little cabin, he felt his heart thump. The cockpit equipment had the bolted-together look of every test airplane Deeke had ever flown. Its hard-wired analogue instruments struck him as startlingly old-fashioned, though, in this age of glass cockpits. And the whole thing was generally scuffed and worn, despite its refurbishment. This X-15 model had been the first to fly in the test program, and the last. And it showed.

But now, sitting in this familiar cocoon, it was as if thirty years had fallen away from him; he felt young again.

He was surrounded by control panels. The front panel, dominated by a big eight-ball attitude indicator, was encrusted with barometric instruments to help with control and guidance. But for most of the flight the X-15 would be outside the sensible atmosphere, and such instruments were useless; he would have to rely on inertial data, computations performed by the onboard processor.

For atmospheric flight there were control rudder pedals and a control stick to his right-hand side, which moved the aerodynamic control surfaces. There was also a center stick, but in the course of the flight program it had become a macho thing never to touch that center stick but to rely on the side stick and pedals. And then on the left-hand instrument panel was mounted another hand controller, to operate the manual reaction controls: the little rockets which controlled attitude outside the atmosphere.

X-15 was built to fly like an aircraft when it had to, and as a spacecraft when it had to.

The crew closed the canopy.

The canopy was a solid box, save for a mailbox window to the front and the sides. Deeke was sealed in, inside this little bubble of nitrogen, unable even to lift his faceplate to scratch his nose. All he could smell was the cool oxygen in his helmet;

all he could hear were the intermittent crackles of radio voices. Deeke was in a world over which he had complete control. He could make it hotter or cooler, brighter or dimmer; if he wanted he could even shut out the radio voices with his volume control. He was secure in here, safe. He felt himself receding deeper into the recesses of his own mind, his memories, and it was a nice place to be, excluding the complexities and doubts of the murky future outside.

Now the bomber's engines started, and Deeke could feel the deep thrumming transmitted to him through the connecting bomb shackles.

The B-52 began its taxi to the duty runway. He could hear little of the noise of the plane's big engines, the nearest just feet away from his head. Ground vehicles drove alongside, eight or ten of them, their headlights making great elliptical splashes of light over the dark tarmac. It was a rough ride for Deeke, with a lot of hard, jarring vibration to his spine. Probably the wheels of the B-52 had got out of the round during the long wait.

The control crew called out a brisk takeoff clearance.

The B-52 began its takeoff roll. It soon outstripped the ground vehicles, and the runway lights whipped away to either side of Deeke.

Then the lights fell away beneath him, and the ride smoothed out.

In the Flight Control Room in JSC's Building 30, Barbara Fahy stood up behind her console, and surveyed her controllers. As they waited for the point, eight seconds into the ascent, where they would take over the management of the flight, the controllers cycled through their displays and spoke calmly on the loops to each other, to their back room teams, and to her. There was an atmosphere of competence, of calm.

Each of the controllers had a little plastic Stars-and-Stripes on his or her console, a memento of the mission, America's last manned spaceflight, in this year of Our Lord, 2008. The STS-

147 mission patch was high on the wall of the room, a big disc bearing a stylized planet Saturn with a Shuttle orbiter looping through the rings. It was only the second mission patch not to bear the names of the crew: the first was *Apollo 11*.

The launch events unfolded, eroding away to the moment of ignition.

There were no malfunctions, no holds. She tried to put aside her gnawing anxiety.

Jackie Benacerraf was almost late for the launch.

She'd flown into Orlando and stayed overnight, and then driven out to the Cape straight along Interstate 50. But that was the wrong way; she was turned back by a guard on the road, and she had to go over a bridge to the south and drive north along Merritt Island. Then, for the first time, she got caught in traffic.

The commentators had predicted a big turnout to watch this last Shuttle launch. It would be *Apollo 17* all over again, the old-timers predicted. The nostalgia factor. Well, there was some heavy traffic here, but nothing like the density she'd expected.

But there were some roadside parties, young people glittering with image-tattoos, writhing to arrhythmic rock, draped in softscreen flags. They looked like beings from the future, she thought, brought back in time to this site of monumental 1960s engineering.

Maybe it really is over. Maybe people really don't care any more, she thought.

At last she got into the Space Center, by Security Gate 2 off U.S. 3. There was an orderly demonstration here, mounted by a creationist group from Texas called the Foundation for Thought and Ethics. Here was Xavier Maclachlan himself on a soapbox, all jug ears and ten gallon hat, steadily denouncing the manned space program for the sake of the cameras.

At an office at the gate, after queuing, she picked up her orange STS-147 media badge.

She parked in the big lot at the foot of the stupendous Vehicle Assembly Building. When she got out of the car, with her camera around her neck and her softscreen rolled up under her arm, she heard the voice of the public affairs officer drifting across the lot, from the big speakers close to the press stand . . . *T minus four minutes and counting. As preparation for main engine ignition the main fuel valve heaters have been turned on. T minus three minutes fifty-seven seconds and counting; the final fuel purge on the Shuttle main engines has been started in preparation for engine start* . . .

Four minutes. Jesus, she'd cut it close.

She spent a moment looking up at the VAB: that gigantic block, taller than a twenty-story tower, was as impressive, still, as when it had been built back in the 1960s. But it was showing its age, like the rest of the space effort. Its exterior was stained by the weather, and the big Stars-and-Stripes, painted on the building's flank during the Bicentennial, was faded and had run.

She locked her car and hurried past the network TV buildings, with their glittering glass carapaces, to the press stand. The faded wooden bleacher was no more than a third full, last mission or not. There were a couple of guys in the front row doing radio feeds. A hundred yards away there was a portakabin press office, but it turned out that the mission timelines and info packs hadn't arrived yet.

Her mother had fixed her an invite to the grander family viewing area, on the roof of the administration building. She'd decided she'd rather be here, in this battered old press stand, with working people, rather than drink with faded celebrities.

She sat near the front of the stand. She was looking east. The sky was overlaid by lumpy, broken gray cloud. Before her was a big old-fashioned TV monitor showing a grainy image of the interior of the orbiter flight deck—an image of her mother the astronaut, for God's sake—intercut with shots of the Firing Room here at the Cape containing the controllers who would run the first few seconds of the launch, and Mission Control at Houston, who would take over later.

She looked around. The VAB was a big, visually dominating block over to her left. On a patch of grass before the press stand there were the press portakabins, a big rectangular digital clock, steadily counting down, and a flagpole. Beyond that was a stretch of water, the barge canal from the Banana River leading to the VAB. Behind the canal was a treeline, and beyond that, straight ahead of her, she could make out the two great launch complexes: 39-A to the right, forever empty now, and 39-B to the left, with *Endeavour.*

The launch complex looked gray, colorless, like a piece of some industrial plant. Beside the gantry there were big hemispherical fuel tanks, and a water tower. And she could see *Endeavour*, the gleaming white of the orbiter against the orange of its External Tank and the battleship gray of the gantry. She could make out the orbiter's tail, wings, windows.

It looked, she thought, surprisingly beautiful, like a 1950s vision of a spaceplane, somehow futuristic. The curve of the wing was especially striking at its joint with the body, the only curve in the mountain of engineering, graceful against the blocky industrial gantry.

To Jackie's right there were more pads, stretching off to the south, towards what they called ICBM Row, a whole line of launch complexes facing the ocean. Among them were the pads which had launched the early Mercury and Gemini manned shots. Most were disused, dismantled. Already museum pieces.

She could have brought the kids today, but neither of them had been interested. Both of them had preferred to stay behind for some out-of-school trip to a Disney-Coke net Island.

That was fine by Jackie. She didn't want to confront them with the reality of this. Her kids had been forced to say goodbye to their grandmother; what the hell could Paula expect from them?

☆   ☆   ☆

Gareth Deeke was suspended beneath the wing of a B-52, high in the brightening sky over the Atlantic seaboard.

His head was enclosed snugly by the cockpit canopy. There was only just room for his helmet, and every time he moved, he brushed or banged his skull on a pad or the canopy structure. As the mailbox windows were right next to his head he had good vision ahead and sideways, but the widening fuselage beyond the windows restricted his downward vision. Because of the placement of the windows and the fuselage, he could see nothing of most of his airplane, the wings and nose, or indeed the ground.

On most planes, the airframe could be used as a reference platform. Not in the X-15. It was disconcerting, as if he was suspended in the air in this glass bubble, as if his controls were connected to nothing at all.

At twelve minutes to launch he started to activate the X-15.

Inside the B-52 an engineer was working a panel. "Okay, Linebacker, you want to reset your altitude? I've got just a hair shy of a thousand feet per second velocity and maybe three hundred feet up. Eleven minutes to launch."

"Rog," Deeke replied. "Attitudes look good."

"Do you want to try your controls again, Linebacker?"

Deeke worked his stick. "Here's roll, pitch, and rudder."

"Try your flaps."

"Okay, flaps coming down."

"Confirm that."

"And back up."

"We see flaps up."

"My aux cabin pressure switch is on. The inertial platform is going internal."

"That's nominal, Linebacker," the ground called.

He went into a stability augmentation system check. Then a generator reset. A hydraulic press check. And an electrical press check . . .

His launch light came on.

Everything was looking good. By God, it looked as if not even a malfunction was going to curtail this incredible flight.

"Five minutes."

The ground instructed the B-52 to turn further eastward. Thus far the ground path had been a broad circle inland. Now, Deeke knew, the B-52 was going to line itself up with the ground path of the Shuttle, which, after launch, would be driving eastward towards its orbital path.

The B-52 crew called, "Two minutes."

"Okay," Deeke said, "data is on. Tape to fifteen. Push to test ball nose. Looks good. Alpha is still about one degree, beta is about a half degree right."

"Calibrate, Linebacker?"

"Confirm, I got a calibrate."

"One minute to go," the B-52 said. "Picking up heading."

One minute. Now he had to activate the engine.

"Emergency battery on. Fast slave gyro on. Ventral jet armed . . ."

Even now, Deeke half-expected to be called back.

The call didn't come.

"Prime switch to prime. Igniter-ready light is on. Precool switch to precool." Now the priming sequence had commenced, and the precool switch increased the flow of lox to the turbopump.

"Coming up on ten seconds. Pump idle."

When Deeke pressed his pump-idle button, the rocket engine's turbopump came up to speed and forced propellants into a small chamber called the first-stage igniter, where they were burned by a spark plug. The igniter acted like a blow torch, firing the propellant and oxidizer into the main combustion chamber.

Deeke heard a deep, bass rumbling.

The X-15's flight path today was based on the old high-altitude profile used at Edwards. The only powered portion of the flight was the short rocket burst at the beginning, just after launch from the B-52, driving the bird into a steep climb out of the atmosphere. Then would follow a ballistic, unpowered trajectory up to a peak altitude, and a steep fall back into the atmosphere.

Thus, Deeke would leave the atmosphere and would be weightless for several minutes. This flight was basically a short-duration spaceflight, comparable to the first suborbital Mercury lobs by Alan Shepard and Gus Grissom, but fully under Deeke's control.

Not that it was recognized as such, by NASA.

Maybe today would be a kind of vindication, Deeke thought.

And now, the moment was approaching.

"Everything looks good here."

"Manifold and lines looking good. Launch light going on."

Still no cancellation.

"And we'll call that three, two, one, launch—"

"Three minutes. Orbiter main engines gimballed to launch positions. T minus two fifty-five. External Tank oxygen vents closed. Pressurization of the tank has started. You're configured for lift-off. Two minutes. Set APU to inhibit."

Libet turned a switch. "APU auto shutdown to inhibit."

"Sound suppression power bus armed."

Angel said, "Visors down."

"Launch crew calls Godspeed, *Endeavour*."

"Thank you for that, Marcus."

Benacerraf pulled closed her big faceplate. It clicked shut, and the whir of the cabin's pumps and fans was muffled.

"*Endeavour*, control. Thirty-five seconds. Software mode 101 loaded. Hydrogen tank at flight pressure. APUs have started in the Solid Rocket Boosters. Go for redundant set launch sequence start. Twenty-five seconds. Smooth sailing, guys. *Endeavour*, control. You are on your on-board computer. Software mode now 102."

"Copy that."

Now the GPCs, the redundant general purpose computers on board the orbiter, had taken control of the launch sequence. Only one more command, for main engine start, would be sent from the ground.

Bit by bit, Benacerraf thought, *Endeavour* was cutting her ties to Earth.

Angel read off the continuing prelaunch events from his displays. "Pyrotechnics armed. Sound suppression system activated."

"Fifteen seconds," Libet said.

"SRB pyro initiation controller in its voltage limits . . . We got a live SRB destruct system."

"*Endeavour*, we have a go for main engine start."

"Rog," Angel said. "Time to kick those tires and light that fire. Eight seconds. Position vector loaded . . ."

The geographic location of the launch pad had been turned into positional data inside the orbiter's computers. *Endeavour* had become aware of its location as an object in three-dimensional space, only temporarily and accidentally clinging to the surface of a planet.

Angel said, "Engine flares ignited. Five, four. We have main engine start."

There was a remote bang, a premonitory shudder.

"There they go, guys," Angel shouted. "Three at a hundred."

The orbiter cabin creaked. Benacerraf could feel the displacement of the twang, through all of two feet: the Shuttle stack, pinned to the pad by posts at the base of its SRBs, flexed forward as it accommodated the thrust of its main engines.

Angel and Libet spoke at once. "Main engine pressure above ninety percent, all three." "Engine status lights all green." "Two, one. SRB ignition."

☆   ☆   ☆

For a few seconds, Jackie could make out a shower of sparks, bursting from the nozzles of the orbiter's three main engines. Now a mist of propellants—liquid hydrogen and oxygen—was injected into the sparks, and a bright clear white light erupted at the base of the orbiter, and white smoke squirted out to either side.

The SRBs ignited. The plume of yellow light from the solid rockets was bright—dazzling, like sunlight, liquid light. There was a brief flash, as pyrotechnics severed the hold-down bolts pinning the stack to the pad.

The stack lifted off the ground, startlingly quickly, trailing a column of white smoke which glowed orange within, as if on fire. The movement of the huge Shuttle stack seemed impossible, as if a piece of a cathedral had suddenly taken leave of the Earth.

At the moment of launch there was a kind of release among the press flacks gathered in the stand. As one they stood, and there was clapping, cheering.

Jackie lifted her face to the rocket light that, for a few moments at least, was banishing the gray of winter.

It was, she conceded, a shame the boys weren't here to see this.

And then the noise came, not a single roar but a succession of coughs and barks and crackles, like the popping of some immense oil fire. The ground shook, a rattling she could feel through her feet, on the bleachers.

To Benacerraf it was a shove in the back. It wasn't a sharp spike of thrust—the Shuttle was much too heavy for that—more like riding an elevator of immense power, suddenly hurling her upward, but an elevator that would keep on going until it burst, cartoon-style, through the roof.

The cabin shook violently, and the noise engulfed her. The cockpit was filled with yellow-white light, diffused from the rockets' glare, eighty feet below her. She could see chunks of ice, breaking off the hull of the External Tank, clattering against the pilots' windows.

The mood of quiet calm which had characterized the pre-flight prep was dissipated in an instant. She was riding a rocket, and it felt like it.

A new voice came on the loop. "*Endeavour*, Houston. Launch tower cleared. Eight seconds. All engines looking good."

"Copy that, Marcus." Angel's voice sounded thin, and it trembled with the vibration.

Mission Control at Houston took control of the flight once the Shuttle stack cleared the launch tower. Marcus White, voluntarily brought out of retirement once more, was the capcom there today. It had been done as a PR stunt—a Moonwalker in Mission Control—by the NASA PAO, desperate to milk this last moment of attention for all it was worth. But to Benacerraf, immersed in noise and vibration, it felt comforting to have White's gravelly tones on the other end of the line.

"Eleven seconds," Angel said. "Initiating roll maneuver."

The orbiter went through a hundred and twenty degree roll to the right and pitched over as it climbed, to ease the aerodynamic loads on the complex stack.

Thus, thirty seconds after launch, she was suspended upside down, and hanging from her straps. The ground was visible above the heads of the pilots, receding quickly. Like her first flight, Benacerraf was surprised by the violence and speed of the maneuver.

"Shit hot!" Libet shouted.

It was like being shot downward, out of a cannon; it felt as if the X-15 had just exploded off the hooks.

The violence of the moment was bracing, exhilarating, an intrusion of reality. My God, he thought. It's real. We're really doing this.

Immediately the plane began to roll to the right. X-15

always had a tendency to do that, because of flow effects around the B-52's launch pylon. He worked the left aileron to compensate.

He was basically in free fall right now, falling away from the B-52.

He felt adrenaline pump crisply into his system. It was time. He pressed his launch switch.

There was an explosive noise, like a shout. The main combustion chamber had ignited.

The bird was hurled forward.

He was pressed back, hard, into his seat and headrest. Another memory he'd suppressed. And he started to develop tunnel vision, with blackness shrouding the periphery of his view. He tried to remember what kind of instrument panel scan pattern he used back then. So much he'd forgotten.

The engine noise built up into a banshee squeal.

He rolled his wings level and pulled his nose up to a ten-degree angle of attack. The acceleration swiveled around, from the eyeballs-in of the launch to eyeballs-down at pullup. He felt as if he was climbing straight up, or even going over onto his back. He knew he had to discount the sensations, and just watch his instruments.

The B-52—flying at Mach point eight—just fell away behind him, as if it wasn't moving at all.

The rocket engine was putting out full thrust. Now, for the next eighty or ninety seconds, it was Deeke's job to ride this bull, to keep X-15 on the track that had been programmed for it on the ground.

Soon he would be accelerating at multiple Gs, which meant adding ninety miles per hour every *second*.

He'd forgotten how impressive an aircraft X-15 was.

"Should be coming up on alpha," the ground said.

Seven seconds. Deeke turned three degrees to the right to correct his heading. He kept one eye on the cockpit clock. Nine seconds. Ten seconds. Timing was everything in an X-15 flight. He checked his angle of attack, angle of sideslip, roll attitude, rate of climb.

Fifteen seconds. The acceleration looked nominal, still under two G. He watched his pitch attitude vernier needle, which was starting to come off its peg. Here it came, at eighteen seconds, moving towards the null position. At twenty seconds the needle was centered and he eased off on his angle of attack, to maintain the planned twenty-five-degree climb angle.

"You should be on pitch attitude now," the ground said.

"Rog. Track looks real good. I feel as if I'm back in the saddle again. I wish I could do a barrel roll."

"Rog that," the ground said anonymously.

Yeah. You aren't here to enjoy this, Linebacker.

At fifty thousand feet he shot through a layer of gray, hazy cloud. He emerged into a blue, infinite sky. The sun was still low, and it cast shadows on the ocean of cloud beneath him, which obscured the Earth.

He looked ahead, half expecting to see the Shuttle's vapor stack, ahead of him; but his tipped-up windows showed him nothing but sky.

The handover from the KSC Firing Room had been as smooth as Barbara Fahy could have asked for. She didn't even have to say anything. The ascent, complex and dangerous as it was, was just a process, she reflected, something they had handled more than a hundred times before, unfolding now with the inevitability of the logic of a well-tested software program.

Only the brilliant rocket light on the projected display at the front of the room gave any hint of the violence of the events the FCR's devices were monitoring.

Even so, Fahy found it difficult to breathe.

. . . Now a new voice sounded in her ear. It was the range safety officer. It seemed that some unknown aircraft had wandered into the exclusion zone around the ascent profile.

☆   ☆   ☆

Benacerraf looked ahead, out of the window beyond Angel. A layer of cloud hurtled at the orbiter like a wall. *Endeavour* shot through in a second, and emerged under a deep blue, dome-like sky.

Angel closed switches, configuring the attitude indicator before him.

"There's Mach point nine," Libet said. "Okay, Mach one. Going through nineteen thousand."

Forty seconds, Benacerraf thought, to reach the speed of sound from a standing start.

"Forty-four seconds."

"Houston, *Endeavour*. Max Q. Into the throttle bucket."

Max Q was a moment of danger, Benacerraf knew, the moment at which the Shuttle stack's gathering velocity, coupled with the still-high density of the air, exerted maximum aerodynamic pressure on the airframe. The main engines had briefly throttled down to relieve the pressure.

"Copy," Marcus White called. "Fifty-seven seconds. *Endeavour*, Houston. You are go for throttle up."

"Copy that. Throttle up."

"Wow," Libet said, "feel this mother go."

"Sixty-two seconds," White said.

"Thirty-five thousand," Angel said. "Going through Mach one point five."

"Here we go," Libet said. "SRB pressure is dropping."

Already the solid rocket boosters were burning out.

"One minute fifty," White called up. "Twenty-one miles high, eighteen miles down range."

"Houston, *Endeavour*. Pressures less than fifty psi."

"Copy."

"SRB burnout."

As the solid boosters died, it felt to Benacerraf like a dip, as if the Shuttle was suddenly falling out of the sky, just for a second. But then the acceleration built up powerfully once more.

"Ready for SRB sep."

"Roger."

There was a bang and a bright flash, beyond the orbiter's panoramic windows, as the boosters' separation motors ignited. It was as if she flew through a fireball.

"Okay, Linebacker, we have you right on track, on the profile."

"Rog."

Thirty-one seconds. The rocket burn roared on. Deeke worked his way around checks of his engine instruments, hydraulic pressures, generators, APU temperatures, stabilizer positions, cross-checking his altitude and velocity and rate of climb.

Thirty-five seconds. He shifted in his seat slightly, trying to get more comfortable; the G was already above two and was climbing fast.

"Stand by for eighty-three thousand feet."

"Rog, eighty-three thousand." Now his altitude too was piling up rapidly.

"Do you still read us, Linebacker?"

"Affirm."

"Coming up on a hundred and ten thousand."

"Hundred and ten, affirm."

"On the profile, on the heading. On the profile."

A minute fifteen.

He was already above the bulk of the sensible atmosphere. Ahead and all around him, the sky started to turn from a pearl blue to a deeper, dark blue. His vision seemed to stretch to infinity, to the gently curving, blue-white horizon; there was very little dust or mist above him.

The G forces were reaching their peak now—constant thrust combined with reducing aircraft mass to drive the acceleration higher—he was almost up to four G. This wasn't excessive, Deeke knew, but it hurt his aging chest; he felt he had to fight to take a breath.

"Stand by for shutdown."

"Standing by."

The airframe popped and banged, its skin panels buckling and cracking as he climbed through four G. He'd heard such noises before. The pilots used to call it the oil-can effect. Outside air would work its way into the aircraft through small gaps in external doors or panels; the air was like a torch at high speeds, and would burn electrical wiring, aluminum internal structure and metal tubing, and smoke would waft into the cockpit.

But the X-15, even after decades in a museum, was a tough old bird.

A minute twenty-three. Deeke closed the shutdown switch.

The roar of the engine tailed off into a high-pitched, hog-calling squeal, then ceased.

Suddenly he was weightless; he was thrown forward against his restraints, and he felt his stomach lurch within him.

He was gliding, at almost five Mach, a stone hurled from a catapult.

Now Deeke took his left-side stick, to work the RCS manual controls. He dipped the nose of the X-15.

The horizon rose over the lip of the mailbox window before him. My God, he thought. I'm too damn old for this.

Earth was a brilliant blue floor beneath him, set beneath a darkened sky. To his left and right, he could make out the whole of the eastern seaboard of the U.S., from New York bay to his left, Florida obscured by its ragged coating of cloud below him, and to his right, set in the glittering blue skin of the ocean, a lumpy, brown-green mass that must be Cuba. He was still climbing, thrown by the rocket thrust out of the atmosphere like a stone. The curvature of the planet was clearly visible, as was the layer of denser atmosphere that surrounded it.

And, directly ahead of him, a pillar of orange-white vapor came climbing out of the atmosphere, filled with bright sunlight, arcing gracefully away from him. At the tip of the pillar there was a jewel of yellow-white light, a droplet of brilliance brighter than the sun itself.

The stark simplicity of that thrust out of gravity's bonds was unbearably beautiful, astonishing, like a direct challenge to God.

Through gaps in the cloud Jackie could see the solid rockets fall away from the stack, still trailing dribbles of smoke and flame. There was a ragged cheer from the stand behind her.

Once started, the solid rockets couldn't be stopped or throttled down, unlike liquid boosters; once the solids were lit, the orbiter—and its crew and that huge explosive tank of hydrogen and oxygen strapped to its belly—were just along for the ride, until the SRBs expended themselves.

So getting rid of the SRBs was a good sign. And—

And suddenly there was a second contrail in the sky, spider-web thin, climbing up from the southwest.

She heard some muttering from the press stand behind her. "What the hell can that be? A chase plane?"

But there were no chase planes during a launch. The whole area was supposed to be kept clear.

It was difficult to follow the track, through the breaks in the cloud deck. But it looked to Jackie's inexpert eye as if that second trail was heading straight for the climbing Shuttle stack.

"NASA have confirmed SRB sep, Linebacker."

"Rog."

At this point in its ascent profile *Endeavour* was climbing towards Mach Four, Deeke knew—but even so the X-15 was outrunning it. It was the only aircraft in the world which could have done so.

Now there was one more decision point, one more gate to pass through.

It took one more second for the confirmation to come.

"Linebacker, you are go to deploy. Repeat, go to deploy."

The pure oxygen in his helmet seemed to have turned his mouth dry as Mojave dust.

"Linebacker, do you copy? You are go to deploy."

". . . Affirm, Canaveral. Copy that. Go to deploy."

There was one major addition to the X-15 control panel, a small flip-up softscreen display. Deeke reached forward and lifted this now. It showed a schematic gunsight, and a bright starburst, representing the Shuttle, over to the left of the screen.

He took the RCS control in his left hand. The reaction control system was a set of simple hydrogen peroxide rockets. Deeke used the system in bang-bang mode, where he just pulsed the RCS rockets by shoving at the control stick. When he didn't get the response he wanted, he applied another impulse. And he took care to move in just one axis at a time, to keep control.

In stages, blipping his RCS, he turned the nose of the X-15 as it soared through its ballistic profile. All Deeke had to do now was to center the Shuttle starburst in the little toy gunsight.

Point and shoot.

After a couple of minutes, still closing on *Endeavour*, he got the starburst centered.

It was a firing solution.

The digital display came up with a small qwerty keypad, for him to punch in an enabling code.

He held his gloved hand over the pad.

His whole life hung on this moment, the actions he took in the next few seconds.

Somehow, although he'd rehearsed it, in simulations and in his head, he'd never quite believed he'd have to face this. All he'd really wanted was a way to get back into the cockpit of an X-15, one last time, before he subsided into old age.

"Canaveral. Do I still have go for deploy?"

"Linebacker, you have go for deploy. Repeat—"

"Affirm."

He thought of the blank faces of the ground crew and suit techs, of Hartle sitting like a spider in its web at the heart of Cheyenne.

What right did Deeke have to entertain doubts? What right did he have to oppose such certainty?

His hesitation melted away. He tapped in the code with confident keystrokes. He could barely feel the pad through his thick gloves.

He felt a solid clunk beneath him. That would be the pyrotechnic bolts severing the ASAT from its berth in the belly of the X-15, and pushing it away.

It was done.

For a moment he heard and felt nothing else. The X-15 continued to arc upward through its ballistic profile, climbing towards its peak altitude of two hundred thousand feet. His attitude was drifting off a little; he would have to correct it . . .

There was a burst of yellow-white light beneath him.

He could see a slim pencil, trailing a blob of fire and billowing smoke, white and clean, like the smoke from the Shuttle's own solid rocket boosters.

Deeke corrected his attitude drift with blips from his RCS. He lifted his nose, so that the horizon was hidden by the sill of his window. He didn't particularly want to witness the last act of this drama, when it came.

He closed up the little digital pad; it had served its purpose, and had no further function.

The ASAT arced away from him, towards the sunlit horizon, over the lumpy cloud.

"Smooth as glass, Houston. To software mode 103 . . ."

With the solid boosters discarded, *Endeavour* was driven upward solely by her main engines, the External Tank feeding propellants through its connecting pipes. The ride became easier; liquid boosters provided a much smoother thrust than solids. The whole stack seemed to purr, like some huge sewing machine, every part working in harmony with the rest.

Benacerraf found herself grinning, the exhilaration of the launch getting to her.

Way to go, she thought. *Way to go.*

The ASAT, developed by Boeing in the Reagan years, had been in storage for two decades.

Now, called upon at last, it functioned perfectly.

It was actually a three-stage solid-propellant rocket. It controlled its attitude using three large movable fins on its tail. It carried an infrared sensor and eight small telescopes to help locate its target. It was intelligent, to some degree, containing an on-board computer and a laser gyro.

The first stage fell away, and the smaller second stage burned briefly, accelerating the ASAT to many multiples of the speed of sound.

Then the second stage was discarded.

The ASAT was designed for airborne launch, primarily from an F-15, and was actually capable of knocking satellites out of low Earth orbit. So it was overdesigned for this particular mission. That was not seen as a problem, by the mission planners.

The final stage of the ASAT was basically a smart projectile, which would use the momentum imparted by the rocket boosters to hurl itself at its target. It spun itself up now, and used the fifty-six small rockets in its outer hull to obey its guidance system and keep it on its course. It carried no explosive; it was designed to destroy its target by direct collision, impacting with the force of a shell from a battleship's main gun.

It closed rapidly on the infrared glow it perceived before it. But the target was large, complex, with many sources of heat; accuracy would be difficult to achieve.

☆   ☆   ☆

There was a bang: loud, deep, solid.

The flight deck shuddered, over and above the usual rattling of equipment and loose gear.

Benacerraf was startled. She remembered nothing like this from the sims, or her first flight.

Libet turned to Angel, her mouth open. "What was that?"

Marcus White called up with a routine message. "*Endeavour*, you have two-engine transatlantic abort capability."

Angel said, "Copy, two-engine TAL." His voice was flat, the response automatic; Benacerraf could see that his attention was focused on a main engine status display. "Houston, *Endeavour*. I think we might have a situation here. I'm reading a climb in the fuel pump operating temperature, on main engine number one."

"*Endeavour*, Houston. Say again."

"I have a multisensor fuel pump temp rise on engine one."

"Copy that, *Endeavour*. Stand by . . ."

Tell me this isn't happening, Barbara Fahy thought.

In her mind she replayed those final, stunning pictures from the big FCR screens, over and over again: the remote, blurred image of the Shuttle stack still rising smoothly, with the SRBs slowly diverging—and then that shocking incursion from the edge of the picture, a second contrail that had cut obliquely across the complex shape of the orbiter.

Some asshole *shot* at us.

I still can't believe this is happening, she thought. Who the hell would try to shoot down a Space Shuttle? The Chinese, maybe?

The controller called Booster was trying to get her attention. "Flight, Booster. *Flight*."

She tried to reply; she felt her mouth working, but no sound emerged, as if the components of her body were becoming disengaged, the systems breaking down.

At last she forced out a word. "Go."

"Confirm that temperature rise in the center engine. If we pass through nine hundred fifty we're heading for an auto shutdown. We're working on the hypothesis that there's been a collision of some kind, probably with one of the discarded SRBs. We——"

"No. Booster, that's wrong."

"But——"

Somehow it made it easier for her that she wasn't the only one, here, who couldn't believe this. "We all saw it, damn it. Someone just drove into us. We've been hit a glancing blow by some kind of projectile. Prop, Egil, DPS, are you working with Booster on this?"

"Confirm, Flight."

"Flight, capcom. What do I tell the crew?"

She took a breath. "Stand by, Marcus. Let's just keep monitoring. We haven't lost anything yet; we still have all three engines."

But, she wondered, for how long?

To Benacerraf, it was like a rerun of the disintegration of *Columbia*'s final mission, the slow, almost laborious unraveling of catastrophe. Not again, she thought. Dear God, whatever happens, I can't go through that again.

Angel turned to Libet, and Benacerraf could see him clench a fist, big knuckles white. "Houston, we heard a bang, just after SRB sep. A loud bang. We have a real issue here." His voice had a sharp edge.

"We're working on it, Bill," Marcus White said. "Four minutes twenty. You have negative return. Do you copy?"

That routine call meant that, whatever the emergency, the abort option of returning to the launch site—in a drastic powered maneuver that would have pointed the Shuttle back towards Canaveral and used its main engines to slow it—was no longer available.

And it was a reminder that the events of the launch were continuing around them, bang or no bang; that Benacerraf was still trapped here, inside this slowly exploding bomb.

Angel said, "Houston, I'm watching this damn engine temperature reading here. It's still climbing. Over nine twenty degrees—"

"We're copying, *Endeavour*. Hold on that. *Endeavour*, Houston. Negative TAL now."

"Copy, negative TAL."

Another abort option had passed out of operation. Now it was impossible for the orbiter to attempt to cross the Atlantic and land at the emergency airstrip, at Zaragoza in Spain.

"Four minutes fifty seconds," White said. "We're still with you guys."

Despite the situation, his tone was even, deep, immensely reassuring to Benacerraf. *This is a man who has been to the Moon,* she thought. *Marcus won't feed us bullshit. He will make sure we're okay.*

Angel was hunched forward, against the acceleration, studying his main engine temperature gauge.

If only, she thought, *White was here in the cabin with them.*

Angel said, "Okay, the center engine has gone through its red line. Do you copy? Nine hundred fifty centigrade. And—"

Benacerraf felt an immediate decrease of acceleration, a lessening of the Gs that pressed her against her seat. The flight deck was filled with a loud, oscillating tone. Four big red push-button alarm lights lit up on the instrument panels around the cabin.

Angel pushed a glowing button on a central panel, above a CRT, to kill the alarm. "Master alarm," he snapped.

I know, Benacerraf thought bleakly.

Just to the right of the lowest of the cockpit's three CRT screens was a small cluster of three lights. They were main engine status lights. Benacerraf saw that the centermost light had turned red.

"We lost the center engine," Angel called. "It got too hot and shut itself down."

"We copy, *Endeavour*," Marcus White said. "*Endeavour*, Houston . . ." The capcom fell silent.

"We're waiting," Angel said heavily.

Deeke tried to keep from looking out of the cockpit.

What would he see? —a cloud of dispersing liquid oxygen from a ruptured External Tank, the bright orange glow of RCS hypergolics, fragments of the orbiter wheeling out of the plume, like another *Challenger*?

Had it worked?

. . . He approached his peak altitude. Deeke began to push his nose down, with RCS blips, so that he climbed to the top with a ten-degree nose-down attitude.

In the moment of stasis at the top of his trajectory, he saw the Earth, spread out before him, through his mailbox window.

The world was very bright, like an inverted sky. Under the nose of the aircraft it curved away, in all directions, as if he were poised above some huge blue dome. Out ahead, he could see the ocean, a deeper, bluish gray color. The atmosphere was clearly visible, as a layer of blue haze over the Earth. Above him there was only blackness.

It was extraordinarily beautiful.

My God, he thought. What have I done?

He probed his soul for remorse.

His main regret, actually, was that he would surely, in any conceivable future, never again fly like this, never see the Earth from this extraordinary altitude, spread out like a bright blue quilt.

As he went over the top, the change was rapid; the flight path changed from a climb of plus thirty degrees to minus thirty in minutes.

The deep ocean receded from him as he fell. The lighter blue of the coastal waters expanded below him, coated with lumpy cloud. The air seemed to reach up and clutch at him.

The black nose of the X-15 began to glow as the plane dipped back into the thickening atmosphere. The sensation of speed returned, and negative Gs piled on, soon climbing to four or five.

Deeke pulled X-15 up through twenty degrees. He could feel the aircraft fighting him. The leading edges of the wings glowed a bright cherry-red; now, at the climax of the reentry, the heat of air friction was dispersing around the airframe, raising its average temperature above a thousand degrees. But here, in his little aluminum shell, Deeke could feel nothing but the brutal eyeballs-out deceleration. He felt blood pool in his arms, painfully.

Canaveral said, "Ease it on over. Watch your nose position, Linebacker. We have you low on altitude. Bring it back up. Pull your nose on up, Linebacker."

"Okay, it's coming up."

"Turn left three degrees. Left three degrees."

"Rog."

"Speed brakes in. And maintain your altitude, you're still a little low, Linebacker."

"Rog."

"Okay, you're about ten miles from your checkpoint. You're looking very good here, Linebacker."

The calm, competent dialogue went on, routine and almost meaningless.

Nobody had said a word since he'd deployed the ASAT. He still didn't know whether he'd succeeded or not.

Just get onto the ground, Linebacker. Time enough for all that later.

The flight dynamics engineer, Fido, was talking steadily in Fahy's ear, outlining available abort modes to her.

The RTLS and TAL modes were already unavailable to her.

But they could lengthen the burn of the remaining engines and the OMS, and so reach some kind of orbit. That was an Abort to Orbit, ATO. It had actually been flown before. Later, an abort once-around would be available, with *Endeavour* completing a single circuit of Earth, and reentering immediately.

The ATO gave some chance of salvaging some of the mission's objectives. And getting *Endeavour* up, intact, into some kind of orbit would provide time to figure out what in hell was going on here, and what resources she had to work with.

But an ATO would be a gamble. She would have to hope that the remaining main engines kept working nominally for the rest of the ascent. And as Booster kept pointing out, there was no guarantee of that.

Someone shot *at us, damn it. I can't believe it.*

The launch sequence was unfolding rapidly, a ticking clock. In the next few seconds, she had to make the decision: to abort or not, and which mode.

Again that strange feeling of decoupling settled over her, as if she was paralyzed by her anxiety, as if she could no longer make her body function in conjunction with her will. She wanted to just sit here, listening to Fido's brisk voice outlining the technical options.

It's as if I was hit by that damn missile, whatever it was, rather than the Shuttle. We're all just flawed, limited beings, struggling to cope with these monstrous machines we create, and failing.

I can't do this any more, she thought.

But I must.

She thought about her assets. After all, the Shuttle's main engines were the most complicated ever built. They were throttleable, and had to deliver high thrust with great efficiency. They had inbuilt control systems, so they could monitor their own performance. They were heavily over-engineered, made to be rugged for multiple reuse. Each of the engines on *Endeavour* today had flown a dozen or more times before, on

different orbiters, running up thousands of seconds of hot-fire
time each.

The hell with it, she thought. Those engines are tough. No
asshole is going to shoot us down. Especially as they all but
missed.

She felt determination gathering in her, dispelling her doubts.
She turned to Marcus White, her capcom.

When White came back on the loop, he sounded more decisive.

"*Endeavour*, Houston. Abort to orbit."

Angel glanced at Libet. "Say again, Marcus."

"*Endeavour*, Houston. We're going to abort to orbit, Bill."

"About fucking time," Angel said.

He reached down to a small panel close to his right hand,
and turned a rotary switch from OFF to its extreme right position, ATO. Then, on the same panel, he pushed a button to
confirm the abort. Now they had a course of action ahead,
Angel looked as if he was actually enjoying this, as if he was
already thinking ahead to the sea stories he could spin out
of it.

He was one unimaginative asshole, Benacerraf thought
angrily. And yet right now, her life was in his hands . . .

"Uh-oh," Libet said.

"What? What now?"

"I got temperature rises in the remaining main engines."

"Which one?"

"Both of them, Bill. Look here."

"Oh, shit."

Benacerraf tried to remember what the procedure would be
if they lost another main engine now. She had a sinking feeling
that there wasn't one.

Is this how, after all, human spaceflight is to finish, for the
foreseeable future?

Beyond the pilot's windows, the sky was growing dark.

"*Endeavour*, Houston. We copy your temperature rises, Bill.

Here's what you have to do. We want you to override the main engine auto shutdown."

"Say again."

"Override the shutdown. Don't let the engines shut themselves off."

Angel and Libet hesitated for one second. Then they began to work switches.

The first engine had shut itself off when its internal multisensor noted the pump operating temperature exceeding its safety limit. Perhaps Mission Control was speculating that the readings were flaky, that identical temperature rises in the other pumps were unlikely. If that was so, then a well-meant auto shutdown of a perfectly functioning engine might be the greatest hazard facing the crew.

On the other hand, if the sensor readings were not ratty—if the operating temperatures in those pumps really were rising as the data showed—then probably, before they reached orbit, one of the pumps would blow itself to pieces. And that would finish *Endeavour* anyhow.

After all, they had all heard and felt that bang. There was more than just a telemetry problem here.

Fahy, Benacerraf sensed, was taking a hell of a gamble.

Maybe she is compensating, still, for what happened with *Columbia*. Even overcompensating.

But what choice do I have but to trust her?

"Okay, Houston, *Endeavour*. Auto shutdown disabled. Now what?"

"*Endeavour*, we're going to ask you to burn your remaining two main engines for an extra forty-nine seconds. And the OMS one burn will be extended. And augmented with an aft RCS burn. Do you copy all that?"

Benacerraf had scribbled down the instructions on a scratchpad. "Forty-nine seconds, then an extended OMS. We have that, Houston."

Meanwhile the orbiter continued its climb.

They were eighty miles high, and moving at Mach fifteen.

Now Benacerraf felt the orbiter pitch further over, almost onto its back.

"Okay," Angel said, "we have single engine press to ATO. Houston, *Endeavour*. Single engine press to ATO."

"Copy that, *Endeavour*. We're breathing a little easier down here."

"Keep your pacemaker charged up, Marcus."

Another barrier had been passed. Now, even if another main engine failed, the Shuttle could still continue to MECO—main engine cut-off—with one engine, and so, presumably, achieve some kind of orbit, even if lower than planned.

Benacerraf knew that the risk of catastrophic failure had receded a little.

"Main engine throttle down."

"Throttle down, copy."

"Seven minutes forty. *Endeavour*, Houston. Engines down to sixty-five percent. You're looking good."

"Sure we are."

She could see a muscle ticking in Angel's cheek. He was itching to *do* something, she saw. The launch sequence was so automated that there was almost nothing the crew could do to influence events. They could only sit here, gripping checklists and seat frames, wait while some piece of abort-procedure software flew the craft, hope that nobody had screwed up. No wonder the astronauts had always fought to retain control systems in their ships. Inactivity drove them rapidly crazy.

"Eight minutes thirty-eight," Angel said. "Okay, people. Now we're in the extended thrust regime. Here we go . . ."

According to the original timeline, MECO should have come at eight thirty-eight. They were off the flight profile, then.

"*Endeavour*, Houston. Coming up on MECO at revised time of nine minutes twenty-seven."

"Copy that, Marcus."

"At this time you are go for MECO."

"We're relieved to hear it."

"Coming up on MECO, on my mark."

As the tanks emptied, the acceleration built up to its dynamic crescendo, shoving Benacerraf harder back in her seat.

"Three, two, one. Mark."

The acceleration faded immediately.

Benacerraf was not thrown forward. The force which had pressed her back simply vanished.

She still had a sensation of motion, of high velocity, as if she could feel the huge energy which had been invested in her body and the rest of the orbiter's mass.

Her arms, limp, floated up from her lap before her.

"MECO on schedule," Angel said. "Houston, *Endeavour*. I got me three red engine status lights." He turned and grinned through his faceplate at Benacerraf. "Those balky main engines can't hurt us now."

"*Endeavour*, Houston. Bill, you are go for ET separation. On my mark. Three, two, one. Mark."

There was a remote boom.

"ET sep is good," Angel said. "Beginning minus zee translation."

"Paula," Libet said. She pointed upward. "Look out there."

The orbiter, without its External Tank, was still flying upside down, almost parallel to the Earth's surface. So when Benacerraf squinted upward, she could see the blue skin of the Indian Ocean.

And there, dark and ugly against the ocean, was the bullet shape of the External Tank. The brown insulation foam over its aluminum-lithium lightweight honeycomb shell was battered and badly charred, by the air friction of the ascent and rocket exhausts. It would fall back into the atmosphere to a height of a hundred and sixty thousand feet, where, glowing white hot, its fragments would hail down over an empty slice of Indian Ocean.

"It looks more beat-up than I expected," Benacerraf said.

"Yes. Like it's been in a war," Libet said.

"So it has."

"Software in mode 104," Angel said.

"*Endeavour*, Houston. You are go for the OMS-one burn."

"Copy that, go for OMS-one," Angel said.

Libet worked switches. "Attitude indicator to inertial."

Angel began to punch the relevant navigation software into the computer, using the keypad to his right. Benacerraf, still following her checklist, monitored his keystrokes: ITEM 27 EXEC.

The small orbital maneuvering system lit up with a crisp jolt, a dull roar.

"We're going to come out of this low," Libet said.

She got no reply. There was silence, on the ground, on the flight deck.

The burn seemed, to Benacerraf, to go on and on.

White called from the ground, "Coming up on OMS cut-off. On my mark. Three, two, one. Mark."

The gentle thrust died.

In the FCR there was a burst of clapping.

Endeavour was in orbit.

Barbara Fahy thumped her clenched fist against the surface of her workstation. She felt a surge of savage, exultant joy. She had acted; her decision had been correct, and had maybe saved the mission.

She wished she could get her hands on whoever had shot at her orbiter. She felt she could destroy them herself, with her bare hands, unleashing primitive, savage energy.

She tried to calm herself down. She started to talk on the voice loops, calling her controllers to order. There was still a hell of a lot of work to do, not least the planning of the next big burn, the revised OMS-two burn.

But, even as she forced her mind to work analytically once

more, she clung to the memory of that wild moment of exulta-
tion.

Jackie stayed in the press stand, listening to the fragmentary,
incomplete announcements from the NASA PAO. It was as if
she was somehow connected to *Endeavour*, that huge pile of
metal to which she'd been so close, just three miles from it,
before its explosive launch into space—as if she had to stay
here until the crew were safe, as though if she moved away she
would somehow break the spell that was somehow preserving
the crew, her mother's life.

In the distance she could hear cars, the squeal of brakes and
tires. The car park around the VAB was filling up, and there was
a lot of activity in front of the TV networks' big glass-fronted
studios. More press were hurrying here, and presumably to the
other NASA centers around the country, now that the launch
had turned into some kind of genuine news story.

They finally did it, she thought. She'd understood, technically,
only a fraction of what she'd witnessed today; but the meaning
was clear.

At last, the military-industrial complex of the United
States—the sprawling, interconnected mass of semi-covert
interests and alliances out of which the space program had
been spawned in the first place—had turned in on itself, and
was consuming its own children.

The column of smoke and vapor from the launch still towered into the sky, dwarfing everything, dwarfing even the VAB
itself. It broadened and twisted as the off-shore winds pulled
slowly at it.

I always knew this was a dumb idea, Mother.

"Seventy thousand feet."

"Okay, all out."

"Keep on coming downhill, looks real good. The strip is off
to your ten o'clock, do you have it in sight?"

"Yep."

"Coming through Mach two now, real nice. Keep your brakes out. Okay, you can bring the brakes in now, have you about ten miles out. One point five Mach. What's your attitude, Linebacker?"

"Coming through forty-five now."

"You're about six miles out of high key here, Linebacker."

"Rog."

"Velocity one point two Mach. Watch that angle of attack."

"Rog."

Deeke was flying an unpowered aircraft now. He was facing perhaps the toughest moment of the flight, an unpowered deadstick landing. And this wasn't Edwards, on the tabletop of the Mojave, with its hundreds of miles of surrounding glass-smooth dry lake beds. He would get just one chance at this.

But he had always been a pretty good stick and rudder pilot. He wasn't really concerned.

In fact, he'd rather the flight never ended.

At thirty-five thousand feet he reached the high-key position. He was now directly over his landing site, and he would go through a three hundred and sixty degree spiral, to line himself up for the runway.

He rolled into a broad left turn, using a thirty-five degree bank. Now, from his side window, he could see Merritt Island set out below him, like a flat, brown map overlaid with the long straight lines of highways and the Canaveral AFB, surrounded by flat, shining water. And there was his runway, fat as a goose, right under him where it ought to be.

He glanced up. He caught a glimpse of a vapor plume to the north, still lingering around Launch Complex 39-B.

He descended smoothly and steeply, hanging on his speed brakes. The X-15 seemed to drop like a brick; he decided he'd done too much flying in commercial aircraft, with their baby-gentle descent profiles.

At some point the ground metamorphosed from a flat landscape far beneath him, into a complex three-dimensional world. The runway stretched off before him, converging, comfortingly infinite.

He pulled the X-15 out of its dive, coming level at about a hundred feet above the ground. He extended the landing flaps, and brought up the plane's blunt nose, scorched and blistered from the reentry.

Just feet above the runway, still moving at more than two hundred miles per hour, he pulled a T-handle to the lower left side of his instrument panel. He heard a solid bang under his feet: the landing gear dropping into place.

"Flaps down," he said.

"Rog, flaps look good, gear looks good. Fifty feet, ten, five."

The rear skids hit the ground first, sending a cloud of dust up into the cold January air. The initial touchdown was smooth, and the nose wheel held aloft for a few seconds. Then the nose thumped down, hard enough to give Deeke an eight-G jolt. For a moment he thought the nose gear must have failed; he'd forgotten how close the cockpit was to the ground in the landing attitude. The X-15 was a low-slung aircraft; his head was no more than five feet above the ground.

"That's a beauty, Linebacker."

He pulled back on the stick. It was an old trick: hauling back on the control stick increased the friction with the ground, and slowed his slide more quickly.

A mile from the touchdown point, the X-15 dragged to a halt.

"How about that," he said.

"Yeah. Real nice show, Linebacker."

He checked his timer. The whole flight, from his launch from the B-52, had lasted just five hundred and eight seconds. Less than nine minutes. It was hard to believe; it felt much, much longer.

Recovery vehicles converged on him, a dozen of them, like, he thought, vultures after a corpse. A recovery helicopter flapped overhead, thirty feet up, seeking fires or propellant leaks. Then it landed, and dropped off two technicians in protective suits. They came running towards the cockpit.

He sat in his warm cabin, breathing hard. When he lifted his arms, he found them shaking, as if the muscles were depleted, and he felt sweat pooling at his collar. He was definitely getting too old for this.

He remembered landing at Edwards after his first familiarization flight. Most of the project's staff, and PR people and a few family, had been out there on the lakebed. Later, Deeke figured he had shaken over a hundred hands, out there in the dry sunlight of the high desert, while the chase planes did salute rolls overhead. And then they had all returned to Rosamond to sink a few Baltics. It had been one hell of a day, the height of his sunlit youth.

He wondered if anyone would shake his hand today.

There were military police vehicles on the fringe of the recovery convoy, holding back while the technicians moved in on him.

The first tech opened up the canopy, and began to secure the ejection seat. Fresh, cold air pushed into the cockpit; Deeke breathed of it deeply.

To the north, that tower of vapor still dominated the horizon, misshapen, slowly dispersing.

Endeavour, still inverted, was crossing the equator.

Benacerraf looked up. The glowing skin of Earth scattered rich, cool light over the consoles and equipment of the cluttered cabin. Thunderclouds, ten miles high, were piled up along the equator; visibly three-dimensional, they seemed to reach down from a solid sky, clutching at the wounded orbiter.

My God, she thought. I'm still alive. I survived it. Again.

"We're working on a revised OMS-two for you, Bill. Hang in with it. In the meantime, you want to proceed with your checklist?"

"Rog."

"APU auto shutdown enabled. Boiler controller off. APU control off."

"OPS 105 PRO. Gotcha."

"ET umbilical door mode to manual. Left and right door, left and right door latch switches . . ."

"Houston, *Endeavour*. You want to tell us where the hell we are?"

"You're in orbit, guys. Ah, seventy by seventy-one miles. Congratulations."

"Jesus. We're hardly out of the atmosphere," Angel said.

Benacerraf knew he was right; at this altitude atmospheric drag would soon haul the orbiter back to Earth, whether the crew chose to come or not. And they had a way to climb to get to the rest of the cluster, built around *Discovery*.

But they would overcome all that. She felt a huge relief.

Angel whooped. "I guess we had a horseshoe up our ass the whole time, huh."

Book Three
CRUISE
A.D. 2008–A.D. 2014

*C*assini **was traveling** at three miles per second: more than four Titan diameters every hour. And as *Cassini* climbed out of the heart of the Saturn system, Titan itself lay dead ahead, a featureless, orange-brown ball, dimly lit by the remote sun.

As Titan approached, a human passenger on *Cassini* might have been exhilarated, or terrified, by the probe's plummeting towards the moon.

Cassini was a survivor. It had endured a two-billion-mile cruise through some of the most hazardous sites in the Solar System to get here. It had even survived Earthbound attempts to cut its funding, to abandon it to its fate, here among the moons of Saturn.

Cassini had already completed sixty orbits of Saturn. The orbits, pumped and shaped in three dimensions by Titan flybys, had periods ranging from a hundred days to ten, Saturn closest approaches ranging from three Saturn radii to seven, orbital inclinations ranging up to sixty degrees above Saturn's equator.

There were more than thirty close Titan flybys during the tour. *Cassini* had even grazed Titan's atmosphere, scooping particles of the thin, high layers of air into its mass spectrometer. The flybys had brought *Cassini* as close as six hundred miles from Titan's cloud tops, passing at a speed of twelve thousand miles per hour.

Mission planners on the ground had eked out the spacecraft's remaining propellant supplies and power in order to keep *Cassini* functioning effectively as long as possible. Perhaps, the planners dreamed, *Cassini* could survive through a single complete Saturn year, while Earth traveled around the sun thirty times. It could even slingshot off Titan to head for another planet, or an asteroid.

But now *Cassini* had a new mission: an assignment which, ultimately, it could not survive.

Humans were coming to Saturn. And *Cassini* would have to serve them.

It was January 18, 2008.

Communications from the surface of Titan would not be easy, for human colonists there.

As Titan kept the same face to Saturn at all times, a colony would be out of line of sight of Earth for half of each sixteen-day orbital period. That compounded the problems of Saturn's billion-mile remoteness from Earth, and the difficulties of superior conjunctions: those periods, occurring once a year, when the geometry of the orbits of Saturn and Earth was such that the sun got between the Earth and Titan.

What the colony would need was a relay satellite in orbit around Titan. The human mission could have brought along its own relay satellite, and left it in orbit after its crew descended to the surface.

It would prove cheaper to use *Cassini*.

Cassini was to be placed in Clarke orbit around Titan, a synchronous sixteen-day orbit, so that it hovered above the ground station continuously. That way the satellite would be in line-of-sight with Earth almost all the time, save for those brief periods when it was eclipsed by Titan, or Titan passed behind Saturn, or when a superior conjunction made communication impossible in any case.

Cassini had on board an electronics package called the Probe Support Equipment, which had been designed to enable it to pick up data from the *Huygens* probe during its descent to Titan's surface, and later downlink the data to Earth. And now this old piece of hardware and computer software, used only once, could be used to communicate with a surface human colony.

But to be captured by Titan, *Cassini* was going to have to

shed most of its twelve-thousand-mile-per-hour approach velocity.

There was no way *Cassini*'s rocket propellant—tanks of hydrazine and nitrogen tet—could deliver such a velocity change. Even at the start of its tour, the total the propellants could have delivered had been about five thousand miles per hour; now, they were much depleted.

So *Cassini*—aging, space-soaked and battered, short on energy and fuel—was going to be dipped into Titan's atmosphere, and aerobraked.

For *Cassini*, which had never been designed for such a mission, there were some drawbacks.

Principally, it had no heatshield. And it had no aerodynamic surfaces for control. *Cassini* had the typical angular, nonstreamlined look of a craft designed for the vacuum of space. Now, it would have to function as a mixture of entry capsule and aircraft.

As Titan neared, it began to open outward, turning from a socked-in ball to a wall of cloud, its scale overwhelming the hardy probe. *Cassini* was not heading for the heart of Titan's face, but was passing the moon tangentially: aimed, roughly, at the edge of the atmosphere.

Cassini's temperature rose rapidly as it encountered the first wisps of Titan air, nitrogen and methane and hydrogen.

Cassini plunged into the atmosphere of Titan with its lower equipment module, and its cluster of engine nozzles, leading; the umbrella-shaped high-gain antenna followed behind, acting as a kind of keel to keep the spacecraft stable.

Cassini was traveling at many multiples of the speed of sound. The temperature of the spacecraft's structure rose rapidly, and a thin bow shock of plasma, glowing gray-white, formed ahead of the craft's squat, angular prow.

The onboard processors monitored the spacecraft's status. Internal thermometers noted the temperature rise within the body of the craft, and accelerometers recorded the reduction in velocity. If the velocity drop was too great, or the spacecraft began to overheat, the processors would fire the main engines. That would boost the spacecraft rapidly back out of the atmosphere, to the relative safety of space.

But *Cassini* would leave the atmosphere with most of its velocity intact. On this first entry *Cassini* would not even shed enough speed to be captured as a satellite of Titan; for now it remained in orbit around Saturn, although on a lower-energy trajectory, and must return to Titan for more aerobraking. Eventually, after several passes, the craft would shed enough energy to enter an elliptical orbit around Titan. And at last, using a combination of aerobraking and engine burns, *Cassini* would circularize its orbit and take up its position over Titan's equator.

Later, the craft could be moved to station-keep over the eventual human colony's position.

Many engineers on Earth gave low odds for *Cassini* to survive so many Titan passes. But in any event that was for the future, many months away.

For now, *Cassini* blazed in the thin, high air of Titan, a man-made meteorite, dragging a straight yellow line across the orange face of Titan's cloudscape.

Even during this first atmospheric pass *Cassini* suffered some damage. Many of the covers of its sensors were corroded; its ability to function as a science platform was already degraded.

But much of its yellowed paint and pitted, blackened insulation blankets had been stripped away, the underlying metal surface exposed, gleaming. That was going to give the mission controllers, in the future, some heating problems. But the spacecraft itself looked young again, its scoured-clean surfaces shining.

Cassini, in fact, looked as if it had just come out of the clean room at JPL.

Day 80

The human spacecraft *Discovery*, laden with fuel tanks and habitation modules and antennae, sailed away from Earth, towards the sun.

Discovery was an airliner shape suspended in black infinity, the radiators of its payload bay doors gleaming in the harsh, flat sunlight. The orbiter looked much as it had done in Earth orbit, save for the wings—reshaped for Titan's atmosphere—and the removal of the tailplane.

Beyond the leading edges of the wings supplementary tanks protruded massive, blunt-nosed cylinders swathed with reflective insulation blankets. The tanks carried the fuel for the final big OMS burn that would place *Discovery* into orbit around Titan.

In the payload bay was lodged a lumpy Space Station habitation module, with its front end docked to the orbiter's big crew compartment, its rear fixed to a docking node. Designed for low Earth orbit, where it would have been protected by the Earth's magnetosphere, the hab module had been crudely toughened up with layers of aluminum to provide radiation shelter for the crew. The water tanks were clustered around the walls, too, making the interior of the hab module the nearest thing the crew had to a storm shelter in case of a violent radiation event, like a solar flare.

The docking node, too, was scavenged from the Space Station program; it was a squat, compact cylinder, every face sprouting docking nodes and airlocks.

Two Apollo Command Modules were stuck on the side of the docking node like suckling aluminum piglets.

Behind the node was the CELSS farm: it was an adapted Spacelab module, filled with the racks and lamps of the crew's little hydroponic homestead.

And behind the farm, heavily shielded, was the cluster of fission generators. They were heavy, reconditioned Soviet-built antiques, of a design called Topaz. Each Topaz was a clutter of pipes and tubing and control rods set atop a big radiator cooling cone of corrugated aluminum, that looked like a hollowed-out Mercury spacecraft. The whole thing was perhaps five yards tall. The Topaz, intended to power ion rocket deep-space probes, was the only fission-design that had flown in space.

The launch of the reactors, aboard *Endeavour*, had been one of the most controversial aspects of the mission.

All the modules in the payload bay were swathed with gold-colored sun-shielding insulation blankets; they looked like presents wrapped up for Christmas. And the orbiter's big, filmy high-gain antenna had been oriented to provide some shade from the approaching sun: the double-hide maneuver, the mission planners called it. But after three months' exposure to the strengthening sunlight, parts of the blankets had already baked and turned black.

In the sunlight, the payload bay was brilliantly bright, and the sky beyond was black and empty of everything except the fiery disc of the sun itself.

Discovery coasted, unpowered, on its long trajectory towards the sun. *Discovery* had left Earth behind, and entered a realm governed only by the simplest of laws, gravity and Newton's laws, utterly predictable.

Shadows shifted steadily across the cluttered payload bay as the orbiter went through its slow thermal roll.

Life in Microgravity:

Benacerraf had a lot of trouble sleeping.

When her little alarm watch sounded she was already awake, her eyes crusty and sore. She wriggled out of her sleeping bag;

it was a little tight at the neck and she had to squirm.

Wearing just her underwear, she emerged from her private compartment into the bulk of the hab module.

Nobody was around. That suited Benacerraf; she liked to have a little time alone, to start the day. Right now, though, according to the schedule, somebody should be using the centrifuge; but she couldn't feel the characteristic rhythmic judder of that big, heavy arm going through its six-revs-a-minute cycle. She made a mental note; somebody was goofing off.

The hab module looked clean, intact, its systems humming and whirring. The module was cylindrical, sized to fit into a Shuttle orbiter cargo bay. But inside, the module had a straightforward square cross-section, with flat walls, ceiling and floor, and rounded edges. The color scheme was a cool Earthlike blue, and the lighting was designed to provide plenty of up-down clues. Benacerraf, prone to dizziness and vertigo, appreciated that aspect of the design.

The gaps between the flat walls and the curved hull housed racks—ORUs, orbital replacement units—which could be folded out and replaced. The design rule was that life support and emergency systems and supplies were housed in the ceiling and floor, and systems the crew would use routinely were located in the walls. And strung out along the length of the hab module were the crew quarters, a health care bay, a galley area, and wardroom and hygiene facilities.

Briskly, she used the waste management facility. This was a little booth containing a Shuttle-technology commode, with pin-down bars over her thighs, and a unisex urination cup, color-coded for her use. When she closed the switch, fans started up with a rattling whine. Her urine was drawn away by a current of air, for storage and reclamation.

Benacerraf was proud of the work that had been done on the hab module, under her supervision, at Boeing's Station assembly facility at Huntsville. They had stripped out the equipment racks, floors and utility systems; they'd taken the thing right down to its structural subassemblies and started again. They even stripped all the paint off, until it looked like it had just come out of the horizontal boring mill. They ran structural tests to check decade-old welds, and pressure and leak tests, and fixed a thousand strain gauges to measure stresses.

Then there was a whole series of modifications. They had adapted a hab module—intended as part of a frequent-resupply low Earth orbit station—to serve as the core of a many-year deep space mission. They had reconfigured the systems to take power from a couple of reconditioned Topaz fission reactors, for instance. And they had restructured the module to put shielding material around the hull, like water tanks. It was a lot of work; the engineers had to redesign and rebuild on the fly.

But for Benacerraf it had been a kind of relief, after a decade of frustration. So much fine work had been done on the Station components, only for them to be left standing around in assembly facilities. She had been involved right back when they put together the external structure of the first lab module, back in 1995. Three thousand one hundred inches of weld, all of exceptional quality. You couldn't buy quality like that. You had to earn it. It was good to see this fine work put to use.

When she was done she made her way to the personal hygiene station, where she washed her hands, face, armpits and crotch with a sponge. The sponge, and the excess water she shook off, she stored so that her hygiene water could be reclaimed.

At the little galley, she prepared a quick breakfast: precooked apple sauce, rehydratable granola, beef jerky and breakfast roll; and to drink, chocolate instant breakfast and an orange-grapefruit squash. She had to put the granola bag into a little tray, which slid into a slot in the galley wall to inject the bag with water. She piled the food up on a tray, sticking it down with Velcro pads.

She ate in a kind of Japanese style, with the food close to her face, and she spooned it into her mouth in smooth, graceful arcs. She worked with care. If she jerked the spoon, the glob of food would just fly off, and end up on her face, in her hair, on the walls. And when she sipped her drink, she took care to blow the excess liquid back into the container, or it would come slithering out of the straw and go floating around the module.

She didn't feel hungry, but she made herself finish the food. Suppressed appetite was some artifact of microgravity, an illusion. She tried to add salt and pepper to give a little flavor to the meal. But the diluted salt tended to clog the nozzle of its dispenser. Once Angel, frustrated, had squeezed the dispenser so hard it burst, and they spent two days picking salt off the walls of the hab module. And the pepper, in traditional particle form, just floated off around the hab module rather than settle on the food. The crew had anticipated this and had brought along a lot of spices and condiments, like horseradish and soy sauce and Tabasco sauce. But already these were becoming depleted, and they were trying to ration themselves . . .

She let herself drift in the air as she ate, her eyes unfocused. She felt herself relax into what the surgeons called the "neutral G" position, with her legs pulled up a little, her shoulders bent into a crouch, and her elbows bent. She was floating like a fetus, in the warm blue womblike interior of this hab module.

Right now they were still living off Shuttle-class consumables, but they would be replaced by produce from the CELSS farm as soon as was practicable. Already, their waste was being stored, and would be cycled through the hydroponic farm, so as to close the matter loops of their life support system.

But they would still have to supplement their diet with stored food—this disgusting beef jerky, for instance—to acquire amino acids and other substances not available from the farm's vegetables.

When she was done, she rinsed off her tray in the housekeeping and laundry area. The water she used was sucked away by a vacuum pump, for further recycling.

It was Benacerraf's day for fresh clothes. She went to her personal locker in the wardroom area. She pulled out her underwear drawer. The clothing did the usual zero-G jack-in-the-box trick, bursting out of the drawer and into the air around her face. It took her a couple of minutes to stuff it all back in the drawer and strap it down, picking out items to wear today. Then she opened her main clothing drawer and picked out a T-shirt and trousers.

She went back to her quarters.

She stripped naked and examined herself briefly, with the help of the little mirror of polished aluminum on the wall. Her face had become puffy, especially around the eyes. The girth of her waist and chest had increased. The blood was pooling in her chest, where it restricted the capacity of her lungs, and in her back, where it was absorbed by the spongy discs between her vertebrae, making them thicker and pushing the vertebrae apart. As a result she was an inch or two taller than she had been on Earth.

She inspected her legs with some interest. Legs were pretty much useless in space, serving only to bump into obstacles. And after eighty days, her legs—skinny, pale chicken legs, drained of fluid—were covered with bruises and cuts, in various stages of healing. But she was getting better. Actually she rarely moved faster than a couple of feet per second; she found it was more productive, in microgravity, to aim for precision rather than speed.

She got dressed.

The clothes were dull: T-shirts, jackets and trousers made of golden-brown Beta-cloth—selected because it was fireproof—with 1970s-style turtlenecks and elasticated cuffs. The others griped about the dull, scratchy clothes, but Benacerraf didn't mind. These designs actually went back to Skylab; the clothes were tough, would stand repeated washing, and they were available, just lying around in a store at JSC.

Getting dressed was always an unexpected struggle. The clothing tended to wriggle away from her. She had to work her stomach muscles to drag her feet up close to her chest to pull on a sock or a shoe, and when she'd finished it always felt as if she had given those muscles a tough workout.

The gold-brown outfits were fitted with pockets all over, along both sleeves and legs; and in them she stowed everything she was likely to need during the day—flashlight, pad, pencils, Swiss Army knife, scissors. She popped the pockets shut methodically; if she didn't, the smaller items were likely just to drift out.

She emerged from her quarters and stuffed her used clothes into the laundry bag.

Her most important daily task was to check the status of the life support systems. So she made her way to the control panel.

Every year, a healthy human would consume three times her body mass in food, four times in oxygen, and eight times in drinking water; and would, besides, excrete the same mass in urine, feces, carbon dioxide and water from respiration and perspiration. The only way *Discovery* could sustain a six-year mission to Titan was by closing as many of its mass loops as possible, to support the slow-burning human metabolisms it shielded, to clean up and feed back waste products.

In a way, *Discovery* constituted the ultimate life support technology testbed.

Benacerraf started with the water management system. Their urine, pretreated with acid, had its water distilled out, reducing the urine to a gooey solid. The water was treated with ozone and charcoal filters before being used again, and anyway went into the hygiene supply first, rather than coming straight back to the drinking water. The still had to be rotated to enable phase separation in microgravity, and the rotation tended to disrupt any experiments requiring stability the crew attempted. And every so often the evaporator had to be evacuated and cleaned out, and the fluids pump replaced. A delightful job. Right now, however, the still seemed to be functioning well.

Waste water from other sources—hygiene, the laundry and the air condensate—was cleaned up by a series of filters and packed columns of activated charcoal and resin beds. The filter beds had to be replaced periodically. Then there was a biocide injection system, and a series of automated systems that monitored the quality of the water—for acidity, ammonia, organic carbon content, electrical conductivity, microbial concentration, color, odor, foaming, and heavy metal concentrations—before it was returned to its stainless steel tanks . . .

She looked over the air management system. The steps here had to mimic some of the processes of life on Earth: carbon dioxide had to be removed and reduced from stale air; oxygen had to be generated, and trace contaminants monitored and removed.

The carbon dioxide was removed by passing the air over filter beds containing solid amines, steam-heated. A Sabatier reactor combined the extracted carbon dioxide with hydrogen, to produce methane and water. The Sabatier was a nice reliable design which needed hardly any maintenance. Oxygen was produced from the water by electrolysis, a process she remembered from her own high school days, where an electric cell broke up the water molecules into hydrogen and oxygen. The oxygen fed back into the air supply, and the hydrogen was passed back to the Sabatier reactor. The electrolysis technology was so simple and mature that there was hardly anything which could go wrong with it.

Carbon dioxide in; oxygen out. It was a neat, robust system.

The trace contaminant control was built into the ventilation. A lot of crap could build up quickly in the closed cycles of the hab module. So there were particulate beds to separate dusts and aerosols, activated charcoal to keep out heavier contaminants, chemisorbant beds to remove nitrogen, sulphur compounds, halogens and metal hybrids, and catalytic burners to oxidize anything that couldn't be absorbed.

She checked through a few more ancillary systems: composition and pressure control, the heat exchanger slurper that controlled temperature and humidity . . . The whole system was monitored and controlled in real time by a complex of sensors, including a mass spectrometer and infrared detectors.

She checked the SCWO reactor, the supercritical wet oxidation system. The SCWO was a remarkable piece of gear. Inside, slurry was heated to four hundred and eighty degrees Centigrade and two hundred and forty atmospheres, conditions where water went supercritical. It was like liquid steam. If you jetted in oxygen, you could get an open flame, under water. The SCWO would burn anything, any waste they threw into it: crap, urine, food scraps, garbage, mixed up with organic wastes and water. Out came steam, carbon dioxide, and a whole bunch of nitrates—compounds of nitrogen they could use in the farm.

It looked to Benacerraf as if the temperature control inside the reactor had been a little variable. That was a worry; not everything that happened inside that reactor was well understood. The SCWO was a relatively new technology—the reactor and its backup fitted in *Discovery* were actually upgrades of breadboard prototypes. There were safety concerns around the high temperatures and pressures in the reactor, and corrosion of the pressure chamber. That corrosion could leak metals into the liquid effluent, which could then end up in the food chain.

In a way she was relieved to find something wrong. It proved the monitoring systems were working, and that she was maintaining her own attention as she worked through this daily inspection routine. Bill Angel was on SCWO duty this week. Good; Bill was mechanically adept, and might be able to do something with the malfunctioning reactor. She made a note, and moved on to the next system . . .

Thus, with this string of clanking and banging mechanical gadgets of varying sophistication and reliability, with a stream of endless small details, the crew of *Discovery* sustained the stuff of their existence.

Her last chore, before starting the day proper, was to check the vent grilles, the dark screens that led to the air conditioning system. Not being able to put things down and find them again was the single biggest handicap, as far as she was concerned, about living in microgravity. If you let some small item drift off, you really had no clue as to which direction it might have taken, and you just had to be patient and wait the couple of hours it usually took for items to fetch up against the grille.

Today she found a syringe, a one-inch bolt, a couple of small bags, a rule, and several scraps of paper. She had a system for this; she saved the stuff that looked useful in one pocket, and the detritus in another.

She tried to get a little science done.

There was a telescope mount, equipped with lightweight cameras for observing the sun at a variety of wavelengths: hydrogen alpha emissions from the sun's surface, ultraviolet and X-ray photography of ionized atoms, solar corona and flare imaging systems. No human crew had ever before ventured so close to the sun, nor would again for a hell of a long time.

But the science was hardly high quality. The equipment in the telescope mount had been improvised from left-over spare parts from unmanned missions, like *Soho* and *Ulysses*. And besides, *Discovery* wasn't a good science platform. The camera tracking gear had to compensate for the spacecraft's slow barbecue-mode rotation. And *Discovery* was just too unstable, with five humans, hundred-and-fifty-pound water sacks, lurching massively around its interior. It was G-jitter, in the jargon, sometimes amounting to five or ten percent of G. Even a cough would exert fifteen or twenty pounds of force, and a squirt on a water spigot would jar the cluster enough to jolt the crosshairs of a camera from the center of the sun. And of course the use of the centrifuge shook the whole cluster around so much it made any kind of sensible experiment more or less impossible.

Meanwhile the crew themselves were the subject of endless experimental studies; the bodies of the crew of *Discovery* would, she knew, write the textbook for the next few decades on the long-term effects of space travel on human physiology. But the studies were distorted by the fact that the crew were doing their utmost, with varying degrees of enthusiasm, to combat the effects of microgravity, radiation and the other hazards of the flight. If the studies had been true science, she reflected, you'd have some kind of control: one crew member who didn't take any exercise or other precautions at all, for instance.

There were rumors that the Chinese, in the course of their expanding space program, were doing just that. But for Americans, of course, that was just unacceptable.

The voyage of *Discovery* was becoming, she thought, a clinching argument against humans in space, for science purposes.

Anyhow, the truth was that the science stuff had essentially been tacked on to give them all something meaningful to do, while their twenty-six-hundred-day mission wound through its dull course. Nobody on Earth was waiting with bated breath for *Discovery*'s dazzling streams of data.

Exercise time.

She pulled herself through a hatch into the docking node at the aft end of the hab module. Then, another hatch above her head led into the centrifuge cabin. This was a cylinder, only just big enough to hold a single human standing upright, its walls cluttered with equipment and punctured by small round portholes. It was fixed to a robot arm, derived from the Shuttle's old remote manipulator system.

When she had sealed up the hatch behind her and given the cabin's rudimentary systems a check-out, the cabin detached from the docking node and the arm swung it out and away from the body of the orbiter.

The arm began to pull the cabin through a circle, twenty-five yards in diameter. The cabin creaked, a little ominously, as the arm picked up speed, and she could feel the metallic swaying of the stiff arm as it spun up.

When it got up to speed the cabin would swing around, like a bucket on a rope, at the best part of six revolutions a minute. That would give her an illusion of gravity, generated by centripetal acceleration, of the best part of a G.

She peered out the windows.

Benacerraf was orbiting in a plane a few feet above the orbiter's payload bay, with its shining insulation blankets, its complex shadows, the empty blackness of space beyond.

As the centrifuge picked up speed, the Universe started to wheel around her, so she closed up the windows, pulling down compact little aluminum blinds. Enclosed, she could feel her feet pressing more firmly against the floor. There were handrails here, painted green, and she hung onto them now.

Experimentally, she moved her head, this way and that. Immediately, waves of nausea and giddiness swept over her.

The trouble was, this wasn't true gravity, but centripetal acceleration induced by the spin. There was also Coriolis force, the sideways push that produced weather patterns on the rotating Earth. It was fine as long as she didn't move. But if she moved her head in the direction of the spin, Coriolis pushed back with a force of a fifth of a G. And if she moved it in the opposite direction, her head felt lighter by the same amount. If she were to try to climb up, the Coriolis would push her sideways. And so on.

There were other problems, too. There was a variation, like a tide, of the size of the force along the length of her body; her head was a good deal closer to the axis of spin than her feet. The centrifuge's arm couldn't have been much shorter than it was, or that difference would rise above a few percent, and cause damaging hydrostatic pressure differences in her tissues.

There were two fold-up exercise devices in here, a cycle ergometer and a treadmill, both folded away against the wall. Moving carefully, she reached down now and pulled out the bike.

The fake gravity was still so low that she had some trouble starting; her pedal motions tended to lift her off her seat. She had brought a pillow which she braced now against the ceiling of the cabin, and wedged herself in place with her head. She held tightly to the handlebars. Her feet were in pedal straps, so she could pull down with one pedal while pushing with the other, and that helped keep her in place.

Nobody had run a mission in microgravity much beyond a few hundred days. Nobody knew for sure what the impact of very long term exposure to microgravity would be, or if any of the countermeasures they were taking would work. And nobody had tried to live for years under one-seventh G, as they would have to on Titan. The surgeons didn't know if that was even survivable. For sure, the crew had to expect a long-term loss of bone mass of maybe a quarter, even after they had reached Titan.

Exercise, which would help combat the other damaging microgravity deconditioning processes—muscle atrophy, bone marrow loss, reduction in T-lymphocytes—was no use with the real showstopper, the cumulative loss of bone calcium. And although the crew would be treated with osteogenic drugs—and there was hopeful talk, which had so far come to nothing, of finding ways to stimulate bone growth with electromagnetic fields—the surgeons on the ground had agreed that the only practical solution was to remove the cause: to restore the crew, periodically, to gravity.

So this centrifuge had been improvised. Every crew member was supposed to work out in here, in conditions of nearly a G, for several hours a day.

She didn't really object to the exercising, uncomfortable as it was. Unlike some of the others. It got a lot of the stiffness out of her underused muscles, especially her legs. It was as if her body had an agenda of its own, every now and again demanding that she give it some work to do. And she enjoyed the glow of rude health she experienced after a tough work-out.

It made her look better, too—more like herself—because the extra flow of blood to her legs reduced the puffiness around her eyes.

Anyhow, she thought, it was better than rickets.

And she enjoyed the privacy of this snug, enclosed little bay, the isolation from the others.

As she worked, she thought about her crew.

Rosenberg seemed relatively content with his restricted life: pursuing his own research, bitching at the others when some disturbance wrecked one of his careful experiments. But he was drawing inward, she thought.

So, too, was Nicola Mott. Mott seemed moody, perhaps depressive, ground down already—despite her experience on Station—by the dullness of the interplanetary trajectory, without even the glowing skin of Earth sliding past the windows as a distraction.

But Siobhan Libet, who of all of them was closest to Mott, seemed to be hanging on to her cheerfulness—her sense of wonder—longer than the rest, and she seemed to be doing a good job of keeping Mott back from whatever abyss of depression was threatening her.

Then there was Bill Angel: tough, competent, but restless—a pilot, Benacerraf thought, without any piloting to do, for two thousand days. Of all of them it was Angel who had most rebelled against their daily regime, bitching at the others and Mission Control in Houston. He was a monkey rattling the bars of his cage.

And as for herself, Benacerraf tried to avoid too much introversion, as she had throughout her life. She, like Angel, felt the chafing frustration of being stuck in here with nothing meaningful to do.

Early in the mission, during the euphoria that had followed their hair-raising launch and injection onto this long interplanetary trajectory—and the delight of becoming the first humans to leave cislunar space—they had all been a lot more sociable with each other. They had made a point, for example, of planning meal times to be together.

But that had worn off as soon as the dull daily slog of the mission unfolded.

She'd read of Antarctic scientists who, after a winter snowed into their huts, would throw open the doors as soon as spring came, and just walk off, heading so far into the distance, away from each other, that they might disappear over the horizon.

The crew of *Discovery*, in their space-going shack, faced a winter that would last six long years. As far as Benacerraf was concerned, anything that they found to help them all endure that and keep from driving each other crazy, like fragments of privacy and broken-up shift patterns, was fine by her.

She pressed her eye to the coelostat eyepiece. The coelostat, an old British invention, was an arrangement of spinning mirrors that compensated for the whirl of the centrifuge, and the barbe-cue roll of *Discovery*, to deliver a reasonably steady telescopic view.

She had the coelostat centered on Earth and Moon. The image was slightly blurred, and prone to drift.

Discovery's trajectory was a complicated double orbit around the sun, in which she would complete two passes past Venus, and then a final close approach to Earth, coming within a few hundred miles of the surface, achieving powerful gravity assists each time.

Only then, after two years, having accumulated the velocity its chemical rockets could not impart, would *Discovery* leave the inner Solar System behind, and be hurled towards Jupiter—for a further assist—and on to Saturn.

Thus, right now, *Discovery* was spiraling in towards the sun, on its way to the first rendezvous with Venus. But the energy provided by its injection burn was so low that the ship's orbit was pretty much tracking that of Earth around the sun, draw-ing almost imperceptibly away from the home world, in towards the solar fire. So even now, after eighty days, Earth and Moon showed fat, gibbous discs, their faces turned in parallel to the sun. The blue-white of Earth was much brighter, almost overwhelming the faint brown sheen of its smaller companion.

Benacerraf could still study Earth. She was looking at the

area from Tibet across Mongolia: northern China and the Gobi desert, one of the bleakest, most barren parts of the planet.

Her perspective was evolving, as Earth receded.

She'd tried to follow, even participate in, the inquisitions that had followed the *Endeavour* launch. The country had gone into a kind of weary agony when it had been discovered that the X-15 operation had been mounted by a rogue USAF faction, and heads were rolling. There seemed to be a mood of sourness among the public, engendered by the X-15 incident, as if NASA and the USAF were all of a piece. And besides—as Jackie had predicted—the public had rapidly grown bored with the unchanging news from space.

Xavier Maclachlan was growing ever stronger, his lead in the polls consolidating. Jake Hadamard was already fighting a rearguard action to maintain the RLV and other programs he had started, in the wake of the *Columbia* crash.

It became steadily harder to believe that there would ever be a meaningful attempt at a retrieval.

But it was too late to turn back. Benacerraf had committed herself to traversing this long dark tunnel, leading only to the frigid wastes of Titan. And she suspected she'd always known in her heart of hearts it would turn out this way.

But it grew harder to care, as the radio voices grew fainter, buzzing like wasps in a jar. Even Jackie's irregular, begrudged messages seemed to be losing their power to hurt her.

Earth was irrelevant, now; America was simply the crucible within which this mission had been forged. She was glad to leave it all behind, she was deciding; in many ways she preferred her new life here, cooped up in this handful of dimly lit, sour-smelling compartments, the confines of the ship her only reality, the cool logic of Newton's laws her only constraint.

After a time, she pushed away the coelostat eyepiece.

She cycled for her regulation four hours.

Discovery was moving at a little more than Earth's escape

velocity, seven miles a second. So, Benacerraf figured, while she had been cycling *Discovery* had crossed around a hundred thousand miles: nearly half the distance between Earth and Moon. It would be something to radio back to her grandsons.

With a shuddering whir, the centrifuge began to slow. Soon, the cabin had snuggled against the docking node.

The day eroded to its close.

Her sleeping restraint was just a bag fastened against the wall of her quarters, her little rounded-door compartment on the starboard side of the hab module. Sometimes she was cold, because the sleep compartments were ventilated to the point of being draughty. There wasn't much choice about that, because otherwise, in the absence of convection, she could suffocate in the lingering carbon dioxide of her own breath. But at first she'd found the ventilation stream was blowing up into her face, into her mouth and nose, making her feel chilled to the bone. So, defying the local vertical, she'd turned her sleeping bag around. But now the draught tended to blow up into her sleeping bag, making it billow around her, and dissipating the warmth generated by her body . . .

Besides, the hab module was full of noise.

She wasn't disturbed by the whine of the pumps and fans of the air conditioning system. That was a comforting, surrounding susurrus. But as the sun approached, the heat made *Discovery* expand and contract, popping and banging like a tin roof. And whenever *Discovery*'s RCS thrusters fired, making some automated tweak to the trajectory, it sounded like machine gun fire.

She'd adapt, she expected. She had, after all, two and a half thousand days to get used to this.

To unwind, she read her book.

It was science fiction, a lightweight paperback. There were whole libraries stored on CD-ROM, of course, but she'd never gotten used to reading online, even on softscreens. She'd brought this book, and a handful of others, along with her in her Personal Preference Kit.

(. . . Actually the books had had to be tested for their flammability; she'd had to give up a couple of her precious old paperbacks, to let engineers at JSC set fire to them. Oddly, books didn't burn so well. The engineers called them ablators. Each page had to be on fire before the next inward reached its scorching point, and so the books would protect themselves, shedding heat by discarding pages, like a spacecraft entering an atmosphere . . .)

The book was *2001: A Space Odyssey* by Arthur Clarke, a yellowing paperback from 1971. She wasn't a sci-fi buff, but this book had always been a favorite.

It charmed her that this wonderful old book also featured another ship called *Discovery*, heading for the moons of Saturn. But Clarke's nuclear-powered *Discovery* was all of four hundred feet long, and in its pressure hull, a spacious hall thirty-five feet across, a carousel rotated fast enough to simulate lunar gravity. (Too small, she thought wistfully; Poole and Bowman would have been knocked sideways by Coriolis, and spent their lives throwing up.)

The truth was, she thought sadly, 2001 had come and gone, and the book, like the work of Wells and Verne before, had mutated into a period-piece, a description of a lost alternate world. But at least, she thought, she had been spared Hal.

She let go of the book. It drifted off into the air like a yellowing bird, and the residual strength of its cracked spine closed it up, losing her place.

It had been a pretty good day. She'd managed to get through the whole of it without encountering the others once.

She closed her eyes.

In the end, the launch actually brought Barbara Fahy some favorable publicity.

NASA's PAO presented her as the woman who had lost *Columbia*, but who had redeemed herself by making the right decisions when rogue USAF officers had tried to shoot down *Endeavour*. It was a neat feel-good story. Even if not everyone agreed that those USAF assholes had gone rogue.

Hadamard promoted her out of Building 30, to a more senior program management role. But she found her time occupied by PR: TV interviews and newspaper profiles and goodwill tours.

Hadamard even asked her to accompany him to China.

Thus she found herself as part of a NASA-USAF party, headed up by Hadamard, on a goodwill visit to the Xi Chang launch center. Incredibly, Al Hartle came along, the notorious Chinese-basher who everyone suspected was at the heart of the X-15 plot. But Hartle was a close ally of Xavier Maclachlan, and in exercises like this, many constituencies had to be pacified.

They were flown into the sprawling city of Chengdu, at the heart of the green and mountainous Sichuan province, and then driven in a fleet of air-conditioned limousines towards the launch center. There, they would be met by Jiang Ling, the first of China's dozen or so astronauts, who Fahy had gotten to know a little during her trip to Houston three years earlier.

Looking around the car at her companions—Hadamard's passive stare, Hartle's ferocious, paranoid bald-eagle scowl— she suspected that none of them really wanted to be here. This "friendship" tour was an empty gesture.

But the gesture was the whole point.

The White House had more or less forced this trip on NASA and the Air Force. Every poll indicated that Maclachlan was going to storm the election at the end of the year, and after that all bets were off; the outgoing Administration wanted to do whatever it could to cement Sino-American relations while it had the chance, before Maclachlan started building walls around the nation. Fahy applauded the motive; one look at Hartle's body language today was enough to show her how fragile any kind of China-U.S. accord was likely to be.

But the huge reality of China soon began to overwhelm Fahy, diminishing the internal calculations of the Americans to absurdity.

The heart of Chengdu was impressive, but the city was choked by a huge shanty-town, a constricting girdle of wood and paper shacks. Children sprawled by the roadside. They stared at the cars, their bare bellies swollen, their palms lifted to their pretty, empty faces in the universal sign for "please."

Out of the conurbation itself the convoy entered the eternal Chinese countryside. Fahy caught high-speed glimpses of peasants, scratching at the soil, as their forebears must have done for centuries. China was *crowded*: everywhere there were more people than she had expected—impossibly many of them, working in the dried-out paddies or stumbling along the fringe of the highways or squatting by the road.

Fahy was stunned by her glimpses of the immensity of the Chinese landscape, the huge human resources of the nation.

Like most modern Americans, she had never set foot outside the U.S. before, even though she had worked on a mission to another planet. But she was shamed to find how little she had really seen and understood of her own world.

The space center itself was little more than twenty years old. It had been designed as China's door to geosynchronous orbit, using its Long March fleet. The center was cupped by green-clad hills. The sky was blue, the air fresh and clear; the party were taken around by car and golf-cart buggy.

There were buildings for the horizontal assembly and checkout of Long March boosters, payload preparation bays, and a string of compact-looking launch pads, strung out along a rail line. Fahy endured the usual mind-numbing visits to propellant charging and draining facilities, cryogenic handling systems, pyrotechnics stores, the launch control center.

There was a heroic-pose statue of Jiang Ling. But there was

no sign of any memorial to Chen Muqi, the third Chinese to be launched—officially—who had been killed when his oak-resin heatshield failed during reentry.

They were shown a proud display of China's proposed Moon landing system. The Chinese weren't planning to build a huge Saturn V-class booster. Their strategy would be based on smaller boosters and Earth orbit rendezvous: assembly of the Moon ship in Earth orbit. There was a little plastic mock-up of structures on the Moon's surface: a proud lunar lander, hauntingly like the Apollo Lunar Module of four decades earlier, a compact surface shelter half-buried in the regolith, the Chinese flag surrounded by four or five toy astronauts.

Despite setbacks, the Chinese still claimed they believed they could achieve all this by 2019—the fiftieth anniversary of *Apollo 11*. Al Hartle growled at this, looking chagrined.

Fahy saw no reason to suppose the Chinese couldn't achieve their target. Especially since the Chinese were adopting a strategy which some argued the Americans should have followed all along: to drop any attempt at perfect reliability, to accept lower-cost, more practical solutions—and the heroic deaths that would inevitably accompany them.

Such losses seemed to be acceptable here.

The party was hurried quickly away from any areas of technical sensitivity; the tour was actually, she thought, as shallow as a tourists' visit to the Cape.

She grew bored, restless. She disliked spending her time as a mute geopolitical symbol.

Still, the launch site snagged her attention. Surrounded by mountains—by oxygen, by green growing things—it seemed a place of hope and renewal to her, a port to the future: a real contrast to Canaveral, suspended as it was between land and sea and space, subject to endless entropic degradation.

The party was whisked away by air to Shenzhen, a new city that had grown out of a border stop between Canton and Hong

Kong. They were loaded into a fleet of fresh limousines, and Fahy found herself sharing a car with Jiang Ling.

The road south from Canton followed the Pearl River delta. There was development everywhere—gas stations, snack stands, car repair shops, stores, flophouses, restaurants, factories. Further away from the road Fahy could make out shanty-town clusters, washing up the hillsides like a gray tide. Some patches of green showed, but there were huge gashes in the red earth where new construction was being prepared. The journey was uncomfortable: hot and dusty, the road pot-holed and trash-strewn and full of expensive-looking cars, businessmen behind tinted windows making deals via image-tattoo phones on the backs of their hands as they drove, one-handed.

Jiang Ling apologized for the road. "There is a new highway to link Shenzhen and Canton." Her English, learned since her historic flight, was clipped and precise. "But the highway is even more congested, generally at a standstill. There is another to link Shenzhen with Shantou, another of the SEZs here in Guangdong province—"

"SEZ?"

"Special Economic Zone."

"Oh." Deng's old idea. Commercial enclaves; forward outposts of contact with the capitalists.

They reached a checkpoint, like a customs barrier. Tough-looking young soldiers checked papers passed up by the driver. To left and right a fence, of concrete and ditches and barbed wire, extended as far as Fahy could see.

Jiang caught Fahy looking. "A wall, eighty-six kilometers long. Not everyone, you see, can share in the benefits of the SEZ. Even today."

The car glided on.

Shenzhen was a city of broad boulevards lined with high-rise apartment blocks, office buildings, luxury Western-style joint-venture hotels. The car entered a jungle of neon and softscreen signs announcing bars, discos, karaoke clubs, restaurants, fast-food joints; but in amongst the ads for Microsoft and Disney-Coke and Nike and the other Western giants, Fahy saw—translated for her by Jiang—stern admonitions to buy from the China National Cereals, Oil and Foodstuffs Corporation, and the China No. 2 Automobile Plant United.

On the seat back before Fahy a softscreen was tuned into some local channel. At the center a girl sang a brash, upbeat pop song—it sounded dated to Fahy's inexpert ears—and her face was surrounded by multiple ads, thumbnail images of faces and products, flickering on and off, Cantonese voices shouting their messages like so many quacking ducks. Jiang began to sing along with the jingle. ". . . *The red in the East raises the Sun / China gives forth a Mao Zedong / He works for the happiness of the people / He shall be China's saving star / The East Is Red!*" She laughed, like a child.

Revolutionary songs, Fahy thought, to a boogie beat and wah-wah guitars.

The convoy stopped at the Century Plaza Hotel. Hadamard, Hartle and the others ducked quickly into the lobby through the smoggy air, their heads averted from the Shenzhen cityscape. Jiang and Fahy followed more slowly.

The lobby was cool, glittering, anonymous. There were expensively dressed girls—and some boys—hanging out here, sitting at low tables and smoking, sparkling displays playing over their image-tattooed cheeks.

Jiang caught Fahy's arm. "The others are planning to play golf later—"

"Where?"

"At Augusta. Or rather, in a VR sensorium in the basement of the hotel . . . Would you prefer that we slip away, see something of the rest of the city?"

Fahy frowned. "You mean a VR tour?"

Jiang smiled. "Actually I meant—ah—RL. On foot."

The prospect terrified Fahy. But she didn't feel she could refuse.

And so they walked out.

Shenzhen hit all her senses at once.

There were five-star hotels, and revolving restaurants, and a stock market. There were huge billboards, maybe half of them animated, all of them acoustic, bellowing out ads. There was construction everywhere, buildings rising like fragile plants from cages of bamboo scaffolding; huge robot piledrivers hammered, and dust and rock fragments billowed out in peals of concussive noise. Cars and bicycles jostled in the crammed streets.

Jiang, hidden behind softscreen one-way glasses and a smog-excluding facemask, kept hold of Fahy's arm, and guided her away from the worst hassles. But still she saw prostitutes everywhere, painted girls in miniskirts or tight pants lining the curbs. There were child beggars in rags, running after cars, babies flapping like dolls in their arms. There were groups of young men wearing flashy softscreen-rich Western clothing, modish moustaches and elaborate coiffures; some of them wore rumpled, denim Mao jackets.

Over a main artery there was a huge softscreen picture of the Helmsman of the Nation, China's antique revolutionary-era leader. The image of his masklike, cracked face repeated a phrase over and over, which Jiang translated: *Stick to the Communist Party's line, one hundred years unwavering . . .*

There were few foreigners, little evidence of ethnic diversity. Everywhere, short, skinny people stared at Fahy, curious and hostile.

Jiang leaned close to Fahy and murmured in her ear. "What do you think?"

Fahy lifted her smog mask. "I feel like I've arrived in hell."

Jiang Ling laughed. "Perhaps you have. There are no cathedrals here. Shenzhen is a new city. There is nothing to do here but eat, buy sex, and do business."

"There are so many people . . ."

"Of course. The city is a magnet for those from the country. It has always been thus. And besides, the countryside is failing."

"Failing?"

"The country is suffering a severe water shortage. You must realize this is a global phenomenon. The Earth offers us only a finite amount of fresh water each year. Global warming is depleting the supply. And as the population and water usage grows, we may soon pass a fundamental limit . . . In China, much agriculture is water-intensive. The rice paddies, tended for a hundred generations, are drying out. So what is there to do? Life in a Shenzhen dorm—ten to a room, stinking metal bunks, locked in to mitigate against theft may be horrible, and prostitution may be morally foul. But it is better than starvation in a parched field. And then there are the plagues. Tuberculosis is the worst—"

Fahy couldn't help but flinch at that.

Jiang's hold on her arm tightened. "Don't worry. There are monitors at the border fence, and medical patrols within. The TB is excluded from the city; cases are rare."

"I wasn't thinking about my own safety," Fahy said, but she was lying. "There must be solutions to the water problem," she said. "Dams, river diversions—"

"For many years such schemes have been proposed," Jiang said. "There is a scheme to dam the Yangtze below the Three Gorges, for example, and another to divert half the Yangtze's waters to the arid north. But the West has been reluctant to invest in such projects. Environmental concerns are raised, for example."

"That must be valid."

"But perhaps also there are ulterior motives: a continuing desire to contain China, to restrict its growth, using environmental factors as a pretext." Jiang's face, masked by her colorful softscreen glasses, was unreadable, betraying no resentment; her voice was even.

They walked near the river, the Lohu, and the stink of hydrocarbons from the polluted water made Fahy think of the surface of Titan.

☆   ☆   ☆

Jiang led her to a park called Splendid China. This was a kitschy theme park with models of Chinese wonders, like the Great Wall and Tiananmen Square and the Potala Palace in Tibet. This was what passed for Shenzhen culture, said Jiang.

They walked past a little model of a Long March, and a toy *Lei Feng* Number One suspended on a wire.

Jiang laughed at this. "I can buy myself here, as a doorstep god," she said. "How strange life is!"

They called into a tea shop; they sat in comparative comfort and sipped hot jasmine tea—decaffeinated, Jiang assured her.

An old man went by taking his canary in its cage for its constitutional. He encountered another owner on a small grass space outside a broken-down apartment building; they held up their birds, and stayed silent, while the birds sang to each other. Somewhere, the voice of a sim-Elvis—probably pirated—was crooning a song called, said Jiang, *Ah, Chairman Mao, How the People from the Grasslands Long to Behold You.*

Fahy studied Jiang, discreetly. The slim girl she had met back in Houston in '05 was still there, she thought, but now Jiang looked much older: strained, disoriented.

"You look tired, Jiang Ling," she said.

Jiang smiled. "Three years of touring the world. Perhaps one day I will be allowed to return to my first love."

"Flying."

"Yes." Her face worked. "But I understand I am too valuable in my symbolic role. How I envy you."

"Me?"

"You worked on the voyage to Titan. You showed vision and perseverance. And now, the fact that you are prepared to continue with your work even after the latest setback—"

"You mean the RLV deferment." Hadamard had been forced to accept another scaling-down of the Shuttle replacement project, another deferment of hardware delivery and testing. The current funding problems were the result of preliminary maneuvering in Congress as the members tried to position themselves for the new climate to come when, as expected, Maclachlan took the White House later in the year.

The current scenario showed a Titan colony being resupplied by payloads delivered by a series of unmanned boosters—Delta IVs or Protons, probably—while some new manned capability, based on a Shuttle II, was developed, so they could be retrieved. But that possible retrieval date was receding further and further into the future. And if Maclachlan was elected—and did everything he said he would—it was quite possible even the resupply strategy would be allowed to wither altogether.

Fahy refused to believe the dire worst-case predictions mouthed in the NASA centers. Was it really possible that some future Administration would actually choose to *abandon* Americans, on a remote world, without hope of retrieval or resupply? . . .

Despite brutal controls, China's population had grown to one and a half billion—a quarter of all the humans alive. Of those, a billion lived as peasants in the interior. And, it was estimated, as many as a hundred million lived in squalor and poverty in the shanty-town fringes of the glittering cities.

More than a billion people, she thought, living in a cage, imposed by the continuing technological dominance of the West, and the rigid grip of the aging Party hierarchy.

As long as the cage held, maybe things could persist. But it was all so damn unstable.

China was not what she expected. China was *different*. China wasn't just another geopolitical foe, like the Soviets used to be. It seemed to Fahy, sitting here in this tea shop, that China was the huge soul of humanity, its grandeur; and now that soul was waking, and America, with its tin-foil technology and rocketships, seemed remote and fragile, a land of fools.

The future was bewildering. Not for the first time she wished she was traveling with Paula Benacerraf, leaving this huge, messy planet for the clean simplicities of spaceflight.

A group of young people moved into the restaurant. Their faces and hands were invisible, as if made of glass. They sat in silence at their table. They wore plain Mao suits and caps. Their exposed flesh must be uniformly coated with image-tattoos which, thanks to some smart arrangement of microcameras, projected images of the background to each piece of flesh, so that their heads and hands looked invisible. They were even wearing softscreen contact lenses over their eyes, and their heads must be shaven of hair and lashes and beards.

Of course the illusion wasn't perfect; there was a vague sense of shape and form in the diffraction of light through the imaging systems, and whenever a hand or face was moved too quickly the imaging systems would lag, and the illusion would be briefly lost. But perhaps those imperfections, Fahy thought, merely added to the oddly repulsive fascination of the adornments.

She pointed them out to Jiang, who looked surprised.

"You've not seen this before? It is a new cult among the young. The Nullists. The cult of non-existence of the self."

"Good grief . . . I thought I'd seen everything. What is this, some kind of protest against the net clampdown?"

"You are being parochial, Barbara. Remember, we never enjoyed the brief freedom of the net indulged by the West. No, it is, I think, a consequence of the way we explain ourselves and our world to the young. Science and economics: science, which teaches that we come from nothing and return to nothing; economics, which teaches us that we are all mere units, interchangeable and discardable. Science is already a cult of non-existence, in a sense. The most extreme adherents coat their bodies in image-tattoos, hiding themselves utterly. The Nullists are a strange mixture of scientific and Zen influences."

"Good grief. It's the Church of God the Utterly Indifferent."

"Pardon?"

"I'm sorry. An old Kurt Vonnegut book. I haven't seen this before."

"But the world is a small place. I'm sure it will spread to the US . . ."

Fahy thought again of Xavier Maclachlan, of the anti-science mood he seemed determined to tap.

Jiang said, "What does the Nullist phenomenon say about the world we are constructing for the young, Barbara?"

Fahy looked out, at bustling Shenzhen. "Perhaps that it is hell indeed," she said. She looked up; the Moon was rising, its face still bearing American footprints—battered and lifeless. "And there is no escape."

The two of them left the tea shop and walked back towards the hotel.

In the distance, a couple of blocks away, she saw some kind of disturbance. A pack of children were attacking a sack of what looked like food—tangerine fruit, maybe. They attacked the pack like animals, she thought; their hunger was not feigned. Adults were joining in, beating at the children with sticks. She caught a glimpse of running police, the distant crackle of gunfire.

Day 169

Siobhan Libet pulled herself out of the hab module, and crawled through the flexible access tunnel into the farm.

The CELSS farm—CELSS, for closed environment life support system was a basic pressurized cylinder sixteen feet long and fourteen across, fitting neatly into *Discovery*'s payload bay. It had been improvised from a couple of old Spacelab modules. Spacelab was the pressurized workshop provided by the Europeans for flying aboard Shuttle. Now that Spacelab wasn't going to fly any more, the redundant hardware had been turned to better use.

As she closed the hatch behind her, Libet felt an immediate sense of coziness, of warmth, of brightness. The pressure was high in here. The glow of the banks of lights was warm on her face, and the air seemed thick and humid and full of the smell of chlorophyll, of growing things; it was, simply, like being inside a compact greenhouse.

The equipment racks and data processing consoles of the old low-Earth-orbit experimenters had been stripped out, and replaced by three racks of plants. The racks were thick, with fat pipes carrying nutrient solution that flowed beneath them. Fluorescent tubes were poised above each of the racks, flooding the place with a cool white light, and bundles of fiber-optic cables brought light to the darker corners of the farm. The racks were immersed in pipes and cabling and sensors, and there was a constant hiss of fans and extractors, a warm gurgling of fluids through the pipes. There was a gap down the center of the racks, just big enough to admit a human to work.

Looking into the farm racks was a little like looking into a huge refrigerator, the green of the growing plants somehow dulled and coarsened by the flat white light of the tubes. As technology, the whole thing always looked strangely primitive to Libet.

But it was working, after a fashion. Plants, green and spindly, strained upward towards the lights, from the plastic surfaces of the racks. This was a salad machine, in the jargon, the best-studied form of closed life support system; the other choices had been a yogurt box—algae—and a sushi maker, a fish farm.

There was a locker close to the hatch. When Libet opened it, the usual jack-in-the-box effect shoved out a lightweight coverall, gloves, a hat and a small toolkit. She pulled on the coverall and hat, and donned the gloves. Humming, she prepared to work.

☆ ☆ ☆

It was actually Bill Angel who noticed the SPE problem first.

Inside the hab module he was working—in conjunction with the ground—through a check of *Discovery*'s navigation systems; and, as usual, he was royally pissed off.

He was finding life in *Discovery* a lot more irritating and frustrating than he'd expected. His uppermost beef today was that nothing ever seemed to be stowed in the right place. There was supposed to be a computer tracking system, at JSC, that would keep track of every item on the ship, but that had soon broken down when his asshole crewmates insisted on not putting stuff back where it belonged. As a result he spent half his precious time raking through drawers and lockers, and every time he opened a drawer all the crap would come spilling out all over the place and he'd have to hunt it down and ram it back . . .

Ah, the hell with it. At least the work he was doing today had some intellectual meat to it.

But he was having problems with the navigation systems.

The point of navigation, and the mid-course burns called trajectory correction maneuvers—TCMs—was to keep the spacecraft on its planned trajectory for the duration of the flight. For six years, *Discovery* was going to coast, mostly unpowered, all the way to its rendezvous with Saturn. The way Angel thought of TCMs, it was like cheating at pool. It would be much easier to sink a long shot if, after the ball had been struck, you were allowed to nudge the ball a couple of extra times with the cue stick as the ball headed towards the pocket. Well, that was the idea of the TCMs; without those small adjustments the spacecraft would miss Saturn by many millions of miles.

But it all depended on precise navigation.

There were actually three navigation techniques in use on *Discovery*: doppler, ranging, and optical navigation. The first two could be run from Earth. Doppler was a way to measure the speed the ship was approaching or receding from the Earth, and ranging exploited the finite speed of light to measure the distance from the spacecraft to Earth. When used together, *Discovery*'s position and speed could be determined very accurately . . .

But not accurately enough, over the billion miles *Discovery* was to travel. The only way was to navigate from the spacecraft itself, by the stars.

There was a kit of hand-held gear, a sextant and low-power optical telescope, and there were camera systems. The most basic systems—and the most heavily used—were the simple light-sensing star trackers that had been installed around *Discovery*, in the wings and boattail and nose. Without intervention from the crew these could fix on the sun and Earth and maybe a fixed star, like Canopus, allowing *Discovery* to triangulate its position.

But today something was wrong; the star trackers kept losing their locks.

Angel—ill-tempered, impatient—probed at the problem. The trackers seemed to be picking up a lot of false images, whole constellations of them, that made it impossible for them to recognize their stellar targets. That wasn't so unusual in itself—the spacecraft was habitually surrounded by floating chunks of debris, flecks of paint or insulation that had broken away, all of which glittered like stars in the intense sunlight—but it was unusual for such a flood of false readings to hit all the trackers, all at once. Maybe something had come loose in the cargo bay, he thought.

Then the word came up from the ground.

"*Discovery*, Houston . . ." They didn't wait out the time delay for his reply. "We've been looking at your anomalous tracker readings. We figure that what they're seeing is Cherenkov radiation. Repeat, Cherenkov . . ."

Oh.

Angel knew the implications.

When a high-energy subatomic particle hit a star tracker, it could rip through the tracker's glass window faster than the speed of light in the glass. There would be a kind of optic boom—a blue flash, a burst of Cherenkov radiation, a spark confusing the sensors.

Cherenkov radiation meant that from some source, heavy, fast-moving particles were scouring through *Discovery*.

Angel acknowledged the message, and asked for a confirmation.

Most of the plants were growing hydroponically, with their roots bathed in a liquid nutrient solution called Salisbury/Bugbee. As a backup, others were growing in an experimental soil substitute based on zeolite granules impregnated with potassium and nitrogen and other nutrients, like little time-release pills, with enough nutrients to last years.

In the hydroponic racks, plant stems protruded through little holes in plastic sheeting, straining up at the artificial lights. Water flowed through the solution and air bubbled up from below, while carbon dioxide was pumped in over the plants and oxygen sucked away by a miniature air conditioning system.

Libet's main job today was to pull out the plastic irrigation nozzles from a couple of the racks, which had become clogged. She had to disassemble the base of the rack to get to the nozzles. She opened up her toolbag. Pliers, small hammers, screwdrivers and spanners came floating out at her face, chiming gently against each other. She retrieved the tools, picking out the screwdriver she wanted, and went to work on the rack. Soon she had a handful of screws, nuts, washers and other small parts from the rack. She put all this in a pocket, carefully buttoning it up. When she'd started to work in microgravity she had tried leaving such items suspended in mid-air. But that didn't work in the farm; if you looked away for more than ten seconds or so your nut or washer would go sailing off in the powerful breezes in here.

Anyhow, she retrieved the nozzles; she wiped them out and replaced them. She made a mental note that in a couple of weeks, after the next wheat crop, she would have to clean out the culture media.

If only they were using soil, she mused, then she could take off her gloves and dig in with her fingers; she would need tiny spades and forks, not spanners and screwdrivers. But at least she got to handle the little plants, the green growing things. She breathed on them, enriching their atmosphere with her carbon dioxide.

It had taken a lot of care to select the plants. In typical NASA fashion, plants had been studied in a way traditional farmers would never have recognized, in terms of parameters like edible biomass produced per unit volume, growth period from planting to harvesting, and biologically recoverable calories.

So there was wheat and rice, for calories, starch and protein; white potatoes for carbohydrates, vitamin C and potassium; soybeans for protein and amino acids; peanuts for protein and oil—although the peanuts were difficult to grow and harvest—lettuce for vitamin A and vitamin C.

Wheat was the staple. They got a crop every sixty days. They even had ovens on board (fan-forced—no convection, without gravity) so they could make their own bread. And they were trying out an experimental dwarf spring wheat crop developed in Utah called Apogee, which gave a higher yield.

The warm scent of bread filling the hab module was one of the most pacifying elements of their whole environment.

She turned to her next chore.

Working in microgravity presented its own challenges, as usual. She had to get some kind of foothold, so she jammed her body into the space between the racks using her muscle tension and her legs to hold herself in place. She had a lot of reach— her work envelope, as the mission planners called it, was wider than on Earth, because she could just sway from side to side as she needed to, like seaweed in a current. But her legs, holding her in place, were in tension instead of compression, as they would be on Earth, and she had to take frequent rests to relieve her muscles.

She liked to shut out the noise of the pumps and fans of the nutrient systems and air blowers; she wore earplugs, like today, or sometimes the headset of a walkman. She found that in here she preferred thin, cold, almost abstract music: complex Bach fugues, perhaps, or late Beethoven string quartets. There was something about the voiceless, precise compositions which seemed to complement the lush warmth and visual brightness of the farm.

She was bending the rules by wearing the plugs, though. There was a danger she wouldn't be able to hear the master alarm, if it sounded; there were visual alarms built in here— flashing red lights fixed to the walls—but, from amongst the racks, they were difficult to see.

But Libet figured the danger was minimal. The worst that could happen was probably a micrometeorite puncture—and then she would feel any loss of pressure as rapidly as it happened—or a radiation pulse, a solar particle event. But even so she was safe; the farm was just about as heavily shielded from radiation as the hab module. Plants had higher radiation dose limits than humans, but exceeding the limits would have just as lethal effects. She would just have to wait out a storm in here, for as long as it took.

As she worked, she thought a lot about Nicola.

Niki's depression seemed to be deepening. She went through the work assigned her with no enthusiasm, and not much concentration. And she was having trouble sleeping at night, and was reluctant to wake in the morning. She seemed to have no appetite—hell, none of them did but she was a lot less determined about keeping up her diet and her fluid intake than the rest.

Libet thought she understood. The isolation, the cramped

quarters, the growing unreliability and shoddiness of their equipment—and the utter, utter impossibility of being able to get away from the others—all of that was working on them all in some way, and, it seemed to Libet, they were all changing, adapting to the situation.

Bill Angel, for instance, seemed to be shedding a lot of the bluff humor that Libet had recognized in him on Earth. He had grown an undisciplined black beard—he didn't even look like himself any more and he spent a lot of time bawling out the mission planners and controllers who, he said, were grinding them all flat with their instructions and demands and routines—or Paula Benacerraf over some chore he'd been assigned that he wasn't happy with, like the work on the balky SCWO waste-reduction reactor which still wasn't functioning as it should . . .

All this bull just washed over Libet. Angel was a pilot with nothing to do, just spinning his wheels. He was just finding ways to cope with his situation. Likewise Rosenberg, with his endless, obscure chains of experiments. Ways to cope.

But with Nicola it was different. Nicola didn't seem to be finding the inner resources to handle this. She didn't find anything a comfort any more: the work they did, the entertainment materials they'd brought along.

But at least they had each other.

It had taken the two of them a month to work up the courage—and to get over their space adaptation syndrome—but now Libet and Mott were regularly spending their sleep times in each other's quarters.

It was a small ship, and the rest weren't stupid. She'd intercepted one or two quizzical smiles from Benacerraf, exasperated glares from Bill Angel. Only Rosenberg seemed too sunk in his own world to figure it out.

Sharing quarters designed for one person was pretty cramped, but that was okay for Libet; she seemed to find the closeness of another human body—the warm smoothness of Niki's skin against hers—a great comfort.

Like the farm, maybe: elemental human contact, as a barrier against the huge searing dark outside.

A farm this size needed around sixteen hours work a day: planting, harvesting, wheat grinding, preventative maintenance, adjusting the nutrient solution. So that was work for two people, every day.

Libet did more than her fair share. But then, this was her favorite place in the spacecraft cluster.

She hadn't expected to react like this, to hanker after growing things. She was a city girl. And after all she'd spent months in low Earth orbit, on Station.

But there, right outside every window of Station, had been Earth itself. Here on *Discovery*, between planets, Earth had been taken away. The only object that showed as more than a point of light anywhere in three-dimensional space all around the orbiter was the sun, huge and bright.

Oh, Venus was approaching; in a month or so they would make their first pass past the planet, for the first of the two fuel-saving gravity assists. It would be spectacular. But Venus was just a big white featureless billiard ball, hot and hostile and hidden. Venus didn't count.

The orbiter was like an isolated island, suspended in blackness. And she missed Earth. She missed having that huge sky-bright skin below the craft all the time, complex and dazzling, throwing soft, diffuse light into the cabins. She missed having home so close. She was, she was realizing belatedly, a true creature of Earth; she just wasn't designed to be out here, in all this emptiness, with only the hard, pitiless light of the sun around her.

And so she spent as much time as she could afford here, in this little bubble of light and life, ignoring the huge dark beyond the walls.

Angel pushed buttons to open up the protective doors over the various solar telescopes. The cameras provided images of the sun at a variety of wavelengths, each generated by a different temperature, and so corresponding to a different depth in the star. In the H-alpha wavelength the sun was a fat, roiling sphere of white gas, peppered with black specks that churned, slowly and grandly, like some huge bowl of boiling oatmeal. In the extreme ultraviolet, the sun was a disc of irregular patches of color, without pattern or meaning he could detect. And in X-ray the sun was a fantastic landscape of blue, black and orange, showing up the areas of greatest activity and heat.

As soon as he brought up the X-ray image he could see what the problem was.

There was a big fat dark blue patch, like a bruise, right in the middle of the sun's disc. That was a coronal hole, a part of the solar surface where the corona—the sun's outer atmosphere—was less dense. Magnetic field lines could sprout vertically out into space, gushing out heavy particles at twice the normal velocities, like a hose. And that powerful jet was slamming into the slower-moving solar wind that lay between the sun and the spacecraft, churning it up into vast disturbances with tangled magnetic fields.

And all that shit was coming down on *Discovery*.

Angel hit the master alarm. The hab module was filled with a loud, oscillating tone, and four big red push-button alarm lights lit up on the instrument panels around the cabin.

A second later the automatic flare alarm joined in, triggered by the radiation pumping against the hull of the ship.

Benacerraf came stumbling out of her quarters. She was in her underwear, and Angel could see the curves of her small, blue-veined breasts. Her hair was stuck to the side of her face, and her eyes were huge.

Angel hit a button to kill the alarms.

"What? What is it?"

"SPE," he said. Solar proton event: a solar storm. "We got to get everyone in here."

"Rosenberg is supposed to be asleep, and Nicola is in the

centrifuge." She looked about. "Siobhan must be in the farm—"

"She'll be safe if she stays in there," Angel barked. "You bring Nicola in. I'll talk to Siobhan, make sure she stays put for a few hours."

As he snapped out the orders, he felt exultant. At last, they were going to see some action; at last, after these months of dullness, he could *do* something.

Angel tried the squawk box, but got no reply from Libet. So he went back to the science station to try to get more data on the SPE.

Soon, four of them were here: Angel, Benacerraf, hastily dressing, Rosenberg looking sleepy and confused, and Nicola Mott, still sweating from her time in the centrifuge.

Angel found his gaze wandering over Mott's body, what he could see of it inside her shapeless Beta-cloth clothes. She was sunk in on herself, but she was cute as hell, dyke or not. It would be interesting to make her sweat some other way, he thought.

"How come those assholes on the ground didn't warn us about this?"

Benacerraf shrugged. "They probably didn't know themselves. We're a lot closer in than they are; the storm may not have reached them yet."

He tried the squawk box again. "Damn it. I still haven't spoken to Siobhan."

Mott looked horrified. "Then she mightn't know what's going on. Maybe I should go find her. You know what she's like. She spends hours in that farm with her earplugs in—"

Benacerraf said, hesitant, "The access tunnel isn't shielded. Wait until the storm passes. Anyhow, even if she has her plugs in she should see the alarm lights."

Mott frowned, and started to chew at her fingernail, industriously.

Angel tried the squawk box again; there was no reply. "Ah,

the hell with it. If there's nothing you can do, make the best. Right? I'm hungry. Who wants to eat? Paula, who's on chow detail?"

Rosenberg sounded disgusted. "I'm going back to bed. You asshole, Bill."

The women turned away from him. Benacerraf said, "Keep trying Siobhan, Bill."

Chicken-livered dykes, he thought.

He turned once more to the X-ray image in the monitor, and watched the gray-black coronal hole work its way across the boiling surface of the sun.

When her work was done, Libet stowed away her tools and cleaned her hands with disinfected wet-wipes. She was due for her daily four hours in the centrifuge; her legs seemed to ache in anticipatory protest.

She stripped off her coverall and hat, and stowed them away. She opened the hatch to the connecting tunnel which would take her back to the hab module. The tunnel, a few yards long, was light, flexible.

Unshielded.

She had to dog closed the hatch behind her. The hatch was heavy and tended to stick, and had taken some shifting; by the time she had it closed she was tired and felt ready to rest, briefly, in the tunnel.

She let herself drift in the air, and she could feel her relaxing muscles pulling her into the usual neutral-G fetal position.

She closed her eyes. After the breezy farm, the tunnel was cool and still and comfortable. Maybe she could nap for a few minutes; it wouldn't do any harm.

A line of light streaked across her vision, a tiny meteor against the dark sky of her closed eyelids.

In the farm module, unnoticed, a red lamp was blinking.

There were no alarms in the access tunnel.

☆   ☆   ☆

Benacerraf drifted in her sleeping bag, her reading light on, listening on the squawk box to the reports from JSC.

Solar plasma was buffeting the Earth's magnetic field, making it shudder, and huge electric currents were surging around the upper atmosphere.

The power grid serving the Canadian province of Alberta had gone down. In Britain, the northern lights were visible as far south as London. The Global Positioning System was breaking down; navigational fixes from the GPS satellites were unreliable because of the changing properties of the atmosphere. The Chinese had lost Echostar 3, a communications satellite. The energetic electrons racing around the Earth had caused a build-up of charge; a spark had generated a fake command to turn Echostar's solar panels away from the sun. After a couple of hours, its batteries ran down, and it was lost. The energy of the storm was also heating up the outer atmosphere, making it expand; satellites as high as two or three hundred miles were experiencing a twenty-fold increase in atmospheric drag . . .

She fretted about Siobhan. But there wasn't a damn thing she could do until the storm passed.

Discovery was designed to shield them from the radiation hazards of deep space—hazards from which Earth's magnetosphere and thick layer of atmosphere sheltered the rest of mankind.

The system had to cope with three kinds of ionizing radiation, high-energy particles and photons which could knock apart the atoms of the body as they sleeted through it. There was a steady drizzle of solar cosmic rays—the regular solar wind, a proton-electron gas streaming away from the sun, boiled off by the million-degree temperatures of the corona and galactic cosmic radiation, GCR, a diffuse flood of heavy, high-energy particles from remote stars, even other galaxies, which soaked through the Solar System from all directions. And then, in addition to the steady stuff, there were SPEs—solar proton events, the kind of storm they were suffering now, intense doses of radiation which persisted for short periods, a few hours or days.

Astronauts tended to think of solar and galactic radiation as career-limiting, and SPEs as life-threatening.

Discovery's aluminum shell would shield them from the worst of the effects of GCR, reducing their cumulative six-year dose, anyhow, to maybe three hundred rem. That was high—and significantly increased the risks they all faced of cancer and leukemia later in life—but within the four hundred rem advisory career limit.

Of course it meant they wouldn't be able to sustain another six-year journey home again, without improved shielding.

But to shelter from an SPE they had to retreat to their storm shelters, either the hab module or the farm, with their heavy plating of aluminum and water tanks clustered around the walls.

If—just if—Siobhan was caught in the storm, she could expect a dose of a hundred rem. At least. That would give her nausea, vomiting for a day or so, fatigue. And some long-term damage to the more sensitive parts of her body—the gonads, lymphoid tissues.

If Siobhan was unlucky her dose might rise five times as high.

And anyhow, there was no safe lower limit, Benacerraf knew. However small the dose, you were at risk.

To Benacerraf, huddled in her cabin and waiting out the storm from the sun, it felt as if the metal walls of the ship, the elaborate precautions and dosimeters they had taken, counted for nothing, as if *Discovery* was no more protection than a canvas-walled tent, in this storm generated by huge and remote and impossibly violent events. She had never felt so far from the protective embrace of Earth.

The *Discovery* crew truly had stepped outside the farmhouse door.

☆   ☆   ☆

In the access tunnel, Libet started awake.

She could see more flashes, within her eyeballs: little streaks and curves and spirals.

She knew what *that* meant, of course: the flashes were caused by heavy particles, lacing into the matter of her eyes. She thought she could feel the radiation sleeting through her, warm and heavy. Those heavy nuclei would be ramming into the molecules of her body, smashing away electrons in little cascades.

Hard rain, she thought.

She really ought to open the hatch to the hab module, she thought. But, as she peered up through eyes that were laced with flashes and spirals, it seemed a long way away, and an awful lot of effort. Maybe soon.

And anyhow she was starting to feel ill. Nauseous, a little giddy, tired. Maybe it was space adaptation syndrome back again.

And she thought she could smell ozone, like a beach.

She closed her eyes again, and drifted like a fetus in the air.

Poor Niki, she thought.

The flashes and spirals continued, as if a shoal of some tiny fish were swimming through her head.

Day 325

The blood trickled sluggishly out of Angel's arm.

As he tended the donation bag, Rosenberg couldn't tell what Angel was thinking.

Bill just didn't seem the same guy Rosenberg had got to know down on Earth. Floating around up here in the usual semifetal position, so many of his gestures and postures had changed: he would never sit with his legs crossed like he used to, or stand with his hands on his hips, or cross his arms . . .

Microgravity had even messed up their body language. Rosenberg just couldn't read Angel any more.

It sure didn't help them all get along, cooped up in here.

Now Rosenberg watched, irritated, as the clear plastic bag suspended from Angel's arm slowly filled up. "Clench, God damn it, Bill."

Angel's fist closed harder around the little rubber grip, and the dripping flow of blood accelerated a little. "Fuck you, double-dome. You should be grateful. I got better things to do than bleed myself to death to preserve that shriveled dyke in there."

Paula Benacerraf came out of her quarters and joined them in the common area of the hab module. She looked as if she had been sleeping; her face was slack and baggy, and she was struggling into a grubby T-shirt. They were all wearing stinking, dirty clothes right now, because the laundry was malfunctioning again—clogging and leaking water—and none of them had had the will to fix it. "I think we've all heard what you have to say, Bill, a dozen times."

"Oh, you have. Then screw you." Angel pulled the loose bandage off his arm, and began to tug at the needle protruding from his skin.

Rosenberg said, "Hey, leave that alone. You're not done."

"Yes, I am." The needle came loose, and Rosenberg hastily swabbed at the puncture wound in Angel's flesh. Angel glared at him, his eyes wild above his tangle of floating, grayed beard. "This isn't a God damn nursing home. We don't have the resources for this. I say we cut our losses."

Rosenberg held up the half-full bag. "Paula, he didn't complete the donation."

Benacerraf looked at him from eyes sunk in pads of puffy flesh. "Make it up from stores, Rosenberg."

Rosenberg kicked off the wall and caromed in front of Benacerraf, thrusting the bag in her face. "Don't you get it? We don't have any stores. This is all there is."

"Make it up," she said wearily. Without waiting to see if he complied, she pulled herself along the hab module to the waste management facility.

Angel snorted contempt, and went into his own quarters, slamming the door closed behind him.

Rosenberg was left alone in the common area, his own anger surging. He threw the bag of blood against a wall. It bounced off, soggily, and began drifting away from him, the viscous blood undergoing complex, slow-motion oscillations.

After a couple of minutes, his heart still rattling with anger, he scooted along the module to retrieve the blood.

Rosenberg's personal theory of Angel was that he was the kind of bad-mouthing asshole who would always bitch at any leadership shown by anybody else, but would always be unwilling to take any real responsibility for himself. He reacted, not acted, and in the meantime made life a living hell for the rest of them stuck here with him.

But strictly speaking, of course, he was right about Libet.

Rosenberg was a biochemist, but he was also doubling up as the nearest thing *Discovery* had to a doctor. He'd done a crash basic medical training program. At the time he hadn't taken it all that seriously: as the only crew member with any real grounding in the life sciences, he was the logical choice, but somehow he'd never thought he'd have to put any of this into practice.

But here they were—still inside the orbit of Earth, with a deep space maneuver and their second Venus flyby still to come—and not even one of the six years of the mission elapsed. Yet already one of the crew was basically hospitalized.

The purpose of the crew's med training had been to enable them to prevent biological death. They had all rehearsed in resuscitation procedures: mouth-to-mouth, sternum compression to get the heart pumping, electroshock paddles, endotracheal intubation, cricothyroidotomy, tracheostomy. They had even—back in the remote early days of the mission when they had all still been talking to each other—tried to rehearse such procedures under microgravity conditions. It had soon become comically obvious that grappling with a limp crewmate in microgravity was physically awkward, distasteful, almost grotesque. And many of the steps in their manuals—*tip the victim's head back at forty-five degrees*—no longer made any sense . . .

Anyhow, the theory of their training was that if they could just stabilize whatever situation came up, there would be time to wait for radio waves to crawl across the Solar System and bring advice from the medics on the ground.

But they simply weren't geared up to nursing anyone—even one person, twenty percent of their crew—long term. This was a marginally capable interplanetary craft, not a convalescent home.

The blood had been the first, and most visible, stock to be diminished; the almost daily routine of drawing blood from the crew who were already weakened by their own reactions to microgravity had jammed the cost of maintaining Libet's life in the faces of everybody on board.

Then there were the drugs. There was a pretty wide range of products in long-term storage. They had intravenous fluids, whole blood, crystalloid solutions: both saline and normal serum albumin, morphine sulphate, lidocaine, digitalis preparations . . . But the difficulty they faced now was that Libet had already absorbed a lot of the resources they'd started out with. And that had caused growing resentment among everybody else. Including, Rosenberg admitted, himself. *Why the hell do we pour this stuff into Libet? This is all we have to keep us alive for the next decade or more . . . Anyway, getting caught by the flare was her own damn fault.*

He tried not to think about it. There were other problems to face.

He dug out his softscreen, with his copy of today's checklist. He was scheduled to put in a little time in the centrifuge himself right now. But he could feel the steady whir of the arm as it rocked the spacecraft. That was Nicola Mott; even as Libet declined, Mott seemed to be taking an obsessive interest in her own health, and was putting in extraordinary hours up there.

He listened for a moment to Mott wheeling overhead, grimly fighting back the tide of microgravity changes. Whump, whump.

According to the checklist, Mott should have been putting in some time in the farm. Rosenberg decided he might as well cover for her.

He pulled himself through the hab module hatchway, along the little flexible access tube, where Siobhan had gotten her dose, and into the CELSS farm. He pulled on the protective gear—now, after months, rank with the sweat of others—and began to work around the racks of plants.

He didn't like it in here.

Most of Rosenberg's work, though on living systems, had been at the microbiological or biochemical level. The fact was, he hadn't had much contact with living creatures, human or otherwise, and he found these ranks of straining plants a little sinister.

Overall the hydroponic system was working as it should, and he could see that many of the plants had the large leaves and small roots characteristic of such a facility. But he could also see, at a glance, there were the usual mechanical problems with the facility: clogged irrigation nozzles, a couple of failed fans, a suspiciously dark hue to the solution in one tank, indicating maybe a problem with the nutrient mix. And here was one place where the solution looked aerated, full of fat, sluggish bubbles which clung to the roots of the plants. Aeration was bad. The roots had to stay in contact with the solution to prevent dehydration and nutrient starvation, and to Rosenberg those plants looked, even to his naked, inexpert eye, undernourished.

There were more fundamental problems. Within the muddy hydroponic nutrient he could see roots growing—not downward—but in straight lines away from the seed plate, and at bizarre angles to the shoots. And in these late-generation growths, healthy plants were dotted among many unhealthy and abnormal growths.

It wasn't a surprise to Rosenberg that after billions of years of adaptation to a gravity well the plants were having trouble with microgravity. There were gravity-related mechanisms that controlled branch angles and leaf orientation, and gravity dominated plant cell growth, elongation and development. Without gravity, the physical stresses and loading on cells disappeared. In fluids buoyancy was lost, and gas-filled volumes and vesicles would not move as they should . . .

He could see that some of the wheat crop would need reseeding. Several generations since leaving Earth, the yield of the crops was reducing, and although he could see no gross morphological defects there was some evidence of discoloration and perhaps malformation of the stem growth. He reached into the trays and took out a couple of stems as samples. He was sure he would find problems in cell division, nuclear and chromosomal behavior, metabolism, reproductive development and viability.

He understood, deep down, that it had always been a gamble that they could make this little farm work, and they were just going to have to work their way through the problems as they came up. The truth was, nobody knew what the long-term effects of microgravity and GCR would be. The handful of experiments on biological systems in space—in *Salyut*, *Mir*, and a few unmanned satellites—had not shown up enough data to provide much insight. Still, he thought, it was a shame to see the farm degrade from the triumph of the earliest months of the mission, when it had returned satisfying yields.

Libet had been the most assiduous farmer; her absence, here, among these fragile green things, was keenly felt.

In his softscreen he made a brief list of the main problems he found, to raise at a crew meeting later, and he began to strip off the protective gear.

☆   ☆   ☆

Back in the hab module he had to climb past the wreckage of the laundry, which, it appeared, Benacerraf had been disassembling. The front cover was drifting loose, and he had to shove it aside to get by. It took a little experimentation; if he pushed away from the line of its center of mass the cover just spun, or oscillated in space. There was also other debris from the half-finished job, mops and small tools and a little clear plastic bag of nuts and washers, cluttering up the air.

He looked absently inside the laundry. Benacerraf had opened up the exit vents, and he could see there was some kind of growth in there, what looked like a black algae, coating the walls and vent grilles. He'd found some of the same growth himself on the shower curtain. Microorganisms tended to flourish in the habitable compartments, surviving on free-floating water droplets in the air.

But the problem was deeper than that. Their miniature biosphere had fundamental problems of scale. It was poorly buffered; the biota were connected with a much smaller reservoir of biogenic materials than on Earth. Carbon dioxide, for instance, was recycled through the *Discovery* system in a few hours or days, compared to several years on Earth. So minor imbalances could significantly affect the composition of the buffer in a short time, and imbalances could run away rapidly.

This algal growth was a typical, relatively harmless, example. The others bitched about scraping this stuff out of the shower, but things could get a lot worse: if, for instance, the levels of cee-oh-two rose or fell away from nominal too dramatically, the whole life support system could crash altogether.

Nobody knew what was really going on in here, and they just had to cope with it as best they could. Rosenberg felt he understood this, that he'd understood it before he got on board *Discovery*. It was part of the life he'd chosen.

As he waited for his mail to open on the softscreen he listened to the continuing slow rattle of Mott in the arm. He wondered if he ought to get her down out of there. These long periods in the arm wouldn't do Mott any harm, but if she started giving them all an excuse not to do their hours in there she could damage them all . . .

One of his messages, from the surgeons on the ground at JSC, was a little worrying.

They had been monitoring the routine electrocardiogram readings Rosenberg had been sending down the loop. All five of them had suffered minor heart irregularities over the last twenty-four hours. Rosenberg himself had suffered a so-called bigeminy rhythm, in which both sides of the heart contracted at once. Rosenberg thought he could feel his own heart thumping now inside his chest, huge and vulnerable, as he tried to digest this piece of information. He checked the time of his bigeminy. He didn't remember anything wrong, except maybe feeling tired. He frowned. He'd have to look into this later; the surgeons wanted more EKGs taken of all the crew, and they had a number of suggested causes for the irregularities . . .

He moved his analysis of the farm plant samples up his mental priority list. He was becoming convinced many of the problems with the biosphere could be related to deficiencies or surpluses of trace elements. The plants, on analysis, would be a good check of such problems.

He looked again at his checklist.

He couldn't find any excuse to avoid his patient any longer.

Siobhan Libet was slung in her sleeping bag, and her cramped little quarters had been made over as a kind of miniature hospital ward. The place was cluttered, but it was clean and smelled fresh, if a little antiseptic. That was thanks to Mott, Rosenberg knew. As far as he was aware neither Benacerraf nor Angel ever ventured in here.

Libet was unconscious. She'd been that way for three days now.

He pulled the door closed behind him, and started his examination.

Siobhan's problems were multiple, and linked.

The effects of microgravity were marked in Libet, who, after all, hadn't been able to get to the centrifuge for a hundred and sixty days. Her skeletal muscles were deeply atrophied. The wasting of her cardiac muscles seemed to have stabilized at about eight percent. That was higher than the crew's average, and Rosenberg worried about eventual cardiac arrest. Libet's hemoglobin was down by fifteen percent, enough to mark her out for treatment, on Earth, as an anemic. That hemoglobin count meant less oxygen being carried to the debilitated heart and skeletal muscles.

Her white cell count was down too, so her ability to fight off infection was reduced. Rosenberg was administering interferon to her, a protein involved in the immune system—production of which was also suppressed.

A couple of simple tests showed him that Libet's flexor muscles had lost around twenty percent of their strength, the extensors twenty-five percent. Even the cell structure of her muscle fibers was changing, he knew; microgravity was working on her right down to a microanatomical level.

Libet's bone calcium continued to wash out in her urine, at a half percent a month. Rosenberg thought there was a danger of her inner spongy bone, the trabeculae, vanishing altogether, without hope of regeneration. He didn't have any way of monitoring the build-up of some of that calcium in Libet's kidneys, which could lead ultimately to kidney stones. And on top of all of that, Libet was working her way through the classic symptoms of acute radiation sickness.

In the first few days after the solar storm incident Libet had suffered from nausea, pain, a loss of appetite, extreme fatigue, vomiting. After a couple of weeks she had started to suffer diarrhea, hemorrhaging from the mucous membranes in her nose, mouth and other parts of her body, and hair loss, from patches all over her scalp.

Libet had taken a dose of around five hundred rem. The

textbooks said her chances of survival in the short term were less than fifty percent; and in the long term—when effects like cancer had time to work through—even more marginal . . .

He suspected she'd done well to survive so long, even to stay conscious.

He looked at Libet's face. He could see tears leaking steadily, and when he raised a lid, her eye was bloodshot. That was partly due to the changed fluid balance, and partly to the dustiness of the air: in microgravity, dust didn't settle out. The eyes produced tears, and blink reflexes cut in, intended to wash foreign bodies off the eye, into the lacrimal duct and into the nose. The nose was supposed to run, then, to wash the particles out of the system. But in microgravity there was no gravity feed to the lacrimal duct. The blinking could only redistribute particles over the eye; Libet's cornea was, as a result, red and scratched. And the particles which were forced into Libet's lacrimal duct did not run out of her nose, because her nose was almost stopped up by excessive mucous secretions.

If she ever pulled through this he didn't want Libet to emerge with eye damage. So he had set Mott the task of bathing Libet's eyes, and treating them with various drops . . .

Complex, messy, unanticipated problems.

As he worked, Rosenberg thought about death.

If—when—Siobhan Libet died, it would be Rosenberg who would have to sign her death certificate.

He would have to perform the autopsy.

He would have to provide standard and X-ray documentation, and subject tissue samples to toxicologic, bacteriologic and biochemical analysis; he'd have to take samples from the liver, a kidney, the brain, a lung, cerebrospinal fluid, vitreous humor, hair, skin, spleen, and the skeletal muscles . . .

The legal position wasn't very clear.

NASA spaceflight crews were judged to be federal agency radiation workers, and so were covered by Occupational Safety and Health Administration radiation protection measures. But

those measures had not been drawn up for spaceflight, and
NASA had prepared its own standards for crew dosage. As far
as he could make out, because of get-out clauses, there were
actually *no* radiation exposure standards for human exploration
missions.

For sure, though, they hadn't adhered to the ALARA principle that the standards laid down: exposure As Low As
Reasonably Achievable.

If the law suits started flying, Rosenberg might even be
asked to preserve the body. That would mean, as far as he could
see, mummification.

Jesus. What a situation.

In the course of his med training, Rosenberg had had some
preliminary introduction to psychology. It wasn't exactly a subject he was interested in, but what he had learned had pretty
much confirmed his preconceptions about NASA: that the psy-
chological preparation of NASA crews, including this one, was
pitiful.

Nobody had figured out how they should respond to a situation like this. What *would* they do if someone died? Hold a service? If so, what denomination? And if they had to store the
evidence, what were they supposed to do with the mummified
body?

Maybe the worst problem was that the five of them had,
prior to Libet's accident, come to some kind of accommodation with each other, and with their situation. But the injury to
Libet during the solar storm, and now her likely death—the
loss of her skills, her muscles, her dedication to the farm, her
contribution to the collective personality of the crew—was
likely to destabilize them all, he feared.

Or worse. It might destroy them altogether.

. . . In sleep, her skin was smoothed out, almost glowing in
the soft light of her cabin's reading lamp. She looked young,
trouble-free, save for the occasional grimace, pain echoes
which crossed her face.

It was an odd thing, but he'd never really gotten to know Libet, in the years they'd spent together training for this mission, even the months they'd been cooped up together in this hacked-up Space Shuttle. To him she was a kind of sketch, a collection of barely understood traits: her readiness to laugh, her obvious sense of wonder, her youthful impatience to fly in space, her relationship with Mott.

But then, he hadn't really gotten to know any of the rest of the crew, except in so far as their interests crossed his own. It was only now, when he had been forced more or less to suspend his own work on the Titan data and had been reduced to a kind of low-level nurse for Libet, that he had started to see her as some kind of human being.

There was a person in there, he realized now: an interior presence as deep and complex as his own, inside this shell of damaged flesh. And she was suffering.

He hadn't quite understood his own reaction when he saw how Mott, in her distress, held Libet, and how Libet responded to her. He had been baffled, angry, as if Mott was intruding.

It was a funny thing, but it was as if, out here, so isolated from all but this ill-assorted handful of people, Rosenberg was starting to gain some kind of psychic connection with his fellow humans, for the first time in his adult life. And it wasn't all that hard for him to figure out why he had gotten so angry at Nicola Mott, Libet's grieving lover.

It was because—in a stupid, unworthy way, now that she was utterly dependent on him—he was falling in love with Libet himself.

Rosenberg was jealous.

When he got back to the common area, he found Angel and Benacerraf screaming at each other.

Paula had algal growth smeared over her cheek. "Were you aware of this?"

"Aware of what?"

"What he's been taking." She stabbed a finger at Angel, who loomed in the air beyond her, his beard floating, his body hunched over in the shape of a huge, brown-jacketed claw.

"Are you talking about drugs?"

Paula seemed to be trembling, so extreme was her anger. "God damn it, am I supposed to watch over every damn thing on this fucking ship? Rosenberg, you're the surgeon up here. You got a responsibility for this stuff."

"Woah." Rosenberg held his hands up. "Back off, Paula. As far as I'm concerned all I have is a field assignment. I'm no doctor, and I sure as hell will not accept sole responsibility for our medical supplies." Now it was his turn to point at Angel, who laughed at him. "If that asshole wants to shoot himself up, that's his responsibility. There's no lock on the cupboard, and I'm not prepared to hold any key—"

"Fuck this," Angel snapped now. "Look, Benacerraf, I'm not taking any orders from you over this."

"Then you can take them from NASA."

"NASA are ten million miles away," Angel yelled. "We're on our own out here. Don't you get it?"

Benacerraf tried to face him, but they were both bobbing in the air as they gestured, their centers of mass adjusting as they threw their arms back and forth. It added an air of absurdity to the whole situation, and was maybe even extending the row.

"Steroids," Rosenberg said.

They turned to look at him.

"Anabolic steroids. That's what this is about, isn't it? He's taking steroids, against microgravity wasting of his bones."

"Steroids," Benacerraf said, "and fluoride to promote calcium growth. That's what I've been able to trace anyhow."

Angel shrugged. "Sue me," he said. "It's a hell of a sight easier than those dumb hours in the arm."

"It doesn't work," Rosenberg said. "What is it you're using, the nandrolone? Look, steroids work by increasing muscle strength, not by acting directly on the bones. The stronger the muscles, the more stress they impose on the skeleton; and your skeleton adjusts itself until it's just strong enough to withstand muscle stress. But here's the catch, Bill—you still have to do your exercise to get the benefit. Don't you get it? And as for the fluoride, that really is dumb. You'll start getting calcification where you don't want it. And—"

"Up your ass, double-dome," Angel said savagely. "You're no doctor. What do you know?"

Rosenberg shrugged. "Fine. Your choice. Don't come to me when your tendons ossify."

"Fuck you," Angel said. He pulled himself into his quarters, and slammed the door closed behind him.

Now that the shouting had stopped, the routine noises of the hab module became more apparent: the whir of the high-speed fans, the hiss of the vents, sixty decibels of white noise.

For a moment Benacerraf hung there in the air, her legs drawn up towards her chest. Her breathing was rapid, her face flushed, her eyes, over puffed cheeks, red-rimmed and irritated. Rosenberg wondered vaguely about the state of her heart. "Rosenberg," she said now, "I want you to take responsibility for this. I want you to find a way of locking those damn drugs away from Bill."

He didn't respond.

He had no intention of locking away anything. He sure wasn't going to intervene in some argument between Benacerraf and Angel, for the benefit of a control freak like Benacerraf.

Anyhow, he figured, he had enough responsibility already.

He got away from Benacerraf. He made his way past the debris of the laundry, and in the galley he tried to find something easy to fix for lunch.

Hadamard was in Washington during the inauguration of
Xavier Maclachlan, after his wafer-thin win in the 2008 election.

Maclachlan called it a "liberation of the capital."

Armed militia bands came in from Idaho and Arizona and
Oklahoma and Montana, to fire off black-powder salutes to the
nationalist-populist who promised to repeal all gun control
laws. In the crowd, Hadamard saw a couple of Ku Klux Klan
costumes, a sight he thought had gone into an unholy past.
Come to that, there was a rumor that a former Klan leader was
being made ready to become a future White House chief of
staff. And in his speech Maclachlan appealed to the people to
end what he called the "Israeli occupation of Congress" . . .

And so on.

As soon as Maclachlan lifted his hand from the Bible, U.S.
peacekeeping troops in the Balkans and Africa started to board
their planes to leave. Foreign aid stopped. The U.N. was being
thrown out of New York, and there was a rumor that Maclachlan was planning some military adventure to take back the canal
from Panama.

Army engineers set in place during the handover from the
last Administration started to build a wall, two thousand miles
of it, along the Mexican border, to exclude illegal immigrants.
While it was being built, troops brought home from peacekeeping abroad were operating a shoot-to-kill policy.

There was chaos in the financial markets. Maclachlan had
withdrawn the U.S. from the North American Free Trade
treaty, from the World Trade Organization, from GATT.
Reviews of the country's membership of the World Bank and
the IMF had started—arms of an incipient world government,
Maclachlan said, designed to let in the Russians. He had raised
tariffs—ten percent against Japan, fifty percent against the
Chinese—and world trade collapsed.

The Chinese, particularly, screamed. And so Maclachlan sent
the Seventh Fleet to a new station just off the coast of Taiwan.

Meanwhile all the strategic arms treaties with Russia were torn up, as Maclachlan ordered his technicians to dig out the blueprints for Reagan's old dream of SDI. In fact, Maclachlan wanted to go further. He was inviting ideas for what he called his "da Vinci brains trust." The press was full of schemes for fantastic new weapons: smart remote sensors; dream mines that could shoot at passing traffic; smart armor that would use explosive tiles to deflect incoming projectiles; maybe even an electrical battlefield in which electricity-propelled shells would be zapped in by low-flying aircraft.

And back home, Maclachlan had cut off any remaining programs which benefited blacks and other minorities, and any funding that appeared to support abortion, which had been made illegal in any form.

Xavier Maclachlan was a busy man, and he was fulfilling his campaign promises.

Jake Hadamard was still in his job at NASA, trying to maintain support for the Titan mission, still coping with the fallout from the *Endeavour* launch. Not that anybody seemed to care much about that any more. The scuttlebutt, in fact, was that Maclachlan was lining up Al Hartle as Hadamard's replacement. Maclachlan couldn't have sent a clearer signal as to what he thought of the X-15 incident.

Hadamard had thought he could work with Maclachlan. All his life, Hadamard had put himself, his career, first; he'd thought he could work with anybody.

Maybe he'd been wrong.

He thought Maclachlan was causing a lot of people a lot of misery, needlessly. He was stirring up hate that might rebound on him. And he was taking one hell of a risk by enraging China like this.

Hadamard felt afraid of the future. But his greatest fear was that Maclachlan might actually be right. What if his protectionism and military bristling actually gained back the advantage for the U.S., as they all entered the second decade of what the commentators were calling "China's century"? What if his own, Hadamard's, vestigial moral doubts were exposed as the confusion of a weakling? What then . . . ?

The future, his personal future and the nation's, was more cloudy than ever before.

Marcus White asked to meet him at the KSC Visitors' Center. He parked his car and walked through the Kennedy rocket park. Hadamard remembered how you used to be able to see the rockets as you approached the Visitors' Center, sprouting from the far side of the freeway, white and silver, like the ash-coated stumps of burned-out trees, tied to the ground by their stay-wires.

Now, though, those silver treestumps were almost all fallen; those that hadn't been dragged away to be dismantled lay against the hot ground like discarded matches.

He was early.

The old Visitors' Center was deserted—the ticket booths closed up, the once-sparkling VR displays of the Moon and Mars just empty stages—but the main work of dismantling the place hadn't yet begun, and as Hadamard walked the click of his patent leather shoes on the floor echoed.

He walked around the old-fashioned displays of real hard-ware: Gemini, Mercury, Apollo. The Mercury capsule—America's first manned spaceship—was just a cone of corrugated metal, packed with equipment, enclosed in a glass sheath; the controls were glass and Bakelite and metal toggles, clunky and crude. It was hard to see how a man in a pressure suit could get inside there, let alone fly the thing into space.

Even the Apollo Command Module seemed small, dingy and primitive: impossibly cramped, with the metal frames of those three couches jammed in together. The interior finish had faded to a muddy yellow. There was big chunky machinery on the hatch, and tiny, thick windows, and Velcro patches everywhere.

"I know what you're thinking."

The gravelly voice in his ear made him jump. He turned. In the dimmed lights he made out the tough leather face of Marcus White.

"I know what you're thinking. How the hell did they go to the bathroom in there? Well, I'll tell you. You had to strip naked, see, and then take this plastic bag and clamp it to your ass. And when the turds came out you had to hook them down into the bag with your finger, through the plastic. No gravity; nothing to make stuff fall by itself, right? And then——"

Hadamard forced a smile. "Marcus," he said, "I know how Apollo astronauts went to the bathroom."

"So you came to see these old birds before they are taken out for scrap?"

"They're not being scrapped, Marcus," Hadamard said patiently. "As you know. They'll be put in storage, here at the Cape or at Langley or Vandenberg. It's just——"

"I know. Nobody wants to see this old junk any more. Right? So, you believe that too, Jake?"

Hadamard shrugged. "Hell, I don't know any more, Marcus. Most of the population is too young to remember Apollo anyhow. And the opinion polls say most of them don't believe it ever happened, that it was all faked, a Cold War stunt. Attendances here have dropped right off. What do you want to see me about?"

White let his mouth drop open. "You don't know what's going on here—you, the big cheese?"

"I don't get to hear everything."

"Sure. Not since Maclachlan took the oath, right?"

Hadamard stiffened. "So tell me."

White made an odd, growling sound at the back of his throat. "I'll show you. I was called in to do a VR recording. For the new arcade. They called us all in, those who are left alive. Pete, Neil . . . Quite a reunion."

"Sounds like fun."

"Not really." They walked on, past more mummified, dust-covered 1960s hardware. "You know, I see these guys once every five or ten years. And all I can think is, once you could bounce around on the Moon as light as a feather, and now, my God, look what all this gravity has done to you . . .

"Anyhow, come on. You won't believe your fucking eyes."

The new arcade was a lot smaller and more compact than the old, sprawling Visitors' Center—it had an atmosphere more like a chapel, in fact, as opposed to the old center's VR whizz-bang. There were no Geminis suspended from the ceiling, no wax dummies of spacewalking astronauts, no Jim Lovell space-suits or Lunar Rovers on faked-up moonscapes. There were a few simple decorations—abstract paintings of the Earth, Moon and stars—and a discrete row of VR booths, almost like confessionals.

White pulled back the curtain on the first booth. It showed a simulated Buzz Aldrin, as he'd been when aged around seventy: tanned, seated, relaxed in a sports shirt and slacks. As the curtain opened he went into action.

. . . I remember reading about Edmund Hillary and Sherpa Tenzing when they got to the summit of Everest, in 1953, the VR said. *They just had a few minutes on the peak. Hillary acted like a conqueror. He took pictures down the sides of all the ridges, to prove to everyone that they had made it. But Tenzing knelt down and hollowed out a little place in the snow, and filled it with offerings to his God. You see, for him, it was more like a pilgrimage.*

If anyone was going to top that for a pilgrimage to a strange and remote place, it was Neil and me.

We had a quiet moment, after we'd settled down from the post-landing checks. In my Personal Preference Kit I'd packed away a little flask of wine, a chalice and some wafers. There was a little fold-down table just under the keyboard that worked the abort guidance computer. I keyed my mike, and said something like, "This is the LM pilot. I want to ask everybody listening in, whoever and wherever they may be, to pause for a moment and contemplate the events of the past few hours, and to give thanks in his or her own way." So I poured out my wine; I remember how slowly it rolled out of the flask in that gentle gravity, and curled up against the side of the cup. And I read, silently, from a small card where I had written out a quote from the book of John: *"I am the vine and you are the branches / Whoever remains in me and I in him will bear much fruit / For you can do nothing without me . . ."*

"Are these recordings?" Hadamard asked.

White shrugged. "Some recordings, some cleaned-up and digitized, some straightforward faked-up sims. The story about Buzz's communion on the Moon is true, though. Look at this next one." He pulled back a second curtain; another spectral simulation popped into life.

My name is Jim Irwin, and in 1971 I traveled to the mountains of the Moon. I was captivated from my first footsteps off the LM, when I nearly tipped over, and found myself staring back up at the sparkling blue of Earth. When I stepped into that distant, untrodden valley, I felt buoyant, elated; I felt like a little child again. The Lunar Apennines weren't gray or brown as I had expected, but gold, in the light of the early lunar morning. Golden mountains. They looked a little like ski slopes, actually. Others called that place stark and desolate; I have to say I found it warm, friendly, welcoming. The mountains surrounded our little base like a hand cradling a droplet of water, of life. I felt at home on the Moon . . . At one point we had a problem deploying our ALSEP, our science station, that we had never encountered in training. The cord that was supposed to deploy the central station broke. Well, I prayed for guidance; as I often did during those three days, I recited a phrase from the Psalms which goes: "I will lift up mine eyes unto the hills / From whence cometh my help? / My help cometh from the Lord." And you know, I knew straight away that the answer was to get down on my knees and to pull that cord with my hands. And it worked. I had this glow inside me; I felt we could solve anything that came up, that nothing could go wrong. I sensed that God was near me, even in that remote place . . . I knew then that God had a plan for me, to leave the Earth and to come back to share the adventure with others, so that they could be lifted up in turn . . .

Irwin looked thin, pale, wasted to Hadamard; two decades after his return from the Moon, Irwin had died of a massive heart attack.

White was looking into his face, waiting for a response.

Hadamard spread his hands. "Maybe this isn't so bad, Marcus. After all, maybe we've been too hot on the technology, rockets and capsules, for all these years. Maybe we neglected the spiritual side too much. This is just a—course correction."

"Bullshit," White growled. He stalked forward and pulled another curtain.

. . . I could see the crescent Earth rise, glowing, through the windows of the Command Module. We were returning home. The pressure was off after the Moonwalk, and we could relax and try to make sense of what had happened to us. And as I worked, just routine stuff keeping the spacecraft going, I was filled with a kind of gentle euphoria, a great tranquillity, and a sense that I understood. It was as if I had suddenly started to hear a new language—one spoken by the Universe itself. No longer did the Earth, or anything in the Universe, seem random to me. There was a kind of order—I could feel it out there—all the worlds of the Solar System, the stars and galaxies beyond, all moving like clockwork together. It was a sudden revelation, you must understand; one moment I was a detached observer, stuck in my head as if inside some kind of armored tank of flesh and muscles—just like you must feel— and the next I could see, for sure, that I was part of it all. And as I worked on I had a sense of being outside myself—as if I was a robot, and somebody else was turning the knobs and tracing down the checklists. I knew I had been enlightened, although right there I didn't know how or why; I guess I have spent the rest of my life figuring it out. But I knew, even then, it was the most important moment of my life; it even overshadowed walking on the Moon itself . . .

White seemed to be grinding his teeth; big animal muscles worked under the silvery stubble of his cheeks. "They're calling this display 'Testimony.' They want a contribution from each of us, the Moonwalkers, the story of our spiritual revelations on the Moon, or in space. For the guys who died, like

Irwin and Tom Lamb, they're assembling VR sims using old interview clips and autobiography stuff."

"You won't cooperate?"

"Like hell I will. Jake, believe me, it just wasn't like that. It was about getting through the checklist, and not screwing up. No damn hand of God helped me wipe my butt in one-sixth G . . ."

Hadamard shrugged. "I guess this is what you get if you out-source your visitors' center to the Foundation for Thought and Ethics."

"That bunch of fucking creationists?"

"They have buddies in the White House now, Marcus. Look, you just have to go with the flow on this one. It's a sign of the times. Maybe we're entering a more spiritual age."

"Come on, Jake. You don't believe that. This is all just Maclachlan and his tub-thumping fundamentalism. We're going to get dragged back to the fucking Dark Ages if we go on like this. You know they're teaching creationism again in the schools?"

"I know." Hadamard sighed. In fact there was more, proba-bly unknown to White: for instance NASA press releases were already being "vetted" by a monitor appointed by the Foundation for Thought and Ethics, for any antireligious "bias"; the archive of images garnered from the Hubble space telescope and other satellite observatories was being "purged" of any images which might directly support theories like the Big Bang, in a manner which was not conducive to a "reasoned response" from proponents of alternative "theories" . . .

"So it goes, Marcus," Hadamard said gently. "I guess you heard about the RLV."

"Yeah."

The final cancellation of the much-delayed, budget-strangled Reusable Launch Vehicle program had been one of Xavier Maclachlan's first executive decisions.

"I'd like to think," White said heavily, "that the decision was made over your head."

Hadamard made, routinely, to deny that—then hesitated. "Effectively. I didn't have much choice, after the President and his budget chief got together to beat up on me. The basic argument is the need to free up federal funds to counter the secession threats from Washington State and Idaho. Not to mention Nevada, if Maclachlan goes ahead with his threat to shut down the godless gambling in Vegas . . . Maclachlan thinks that the whole point of us launching off the Titan mission before he got elected was so we would have a peg to hang the RLV program on. He thinks we tried to pre-commit him to an expenditure of billions on space, year on year ongoing, before a vote was cast in the '08 ballot. So he just shut the damn thing down."

"So we don't have a way to retrieve those guys. My God. A year out, and we already abandoned them."

"That's not the official position. That's not *my* position. I have study groups in all the centers working on retrieval options without a new RLV. But I admit I had to fight even to ensure the resupply Delta IV launches . . . Marcus, space just isn't where the President wants his head to be."

"But at least you argued against the shutdown," White said evenly. "Maybe you're more than the paperpushing fucker we all thought you were, Jake."

"Thanks a lot," Hadamard said drily.

The thing of it was, White was right. Hadamard *had* argued against the decision, and he probably had damaged his career prospects in Maclachlan's eyes, and he'd gained nothing in the process.

He was still trying to figure out why he'd done it.

It sure wasn't anything misty-eyed to do with the safety of Our Men and Women in Space. To hell with Benacerraf and the rest, frankly; they had known the risks, technical and political, when they climbed on board that last Shuttle.

For Hadamard, it was something deeper than that.

Hadamard found himself resisting Maclachlan, on whatever turf he could defend.

It all seemed to be becoming symbolic, for Hadamard. *My God, Jake,* he thought. *I think you're growing principles, in your old age.*

But White was still talking. His praise, Hadamard thought drily, was less than unqualified.

"Of course you got it all wrong," White said.

"How so?"

"Going to Titan in chemical rockets *is* a truly dumb thing to do. I supported Paula's suggestion, because it was all we had. And I thought it would be the start of the future, not the end."

"So what we should be doing is—"

"What we should be doing is building for the future. An integrated program. With this Chinese scare we had the chance to change hearts, to thrill and terrify, to lead America to space . . . We should be building the new RLV, and launching fission rocket stages to orbit, and going to Mars and back in a fortnight. We need an integrated vision of the colonization of the Solar System: Earth orbit, the Moon, Mars, beyond. It's not impossible, technically. It's just will, and politics. Politics is just paperwork. And this country has carried through great, world-changing projects before. Look at World War Two. And . . ."

Hadamard let the old man talk for a while, until he ran dry.

Then he said, "We've been here before, Marcus. In the 1950s we dreamed of Tsiolkovsky: the orderly conquest of space. But in the 1960s, what we built was Apollo. That's the kind of species we are, it seems. And the smart guy, the guy who achieves things, is realistic—about what we're capable of, what we're willing to do—and works in that framework."

"Like Jim Webb."

"Like Jim Webb. In the middle of the Vietnam war, after his President was shot out from under him, Jim Webb got *you* to the Moon. He did it by playing hard politics, and he couldn't have achieved any more. And in the same way, with forty-year-old technology and Maclachlan coming down my throat—"

"You sent us to Titan."

"Hell, yes. I know it's not ideal, the smartest thing. But we ain't so good at doing the smart thing, Marcus. You have to do what you can. Anyhow, would you rather *not* be going to Titan? Would you rather you hadn't had those three days up there on the Moon?"

"No. Of course not," White rumbled. "It's just I'd rather have had half a lifetime . . ."

"That wasn't an option," Hadamard said severely. "We do what we can."

They walked on through the rest of the half-finished center. White's temper didn't improve, as he picked out more VR highlights for Hadamard: Ed Mitchell's cislunar ESP experiment, endless items from NASA apocrypha—"sightings" by astronauts all the way back to Armstrong of UFOs and alien bases on the Moon, a reconstruction of the supposed "lost" transcript of the last couple of minutes of the *Challenger* disaster, with its terrified astronaut's voice reciting *The Lord Is My Shepherd* . . .

White was getting very upset, the muscles and veins in his neck standing out like steel cords.

"You know, when I was a kid, Titan was just a point of light in the sky, like thousands of others. Now, we've landed a probe there. It's a new fucking world. We have maps of the surface. We have a crew on the way to land there, for Christ's sake. But if Maclachlan and the Foundation for Thought and Ethics and all those other assholes have their way, in another hundred years Titan will just be a dot in the sky again. How the hell can we lose all that knowledge, Jake?"

Hadamard said, "But you walked on the Moon. Whatever else happens, they can't take that achievement away. Not for all time."

White studied him. "You *are* changing, paperpusher."

"Or maybe the world is changing and leaving me behind." He took White's arm; he could feel bunched muscle, still hard, through a light cotton sleeve. "Come on," he said. "Let's get out of here. I'll buy you a beer."

They walked out, towards Hadamard's parked car.

In the rocket park, a wrecking crew was hauling down the Atlas-Mercury. It was a slim silver cylinder topped by the dark cone of a Mercury capsule, the configuration that had taken John Glenn to orbit. The Atlas left the vertical with a groan of tearing metal.

Day 504

When Siobhan finally died, Mott realized that she had no framework for coping. She had no prayers to say, no hymns to sing, no rational or social structure which could accommodate death.

But then, the rest of the crew didn't know how to handle this either.

Bill Angel argued for breaking down Siobhan's body and using it as nutrient in the farm. "She always wanted to be a farmer in the sky," he said, his face hard. "Now she can be. Just dumping her body overboard means losing raw material, a loss we can't afford." He stared at Mott, as if challenging her. "We're on the edge here. Life must go on. Our lives."

He'd actually had some endorsement for that, from the surgeons on the ground. Although they would have wanted Siobhan's flesh and bones treated before being ground up for consumption by the plants.

Benacerraf opposed it, and Mott and Rosenberg backed her up.

At last they came up with a solution they could all accept.

Benacerraf clambered into her EMU, her EVA suit, and hauled Siobhan's body out of the airlock and into the orbiter cargo bay. The body was wrapped in a Stars and Stripes—a flag that should have fluttered over the ice of Titan—and bound up with duct tape and Beta cloth.

Benacerraf braced herself in the payload bay and just thrust that body away from her, letting it drift away.

Benacerraf, floating in the payload bay, said some words, her voice a crackle, distorted by static.

"I want to read to you what Isaac Newton wrote to John Locke, on looking into the sun. I think it's kind of appropriate . . ."

In a few hours I had brought my eyes to such a pass that I could look on no bright object with either eye but I saw the sun before me, so that I durst neither write nor read but to recover the use of my eyes shut myself up in my chamber made dark for three days together and used all means to divert my imagination from the sun. For if I thought upon him I presently saw his picture though I was in the dark. But by keeping in the dark and employing my mind about other things I began in three or four days to have some use of my eyes again and by forbearing a few days longer to look upon bright objects recovered them pretty well, though not so well but that for some months after the spectrum of the sun began to return as often as I began to meditate upon the phenomenon . . .

"I think that sums it up," Benacerraf said gently, her voice scratchy on the radio loop. "Siobhan looked, too long, into the face of the sun. We won't forget her."

Mott sat at the window of the flight deck and watched the body ascend past the shadow of the high-gain antenna. In the ferocious glare of trans-Venusian sunlight, it exploded with brilliance.

At last it was lost in the sky.

Mott tried to come to terms with all this, with her loss.

Part of her was frankly glad that it wasn't her, Mott, who had been caught in that access tube. And another part was guilty as all hell about *that*.

But mostly, when she looked into her own soul, she found only incomprehension.

It proved impossible to forget Siobhan, to restore life to normal. Bizarrely, grotesquely, Siobhan hadn't actually departed so far. The small impulse that Benacerraf had imparted to the body had done little more than send it on a slowly diverging, neighboring orbit to *Discovery*'s. Poor Siobhan was still tracking *Discovery* on its complex path around the sun.

It was as if Siobhan had never gone away. As if her absence, the hole she left behind, was a real thing, which pursued Mott, no matter what she tried to do: the hours of grueling exercise she burned up in the arm, her work in the corners of the cluster like the farm or the Apollos, the time she tried to lose in the emptiness of sleep.

After a time, Mott realized, she was barely functioning, so far sunk was she in black despair.

Barbara Fahy, recently appointed head of the Office of Manned Spaceflight, heard the news on a copied e-mail, passed down the chain of command from Jake Hadamard. Al Hartle—now working as a senior adviser to the President—was trying to block the release of the Delta IV boosters for the resupply of the *Discovery* crew.

Fahy couldn't believe it. But she checked with Canaveral and Vandenberg. The payloads that had been under preparation for the first Delta IV launches—consumables and other equipment to follow *Discovery* to Titan—had already been stood down, and were being disassembled and placed in storage.

So it was true.

She called up Hadamard, in his office at NASA Headquarters in Washington, D.C. In the image in her softscreen, Hadamard looked tired, his face slack.

"Yes," he said. "Yes, it's true. I would have told you in person, but——"

"But what? You couldn't stand to face me?"

"I don't know, Barbara. Hell." The screen flashed up a blasphemy-filter warning.

"Jake, I didn't want this job in the first place. How am I supposed to carry it through if you don't keep me informed?"

"Washington's a tough place right now. Do you really want me to involve you in every battle I have to fight?"

"If it involves the lives of our crew," she said, "the only crew we have up there, then, hell, yes, I do." *Blasphemy warning.* She poked reflexively at the softscreen, but there was no longer any way to turn off the obscenity filters. "We've already stranded them up there, without hope of retrieval. If we cut the resupply—"

"I know the implications," he snapped. "I'm not a fool, Barbara. But right now there doesn't seem to be anything I can do about it. I can't win every battle. I have to pick my ground."

"What ground is more important than this, the lives of—"

"I have to make that judgment," he said, his voice laden with stress. "Look, I have a head-to-head with Hartle at nine A.M. tomorrow. In my office. I want you here."

"Why?"

"It's better if you find out then."

"What shall I prepare?"

He smiled. "Just bring along the look you had on your face when you called me up. Use it on Al Hartle, instead of me . . ."

On flights into Washington nowadays, the airlines gave out smog filters and compact respiration packs, as standard to every passenger. And when Fahy reached the limo sent for her, outside the terminal building, the cloudless sky was so smoggy it was actually a little orange.

Maybe that was an omen, she thought. Titan weather, come to Earth.

Hadamard's office was long, plush, old-fashioned, in the NASA Headquarters building.

When she arrived, Hartle was already there, with an aide, a thin officer in a sober blue uniform. He introduced himself as Gareth Deeke. He nodded curtly at Fahy, a small grin on his mouth, as if amused to see Fahy here. His eyes were hidden behind big insectile mirrored shades.

Deeke had unrolled a softscreen and plastered it over the office wall; it was filled up with a glowing, full-color map of the Pacific rim. This was, as far as Fahy could figure, some kind of military strategic briefing.

This might still be Jake Hadamard's office, she thought, but it sure as hell wasn't Jake's agenda any more.

Deeke resumed his briefing.

". . . This is the Asian century," Deeke said. "Our analysts were predicting that twenty years ago, and it sure has come true. We can't assume our geo-economic dominance is going to last a lot longer; we are going to enter a period in which we are just one of a number of players around the rim of the Pacific. We face Japan, Korea, Vietnam, several others, and the powerhouse of the whole area—"

"Red China," Hartle said softly. "Red fucking China. Now the biggest GDP in the world, the fastest economic growth, the fastest military expansion: six million men under arms, ten thousand combat aircraft . . ."

Graphics of China; schematic starbursts around its periphery. Deeke said, "We know that China has a whole series of expansionist aims around its borders, by land and sea, some of which it has pursued for decades. Recently Chinese gunboats have been taking offensive action against PetroVietnam-Conoco oil rigs *here*, in the South China Sea, southeast of Ho Chi Minh City. I don't need to remind you that China and Vietnam fought a border war in 1979. This whole area is criss-crossed by shipping lanes; any conflict between China and Vietnam could draw in Malaysia, Taiwan and the Philippines.

"Look up here," he said, tapping another part of the map. "Vladivostok, the heart of what the Russians call their Pacific Maritime Territory. It was ceded by Beijing to the Russians in 1860, when the French and British were at China's throat. Well, the Brits and the French have gone now, and China wants its province back. This is a key area. At stake is China getting hold of a port in the Sea of Japan; right now, you can see they are landlocked by Russia and Korea. And besides, the population density on the Chinese side of the border is three times that on the Russian side. It must look tempting . . .

"Item three," he said, and he brought up another map. "Taiwan. The CIA thinks this is the main flashpoint area in the whole region. The Red Chinese have always claimed that any effort by Taiwan to achieve formal independence would justify them going to war. Currently the Taiwanese are pressing no such claim. But now we think the Chinese are preparing for a more significant push.

"We've seen exercises by the People's Liberation Army on the mainland. Violations of Taiwanese airspace by Chinese military jets. Missile launches, impacting the ocean within Taiwanese waters. Blockades, particularly around the big ports, Keelung and Kaohsiung . . . It's a classic pattern. They did all this in the '50s, and again in the '90s. This time, we think they mean it. And there appears to be a faction within the senior and military Chinese leadership which believes that the U.S. would not intervene in the Taiwan Strait, no matter what happens there."

"But why would the Chinese do this?" Fahy asked. "Why now?"

Hartle turned to her. "To see that, Miss Fahy, you have to understand the psychology of the very old men who run Red China. Have run that country for decades, in fact."

She looked into his leathery face, the rheumy blue eyes embedded there. Nobody better placed to figure that psychology than you, General, she thought.

"The Party still has a grip on China. For now. But those wizened old dwarfs in Beijing can feel their grip slipping away. They fear *koan*—a return to chaos, which they see as fundamental to China's former weakness—more than any other condition. And we have every indication that *koan* is indeed descending on the country."

Deeke said, "Some of the new economic growth areas are pushing for more independence from Beijing. Nobody really knows what's happening in the heads of the young people over there, in the new cities. And the influence of Communism in the rural areas has been waning for decades. In its place, you have all sorts of crazy cults and beliefs. There's the cult of Wu Yangming, who was shot as a rapist fifteen years ago. He called himself a Holy Emperor, the reincarnation of Jesus Christ. Death didn't stop him; Wu alone has a million followers. Some of these cult types are organizing using the methods Mao Zedong used during his insurrection—and his revolt worked, remember."

Hartle said, "Think of it. A billion fucking peasants, still poor, their rice paddies drying out, all going crazy about their gods, consulting the *I Ching . . . and organizing.* What a tinder-box."

Deeke said, "The leadership need some way to reassert their grip. A symbolic act, a show of strength. The space shots didn't quite hack it, it seems. Maybe a war with Taiwan will do it."

Hartle said with an almost comical darkness, "We must not allow the emergence of a great power on the Asian continent. We don't want to spend the rest of the millennium paying trib-ute to the fucking Red Chinese. If the Red Chinese resent that, fuck them. But if they try to break out—go for Taiwan, for instance—we have to be ready . . ."

Fahy scowled. "I thought we were here to discuss the space program."

Hartle studied her, analytically. "Here's a quotation for you, Miss Fahy. I wonder if you recognize it: *You may not be interested in war, but war is interested in you.* You know who said that?"

"No . . ."

"Trotsky. War has come looking for us, young lady." He eyed her. "You run the Office—"

"Of Manned Spaceflight."

"Well, there ain't going to be any more manned spaceflight,

Miss Fahy, so I guess you're out of a job. But we hate to lose good people. Maybe you're just the person we need for our new program."

"What program?"

Hartle nodded to Deeke, who tapped his softscreen once more. A new schematic came up: blown-up images of bacteria, DNA strands. Deeke launched into his new spiel. His slickness unnerved Fahy; he was like a machine, utterly subservient to Hartle, without anything to say for himself.

He said now, "The Chinese are not short of people, and have always accepted the human wave—attrition, mass slaughter—as an acceptable form of warfare. The First World War should have been a Chinese war."

"So," Hartle said, "we need a new deterrent."

Hadamard frowned. "What?"

"A bio-weapon." Hartle smiled. "Jake, Miss Fahy, we seem to have reached a plateau in mechanical engineering, but those biological lab boys have made remarkable progress in the last couple of decades. Now that the human genome map is complete, new possibilities have opened up for us. It's possible to distinguish the DNA variation between different racial and ethnic groups. What I'm saying is, the lab boys can develop an agent which will kill only a specific group."

"My God," said Fahy. "Such as?"

"Such as the Han Chinese. Miss Fahy, with such a weapon— delivered by some small-scale missile launcher, which is where we need NASA technicians—we could lop off the head of the Red Chinese flower. Or threaten to, which is equivalent."

"You're crazy," Fahy breathed.

Hadamard said, "Now, Barbara——" He steepled his hands. "Al, I think we've gone far enough. NASA is still a civilian agency. Dedicated to the exploration of space and the dissemination of information to the public, and the world. And so forth. You cannot expect us to contribute to any such program as this . . ."

Hadamard, even to Fahy, sounded weak, unconvinced by his own words.

"He's right. You can't tell us what to do," she said to Hartle. "No matter what Maclachlan says. Your authority has limits."

Hartle seemed unfazed. "Jake, excuse me. Have you told her?"

Fahy frowned. "Told me what?"

Hartle said, "As of seventeen days hence, I will be Administrator of NASA. Changing times, Miss Fahy."

Hadamard looked across at Fahy and shrugged. "It took fifty years, but in the end the Air Force won. I'm sorry, Barbara."

Hartle grinned at Fahy, and she could see antique fillings in his teeth. "Let me tell you what my first orders are going to be, just so you can start to prepare, Miss Fahy. NASA has been a sink of national resources for decades; now we're approaching a time of unparalleled crisis, and that is going to stop."

Hadamard said, "Meaning?"

"Meaning, no more of this science crap. Item. The Deep Space Network can go. Item. All those science satellites, the observatories—"

"Some of them have been up there for decades," Fahy said. "The Hubble space telescope is the most successful—"

"If there are decades' worth of data in the can," Hartle said, "there shouldn't be too much objection when I turn off the tap, should there?"

"It doesn't work like that, Al," Hadamard said mildly.

"What doesn't? Science? Fuck the science, Jake. I guess you hadn't noticed, here in this ivory tower of yours, but science isn't exactly the top priority of this Administration. Six months from now, the only U.S. satellites I want operating up there are those with military or commercial potential—comsats, Earth resources, reconnaissance. Item. The Delta IV boosters currently assigned to these asshole deep space resupply missions will be switched to military missions, which was the primary

function of the Delta IV program in the first goddamn place.
Miss Fahy. You got a problem with any of that?"

"Yes," she said, flaring. "Yes, I have a problem. Damn it,
General——"

"Nobody forced that fucking crew of yours, that bunch of
dykes and ecologists and has-been pilots up into space," Hartle
said. "Did they? They knew the risks when they accepted the
assignment."

"They didn't accept the risk of being shot down."

Hadamard said wearily, "Barbara . . ."

Hartle studied her, as if pitying her. "You know, I truly
believe you haven't taken in a word that's been said this morning, Miss Fahy. Let me spell it out again. The time for your Buck
Rogers space cadet stunts is over. The loss of your crew—if
that happens—is regrettable. But it was their choice. We've
been pouring billions every year into this fucking circus stunt.
Well, Miss Fahy, I now have a clear mandate from the President
to put a stop to that. And it's the first thing I intend to do."

"Let us keep a dish," Hadamard said suddenly.

Hartle looked at him. "Huh?"

"A deep space dish. Let us keep Goldstone open, at least.
That way, at least maybe we'll be able to listen to *Discovery*.
Better PR, Al."

Hartle's eyes narrowed. "What the hell," he said. "Keep the
fucking dish; what can that cost?"

Hadamard nodded, avoiding Fahy's eyes.

He'd won a small victory, Fahy saw, extracting such a relatively inexpensive concession in this, Hartle's moment of triumph. Maybe this was his main objective for the meeting, in
fact. Maybe he brought me in here as a kind of diversion, to
soak up Hartle's fire.

I should be so political, she thought.

But I'm not.

She asked, "Who is going to tell the astronauts? You,
General? The President? Who will tell their families?"

Hartle grinned easily and stood up. "I'll leave that to old Jake here; he's still the man holding the ball until next month. And you, Miss Fahy, will start working on delivery systems for those biobomb options we outlined."

"I quit," she said impulsively. "You'll have my resignation on your desk the day you walk in here."

He walked over to her; he stood before her threateningly, a squat pillar of silver hair and grizzled skin and tough, aged muscle. "And you'll have it back up your ass, corners first, a day after that. This is a time of national crisis, Miss Fahy; quitting is not an option. For any of us."

He turned and left. Deeke rolled up his softscreen, nodded to Hadamard, and followed.

Hadamard, staring at the floor, seemed to have nothing to say. Framed in the window behind him, a slab of orange Washington sky was brightening to a washed-out glare.

Day 680

On *Discovery*'s flight deck, Benacerraf sat strapped into the left-hand commander's seat. She was wearing her usual grubby Beta-cloth T-shirt and shorts. The flight deck was homey, like a little den, glowing with the fluorescent glareshield lights, and the multicolored light of the instruments panels. Benacerraf always felt comfortable in here: at home, in the environment in which she'd spent so many hours training and flying. Anyhow, the flight deck, with its big windows, made a pleasing change from the shut-in squalor that the hab module had become, and the stinking cabin of the centrifuge.

Especially today, she thought. Because today, for the first time in nearly two years, Earthlight was streaming into *Discovery*.

Thirty minutes from closest approach, Earth was a fat ball that looked the size of a dinner-plate held at arm's length.

From Benacerraf's point of view, behind the big picture windows on *Discovery*'s flight deck, the planet was a gibbous disc, close to full, suspended over the roof of the cabin. The orbiter would fly past Earth with her belly away from the planet, and her payload bay turned to Earth, to give the instruments there a good vantage.

Discovery was barreling in at around twelve miles per second—fast enough to cross the continental United States in five minutes, fast enough to traverse the diameter of Earth itself in eleven minutes.

The hemisphere turned to the sun was coated with land: it was noon somewhere over central Asia, and much of the Pacific must be in darkness. She could see the mountain-fringed plateaux broadening out from Turkey, through Iran and Afghanistan, to the great Tibetan plateau. The plateau was cut off from the rest of India by the still higher Himalayas. To the south and east of this plateau were the great river valleys of Asia, crammed with humanity. Masses of stratus clouds were piled up behind the mountains; she could see how the mountains, protruding through the vapor layer, were causing disturbances in the clouds, like waves, along a front a thousand miles long.

Benacerraf—parochial to the last—felt a stab of regret she wasn't going to get to see more of the continental U.S.

There were few signs of human life, even from here.

She knew that the old Apollo astronauts had been struck by the beauty and fragility of Earth from space. It hadn't hit Benacerraf like that at all. At first glance Earth was a world of ocean, desert and a little ice, half-covered by cloud. The areas colonized by humans seemed tiny, dwarfed, little rectangles of cultivated ground clinging to the coasts, or the banks of rivers, or timidly at the feet of mountains. Almost all of the Earth was empty, too hostile for man; humans clung in little clusters to the fringes of continents, like some feeble lichen.

To Benacerraf, the view from space showed her not so much the delicacy of Earth, but the tenuous grasp of humanity, even on this single planet, even after four billion years of life's adaptation, down there at the bottom of that murky gravity well.

Humans were restricted to a shell around the surface of Earth, no thicker than an hour's car ride. In the depths of interplanetary space, where Earth and Moon were reduced to faint specks, man had left no mark but a handful of aging spacecraft, a thin hiss of radio static . . . and *Discovery*.

The Universe was huge, empty, dead. It knew nothing of mankind and all its works. Benacerraf had traveled beyond Venus; she had seen that for herself. Here she was scooting over the surface of Earth itself, and she still thought so.

At such times, the thought of life aspiring to anything but to cling to the surface of that big ball of rock down there seemed absurd.

She was alone up here, on the flight deck. She didn't even know where the others were right now.

It made you think, if the four of them couldn't stand each other enough to be together even for the few hours of this flyby of the home world.

But she was going to stay up here. It was, after all, one hell of a view. And she had a duty to perform.

Discovery was passing behind the planet, crossing over its night side, so from Benacerraf's point of view the fat gibbous disc began to narrow, soon approaching a crescent.

The crescent thinned rapidly as it grew, as if the light were bleeding from its tapering horns. Soon it was so huge that Benacerraf had to crane her neck to see its full extent.

And then, with a flare of gold and red, the sun passed beyond the horizon.

Discovery, flying over oceans, plunged into Earth's huge shadow. Now, the spacecraft inhabited a new landscape, which revealed itself to Benacerraf as her eyes dark-adapted.

Over the night hemisphere of Earth, a huge aurora glowed.

It was a curtain of green light that appeared to extend from the fleeing spacecraft all the way to Earth's horizon, at the pole. Beneath, the aurora blended in with the airglow, the luminous gas layer high in the atmosphere excited by the sun's radiation. And Benacerraf could see noctilucent clouds, very high decks illuminated by the airglow, like the surface of a thin, milky sea. Above the aurora, very faint, she could see streamers, very thin striations which seemed to extend down from much higher altitudes, spokes aligned with the Earth's magnetic field.

The aurora's curtains and folds seemed to be on the same level as *Discovery*—the orbiter was near its closest approach now, just a couple of hundred miles above the planet—and Benacerraf had a rare sense of motion, of speed, of sailing through some invisible sea, populated by these bergs of cool light.

It was the most beautiful thing Benacerraf had ever seen. And a hell of a relief from the bleak emptiness of interplanetary space, where it never felt like she was going anywhere. Damn, damn. How could I abandon all this?

Discovery was revisiting Earth for its final gravity assist before Jupiter; Earth was, in fact, the most massive object between the sun and Jupiter.

By passing so close to Earth—coming within a couple of hundred miles of its surface—*Discovery* had become briefly coupled to Earth, like, Benacerraf thought, a child grabbing hold of a merry-go-round propelled by the strong arms of its father. When *Discovery* flew on, it would have picked up energy from the encounter—the equivalent of thousands of pounds of additional fuel—and Earth's store of energy would be reduced; forever after the planet would circle the sun a little slower.

Benacerraf remembered a Public Affairs Officer trying to explain this at a JSC briefing, a couple of months before the launch. A reporter asked if the resulting slowdown in the Earth's orbit around the sun would do harm to the environment. On the podium, there were the usual shaking of heads and rolling of eyes. Then Bill Angel had said, mockingly, that NASA would just have to launch another spacecraft and make it fly by Earth on the opposite side . . .

General laughter.

It had left a sour taste in Benacerraf's mouth. That reporter had been entitled to a better answer than that. There was too much bullshitting of the ignorant, when it came to science and engineering, she thought. You only had to look at the history of the civil nuclear power program to see that engineers didn't deserve any kind of implicit trust, that they had a duty to answer as fully as possible every question and concern from the public, however dumb it might seem.

And anyhow, Angel's answer had been wrong tactically; because after that the questioning had gotten very hostile, for instance on what contingency plans NASA had to shoot *Discovery* down if something went wrong—if the ship came barreling in towards a collision with Earth, with the payload bay full of uranium . . .

And maybe all that arrogance had contributed, in the end, to the decision to dump Benacerraf and her crew: to cut off the retrieval program, even to close down the resupply missions.

Benacerraf and the others had half-expected such a sentence from the beginning, she suspected, even as they'd formulated the unlikely mission profile, over Chinese food in her house at Clear Lake. And, oddly, it hadn't seemed so hard to take when the news first came in, as they sailed around the sun at the boiling heart of the Solar System.

But now, so close to Earth, it was much more difficult. To sail over that blue-glowing landscape, so close, to be within a couple of thousand miles of Jackie and the kids—and not be able to reach them—was pretty much unbearable.

For this closeness was an illusion. She was separated from Earth now by intangible barriers of energy and velocity, as impenetrable as the huge distances of the Solar System. There was no way *Discovery* could shed all its hard-won kinetic energy, and allow them to sail safely home.

Benacerraf was not going home, ever again. Her only destination now was Titan, a cold dark hole, out on the chilly rim of the System.

Suddenly, the sunrise was approaching, far ahead, at the rim of the roof which the Pacific hemisphere had become.

A blue streak, deep and beautiful, spread around Earth's huge curve. Then a golden brown began to seep into the light. Abruptly the gold flooded out the blue, becoming as bright as rocket light, and spreading around the horizon; a fingernail arc of the sun appeared at the horizon, and the shadows of clouds fled across the ocean towards Benacerraf.

Bright white light flooded the cabin, as the sun hauled itself over the limb of Earth.

It was, Benacerraf realized, almost certainly the last Earth sunrise she would ever witness.

. . . There was a sharp tap, directly in front of her, making her jump.

Holy shit, she thought. It had sounded for all the world like a fingernail on the window.

She released her restraints and pushed herself out of her chair, head first towards the window before her.

She could see a tiny crater there, maybe a sixteenth of an inch in diameter. It picked up the flat sunlight coming over the ocean, and gleamed like a raindrop on the outside of the glass.

She knew she was in no danger. The exterior window was a half-inch thick, and two further panes lay behind that; there was a total of two inches of glass between her and the vacuum.

Maybe this little dink had been caused by something natural, a micrometeorite. Maybe. On the other hand, *Discovery* was flying right through the altitude where the maximum density of man-made debris had accumulated: bits of broken-up satellites, droplets of frozen fuel, nuts and bolts. She was willing to bet that if she dug down into that little pit, she'd find a flake of some cheap Chinese paint, or a droplet of frozen urine from the *Mir*.

A minute after closest approach, Earth had receded by seventy miles, and Benacerraf could see the planet falling away; a couple of minutes after that and *Discovery* had risen more than a thousand miles above the surface. As Earth closed over its own spherical belly of silvery ocean, Benacerraf felt a stab of loneliness, of loss.

Earth receded, now, as dramatically as if she was rising in some kind of high speed lift. The huge, delicately edged crescent of blue and white opened out rapidly, the sky-bright sunlit side expanding into the darkness. She could see how rapidly she was moving; the clouds piled up over the equator seemed to flow steadily into her view as *Discovery* flew on. After perhaps fifteen minutes the orbiter had receded to about a full Earth diameter, and suddenly she could see the half-shadowed disc of Earth, contained in her window, hanging over the payload bay like some unlikely Moon . . .

And, over the night side of Earth, Benacerraf saw a bright streak of light: a flare, hair-thin, its length of perhaps a few hundred miles dwarfed by the carcase of the planet.

The light died, as rapidly as it had formed.

She felt her mouth draw into a smile.

That was what she had been waiting up here to see. Now, *Discovery* would sail on alone; now, perhaps, Niki Mott would be able to get some sleep.

After sailing with *Discovery* around the sun, Siobhan Libet had made it home.

When he got off the plane at Sea Tac, Marcus White found a long queue at passport control. He stood in line like everyone else, ignoring the pain in his back and his rebuilt hips and his osteoporosis-stricken legs and the pressure from his bladder, which seemed to hold no more than a shot glass these days.

The thing of it was, he felt just the same as he ever did, inside; he was just stuck inside this decaying, betraying husk of a body, getting slower all the time, in a world that was moving past him ever more quickly.

There was a huge screen up ahead, Frank Sinatra and Katharine Hepburn starring together in a new gender-reversed version of *Casablanca*, and everyone else in the line seemed to be goggling up like mesmerized sheep at sim-Sinatra's digitized face.

The line shuffled forward. His attention drifted.

. . . *Sometimes he thought he could see that light-drenched landscape again: the glowing regolith under the black sky, his own reflection in Tom's mirrored visor, breaking through the washed-out reality of the present . . .*

Some guy poked him in the back. He'd been holding up the line.

He remembered something that Chinese kid, Jiang Ling, had told him during her visit a few years back. In China, for all its faults, things were different; in China, they were aiming for economic growth, but without dumping the family en route. Jiang talked about how it was her duty to protect her parents, her surviving grandparent.

He could see it in the faces of people around him, even here, in this goddamn line: they looked on him as just an obstruction, an irritation.

Meanwhile that prick in the White House, Maclachlan, was talking about "radical solutions to our demographic problems" . . .

Happy booths, they were calling them. Sometimes, when White thought about it, he got scared. But Geena was long dead, and his son, Bob, had a family of his own, who White hardly ever got to see. Most of the time, he couldn't give a fuck.

At last he got to the front of the line. The clerk was just a kid; her face was so covered in image-tattoos she almost looked like one of those fucking Nullists who were making life miserable for everyone. White took the opportunity to vent off a little steam at her. Maybe Washington was a different country now, but as far as he was concerned it was a joke to have to produce a passport—even the new type, a shiny patch tattooed to the back of your hand—just to get from Houston to Seattle.

The clerk just tolerated him; she had, of course, no reply to offer.

Outside the terminal he caught a cab, and gave the driver Jackie Benacerraf's address, just off 23rd Avenue, in the Capitol Park district.

Seattle was bright, clean, growing; the air seemed clean and fresh, and he felt he might have been able to smell the scent of the woods. He didn't even need the brolly he'd brought, against the habitual drizzle.

It was a city he'd always liked; a long, skinny town sprawling along an isthmus, a tongue of land, with its parks and waterways and its neat views of mountains and lakes. He'd come out here years ago, during Apollo, to visit Boeing for training and familiarization and glad-handing; they'd been responsible, back then, for the development of the Saturn first stage. He recognized a lot of the landmarks he'd gotten to know then. But there was a lot of construction going on, and it seemed to White that everywhere he looked he saw plump Asian faces: Chinese, Japs, Malaysians. And the walls, even of the older buildings, were covered with those huge new softscreen billboards, pumping out ads and infomercials and online soaps day and night, so that it was somehow hard to make out the shape of things, the sweep and structure of the city, and he could have been anywhere.

New Columbia, they called it now: an amalgam of Alaska, Washington, Oregon—all seceded from Maclachlan's imploding U.S. with the old Canadian provinces of British Columbia and Alberta. On its formation the new nation had instantly become an economic giant, with a massive trade surplus and a lot of assets: Alaskan oil, Albertan natural gas and wheat, Washington's nuclear, aerospace and software industries, Oregon's timber and high-tech industries, a string of massive ports serving the Asia-Pacific trade, not to mention a highly educated workforce.

He was a long way from what was left of the old U.S. of A now, he thought, all that smoggy old development on the East Coast. This was a modern Pacific nation-state, prosperous, aggressive.

He shook his head. He hated to find himself thinking like an old fart. His real trouble was not that Seattle wasn't part of the USA any more, but that it wasn't the 1960s. The young people were remaking the world, and Earth was becoming an alien planet to him: more alien, in fact, than the Moon, if by some magic he could have been transported back there.

Still, he thought, if you had to go to somewhere that had seceded, he still preferred Washington State to Idaho.

At Jackie Benacerraf's house, it only took a minute to be allowed in through the security barrier, although he had to present his passport tattoo to the cameras. A kid, a little boy around ten, let him into the house itself, and directed him to the living room where he'd find Jackie.

White dropped his bag in the hall. The house was big, sprawling, bright, but messy. Softscreens were playing in every room, mostly kid's stuff, pop videos and animations. It was a clamor of noise and imagery to White, but it didn't seem to faze the kids, two of them, Fred and Ben, Paula Benacerraf's grandchildren, boys who ran around and wrestled and seemed to be doing pretty much what White had gotten up to when he was nine or ten. But the kids looked odd, to White, with their image-tattoos and pierced cheeks and ears and shaved-off, sculpted hair. The younger one, in fact, was pretty much coated with image-tattoos, like a Nullist, but he was too young to hold still for long enough to let the processors turn his flesh invisible.

It ought to be possible to exert some kind of control, he thought. These kids ought to be playing softball in the yard, not dressing up like high-tech Barbies, playing with the designs on each other's faces.

We got decadent, he thought. Like ancient Rome. No wonder the Chinese are beating the pants off of us economically.

In the living room, Jackie Benacerraf was sitting on the floor. She was surrounded by softscreens and books, which she was pawing through and tapping desultorily. On the wall, apparently unnoticed by Jackie, a softscreen bore the image of Paula Benacerraf's face—pale, a little haggard, her gray hair floating around—against a dimly-seen background of clunky, beat-up hab module interior. Paula was talking quietly, describing how the surviving crew all were, what they were doing, their daily routine, their science observations.

Jackie looked up at White. She smiled, but it looked forced. "Hi. You didn't need to come out, you know."

He shrugged, standing there awkwardly. "It's not a problem. I thought somebody ought to."

"Yeah." She stood up, a little stiffly. She looked to have aged, too, to White. How old was she now? no more than thirty, surely . . . Her face had lost a lot of its prettiness, he thought sadly; her skin already looked slack and lifeless, her eyes deep-shadowed, and he thought she was putting on weight, though the black, softscreen-sequined kimono she was wearing masked a lot of that. Her hair was a close-cropped black fuzz, and there were pale patches on her cheeks where she had had old image-tattoos removed.

"So," she said without enthusiasm, "you're here. You want a meal? Are you hungry?"

"No. I ate on the plane. A coffee would be good, though."

She smiled. "Let me guess. Black, sugar, caffeine."

"Almost. I take it white. You have any cream?"

She pulled a face. "Are you kidding? Take a seat."

He sat on the end of a sofa. He had to clear a space, move aside some softscreens and books. The cushions were too soft, and he knew he would have trouble getting up later; but it was, he admitted to himself, a relief to sit down again.

He heard her banging around, the hum of a microwave. "We're all out of caffeine," she called.

"Forget it. I'll take it as it comes."

Paula Benacerraf kept on talking.

. . . You have to try not to worry. We aren't in despair; no way. The whole point of this trip was to figure out how we could become self-sufficient up there. Now, that just has a little extra sharpness. And we have Rosenberg, who's a bright guy, and you can be sure when we get to Titan we'll be doing our best to figure out how we can use the local resources to . . .

The quality of the image was poor; big blocky pixel faults crawled over Paula's face like organized, repetitive insects. Benacerraf's personal message would have been recorded, digitally compressed, and then fired off in a brief pulse from *Discovery* to Goldstone, probably as filler along with another data stream.

He understood how hard it was for Paula to express herself in such a situation. Space was a mixture of the bland—the endless dull routine, the business of survival—and the deadly. And in the midst of all the routine stuff, how could you talk of your fears, without sounding lurid and indulgent? But if you didn't, how could you communicate with the folks at home?

Damn, damn. Paula Benacerraf was an impossibly brave woman, and she had been betrayed, by NASA itself. The anger, the near-grief he'd been nursing since that asshole Hartle had started issuing his draconian edicts came bubbling to the surface once more.

He turned away, looking for distraction.

Under the layers of softscreens the walls were just plaster, he saw, white-painted. Nobody decorated their home any more, he thought, save for throwing up these damn screens. Jackie's home was a kind of shell of shifting light shapes, like an underwater cave, nothing permanent, nothing worthwhile, nothing owned.

No wonder the kids these days are going crazy, he thought.

He flicked through Jackie's softscreens, until he found some news, an online edition of the *Seattle Times*.

Lousy economic figures once again: the depression seemed to be deepening, with more trade barriers going up around the world, capital fleeing from one country to another. Australia was the latest to have run into the buffers. There were pictures of queues for some kind of new-millennium soup kitchens in Sidney and Melbourne, starving kids in the outback, swollen pot-bellies that made White think of pictures of Africa rather than anywhere with an Anglo-Saxon background.

He had been born during one great depression, he thought; maybe he was going to die during another.

There was more trouble from the Nullists, this time some kind of pipe bomb in New York. And the negotiations between Washington, D.C., and Boise over the future of the nuclear silos were getting stalled again, and there had been some kind of border-crossing incident near Richmond, Utah . . .

Here was a piece on the new Pope—some Italian cardinal called Carlo Maria Martini, who'd taken the name John XXIV—coming to visit Idaho, the first major figure from the outside world to do so. Maybe some of the conspiracy nuts were right: the guys who thought that Idaho, Christian-Fundamentalist as it was—even more extremely so than Xavier Maclachlan's America—was being funded in its secession by the Catholic Church, which, in the wake of the uprise of fundamentalism all over the planet, seemed to be trying to reemerge as a global force.

It wasn't impossible, as far as Marcus White was concerned. He was even prepared to believe that the Catholics had been working, covertly, with Islam for years, in defense of common precepts on sexuality and reproduction. Some said it went all the way back to John Paul II, the last Pope but one . . .

The news drizzled on, depressing, a series of high-tech images of timeless human foolishness and misery.

It seemed to Marcus White beyond dispute that the world was going to hell in a handbasket. But then, maybe every old geezer who ever lived thought the same way.

Jackie came back in, carrying a coffee and a can of diet soda for herself. She sat with him, at the far end of the sofa, her gaze drifting around the junk in the room.

White killed the softscreen. He sipped the coffee gratefully; it was bland, lacking the charge he felt he needed from the caffeine, but at least, he thought, he should get a boost from the sugar.

She said, "I don't really understand why you're here."

"You don't? . . . Barbara Fahy asked me to fly over. It's a kind of tradition, at times like this."

"Times like what?"

He frowned. "Your mother's situation."

"Her situation." She smiled. "The truth is, NASA has abandoned my mother, left her to die up there. Why not just say it?"

He said doggedly, "It's a tradition to send an astronaut, or an astronaut's wife, to break news like this. The theory is we understand how this feels, better than anyone else."

"You aren't breaking the news," she said mildly. "I heard already." She pointed to Paula's image, ignored, still working through its message on the wall. "I got a notification from Al Hartle's office. In fact I heard it first from the net news, the public stuff . . ."

He grunted. "It wasn't headline. How did you—"

"News gophers, of course," she said. She smiled, a little more kindly. "You really are behind the times, Marcus."

"Whatever." He felt irritated, to his shame a little petulant. "Well, I guess I shouldn't have come. It's a tradition, is all."

"I'm sorry," she said quickly. "I don't mean to be so sharp.

It's just that I have my head full of other stuff. Here. Look at this junk."

She picked up one of the softscreens; it was scrolling through some kind of text, with diagrams, on religion.

He scanned it quickly. It was—he read, bemused—a modern rework of the *Summa Theologiae* by St. Thomas Aquinas, issued by the Foundation for Thought and Ethics.

"It's what they're teaching the kids at school now; by law, every parent has to learn this stuff too."

He said, "The Foundation was the group behind Maclachlan."

"Yeah." She smiled, tiredly. "In New Columbia, we might have busted away from Maclachlan's politics and economics, but I'm afraid we took his theology with us . . ."

The *Summa*—the original written in 1266—was a kind of theological Theory of Everything, White read. It united Christian practice with Aristotelian physics. White read about transubstantiation, for instance: the moment in the Catholic Mass in which the bread and wine held by the priest became the body and blood of Christ. The stuff might still look like bread and wine, but—according to Aristotle—the form and the substance of every object were different. And at the moment of transubstantiation, while the form was unchanged, the substance of the bread became that of Christ's body . . . And so on.

"It makes a kind of logical sense," Jackie said. "It just isn't science. Which is why they've started teaching Aristotelian physics in the schools."

That gave him a double-take. "Woah," he said. "You're kidding."

"No," she said. "The kids these days are getting the whole shebang. Even the cosmology: the spheres of Moon and sun, the fixed stars beyond . . . Technology is allowed to continue as long as it's limited to practical, Earth-bound applications. Even low Earth orbit satellites are okay, because they are beneath the sphere of the Moon. But we're not supposed to look up at the sky, for fear of getting scared. In greater Seattle, they've even banned telescopes . . . Xavier Maclachlan is putting us back at the center of the Universe, Marcus; he says he wants to heal the spiritual dislocation that science has caused." She shrugged. "There are compensations. Aristotle taught the interconnect-edness of everything; that's not a bad thing for kids to learn. Look at the environment. Besides, who am I to say Maclach-lan's wrong, if it does make people happier?"

"It's not right, damn it," he growled, shocked.

"But you have to face the facts, Marcus," she said. "To most people the Earth might as well be flat anyhow. The sun might as well be a disc of fire floating round the sky . . ."

"But I walked on the Moon."

Her face hardened. "Not too many people care about those old Moonwalks nowadays, Marcus. Anyhow, you can see why I can't make too much of a fuss about Paula. She's gone to a place which—according to what my kids are being taught—doesn't even exist."

After a time, they ran out of things to say.

White stared into his coffee cup. The milk substitute, what-ever it was, had created some kind of scum that swirled around on top of the coffee's meniscus; when he drank, he tried to fil-ter the shit through his teeth.

The two boys just ignored White, carrying on with their busi-ness as if he wasn't there. There had been a time when it was dif-ferent. There had been a time when any ten-year-old kid would have been as thrilled as all hell to have a Moonwalker come visit.

Paula's message ran out. At the end, Benacerraf seemed to be trying to say something a little more personal—*I love you, I miss the kids*—but her face just hovered on the wall, mute and distressed and inarticulate.

At last, to White's relief, the image faded to black; the softscreen filled up with some kind of cartoon.

Jackie, awkwardly, offered to put him up for the night. It was a genuine offer but not exactly heartfelt; he found it easy to turn down. He would take a cab back into the city and find a hotel, fly home tomorrow.

When the cab came she walked him to the door; he emerged into the fresh sunlight.

He said, "I got a feeling I wasted my time here."

"No," she said, distracted. Then she seemed to be trying to make more of an effort. She put her hand on his arm; her fingers were light, as fragile as dried twigs. "No. I'm sorry you feel that. I'm grateful you came. I know you were trying to help."

"In my old fart way."

"I didn't mean that."

"Sure you did."

A shadow drifted across them, like a cloud. Together, they looked up, White shielding his rheumy eyes against the low afternoon sunlight.

It was an aerostat: a filmy bubble a mile wide, a geodesic sphere overlain by a translucent film that caught the sunlight, like a huge soap bubble. The shell, buoyed up by the heated air inside, was tinged with the green and yellow of crops, growing in the rich high-altitude light. And the base trailed what looked like spiny tentacles; they were electrostatic chargers, generating and scattering ozone. White could just make out the huge Boeing logo, and the ocean-blue flag of New Columbia, painted on the side.

To White, it was just another fix of disorientation. The whole floating factory-farm looked like some huge jellyfish: an alien invader, maybe, drifting through the tall blue sky of Earth.

Jackie looked up at him, her eyes empty, the tattoo scars on her cheeks a washed-out pink in the sunlight. "I lost my mother years ago. Or maybe she lost me. The fact that she's still alive up there, floating around halfway to Jupiter in some metal coffin, is just—" She hunted for the word. "Theoretical."

He tried to think of something to say, some way to get out of this situation.

You're too old, Marcus, just too damn old.

Day 1181

Alone in the humming calm of the flight deck and with her feet padding at the Teflon sheet—with all the lights subdued save for the small instrument glows, surrounded by the soft sounds of her mother's voice, her own breathing and the high-pitched whir of the pumps—Nicola Mott stared upward at the moons of Jupiter.

The crop yields continued to fall, and the transmission of mutations to successive generations was rising. Some plants, like the strawberries, refused to flower altogether. Rosenberg had talked about the reasons for this—inappropriate cell structures, poor fluid transmission—but Mott just tuned him out. The science really didn't matter right now; in a sense, it never had.

They just had to find solutions with their available resources. Ways to survive.

So they were improvising. Rosenberg had designed a new plant growth unit to work in the centrifuge arm, where the plants could be subjected to a high percentage of a G for most of each day. That meant transferring some of the farm's equipment lamps, the air blower system, racks and nutrient baths and reservoirs into the cramped arm cabin.

It was a long and difficult job, to which they were all having to contribute, under Rosenberg's reluctant supervision. It wasn't going to be a complete answer; the growing area inside the arm would be nothing like sufficient to fulfill their needs. And the arm wasn't shielded from radiation so well as the farm itself. But Rosenberg's hope was that stronger growths in the arm, coupled with at least some provision from the original farm, would close the gap in their requirements, before they started to go hungry.

The biggest drawback was the loss of the centrifuge for the crew.

They had reinstalled the exercise cycle, up on the flight deck, where there was still a little room. But not the treadmill.

That pissed Nicola Mott. It had been proven, all the way back to Skylab, that a treadmill was a much better way of exercising a range of muscle groups than a cycle. In her opinion it was just another example of the crew's collective laziness and incompetence, which would lead them all, ultimately, into disaster.

Anyway, she had got on with devising her own solution.

She improvised a treadmill. It was just a slippery sheet of Teflon that she bolted to the floor of the flight deck, behind the pilot's seat. She could balance herself with a hand on the seat in front of her, and just walk along, her feet slithering on the slippery pad. She wore socks, so her feet could slide more easily. It wasn't as effective as the real thing; too often she stubbed a toe on the bolts that held the Teflon in place, and because she couldn't vary the resistance, generally it was muscle fatigue that stopped her working. But she found if she worked at it long enough her calves, tendons and toes got a real workout.

And so, here she was. She had slapped a softscreen on the wall, and as she worked she listened to a message from her parents, relayed from their home in Cambridge, England. She didn't trouble to watch too carefully; the quality was low because of reduced capacity anyhow, and her father was prone to providing her with badly-shot home movies overlaid by her mother's slow, monotonic speech. Right now, for instance, there was a shaky pan of the new rice paddy fields around Ely in Cambridgeshire.

. . . *You remember your cousin Sarah,* her mother said. *Came down with CJD, didn't she. She was only twenty-two. Such a pretty girl. She chose the euth clinic, you know, even though Mary—your aunt Mary, you know, her mother—said it was un-Christian. What a mess the whole thing is. Of course we don't have blood donors now, all our transfusion blood is flown in from abroad, and the Tories say the government's blood tax is too high. Quarantine, they call it. The French were the first—typical bloody French, your father says—when they poured all that concrete down the Channel Tunnel. Oh, John Major died. There was a program on the telly. I didn't realize he was the last Tory Prime Minister, who'd have thought it . . .*

Her mother's face, on screen now, was a ruin, the left side imploded, cratered. She had come down with a prion disease related to Creutzfeld-Jakob, non-fatal but disfiguring, the prions steadily sculpting the soft cells of her flesh.

It had taken Mott herself a hell of a lot of tests to be proven fit to come to the States, to get into NASA.

She had come a long way from Cambridgeshire.

. . . Everything was different here.

Discovery was now five hundred million miles from the sun—five times the distance of Earth from the parent star. As the mission had unfolded the inverse square law had worked inexorably at the sun's radiation and size; from here the sun was still brilliant—at magnitude minus seventeen, much brighter than any star or planet seen from Earth—but its disc was tiny, like a flaw in the retina, like a distant supernova, like nothing she had seen from the surface of Earth. The light it cast had a strange quality, too: almost the light of a point source, the shadows stretching over the orbiter long and sharp.

Even the sun was different here, transmuted into something alien by distance.

As *Discovery*'s separation from Earth had grown, and the lag of radio signals from Houston had risen to an hour and a half round trip, it was as if their tenuous link to home had stretched, broken.

Now Earth was just a spark of blue light close to the shrinking sun, the place the high-gain antenna pointed. And those remote voices, from Mission Control and in the back rooms of Building 30 at JSC, with their detailed reams of advice and instruction—trying to control the crew, as once they had choreographed Moonwalkers, step by step—seemed to have little to do with their situation, here, suspended in extraordinary isolation in this outer darkness.

It was taking a while to sink in, after four decades of the culture of the ground control of spaceflight, but out here, as they sailed past the moons of Jupiter, the crew of *Discovery* was truly alone. There was nothing to fall back on but what they had brought along with them, for better or worse, and whatever ingenuity they could apply.

Your father's talking about a holiday. He wants to go to MegaPower—you know, the turbine tower, that Dutch monstrosity in the North Sea. Apparently they have restaurants and a hotel and shop, four miles high. All covered over, of course. Fancy that. But I wouldn't trust it, not after the leak of that huge cloud of ammonia last year . . .

Directly above her head Mott could see the half-disc of Jupiter. It glowed salmon-pink in the flat sunlight. *Discovery* was coming no closer than two million miles to the planet—twenty-five Jupiter diameters—but even so the giant world showed a sizable disc, like a big pink coin held at arm's length, four times the size of the Moon in Earth's sky. On the sunlit hemisphere she could make out the stripes of the ammonia ice cloud bands, brown and white and orange stripes, streaked and curdled with turbulence along the lines where they met. She couldn't see the Great Red Spot, and that was a disappointment. But Jupiter's day was only ten hours or so; perhaps the planet's disc would stay visible long enough for the Spot to be brought into view.

And Mott could see some of Jupiter's moons, strung out in a line parallel to the equator of their parent.

Io—a little larger than Earth's Moon—lay between its parent and the sun, about two Jupiter diameters from the cloud tops, its illuminated hemisphere a sulphur-yellow spot of light. Ganymede, twice as far from Jupiter as Io, sat behind its parent, its ice surface glittering white. Europa and Callisto, the other large moons, were harder to spot; eventually she found

Callisto as a bright white spark against the darkness of Jupiter's shadowed hemisphere.

It only took Io, the innermost of the large satellites, a day or so to travel around its orbit around Jupiter. If she stayed up here long enough, Mott would get to see the moons turn around their parent in their endless, complex dance . . .

The compact Jovian system was oddly charming. Like an old-fashioned orrery, a clockwork model of the Solar System. But Jupiter was eleven times the diameter of Earth. And its moons, if freed from Jupiter's grip, were large enough to have qualified as planets in their own right. Ganymede—out here, a spark dwarfed by Jupiter—was the largest moon in the Solar System: larger than Titan, larger, in fact, than the planet Mercury.

In a window frame of this beat-up Shuttle orbiter, she could see five worlds, clustered together in one gigantic gravity well.

But, she thought, there was no life here, not even—as far as anyone could tell—on that slush ball Europa. There was no life for a half-billion miles in any direction, save within the battered walls of this spacecraft, the bubble of air which sheltered her.

Damn it all. She wished Siobhan could see this. That remote death, back in the heart of the Solar System, was losing its power to hurt her now. But still, what a waste, what a meaningless, cruel waste.

No, I want to go to the hedgerow museum in Hampshire. Apparently they still have some ptarmigans there, the last ones. Oh, I have to tell you, you wouldn't believe the price of potatoes in the shops. All the sweetcorn you could ask for, but it's not the same . . . We know you are still missing Siobhan, love. We know you two were pals. You take care of yourself, and try not to fret about it all too much . . .

Pals. Her parents had never known—or had preferred not to know—about Libet's true relationship with their daughter. Her parents had been young in the 1970s, hardly the Victorian era. Mott wondered if there was something in the human genome which dictated that no generation could accept the sexuality of its offspring.

But, out here, it hardly seemed to matter, like so much else.

Discovery's path—whirling around the inner planets, and then out past Jupiter to Saturn—was actually similar to that of *Cassini*, which had come this way more than a decade before. But since then Jupiter and Saturn had wheeled through their grand orbits, of twelve and twenty-nine years, and they weren't in such a favorable position for *Discovery*'s slingshot as they had been for *Cassini*. *Discovery* needed to come in a lot closer than *Cassini*, to extract still more energy from Jupiter, the most massive planet in the Solar System.

But that meant the orbiter had to penetrate deep into Jupiter's magnetosphere.

Mott knew she, and the rest of the crew, were paying a price. Jupiter's magnetic field was ten times as powerful as Earth's, and its magnetosphere—the doughnut-shaped belt of magnetically trapped solar wind particles—stretched fifty Jupiter diameters, far beyond *Discovery*'s current position. Right now heavy solar wind particles, electrons and hydrogen and helium nuclei, which circled, trapped, in Jupiter's magnetosphere—ten thousand times as energetic as those in the Van Allen belts of Earth—coursed through the fabric of the ship, and her body.

Arguably this place, the magnetosphere of the most massive planet, was the most hostile section of deep space in the Solar System. And here she was, staring out the window at it.

Mott stayed on the flight deck as long as she could, exercising in Jupiter light.

She slowed her pace on the treadmill. She hung onto the pilot's seat for a moment and let her aching legs drift, deliciously, in the balm of microgravity, bearing no weight at all. Then she swiveled and pulled herself to the instrument panel at the back of the flight deck, and looked out over the orbiter's instrument bay.

Discovery was passing Jupiter with its payload bay turned up to the giant planet and its system, instruments straining, the big high-gain antenna pointing at remote Earth, lost now in the glare of the sun. The point-source sun and pink Jupiter, at right angles to each other, cast complex multiple shadows over the blocky, blanketed equipment in the payload bay, and over *Discovery*'s curving wings.

It was impossible to reconcile the awesome spectacle up here with the squalor and crap of their lives inside the space-craft—the shitty, failing systems, the endless slog of their daily lives.

But there had been no other way to get here, to see this.

She toweled off her sweat, wrapped up her softscreen, and went back to the hab module.

Rosenberg clambered into Apollo Command Module CM-115, through the tight little docking tunnel in its nose, past the compartments containing the drogue and recovery parachutes and their mortars and the forward reaction control system.

He came down into the big pressurized crew compartment in the mid-section, descending on it from above. There were three couches in there, side by side on their backs. They were just metal frames slung with gray Armalon fiberglass cloth, so close together he was sure it wouldn't be possible for three adult humans to pack in there without rubbing shoulders, elbows and knees against each other.

Rosenberg wriggled into the center couch, the Command Module Pilot's. He spread out his manuals on his knee.

He was here as part of his in-flight training program. He was never going to be a pilot, but he had to learn how to fly an Apollo—in case of contingency—all the way to the surface of Titan.

The Command Module was like a small aircraft, upended, its interior coated with switches, dials and cathode ray displays. The lights were subdued, the glow in the cabin greenish from the CRTs. Directly in front of him there was a big, gun-metal gray, one-hundred-and-eighty-degree instrument panel, glistening with five hundred switches. There were control handles on the commander's couch armrests: the attitude controller assembly on the right, which was used to control the reaction thruster assemblies, and the big thrust-translator controller on the left, which could be used to accelerate the craft forward or back. For this unique mission, the attitude control would also be used to direct a paraglider, a shaped parachute which would guide Apollo down to a safe landing on Titan's slushy surface.

There was a smell of plastic and metal; all around him the fans and pumps of the Command Module clicked and whirred.

The windows seemed small and far away; he was pretty much surrounded by metal walls, here, and even though the side hatch was still open, he felt closed in.

The Command Module showed Apollo's priorities: it had been built to keep people alive, not to let them sightsee, or do any of that fancy science crap en route to the Moon.

He turned his attention to the instrument panel.

There were toggle switches, thumb wheels, push buttons, rotary switches with click stops. The readouts were mainly meters, lights and little rectangular windows. There were tiny joysticks and pushbuttons: translational controllers, to work the Command Module's clusters of attitude rockets. He experimented with the switches. They were protected by little metal gates on either side, to save them being kicked by a free-fall boot. He worked his way across the panel, practicing flipping the dead switches, getting used to the feel of them.

There were little diagrams etched into the panel, he saw, circuit and flow charts. He consulted his manuals. All the switches were contained by one diagram or another. Once he started to see the system behind the diagrams, he began to figure the logic in the panel, how the switches clustered and related to each other.

He surveyed the cabin, checking he understood the contents of the lockers.

The equipment bay beyond the left-hand couch contained components of the environment control system, including the control unit. The bay in front of this held more life support equipment such as a water delivery system, and doubled as a clothing store. The right-hand bay contained more food, and the extremely clunky Apollo-era waste management systems: plastic condoms, and bags within which you had to catch and treat your turds. In a bay ahead of this Rosenberg found medical kits, survival gear and modern-looking camera equipment. In the aft bay, beneath the couches, were components of pressure suits.

If you docked with a Lunar Module, Rosenberg learned, you stowed your docking probe in that aft bay, and the circular tunnel cover in the left-hand bay . . .

In the lower bay at the foot of the center couch he found guidance and navigation electronics. Communications equipment was also crammed in there, along with batteries, food and other equipment.

There was also a tiny, beautiful sextant and telescope, for navigating between Earth and Moon.

CM-115 had been built four decades earlier, to fly to the Moon. But now it had been rebuilt, to some extent. CM-115 had been upgraded to stand a space soak of six years. Its attitude control system was to be based on nitrogen, which would not degrade in space. Hydraulic systems, which might freeze, were replaced by systems of wires and electric motors. The cooling system had been replaced by a water-based design, because chemicals in the old system like glycol were corrosive and couldn't be stored over long periods. A thermal blanket cocoon had been fitted over the Command Module's heatshield, to protect it from micrometeorite damage. The life support systems—some of which dated back to the Mercury era—had been upgraded to Shuttle technology. And so on.

The main challenge, in learning to handle this thing, was going to be the computer system.

Rosenberg spread a softscreen over his knee, opened up a manual, and began to poke at the Command Module's DSKY—

pronounced "disky"—the little computer touch-control pad.
The technicians had torn the heart out of Apollo's computers,
but had to leave the same interface. Anything else would have
meant pulling the ship apart, and nobody had the confidence to
do that.

The DSKY was not a softscreen—not even much like the
keyboard, mouse and monitor technology he had grown up
with. There was just a block of status and warning lights labeled
PROG and OPR ERR and UPLINK ACTY and COMP ACTY . . . He began
to study their meanings.

Tentatively, he started to punch the keypad. The pad wasn't
even qwerty; it contained a blocky numeric pad, with addition
and subtraction signs, and eight function keys with tiny lettering: VERB, NOUN, ENTER, RSET, PRO, others. The keypad was used
to construct little command sentences, to communicate with
the computer. There were about a hundred verbs and nouns he
would have to know.

He practiced loading a rendezvous program. He touched
the surface of his softscreen, and a little prompt panel opened
up. He told the computer he wanted to change the program: he
pressed the VERB function key, and then 3, 7, ENTER. He gave it
the new program: P31, a rendezvous mode. 3,1, ENTER. He
asked for data. VERB 0, 6; NOUN 8, 4. Five-digit numbers flashed
up on the display area. That was the velocity change he'd need
for the next maneuver.

The display could show decimal numbers, angles, octal
numbers, time . . . He could only tell which was which by con-
text, following his checklist.

The flight load had dozens of programs. Rosenberg would
have to learn which was which, learn to select them without
thinking. There wouldn't be much help for him, if he had to
run this stuff in anger. But then, nobody said it would be easy.

And besides, he was kind of enjoying this. It was like solving
a series of little logical puzzles.

They nearly didn't have computers in the old Apollos at all, he'd learned. Not everyone had agreed they needed them for navigation and rendezvous; ground control could cover all of that. Two arguments got computers in here. The first was the Russians. What if those Soviets tried to disrupt communications with Houston? The astronauts needed some way to get around the jamming by doing their own calculations. And the second was that NASA wanted to prepare for longer-duration missions, such as the flights to Mars that had never been funded: far enough away, you can't afford to wait out the minutes, or hours, it might take for some number to come up from the ground; you needed a local processing ability.

Fear and dreams, he thought, that's what had driven the computer technology, and everything else about Apollo, and maybe now the Titan mission as well. Fear and dreams.

The DSKY system was so counter-intuitive it was going to be tough to learn. But he had six years to study it, en route to Titan; if he ever needed to fly this ship he'd be able to play the crummy little gadget like a piano.

And anyhow he enjoyed the work. He enjoyed being tucked away, alone, in this humming little cabin with all its gadgets, occupying his mind with creaky old computer codes. It was a break from the complexities of life support, and his ambiguous and increasingly unwelcome role as ship's doctor, and the sour relationships that prevailed in the hab module.

And besides, Rosenberg found himself being slowly seduced by the Apollo.

He loved the endless lockers, the compact equipment, the careful design and storage, the way everything was tucked away.

When he was a kid, he'd built himself a den cum spaceship something like this. It was just a plastic tent hung up inside a climbing frame. He had little food boxes in there, and stocks of soda, and a rolled-up Army-surplus sleeping bag in one corner, and a couple of boxes of cold lights. He'd landed on a hundred planets in that little ship, all of them contiguous with his mother's backyard. He would peer through muddy plastic portholes, then creep out of his ship with his torch and his walkie-talkie and explore; but the main joy was to huddle back in the safety of his den, cocooned by his material and equipment, the stuff of his portable world, and write up his log.

Sad little bastard, he thought bleakly.

Anyhow, what was Apollo but the apotheosis of all dens?

And what did that say about Isaac Rosenberg? By launching himself off on this endless spaceflight, was he braving a new frontier, or retreating to some cozy fantasy of his lonely childhood?

It was best, he had learned much earlier in this mission, to avoid self-analysis.

Sitting alone inside the quiet Apollo, he worked his way through his manuals, learning how the old spaceship was flown.

Benacerraf had instituted a weekly crew meeting.

They were facing so many problems now, she figured they couldn't afford to indulge in their habitual acrimonious isolation from each other. They had to discuss their problems, come up with solutions, parcel out pieces of work.

Much as she hated the idea herself.

And so, now, the four of them hooked legs or arms around stanchions and struts, their postures taking on the stooping crouch of the neutral-G position.

They looked, Benacerraf thought, like four birds of prey, perched on some metal branch.

". . . We traced the root cause of the heart arrhythmia problems," Rosenberg was saying, reading from a softscreen which was suspended in the air before him. The computer folded softly like a bird's wing, the letters and numbers shimmering across its surface. "It was a trace element deficiency."

Benacerraf said, "What trace element?"

"Potassium. You find it in sea water and in various salts, like carnallite and sylvine. Potassium is essential in the biocycles. Its salts are used as fertilizers in the farm's nutrient solution, which—"

"Cut to the chase, asshole," Angel said mildly, his eyes closed.

Rosenberg said, "In the potable water we have a limit of three hundred forty milligrams per liter. We've actually been recording a level of a tenth that." He scratched his face. "The problem is partly the excess peeing we all do. Potassium, along with other stuff, gets flushed out of the system. So it has to be replaced. Now I'm spiking the potable water with electrolytes, specifically potassium, to restore the balance."

"So will we have long-term heart problems because of this?" Mott asked.

"Probably." Rosenberg shrugged. "But this is not a regime in which we're aiming for a long and healthy old age anyhow. I wouldn't worry; it's just another bogeyman to bite us, in a long line with all the others."

Benacerraf found Rosenberg's thin voice fantastically irritating, as he droned through his lists of facts. "So tell me what caused the deficiency in the biocycles."

"It has to be the SCWO," Rosenberg said, his eyes studiously on Benacerraf's face.

Angel showed no reaction, his face hidden by his beard.

Rosenberg doesn't want to take him on. So, Benacerraf thought wearily, it's up to me to confront this asshole again, to take on the burden of responsibility for us all.

"Bill, the SCWO is your baby. We've been having problems with it for years. And now this potassium crap."

Angel shrugged, his body moving minutely in the air as his center of mass shifted. "What do you want me to tell you? Look, we knew when we launched that the SCWO was immature technology, a risky piece of equipment to haul along. Basically the damn thing works. Hell," he said, leering casually at Mott, who looked away, "you know that, or we'd all be knee-deep in Rosenberg's pale shit, right? But we still get a lot of corrosion of the surfaces in there—it's a hostile environment, and there are a shit-load of toxic gases which—"

"Bill, I've been relying on you to fix it. And now I hear this."

"I've nursemaided the damn thing halfway to Saturn already," Angel snapped. "I'm a pilot, not a plumber."

"You have to get it *right*, Bill. Right to the last decimal place, of the last trace element. That's what it takes." She felt herself slipping into peevish anger. "Don't you see that? Why should I have to tell you what to do, how to do it? Why can't I trust you to do your job? . . ."

She noticed Mott folding her arms over herself, and rolling her eyes, escaping inward.

Damn it, she thought. We set ourselves the trap again. And I fell into it.

Angel was still blustering, justifying his negligent work on the SCWO. And Rosenberg, unfortunately, was going into lecture mode. He put his hands to his temples, his own long hair and wispy beard drifting around his face, and he started telling Angel stuff he already knew: about the instability of their miniature biosphere, the lack of buffering reservoirs of essential elements like potassium, the way the balance had to be monitored and adjusted constantly by the crew . . .

Angel started yelling back at Rosenberg, who just closed his eyes and droned on. Their voices seemed amplified in the dingy metal tube of the hab module.

Benacerraf knew she needed to find some way of defusing the situation. But, she thought wearily, why me? Why is it always me who has to be the peacemaker, to eat shit, to make Bill calm down and force Rosenberg to look up from his softscreen and dry Nicola's eyes over her girlfriend— *why me?*

The meeting broke up, acrimoniously, with no real outcome. Mott went to her sleep compartment, Rosenberg to the farm. And Angel . . .

☆   ☆   ☆

Benacerraf watched, discreetly, as Angel took up position near
the water spigots of the galley. And, with his skinny, spindled
legs folded under him, he started to play with water. Angel took
a syringe now, for example, and filled it with water from a
spigot. When he pressed the plunger, slowly and carefully,
injecting water into the air, a small bubble grew from the needle's tip. He jerked the needle away and the water took the
form of a tiny planet, floating in the air. Angel worked his needle and produced a whole set of the little water globes, drifting
in the air around his head.

Then he took smaller syringes from a set he'd improvised
from medical waste, and injected the bubbles with iodine,
grape juice, diluted orange juice, to stain them blue, green, yellow, red. Soon he had a whole Solar System, Benacerraf
thought, with a miniature Mars and Earth and Jupiter, floating
around his bearded head as if around a sun. Angel's eyes followed the little spheres, entranced.

Now Angel tried to herd his little water planets together,
with his open palms. The water spheres were clammy to the
touch; if Angel was gentle they bounced away from his palm as
if coated with some fine elastic membrane, but if he wasn't so
careful the balls of water would cling like some jellyfish,
spreading over the surface of his palm. With one such glob
dangling from his palm, he shook his hand gently, up and down;
the spherical cap rippled symmetrically, clinging to his skin.

In microgravity, water's surface tension became dominant,
and tried to haul it constantly into the shape of a sphere. But
with a little ingenuity a lot of bizarre shapes could be conjured
out of this most basic of materials. And it fascinated Bill Angel.

Angel spent hours turned in on himself like this, with his
syringes and lathes and bizarre, oscillating shapes. And as he
stared into the shimmering meniscus of some new sphere or
torus, he seemed, to Benacerraf, to be peering into some world of
his own, a private place the others couldn't share, a place he could
escape to, as if the water forms were projections of his own mind.

Rosenberg had his own theory about Bill. So he'd told her privately. He thought Bill was aging too quickly. There were studies that showed how cosmic rays caused irreversible damage to nervous tissue. For instance, the response of nerve cells to muscarinic neurotransmitters, which helped muscle-controlling neurons communicate, deteriorated. Maybe this was happening to Bill, Rosenberg speculated. Maybe space was turning him into a decrepit old man, before their eyes.

She suspected Bill had gotten wind of this, in fact. He had taken to sleeping at one end of the hab module, surrounded by big batteries with lots of nickel and cadmium, which gave him good shielding. But it was probably too late.

Benacerraf was no expert on abnormal states of the mind. But she hadn't tried to discuss this with Mission Control. She wasn't sure who would be listening any more anyhow. And on a planet where local wars were flaring over water management problems, the image of gaunt Americans playing head games with the wet stuff on some dumb Buck Rogers mission halfway to Saturn would not play well with the public.

On and on Angel fiddled, while *Discovery*, cradling its little nest of light and warmth, sailed further from the sun.

Around the U.S. carrier *Independence*, the Pacific stretched to the horizon, as flat and still and steel-gray as the deck of the carrier itself, its sluggish waves reflecting the cobalt blue of the cloudless sky. Even the rest of the battle group was out of sight, over the horizon.

The sun was low, the light harsh, and Gareth Deeke was grateful for his cap and sunglasses.

A single aircraft stood ready on the deck: a McDonnell-Douglas F-28, its slim form sixty feet long, its delta wings all but obscured by the snaking hoses of the fueling tankers—

kerosene and hydrogen peroxide—which surrounded it. The
F-28's thermal shield, plated over its upper hull, gleamed white
as snow in the Pacific sunlight.

The F-28 was Deeke's aircraft.

The *Independence* was four hundred miles from the Chinese
coast, and two hundred miles from Taiwan, to the southeast of
the island. And it was a matter of hours—less, perhaps—from
the initiation of a U.S.-China war. But, suspended in this
instant of calm, the ship could have been anywhere, Gareth
Deeke reflected, anywhere on the surface of this watery planet;
and it could have been transported to almost any time in the
last half billion years.

He was pretty much alone up here, save for the service
techs. He'd been here for a time, but he wasn't bored. He was
standing on alert. He had stood on alert many times before, in
his long career.

He had a choice of being up here or going down below, to sit
with the other pilots and chew on pizza and mixed vegetables
and watch softscreen CNN reports on the progress of the
Chinese preparation for invasion.

His preference was clear.

Besides, he didn't exactly mix easily with the others. They
respected his ability and experience, but most of the guys, with
one eye on their own careers, shied away from a man with a
past as tainted and complex as Deeke's.

It didn't trouble him. At least, not away from the cramped
confines of his quarters, where he had too much time to think.
He wasn't troubled by anything here: up on the flight deck, in
the salt air.

A shadow flickered across the deck. Deeke looked up.

It was a Condor, an unmanned surveillance plane built by
Boeing. The Condor was a light, subsonic craft with a single tur-
bofan engine. It was big, with the wing span of a 747, and it could
hover at sixty thousand feet for a week without replenishment,
scanning the ground with high-resolution radar and electro-

optic sensors. Condors—and their smaller cousins the Dark-Stars—had become a common sight in areas of tension like this, wheeling through the air like expectant birds of prey . . .

There was a low beeping.

He lifted his wrist. A softscreen patch on the back of his hand was scrolling with symbols.

The Chinese ships were leaving harbor. It had started. Deeke grinned.

He turned on his heel and headed for the personal gear room.

The hot war had started two weeks ago; Deeke had followed it closely, expecting his call.

Taiwan's president, after his latest reelection, at last came out openly in favor of a declaration of formal independence from Beijing. China responded immediately, and the Taipei stock market hit the floor.

It took three days for Beijing to assemble a hundred thousand troops in the embarkation ports in the provinces of Zhejiang, Fujian and Guangdong. Taiwan put its armed forces on their highest level of alert and mobilized its reserves, and asked the U.S. for arms shipments under the Taiwan Relations Act.

The next day, Taiwan naval patrols in the Strait had been fired on by Chinese "fishing boats." They returned fire, and China proclaimed that a "hostile act against ordinary Chinese people." In response, China announced a naval blockade of all the tankers ferrying oil to Taiwan.

Air battles started over Taiwan, mass flights of ancient Chinese Russian-built Sukhois against Taiwan's more modern Western-built F-16s and Mirage 2000-5s. The technology was a mismatch, but the numbers were telling: after a couple of days China had achieved a tentative control of the air over the Strait.

The Great Helmsman himself had appeared in Tiananmen

Square to announce that if Taiwan didn't capitulate, the invasion would begin.

Maclachlan responded by saying that an invasion of Taiwan would amount to a declaration of war with America. And besides, China's control of the Strait didn't amount to a hill of beans, said Maclachlan; not with the U.S. carriers, and F-15s in Okinawa, ready to join the action.

Anyhow it didn't seem likely the Chinese could secure a beachhead, even without the U.S. coming to the aid of Taiwan. And a failed invasion could cost fifty percent casualties.

But the Chinese had nukes, and ICBMs. They could simply wipe Taiwan off the face of the Earth.

Nobody was too sure about what the U.S. would do in that circumstance. Did the Americans, asked the Great Helmsman, care as much about Taiwan as about Los Angeles?

The Chinese would have to be dumb, or desperate, to take such a step. But they were indeed desperate, Deeke thought.

For decades they had watched the U.S. cozying up to India, recognizing Vietnam, selling F-16s to Taiwan, forging alliances with Japan, trying to work for a united Korea under Seoul allied to the U.S.

From the Chinese perspective, it looked like a ring around China. Which, of course, it was.

And besides, there was one way the Chinese could win . . .

Which was why Deeke was here.

So matters stood. Now, they were all waiting.

Deeke emerged in his flight suit, with an oxygen mask, straps everywhere, a parachute on his back, survival kits for several environments tucked into pockets, emergency oxygen, intercoms.

He walked up to the F-28.

Close to, the plane looked something like a miniature Shuttle orbiter, with the underside of its fat delta wing coated with black silica-based thermal protection tiles, and the upper hull layered with a gleaming white felt blanket, patched with black around the attitude control nozzles. The felt blanket gave the plane an oddly clumsy look, he thought; it lacked the metallic sleekness of the hulls of conventional aircraft. But that blanket was plastered with USAF logos, and his own name and rank, picked out under the canopy.

The F-28 looked what it was: a plane built for space, America's first rocket plane since the X-15.

Although the basic rocketry would have been recognized by von Braun, in every other way the F-28 was a child of the twenty-first century.

The concept was based on proposals touted in the 1990s by space enthusiasts for a fast-turnaround, relatively cheap, single-stage-to-orbit military spaceplane. When Xavier Maclachlan came to power, and after extensive lobbying by the USAF, he wasted no time in pulling Lockheed Martin out of NASA's doomed RLV development, and ordering the accelerated development of what became the F-28 for the Air Force.

Needless to say, it had come in way over budget. But even so the cost was manageable. The F-28 was designed to work with existing runways, fuel distribution systems, non-specialized hangars and standard handling equipment . . . The only novelty was the use of kerosene and concentrated hydrogen peroxide to burn in the plane's five engines, to give the F-28 a high power to weight ratio.

The cost of the whole project had been about equivalent to two Delta IV launches, less than the cost of a single Shuttle launch. For that price, the USAF had gotten itself a whole new aerospace craft.

Gareth Deeke was just grateful that a new chain of command—via Hartle, up to President Maclachlan—had brought him and his skills and experience here, to head up the USAF's newest battle wing. The USAF didn't have so many rocket-plane pilots that it could afford to ignore a man like Gareth Deeke, age or not.

Two techs helped him climb up and lower himself into the cockpit of the F-28. The rocket plane's white-tiled walls were only just wide enough for him to squeeze in.

The elemental countdown dialogue with his controller inside the carrier began as soon as he strapped into his seat; around the plane, the stubby, shielded fueling tankers withdrew.

"Data on," he said. "Generator reset. Hydraulic pressure, check. Electrical pressure, check. Rudder, check . . ."

"One minute, Gareth."

"Rog. Master arm is on, system arm light is on . . ."

"Ready for the prime."

"Prime, igniter ready. And precool, igniter and tape . . ."

"Thirty seconds."

Inside the craft, there was little similarity with 1970's Shuttle technology. This cockpit was high-tech: the walls were coated with softscreens, which reconfigured to suit each successive flight phase, and his helmet offered head-up and virtual imaging, overlaid on his view through the canopy. Now, the systems worked him calmly through the final preparations.

". . . Fifteen seconds."

"Pump on," Deeke said. "Good igniter."

"Five seconds. Looks good here, Gareth. And three, two, one."

Deeke braced.

The noise of the F-28's five rockets rose to a roar.

In his glass bubble Deeke was slammed in the back, suddenly cocooned in light and noise and vibration. The carrier deck whipped away, exposing the gray, bone-hard surface of the ocean. The plane swiveled back, pitching suddenly upward, so that he lost sight of the ocean.

The F-28 rose almost vertically. Twisting his head, he glanced down: the carrier was already lost, remote, a patchwork of blue gray adrift on the wider hide of the ocean.

Then, in a few seconds, the sky faded down to a deep pearl blue.

At thirty-five thousand feet he leveled off. The plane was a little isolated island of reality, gleaming white felt and warm air and hard surfaces, up here in the mouth of the sky.

There was a tanker aircraft waiting for him here. The F-28 carried a full load of fuel, but it needed replenishment of its heavy oxidizer for its final leap into space. With practiced ease, he slid the replenishment nozzle mounted in the nose of the plane into the dangling cup trailed by the tanker. The replenishment took just three minutes.

When it was done, the tanker pulled away.

Deeke hauled the nose of the plane upward. The rockets howled again, and the Gs rammed him hard into his seat; his head was pushed into his shoulders, and his vision tunneled, walled by darkness.

There was the mildest of vibrations as the craft went supersonic, and then the ride got a lot smoother, the noise of the rockets dying to a whisper. The cockpit now was a little bubble of serenity, of cool, easy flying; meanwhile, he knew, sonic thunder was washing down on the ocean below.

Eighty thousand feet. He moved the throttle to maximum thrust, and he was pushed back into his seat by four and a half G. He was already so high he could see stars above, in the middle of the day; so high there were only a few wisps of atmosphere, barely sufficient for his plane's aerodynamic control surfaces to grip.

Ninety thousand feet; thirty two hundred feet per second. The Pacific spread out beneath him, the shining skin of the world.

There was a rattle of solenoids, a brief squirt of gas beyond the cockpit. His reaction control thrusters had activated.

The rockets shut down with a clatter.

He was thrust forward against his restraints as the acceleration cut out, and then he drifted back again.

He had gone ballistic. He was weightless inside the cabin, and it felt as if his gut was climbing up out of his neck. Up here, coasting in near-silence, he lost all sensation of speed, of motion.

He was fifty miles high. The sky outside his tiny cabin was a deep blue-black, and the softscreen displays gleamed brightly. He could see the eastern coast of Asia all the way from Japan to the Philippines, with the distinctive teardrop shape of Taiwan directly beneath him; it was all laid out under him like some kind of relief map. Up ahead the Earth curved over on itself, looking huge and pregnant, and at the horizon's rim he could see the thick layer of air out of which he'd climbed.

Just like the old days.

Then there was a final kick from his rocket engines, the injection into space.

On orbit, he opened the F-28's payload bay doors.

The payload deployed automatically. It was a small, complex satellite with a compact rocket booster. As it unfolded from the narrow payload bay the satellite looked like a fat, ungainly toy, illuminated from beneath by the glowing blue skin of Earth.

A spring mount pushed the satellite away from the F-28. Then the main solid-rocket booster pack opened up; Deeke could see orange smoke and debris gush from the fat, squat nozzle.

He watched the satellite arc away, upward, directly away from Earth. It was heading for geosynchronous orbit, to hover over Borneo.

Thus, less than twenty minutes after receiving the order to launch, Deeke's mission was complete.

The satellite was a derivative of Aquacade technology. It was a communications link, one of the final pieces in the U.S. forces' electronic coverage of the battle zone around Taiwan. It would enable other satellites—Milstar communications birds, Keyhole surveillance craft, others—to communicate directly with each other, rather than via signals to ground stations. The satellite-to-satellite links would make the system virtually impregnable to Chinese attempts at jamming or interception.

The only real Chinese threat to the U.S. forces, in fact, was their stock of cruise missiles: the M-12 intermediate-range weapon, originally a derivative of the Scud but now heavily upgraded, and generally recognized as China's best piece of kit.

But with the surveillance systems successfully deployed, no M-12 would be able to get more than twenty miles from its launcher without intelligence on it being fed down to the battlefield. Deeke doubted, in fact, that a single cruise would get through the anti-missile batteries.

Information was the key to this war. Information flowed throughout the U.S. and Taiwanese forces. Every ship, every land vehicle, every infantryman, airman and sailor was suffused with computer technology, linked directly or through the satellites. The forces, joined by the technology, were like a single organism, ready to respond as if united by a central nervous system.

There were, in fact, more warriors in this conflict deploying computers than firing weapons.

The Chinese, with their crude human-wave strategies and resources, had only the rudiments of this technology. It was like a conflict between time travelers. As if a Roman legion had taken on a band of Australopithecines.

The war might take some days to play out yet, and no doubt many lives would be lost. But for China, Deeke reflected, it was already lost. The containment was going to continue.

He cleared his helmet of its displays. For a few seconds, he allowed himself to look out through the sparkling clearness of his canopy.

Here—for the next few minutes anyhow—he was suspended between the curve of Earth below, the stunning blackness above. His mission was achieved, his fuel spent.

He felt an odd stab of emotion. It's so beautiful, he thought. So beautiful.

Below him, hundreds of thousands of men were swarming like ants to meet each other in a conflict that would be all but invisible from this height. Across the thin sky of Earth, aircraft and missiles scratched contrails; far above him, twenty-two thousand miles from Earth, artifacts of the most advanced nation on the planet clustered, to observe and monitor and warn.

And right now, there were four human beings—four Americans—suspended between Jupiter and Saturn, engaged in the most extraordinary adventure yet conceived by man. And his role in that adventure had been to try to shoot them down on takeoff.

But space travel was an absurdity. The journeys were magnificent, but there was nowhere to go, nothing but a series of lethal landscapes, floating like islands in the sky.

And if the U.S. had reached for the stars, like a soaring tree, its enemies—first the USSR, now the Chinese—would have had no hesitation in spreading over the face of the planet to cut away its trunk.

Gareth Deeke had no doubts as to the strategic correctness of the massive U.S. military investment of the last fifty years. No doubts, in the end, about his own role in the ludicrous Titan adventure. Military spending had caused the Soviet Union to implode, with barely a shot being fired; now it would enable the U.S. to contain China indefinitely.

Space had nothing to do with humanity. Down there, in the eternal blood and mud and dust of the two-dimensional battlefields of Earth, was where history was shaped. It had always been thus, and would always be thus.

And it was possible, he thought, that over Taiwan this day, the shape of the planet's destiny for the next century might be determined.

He closed the payload bay, and, briskly, he prepared his ship for reentry, and the long glide home to the salt flats around Edwards Air Force Base in California.

Day 2460

Six years and nine months after its launch, the human space-craft *Discovery* reached the moons of Saturn.

The etiolated crew prepared for SOI: Saturn orbit insertion, the long rocket burn which would embed them forever in the gravity well of the giant, remote planet.

They had arrived, Paula Benacerraf thought, at the desolate rim of the Solar System.

"Okay," Nicola Mott said. "Twenty minutes to the burn. Let's go to auxiliary power unit prestart."

"Rog." Benacerraf consulted the checklist strapped to her leg, and began throwing switches on the panel to her right. "Boiler nitrogen supply switches to on, one, two, three. Controller switches on, one, two, three. Power heater switches to position A, one, two, three. APU fuel tank valve switches closed, one, two, three."

"Copy," said Mott. "OK, APU prestart complete."

"Good . . ."

Benacerraf—sitting to Mott's right, in *Discovery*'s pilot's seat—closed her visor. Sealed inside her orange pressure suit, she was cocooned in a little bubble of sound: the hum of fans, the hiss of oxygen over her face, her own slightly ragged breathing. She heard Rosenberg's voice as a crackle over the speakers in her Snoopy hat.

"Visors closed," he said. Rosenberg was sitting behind Mott and Benacerraf, in the flight engineer's seat.

Bill Angel was the only member of the crew not on the flight deck; he was back on the orbiter's mid deck.

"Bill?" Benacerraf called. "How about you? Bill, do you copy about the visor? Respond, Bill, you asshole."

"Copy, copy. Jesus, Benacerraf, give me a break." On the loop now there came the sound of humming: fragments of song, mostly unrecognizable, jumbled up and reassembled as if at random.

"I'll take that as a rog," Benacerraf said.

Rosenberg laughed. "He won't close his suit. He told us so; we ought to believe him. Who cares? Let him play with himself all the way through the burn. Let him—"

"Can it," Benacerraf said sharply.

Crazy or not, Benacerraf didn't want Angel's death on her conscience. And besides, there were no scenarios which showed how just three of them, of the five nominal crew, could expect to survive on Titan's surface. Angel was a resource she needed, and she had to protect him.

For now, however, they had a checklist to get through.

One step at a time, Paula.

"Load the SOI software, Niki."

"Rog." Her gloved fingers clumsy, Mott entered a sequence of commands into the computer keyboard. OPS 702 PRO. This was a chunk of a new software mode written by the ground crews and loaded up into the Shuttle's guidance computers. OPS 7: software to control SOI, Saturn Orbit Insertion.

The light was changing. Benacerraf looked up from her checklist.

Mott said, "Time for the maneuver to the burn attitude. Track me, Paula."

Benacerraf glanced at Mott. She could see Niki's face framed inside her white helmet: calm, almost expressionless, a hint of fear about her eyes.

She reached over and, briefly, closed her glove over Mott's. "You'll be fine, Niki. Just like the training."

"Sure." Mott laughed weakly. "Just like the training."

Neither Mott nor Benacerraf had piloted a Shuttle before, though both had worked as flight engineers. If the prelaunch plans had worked out, Bill Angel and Siobhan Libet would be sitting here now, as prime orbiter commander and pilot.

But Libet was long gone. And, after a lot of agonizing—and solitary, time-delayed conversations with the ground—Benacerraf had taken the decision that Angel couldn't be trusted near the controls of the orbiter any more.

So, absurd as it was, Mott and Benacerraf had to pilot *Discovery* through its most crucial maneuver since leaving Earth orbit. All the good pilots were nearly a billion miles away, or dead, or half-crazy.

Mott reached forward. "Flight control power switch to on."

"Copy that," said Benacerraf. "ADI ATT switches—"

"Attitude switches to inertial, panels F6 and F8. ADI error to median. ADI rate to median . . ."

Mott reached for her hand controller, and pulsed the RCS jets. Benacerraf could hear the hard click of solenoids, feel the soft shudder of the little jets as they shoved at *Discovery*'s mass.

The light started to change.

As *Discovery* turned, the sun was crossing the window, right to left. It was a shrunken disc. Pale, yellowish light played directly into the cabin, the window struts casting long, sharp shadows over Benacerraf's lap. False images sparkled in the scuffed plexiglass of her helmet visor.

Diminished since Jupiter, the sun was still more brilliant than any star or planet seen from Earth, ten thousand times brighter than a full Moon. It was a little like looking directly into an approaching headlight.

And now the limb of Saturn, a thin crescent, reached into the window frame. Precise and huge and intimidating, it reared up before the sun. It was a yellow arc, obviously flattened from the circular, blistered with turbulence. The colors were subtle, and she found she had to shield her eyes from the glaring yellow and white and green of the orbiter's instrument lights.

Saturn was no gaudy pyrotechnic display, but an autumn-color sculpture wrought of the soft light of the remote sun. It was, Benacerraf thought with a shiver, utterly unearthly.

Mott had to turn the orbiter so it was flying tail-first. *Discovery* had accelerated as it had fallen into Saturn's gravity well. Already deep within the planet's magnetosphere the spacecraft was now plunging towards Saturn itself; it would make its closest approach over the dark side of the giant world, just a sixth of a Saturn radius above the cloud tops. And there, at the lowest point in the gravity well, the SOI burn would be initiated.

After a six year space soak, the orbiter's OMS engines, the small orbital maneuvering system, had to burn for a hundred minutes, sucking fuel and oxidizer out of the big supplementary tanks that were strapped to the orbiter's wings, like two fat bomb pods, slowing the craft into a looping, five-month orbit around Saturn.

The burn had to work. Otherwise, *Discovery* would not shed enough velocity to be captured by Saturn's gravity. They wouldn't make it to Titan. Not only that, the orbiter would be hurled onward in an involuntary slingshot, towards the stars.

Benacerraf had privately calculated they might make it one-tenth of the way to the orbit of Uranus, the next giant planet, before their consumables finally gave out.

And—although it hadn't been expressed—she was sure nobody had forgotten that it was the OMS burn which had been ultimately catastrophic on *Columbia*'s last flight.

But whether they survived all this or not, this battered old space truck had come a hell of a lot further than had been dreamed by those old guys who had devised the Shuttle in the 1970s.

Saturn drifted out of the window frame.

"Maneuver to burn attitude complete," Mott said.

Benacerraf forced her attention to the checklist, and to the instruments on the panels before her. She compared the attitude shown on the CRT display with that given by the eight-ball, the attitude direction indicator. They matched each other and the predictions in the checklist, to several decimal places.

"Good work, Niki," she said. "Maneuver complete, confirm."

"All right," Mott said evenly. Under strain, she was visibly turning her attention to the next obstacle.

One step at a time, Benacerraf thought.

Mott said, "Let's go for single APU start."

"Rog. Number one APU fuel tank valve to open. Control switch to start/run, number one APU."

"Confirm hydraulic pressure indicator one is green," Mott said.

"Hydraulic circulation pump switches to off, one, two, three."

". . . Okay, we have single APU start."

"Good. We're doing fine, Niki. Now. Arm the engines."

Mott reached forward, and over her head. "Auto pilot to auto. OMS helium pressure switches to GPC, left and right engines. OMS engine switches to arm." She looked across at Benacerraf. "Engines armed."

"Good girl."

The routine, the checklists and procedures for just another OMS burn, was comforting. It allowed her to forget what they were doing here: firing rocket engines to go into orbit around *Saturn*, for God's sake.

"One minute to the burn," Rosenberg said.

Mott reached forward to the computer keyboard. She pressed the EXEC key, and the computer began its countdown to the burn.

. . . And suddenly, light exploded into the flight deck, for *Discovery* was sailing above the plane of Saturn's rings.

To Benacerraf the rings looked like a broad sheet of colored light, as if *Discovery* were a mote of dust flying high above some elaborate laser display. This close, it was impossible to see their full extent; Benacerraf could see only a portion of the ring disc framed in her window. Though the lighting was dim, the different bands within the rings were clearly visible, distinguishable by their faint, yellow-brown colorations, separated by dark gaps.

"Incredible," Rosenberg said. Benacerraf could see the rings reflected from his visor, precise stripes of smoky, washed-out light. "It looks like an artifact, doesn't it? Something *made* . . . But if those rings were transplanted home, they would fill up the space between Earth and Moon. Think of that. And look." He pointed. "You can see a moon, buried in there in the structure. That's the E ring; the moon must be Enceladus, I think. See how bright it is?"

After some searching she made out the moon, barely discernible as an icy spark, suspended in one of the dark ring gaps.

The giant shadow of Saturn, blunt and physical, lay across the rings, casting a precise terminator across their structure: perhaps the longest straight line in the Solar System. Earth itself could have rolled around that ring disc, like a ball bearing on a plate. Space here was filled by huge shapes, Benacerraf thought, like gigantic machinery.

Mott said, "Ten seconds to the burn. Five, four, three, two, one."

The orbiter shuddered, and Benacerraf thought she could hear a remote bass roar, transmitted through the structure of the craft.

"Ignition," Mott shouted.

"Copy OMS ignition."

"Building up to full thrust. Point zero five G. Point zero eight. Zero nine. Stabilizing there . . ."

Benacerraf felt herself sink back into her seat. It was as if the orbiter was tipping up, and she was lying on her back in her couch. The metal of her couch, folds in the fabric of her pressure suit, dug painfully into her flesh. And now there was a dark fringe to her vision, as if she was looking along a tunnel. The colors seemed to leach out of the control panel before her.

My God, she thought. I'm graying out.

She was experiencing acceleration, for the first time since

the CELSS farm had been transferred to the centrifuge, more than three years ago.

The checklist fell from her lap against her chest, landing with a thud that knocked the air out of her. Her arms were across her chest, and she could feel where they lay, like concrete beams compressing her lungs, her gloved hands huge and massive. And her internal organs, her heart and guts and lungs, were settling out, moving to some new equilibrium inside her. She couldn't have moved, reached up to a control, to save her life.

And this is only a tenth of a G. We'll be incapacitated on the surface of Titan. Even if we survive the reentry.

"Holy shit," Mott said. Her voice was remote, weak.

Benacerraf tried to turn her head to see Mott, but her skull felt as heavy as a ball of concrete. "Take it easy, kid," she said. "*Discovery* can fly itself; we don't have to do a damn thing."

The burn went on and on.

Discovery sailed into the shadow of Saturn. The darkness seemed cool, immense, deepening their isolation. It was the first time in six years that the orbiter had not been bathed in sunlight.

And now, with the instruments in the payload bay gaping at the planet, *Discovery* fell through the plane of the ring system. The rings were less than a mile thick, and at *Discovery*'s interplanetary velocity, the plane was crossed in a fraction of a second.

Benacerraf, staring back along the path of *Discovery*, could see the shadowed rings above her. They were a huge roof of darkness, occluding the patchy stars. Here and there she thought she could see a gap in the ring system, a fine circular arc, full of stars. The bulk of the planet was to her right, a flat-infinite wall of shadowed cloud, just a sixth of Saturn's radius away.

Discovery was a fly circling the flank of an elephant.

And now, as her eyes continued to dark-adapt, she saw that

there was a patch of light tracking over the shadowed ceiling of the ring system: a diffuse circle, like the image of the sun seen through fog. It seemed to be matching the movements of *Discovery*.

It was the light of *Discovery*'s engines—the burning of monomethyl hydrazine and nitrogen tet, hauled out here all the way from Earth, reflecting from the icy rings of Saturn.

Then, as *Discovery* fell beneath Saturn's equatorial plane, the diffuse glow faded out—

There was a bang, sharp, muffled by the thickness of her helmet.

It was gone so quickly she wasn't sure if it had been real.

"Niki. Did you hear that?"

"No." Mott hesitated. "But I felt something. A shudder."

A bang, a shudder. Put it together, Paula.

Benacerraf felt fear gather like a sharp knot in her stomach. But she was helpless, trapped in her seat by this minuscule gravity.

The sounds of the cabin, the whir of the pumps and fans— already subdued by the helmet around her head—died away.

"We're losing pressure," Mott said, her radio-transmitted voice full of wonder.

Rosenberg started yelling. "Bill, close your eyes! Bill, if you can hear me, close your eyes!"

. . . Light seeped into the cabin. Above Benacerraf, the ring-plane terminator was sliding into view, a geometrically straight line that could have stretched from Earth to Moon. The subdued gold-brown light of the rings soaked over her face.

Rosenberg, with no reply from Angel, quit yelling.

"What the hell happened, Rosenberg?"

His voice was fragile. "We got hit by a ring fragment."

"But we'd already passed through the plane of the damn rings. And besides, we aimed for a gap."

"But the rings we see are patterns imposed on a complex,

chaotic cloud of particles or dust and ice. This is a crowded part of space, Paula. We only came this deep because we needed the benefit of a low periapsis. We gambled we wouldn't hit anything on the way through."

"Lucked out," Nicola Mott said.

Rosenberg pointed out, "Bill isn't answering."

"How long until the burn's done, Niki?"

"Eight more minutes, Paula."

Rosenberg said, "Look, we have to go down and help Bill. Vacuum exposure will kill him."

Mott said, "Sit still."

"She's right," Benacerraf said wearily. "If you try to get out of your couch you'll just fall the length of the cabin. Rosenberg, we have to wait."

"If we wait, we'll find him dead," Rosenberg said. "Damn it, Paula. If Bill is dead I hope you can live with yourself."

Benacerraf felt herself smile, tiredly. And there's my function on this flight, she thought. *Blame Paula*: not that asshole Angel for endangering his own life by his madness and stupidity, not the confluence of forces which delivered us to this perilous point in space and time in such a fragile craft, not the malevolent God who put that fragment of primordial ice right in our path in the middle of the one and only traverse, by humans from Earth, of the rings of Saturn . . .

At last the burn died.

"Good burn," Mott whispered. "Residuals were less than three tenths, on all axes."

"Welcome to Saturn," Rosenberg said drily.

The mid deck, like the flight deck, was in vacuum.

The chunk of ring material had entered the mid deck at about waist height in the middle of the left hand wall, close to the galley. They found a neat round hole in the panel there, almost big enough for Benacerraf to push her finger into. And there was a matching hole in the floor, a few feet away, as if the particle had slanted down like a sniper's rifle shot through the cabin.

In fact, they had been lucky, she realized. It was a clean impact. A grain the size and speed that hit them could have done a lot more damage than just puncturing the pressure hull so cleanly.

Ring material. At least, thought Benacerraf, it was more glamorous than the particle of flaked-off paint or frozen cosmonaut urine that had zapped them during their Earth flyby.

It was simple to slap patches over the damage; soon the air pressure in the mid deck was restored.

They found Angel sitting strapped into his fold-up seat. He had his pressure suit helmet on, with the visor closed; but the helmet wasn't locked correctly at the neck. He was unconscious. Benacerraf could see his eyes were closed, his face contorted. And there was some kind of fluid, smeared over the inside of his visor, making it difficult to see inside.

Rosenberg peered into Angel's helmet, and shrugged. "He must have been exposed to vacuum for a few seconds, low pressure for a while longer. We got to get him out of here."

They manhandled Angel through the airlock at the rear of the mid deck, and into the hab module. Then the three of them went into the resuscitation routines they had rehearsed on Earth.

With Benacerraf and Mott holding Angel's limbs, Rosenberg checked for breathing, then braced himself against a wall and pumped four mouth-to-mouth breaths into Angel's lungs. There was no response, so Rosenberg had the women move Angel around so that he could push his arms around Angel's thorax and under his arms. He grabbed Angel's elbows and worked them like a bellows, up and down, four times.

"All right," he said, breathless. "Now we got oxygenated air in his lungs." He looked exhausted, his glasses sweat-streaked, as if he might pass out himself. "Now, the heart." He felt for Angel's carotid pulse. "Nothing. Niki, you're stronger than me. Come around here."

Mott pulled herself behind Angel. She placed her left hand fist in Angel's sternum and grabbed the fist with her other hand. She pulled Angel's back against her chest, then compressed his sternum, hauling him hard towards her, counting. "One. Two. Three . . ." The idea was to squeeze the heart between the sternum and the thoracic vertebrae, and so push oxygenated blood through Angel's body.

At a count of twelve, Angel shuddered. He coughed, his throat dry and ragged.

Later, Benacerraf was at a squawk box, listening to the insectile voice of a capcom, the words eighty minutes old. The capcom was enthusing about the images they had received during the Saturn closest approach. Already NASA was receiving requests for the commercial rights, and there were believed to be hundreds of illegal hacked-up VR copies running through their cycles even now, out in the net.

She stared into a monitor.

Discovery was receding from Saturn now, skimming back, briefly, towards the sun, and the planet was once more turning its full face to the spacecraft. The cloud bands were sharply distinguished, though more subtle and yellowish than Jupiter's. Along the fringe of one band at the equator Benacerraf could see turbulence, oval clouds like cells. The rings themselves cast a shadow, a thin, complex line, over the milky equator of Saturn's daylit hemisphere. The shadow was curved, an exercise in projective geometry. And the rings had a lacy, tenuous appearance, so that she could see the curve of the bright limb of the planet through their structure.

There was *nothing* to compare to this experience.

This was not, she thought, even like traveling from Earth to Moon, from one closed-up sphere to another. They had journeyed for years, into the huge outer wastes of the Solar System, and entered orbit around this metahuman artifact, this structure of rings and spheres that could fill up the Earth-Moon system.

It is the dream of a million years, she thought, to be here and see this.

Rosenberg drifted in, and took her through Angel's injuries.

". . . Paula, you have to understand the human body is not designed to withstand vacuum. Basically the internal pressure turns it into a kind of low-tech bomb. All Bill's internal material tried to escape, through his skin, the orifices of his head and body. Bleeding everywhere. His lungs are torn. His blood vessels have been leaking. A few more seconds and he would have drowned in his own blood. His blood must have been close to boiling in his veins."

"Will he live?"

Rosenberg shrugged. "Sure. For a while. We all will, for a while. But if he was at home he'd be hospitalized."

"We aren't at home."

"And, Paula—"

"What?"

"His brain was starved of oxygen. I don't even know how long for."

That helps, she thought bleakly.

"What was that fluid, on the inside of his visor?"

"The clear stuff?" His face was neutral. "Oh, that. I did tell him to keep his eyes shut. His left eye ruptured, and—"

Benacerraf felt bile pool at the back of her throat. She made it into the waste management area in time to throw up, violently, into the commode.

She wiped her mouth on a wet-wipe, the antiseptic stinging her tongue.

In his quarters, Angel was waking up. He was starting to scream.

Book Four
GROUND TRUTH
A.D. 2014–A.D. 2015

Voyager One **flew high** above the plane of the ecliptic, that invisible sheet in space which contains the orbits of the major planets of the Solar System.

Voyager was a spindly dragonfly construction, of booms and struts and instrument platforms, and a huge antenna which pointed back at Earth. Built around a compact ten-sided box, it weighed about a ton, and was big enough to fill a small house.

During its long mission, it had visited both the Solar System's largest planets, Jupiter and Saturn. The gravitational fields of those worlds had flung *Voyager* onward at such a high speed that it had broken the bonds which once tied it to the sun.

Now, *Voyager One* was racing across space at a million miles per day, heading for the stars.

But in the year 2014, an expected command from Earth did not arrive.

Voyager had been designed to operate during an extended lifetime and at a great distance from Earth, with an hours-long downlink-uplink communications round-trip time. Since contact with the ground would not be continuous, the spacecraft could know if it had lost contact with Earth only if it missed an expected command. So the software embedded in its engineering flight computer contained a command loss subroutine.

When the command did not arrive on schedule, an internal alarm went off.

The computer went into an algorithm designed to protect the spacecraft and its mission.

First *Voyager* was placed in a stable, passive state. Then, for two weeks, *Voyager* waited for the ground control to solve whatever problem had arisen on Earth, and to send the spacecraft a new command sequence. The basic design assumption was that the control centers would be sending a stream of commands, frantically trying to get the spacecraft's attention.

When no command sequence was received *Voyager* assumed the fault was with itself. It went through an emergency routine, in a bid to reestablish contact with the Deep Space Network stations.

The procedure worked in a loop. First the computer tried to figure out whether the craft's radio antenna was still pointing at Earth. *Voyager* had sensors to detect the sun, and fixed, bright stars like Canopus; it knew where it was in three-dimensional space. The craft was smart enough to know where Earth should be, relative to the fixed stars, at any moment during the extended mission.

So the software checked the angles, and the antenna was pointed at Earth.

Still no commands were detected.

Voyager's next assumption was that its radio receiver was dead. So it shut down its primary radio and turned on its backup receiver. It broadcast telemetry to Earth, indicating what it thought might have happened.

There was no response from Earth.

Voyager went back to the beginning of the loop, and began the reacquisition process once more . . .

It could not know there was nobody on Earth who was listening, any more, to voices from the sky.

The Space Shuttle orbiter *Discovery* sailed over the equator of Titan, five hundred miles above rust-brown cloud tops. It was flying with its payload bay facing the clouds, and its instruments, battered by their billion-mile flight, peered down at the hidden surface. The blunt heatshields of two Apollo capsules, facing Titan, glowed in the light of the world they had come so far to challenge.

☆   ☆   ☆

Nicola Mott sat in the flight deck commander's seat, loosely strapped in.

Titan hung above the flight deck windows, above her head.

From pole to pole, she could see no differences, no details in the drab burnt-brown clouds, no breaks, no structure. There was perhaps a subtle shading, the south hemisphere a little lighter than the north. But the light was so uncertain that Mott couldn't be sure. And Titan was dark, darker than the enhanced *Voyager* and *Cassini* images had led her to expect, a deep dull brown rather than orange.

It was almost like the flybys of Venus again, Mott thought. Here was the same perfect sphere, the billiard-ball-smooth sheen of haze and cloud, hiding any glimpse of the ground. But the light of the sun was less than a hundredth its strength at Venus; the clouds of Venus had been dazzling white, almost blinding, like sheets of sunlight. Titan looked almost spectral, somber, the ochre hue of its clouds drawn from the palette of some obsessive, gloomy painter.

And Titan was a small world. Its curve was evident, much more so than Earth from low orbit, and its orange-brown belly protruded at Mott, shaded, obviously three-dimensional.

Discovery rolled into another two-hour sunrise.

Mott watched the sun lift through the cloud layers. The thin light, occluded by the air, gave her glimpses of structure: onion-skin layers deep in the clouds, perhaps the glimmerings of faint outer shells, beyond the bulk of the atmosphere.

And Saturn rise was . . . remarkable.

The planet was like a sculpture of glass, two or three feet across, held at arms's length. Saturn itself was a fat ball of milky yellow crystal, at the heart of a plate of shining rings. The rings—contained well within the orbit of Titan—were tipped up, from Mott's perspective; they emerged from darkness on the face of the planet, and formed a thin, banded ellipse. Looking along the rings, Mott could see other moons, a string of glowing crescent-beads.

Under the clouds of Titan the sky would be hidden. It was going to be hell to know that *Saturn itself* was suspended above the clouds, as motionless as Earth in the black sky of the Moon, and yet forever invisible.

The hatch opened. Benacerraf and Rosenberg came bustling onto the flight deck, up the tunnel from the orbiter's mid deck. Through the open access-way to the mid deck—through the airlock and the connecting tunnel to the hab module—Mott could hear the aimless crooning of Bill Angel, blind and alone. His gull-like cries were diminished by distance; sound didn't carry well in the reduced pressure of the hab module.

Mott said, "What do you want?"

"We have to talk," Rosenberg said.

Benacerraf looked at Mott and shrugged.

Mott, reluctantly, released her restraints and pulled herself across the cabin.

Rosenberg said, "We have to discuss Bill. How in hell are we going to get him to the surface?"

Benacerraf sighed. "Damn your logical mind, Rosenberg."

But it's a non-question, Mott thought. She avoided the eyes of the others; she stared at the dull ochre Titan highlights on the instrument panels. She said, "Logical, maybe, but he's starting from an assumption."

"What assumption?"

"That we take Bill down at all."

There was a long silence.

The three of them drew closer together like conspirators, Mott thought, their hair drifting in the sluggish currents of the air. They were gaunt, withered by years of microgravity and a lousy diet and canned air; they must look like three witches, gathered around some spell-book, plotting the fate of another human being.

Benacerraf said at last, "There is nowhere to leave him. We're taking *Discovery* down too, remember."

"I know," Mott said. "That doesn't alter the suggestion."

Rosenberg raised graying eyebrows. "Right. And *you'll* be the one who will shove him out the airlock."

Mott opened her mouth to reply.

Benacerraf said, "This isn't doing us any good. Niki, Bill Angel didn't ask to finish up as he has. He's just turned out to be the weakest of us, is all. It could have been any of us. And now, he's a billion miles from the nearest person who can help him. Save for us. So we take him down."

"Anyhow," Rosenberg said, "you know what Houston says. Maybe being returned to a stable gravity environment will help bring Bill out of this. He's always going to be disabled, of course. But he was a competent astronaut. Maybe he can still be useful."

"And you believe that?" Mott said mildly.

"Enough," Benacerraf snapped.

Mott thought about pushing it.

After six years, she was sick of Benacerraf's peevish bossiness. One day, perhaps, she was going to have to challenge the authority that Benacerraf assumed so easily. But now wasn't the time.

"Which returns me to my original question," Rosenberg said. "How do we get him to the surface?"

Benacerraf frowned. "Each Apollo can hold one, two, three—even all four of us if it has to. Logically, we ought to split evenly between the capsules: two and two."

Rosenberg shook his head. "I got to advise against that. We know little enough about this Titan entry as it is, and we're not sure how the Apollos will behave, after a couple of decades in store and six years of space soak. Anything could happen. Who would want to be alone in a failing Command Module with Bill Angel?"

"Even if he was sedated?"

"Even so. Paula, the entry is going to take hours, remember."

Mott said, "We could all four of us ride down in the one capsule. It wouldn't be comfortable, but with a couch installed in the lower equipment bay—"

"Again, bad idea," Rosenberg said. "We ought to go down separately. If one Apollo has a bad landing, we only hurt half the crew; the rest are on hand to help."

"But," Benacerraf said, evidently irritated, "that logic leaves us with only one combination. *One and three*: one person alone, and two of us sandwiching Angel. Hardly an ideal."

"Well," Mott said angrily, "it might not be what we planned. But it's what we're left with. We never planned for Siobhan to get herself killed—"

"Nicola. The one alone. It has to be you."

That hadn't occurred to Mott. "Tell me why," she said.

"You're the nearest thing to a pilot we have left. I could trust you to fly that Apollo down alone, but not myself or Rosenberg."

To fly down to the surface of Titan, a new world, alone . . . She felt an odd mixture of exhilaration and sheer, unadulterated fear.

It would be the first time the crew had been separated, since the launch day.

The three of them gathered a little closer, watching each other, as if in awe of how far they had traveled together, of what they were planning now.

"All right," Mott said. "I'll do it."

Both Rosenberg and Benacerraf, simultaneously and apparently on impulse, reached out towards her. Physical contact had become a major taboo for them all; but now they held onto each other's arms, feebly hugging.

Benacerraf said, "We don't have anything to fear. We can do this. We'll be there for you when you land."

"Sure," said Mott. "See you in the mud."

Rosenberg tugged at his wispy beard. "We need another name. A call-sign for the base camp, the landing site of the orbiter . . . You know, in Greek mythology the Titans were a family of giants, the children of Uranus and Gaia, the sky and the Earth. Before the gods, they sought to rule the heavens. You'll know some of their names: Rhea, Tethys, Iapetus, Hyperion, Phoebe. And others—Cronos, the leader, Oceanus, Coeus, Crius, Mnemosyne. Their stronghold was Mount Othrys, a counterpart of Mount Olympus."

"Oh," Benacerraf said. "Hence the Geological Survey name for our friendly ice mountain down there. So what happened to the Titans?"

"Cronos overthrew Uranus, his father. But then there was a ten-year battle, between the Titans and the gods. Zeus beat out Cronos by bringing in Hundred-armed Giants—the Hecatoncheires—as his allies. Then the Titans were imprisoned, for eternity, in Tartarus. They were locked behind huge bronze doors, and the Hundred-armed Giants were appointed jailers—"

"Tartarus? Where's that?"

Rosenberg pulled a face. "You don't want to know. A place as far below Hades as Hades is below Heaven."

Mott stabbed a finger at Titan. "Then that's the name for our colony. Where we're going to have to live out the rest of our lives. Underneath all that orange shit. *Tartarus.*"

Nobody disagreed.

The rusty light of Titan, washing from the hab module's multiple monitors, made their skin look old, pallid.

Mott lay on her back in the center couch of Apollo Command Module CM-115, now known as *Jitterbug.*

She was alone in here. She was wearing her orange pressure suit. Cool air washed over her face, inside her helmet, bringing with it a smell of plastic and metal; all around her the fans and pumps of the Command Module clicked and whirred. It was a mundane, comforting noise, louder than a Shuttle orbiter or the hab module, somehow more obviously mechanical; it was like being inside some huge, elaborate clock.

She looked ahead, through the small docking windows set in *Jitterbug*'s nose.

She was sailing backward over the orange-brown cloud-sea of Titan. She was in Titan's shadow, but some light was diffused forward by the thick atmosphere, so that the clouds before *Jitterbug* were a blanket of rusty oranges and browns, fading into curved darkness far ahead of her.

And now, in her side windows, the sun rose, a spot of light like a helicopter searchlight, rising up from the blurred haze, the multiple layers of atmosphere she would, today, traverse.

It was probably the last dawn she would ever witness.

"Hey there, *Jitterbug*."

It was Benacerraf. Mott flicked the switch on her microphone wire. "I hear you, *Bifrost*."

"I can see you, fat as a goose."

She twisted in her couch. And there, framed by the small window to her right, was *Bifrost*. The familiar cone profile of the second Apollo, illuminated by Titan light, was unmistakable.

In space, the various upgrades were obvious. No attempt had been made to refurbish the Apollos' old ablative heat-shields. The base of *Bifrost*, which would take the brunt of the entry heating, was coated by black silica-based tiles, the same material used on the undersurface of the Shuttle orbiters, bonded to an aluminum honeycomb beneath. And the upper conical surface, which would reach much lower temperatures, was coated with white Nomex felt tiles. The black and white finish, punctured by windows and the gaping mouths of reaction control nozzles, gave *Bifrost* an oddly modern look, Mott thought, compared to the baroque silver hulls of the old Moon-mission designs.

Strapped to *Bifrost*'s base there was another novelty. The classic fat silver cylinder of the Apollo Service Module was replaced by a squat tube six feet long—about half the length of the Command Module—with a fat, flaring nozzle. This was a PAM-D-II, a payload assist module. It was a Thiokol solid rocket booster which had been used as an upper stage for launching satellites from Shuttle and Earth-orbit flights. It was strapped to the center of *Bifrost*'s heatshield by metal straps, which would be severed by pyrotechnic bolts. The PAM would be used to knock *Bifrost* out of orbit . . .

Discovery had already been flown down, under automatics, to the surface. So here were two Apollo Command Modules, flying in formation around a moon of Saturn.

"Okay, Niki," Benacerraf called over now. "You ready for your preburn checklist?"

"I got it." The checklist was Velcroed to the instrument panel in front of Mott.

"Thrust switches to normal."

Mott closed her switches. "Thrust switches normal."

"Inject prevalves on."

"Okay. Prevalves on."

"One minute to the burn, Niki. Arm the translational controller."

"Armed . . ."

The crews had agreed that Mott, alone in *Jitterbug*, would be walked through her entry burn first, with the aid of Rosenberg and Benacerraf. *Bifrost* would descend an orbit later, two hours after Mott.

Thus, Mott would be the first human to land on Titan.

She had been given the mission's remaining flag to set up, a plastic-coated Stars and Stripes, neatly wrapped in a little cellophane bundle. And on her chest was stitched a tiny Union Jack.

"Thirty seconds," Benacerraf said. "Thrust-on enable, Niki."

Mott unlocked the control and gave it a half-turn.

"Fifteen seconds. That's it. You've done it, Niki. Sit tight, now."

Sit tight. Sure. And what if the PAM-D doesn't fire, after six years of space soak? The PAM-Ds were pretty reliable, but had been known to fail, even in Earth orbit, a couple of hours after leaving the KSC pad. And nobody was sure what would happen if those straps failed to sever, and a Command Module finished up carrying a PAM-D, partially expended, through the fires of entry.

She braced herself for the kick in the back.

"Two, one."

There was a bang, a rattly thrust which pushed her into her couch. It had the crisp, crude sharpness characteristic of solid rocket burns. The push felt enormous, but she knew it was no more than a half-G.

There was a green light before her.

"Retrofire," she said.

"Copy the retrofire, Niki. See you on the ground. Don't mess up the place before we get there."

"I won't."

The burn lasted thirty seconds, yellow rocket light flaring from the PAM-D nozzle ahead of *Jitterbug*.

The thrust died.

She heard a thump of pyrotechnics, a clatter against the hull, like birds hopping over a tin roof. It was the straps holding the PAM-D against the heatshield; they had burned through, and the PAM-D was discarded. After a few seconds she could see it through her window, a squat cylinder spinning away over the orange clouds, shiny straps dangling, abandoned after being hauled across two billion miles for its half-minute of service.

Jitterbug was still in orbit around Titan. But Mott's orbit now would take her dipping deep into the outer layers of Titan's thick atmosphere. And there, she would lose so much energy that she would not be able to climb out again.

She was, she knew, committed.

"Godspeed, Niki," Benacerraf called distantly.

Six hundred miles above the surface of Titan, on the fringe of the deep, massive atmosphere, Mott felt the first brushes of deceleration. The couch frame dug into her microgravity-softened flesh.

In her window, she could still see Saturn, like a gigantic, gaudy toy.

There was a rattle of solenoids. Outside the windows, to her left and right, there were little flashes of light. That was the gas of the RCS clusters, flaring against the air of Titan. The onboard computer was trying to keep *Jitterbug* in its forty-mile-wide reentry corridor, before the air thickened so much that the reaction control system was disabled.

A light came on before her. It was the oh-five-G light, the measure of the first feeble tugs of deceleration.

Five hundred miles high, Mott passed through the first haze layer. It was a shell of faint rusty light, which seemed to coalesce above her, blurring Saturn's image.

It ought to be a gentle entry. CM-115 was entering the atmosphere from low circular orbit around Titan. It would have to shed a mile per second against atmospheric friction. That compared to the Earth-orbital velocity of five miles per second survived by the Shuttle, Gemini and Mercury, and with the even greater seven miles per second survived by Apollo capsules returning from the Moon. The peak deceleration, in the next few minutes, ought to be no more than one and a half G. That was eminently survivable by an Apollo—even a Command Module that had been in storage for most of Mott's lifetime . . .

The pressure mounted, climbing fast, impossibly quickly, slamming her into the couch. Titan's thin, cold upper atmosphere was hauling at *Jitterbug* in earnest.

. . . Assuming, of course, the theoretical models of Titan's atmosphere were right. And Mott, after six years in microgravity, for all her exercising, wasn't as robust as she used to be.

A pale, gray-white glow began to gather at the base of the window. It was plasma, the atoms of Titan's air smashed to pieces by the passage of this intruder from Earth, gathering in a thickening shock layer beneath the Command Module. The air of Earth produced a pinkish, almost welcoming glow on reentry. But the light of Titan's plasma, a thin mix of ionized nitrogen, methane and argon, was a cold pearl-gray glow.

Even the plasma was alien here.

Benacerraf was still speaking to her, she realized belatedly. She tried to call back, to acknowledge; but Benacerraf's voice was breaking up in static as the plasma shell engulfed *Jitterbug*.

A hundred and eighty miles above the surface, the deceleration peaked. Mott lay on her back, buffeted, compressed, while the cabin equipment rattled around her. She was deep in the atmosphere, moving at Mach twenty. The weight on her was huge, crushing, worse than anything she had imagined in six years of anticipation of this ordeal. The surges in deceleration seemed astonishingly abrupt, violent. She could feel her internal organs sliding over each other, flattening against her spinal column. Her limbs felt as brittle as twigs, her muscles as limp as wet string; she didn't dare move a limb. She didn't seem to have the strength to draw in a breath, and she felt panic creeping over her as the oxygen in her lungs grew depleted.

The colors leached out of the big clunky control panel in front of her, and walls of darkness closed in around her vision. It was hard even to blink, to relieve the dryness of her eyes. Her mouthpiece felt like an iron bar being forced against her jaw. Unable to see a chronometer, she tried to count, to reduce this experience to a finite time that must pass. *A thousand and one. A thousand and two . . .*

She couldn't concentrate. She lost count. She wasn't even able to maintain the rhythm of the count.

Starved of blood and oxygen, her brain was closing down.

The darkness at the fringe of her vision closed in, like sweeping curtains.

Then, as suddenly as it had mounted, the pressure faded. The weight on her chest was lifted off. She sucked in air, her chest expanding against emptiness.

The glow of the plasma was fading. Beyond *Jitterbug*'s window there was a rusty orange glow. Already she was deep within the air-ocean of this drowned moon; above her was a hundred miles of murky aerosol haze, a hundred miles of cigarette smoke.

For the first time in six years, Mott's sky was no longer black.

The fiery entry phase was already over. The G meter read nought point one four—Titan gravity, one-seventh of a G. Three minutes after leaving orbit she was falling, alone, towards a hidden landscape, at nine hundred miles an hour.

Now, the first drogue parachute should deploy. It would burst from the parachute compartment in *Jitterbug*'s nose with a pyrotechnic bang, blowing away the apex cover of the compartment, and then open with a snap . . .

Nothing happened.

She checked her mission timer and G-meter against the checklist, still fixed to the control panel before her.

The drogue should have opened by now. If the drogue didn't open, neither would the main chutes.

Shit, she thought. What did I miss?

She punched the manual drogue deploy button.

After a few seconds she heard the bang of the drogue's pyrotechnics. The drogue chute hauled at the capsule, jolting her hard into her couch.

Jitterbug's velocity slowed—in thirty seconds and five miles—to three hundred feet per second, well below the speed of sound.

A hundred miles up, the air temperature outside was minus 120 degrees C.

Another bang. That had to be the mains, the three eighty-footer ringsails which would lower *Jitterbug* gently to the surface of Titan. Through the little docking windows above her Mott could see the main chutes as they unfolded, streaming upward lazily in the thickening air. The chutes were unbleached, to save weight; they were yellow, like three big dirty jellyfish.

Jitterbug became a huge pendulum, swinging on a wide, slow path, suspended beneath the mains, in Titan's feeble gravity taking all of forty-five seconds to complete a cycle; it was a slow, comforting rocking.

She felt her heartbeat slow, the moment of panic over.

What did I miss?

The Command Module was supposed to be controlling its own sequence of operations, now, as it went through its cycle of pyrotechnic explosions and parachute deployment. The main Arming Timer fired the pyrotechnics in a hard-wired sequence keyed to deceleration measured by a G-switch. The idea was to improve reliability, to provide a hardware-managed timelining that was independent of the Command Module's computer processor and software.

That was the idea, anyhow. She scanned back up her checklist.

. . . Oh.

She had been supposed to enable the whole system by throwing a couple of switches, to start the Titan landing system and disable the reaction control shutdown. She should have done that just after emerging from the heavy deceleration of the entry phase.

She hadn't. Maybe if she hadn't been alone, she wouldn't have missed it.

So far it all seemed to be working, however. Except for her human error. Everything—her life—depended on how robust the reworked systems now proved to be, in the face of that mistake.

She heard a rattle of solenoids; the capsule jerked about, startling her.

It was the reaction control thrusters. They were still firing, trying to damp oscillations in the vehicle's attitude, their action futile so deep in the atmosphere. It shouldn't be happening. The RCS should have been disabled, at the start of the auto sequence that she'd missed.

She snapped the RCS switch to OFF. The solenoid rattle died immediately.

The fact was, she was off the nominal program, now.

By failing to enter that command to start the new customized automated sequence, she was having *Jitterbug* follow fallback paths. Fifty-year-old logic paths, designed, originally, for entry into Earth's comparatively benign atmosphere. And although those logic paths had been tested out, there was no way they could have been made as safe as the primary path . . .

She felt a flicker of unease.

For fifteen minutes *Jitterbug* drifted under its main chutes, its speed gradually dropping. It was as if she was suspended above the surface of Titan in the metallic gondola of some balloon.

She monitored the Command Module's clunky systems, waiting for the next glitch, the next anomaly.

She tried the periscope display. This was an oval piece of glass about a foot across set in the middle of the instrument panel before her. The periscope gave her a fish-eye view of the surface, looking down past the scorched white tiles of the hull:

A layer of thin white cloud, like cirrus, came ballooning up around her. Methane ice. Once through that, she looked down on a rolling, unbroken layer of thick, dark methane-nitrogen clouds, hiding the murky ground below. The clouds were almost Earthlike: fat, fluffy cumuli . . .

She could turn the periscope this way and that, with a little joystick in front of her. She imagined the tiny lens poking out of the hull and swiveling, above her head. The periscope had actually been cannibalized from an antique Mercury capsule, one of the original production run, which had been designed without windows; the periscope had been installed after protests from the astronauts to give them a view.

Even the effort of twisting the joystick seemed to deplete the muscles of her hand. It was going to take her a good while after landing before she had acclimatized enough to clamber out of her couch and try cracking the hatch.

After fifteen minutes the Command Module's velocity was reduced to a hundred and twenty feet per second, and she was ninety miles above the surface. Now, with a crack of pyrotechnics above her, the main chute was jettisoned.

For an instant she was falling freely.

And then the final chute, the paraglider, opened up; and she was jolted back into her couch once more.

She let out her breath. She was through another command sequence which hadn't gone wrong. Maybe she would live through this yet.

The paraglider was just a shaped canopy, marginally steerable. It was another old idea, that had been tried out for Gemini. Thus, a Gemini paraglider and a Mercury periscope should let Mott fly an Apollo capsule, like Dumbo, down to the wreck of a Shuttle orbiter, a billion miles from home . . .

Fifty miles above the ground, *Jitterbug* was immersed in thickening orange petrochemical haze. But the sun was still plainly visible as a brilliant disc, surrounded by an aureole, a yellow-brown halo.

Mott swiveled her periscope until Saturn was fixed at the center of her oval window. But already the water-color yellow wash of Saturn's surface was becoming fainter, obscured by the uniform brown smear of the smog. She stared into the periscope until at last the planet's fat, elliptical outline was lost, as if fading out on a poorly tuned TV screen, and the cloud closed over.

The sun, she saw, had vanished too. She had watched her last dawn, her last sunset. She was stuck down here, for good or ill.

Forty miles high, *Jitterbug* fell out of the condensate haze, into a layer of clearer air. Then, at thirty miles, it penetrated the fat methane clouds. The temperature was close to its minimum here, at minus two hundred degrees Centigrade. The clouds were dark, brooding, as if stormy. Deep within the clouds, the cabin grew dark, and the lights of the instruments on the panel before her seemed to glow brighter.

Suddenly the altimeter kicked in. She was at a hundred and fifty thousand feet, it said. Feet, not miles: the measure of an aircraft, ballooning down through Titan's atmosphere.

Jitterbug emerged from the base of the clouds, which now hid the orange sky.

Gradually, through mist and scattered cloud, for the first time, Titan's surface became visible to human eyes.

. . . Fluffy clouds of ethane vapor lay draped over glimmering circular lakes, which were cupped in continents of water ice. The liquid in those lakes was black to her vision, the round ponds puncturing the redbrown carcass of Titan like neat bullet-holes. It might have been a high-altitude view of Earth's surface, though rendered in somber, reds and browns, a twilit panorama . . .

She reached out and took hold of a handset on the panel in front of her. The handset controlled the paraglider, by tweaking at its cables. Using this she ought to be able to fly the Command Module right in to the orbiter, with an accuracy of—the designers had told her—a hundred yards or so. And in the limited VR sims they'd set up, she'd consistently scored better than that, getting down to within thirty or forty feet of the target.

But first she had to spot her target, the orbiter on the surface.

She peered anxiously into the periscope. The surface of Titan—in the fish-eye view, bulging towards her—was resolving into a landscape of mud and crater lakes. The smaller lakes, a couple of miles across, were simple circles. But she could see central peaks protruding from the centers of some of the larger lakes, their shores washed clean of muddy slush.

And now *Jitterbug* drifted over a pair of giant craters, each perhaps fifty miles across. In one of these the central peak seemed to have broadened into a dome, so that the ethane pool was contained in a thin ring around a central island. But she could see a pit at the center of the dome, itself containing a small pool, so the whole structure had a bull's-eye shape, with the solid circle and band of dark fluid contained by the circular crater rim. And in the second of the big craters, the outer annulus of fluid seemed to be heaped up against one wall of the crater—perhaps by some tidal effect—so that the lake was in the form of a semicircular horseshoe.

The landscape was strange, even the shape of the lakes bizarre.

This is Titan, she reminded herself with a shiver. *You are a billion miles from home. And there's nothing in human experience to guide you as to what you'll find here.*

The Command Module shuddered, the hull groaning.

She gripped her seat, hard. She could feel the hard metal frame through the thickness of her pressure suit gloves. The Command Module felt fragile around her; it was like being inside some flimsy aluminum bathysphere, descending into this murky orange ocean.

Now she was suspended over a mountain range, wrinkles in the glimmering surface. The peaks were exposed, dark gray water ice bedrock, and the uniform orange coating of the lower ground lay in streaks that followed the contours of the mountain, like snow runs.

The area looked familiar from Rosenberg's *Cassini* maps. She turned the periscope, jerking it from one side of the ship to the other.

There. A little way away from the range was a crater lake, the muddy liquid pooled in the shape of a cashew nut.

It was Clear Lake: just like the radar images. And Mount Othrys must be somewhere in that range below her.

. . . She caught a glimpse of white, embedded on the dried-blood surface like a splinter of bone protruding from a wound.

It was a delta-shape. *Discovery*.

She grinned fiercely, her spirits rising for the first time since Saturn had disappeared. She wouldn't even have to steer the paraglider much; now all she had to do was glide her way down this last ten thousand feet and—

There was a snap, somewhere in the wall high above her.

Murky air billowed into the cabin, above her face. There was a stink, of swamps and marshes and . . .

And methane. Titan air. And, mixed in with it, the sharp tang of nitrogen tetroxide, oxidizer from the RCS.

She couldn't believe it; she sat staring as the orange mush billowed down towards her. Following some antique command, the cabin pressure relief valve had opened. The valve was a two-inch nozzle designed to let in warm Pacific air, for returning Moon voyagers. It was *not* supposed to open on the way down to Titan.

It was the failure she had been waiting for. This had to be some consequence of her failing to follow the correct automation sequence earlier. Another untested logic path. But why the hell hadn't that damn valve simply been welded shut?

It was a multiple failure. Multiple failures always got you, in the end.

And while she lay here and thought about it, she had sucked in a lungful of freezing, toxic Titan air . . .

She closed her mouth and eyes and pulled her faceplate down. It snapped into place, and she felt a cool blue blast of oxygen on her face. She breathed out, trying to empty her lungs. But that, she realized, was only going to start the methane and nitrogen tet circulating in her life support.

The stink of swamp gas was overwhelming. And the nitrogen tet seemed to be burning at her lungs and eyes; she could barely see.

She considered trying to find some way to close that relief valve. But now she could barely see the instrument panel.

Anyhow, maybe it was better for the oxygen in the cabin to be overwhelmed by Titan air. If that methane caught a spark, *Jitterbug* would explode.

She was coughing, her throat and lungs aching.

The descent was nearly over, anyhow.

The cold air of Titan wrapped over her limbs. She found herself shivering already. When she got to the ground, she'd have to move quickly to get to the heated EVA suit. She rehearsed the moves she would make. Stand up, as best she could, and reach under the couch for the big net bag there; haul out the suit . . .

Jitterbug crashed into the tholin slush.

The fall was no more severe than if *Jitterbug* had been dropped on Earth from five or six feet. But to Mott it felt like a huge impact, an astonishing eruption of agony throughout her bruised body.

. . . And now the Command Module tipped to the right. She could feel the roll, see the orange-black landscape wheel past the windows. Perhaps the paraglider hadn't come loose, and was dragging *Jitterbug* over. Or perhaps she had landed on some kind of slope, a crater wall maybe, and was rolling.

Orange-brown mud splashed across the glass of the windows to her right, and turned them dark. Mott found herself hanging there in her straps, with cabin trash raining down around her: bits of paper, urine bags, discarded washcloths. The Stable 2 position, she thought. Upside down. One whole side of *Jitterbug* must be buried in the icy slush of Titan.

For a moment there was stillness, a cramped creaking as the hull cooled.

Then a window to her right cracked in two. Orange-black slush forced its way into the cabin, flowing, viscous.

Mott, suspended, began coughing again.

She was stuck in her seat. She couldn't move. She was going to freeze. Help was two hours away, or a billion miles, depending on how you looked at it.

When the Titan slush lapped against her legs, she could feel the cold of it seep into her bones.

No footprints and flags for me, after all. But I got here. I got to touch Titan.

The slush was rising. It would reach her head in a few seconds. She tried not to struggle.

So quickly, it was over.

Heat and cold, she thought; fire and ice. That's what separates Siobhan and me: fire and ice, at the extremities of the Solar System—

The slush forced its way through her faceplate, driving shards of plexiglass before it.

After its muddy splashdown, Command Module CM-115A settled deeper into the icy slush of Titan, its aluminum hull creaking as it cooled.

A wall-mounted camera peered at Benacerraf, as she lay in her couch, making history. She felt flat, deflated, battered by the events of the entry, the loss of contact with Nicola.

But she had her role to play.

She said, "Houston, *Bifrost*. Tartarus Base here. We have landed."

"Amen to that," said Rosenberg.

Without enthusiasm, she imagined how their words would be collected by *Cassini* and hurled across eighty light minutes, dispersing and growing fainter, to whoever on Earth was left to listen . . .

She turned her head. Every neck muscle ached; her head felt like a sack of water, ungainly and heavy, strapped to the top of her spine.

Rosenberg was sitting in the left-hand couch, Benacerraf the right. Angel was sandwiched between them in the center

couch, his bony body swathed in its bubble of orange pressure
suit, pressed up against Benacerraf. He was apparently at
peace, Benacerraf thought, his sedated madness contained for
now within the orange high-technology bubble of his suit.

The window to her right was already frosted, the condensation from their breath and sweat frozen against the glass.
She could see little of the landscape, in the murky twilight
beyond. Even after just a few minutes on the surface, the
tholin drizzle had coated the windows of *Bifrost* with a thin,
purple-brown, organic scum; it streaked down the window
like leaking oil.

The contrast with the warm, brightly-lit, mundane interior
of the Apollo was marked; to leave here, she thought, would be
like stepping out of your mom's kitchen into a stormy night.

But Rosenberg seemed to feel differently. Elated.

"We're here," Rosenberg said. "My God."

"Yes. We're here. But do you really think anybody gives a
damn any more?"

"I do," he said, his tone defiant. "I do. We achieved what we
set out to achieve. This is *Apollo 11*, all over again." He turned
to face her; there was a smile on his face, framed by his open
visor. "This is history, Paula. There's a new world out there.
You'll be the first: the first since Armstrong—"

"No," she snapped. "Nicola was the first, whatever has happened to *Jitterbug*. Don't you ever forget that."

Rosenberg turned away, and for a moment there was
silence, broken only by the hum of the Command Module's
systems.

She released her restraints.

The Apollo Command Module wasn't designed to land anywhere but Earth. So, it didn't have an airlock. When
Benacerraf opened the hatch, all the Earthlike air inside the
cabin was going to be lost, to be replaced by Titan's methane-
laced nitrogen. So all three of them, Angel included, would

have to be in their EMUs their extravehicular mobility units, their surface suits.

Therefore, by remorseless logic, Benacerraf and Rosenberg were going to have to strip and dress Angel.

Benacerraf got hold of the frame of her couch and pushed herself upright. The Command Module was so small her head was almost brushing the instrument panel above her.

There was a dull ringing in her ears. The colors leached from the instrument panel, and everything turned a dull golden-brown.

"Oh," she said. "Oh, wow."

Rosenberg was sitting up too, his face gray. "Just take it easy, Paula. Sit for a while. Let your body figure out which way is up."

"This one-seventh gravity is a killer, huh."

She could feel her heart laboring to pump blood up this unaccustomed gravity gradient. And this, she thought dismally, was with the assistance of the G-suit that was still compressing the slack blood vessels of her legs.

Slowly—after maybe ten minutes—the ringing subsided, and the colors returned. Her heart was still hammering, though.

Benacerraf knelt on her couch. With Rosenberg's help she reached over Angel, and hauled him off his couch and onto her own. His space-attenuated body weighed an effective thirty or forty pounds, she estimated. But even so it took real effort, by both of them, to wrestle him around the cluttered little cabin.

When Angel was transferred, she released latches and folded up his center couch, and stowed it away in the lower equipment bay, the roomier space beneath the couches. Now she was able to stand. With Rosenberg beside her, she began to work on the inert Angel.

She twisted off Angel's helmet and gloves and boots. She detached the umbilical tubes which connected his suit to the cabin's life support supplies, and pulled off his boots. Then, with Rosenberg, she hauled the heavy, elasticated pressure garment off Angel's limp, unresponsive limbs.

Underneath, Angel was already wearing his basic thermal underwear, with his Heating Garment over the top and a G-suit—inflatable rubber trousers—over that. Benacerraf began to strip off the G-suit.

Next she had to fit Angel's urine collector, a huge, unlikely condom.

She took a deep breath. She reached down and pushed her hand inside Angel's underwear. His groin was warm and faintly damp, she found, disgusted. She pulled Angel's penis out of his underwear.

Rosenberg laughed. "Where no man has gone before."

"Shut up, Rosenberg."

As she tried to push the condom over Angel's penis, he started to move. He was grinding his hips. She looked into his face. His ruined eyes were closed, of course, but there was a grin stretching his lips; a thin sheen of saliva glistened on his lower lip.

He was getting an erection; his grinding was pushing the penis against the palm of her hand.

She snatched her hands away. "Shit," she said.

Rosenberg laughed again. "Hot mike, commander."

"Fuck you, Rosenberg. Bill? Bill, can you hear me?"

Angel crooned wordlessly, rocking his head to left and right.

Rosenberg pressed an infuser to Angel's neck. Angel subsided, almost immediately. "Old bastard," Rosenberg said without malice. "The only bit of him that still works is his libido."

"And how," Benacerraf said, "are we going to get rid of *that*?"

At Angel's groin, the erection sprouted like a miniature flagpole, the veins thick.

Rosenberg grinned. "I always thought Bill was all hat and no horse."

"It's not funny, Rosenberg."

"Don't worry." He reached down to a storage compartment and pulled out a stainless steel spoon. He pressed its bowl against the frosty glass of the window behind him, and tapped the tip of Angel's glans with the chilled bowl.

Angel grunted and stirred.

The penis sagged immediately, like a deflated balloon.

"A nurse's trick I picked up during my med training," Rosenberg said. "Never thought I'd have to use it. And now I'm going to mark this damn spoon, to make sure I *never* eat with it."

Grimacing, Benacerraf reached down once more and tucked Angel's penis briskly into the condom.

With Rosenberg's help, she lifted Angel into his Beta-cloth outer garment. The sleeves and neck were terminated with steel rings that would snap onto Angel's EVA gloves and helmet. Now she fitted a tube over his condom attachment; there was a bag sewn into the outer garment to store a couple of pints of urine. Angel was already wearing a kind of diaper—an absorbent undergarment—that would soak up any bowel movement he couldn't defer.

Benacerraf hoped like hell he would defer. Wiping Angel's ass for him was one chore she hadn't yet had to endure, one aspect of Angel's descent into hell where he'd managed, so far, to hang onto a little dignity.

Benacerraf hauled Angel's PLSS—his Personal Life Support System, his backpack—up from storage lockers under the couches. The pack was a big, massive box coated in Beta-cloth. Here it weighed just twenty pounds, but she could feel the mass of the pack, its Newton's-laws inertia undiminished; she had to handle it carefully to avoid battering the control panels. Rosenberg leaned Angel forward, and Benacerraf lifted the backpack over him and strapped it in place round him. The packs were adapted Shuttle technology, with lightweight batteries for power, air and water circulation pumps and fans, and lithium hydroxide canisters for scrubbing out carbon dioxide. Not much more advanced than the packs which had sustained men on the Moon. The suits would support EVAs of seven or eight hours, if they were lucky.

Next came the fitting of Angel's umbilicals, hoses for air and water for the heating system. Rosenberg and Benacerraf worked across Angel's chest, locking each hose into place, double-checking each other's progress. "Locks checked, blue locks. Locks checked, red locks. Purge locks, double-locked . . ."

The surface of Titan represented a new challenge for EVA suit designers.

All previous EVAs—in Earth orbit, or on the Moon—had been in a vacuum. And the main challenge had been to surround the astronaut with an atmospheric pressure which, if not equivalent to Earth's, was at least sufficient to sustain life. So the astronauts wore pressure garments, bubbles inflated with oxygen.

On Titan, it was different. On Titan, the air was thick—thicker, in fact, than on Earth. The air wasn't breathable, and the astronauts still needed an Earth-equivalent air supply. But there was no need for pressurization against vacuum; the suits in that respect were a little more like deep-diving suits.

There was another novelty.

In the vacuum of space, the problem was keeping the astronaut's body cool. Solar heat could be reflected by white overgarments, and sufficient heat of the astronaut's own body could be retained by insulating layers; the trick was to wrap the body in a cooling garment—tubes of water to carry body heat away, and then radiate it into the vacuum.

Here on Titan, there was no vacuum. In the thick air conduction and convection would work rapidly to carry away heat. The main problem on Titan, in fact, was the deadly cold. If that frigid slush or the thick, sluggish air above it came into anything close to direct contact with an astronaut's flesh, life heat would be sucked away with frightening speed.

To combat the cold, the Titan suit was built on a Heating Garment—a sexless, skintight piece of clothing laced with wires and water pipes. The wires would heat the flesh, and the air which ran over it. It was like wearing an electric blanket. And the water in the tubes had high heat capacity; it would form a heat-retaining shell around the body. And over the heating suit the astronauts would wear layers of soft, insulating clothing.

The final outer garment was crude—much more primitive than the pressure suit—just layers of white Beta-cloth, fiberglass filaments coated with Teflon, with heat-retentive insulating material between, the chest unit studded with umbilical connectors and controls.

She fixed on Angel's Snoopy hat, his flight helmet with its radio earphones and microphone, and over the top of that Rosenberg lifted Angel's hard helmet with its visor, and twisted it into place against the seal at the neck. The last pieces of the suit were the gloves; these were close-fitting, and snapped onto rings at Angel's wrist.

Now Rosenberg flicked a switch on Angel's chest panel. Benacerraf could hear the soft, familiar hum of the pumps and fans in Angel's backpack, the whoosh of the oxygen-nitrogen mix inside his helmet.

Rosenberg and Benacerraf worked through suit checks. There was a panel on the front of Angel's chest which gave a digital readout of oxygen and carbon dioxide and pressure levels, and various malfunction warning lights. She could see Angel's oxygen pressure level stabilizing.

Rosenberg nodded, satisfied.

Benacerraf sat back on the cabin's right hand couch and peered into Angel's helmet. Once again, they had got Bill sealed away, locked into his own self-contained world, as if within a private spacecraft, his degeneration concealed by the gleaming white Beta-cloth layers.

Benacerraf and Rosenberg got into their own suits.

A half-hour later, when they were done, they studied each other.

Their names were stitched on the chests of the shining white suits, and the NASA logo and the Stars-and-Stripes were proudly emblazoned on their sleeves; they wore bright blue overboots, blue gloves. In the bulky suits, hardly able to move in the cramped cabin, they looked faintly ludicrous, like three snowmen, Benacerraf thought.

Rosenberg checked his suit display, and the status of the Command Module from a control panel.

"For the record," he said, "we have a go for vent."

"Affirmative," Benacerraf said. "We're all sealed up. Go for vent."

"All right." Rosenberg closed a switch on the wall.

Vents in the base and apex of the Command Module opened up. There was a harsh hiss.

There was a muddy brown swirl around Benacerraf's feet. The thick air of Titan was forcing its way into the lower-pressure cabin of *Bifrost*. She watched the little dials on the instrument panel, yellow and green and red, bright primary Earth colors. The smog of Titan dimmed them, washing the dials over in an orange-brown murk.

"Okay," Rosenberg said. "Everything is go. We are just waiting for the cabin pressure to equalize with the exterior sufficiently to open the hatch . . ."

His voice is becoming stilted, Benacerraf thought. He's speaking for the camera. For the history books.

The hiss died away.

Rosenberg checked his gauges. "That's it," he said. "One and a half bars; pressure has equalized. You should be able to open the hatch now, Paula."

Her heart thumping, suddenly conscious of the camera on her, Benacerraf turned.

Apollo's hatch was a rectangle, two feet high and three wide, behind the center couch of the cabin. There was a window in the middle of it, already stained with tholin smears.

Benacerraf pulled at the hatch's single handle. She could hear the twelve locking latches click open. The hatch swung outward, easily.

The open doorway framed a rectangle of mud-brown ground, laced by some darker substance. The Command Module seemed to have sunk into the slush, almost to the depth of the door frame.

She looked back at Rosenberg, who was standing between the two couches, watching her. Angel still seemed to be unconscious, sprawled like a flaccid white balloon on the right-hand couch.

Rosenberg took a camera down off its bracket on the wall, and focused on her. He said, "You ready for your one small step?"

It was what Tom Lamb had once said to her, floating in the light of Earth, long ago.

"Let's do it."

To get out of the narrow hatch, Benacerraf had to turn around and crawl out backwards. Rosenberg, keeping the camera focused on her, guided her. "You're lined up nicely. Come back towards me . . . Okay, put your foot down . . . you're doing fine . . . A little more."

At last she found herself with her head outside the conical hull of Apollo, one foot on the floor of the capsule, and the other resting on the edge of the hatch.

She looked around.

It was *dark*.

Darker than she'd expected, like a late, murky evening. The *Huygens* images and *Bifrost*'s own monitors, light-enhanced, had fooled her.

The ground was a plain, slightly undulating, thick with slush. A reddish-brown color dominated everything, although swathes of darker material streaked the landscape. The Command Module sat squat, a metal tent on a muddy, empty plain. The slush must be deep, she thought; even here, at the center of *Bifrost*'s splash crater, no bedrock water ice was exposed.

She couldn't see the horizon through the dense, smoggy air. She knew that if she could crack her helmet, the air's cargo of hydrocarbons would have made it smell like an oil refinery.

She lit up her helmet lamp. A pool of white light splashed on the ground. Organics glistened on the surface of the slush, moist, like flayed human tissue.

Rosenberg passed her the TV camera. She fixed it to a bracket which folded out of the exterior hull of Apollo. Rosenberg tested the camera on a monitor inside the Command Module. "Okay, the picture's good," he said. "A little dark and drab maybe, but nothing that a little image processing can't fix."

She said, "I'm in the hatchway. The Command Module has sunk into the surface through several inches, before the slush compacted to stop it. I can't see any exposed ice. The basic color of the slush is a deep orange, or brown, but it's laced with purples and blacks. Organics, I guess. It looks like nothing so much as mud—Houston gumbo, with a little industrial waste laced in."

"It's called tholin," Rosenberg said drily.

"Yeah. And 'tholin' is Greek for mud," she snapped back. "Gumbo it is. All right. I'm going to step out of *Bifrost* now."

She lifted her left foot off the door frame, reached out, and pushed it into the Titan gumbo. She tested her weight. She could feel the slush compacting, but even so her foot sank in several inches.

She tried to lift her foot out. The gumbo was clinging, heavy, and as it came free her boot made a sucking sound that carried through her helmet.

She left behind a saucer-sized crater, into which the gumbo oozed slowly. There was no distinguishable footstep—

unlike Armstrong's, she thought wistfully, which ought to persist in the crisp lunar dust for a million years. And when she tried to dig a furrow in the gumbo with her toe, she created a shallow valley that filled in almost immediately, without leaving a mark.

There was already tholin, splashed up from her tentative explorations, staining the white fabric coating her legs.

She replaced her left foot, and then lifted her right foot out over the bottom of the hatchway and planted it in the gumbo, still holding onto the hatchway with both hands.

She let the gumbo take her weight.

She sank a few inches. But then the combination of the slush's consistency and her own lightness in this one-seventh gravity stopped her falling further.

She let go of the door frame, and she was standing on Titan.

She took a couple of steps forward. Once again she found it a real effort to lift her feet out of the clinging, sticky slush.

A breeze, fat and massive, buffeted her; the thick air moaned around her helmet.

She knelt down, pushing against the resistance of the suit, in the slush. Where her knee took her weight she could feel the diamond patterns of the wires and tubes sewn into her heating garment, and the chill of the slush penetrated to her flesh and bone. The orange-brown, sticky gumbo lapped over her legs, coating the pristine whiteness of her Beta-cloth suit. The ground was streaked, complex, inhomogeneous, full of chemistry.

She felt a sudden, visceral thrill; suddenly she knew the rightness of what they had done, to come here. This was no dead world, of rocks and geology, like the Moon. This material had been *processed*, for four billion years. She could tell, just looking at it. Save for the home world itself, this must be the most Earthlike world in the System.

She reached down, and dipped her blue gloves into the

slush. The sticky gumbo dripped down through her fingers, like ocean bottom ooze.

She said: "This is the stuff of life."

She took some experimental steps forward, walking away from the Command Module.

There was none of the exhilarating balloon-like floating which the Apollo astronauts had been able to achieve, bouncing off the hard surface of the Moon. The gumbo sucked at her feet, and her backpack, while not heavy, was an obvious mass at her back, throwing off her center of balance.

She found it hard to tell where the vertical was. On Earth, tipping a couple of inches either way was enough to trigger the balance mechanisms in her ears. But in this soft gravity she felt she could tilt a long way before her body could sense it; and in the murky gloom, on the dips and folds of the smoothed-out landscape, her visual cues weren't strong. It all added to the feeling of strangeness.

She stopped, maybe twenty feet from the Command Module, and turned around.

The Command Module was a teepee before her, stuck in a broad splash crater. It had very evidently been dropped, from a great height, into the gumbo. The slush had washed up, viscous and sticky, against the lower hull, swamping the lower reaction thruster nozzles; and the powder-white upper surface of Apollo was streaked with purplish tholin deposits. In the open hatchway, Rosenberg was framed against a rectangle of glowing white light; it looked blue-green, in fact, Earth-like, in contrast with the burned orange of the rest of the landscape.

The camera sat on its stand, panning and focusing automatically.

She turned away.

Bifrost had come down in a shallow depression. Towards the horizon, beyond this slushy plain, there were rolling hills. They were the foothills surrounding Mount Othrys, she knew. The horizon itself was lost in gloom and haze.

The peaks were stained dark red and yellow, with slashes of ochre on their flanks, and streaks of gray, exposed water ice at the higher elevations. The landscape looked as if it had been water-colored by an unimaginative, heavy-handed child. There were scars in the hills' profiles, perhaps left by recent icefalls. The profiles looked oddly softened: these were mountains of ice, not rock, after all. Clouds, red and orange, swirled above the hills. The clouds were fat methane cumuli, fifteen or twenty miles high, dark and oppressive.

This is ancient, unmarked terrain, she thought. Despite Rosenberg's hypothesizing, she had the intuition that there had been no life here, no births, no bodies buried under this complex ground.

Bifrost had come down close to the center of the hemisphere that was turned away from Saturn. It was actually a little before local noon. They would have four or five days before Titan's orbit around the primary would rotate the moon so that the invisible sun set, beyond the banks of cloud and haze. Then they would have to endure eight or ten days of darkness, while this face of the moon was turned away from the sun, before the next, protracted "dawn."

So this was midday on Titan: as bright as it would get. It was like a dim twilight on Earth. Standing in the gumbo in this muddy light, in fact, was like being at the bottom of a pond.

In the half-distance she could see a splash of yellow-brown, like spilled paint. That must be *Bifrost*'s discarded parachute. They would have to reclaim that later, she knew; in the years to come—if they were to survive—they would need the cloth, everything they could salvage. Beyond the chutes she could clearly see the white, gumbo-streaked form of *Discovery*, perhaps a half-mile from *Bifrost*. It looked as if the orbiter had dug a shallow furrow in the surface of Titan, when it had come in from orbit for its automated glide landing.

And, a little further away, she saw a bone-white teepee shape. That had to be *Jitterbug*, Nicola's Apollo. She couldn't tell if *Jitterbug* was upright or not.

"Paula. Check your infrared."

Benacerraf pressed the switch on her chest panel which turned her visor into a crude night-vision monitor. This was an adapted bit of military technology.

The world turned brighter, but gray and blotchy, ill-defined in the long wavelengths of infrared. The icy landscape was cold, dark, like a cloudy, Moonless night on Earth.

Bifrost, with its open hatch, was suddenly dazzling bright, a thing of straight lines and rectangles, still intensely hot compared to the thin cold of the rest of Titan's landscape; that bulk of metal, she guessed, would take some hours to dissipate its heat entirely, before it turned as dark, in her new vision, as the ice which was consuming it. When she turned, she could easily see *Discovery* and *Jitterbug*, glowing like diamonds on the ice.

She looked down towards her feet, at her own body. Even through the insulating layers of Beta-cloth she was glowing with heat, her hands and arms clearly visible, shining; in infrared, she looked like an angel descended to this icy world, alight with fire from the inner Solar System.

She lifted her head, tipping back on her heels inside the stiff suit.

The haze in the sky was transparent, in the near-IR wavelengths to which the visor was tuned. And through muddy purple-orange smears on her faceplate, she could see the sun, a coin of white light, rising above complex cloud layers, almost directly above her head. It was surrounded by an aureole, a disc of milky light that looked as if it was constructed of complex layers, like a huge glass onion in the sky, filled with light. There was probably, she thought apathetically, a lot of atmospheric physics contained in this single image.

Saturn, of course, was hidden by the bulk of Titan, forever below the horizon.

When she turned off the IR visor, returning to human vision, the sun disappeared. She was never going to see the sun with her naked eyes again, not even the attenuated star to which Sol had been reduced by their huge distance.

Her visor had gotten streaked with tholin slush, as if she had been caught in some filthy industrial rain. She lifted her right hand and wiped at the visor with her glove, but that just smeared the slush, making it worse.

I'm going to spend most of my life here just keeping my damn suit clean, she thought. And this tholin drizzle is going to be a constant problem. They should have fitted screen wipers to the visors.

She took a deep breath. "I'm going to *Jitterbug* now."

"Copy that, Paula."

She turned towards that distant shard of bone-white, and began walking.

She found herself shuffling through the gumbo, a hunched old woman. Her helmet lamps cast pools of light on the glistening, purple-streaked surface.

"The slush supports my weight, but it is sticky, cloying," she reported. "It's very tiring to lift my legs out and take a fresh step. Like walking on soft sand. I think we're going to have to do something about this, Rosenberg."

"Snowshoes, maybe," he said.

"Yeah. We'll have to think about it."

She could feel the heavy tubes of warm water wrapped around her limbs; the water seemed to slosh as she walked. Actually she liked the feeling; it was as if she was encased in a little shell of Earth-fluid which cradled her, here in the freezing slush of Titan.

But even so she felt cold. She could feel the heating system of her suit trying to work, the hot little chicken-wire diamonds close to her flesh. It didn't seem to be sufficient. Her fingers, especially, seemed chilled, scarcely protected by the gloves; they were going to have to be careful of frost bite.

In fact, the cold seemed to deepen the further she got from *Bifrost*.

She reached *Jitterbug*.

The Apollo lay nose-down in the slush, its scorched base turned up to the tholin drizzle. She could see immediately what had happened. The paraglider had failed to separate, and had pulled *Jitterbug* over. The paraglider's leads were still attached to the apex of the Command Module, and they trailed across the gumbo to the chute itself.

Even so, it was possible Mott was alive in there. Even conscious. Just stuck upside down in her couch, unable to get to the comms.

When she reached the Command Module, she brushed her hand against its hull. The white tiles were scorched from the entry and laced with tholin drizzle; she couldn't feel their texture through the thickness of her glove. She could see some of *Jitterbug*'s windows, exposed above the slush. They were dark. There was evidently no power in there; there hadn't been for some time.

She turned, and leaned against the Module's wall, resting the mass of her backpack there. After her half-mile slog through the slush she was already exhausted, her heart thumping, the space-wasted muscles of her legs like jelly.

She sipped orange juice, trying to calm her breathing, her rattling heart, trying to face the next step.

Pushing through the sticky slush, she made her way around the capsule.

Jitterbug's side hatch was suspended about four or five feet off the ground. The hatch window was dark, revealing nothing.

She was going to have to open up the Apollo, get inside quickly, try to find some way to save Nicola from the cold.

In a pocket of her Beta-cloth coverall she had a wrench. It was the kind used in the Pacific by Apollo recovery crews. With this, she could undog the hatch from the outside.

It was a little odd working in gravity again, after six years. She didn't have to brace herself, or the item she was working on; gravity did all that, providing a magical vertical-horizontal reference frame, like an invisible jib.

The hatch swung open. Too easily. So easily that the hull must be breached, or a window smashed. The air of Titan had gotten into Apollo.

She pushed her head into the hatchway; the top of her PLSS caught on the top of the frame.

Immediately, Mott's head, in its white helmet, was right before her. But Mott didn't move.

The three couches were almost upside down at an angle, parallel to *Jitterbug*'s tilted base. Mott was in the middle couch, unmoving, hanging in her straps. There was Titan slush all over the cabin; it must have forced its way in through a smashed window, a breach in the hull. It had lapped right up, almost to the rim of the hatch. Mott's face and chest and legs were buried in the slush.

Benacerraf pushed her arms into the slush beneath Mott, almost up to the shoulders. She fumbled for Mott's restraint clasps; she could feel barely anything through her thick, insulated gloves, and she had to trace the straps down from their anchors, over Mott's chest, towards her waist.

Her arms and hands were soon very cold. The icy slush of Titan seemed to be sucking the warmth out of her. Well, she thought, this damn moon's heat capacity can beat out mine any day of the week.

At last she got the clasps loose.

Mott fell forward, into the slurping slush, and Benacerraf's arms.

Benacerraf managed to get her hands hooked underneath Mott's shoulders. She began to haul at Mott's limp body, trying to get it through the hatch. But the orange pressure suit kept catching on the narrow frame, and the gumbo sucked back at her, almost willfully.

At last Mott came free, her knees and feet clattering against the door frame.

Benacerraf stumbled backwards, falling over into the slush. Mott's left foot caught in the hatch, and she sprawled grotesquely against the side of the Command Module, her head dipping into the slush.

A cold, deeper than anything Benacerraf had yet experienced, started to work into her back.

She had to get up, or the slush would kill her.

It took a real effort, a haul by her feeble stomach muscles, to pull herself up to a sitting position. She tried to brace herself against the slush, but there was nothing firm to hold onto. She found she had to worm her way around to a crawling position, her arms embedded in the slush up to her elbows, and then drag herself painfully upright. All the time, the mass of the pack on her back threatened to pull her over again.

When she was on her feet again, she was exhausted anew. She looked down at herself. Her arms, legs and much of her chest were smeared with purple-brown gumbo.

She walked back to Mott. She bent and dug her hands under Mott's shoulders again, and pulled her all the way out onto the ice. Her hands left tholin streaks on Mott's pressure suit.

She turned Mott over. Mott's visor was smashed, her helmet full of slush. Benacerraf reached inside and scooped the slush away from Mott's face. Mott's eyes were open. Benacerraf tried to push closed the lids, but they were frozen, even the eyeballs hard.

Rosenberg said, "Do you have her?"

"Yes, Rosenberg. I have her."

Rosenberg fell silent.

There was Titan slush in Mott's mouth. Benacerraf dug it away with a finger. Her gloved finger seemed too fat for Mott's mouth; it was like clearing vomit from the mouth of a sick child.

"So," Rosenberg said. "Then there were three."

"Yes."

"I'm sorry, Paula."

"Me too. Rosenberg, prepare a message for the ground. Her parents . . ."

"Sure."

Benacerraf straightened up and returned to *Jitterbug*. By touch, in a storage compartment behind the head of Mott's couch, she found a spade, and a little packet of cellophane that contained the Stars-and-Stripes. The spade was broad-bladed, like a snow-shovel. It had a handle that telescoped out. She walked a few yards away from the apex of *Jitterbug* and began to dig.

The blade penetrated the gumbo easily, and she could lift big shovelfuls away into the thick air. But the stuff clung to the spade and was difficult to shake off. And the walls of the little trench she dug kept collapsing inwards. It was like digging into wet sand.

She kept going, until she was four feet down.

She scraped gumbo off Mott's chest, exposing the Union Jack sewn there. Then she opened the cellophane packet. She shook out the flag, and laid it over Mott's body. She wrapped it underneath, making a neat parcel. Now the weak gravity helped her; Mott was feather-light, easy to handle, like a small child.

Two flags, two bodies, she thought.

Benacerraf laid Mott in the trench she had dug.

It was easy to fill. She just pushed the mounds of slush back over the body. The bright orange of Mott's pressure suit, the brave red and blue and white of the flag, were soon obscured, claimed by the ubiquitous brown of Titan. The clinging stuff oozed quickly back to smoothness.

Benacerraf rested her shovel against the hull of *Jitterbug*, and stood at the head of Mott's grave.

"No words this time, Paula?"

"She should have been the first," Benacerraf said. "Not me. She should have been first . . . That's all, I guess."

Her exhaustion was immense, crushing, beyond anything she had known before.

"Paula," Rosenberg said. "Let's go open up *Discovery*."

"Yes," she said. Suddenly, standing here in the slush and dark, the idea of the glowing lights of the orbiter's flight deck and the cramped, clean confines of the hab module, the warm growing smells of the CELSS farm seemed welcoming to Benacerraf.

She could see, in the murk, Rosenberg plodding away from *Bifrost* towards *Discovery*, the dangling form of Angel limp over his shoulders.

Jackie Benacerraf sat alone on the floor of her lounge, waiting for the pictures of her mother's first footsteps on Titan.

So far the big softscreen on the wall was blank, save for schematics and timelines and a couple of animated sponsors' logos. But sound was coming through: traditional astronauts' voices, distorted and overlaid with pops and crackles, and with a judder imposed by the lousy bandwidth of the compressed signals.

For the record, we have a go for vent . . . Affirmative, we're all sealed up. Go for vent . . . All right.

Jackie couldn't even tell which voice was her mother's. There they were, the astronauts, solemnly reporting each step as if working on an unexploded bomb. All for the benefit of those who might follow one day.

But, of course, nobody would. Not ever.

Anyhow, it was hard to concentrate. She was worried about the kids.

She was always worried about the kids.

At least Fred had grown out of his Nullist phase, and he was having some of the image-tattoos removed. That was leaving marks on his skin, but the doctors were saying they shouldn't be permanent—unlike hers—because he was still young enough. That skin cancer he'd developed when one of the laid-bare patches had been exposed to the sun was more worrying, but again the specialists said it would clear up . . .

What bothered her more right now was his determination to quit school and go join the Hunter-Gatherers in Central America.

She'd listened to the arguments and lectures until she thought her head would bust open.

The agricultural revolution ten thousand years ago was now pretty much accepted by the academics as a global disaster. So her son told her, anyhow. The archaeology showed the incidence of tooth cavities rose seven-fold; mothers were badly undernourished; anemia became much more common, and so did tuberculosis . . . We were better off, ran the argument, so argued Fred, before agriculture. It was true that farming a piece of land could support ten times as many people as the hunter-gatherer lifestyle, but that didn't buy you much; today there were seven billion people in the world, almost all of whom were worse nourished than their Stone Age ancestors . . . and so on.

Once, Jackie would have been passionate about such arguments, either for or against. Now, all she cared about was Fred.

The governments cooperating in the Central American park scheme—Guatemala, Honduras, El Salvador, and Belize—had pledged to protect and shelter the young Americans and New Columbians flooding down there to—in theory—rediscover an ancient lifestyle. There was supposed to be no regulation, beyond a simple limit on numbers—but, of course, no communication was possible once you went inside.

Jackie pulled at a tuft of hair. All she could do was keep talking, trying to persuade Fred to think again, to wait, to stick with college . . .

It was just like the arguments her mother had had with her.

Maybe she was doomed to turn into her mother, just as her own kids seemed to be turning into *her.*

Okay. Everything is go. We are just waiting for the cabin pressure to equalize with the exterior sufficiently to open the hatch . . .

You ready for your one small step?

Astronaut humor, Jackie thought bleakly.

The irony was, science was making a certain comeback. The environmental problems were becoming so pressing and complex that Maclachlan had re-opened some of the university science labs and departments he'd ordered shut down. Even in Seattle, a clear-plastic uv filter over your lawn was now almost as common as a sprinkler system.

It was as if humans were studying the ecology by testing it to destruction, in a kind of huge, one-off, millennial experiment. Maybe when we've reduced the whole thing to the grass and the ants, she thought bleakly, we'll understand how it all used to work.

You're lined up nicely. Come back towards me . . . Okay, put your foot down . . . you're doing fine . . . A little more.

It was the plankton crash in the oceans that seemed to be scaring the scientists most. The plankton crisis, it was said, might actually make the planet uninhabitable, ultimately. And in the short term the big problem was the rice crop. There was a blight with an unpronounceable name that was laying waste to rice crops all over the planet. The price of rice in the Seattle stores—particularly Italian rice, for some reason—had gone through the roof. In the longer term, it was said, people would soon be starving, especially in the major rice-producing countries: China, India, Britain.

It was all to be expected, said the doom-mongers. Worldwide, humanity got more than fifty percent of its calories from three carbohydrate-rich crops: wheat, rice and maize. Gigantic monocultures, exceptionally vulnerable to disease.

It was all hubris, fourteen-year-old Ben explained to her earnestly. Humanity had been pursuing a gigantic project, the construction of a technosphere, within which the human species could effectively be freed of its dependence on the Earth: iso-lated, like grandmother in her metal ship, Ben said . . .

She let him talk. Jackie had a bigger argument to win with Ben. The destiny of the species was a piece of ground she could afford to concede.

Okay, the picture's good. A little dark and drab maybe, but nothing that a little image processing can't fix.

Now, at last, the screen filled up. In the foreground Jackie could see what looked like the white-tiled hull of a Command Module, splashed with some kind of mud, and a little further away the ghostly form of an astronaut, a bulky suit topped by a visor that returned brief highlights from the cabin lights. Beyond, no landscape was visible, save only a few yards of what looked like orange-brown swamp.

The astronaut seemed to be pawing at the surface with one foot.

It was, Jackie thought, probably her mother.

The picture was full of digital flaws, rectilinear cross-hatchings and missing pixels, so that you could never forget it was artifi-cial. When the astronaut moved about, so poor was the image quality that she trailed ghosts, pale shadows of limbs and head and torso. It was oddly like the films she'd seen of the first, crude television pictures from *Apollo 11*, Armstrong and Aldrin moving around like ghosts up there.

I'm in the hatchway. The Command Module has sunk into the sur-face through several inches, before the slush compacted to stop it. I can't see any exposed ice . . .

Still analyzing, Jackie thought. Still doing science, even out there, a billion miles from home, one little woman scratching at the surface of a whole world. As if any conclusions she came to made a damn bit of difference.

Still, this *wasn't Apollo 11*. Hardly anyone was watching these four-hours-old images. The broadcast, on a minor cable channel, wasn't exactly illegal, but it also wasn't encouraged by the author-ities either. After all, here were these Americans bounding around in a place the current orthodoxy said didn't even exist . . .

What bullshit it all was; what damage space had done to the cause of science, in America and the rest of the world. Twenty-billion-dollar golf shots. Maybe, she thought, we ought to see the space program—not as the culmination of some huge project of science and technology—but as a gigantic, alienating disaster. Maybe if not for the space program, my kids wouldn't be forced to listen to two-thousand-year-old cosmology every day.

If only it had been done *differently*: with imagination and daring and style. NASA's ultimate triumph had been to reduce everything—even the Moon, even Titan—to the dull, the bland, the predictable.

But probably, on the other hand, space had made no difference. Jackie was becoming receptive to a thesis put about by some academics now that science and technology had anyway reached the end of their usefulness. Humans were becoming overwhelmed by their own sophisticated machinery, because the intelligence required to build a certain level of technology was less than that needed to survive it. There were endless examples: all the nuclear-industry catastrophes leading up to Chernobyl, her own mother's *Columbia* crash, even the new airborne AIDS variant . . .

Her mind came back to the kids, to Ben, with a wrench.

To hell with science, the future of the species, the space program. Who is there to tell you what to say when your fourteen-year-old son comes home and says he wants to get pregnant?

Ben said he was gay. He was in love, with a boy a couple of years older. He wasn't a virgin any more, he said. And, he said, he wanted a kid.

Of course that was possible now, with cloned fetuses being implanted directly into the stomach wall of a father. It was even safe, they said, more so than natural childbirth.

Jackie argued against it. She had found herself sounding like her own mother again, and she hated it. You're too young.

Wait. Don't make any decisions now that you can't unpick later. Finish your education . . .

But then, she reflected, if it made Ben happy *now*, maybe she should let him go ahead. *Maybe I should just let Fred go too, go seek a better solution in the jungles.*

She wasn't convinced that to plan for a long and happy life was a rational decision any more. In her opinion, you could forget the plankton and the uv; the most likely thing to end it all for them was a bunch of Chinese ICBMs flying over the Pacific.

Sometimes she fell into despair, when she thought about the future her kids were going to have to negotiate. She hated her own lack of control over that future, her impotence in the face of the huge changes sweeping like winds across the planet.

Her mother, moving about in the dense orange atmosphere of Titan, looked less than human. Like some kind of deep-sea fish.

All right. I'm going to step out of Bifrost now.

Jackie leaned forward. This is it, she thought. This is the peak of my mother's life. Her crowning achievement, her moment in history.

This is the stuff of life, her mother, on Titan, said, and she stuck her hand in the mud.

Oh, God, Mother, I wish you were here.

Rosenberg, suited up, began his daily inspection tour of Tartarus Base. His boots squelched as he dragged them through the icy mud. He walked like an old man, shuffling and huddled over, his helmet lamp splashing yellow light over the glistening slush. He just couldn't get used to working in this stiff suit, where it took an effort to make the slightest movement, and he was always overcompensating, so that he blundered about like a fool, slamming into equipment and the others, sometimes without even realizing it. Dragging the suit around, in fact, even without attempting anything constructive, was as hard work as shoveling snow, or climbing a ladder on Earth.

But he liked the feeling of being embedded in a gravity field once more, after all those zero-G years. He felt as if he *was* somewhere. Oddly, it made him feel less lonesome.

The Base was, if he cared to be charitable about it, looking a little more like a permanent encampment now, and less like a couple of crashed spacecraft.

He walked around the Shuttle orbiter. It looked like a bulky, downed aircraft, all of a hundred and twenty feet long, its cut-down delta wings ploughed into the gumbo. The trail it had dug on landing still stretched off behind it, into the murk that concealed the horizon. But slowly, that shallow valley was filling in: the gumbo was relaxing, seeping back into the trench. Rosenberg had installed markers—just bits of aluminum and plastic from the wreck of *Jitterbug*—at various points along the valley floor and walls; the creep ought to give him a good understanding of the viscous and mechanical properties of the gumbo.

He stepped up onto the left wing. There was gumbo coating the upper surface of the wing, thrown up there by the landing, and a more uniform coating from the tholin drizzle since. But it was a thin layer, and Rosenberg found it a relief to step onto this hard surface, after a few minutes on the uniform gloopy mess that was Titan's ground.

The orbiter's payload bay doors were open, resting on the wings, like folded-back pieces of the hull. After the landings, the crew had discovered the doors had gotten stuck, and they had to be cranked open by hand. Now Rosenberg clambered up onto the curved inner surface of the payload bay door and, his feet clattering, walked along the sixty-feet length of the cargo bay, inspecting its contents.

The payload bay wasn't completely exposed to the elements

of Titan. They had rigged up a crude canopy, of parachute fabric on aluminum struts, over the bay, like a tent; the centrifuge arm held it up to some extent. The canopy caught the worst of the tholin drift, but it was already sagging under the accumulated weight. Some day he was going to have to get up there and knock the crap off, like a suburban homeowner clearing snow from his roof.

The bay was equipped as it had been during the cruise to Saturn, with the big hab module closest to the orbiter flight deck, and then a short crawl-through tunnel to the reworked Spacelab module that had housed the CELSS farm. Behind the Spacelab lay the Topaz reactors, beneath their heavy shielding. The centrifuge cabin on its big swing arm lay across the top of all this, abandoned now. Its dismantling was on Rosenberg's long list of things to do; that big motor ought to be useful for something.

Rosenberg jumped off the wing. Briefly, he enjoyed the childlike sensation of drifting down as slow as a snowflake in Titan's feeble gravity, and settling gently into the slush.

Then he ploughed his way across the gumbo to the nose of the orbiter.

The upper surface of the orbiter's flight deck, the white felt thermal tiles there, was streaked and stained by tholin gunge. *Discovery* looked battered, aged, as if the mushy landscape of Titan were dragging it down into terminal entropy. But if he bent down and looked underneath the chin of the orbiter, at the black thermal protection tiles sheltered there, he could still make out the scorching of entry. This had once been a spacecraft, after all, and here it still showed. Even if the payload bay had been turned into a shanty town.

But at that, he reflected, this was surely a better fate for *Discovery* than to have finished up as a museum piece on the lawn of some fading NASA center.

Later he was going to have to run an internal check on *Discovery*'s systems. They were having some trouble with balky heaters. Fixed heaters had been installed throughout the orbiter's hull, to help insulate the life-bearing hab module at its heart. The heaters responded to commands from the command software and temperature sensors. There were also small radioisotope heating units, mounted on movable mechanisms, that could vary the heat applied to particularly cold areas.

But the heaters ate up a lot of power. Rosenberg had ideas on how they could coat the Base's main components—the orbiter, *Bifrost*—with blocks of water ice, like igloos. That would retain a lot of heat, and enable them to reduce the power output from the Topaz reactors, so extending their life. Maybe they could build airtight tunnels between the components to give themselves more space, maybe even put up independent igloos, sealed somehow . . .

Of course such grandiose schemes depended on getting access to water ice, which was proving a difficulty, on this ice moon. The problem was the tholin slush. As far as Rosenberg could tell they were sitting on top of a gumbo layer at least fifteen yards thick; as far as they'd dug, they hadn't reached bedrock water ice.

When he looked up at the lighted windows of the orbiter's flight deck, he thought he could see the blind face of Bill Angel. But the glass was obscured by purple stripes of tholin, and it was hard to be sure.

He walked over the gumbo the fifty feet to where they had dragged *Bifrost*, their intact Apollo Command Module. Using components from *Jitterbug*, they had fixed up a crude airlock over *Bifrost*'s side hatch. Power cables stretched from *Discovery*, through the slush, to the Apollo. Rosenberg had rigged up the CELSS farm in *Bifrost*, after stripping out the couches and other movable gear. That had given the crew in *Discovery* the extra living space of the old Spacelab module.

Fifty feet further on from *Bifrost* was a small pile of gear, covered by another hunk of parachute fabric. This was salvage from *Jitterbug*, disassembled and hauled laboriously across the

tholin by Rosenberg and Benacerraf. The shell of *Jitterbug* still
lay in the gumbo where it had come down, its base and chunks
of its hull chopped away, the improvised grave of Nicola Mott
close by.

Rosenberg had developed a habit of peering under the stiffen-
ing fabric over the gear pile every day. He did it now. It was a waste
of time, of course. He was on a lifeless world, here: there were no
thieves to disturb the pile, no rats or dogs who would chew the
tarpaulin. And there never would be, as long as he lived.

He walked on.

The closeness of the horizon, his immersion in this perpet-
ual murk, made it seem as if he was stuck inside the close walls
of some opaque orange bubble. Some deep part of his brain, he
suspected, still believed that things must be different a little
further away: a few miles from the camp, maybe over Titan's
close horizon. Some place where there were all the elements he
had grown up with: people and animals and buildings and cars,
and a blue sky with white, fluffy clouds . . .

But it wasn't true.

It was an odd thing, a small detail, but to Rosenberg the lack
of disturbance to the equipment piles emphasized their isolation on this lifeless moon more than any amount of theorizing.

Benacerraf and Rosenberg, cleaned up, sat on the flight deck of
Discovery—away from Bill Angel—and chewed the fat about
equipment problems.

What they were really doing, of course, was not talking
about Bill.

Rosenberg was suspicious of Angel, on some deep level. Bill
seemed to have stabilized since the landing, as the NASA psy-
chologists had suggested he would. But Rosenberg didn't think
the creature in the hab module was Bill Angel any more. The
way he talked, the body language . . . He seemed to be coming
in at an angle to the rest of the world. As if his head was stuck
in some fourth dimension.

Benacerraf shut Rosenberg up when he talked like this. *How come scientists are so precise and picky about their specialties, but always prepared to bullshit about stuff they know nothing about, like psychology?* As far as she was concerned this situation wasn't about trust; it was about management. Benacerraf approved of Rosenberg's plans for their survival. But to achieve those plans they were going to need resources: time, muscle power, intellectual energy. She wasn't convinced that the two of them, alone, were sufficient. She thought they needed Bill Angel to close the design. If they were going to survive here, they had to manage all their resources effectively. And that included Angel. She saw it as her job to manage Bill, the way they were going to have to manage other pieces of equipment, balky or otherwise.

So now Rosenberg sat here and spoke, not about Bill, but about the Sabatier unit. The Sabatier was a simple piece of kit, basically a pipe surrounded by nichrome heaters. The Sabatier cracked carbon dioxide, collected from the life support system, by reacting it at high temperatures with hydrogen, in the presence of a ruthenium catalyst, to produce methane and water. The water was collected in a condenser coil, and the methane was vented to Titan's air.

"I think the catalyst is being poisoned by a build-up of amine vapors . . . The trouble must be further upstream, in the process, at the SAWD." The solid amine water desorption unit removed carbon dioxide from the air by passing it over beads of resin inside steel canisters. Rosenberg started to list the steps he was taking to test this out. He said, "At least the systems are easier to work with, now we have a little more space to move around in. And every damn component doesn't float off into the air every time you turn around . . ."

And so on, a parade of detail.

Benacerraf was chewing on a spindly carrot from the CELSS farm. "Rosenberg, how are we doing overall? What else do we need to do, that we're not doing?"

He clasped his hands behind his head, and rocked back in

his seat. "Let's go back to basics. During the cruise, where we had to rely on nothing but the resources we carried, we tried to close all the life support loops. We recycled all our waste, solid and liquid, and fed nutrients to the plants we grew, and cleaned the air . . . We did well; we survived six years in interplanetary space. But even so the closure was never perfect; we lost about five percent of most materials as they passed around the life support cycle, to leakage, unrecoverable waste, whatever.

"Here on Titan, outside resources are available to us: water, in the form of bedrock ice, nitrogen and methane from the air, hydrocarbons like the ethane and propane we can get from Clear Lake and other compounds, like nitriles and ammonia. That means we can open up some of the loops."

Benacerraf said, "Water. We're still recycling every drop we drink. I can taste the six-year-old piss in it, for God's sake."

"If we could bring fresh water ice into the system we'd cut down the bulk we're recycling by forty-five percent. And that would give us a system much better buffered against instabilities."

"We're going to have to climb that damn mountain, aren't we?"

"It's why we chose to land here, Paula."

She held her hands up. "I know. It's just that mountaineering on Titan seems a much dumber idea down here than it did from orbit. What else? What about all those amino acids you say we need?"

Rosenberg scratched his head. "Well, that's the hole I can't plug right now. We've taken a lot of samples from the air, the tholin slush. No aminos; all I've found is the prebiotic organic stuff I expected. If we're not to be resupplied, there are some trace elements we need as well."

"So what are the options?"

"We go seek aminos on the surface. Some place we haven't looked."

"Like where?"

"The bottom of Clear Lake. Or carbonaceous chondrite craters," he said.

She turned, looking irritated. "I hate having to ask you to explain all the time, Rosenberg."

He shrugged. "Then read up. Carbonaceous chondrites are a kind of asteroid. Cratering bodies in this neck of the woods come in four main groups. There are a lot of icy bodies: loose stuff like comet heads, maybe disintegrated moons. Then the M-type asteroids are metallic, metal-rich and dense. The S-types are silicaceous. Rocky. And the C-types are the carbonaceous chondrites. Water, iron, stone and carbon. If we find a carbonaceous chondrite crater we might find kerogen."

"What's that?"

"A hydrocarbon. A tarry stuff you find in oil shales. It contains carbon, oxygen, hydrogen, sulphur, potassium, chlorine, other elements . . ." He smiled. "It's the nearest thing to a nutritional broth we're likely to find out here. Mom's condensed primordial soup. You know, we can reach a lot of craters with the skimmer, when we set it up."

"All right. When we fix the skimmer, we'll discuss it. What else?"

What else, what else . . .

As the session went on, Rosenberg started to feel hunted, as if everything was coming back to him. Questions, questions. What if he got an answer wrong? It is too much for one person, he thought, this responsibility for all our lives.

But he did his best to answer Paula's questions.

When Paula had gone, he stayed in his seat and stared out into Titan's twilit gloom.

Benacerraf felt pressured as well, of course. Rosenberg just came up with options; Benacerraf had to make decisions about them.

But all the time they were skirting around the biggest issues. There was the problem of Angel, for one thing. And the real limiting factor to their chances of survival, here on Titan: not water, not amino acids, but *energy*.

The run-down of the Topaz suite was the final limiting factor, even if they could bridge all the other gaps in the loops. When the power faded below some critical threshold, the cold was going to get them at last.

Rosenberg had no plans, no ideas, how to get over that.

Rosenberg was the smartest person on the whole damn moon. If he couldn't figure a way out of this, nobody was going to. And then he would die. And not at some remote, far-future date, but here, on this crappy moon, and soon. All of this—the orbiter, Apollo, their neat little gadgets and improvised tools—all of it would still be here, but his spark of consciousness, his unique self, would be gone. It would be like a shell, slowly decaying, presumably buried for good in the drifting slush in a couple of hundred years. Eventually, there would be no sign he'd even existed.

That was unbearable to Rosenberg. He'd come here, in some vague way, to find the future, to find answers, to do science. To escape Earth. But now, *this*. There had to be a way out of this trap, the abandonment by NASA, the dwindling resources, the cold . . .

Beyond the tholin-streaked windows of the flight deck, the gloomy slush-covered ground of Titan stretched off to an orange-stained, concealed horizon. In all the world that Rosenberg could see, under a brown-black lid of a cloudy sky, only a handful of human artifacts—the bundles of equipment under yellow parachute fabric, the stained white conical walls of *Bifrost*—showed any color other than the universal murky orange-brown.

He closed his eyes, for a few seconds.

Then he got up, and went back to work.

Later, Rosenberg went out again, to help Benacerraf in her efforts to deploy the skimmer.

The skimmer—properly, the TGEV, the Titan Ground Effect Vehicle—was a fifty-million-dollar improvisation, put together by Boeing, at Seattle, in under eighteen months. Right now it was still folded up in its palette on the side of the orbiter like a construction toy. Benacerraf had it halfway out, like an aluminum dragonfly struggling to emerge from its chrysalis. Rosenberg helped her haul on the lanyards.

Abruptly the main fuselage sections locked, and four legs popped out at the corners, telescopic tubes with wide orange footpads. With a couple more hauls, they had the skimmer unfolded, and set upright on the surface.

Rosenberg—sweating inside his suit, pulled muscles aching—walked slowly around the craft.

Sitting on its spidery legs the skimmer was a spindly, open-frame box built around a ducted fan, with a skirt of flexible metal mesh draped around its base. The fan's housing curved upward above the center of the craft, a shaped funnel. There were two metal-framed couches in front of the fan, each big enough to accommodate a suited crew member, and there was a simple control box with a joystick in front of the left-hand seat.

Inside the fan housing there was a rotor blade, designed to push the thick Titan air down through the duct and into the skirt, so providing the hovercraft effect that would lift the skimmer off the ground. The fan was run off series-wound electric motors, powered by two big silver-zinc batteries that could be recharged from the Topaz.

The frame was shaved-thin aluminum, to save weight. The skimmer carried its own navigation computer, communications system and cargo space for maps, samples, tool-racks, spare battery. There was even a fold-out tent, so that astronauts could spend a night away from *Discovery* on an extended EVA.

It was a sophisticated piece of equipment. But the skimmer, with its umbrella antennae and fold-up seats, looked in the light of his helmet lamp as if it had come out of someone's hobby shop. Like some backyard Victorian inventor's dream of space travel.

With her hand in Rosenberg's, Benacerraf climbed up into

the left hand seat. She was maybe four feet off the ground; the duct mouth flared above her like a huge crown. She dug a reference card out of a slip pocket, and began throwing switches.

Suddenly bulbs sparkled over the framework, green and red and white, with big, down-pointing floods that splashed light over the gumbo.

"Wow," said Rosenberg. "It looks like a Christmas tree."

Benacerraf said, "I think—"

There was a noise from the duct, a *whump-whump* that carried easily to Rosenberg through the thick air. Rapidly, the rotor increased its speed, and the noise smoothed out to a whir.

From beneath the skirt, a thin sheet of gumbo blasted out across the ground in all directions. It was like a paint-sprayer; it took only seconds for Rosenberg's legs, almost up to his waist, to be coated in crap.

"How about that," Benacerraf called.

Rosenberg shouted, "If you're going to lift that thing, Paula, strap in."

Benacerraf began fumbling at the restraints at her waist.

The whir rose in pitch to a thin whine, and the skimmer shuddered. It lifted off the ground, the skirt billowing beneath it. Benacerraf whooped, and Rosenberg applauded.

If it worked, the skimmer would extend their range of operations hugely. Any kind of surface car was going to be impractical, given the stickiness of the tholin slush. But the ground effect vehicle idea might have been made for Titan, with its low gravity, all this lovely thick air . . . The best way to get around in these conditions.

Except for human-powered flight on Leonardo wings, of course. But that was a little beyond the imagination of NASA.

The skimmer hung with its four footpads suspended about a yard off the ground. Rosenberg thought he could see the murky Titanian air being sucked into the mouth of the duct, particles of aerosol crud marking the airflow. The central duct jerked this way and that, blasting its jet of air for directional control. There wasn't much sophistication in controlling the craft; you swiveled the ducted fan, taking care not to disrupt the air cushion that held the whole thing up, and went where the downward blast took you . . .

But now the skimmer was wobbling from side to side, as if suspended from an invisible wire. Benacerraf was wrestling with the joystick. "It handles like shit," she called. "It's nothing like the training vehicle at Ellington. This is completely unstable. I can feel it. It feels as if it's about to——"

Abruptly the front of the skimmer tipped upwards, and the skirt lifted clear of the ground. A great gush of gumbo came fountaining out from beneath the skimmer, falling in slow, complex arcs back to the ground. With its cushion of air lost, the skimmer slipped backwards, its rear two legs slamming into the ground.

Benacerraf worked to kill the fan, and the skimmer tipped forward, settling at last on all four legs.

The skimmer looked like an ungainly meteorite, fallen to ground at the center of a great radial splash of churned-up gumbo.

As the fan noise died, Rosenberg stepped forward. He checked Benacerraf was okay, and they started to talk about ways to gain control of the stability.

They kept trying. Benacerraf kept taking the skimmer up, until the batteries started to flatten. They didn't manage to get the skimmer to fly more than five yards before, every time, it veered off course and dug itself into the gumbo like a badly thrown frisbee.

Rosenberg had a deep, pessimistic sense they were wasting their time. The design of the craft looked all wrong to him: its center of gravity much too high, the air cushion the wrong shape. With a ground-effect vehicle stability depended on the design of the air cushion, aerodynamic guidance. The Boeing people had done their best, but they just hadn't had the time or facilities to test out their models of how the thing was going to behave in Titan conditions: the air density, the temperature structure, the gravity.

The skimmer was a wipe-out. And that meant that wherever they went, they were going to have to foot-slog it. They'd traveled a billion miles, and now they were here they could go no further than they could walk.

Their options had suddenly closed in even further.

He'd been out a long time; he was tired. He went to the airlock. Once inside and de-suited he started to clean off the gumbo still sticking to his EMU.

Fifty million bucks, he thought.

On the day of the funeral of Chen Tong, Jiang Ling arrived early at Tiananmen Square.

She stepped out of her hotel onto the Avenue of Eternal Peace. She walked west under the canopy of sycamore trees, just budding, that fringed the bright red wall of the Forbidden City. The sky was suffused with a pearl gray.

She reached the end of the sidewalk, and stepped forward onto a checkerboard of cement paving stones. The place was all but deserted. She walked to the center, her footsteps clicking loudly.

The vastness of the Square swept away around her, like a frozen sea of stone.

She turned, and looked around the frieze of monumental architecture that lined the hundred acres of the Square: the museums to the east, the Great Hall of the People to the west, Mao's mausoleum to the south. And at the very center of the Square there was the Monument to the Martyrs of the People, a granite obelisk inscribed in Mao's own hand with the epigram ETERNAL GLORY TO THE PEOPLE'S HEROES.

And to the north there was Tiananmen itself: the Gate of

Heavenly Peace, leading into the ancient Forbidden City. The Gate was a ten-story rampart set in the massive walls of the Forbidden City; it was painted imperial maroon, capped by two tiers of sloping yellow-tiled roofs, the colors still washed out by the dawn gray. Five portals ran through the base of the Gate, and just above—flanked by inscriptions saying LONG LIVE THE UNITY OF THE PEOPLES OF THE WORLD and LONG LIVE THE PEOPLE'S REPUBLIC OF CHINA—sat the massive, familiar portrait of Mao Zedong. The gigantic softscreen image, responding to her presence, appeared to look down on her and smile in welcome. Something inside her melted. On the screen, a blue sky, fluffy with clouds, blossomed into view behind Mao's corpulent face.

Her memories never did justice to this place, she thought. Photographs had a way of making the Square seem as flat and uninspiring as the endless shopping malls and parking lots she had seen in America. But this was *the Square*: the largest public quadrangle in the world, the center of the country's center— the north star, as Confucius would have said, to which all other stars are attracted.

Standing here she was overwhelmed by the physical size of her nation, the history embedded in the ground on which she walked. And she was touched by her own significance, as the first astronaut, her role in the millennial extension of *tianming*, the Mandate of Heaven.

This was, she believed, a sense of oneness which no Westerner could understand: certainly not the Americans, with their endlessly recycled images of the Tiananmen students of 1989, those unfortunate, misguided wretches with their Western clothes and English-language banners.

This was China, after all: for all its faults and problems, founded on a billion souls, five millennia of history; this could never be America.

And today, it was promised, she would meet the Great Helmsman himself. Her heart thumped as it had not when, during her endless tours, she had shaken the hands of presidents and kings. Perhaps, today, she would at last be released from the burden of her ceremonial duties, and permitted to return to what she loved: to fly, to sample again the light-filled glories of spaceflight.

With hope and expectation, she walked forward towards the Great Hall of the People. The early morning cold dug through the layers of her light Mao suit, but soon the sun would rise, and pour orange light and warmth into the remote corners of the Square.

She entered the grandiose gloom of the Hall itself. This was a true monument of socialist architecture, all of a thousand feet long, room enough to seat five thousand banqueting guests. And today, under the glare of TV lights, the focus of all this immense volume was the wizened body of a very old man, which lay draped in a Chinese flag, under a crystal sarcophagus. There was a sea of Party leaders, almost all of them men, lapping in orderly waves in their dark Mao suits around the glittering coffin.

Jiang took her place in line, alongside her mentor Xu Shiyou. Sandwiched between two octogenarian Party stalwarts from the provinces, they filed forward slowly towards the coffin. On a small stage a senior official was intoning a long, lugubrious eulogy over Chen Tong—a celebration of his glorious career, which stretched back to service with Mao himself before 1949—and the Party grandees, one by one, reached the sarcophagus and bowed three times, and then each of them passed on to Chen's widow and shook her withered old hand.

Thus Jiang Ling found herself adrift in the sea of old men.

Many of them were wearing elaborate hearing aids and softscreen spectacles. Some of them were relatively spry, but others were supported by younger people—secretaries, or perhaps nurses—and they shuffled their feet, hardly able to walk. A few of them were even in wheelchairs, laden with oxygen bottles. And yet many had bizarre marks of youth: thick black hair, smoothed skin, sparkling new eyes. One of them—a few places ahead of her in the line—walked stiffly, and with a whir of servomotors, as some rudimentary exoskeleton beneath his Mao suit propelled him forward.

Jiang was startled and repelled. She had had much contact with the leadership since her flight, but always in meetings with one or two officials at a time; never had she witnessed the leadership en masse in this fashion. She wondered what tonnage of transplanted organs, bones, body fluids—manufactured, or excavated from youthful cadavers—had been installed in this crumbling leadership, to maintain its semblance of forward motion and life. Surely, she thought, nowhere in the world was there a government leadership so visibly tired and aged as the one arrayed around Chen's corpse this morning.

At last she reached the corpse, and she stared, with little understanding, at the smooth, embalmed face of Chen Tong.

Now the eulogy was done. The vacated platform was taken by a fat middle-aged man in an off-white Mao suit, fitted with the elaborate collar of an imperial-era Confucian scholar. He was Gao Feng, a singer who had been popular two decades ago.

Xu Shiyou leaned close to her and whispered, his skin smelling of Western cosmetics: "Perhaps Chen Tong was a fan of Gao."

The singer began to croon: *We all have a family whose name is China . . .*

There was a sharp, cloying smell, unwelcome in the stuffy air.

Jiang turned. The elderly Party leader behind her, his face imploded, was leaning on the arm of his aide and staring down at his trousers, from which leaked a slow rivulet of yellow fluid.

Now that the ceremonial was over, the leaders lingered, talking in small groups, their various attendants standing by impassively. It was an occasion without parallel in the West; there were no refreshments—no drinks, even—and no real focus to the gathering. But she could see, from the intensity of body language, the fierceness of expressions, that much business was being transacted here, between these rulers of the far-flung provinces of China.

Xu Shiyou drew Jiang Ling aside. "The Helmsman wishes to meet you, shortly. Now listen to me, Jiang Ling."

She grimaced. "I always do, Xu."

He snorted through his fleshy nose. "If only that were true. But listen now, Jiang, if never again; for this could be the most important moment of your life."

"You say that," she said, "to a woman who has flown in space?"

"I do," he said seriously.

Xu continued to rise in the leadership, in part—she knew—thanks to the connection with herself, which he had been assiduous in maintaining and exploiting, and in part thanks to his own untiring efforts on his own behalf.

Xu had joined the Communist Party in his teens. He had been an electrical engineer, and had worked as a factory adminstrator for fifteen years, before starting to work his way through the ranks in various economic and diplomatic agencies. He was cultivated, able to chat freely in any of his three languages—Russian, Romanian, and English—and, Jiang had observed for herself, he was able to charm and surprise many of those he encountered with his education and facility. He could recite lines from the U.S. Declaration of Independence as easily as verses of T'ang dynasty poetry.

Jiang would not admit to liking Xu Shiyou. Still less did she regard him as worthy of her trust. But she had come to understand, with a cynical analysis that surprised herself, that as long as she did nothing to tarnish her image as a new demi-god, his interests were identical to hers. Therefore, she decided, he was an ally . . .

So she said, "Give me your advice, Xu Shiyou."

"Whatever the Helmsman says to you, you must endeavor to see the world through his eyes. You must suffer with him, sense his fears."

"His fears?"

"Remember this: the Helmsman was born in 1904. Eleven decades ago: think of all he has seen, and suffered, in those years, his long and hard life matching the tortured history of our country. When the Helmsman came of age, China was a mere dish of loose sand, as Sun Yat-sen said: hopelessly divided by warlordism and chronic social disorder. There is, embedded deep in the bones of these, our senior leaders, a fear of falling back into such a state of humiliation and disunity.

"And now, in the twilight of his long life, the Helmsman faces chaos once more," Xu said solemnly. "It is no secret that our losses in the attempt to liberate Taiwan were monstrous. And it is, of course, the peasants in the hinterland who suffered most. It is said that every family in China lost a son or daughter on the beaches of Taiwan. True or not, that has become a symbol, provoking unrest in the provinces.

"The answer to all this, of course," said Xu, "is economic growth. Expansion. But we are contained, by the Americans and their allies. Our technology cannot match theirs. The puppet allies ring us, their satellites watch over us. And hence any conflict in the future like the Taiwan war must, inevitably, end in defeat for us.

"We must face stark facts. Every effort has been made to maintain ample food and decent housing. But the peasants have little spare income, little choice. The farmers see their cousins in the city acquiring private phone lines, houses, cars, softscreens, image-tattoos . . . And meanwhile, all the forecasts predict a worsening of the lot of the peasants, as new diseases spread, as even the water supplies shrivel . . .

"We are becoming desperate."

"And it is the fault of the West."

"Yes," he said. "The West remains corrupt, increasingly decadent, and must ultimately rot from within . . ."

"Yes," she said. In fact she did agree; based on her own observation, she believed this to be true.

"But when we face the West, Jiang, we face a lunatic; a lunatic more powerful than we are, who cripples us with his threat. What we must do is strike at him—hard, a single blow, which will remove his dominance—perhaps for all time."

That confused her. "What do you mean?"

"We must seek a single hammer blow, which might change the shape of human destiny for ten thousand years . . . And that is what the Helmsman will say to you."

An attendant came to call them forward. The Great Helmsman was ready to receive them.

"Be ready, Jiang Ling," Xu said softly. "Be open."

She approached, fear and fascination mixed in equal part.

He was a wisp of a man, she thought, a dried-out husk of a man, overwhelmed by the bulky technology of his wheelchair. She saw medical equipment, discreet, unlabeled black boxes, tucked into the frame of the chair, pipes and tubes snaking up into the Helmsman's clothing. And she thought she could detect the liquid bulk of a colostomy bag under his jacket. A middle-aged woman, dumpy and plain—perhaps one of his daughters—stood at his side, her plump hand protectively on his thin shoulder. Occasionally, as the leaders paid their obeisance, he would react—nod, shake his head, stare—and the companion would lean, bringing her face closer to his, evidently attempting to decipher his meaning.

Jiang was called to approach. She did so, feeling still more nervous than the day she had been called to enter the first space capsule.

He lifted his head. The eyes in that battered face seemed to fix on her. His mouth worked, wordless.

The daughter began to intone, as if resuming a speech suspended halfway through. Without addressing Jiang directly, she spoke of the crimes of the United States, of atrocities committed during the recent conflict against hapless Chinese servicemen on the beaches of Taiwan. The people of the United States were foreign devils, of the type who had raped China repeatedly in the past. And they did not act alone, but in cooperation with their allies—even with their old foe Russia, even with the new young states which had budded off the corpse of the U.S., and which competed with it in other arenas. The world, it seemed, was polarized: China stood alone, ringed by her enemies, and it was ever thus . . .

Now the Helmsman tipped forward, as if rocking. He spoke, and his voice was faint, as if coming from far away.

"Jiang Ling. I dream I am at home, in my villa here in Beijing, with my family and associates. News arrives. On the fringe of the city, there is an odd outbreak of a respiratory disease. Hundreds of citizens present themselves to the hospitals gasping for breath. The first symptoms include vomiting, fever, a choking cough and labored breathing. Antibiotics appear to contain the disease. Without antibiotics, death from hemorrhage, respiratory failure or toxic shock follows in a few days. It kills more than ninety percent of its victims. The doctors struggle to diagnose this bizarre, unusual illness.

"People start to die, in large numbers.

"At last the doctors understand. The disease is spread by spores—spores polluting the air of the city, thousands of them entering the lungs with every breath—and the spores cross the lining of the lungs and travel to the lymph nodes, where they germinate, multiply and spread to other tissues, releasing toxins as they go.

"Public health officials try to understand where the spores come from and which direction they are spreading. But this takes time; and we have no more time. Rumors begin to spread that supplies of antibiotics have run out.

"Other rumors state that only some racial groups are affected by the disease: specifically, Han.

"I appear on softscreens, in Beijing and across the nation, and I caution against panic. But then news is brought to me that even my family has been exposed, even myself . . ."

He seemed to be looking at her, but his eyes were so vague and discolored she could not be certain. "Jiang Ling, I am describing an attack by the anthrax bacillus—or rather, a strain of it genetically engineered to strike at specific population groups. My advisers inform me that it would take a mere two hundred pounds of spores to destroy three million people in a city like this. And, my advisers say, such gruesome weapons are even now under preparation for use against us in secret laboratories in the United States . . ."

Jiang, horrified, thought of the America she had glimpsed: large, complex, confused, fragmenting, frightened. And she thought of some of the Western leaders she had met, for instance the chilling General Hartle: a grisly mirror image of the Helmsman, another old man clinging to the levers of power, continually reenacting the paranoia of his youth.

Was such scheming possible there?

Yes, she decided.

"But," she asked, "what is my assignment, sir?"

The Great Helmsman lifted his hand, his bony wrist protruding from the soft fabric of his Mao suit, his fingers thin as dried twigs, and he beckoned to her.

She stepped forward and, encouraged by the Helmsman's daughter, she leaned down and placed her face close to his. Close up, his skin did not have the alien texture she had perceived from a greater distance; it was clearly human, but brown with age, as brown as the earth, and riven with wrinkles and cracks, distended pores like the craters of the Moon. She had an impulse to reach out and touch it, to feel the faint warmth which must still pump beneath that battered surface.

His eyes, embedded in their black sockets, were like pearls, gray, moist, formless. His breath smelled, oddly, of milk.

"*Yingzhen zhike*," he said. "Poisonous wine. We must drink poisonous wine to slake our thirst. That is your assignment, Jiang Ling. You must sip the wine, now, for all of us . . ."

His voice was as dry, she thought, as the scratch of a leaf along the bed of an ancient Martian canal.

Benacerraf was standing on a shallow, undulating beach. Overhead, gray-brown methane cumulus clouds crowded the sky.

The black meniscus of Clear Lake, flat and still, swept all the way to a horizon that was nearby and sharply curving, dimly obscured by the continuous, burnt-orange drizzle of organic sediment. To left and right, Benacerraf could make out the mountainous walls of the enclosing crater, like lines of steep, irregular hillocks, their erosion channels stained by gumbo streaks, their profiles softened by the slow relaxation of the bedrock ice. Under the uniform orange glow which suffused everything, the lake's liquid ethane sat like a basinful of crude oil, thirty miles across.

The lighting—orange above, black below—and the sharp curvature of this small world were disconcerting. It was as if she was looking through a fish-eye lens, like the Apollo periscope, which made the ground bulge upward towards her, distorted by a rendering in false colors.

She wondered how long it would take for the lack of blue and green in this landscape to drive her crazy.

Rosenberg had been hoping that they might find the tholin washed away, exposing a rim of bedrock water ice, reasonably accessible. It hadn't worked out that way. These ancient, frozen coastlines were eroded by the slow action of waves—in fact Benacerraf could see some evidence of wave action; at the very edge of the liquid there were parallel streaks of crusty, foamy deposit, like the debris of some industrial pollutant, washed up over the raw tholin—but the drizzle of tholins from the air evidently fell more thickly than the waves could wash them away.

This was really just a down-sloping extension of the sludgy gumbo-coated icescape she'd become used to, the purple-brown sheen of tholin continuing all the way to the edge of the ethane lake and beyond.

And yet this was, nevertheless, a beach: one in its morphology with that other beach at Canaveral, a billion miles away, from which she had launched. And there was the same air of disjointedness she had noticed at beaches on Earth—at the interface between two different media, the sea and the land, where erosion and decay worked to reduce mountains and cliffs to a uniform, muddy mediocrity.

And besides, she thought, maybe this wasn't so unearthly after all. A few billion years back—give or take a couple of hundred degrees—it mightn't have been so different to stand on the beaches of primeval Earth, to look out on a similar ocean of sludgy, prebiotic organic soup. It was on a beach like this, she thought, that some proto-amphibian ancestor of mine first crawled out.

She had come full circle.

Rosenberg touched her shoulder; she could barely feel the weight of his hand through the layers of her suit. "Weather forecast for all you nautical types," he said. "Haze."

"Funny, Rosenberg."

"So. You ready to go?"

Ready, she thought, *to go sailing: on a horseshoe-shaped lake of paraffin, for all the world like a character in an Edward Lear poem.*

I want to be back in Seattle.

She padded back up the shallow slope of the beach to the boat. She was wearing snowshoes, as they called them: big curving plates of Command Module hull metal, strapped to her blue boots. The snowshoes kept her pretty much on top of the sticky gumbo. She had worked out a way of walking that involved sliding the snowshoes forward first, as if scraping mud off the soles, to free them of the clinging gumbo.

The "boat" was simply the base of Mott's Command

Module, *Jitterbug*. Benacerraf and Rosenberg had cut away the external shell of the double-skinned Module a couple of feet above the rounded lip of the heatshield. What they ended up with was a round, shallow bowl with a turned-up rim, something like a big dog-food dish, thirteen feet across. The orifices which had once contained the nozzles of reaction control engines were round, gaping wounds in the shallow walls. Rosenberg had plugged all but one of these; to the last he had fixed a steel cable. Atmospheric entry scorch marks still spread from the heatshield lip up and over the low walls of the boat. The wall had been etched with a scale, gradations inches apart, so they could measure the draught of the boat in Clear Lake. Its interior was cluttered up with the equipment Benacerraf was going to need, out on the ethane.

Building the boat—designing it in the relative warmth of the hab module, cutting and shaping the base of *Jitterbug*—had actually been fun, in a home-workshop kind of way. Working those hours with Rosenberg, most of them in a companionable silence, had been among the happiest Benacerraf had known since leaving Earth. For once in this mission they'd had a finite, well-defined goal, and the means to achieve it.

But now that they'd hauled the thing down here to the lake, it looked absurd, flimsy, a lashed-up improvisation. Which, of course, it was.

Benacerraf lined up with Rosenberg behind the boat. In her multilayer suit it was difficult to bend, and she struggled to close her thick gloves around the half-inch-thick rim of the boat's wall. But when they overcame the friction of the gumbo and got up a little momentum, the boat coasted easily down the beach.

The boat slid into the ethane without a splash, and came to rest a couple of feet from the edge of the beach. It bobbed, eerily slowly, and concentric oily swells rippled away from its circumference, fat and massive.

Now Rosenberg wrapped the end of the boat's steel mooring cable around his waist, and stepped back a few yards from the ethane's edge. He kicked off his snowshoes and let himself sink into the gumbo, anchoring himself there. "Okay, Paula. I'll pull you back at the first sign of trouble. The shallows should be okay, but that boat won't be able to withstand any problems in deeper water. I mean, ethane. And, Paula. Whatever you do, don't fall in. Don't even sit down. That ethane lake has a much bigger heat capacity than your ass, it will give you one cosmic case of hemorrhoids . . ."

"I'll bear it in mind, Rosenberg."

She took off her snowshoes, and lifted them carefully back up the beach. Then she hauled on the cable to pull the boat a little closer to the shoreline, to minimize the ethane wading she would have to do.

She stumbled through the shallow ethane to the boat. As fast as she walked, the stabbing cold of the liquid pierced the multiple layers of her heated boots.

She stepped over the boat's foot-high wall, and moved to the center of the boat. The little vessel rocked back and forth with slow grandeur, and she could hear a slow, somber sloshing from the liquid around its hull.

She looked down at her feet. Droplets of ethane fizzed as they boiled away from her boots.

The rocking steadied, slowly.

Rosenberg was climbing further back up the beach, stepping backwards, making sure his footing in the slush was secure. He sent waves rippling up and down the steel cable. The cable moved with languorous, snakelike grace in the low gravity; but it sliced through the low-density ethane liquid as if it wasn't there. And where the cable penetrated the liquid Benacerraf could see a puncture in the heavy meniscus, surface tension hauling ethane up the steel.

Rosenberg pressed a stud on his chest panel to take photographs with the digital Hasselblad mounted there. "The boat is riding well. You've dipped into the liquid by no more than a few inches, under the combined weight of the boat itself, you, and the equipment . . ."

"Just as you calculated."

"Just as I calculated. The density of the ethane——"

"Archimedes' principle applies, even on Titan. I do understand, Rosenberg."

"Sorry. Good luck, Paula."

"Yeah."

Benacerraf stepped to the rear of the boat and picked up the paddle. This was just another piece of *Jitterbug* hull, a curved shovel shape, fixed to a bar which had once been a couch strut. Feeling self-conscious, she leaned over to dip the paddle blade in the liquid.

She waved the paddle to and fro, in the ethane. There was little resistance to her motion, and the blade cut smoothly through the fluid without turbulence, but she could feel how the ethane was being cupped by the paddle.

With painful slowness, the boat inched away from the shore.

She was soon panting with the effort of waving the paddle. As she couldn't sit down she had to lean over the side of the boat to reach the liquid, and that was making her back and arms ache. Her suit was too stiff for rowing, a task for which it had never been designed. And besides, she knew her muscles still hadn't recovered from their extensive space soak. She made a mental note that they would need a longer handle the next time they tried this stunt.

Despite all this, the boat was gliding forward across the oily surface, fat ripples spreading away from its circular bow, the only sound a glutinous gurgle of ethane against the sides.

"That's it," Rosenberg said. "A back and forth motion; that's fine. Remember the viscosity of the ethane is very low. Once you build up some momentum you should just sail on. Just like the air-bearing facility back in Building 9 at JSC, right? Don't forget you have a back-up paddle in case you drop that one.

Don't try to reach in after it. And—"

"Let me row the damn boat, Rosenberg."

He fell silent.

The shoreline receded, the ethane surface between her and solid land growing into a thick black band.

Behind her, the lake's far shore began to protrude over the horizon. It was a shallow, dome-shaped hill, blackened by gumbo streaks.

When she judged she had gotten to a hundred yards out, she lifted her paddle out of the liquid and dropped it at her feet; her back and shoulders were aching, and she moved her arms around, trying to ease the muscles.

The boat continued to sail on over the surface of the oleaginous fluid. It was as smooth a ride, she thought, as if she was a beetle riding a hockey puck over damp ice.

At last she came to rest. The air seemed a little clearer here, in the middle of the lake, perhaps because of the constant dissolving and exsolving of gases from the ethane. It was as if she was embedded in some clear orange resin, with the dark gray methane clouds scattered over her head in their well-defined layer, like shadows on a ceiling.

From this far out she could make out more of the shape of the lake. It was obviously a horseshoe shape, curving around that central mountain—although from here, if she was honest, it was hard to tell if the lake was a true open horseshoe or if it closed over, around the far side of the mountain, into an annulus.

Looking back to shore was like looking across a sheet of blackened glass, to an encrustation of purple ice and foam at the lake's rim. She could see Rosenberg standing patiently, stained with gumbo up to his waist, where the cable termination glittered. Seen from here, Rosenberg was very obviously alone on that primeval beach. His figure was the only vertical in a landscape of horizontals, starkly isolated. There was nobody else standing with him: no houses or buildings or cars behind him on that landscape of soft undulations, no trees, no birds in the sky. And in the frigid, mushy depths below her there was no life she could recognize, perhaps no life at all.

The boat rocked with a slow, soothing gentleness, with a period of maybe five or six seconds. The lake surface was almost a perfect black, its ripples heavy and shallow, free of breakers. Most organic solids, raining down from the atmosphere, would simply sink to the bottom of the lake. But here and there Benacerraf could see scatterings of foam, gray, and purple. Some of that was spindrift, aerosols caused by bubbles bursting on the surface.

She felt her sense of place and time shift around her. It was as if the landscape of Titan was reaching her, through the isolating layers of her suit; she started to get a sense that she was truly *here*, alive and sentient, on this ethane lake, a billion miles from her birthplace. It took moments of stillness like this to understand this, she thought. Moments that the Apollo guys, Marcus White and the rest, were never given, in their hectic, task-crammed timelines. Moments that had come only, perhaps, in the quiet of their sleep periods, as those fragile Lunar Modules ticked and creaked around them. Moments, little fragments of true humanity, they were never encouraged to report. What a pity.

She wondered how long she'd been out here.

She felt as if her sense of time was dissolving, stretching like melted candle-wax. Pendulums would swing more slowly here, like the rocking of her boat, in the gentler gravity. Perhaps some pendulum hidden deep in her own being was slowing, too, in response to this small world.

But now Rosenberg waved. He had set up the small TV camera on its stand, looking out at her. And the portable antenna pointed straight up, to where *Cassini* hovered far above the clouds and haze in its fifty-thousand-mile Clarke orbit.

The comms gear was a reminder that this wasn't some dumb jaunt on a lake. She was out here to look for amino acids and other good stuff. And this was a NASA extravehicular activity, on the surface of an alien world; they had a duty to return data on what they were doing, whether anybody was listening or not.

Anyhow, she thought, this is the first time in all of human history that a grandmother has gone boating on the surface of a low gravity moon. It *ought* to be on TV. Jackie should see this. And the boys, she thought wistfully.

She began the series of experiments Rosenberg had set out for her. The first was a series of sample collections; she gathered up droplets from the lake into plexiglass test tubes, and bottom sediment that she trawled up using tubes fixed to a line.

She started up the tilt meter. This little gadget was something like an electronic spirit level. It contained two vials of a conductor fluid; as the boat tipped back and forth under the influence of the lake's slow waves, the electrical resistance of the fluids in the tubes changed, and could be measured. Next she dipped a refractometer into the liquid to measure its speed of light. The refractometer was a cute thing, a little transparent box with prisms inside it, which she filled up with Clear Lake fluid. She measured the fluid's ability to conduct heat; by filling up a tube with fluid she immersed a platinum wire, and watched how its resistance changed as she passed current through it. She deployed a simple gadget which measured the speed of a sound wave traveling between two piezoelectric transducers. The sound speed would tell a lot about the ocean, and when she reconfigured the gadget, Benacerraf might be able to make a sonar estimate of the depth of the lake, if the grunge-coated bottom proved reflective enough. She measured the ethane's dielectric constant—its ability to hold an electric charge—by filling up a plate condenser with fluid, and measuring its capacitance. And so on.

One of Benacerraf's favorite instruments was a pair of thin metal vanes mounted on a piezoelectric crystal. The crystal drove the vanes, and their resonance depended on the density of the fluid in which they were immersed.

The results of the experiments ought to help determine more about the lake's nature. The lake wasn't a simple pool of ethane. There were fractions of other paraffins—methane, propane, butane, others—as well as dissolved nitrogen, and a slew of higher organics. For instance, the refractive index of the lake fluid was very sensitive to the percentage of dissolved methane.

She had to bend over the side of the boat to work, and soon her back was aching once more. She tried to keep her hands clear of the cryogenic fluid of the lake itself. She worked with tongs and pipettes, as if dealing with some acid. She fumbled a little with her gloved hands.

Her last experiment was a plumb line, pleasingly crude and intuitive, just dropped over the side. The line was loaded with a scrap of Command Module aluminum, and the depth was marked out by simple knots in the steel cable. It was a little hard to tell when the string was fully paid out, so soft and muddy was the bottom. When she estimated the weight had reached a reasonably firm surface, she read off the depth. Ten feet.

She described the result, and what she could see, to Rosenberg.

"That's good, Paula," he said. "The ethane is deposited at a rate of three feet every ten million years. So that makes your lake maybe thirty million years old, which is pretty young for a crater of such size. When it formed, the crater would have had the kind of shape we recognize on the Moon—a shallow saucer, with maybe a central peak. After that, the ethane lake gathered. But the bedrock ice on Titan flows, on the timescale of a few million years. Viscous relaxation. That pushed up the center of the crater into that ice dome you see. So the ethane was shoved into an annulus, a ring around the domed mountain . . ."

"And the horseshoe shape?"

"Saturn's tides. If Titan was covered by an ocean, the surface would be drawn into an egg shape by Saturn's gravity, with the sharp ends pointing towards and away from Saturn. Our isolated lake is a fragment of that egg-shaped surface. It's as if the crater is tipped up a little bit; all the fluid is pushed to one end of the annulus channel by the tidal acceleration."

Benacerraf felt awed. She looked around at the horseshoe shape of the lake once more. Saturn was invisible, but its gigantic influence was everywhere, its gravity field shaping the very nature of the landscape over which she moved. Benacerraf felt tiny, irrelevant, as if cupped in the palm of huge, invisible forces.

On impulse, she bent, stiffly. She got hold of the lip of the boat's wall, and got down to one knee. Immediately she could feel the cold of the hull, and of the mass of ethane below: it was as if the heat was being drained out of her body through the bone of her knee, the layers of her suit, and she could feel the hot, ineffectual triangles of her laboring suit heater.

She leaned out of the boat, and looked into the ethane. Fat ripples, concentric with the circumference of the boat, oozed across the surface of the lake, suffused with the slow time of Titan. The ethane was utterly black, returning no reflection of her helmet, her face. It was unnerving, as if this wasn't a liquid at all; it was as if she was poised over a hole in the world, a pit of black space that stretched down to infinity.

She reached out with a gloved hand. She passed her fingers through the ethane. In her peripheral vision she could see that a warning light flashed on her chest panel.

She pulled her hand out of the lake.

She lifted up her glove. The residual ethane gathered into fat little globules on her fingers and palm; its high surface tension had pulled it into these tight, mercury-like balls. Set against the blue of her glove, this sample of the lake was a kind of dull brown, but not completely opaque, like dirty petrol. She thought she could see particles, swirling about in the interior of the globules, but the light was poor.

Even as she studied the globules they were shrinking. The

boiling point of pure ethane was around ninety below—which was about ninety degrees above the ambient temperature. It was a big temperature jump, but even so, so quickly, the ethane droplets were absorbing the heat which was leaking out of her suit. The rapid evaporation was disturbing, a tough reminder of the fragility of her situation here. And every molecule of ethane that left her hand would carry away a little more of the heat her body needed.

She shook her hand free of the remaining droplets; they scattered from her glove in slow-motion parabolic arcs.

When she looked at her hand again, she found that the evaporating ethane had left a purplish scum on the fabric, in little discrete spots. Complex, prebiotic hydrocarbons: once more, she was immersed in the stuff of life.

"Paula," Rosenberg called now, urgency in his voice.

"What?"

"Take a look up there. The clouds."

Benacerraf had to tilt back on her heels to see.

The methane clouds were still more broken now, and were streaming, across the orange haze ceiling beyond.

"Wind coming up," she murmured. "That was sudden. What do you think, Rosenberg? Fifteen knots?"

"More like twenty, I'd say. And that means waves. Paula, get out of there."

It was probably good advice. Waves on Titan were not like Earth's.

She looked around, towards the center of the lake.

The waves were already coming, radiating out from the domed ice mountain at the heart of the horseshoe. Bred by Titan's low gravity, they were like slow-motion tsunamis: walls of black ethane, each of them at least a hundred and fifty feet tall. It was hard to tell, but Benacerraf estimated the waves were a half-mile apart. They were moving across the surface of the lake at maybe thirty miles an hour—a glacial pace by Earth

standards, where waves of such size would have moved seven
times as fast.

Maybe the boat could ride this out, just float over the back
of those huge, stretching beasts.

Maybe not.

She began to drag her paddle through the paraffin lake once
more, and she could see Rosenberg hauling clumsily on his
cable, his feet scrabbling at the gumbo for footing.

Within a couple of minutes, with a heavy bump, the boat
had grounded against the shore of Clear Lake.

Benacerraf looked back. The waves were heaping up still,
glistening black walls sweeping grandly towards the shore. But
they would break when they reached the shallows.

With Rosenberg's help, she began to haul the boat up the
beach, far enough that the breaking waves couldn't reach.

"Get moving, you old bastard." Bart went around the
room, his white jacket stained by some yellow fluid, and he de-
opaqued the windows with brisk slaps.

It took Marcus White a while to figure out where he was. It
often did nowadays. So he just lay there. He'd been in the same
position all night, and he could feel how his body had worn a
groove in the mattress. He wondered if Bart had ever seen
Psycho. "I thought—" His mouth was dry, and he ran his tongue
over his wrinkled gums. "You know, for a minute I thought I
was back there. Like before."

Bart was just clattering around at the bedside cabinet,
pulling out clothes, and looking for his stuff: a hand towel,
soap, medication, swabs. Bart never met your eyes, and he
never watched for the creases on your pants.

"My father was there." Actually he didn't know what in hell
his father was doing up *there*. "The sunlight was real strong.

And the ground was a kind of gentle brown, depending on which way you looked. It looked like a beach, come to think of it." He smiled. "Yeah, a beach." That was it. His dream had muddled up the memories, and he'd been simultaneously thirty-nine years old, and a little kid on a beach, running towards his father.

"Ah, Jesus." Bart was poking at the sheet between White's legs. His hand came up dripping. Bart pulled apart the top of White's pyjama pants. White crossed his arms over his crotch, but he didn't have the strength to resist. "You old bastard," Bart shouted. "You've done it again. You've pulled out your fucking catheter again. You filthy old bastard." Bart got a towel and began to swab away the piss.

White saw there was blood in the thick golden fluid. Goddamn surgeons. Always sticking a tube into one orifice or another. "I saw my buddy—Tom, you know—jumping around, and I thought he looked like a human-shaped beach ball, all white, bouncing across the sand . . ."

Bart slapped at his shoulder, hard enough to sting. "When are you going to get it into your head that nobody gives a flying fuck about that stuff? Huh?" He swabbed at the mess in the bed, his shoulders knotted up. "Jesus. I ought to take you down to the happy booth right now. Old bastard."

Like a beach. Funny how I never thought of that before. It had taken him forty years, but he was finally making sense of those three days. More sense than he could make of where he was now, anyhow. Not that he gave a damn.

Bart cleaned him up, dressed him, and fed him with some tasteless pap. Then he dumped him in a chair in the day room. Bart stomped off, still muttering about the business with the catheter.

Asshole, White thought.

The day room was a long, thin hall, like a corridor. Nothing but a row of old people. Every one of them had his own tiny softscreen, squawking away at him. Or her. It was hard to tell. Every so often a little robot nurse would come by, a real R2-D2 type of thing, and it would give you a coffee. If you hadn't moved for a while, it would check your pulse with a little metal claw.

The softscreens were still basically TVs but you had to set them with voice commands, and he never could get the hang of that; he'd asked for a remote, but they didn't make them any more. So he just had his set tuned to the news channels, all day.

Sometimes there was news about the program, if you knew where to look. Which he generally didn't.

He'd heard they were doing more EVAs on Titan, which was a hell of a thing, but he hadn't seen a single damn picture about that. Of course it was different back then. When the *Eagle* set down, he'd watched the walk itself at Joan Aldrin's house at Nassau Bay. When Buzz first came on screen she kicked her feet and blew kisses at the screen. Those creaky old pictures, like some kind of silent movie. And then he'd gone on to one hell of a Moonwalk party with some of the guys . . .

But there wasn't even anybody up in LEO nowadays, except a couple of Red Chinese, maybe.

He couldn't find anything about Titan. He folded up the screen in disgust.

He tried to read. You could still get paper books, as opposed to softscreen, although it cost you. But by the time he'd gotten to the bottom of the page he would forget what was at the top; and he'd doze off, and drop the damn thing. Then the fucking R2-D2 would roll over to see if he was dead.

The door behind him was open, letting in dense, smoggy air. Nobody was watching him. Nobody but old people, anyhow.

He got out of his chair. Not so hard, if you watched your balance. He leaned on his frame and set off towards the door.

The day room depressed him. It was like an airport departure lounge. And there was only one way out of it.

Unless you counted the happy booth. A demographic adjustment, Maclachlan called it.

Maclachlan was an asshole. But White couldn't really blame them, Bart and the rest. Just too many old bastards like me, too few of them to look out for us, no decent jobs for them to do.

Outside the light was flat and hard. He squinted up, the sweat already starting to run into his eyes. Not a shred of ozone up there. The home stood in the middle of a vacant lot. There was a freeway in the middle distance, a river of metal he could just about make out. Maybe he could hitch a ride into town, find a bar, sink a few cold ones. But he had the catheter. Well, he'd pull it out in the john; he'd done that before.

He worked his way across the uneven ground. He had to lean so far forward he was almost falling, just to keep going ahead. Like before. You'd had to keep tipped forward, leaning on your toes, to balance the mass of the PLSS. And, just like now, you were never allowed to take the damn thing off for a breather.

The lot seemed immense. There were rocks and boulders scattered about. Maybe it had once been a garden, but nothing grew here now. Actually the whole of the Midwest was dried out like this.

At least this was still the United States of America, though. At least he was still an American. Things could be worse. At least he hadn't become a fucking New Columbian.

He reached the freeway. There was no fence, no sidewalk, nowhere to cross. He raised an arm, but he couldn't keep it up for long. The cars roared by, small sleek things, at a huge speed: a hundred fifty, two hundred maybe. And they were close together, just inches apart. Goddamn smart cars that could drive themselves. He couldn't even see if there were people in them.

He wondered if anyone still drove Corvettes.

Now there was somebody walking towards him, along the side of the road. He couldn't see who it was.

The muscles in his hands were starting to tremble, with the effort of gripping the frame. Your hands always got tired first, in microgravity . . .

There were two of them. They wore broad-rimmed white hats against the sun. "You old bastard." It was Bart, and that other one who was worse than Bart. They grabbed his arms and just held him up like a doll. Bart got hold of the walker, and, incredibly strong, lifted it up with one hand. "I've had it with you!" Bart shouted.

There was a pressure at his neck, something cold and hard.

The light strengthened, and washed out the detail, the rocky ground, the blurred sun.

He was in a big room, white walled, surgically sterile. He was sitting up in a chair. Christ, some guy was shaving his chest.

Then he figured it. Oh, hell, it was all right. It was just a suit tech. He was in the MSOB. He was being instrumented. The suit tech plastered his chest with four silver chloride electrodes. "This won't hurt a bit, you old bastard." He had the condom over his dick already. And he had on his fecal containment bag, the big diaper. The suit tech was saying something. "Just so you don't piss yourself on me one last time."

He lifted up his arm. He didn't recognize it. It was thin and coated with blue tubes, like veins.

It must be the pressure garment, a network of hoses and rings and valves and pulleys that coated your body. Yeah, the pressure garment; he could feel its resistance when he tried to move.

There was a sharp stab of pain at his chest. Some other electrode, probably. It didn't bother him.

He couldn't see so well now; there was a kind of glassiness around him. That was the polycarbonate of his big fishbowl helmet. They must have locked him in already.

The suit tech bent down in front of him and peered into his helmet. "Hey."

"It's okay. I know I got to wait."

"What? Listen. It was just on the softscreen. The other one's just died. What was his name? How about that. You made the news, one more time."

"It's the oxygen."

"Huh?"

"One hundred percent. I got to sit for a half hour while the console gets the nitrogen out of my blood."

The suit tech shook his head. "You've finally lost it, haven't you, you old bastard? *You're the last one.* You weren't the first up there, but you sure as hell are the last. How about that." But there was an odd flicker in the suit tech's face. Like doubt. Or, wistfulness.

He didn't think anything about it. Hell, it was a big day for everybody, here in the Manned Spacecraft Operations Building.

"A towel."

"What?"

"Will you put a towel over my helmet? I figure I might as well take a nap."

The suit tech laughed. "Oh, sure. A towel."

He went off, and came back with a white cloth, which he draped over his head. He was immersed in a washed-out white light. "Here you go." He could hear the suit tech walk away, laughing.

In a few minutes, it would start. With the others, carrying his oxygen unit, he'd walk along the hallways out of the MSOB, and there would be Geena, holding little Bobby up to him. He'd be able to hold their hands, touch their faces, but he wouldn't feel anything so well through the thick gloves. And then the transfer van would take him out to Merritt Island, where the Saturn would be waiting for him, gleaming white and wreathed in cryogenic vapor: waiting to take him back up to the lunar beach, and his father.

All that soon. For now, he was locked in the suit, with nothing but the hiss of his air. It was kind of comforting.

He closed his eyes.

Paula Benacerraf and Bill Angel, two human beings from Earth, were climbing the highest mountain on a moon of Saturn. They were seeking water ice, to supplement their life support systems.

Toiling up the slope in their bulky white suits, and with their sleds sliding across the gumbo, they must look, Benacerraf thought, like two grubs hauling chunks of cast-off exoskeleton over the skin of some huge animal.

Benacerraf's suit felt hot, and chafed at her groin and armpits, and she could feel blisters forming across the soles of her feet. Every step she took in the snowshoes, going up the gumbo slope, she had to angle her feet and dig in to get traction sufficient to haul the mass of the sled another few feet. Her visor was misted up from her breath, and she could feel her heart hammering.

She paused for breath. She leaned into the sled harness—it was adapted from an Apollo couch restraint—and she rested her gloved hands against her legs. Her helmet lamp splashed light over the glistening slope before her.

As he slogged ahead of her up the gumbo slope, dragging his sled, Bill Angel sang some kind of marching song to himself. Just a couple of phrases of it, over and over. It was easy for him to find his way, sight or no sight; he was just following the line of maximum slope. He was already maybe twenty yards ahead of her, and his form was dimming a little in the murky air, although his stained white suit still showed up brightly against the black layer of methane clouds that hid the mountain's summit, and the splash of light of his helmet lamp—she made him wear it as a beacon—was clearly visible.

He was as encumbered by his sled as she was by hers. The sleds were just cone-section panels of Apollo Command Module hull, so big they would be impossible to pull under Earth gravity, even empty as they were right now. But this wasn't Earth. And Angel just marched on, dwarfed by his sled, his legs shoving at the gumbo like pistons.

Rosenberg called from Tartarus, via S-band, his signal bouncing off *Cassini*.

Clumsily, Benacerraf flicked a switch on her chest panel. Rosenberg had rigged up two separate S-band frequencies: one open to the three of them, and the other available to Rosenberg and Benacerraf alone.

On the private band, Rosenberg said: "How's it going up there?"

She lifted up her arm; there was a reflective panel there that let her read her chest panel. She had rigged up her panel so she could cycle it between the status of her own suit and Angel's. "He seems to be doing okay. Heartbeat a little high, maybe . . ." She switched back into Angel's voice loop for a second. "Still, he goes on with the damn singing. Over and over."

"Singing I can forgive. Check your marker."

She looked back down the slope. It was vertiginous—under Titan's weak gravity, this ice mountain had a gradient of maybe one in four for most of this ascent—and they were already a couple of thousand feet above the reference level where *Discovery* sat. The mountain was a flat cone, thrusting out of the landscape. It was maybe nine miles across, two high. An ice mountain as steep as this would have been impossible on Earth because of the higher gravity; the pressure at its base would have melted the ice, and the form would subside, leaving hillocks only a fraction as high. From here, the base of the mountain was hard to see, washed out by the eternal murky haze. She could barely see the last marker she'd planted; it was just a ghostly vertical line of white metal against the dark-stained tholin slush.

From the pile in her sled she dug out another marker—an aluminum strut from Apollo—and rammed it into the gumbo.

When she turned, Angel was almost invisible, still ploughing upwards.

"Bill, don't get too far ahead."

His singing cut off as if she had turned a switch. He stopped moving; he straightened up and turned, as if looking down towards her.

She took a slug of stale recycled water from the nipple in her helmet, and leaned into the harness once more.

When they were side by side, maybe thirty yards apart, Angel started to toil upward alongside her. Singing.

"Where did you learn the song, Bill? The Air Force?"

Again, that switch-like cut-off. "Nope," he said.

"Then where?"

"My father. Dad would take me walking in the hills. I'd scramble along behind him, over scree and bare rock . . ." Angel laughed. "That old bastard would walk me until my feet bled into my sneakers."

Benacerraf frowned. "It sounds kind of hard."

He tilted towards her, and, through his visor, she could dimly make out his sunken eye sockets. "You're not some Freudian, are you, Paula? Did my dad's cruelty make me what I am? Was his ghost there to push me aboard *Endeavour* that last time? Is it his fault I went crazy halfway to Saturn?"

Benacerraf felt out of her depth. Was he really being so self-reflective? . . . or was even this remark just another thread in the tapestry of his irrationality?

She said, "What do I know? All I said was it seems tough, to drag some little kid over the kind of terrain you're talking about."

"Maybe. But I learned a hell of a lot."

"Like what?"

"Like how to endure. You see, you got to have some kind of mantra, to get you through experiences like this, Paula. Crap that just goes on and on. You can sing, you can fantasize about sex, you can talk to yourself. Anything, to take your mind off what you got ahead of you, the pain in your feet and legs."

"It sounds like auto-hypnosis."

"Maybe it is. Mind-traveling, my dad called it. Seventy percent of any climb is mental. If you're going to get through a slog like this, you got to fight the demons inside. Maybe you should take a leaf."

"Maybe," she said.

Within a couple of minutes, Angel had resumed his singing.

She considered switching off his loop. But if she did that, she couldn't tell if he was in difficulty. She compromised. She turned down the gain, so Angel's voice was reduced to a kind of bass insect-whisper.

Soon her shoulders, back, feet and crotch were aching again, and her body was telling her it wanted to stop, now.

Maybe I ought to try it, she thought, Papa Angel's patent balm for the soul.

Always a little further, pilgrim, I will go. Always a little further . . .

Oddly, it seemed to work. Her thoughts started to diffuse, and she entered a kind of orange, mindless tunnel, of pain and effort and tholin slush that stretched on, up the hillside above her.

Always a little further.

After a time, the going underfoot seemed to be getting a little easier. She didn't sink quite so far into the gumbo, and it wasn't so sticky when she tried to lift up her snowshoed feet.

Then, at last, she felt a scrape of some more resilient surface under her aluminum snowshoes.

She stopped, and leaned into her harness. She tipped up her foot and dug at the gumbo with the lip of her snowshoe. There was some pale gray substance, like fine gravel, mixed in with the purple-brown gumbo.

"Hey, Bill," she said.

"What?"

"I think I found ice."

He laughed. "I been crunching over some shit for a hundred yards or more."

She looked up, tipping to balance the mass of her pack.

The slope pitched up before her as steeply as ever. But now

she could see that the purple-brown gumbo layer had been washed away, exposing gray-white streaks beneath. And when she leaned back to look further up the slope, she saw the surface turned into an almost pure white, streaked here and there with tholin rivulets. The white continued all the way up through the orange air, until it disappeared into the lid of gray-black methane cloud which hid the summit of Mount Othrys.

"How about that. Rosenberg, I think we did it."

"You found bedrock?"

"Water ice."

"How high are you?"

Benacerraf was carrying an altimeter, cannibalized from one of the Apollos; she wore it on a chain that dangled from her backpack. She reached around clumsily, and pulled the altimeter up before her face.

"A shade over three thousand feet," she said.

"Good," Rosenberg said.

"Good?"

"Sure. You're well above the limit altitude of the rain. It only rains on the summits, never on the plains. It's just what I would have expected . . ."

"Theory later, Rosenberg," Benacerraf said.

"It's just nice when you figure something, and it works out. Makes the Universe seem a little less scary."

She let herself out of her harness, and made sure her sled wasn't going to slide back on down the gumbo. Then she walked forward, until the gumbo beneath her feet had thinned out, and she was stepping on bare ice. She kicked off her snowshoes, and left them at the edge of the gumbo.

The ice surface wasn't hard; it crunched beneath her booted feet, the noise sharp in the thick air.

She looked around. "The edge of the gumbo is quite sharp," she reported to Rosenberg. "I guess we could feel it thinning out for a few hundred yards. But it's clearly keyed to the altitude and its edge is a definite line. Like a tree line."

"A gumbo line," Angel said.

"The surface isn't solid, here. It's some kind of regolith. The ground here is very fine-grained. Almost powdery, not like ice at all. I can kick it up loosely with my toe, and it is sticking in fine layers to my boots."

"Is it supporting your weight?"

"Yes. But I sink into the surface a little, maybe a half-inch, before it compacts. It's a little like walking on even snow."

"Snow it ain't," Rosenberg said. "We're two hundred degrees below the freezing point of water here . . . What you're walking on is impact-gardened regolith. Ancient ice, smashed to pieces by meteorite and micrometeorite impacts, over billions of years. Like Moon dust, pulverized to a depth of inches or feet."

"But this isn't the Moon," Benacerraf said. "Wouldn't that thick atmosphere shield out the bolides?"

"Yes. But some, the big ones, will still get through. And remember that Titan isn't particularly geologically active; that ice has probably lain there exposed almost since Titan first accreted, four billion years ago."

"That's time for a lot of gardening," Angel said. "Hey, double-dome. We could go skiing up here."

"I wouldn't recommend it," Rosenberg replied drily.

She lifted up her boot. "It has a lot of cohesion. I'm leaving firm footprints here; the regolith seems to take a sharp slope, of seventy or eighty degrees. Cohesion and adhesion."

"Probably from organic deposits on the grain surfaces," Rosenberg said.

"It's going to be easy to walk here," she said. "Much easier than on the gumbo. I guess we can leave the snowshoes behind."

Angel was walking over to Benacerraf. Free of his harness, he seemed to bounce between each step; he floated over the ice like a human-shaped beach ball, she thought, his white suit still streaked with gumbo. He looked like a floating ghost, in the murky light.

Benacerraf stared at her own footprints, crisp and sharp and white, in the virgin Titan ice.

Benacerraf and Angel harnessed themselves up once more, and renewed their haul up the ice slope. The footing was much easier, and the aluminum carapaces of the sleds scraped easily over the crisp, firm ice.

Soon their footprints stretched down the flank of the mountain behind them, partly obscured by the snail-like trails of the sleds.

The whiteness of the ice underfoot was a sharp contrast to the gray-black lid of methane clouds. Through gaps in the clouds overhead she could see the upper haze layers, a uniform orange which seemed lurid to eyes which were becoming accustomed to the Earthlike gray-white of the ice. Again, she had the disorienting feeling that she was traveling through some false-color VR landscape; Angel's suit looked underlit by the white below, the contours of his body shaded by the burnt orange above.

Another couple of thousand feet higher, Benacerraf called a halt. She felt hot and cooped up in her suit. She felt as if she could just open up her faceplate, take a deep breath of this cool mountain air, and rub a little snow in her face.

Angel slowed and stopped. Over the VHF link between them she could hear the rattle of his vacuum-damaged throat, the slurping of water from the nipple in his helmet. Discreetly, Benacerraf checked his suit diagnostics on her chest panel. He was using a lot of consumables, but no more than she was.

"What do you think?" he said at length. "Is the regolith deep enough here?"

"It's hard to tell. It all feels the same underfoot."

"The depth is probably pretty uniform, away from the gumbo layer," Rosenberg said from Tartarus. "It's just, the higher you go, the cleaner it should get."

"This will do as well as anywhere," Benacerraf said. "Come on, Bill. Let's get these damn sleds filled up."

She bounded down the few paces to the side of her sled and lifted out her shovel.

As it happened, the shovel was the same piece of equipment she'd used to bury Nicola Mott.

Using both hands, holding the handle away from her body, she pushed the rounded edge of the shovel blade into the regolith. There was a hiss of metal against ice grains.

The blade sank in easily for a few inches, but resistance built up quickly. When the blade was maybe five inches deep, she couldn't push it any further in. She hopped forward and leaned over the crude handle of the shovel, propping it under her belly with her hands still wrapped around it, trying to use her weight to push the shovel deeper.

She achieved maybe another inch of penetration. In this gravity, her weight didn't count for a lot.

She straightened up, panting, and lifted up the shovel. Some of the ice she'd raised so laboriously just floated off the blade.

She swiveled to the sled, and dumped in the ice regolith. It fell slowly, and rattled as it hit the aluminum hull of the sled.

She straightened up again. "It's not going to be easy," she said to Rosenberg. "When you push in the blade, the regolith compacts after a couple of inches. It feels more like sand than snow—"

"It isn't snow," Rosenberg said.

"Whatever. It's going to take a long time to fill the sleds like this."

"Paula." Bill Angel said. "Try this."

She turned to look.

He was bending, closer to the ground, so that his blade was entering the regolith almost parallel to the surface. "See?" he said. "It slides easy into these looser top layers. Then you can scoop up a big shovelful. I can feel it." He was right, she saw; he was managing to lift big, tottering heaps of the regolith, which he dumped into his sled.

"I guess he's right," Rosenberg said. "You're gathering raw

materials for life support, Paula, not digging for a core sample. Get it whichever way is easiest."

She bent, and started scraping up the regolith the way Angel did it. The first couple of times she managed to come away with piles of loosely-packed regolith on her blade as big and precarious as Angel's. But the constant bending and straightening, against the stiffness of her suit, began to tell on her lower back and thighs.

She turned so that she was working uphill. That brought the regolith closer, and made it a little easier on her back, but it was still difficult, heavy work. Her EMU wasn't made for heavy labor; it was hot, confining, uncomfortable, and she wished again she could take it off.

She thought about Angel. Now he was humming, the same marching tune as before.

Perhaps it was the climb. She felt vaguely exhilarated herself—liberated by the steady exercise, the sense of altitude, the crispness of the icy regolith.

She realized now that she'd never truly gotten over her sense of confinement after being cooped up in *Discovery* for all those years; Titan, with its lousy visibility, socked-in clouds and gloopy, impeding surface, wasn't much of a release.

Maybe the same factors are working on Angel, she thought. Maybe this is working to clear out the contents of his head.

All he needed, she supposed, was a little space.

The light changed, subtly. It became somehow pearly.

She lifted up her head.

Raindrops were falling towards her face.

It wasn't like rain on Earth.

It was methane rain.

The biggest drops were blobs of liquid a half-inch across. They came down surrounded by a mist, of much smaller drops. The drops fell slowly, perhaps five or six feet in a second. It was more like being caught in a snowstorm, with the flakes

replaced by these big globules of methane liquid. The drops
weren't spheres; they were visibly deformed into flat hockey-
puck shapes, flattened out, she supposed, by air resistance.
They caught the murky light, shimmering.

The first drops hit her visor.

Each drop impacted with a fat, liquid noise; their splash was
slow and languid. The drops spread out rapidly, or else collapsed into many smaller, more compact droplets over the
plexiglass. Low surface tension, she thought automatically.
Some of the liquid trickled down the contours of her visor, but
the evaporation of the drops, over such a large area, was rapid,
and each drop dried quickly.

Her face felt a little cooler, she guessed because of the evaporation of the liquid, carrying away some of her heat.

She leaned forward, compensating for the mass of her pack,
and looked down. As it hit the ground, each raindrop broke up
into many smaller drops, which trickled rapidly into the
regolith, rinsing the tholin streaks off the ice.

Bill Angel turned his head this way and that, letting the rain
fall over his faceplate and helmet. "It sounds beautiful," he
said. "Like being a kid again. Lying under a wooden roof at
night, hearing the rain come down . . ."

"Yes," she said. "Yes." And in that moment she felt closer to
Angel than at any time since they left Earth.

"You know," Rosenberg said, "of all the worlds in the Solar
System, only Earth and Titan know rain. I wish I was there."

"Next time, Rosenberg."

She stood in the rain, wishing it would go on forever. Not
for the first time she was lulled into a kind of peace by the slowness of Titan, the paradoxical heaviness of time in this thin
gravity, the slow rhythms of nature here; it was as if she was
shedding the frantic, energy-laden pace of Earth, and becoming
a creature of Saturn twilight.

At last, the slow patter of drops against her helmet stopped.
She felt a sharp stab of regret.

There was still a faint wash of small droplets around her, but these were dissipating quickly. And now there was a mist in the air, a light, yellowish fog; it made the air seem brighter, like the air after a storm on Earth. Angel, standing before her, looked as if he had some kind of halo around him.

She reported all this to Rosenberg.

"That's a rain ghost, Paula. I want you to take a sample . . ."

She dug a sample bottle out of a pocket on her EMU, and opened it to the air. "Why?"

"The rain starts by nucleating around particles in the upper atmosphere. That stuff is usually suspended higher up, and won't reach the surface. But it can be transported down by the weight of the rain, down to lower altitudes. When the rain stops, the last drops evaporate, leaving their cores exposed. The rain ghost. You see? Paula, what we have is a free sample of upper-altitude haze particles."

"Terrific." She stoppered the bottle, labeled it with her propelling pencil (not a pen—ink froze), and put the bottle back in her pocket.

She looked around. The rain had gone: evaporated from her visor, and was absorbed into the ground. Above them, the methane clouds, evidently rained out, had cleared to a scattered, broken layer of dark fragments, revealing an orange glow above.

Save for the lingering rain ghost, it was as if the storm had never been.

"I guess we can go back," Benacerraf said. "The sleds are full."

"Yes," Rosenberg said. "Your walk-back limit—"

"Oh, fuck our walk-back limit," Angel said abruptly. "Rosenberg, how far are we from the top of this mountain?"

Rosenberg said reluctantly, "Give me an altitude."

Benacerraf consulted her altimeter. "Around eight thousand feet."

"That leaves you three thousand shy of the summit. I don't

recommend going further," Rosenberg said strongly. "You're climbing above the planetary boundary layer, and the winds are going to pick up. And in another thousand feet or so you'll be in the methane cloud layer."

"Actually, that shouldn't be a problem," Benacerraf said slowly. "The cloud is pretty broken up after the rain, Rosenberg."

"I can't believe I'm hearing this," Rosenberg snapped. "Maybe the altitude's affecting your oxygen supply."

"Come on, double-dome," Angel said. "Don't be an asshole."

"Bill—" Rosenberg hesitated. "What's the point? You won't be able to see anyhow. I'm sorry to be brutal, but—"

"The point, dipshit, is that I'll make it to the top. The point is, I haven't crossed two billion miles just to stop a few thousand fucking feet shy of the highest point on the moon. Or isn't that logical enough for you?"

"Paula, if you go along with this, you're as crazy as he is."

Anger flared in her. "Drop it, Rosenberg."

They were, she decided there and then, going to climb the mountain.

For today, anyhow, Bill Angel was out of his craziness. And if anything was going to keep him together, this kind of experience was.

Anyhow he was right. Wasn't this exactly the kind of exploration they had come so far to make?

She floated over to Angel. She took his hand. "Rosenberg, I'll leave markers, and give you an altitude every few hundred feet."

"How can I stop you doing this?"

"You can't," Angel said. "So shut the fuck up, and enjoy the ride."

Hand in hand, Benacerraf and Angel began to climb the icy regolith.

With the methane clouds broken up, it was bright enough to walk without helmet lamps.

Free of the gumbo, free of the sled, the landscape opening

up around her, she felt as if she was floating above the surface. She felt the way Marcus White and some of the others had described walking on the Moon. Only the stiffness of her surface suit, the disconcerting mass of her backpack, encumbered her now.

It was like being eight years old again, she thought: her adult cares sloughed away, her body light and compact and the air fresh and new and full of light.

Soon they were in the lower layers of the cloud. It was like being in a thick, dark mist, like smoke from a forest fire. Benacerraf could still see, roughly, where she was, but she was glad to have the slope of the ground for orientation.

After a couple of hundred feet they emerged above the cloud layer, into clear orange air. The regolith here was still pretty much gray-white, cleansed by methane rain. The lighting was orange and gray, surreal, dim like an early dawn, but bright enough they didn't need their helmet lamps to see.

She strode on, into the light.

They came upon the summit suddenly.

The regolith slope foreshortened before Benacerraf, and she realized they were approaching some kind of ridge. She slowed, and pulled at Angel's hand to warn him.

Still hand in hand, they approached the ridge. The slope flattened out, to a broad ledge maybe twenty feet wide. Leaving Angel behind, Benacerraf walked cautiously forward.

She was standing on the rim of a crater, puncturing the summit of Othrys.

"Take it easy, Paula," Rosenberg said. "We don't know how friable that surface is. Don't go close to the edge."

The crater was like a huge amphitheatre, bathed in the ubiquitous orange glow. "It must be four miles across, maybe five . . . I can see the far rim quite clearly. And in the base there is a dome structure. No central peak—"

"It's a caldera," Rosenberg said. "A cryovolcano. Fueled by ammonia-water lava, a remnant of the primeval ocean."

She looked down towards the ground.

The light was bright—better than twilight up here, like an autumn sunset, perhaps. The sky was empty of cloud, save for a scattering of light cirrus clouds around the zenith, probably methane and nitrogen ice.

The methane clouds formed a distinct layer, a thousand feet below her. They were black, fat cumuli with lumpy tops and flat bases, like froth riding on an invisible membrane in the air. The clouds stretched to the horizon, but through them she could make out the ground. It was an orange sheet, punctured by the jet black of ethane crater lakes, like a photographic negative of the Everglades. She thought she could make out Clear Lake, its compact cashew-nut shape far below, all but hidden by cloud and mist.

The horizon was visible, even through the orange haze. It was the dark band where the parallel sheets of sky-haze, methane cloud layer and punctured land met, all around her. It seemed close by: seventy or eighty miles away, she judged. And it was curved, quite sharply, as if seen through a distorting lens.

Titan was visibly round; she had a powerful sense that she was standing on a sphere, that she was clinging to the surface of a small, three-dimensional object, suspended in space, swathed by a thick layer of air.

"Paula." Angel was waiting for her, a few yards short of the summit. "Are we here?"

"Yes, Bill. We made it. We climbed Othrys."

He was standing slumped forward to balance his pack, and with his arms held loose at his sides. It was like an ape's gait, she thought.

And so they were: two clever apes, who had made it to the highest point on Titan.

She walked down, took Angel's hand, and began to lead him to the summit. "It's beautiful, Bill, so beautiful."

His blind face turned, the orange curve of Titan reflected in his visor. The crunch of the regolith beneath his boots was loud and sharp in the still, huge air.

☆   ☆   ☆

When they got back to Tartarus, Rosenberg insisted on passing the Titan water through the life support system's filters to get rid of the remnant tholins. At last, though, he was able to bring Benacerraf a bowl—in fact an EMU visor—brimming full of cool, clear Titan water.

She raised it to her lips.

It was the finest drink she'd taken in seven years, sweeter than wine.

Jiang Ling first saw the asteroid with her naked eyes when Tianming was ninety days out from Earth, ten days from its closest encounter.

At first the asteroid was barely more than a point of light indistinguishable from the remote stars, had she not known where, precisely, to look. But by the day after that 2002OA had grown to a distinct oval shape: almost like a potato, she thought irreverently, battered and irregular. She knew that from now on the asteroid would grow visibly, day by day, and then hour by hour, until at last its battered gray hide filled the small viewing window of her living compartment.

After the closest approach, the asteroid would then recede, just as rapidly.

But that, for her, was only a theoretical possibility.

Every day she performed two softscreen shows: one in Han Chinese for the benefit of her countrymen, one in English for the foreigners. She was allowed to say what she wished, although the Party expressed clear, if rather obvious, preferences.

Jiang adjusted the angle of her big S-band antenna, ensuring it was centered on the fat disc of Earth. Then she positioned herself before the *Tianming*'s single camera, fixed to a bracket on the wall. She had no props or charts or effects; none were necessary. It was sufficient that she simply talk into the camera, smoothly and plausibly, and production crews on the ground would later patch in such illustrations and other footage as was required.

She anchored herself over her table, and prepared what she would say.

. . . In the ninety days since it had been pushed out of orbit by its solid-propellant injection engine, *Tianming* had coasted slowly away from Earth, heading outward from the sun. It had dogged the heels of the home planet, she thought, as a dog will track its owner. Thus she had drifted more than three and a half million miles from Earth, and when the *Tianming*'s slow thermal roll brought the small viewing window into the right direction, she could see Earth and Moon together: twin crescents before the huge glare of the sun, the smaller brown alongside the fatter blue-white, so close to each other she could cover up both Earth and its satellite with the palm of her right hand, upheld before her.

And there was her theme.

She said: "It is precisely three thousand, nine hundred and sixty-seven years since Chinese astronomers witnessed an extraordinary heavenly event.

"The motions of all five naked-eye-visible planets brought them together in the sky. Above the crescent Moon at the horizon, Venus, Mercury, Mars, Saturn and Jupiter were strung out like lights on some celestial road, near the great square of Pegasus. That unique conjunction must have been a transfixing event. It was the beginning of the planetary cycles of our ancient astronomers.

"There has been no other time in the last four thousand years, and there will not be in the next four thousand, when such a spectacle will be visible again. But I am reminded of it now, as I study the Earth, Moon and sun framed together in the window of my capsule. How appropriate it is that a Chinese person should be here, to witness this unique conjunction!"

The joy in her voice was unfeigned. Jiang Ling was happy and proud to be here. She said that in her broadcasts, and she meant it.

The habitable compartments of *Tianming* were small, confining. The craft was improvised, of course, and much of its mass besides was given over to the weapon and its support systems, rather than to her comforts. But she was comfortable here, in this little spinning metal shell in space, and she was not given to claustrophobia.

Her mother told her she was happy in space, and nowhere else. It was true.

Sometimes it struck her as remarkable, however, how everything in the Universe had become separated into two distinct categories, characterized around herself: within a few feet of her body, contained in this compact craft, or else they were millions of miles away.

She continued with her broadcast, and other duties.

Her shelter in space consisted of cylindrical compartments, strung together along a common axis, like a collapsible telescope. Its curved hull was swathed with a powder-white insulating blanket, which shone brightly in the sun. Three huge solar panels were fixed around the module's widest section; they could be swiveled, like the faces of flowers, to trap the sunlight, and they were covered with cells, big black squares neatly aligned.

The smaller cylinders were used for docking with ferry craft and experimental work, and they were crammed with storage lockers, science equipment and control panels. The main body of the craft was called the working compartment, some fourteen feet wide.

There was a small table at which she could sit, by wrapping her legs around a rudimentary T-shaped chair. There were control and instrument panels, and command and signal equipment of the type used in *Lei Feng* spaceships. There were a number of work positions, where she could take measurements of such items of scientific interest as the interplanetary plasma environment surrounding the ship. There was a single, rather small porthole. During the cruise, the *Tianming* was rolled, continually, to ensure a uniform heating by the sun's rays; this had the effect of limiting her useful observations.

To the left and right of the workstations there were controls for the craft's basic systems: air regulation filters and pumps, temperature and humidity controllers, as well as more equipment and biomedical research apparatus.

There was a small galley area, with enough supplies, she was told, for a mission of one hundred days, with a small margin. There was an exercise cycle into which she could strap herself. Her orders were to use this for no less than three hours a day, in order to reduce the risk of muscle wastage and bone erosion.

Beyond the working chamber, inaccessible to Jiang, was a small hemispherical module containing rocket motors and propellant tanks.

Her home in space was brightly lit, compact and cheerful. She felt liberated, after the confines of the *Lei Feng* capsule, within which it had been barely possible to move. Everything was new and clean, even the lavatory section, the drawers full of neatly folded coveralls and underwear. The fans and pumps hummed comfortingly, and there was a smell of freshness—not a natural smell, but like a new carpet, she thought.

She slept in a cupboard, a box little larger than she was. Inside, however, tucked into her sleeping bag with the folding door drawn to, she was secure.

She had brought with her the small brass bell that had accompanied her on her first flight, in *Lei Feng* Number One— how long ago that seemed! As she prepared for sleep, she watched it drift in stray currents in the circulating air, on its curling length of vermilion ribbon, occasionally ringing. The inscribed face of Mao was intermittently visible, like the Moon hidden by clouds.

During her hundred-day flight, she performed science experiments with her space aquarium.

It looked like a suitcase containing two carousels from a compact disc player; but the walls of the carousels were clear, and murky water was visible within. The aquarium contained one thousand mussel larvae, thirty thousand sea urchin eggs and six thousand starfish embryos. One carousel spun up, imitating the Earth's gravity, and the other provided a gravity-free environment. The experiment had begun three hours after departing Earth orbit, when Jiang had injected a sperm concentrate into a container full of sea urchin eggs.

She had used a microscope to observe the effects of spaceflight on urchin embryo development. The study was designed to provide insight into the causes and cures of osteoporosis and muscular dystrophy. And she followed the calcium formation of a mussel's shell, to shed light on the bone depletion suffered by humans in space. The creatures' unusual swimming and feeding patterns, carefully recorded on video, were studied to provide pointers on how the oceans' fish populations might better be managed. Jiang also spent much time studying the embryos of starfish. The purpose was to learn how to predict and control early birth defects in humans. The embryo of a starfish, in early stages of development, was remarkably similar to that of a human . . .

The bioscience program was genuine work. But it was essentially a blind: a misdirection, intended to confuse anyone following her mission suspiciously.

In some senses she was lying, and she felt obscure shame about that: to come all the way out here, fifteen times as far as the Moon was from Earth—an astounding technical feat, especially for a country which a century ago had been an agricultural backwater—and *lie!*

And yet, she felt, on another level she was telling a greater truth, a truth that transcended the exigencies of her mission.

Earth was not alone. Earth and Moon swam together through a sea of objects, of varying sizes, called NEOs: near-Earth objects, also called Earth-crossing asteroids.

The object of Jiang's mission was known as NEO 2002OA, discovered in 2002. It was a mountain-sized rock, covered with impact craters and a regolith—a pulverized surface layer—like the Moon's. It was on a course which would bring it within a million miles of Earth: just four times the distance from Earth to Moon, only some one hundredth of the distance from Earth to sun.

There were three hundred thousand NEOs a hundred yards across or bigger, and some two thousand half a mile across or bigger. Some were rocky, some metallic, others rich in organics.

Earth sat at the bottom of the deepest gravity well between sun and Jupiter. Over billions of years, twenty percent of all the NEOs would impact the planet.

It was undoubtedly true, she had learned, that if humanity was to have a long-term future, leaving the planet and dispersing was the only option. Space travel was no leisure luxury for a rich world, but essential for the survival of the species.

Perhaps, she comforted herself, her mission—successful or otherwise—might spur a greater awareness of the hazardous environment within which humanity had, perforce, made its home; perhaps, in some ultimate long term, she might actually prove the savior of humanity.

Perhaps she might be remembered as mankind's greatest hero.

Rather than as its supreme villain.

Three days from her closest approach, with the asteroid grown massive in her window, she saw the flashes of the drone warheads which had preceded her.

The weapons had emplaced themselves close to the asteroid, though away from its surface. The flashes looked like miniature dawns. They were immediately surrounded by surges of debris from the asteroid's pulverized surface, which rocketed out in well-defined jets, some fragments glowing white-hot.

There was, of course, no heat, no sound, no concussion wave transmitted from the massive explosions—though her heart quailed as she looked into the fusion light.

She carefully observed the explosions, and prepared to compute their consequences.

The mission philosophy was simple. The smallest impulse required to deflect that rocky body was more than could feasibly be delivered by a single weapon. Too large an explosion, besides, could shatter the object, removing its usefulness.

Therefore a string of automated weapons had been launched by *Long March* boosters over the days preceding Jiang's own launch. The necessary impulse would be applied, not by one large detonation, but by a series of smaller ones. *Tianming* was distinguished only in carrying the last—albeit the largest—of the weapon set, to deliver the final tweak to the asteroid's new trajectory.

The mission design offered a chance for more accuracy, besides. The asteroid still had to travel many millions of miles along its new path. The successive explosions could be used to herd the asteroid closer towards the required final trajectory. The last detonation was, of course, the final opportunity for adjustment.

It was explained to Jiang, carefully, that China lacked the facility for sufficiently precise deep space tracking of either the asteroid or an unmanned spacecraft, and the robotic expertise to enable such a craft to navigate itself, sufficiently precisely. Only a human navigator—such as herself—using optical techniques on the spot could make the precise measurements of the deflection achieved of the asteroid by the unmanned probes, and then emplace the final weapon sufficiently precisely to achieve the last elements of the required deflection.

Such was her purpose.

It was also explained, equally carefully, that time, resource deficiencies and mission constraints were such that it had not been possible to provide a separable delivery system for the weapon itself. Nor any return or reentry provisions for the crew. That is, it was necessary for *Tianming* to remain in place during the explosion.

This was a factor which she took into account, in the course of her decision to accept the mission.

To fly in space: to venture once again beyond the atmosphere, to become the first Chinese to venture beyond low Earth orbit, the first Chinese to spend a hundred days in space—for that, she had, to her own surprise, been willing to exchange everything. Her life.

Even her place in history.

Jiang Ling was a spaceflight junkie.

It was even possible, she mused, that had this flight been offered even to some of the one hundred frustrated American astronauts, dispersing slowly from Houston, some of them may have accepted, so great was the lure of returning to the secret place, to space.

And having made her bargain, she would, of course, complete her mission.

It was conceivable that the detonations would be observed from the United States itself, and elsewhere. If they were, the Party had a further plausible cover story, she knew: that the explosions were being used in a scientific analysis of the asteroid's structure.

The light faded rapidly. The debris cloud dispersed quickly—or rather, the asteroid's new orbit took it away from the fragments blown out of it by the weapons.

The dosimeter aboard *Tianming* indicated that the radiation dose she had already taken exceeded nominal safety limits.

Jiang Ling smiled.

She picked up her optical navigation gear—a sextant with a simple telescope—and began to study the new position of the asteroid.

On the last day before closest approach, she found it more difficult than before to comply with the order to complete her three hours' cycling.

For her final broadcast she chose to feature the aquarium. She positioned the camera so that it focused on the apparatus, and then moved so that her own face was in the shot, close to the aquarium. For the benefit of the video camera, she made a show of peering into the microscope; her vision filled with blue water light. She spoke in her broadcast about these little creatures being her fellow passengers aboard *Tianming*.

It was a little corny, but it contained the essential truth. Somewhere in the milky-blue images of squirming sea urchins and eerily human starfish embryos, somewhere in this drop of the primeval sea which she had carried with her, so far from Earth, there was a sense of unity with all life, a hope of salvation.

She was not alone, even here, so far from the planet which had spawned her; she was still as one with all the creatures of the world.

Her greatest regret, in fact—which grew as 2002OA loomed—was that the thousands of creatures in this aquarium could not hope to survive the events to come.

Jiang Ling could no longer see Earth, Moon or sun.

On this, the hundredth day, the dark hide of 2002OA slid past the small window of *Tianming*.

It was as if she was flying over some miniature Moon, she thought. The surface was so pierced and broken by craters of all sizes that it was impossible to tell, by eye, how far away it was; she might have been in an Apollo spacecraft sailing over the surface of the Moon, sixty miles below, or peering through some camera at a plaster mockup, just out of arm's reach.

The spacecraft was in the shadow of the asteroid now, and only the spotlights of *Tianming* illuminated the surface, less than a mile from the craft: she fired her camera through the window, and the digitized photographs of churned regolith were sent immediately to the ground stations.

She heard the clatter of solenoids, felt the judder of the craft as it was pushed by squirts of the automatic reaction control system.

She was beyond the useful reach of her optical navigation; now, the automatic systems of the spacecraft had come into their own—particularly the radar, which would determine *Tianming*'s distance from the asteroid surface, and match it to the ground-based calculations using her astronomical observations of the asteroid's new path.

For optimal yield, the warhead required a standoff detonation, with the warhead placed forty percent of the object's radius above the surface. There, the weapon could irradiate an ideal thirty percent of the surface of 2002OA.

The weapon had been engineered to maximize its production of neutrons, which would be absorbed by the top few inches of the crust. The irradiated shell would heat, expand and spill away, thus imparting a rocketlike stress wave impulse to the asteroid.

From now on, until the mission reached its conclusion, Jiang Ling was a passenger.

She found the thought oddly restful.

She went to her sleeping cupboard, and retrieved the small brass bell. She rattled it, and the small clapper rang against the wall of the bell, and she stared into the corpulent, smiling face of *ta laorenjia*.

She ate a final breakfast. She found the ground crew had

packed a special, final meal: duck, pork with rice, and even a small bulb of *chemshu*, a rice liqueur.

She ate with relish. Then she carefully tidied away the plate and cutlery and enclosed microgravity cups.

It was hard to imagine that in a few minutes none of this familiar cabin and environment would exist; it was right to behave as if that were not so.

According to her mission clock, the final moment was mere seconds away. She had requested that the cabin camera be disabled, and that the radio link be kept silent.

She didn't want a countdown. And she had said her good-byes.

The last person she had embraced, on Earth, was her mother.

A little before detonation, Jiang Ling pressed her fists into the sockets of her eyes.

She saw the complete bone structure of her hands, like an X-ray, drenched in pink light.

There was a moment of heat—

It was Benacerraf who found the methane vent.

She continued to ban any EVA beyond the walk-back limit, despite her mountain-top adventure. Rosenberg had set up a systematic program to take atmospheric and surface samples from the area around Tartarus they could reach in a couple of hours. So he sent Benacerraf in her snowshoes striking across the featureless, dull ground to the northwest. After a couple of miles, as he had instructed, she filled up her little sample bottles and started to return.

As she returned—taking a sighting on the white crest of Mount Othrys, visible as a hulking silhouette through the haze—she came upon a place where the gumbo appeared to have a different consistency, a lighter color.

She stopped, right in the middle of the discoloration patch.

She dug at the gumbo with her snowshoe, and bent down to take a closer look. The light was even worse than usual; they were coming to the end of one of the eight-day-long Titan "days," and the methane overcast was heavy. But even in the dim, dried-blood light, she could see there was something unusual about the gumbo here. It was peppered by big, flattened bubbles. And as she watched, a fresh bubble emerged from under the tholin, spreading and flattening, streaks of color swimming in its surface.

She must have walked right over this patch on the way out. Whatever this was, it was out of the ordinary, surely the kind of thing Rosenberg had them out here looking for.

She bent, awkwardly, and took fresh sample bottles from her EMU pockets. She took a scraping of the gumbo itself, the air above the gumbo, and—with reasonable skill, she thought—managed to insert the plastic needle of a syringe into a bubble without breaking the sticky meniscus, and was able to draw out the uncontaminated gases within.

She straightened up, labeled the bottles, noted her location and walked on.

Back at Tartarus, inside the scuffed, patched-up, shacklike interior of the hab module, Rosenberg was distracted. He was busy trying to rebuild a balky nutrient pump from the CELSS farm, and he told her to store her sample bottles and he'd check them when he had time.

Meanwhile, Angel was having one of his bad days. He raged around the hab module, frustrated at his inability to perform the simplest task unaided. He railed at the equipment, at the assholes at NASA who wouldn't speak to them any more, at his crewmates.

For all the difficulties his presence posed on even the simplest EVA, it was outside the cramped, battered, stale confines of the hab module that Angel seemed most stable. The opportunity to get him outside hadn't come up for a couple of days, though, and now they were likely to be shut in through the eight-day Titan night. And already, Benacerraf thought, they were paying the price.

She made a meal for Angel, and sat him down in the Apollo couches. He rambled about his life, his space missions, his career, his father, even his sexual experiences. She sat and endured.

Listening to him was an easy safety valve.

Rosenberg padded around them in house shoes improvised from Beta-cloth scraps, and got on with his work on the pump. He didn't actually do anything to help her with Angel; it was clear that as far as Rosenberg was concerned, Angel was Benacerraf's problem, a waste of resources who ought to be pushed out the airlock.

It took Rosenberg two hours to get around to those anomalous samples.

Then he came bustling in from the Spacelab, shouting about an immediate EVA.

Benacerraf glanced uneasily at Angel. But he seemed to be heading into one of his inward-looking, passive phases. He was rocking to and fro in his couch, his right leg tapping rapidly, his head turning to and fro. She had learned to read Angel's moods; if he stayed in this state, he was so shut-in it was beyond the power even of Rosenberg's noisy, unstructured ranting to irritate him.

Rosenberg was still talking about going out.

"Slow down, Rosenberg," she said. "You know we've avoided EVAs at night."

"I know," he said. "I know. But this is exceptional. We have an opportunity, right now, and we don't know when it will recur. We'll miss out on it if we wait seven or eight days for the fucking sun to come up."

"What opportunity?"

"Paula, I analyzed those samples you brought back. The anomalous tholin, the bubbling——"

"I remember."

"You know what I found, in the sample you took from within the bubble?" He grinned. "Guess."

"Don't play games, Rosenberg."

"*Methane,*" he said. "Almost pure methane gas. You see?"

She thought it over. "No. No, I don't get it. The air is full of methane. We even produce it ourselves. Why should we care enough about methane to risk our necks out there in the dark?"

"Because of where the methane comes from," he said rapidly. "It has to be from an underground reservoir. There are probably pockets of methane scattered all through the bedrock ice, though not all so close to the surface . . . It has to be an intrusion of the magma, the deep ammonia-water, which is forcing that methane to the surface now. And if that's so, the site you found is one of the best possibilities for finding traces of ammono-analogue biology. Short of dropping into the caldera on Othrys, we—"

"Woah." She held up her hands again. "Tell me slowly."

"*I'm talking about life*, Paula," he said softly. "Titan life: life beyond Earth. That methane vent represents one of our best chances of detecting it. If we sit in here on our butts, we may miss it." He was struggling to be patient, she saw. "Do you get it? I'm not interested in the methane for itself. I'm interested in the ammonia-water magma."

"Because—"

"Because if we're going to find life anywhere, ammonia-analogue life, it's in the fluid of the ancient oceans. Where liquid ammonia is still available, as a solvent. And that's bubbling up out of the ground, a couple of miles away."

Angel turned his ruined face to Rosenberg. "Titan life, huh. So, what use is that? Can we eat the shit?" He shook his head, mumbling irritably, and retreated inward to his crooning.

"Actually," Benacerraf said drily, "he has a point, Rosenberg. This is science, not survival. I don't think we should put ourselves in a life-threatening situation for—"

Rosenberg seemed to snap.

She'd never seen him so angry. He came up and loomed over her, screaming at her. "This is precisely the reason we came to Titan in the first place. We have to be able to do more than sit around in here recycling Bill's piss and waiting to die. Paula, either you come out with me now, or I go out there myself. Right now." There were flecks of spittle on his lip, and behind his glasses his red-rimmed eyes were staring.

She closed her eyes, and wished she was in her wardroom.

She was sick of juggling them, these two assholes, both as difficult as each other in their ways, both demanding that she soak it all up, run their lives for them.

. . . The news from Earth, sent up to them in digital packets by the last DSN dish at Goldstone, was dire. More ecological decay, more flashpoint wars over crop failures and water shortages, more floods of refugees washing across the southern continents, more saber-rattling between the Chinese and Maclachlan's government. In a way, the Chinese issue scared her most. It was like the Cold War all over again. Except that she sensed those old bastards in Beijing *meant it*, in a way the Kremlin never had.

Well, maybe they could actually do some good up here. Maybe news of life outside Earth might actually lift some hearts, down on the bleeding ground. As Rosenberg said, it was why they'd come here, after all.

"You win, Rosenberg. We'll go."

He backed off, trembling.

"But," she said evenly, "it had better be worth it."

Angel, blind face turning this way and that, cackled as he rocked.

They stepped outside the orbiter, emerging into the pitch dark of a Titan night.

Benacerraf insisted the two of them rope themselves together.

Rosenberg laughed at her. "For Christ's sake, Paula. The tholin out west is as flat as a pancake for miles. What are you expecting to happen?"

She confronted him. "I don't know. I've only taken a walk over a methane vent once before, and last time I didn't know I was doing it. If we have to be out here at all, we take precautions. Take the damn rope, Rosenberg."

He made noises of disgust. But he knotted the rope around his waist.

They set off into the deeper dark, northwestwards, preceded by circles of lamplight. Benacerraf led the way, trying to retrace her steps to the methane vent. The gumbo glistened, purple and black, in the white light of the lamps; it reminded Benacerraf of an open wound.

Somehow, Benacerraf thought, it was harder to walk into the dark, with the gumbo sucking at her snowshoes, and only unmarked desolation ahead of her, beyond the circles of lamp light. Her imagination seemed to be populating the empty darkness with vague demons, and she felt a gathering dread at the thought of proceeding further.

Perhaps, she thought with a stab of unwelcome sympathy, Bill Angel feels like this all the time: his isolation on this dead alien world compounded by being lost in the dark.

After a couple of miles, she slowed. "It was about here."

Rosenberg cast about with his lamp. "The surface looks normal to me." He started to unknot the rope at his waist. "We ought to separate," he said. "We'll halve the time it takes if we work independently. Now, if I take the——"

"Keep the rope on, Rosenberg."

"Paula, that's just not logical. It's so inefficient."

"Keep the rope on, or we go back right now. I mean it, Rosenberg. Ammonia life or no ammonia life."

He groused like a kid. "Shit, Paula." But he knotted the rope up again.

They began to search, working in widening circles around

their starting position, the rope stretched to its maximum extent, their lamps throwing elliptical patches across the glistening, sticky gumbo.

It was more difficult than Benacerraf had expected; the colors of the gumbo were different in white, Earth-like lamplight, and the color changes she'd observed before were obscured. Rosenberg took to using his infrared vision. The resolution was poorer than with the naked eye, but perhaps he could detect the temperature changes associated with the methane vent.

After a few minutes, Benacerraf found what looked like a series of small, circular craters, dug into the gumbo at her feet. When she looked more closely, she found the lamplight had deceived her, making her reverse the image in her mind's eye; the "craters" were actually bubbles, pushing slowly up through the gumbo.

"Rosenberg," she breathed. "I think I have it."

He came over as fast as the gumbo would permit. He stood over the bubbling patch. "My God," he said. "You're right, Paula. We did it. What a discovery."

He unloaded his sampling gear from the pockets of his EMU. He took scrapings of the gumbo, and of the atmosphere within and above the methane bubbles. He assembled a hollow tube from sections, to take a core sample. He hoped that the lower levels of the core would contain materials soaked in liquid ammonia.

Benacerraf worked patiently at the core, twisting the improvised handle at the top, coaxing the core into the ground. It was difficult even to hold the handle against the stiffness of her thick gloves. She could feel the unevenness of her gloves' heating elements rubbing against her palm, and soon she thought her fingertips, where they were scraping against the material of her gloves, were starting to bleed.

It took as much effort to drag the core out of the clinging ground as to insert it. When it was free, Rosenberg started to dismantle the core sections.

A thunderous roar, deep bass, sounded through Bena-cerraf's helmet. Benacerraf could feel deep vibrations, as though the source of the noise was right beneath her feet.

Rosenberg said, "I think—"

There was a boom, like a sonic shock.

A few yards to Rosenberg's right, a gray cloud was erupting. She turned that way to focus her lamp light. The cloud was droplets of gumbo, thrown up from the ground, subsiding slowly back to the surface.

The ground had collapsed beneath the cloud, forming a roughly circular crater maybe six feet across. Benacerraf thought she could make out a gush of gas—methane, she guessed—pulsing out of the hole.

"Holy shit," Benacerraf breathed.

"The whole area is unstable," Rosenberg said quickly. He was still working on the core. "We're on some kind of crust over big methane bubbles. The methane venting might become explosive."

Another shudder beneath Benacerraf's feet. The ground shook again, and again. Another hole, bigger than the first, opened up to her right.

"Let's go, Rosenberg."

He was bending to the surface, scooping up the sections of the core sample. "I just need to collect this."

"Leave it, for Christ's sake."

More crumps and bangs; the ground shuddered again. Rosenberg was still fussing with his samples.

"Rosenberg! Move!" She tugged at the rope, yelling at him.

He straightened up, clutching one core sample section which he shoved in a pocket of his EMU.

They started to make their way back out of the vent area, stepping clumsily, casting their lamp light around. They fol-lowed their footsteps back out towards Tartarus; the footsteps showed up as a trail of shallow, infilling gumbo craters.

A gush of methane erupted from the ice, just to Benacerraf's left. She ducked. The noise was so all-engulfing it felt as if the sound was passing both underfoot and overhead.

And then a crater, a distorted circle ten feet across and steaming with methane vapor, opened up between Benacerraf and Rosenberg. There seemed no limit to the depth of the craters in their lamplight, as if the exposed pits reached to the heart of the world.

There was a feeling of hollowness beneath her; she thought she could hear echoes of the imploding ice and gumbo being returned from some huge chamber beneath her. She had the vertiginous feeling that she was crossing some fragile bridge, over a chasm.

The randomness terrified her. With every step she half-expected a crater to open up beneath her, or Rosenberg. Either would probably be enough to kill them both.

Proceeding cautiously, probing with their lamps, skirting places where the gumbo seemed to be bubbling, it took them an hour to cross a stretch of tholin that had taken five minutes on the way out.

Rosenberg took more than a week, working in his miniature lab, to process the samples he brought back from the methane vent. Benacerraf didn't disturb him; Rosenberg was reclusive to the point of secrecy about work in progress.

But he didn't look happy, as far as she could see.

Eventually, after a few hours' work in the CELSS farm in Apollo, she came into the hab module to find Rosenberg dictating into a softscreen.

". . . CH, CN and CC functional groups are evident in the imaginary part of the refractive index, as expected from the gas phase products that are the tholin precursors. Acid hydrolysis yields an array of racemic amino acids, both biological and non-biological, plus much urea. See Table Twelve. Amino acid yields are about one percent by mass of the tholin; their precursors appear to be formed by chain-addition reactions of the most abundant gas-phase species. Two-step laser mass spectrometry reveals ten to minus four grams per gram of two-four ring polycyclic aromatic hydrocarbons; larger amounts of higher PAHs may be present. The volatile component of the tholin was examined by sequential and non-sequential pyrolytic gas chromatography and mass spectrometry; over one hundred products were detected—Table Thirteen—including saturated and unsaturated aliphatic hydrocarbons, nitriles, PAHs, amines, pyrroles, pyrazines, pyridines, pyrimidines and adenine . . ."

Benacerraf placed a hand on his shoulder. "Rosenberg," she said. "Talk to me."

He broke off. Distracted, his thin face lined and unhappy, he shook his head. "Hell, Paula." He went to the hab module's galley and came back with a cup of water; they sat on Apollo couches, side by side.

She was going to have to be patient, she knew. "Tell me."

"Look," he said. "You know the theory. Maybe life formed here, in the ancient ammonia ocean. The ammono life would burn methane in nitrogen, producing ammonia and cyanogen, just as we burn sugars in oxygen and give off water and carbon dioxide. Maybe it still exists in the aqueous ammonia in the mantle. Or maybe it's at least dormant in there, in some kind of spore, waiting to be revived."

"So . . ."

"So I tried to stimulate biological activity in the mantle samples we brought back in that core sample."

"And?"

He rubbed his face, looking defeated. "I found a lot of cyanogen. The stuff ammonia life would breathe out. More than you'd predict from straightforward physico-chemical processes. And a number of other products which I expected as ammono analogues of terrestrial biochemicals. Aminines, which correspond to fatty acids. Ammono-lipids, like ammono-tristearin. Plenty of complex alpha-aminoamidines, analogues of alpha-amino acids. Carbohydrate analogues like polyaminopiperidines. Ammono-nucleic acids, like a guanine analogue. Actually, I've seen a lot of exotic chemistry here; we didn't even know if such compounds would be chemically stable at these temperatures . . ."

"My God," she said. "If I understand all that, then you were right. Evidence of life."

"Yes," he said. "But it's all four billion years old." He got out of his couch, stamped over to the lab area and came back with a small phial of muddy mantle material. "Paula, when I stimulated the organics in here with ammonia and nitrogen, there was no increase in the cyanogen concentration. The stuff is inert. *Nothing is breathing*."

"Then the ammono-biological products you found——"

"They were fossils. Paula, there *must* have been ammono life here once, in the primeval oceans. It had hundreds of millions of years; perhaps it even reached a high degree of complexity. But it couldn't survive the change, the freezing over of the ocean, the plummeting temperatures. All that's left now is what I found: chemical fossils, the decomposed elements of a life that was snuffed out billions of years ago. Just like that old rock from fucking Mars.

"You called tholin the stuff of life." Now he threw the sample to the floor of the hab module. It shattered, and its muddy contents splashed over the plastic. "You were wrong. There is only death here."

So, she thought, this is the end of Rosenberg's dream: in a sense, the reason we all came here, beyond the geopolitics and the thwarted ambitions, and whatever personal flaws impelled us out of Earth's atmosphere . . .

Titan is dead. We're orphans, in the Solar System. Now, there's nothing left for us to do, but endure, and fear for Earth.

The ancient ammonia bubbled, evaporating rapidly, and soon Benacerraf could smell its pungent stink.

. . . Dead, she thought. Or maybe just deep-frozen?

As far as Barbara Fahy was concerned, it only took a couple of hours for the world to fall apart.

She was summoned to Washington. She was to attend a hastily convened briefing on 2002OA with Hartle and other Air Force officers in the Batcave, the Space Command center buried deep beneath the streets of D.C.

She had to fly by T-38—piloted by a sullen ex-astronaut— as air traffic control was out, it seemed, right across the continent, and civilian flights were grounded. As she flew over D.C. she could see the problems, even from the air: whole city blocks without power, fires burning uncontrolled in the poorer areas.

The Chinese, it was whispered, were screwing with our computers. From here on, it looked as if the scuttlebutt was true.

She was whisked by chopper to NASA Headquarters. There another car was waiting for her, and it took her a couple of blocks across town.

The traffic was lousy. All the lights were out. The big softscreen billboards were all dead, too; they hung like black wings on the sides of the buildings lining her route. Even the little image-tattoos on the faces of the street kids had turned black, like burns.

She arrived at another anonymous-looking Government building, and was hurried through heavy security and into an elevator. The elevator was just a box of steel, its surfaces polished. The security was tough even here: there were video cameras mounted on the walls, watching her, and an armed MP standing discreetly at the back of the car.

The elevator fell rapidly. Fahy, clutching her softscreen and scribbled notes, almost stumbled, disoriented; it was like being back in the T-38 again, pulling Gs.

The MP was only a kid, she thought, surely younger than thirty. His blue eyes were black-rimmed, and she wondered if he'd had any sleep recently. He was probably as afraid as she was. More so, because he couldn't understand as much of what was happening as she did.

On impulse, she asked: "What's your name, son?"

He looked at her, puzzled. "Ma'am?" His vowels had the broad richness of a Texan. His hand, she noted, had gone automatically to the butt of his pistol.

"Never mind," she said.

When she emerged from the elevator, she found herself facing a gigantic, intimidating logo: a shield, studded with stars; a stylized planet ringed by solid-looking orbital hoops, a simple delta-wing spacecraft overlaid before it. It was, Fahy knew, the shield of the Air Force Space Command.

The MP hurried her through steel-walled corridors. His heels clattered on the metallic floor, his gun always visible. Fahy had to half-run to keep up.

After a couple of turns she'd lost her orientation. The lighting came from dazzling, gray-white floods embedded in the ceilings, so that the illumination was colorless, flattening. Everyone she encountered looked deathly pale, as if drained of blood. There were no colors here, no smells. It was like being inside a huge machine. The rooms were crammed with information technology: huge wall-mounted softscreens, printers, telecommunications gear; earnest young Air Force officers, many of them bespectacled, labored at terminals.

Machine or not, she sensed panic.

They arrived at a small, compact briefing room. A single table stretched the length of the room; it was oak, its surface polished smooth, a bizarre touch of luxury in this dehumanized cavern.

She had arrived in the middle of a briefing. It was a chaotic hubbub.

Al Hartle sat at the far end of the table. Gareth Deeke sat

alongside him, his eyes hidden by his mirrored glasses. There were several others here, mostly men, mostly heavy-set and middle-aged. Some wore service uniforms, mostly from the U.S. armed forces, but there were also representatives from the military establishments of Canada, Quebec, New Columbia, Idaho. There were even a couple of Russian officers: evidently the embodiment of some post-Cold War strategic tie-up between the U.S. and post-Soviet Russia, a new cooperative understanding as the former adversaries banded together in the face of a newly hostile and baffling world.

Anyhow it was quite an assembly, a representation of the military establishments of two continents.

Around the walls of the room, framing the group at the table, a series of young officers sat at compact workstations, the glow of their softscreens illuminating their earnest, smooth faces. She could see information flowing in continually over the surface of the softscreens, and occasionally scribbled notes were passed to the heavyweights at the main table. Network cables lay across the floor, roughly anchored here and there with duct tape. Jackets had been draped over the backs of chairs, ties were roughly loosened, and a pall of blue-gray smoke hung over the center of the room.

There was a stench of stale sweat, of too much aftershave. Of fear.

Oddly, she found she welcomed the body stink. At least, she thought, you could tell there were living human beings in this place of metal and plastic.

Fahy was waved to a seat.

Hartle clapped his hands, and the hubbub died a little. "Let's try and get some kind of overview here," he said. "Gareth. What's the most significant item we have, in your view, right now?"

Deeke didn't hesitate. "As far as the President is concerned, it must be the Wall Street bomb. The physical damage wasn't important, Al. In fact it was just a suitcase bomb. The point of it was the electromagnetic pulse it delivered. Al, it knocked out everything: bank transfer networks, stock and bond markets, commodity trading systems, credit card networks, telephone and data transmission lines, Quotron machines . . . We're looking at financial chaos, a meltdown of the global finance system. All from one suitcase bomb.

"General, we have two hundred million computers tying us together through an array of land and satellite-based communication systems. We thought we were protected. We weren't. The nodes of our government and commercial computer systems are so poorly shielded that it's been a chicken run for the enemy, or their agents. And in our systems themselves, even the most secure, we have evidence of the work of crackers— malevolent hackers—and cruise viruses, targeted at our vulnerable points. Al, at this moment I don't think we can trust any of the information we do have coming in here, or even our weapons targeting and arming systems."

"All right," Hartle snapped. "What else?"

"We've lost our satellites," another officer said bluntly.

"How? Anti-satellite strikes?"

"ASATs aren't necessary," Deeke said. "It's easier and cheaper to soft-kill a satellite: damage, distort, even reprogram the information it processes and transmits. You can jam, intercept, spoof, hit the ground stations, break into the comms networks . . . Al, this is knowledge warfare. We have to assume that there are troop movements, going on right now. Launches of their CSS-2 IRBMs. Stuff we can't see any more—"

"Knowledge warfare, horseshit. I'll tell you what this is," Hartle said. "This is an electronic Pearl Harbor. The Red Chinese have blinded us. They're doing to us what we did to them over Taiwan, back in '12. We just didn't think big enough, is all; we never thought they would attempt this—"

"And of course we have a rather larger problem," Deeke said mildly.

Hartle turned to Fahy.

"Miss Fahy," he said, glowering at her. "Welcome to hell. Now, tell us about 2002OA."

Fahy, nervous, fumbling, stood up and walked to the head of the table, opposite Hartle. "2002OA is a NEO. A near-Earth object, an asteroid. We have four dedicated NEO search programs. Three in the northern hemisphere, one in the south. The U.S. has been running planet-crossing asteroid surveys for four decades now out of Mount Palomar, Kitt Peak and the Lowell Observatory. The surveys use photographic methods, with some upgrade to electronic methods. Palomar alone is responsible for the discovery of one-third of the NEO population known today. All these observatories are situated in the southwest of North America, and so cannot reach southern declinations. In response, a program called the Anglo-Australian Near-Earth Asteroid Survey was initiated in the 1990s . . ."

"So," Hartle snapped, "where the fuck is 2002OA?"

She fumbled with her softscreen, working through the presentation she had prepared, at last bringing up the image she wanted: a pencil of possible orbits, fanning out from 2002OA's present position. The orbits enveloped the Earth.

"The orbital elements of 2002OA are not precisely determined, yet. For one thing it is only visible from one NEO tracking station, the one in Australia, though we're trying to bring more resources to bear. It's possible, but not certain, that 2002OA will collide with Earth. We certainly can't be specific about where, precisely, in geographic terms. The orbital data is too fragmentary at present to be able to—"

Hartle closed his eyes. "Which hemisphere?"

"I can't tell you that, sir."

Deeke said, "NORAD and NASA are refining their projections all the time, Al."

Hartle said, "But if we can't even figure out where it is heading, how was it possible for the fucking Chinese to aim it?"

Deeke shrugged. "By placing a spacecraft on the spot. By

doing navigation from there, they could achieve much greater precision. Maybe they even sent up a man to do it, General. After all, they aren't scrupulous about spending human lives."

"And what damage is this fucker going to do to us?"

"General, we think the Chinese miscalculated," Fahy said, flicking through the projections her staff had prepared. "2002OA is a big rock. Bigger than they need, if they just wanted to strike at the U.S. We think they intended some kind of glancing blow, or maybe to calve off a piece of the rock. Then we'd face localized destruction, maybe something like a nuclear winter. A Tunguska rock on New York. A Meteor Crater where Washington is. We think that was the plan. But 2002OA is too large. Instead, we may be looking at some kind of Cretaceous-Tertiary boundary impact—"

Hartle turned to Deeke. "What the fuck?"

"A dinosaur killer, General," Deeke said softly.

There was a moment of silence.

Hartle said to Fahy, "So tell me how we shoot down this motherfucker."

She fumbled through her notes. "In general, the strategy for dealing with incoming objects requires spacecraft capable of rendezvousing with a threatening NEO and deflecting it by incrementing its velocity with a delta-vee—that is, an impulse—sufficient to cause them to miss the Earth. There are two generic strategies: remote interdiction, when the collision is predicted several orbital periods away, and terminal interception—when the collision is imminent, with the projectile less than one astronomical unit away—that is, days away from impact—and closing. Remote interdiction requires relatively small delta-vees, terminal interception much larger. In both cases, a deflection velocity is applied sufficient to cause it to drift from its original trajectory by at least one Earth radius. In cases of terminal interception it is best to apply the impulse perpendicularly to the projectile's motion, which imparts an eccentricity to its orbit. The deflection delta-vee required is inversely proportional to the distance from Earth. And because of this—"

"Jesus Christ," Hartle said. His body was unmoving as he watched her, as if carved from granite, his contempt etched on his face.

Deeke said, "Tell us about *Clementine*, Ms. Fahy."

"Right . . ." Fahy scanned ahead through the slides on her softscreen, and began stumbling through a hasty presentation on a space mission called *Clementine II*.

Clementine had been an experimental 1990s deep-space mission cooked up by NASA and the Air Force Space Command. *Clementine*'s primary purpose had been to serve as a test-bed for the performance of advanced defense technologies in deep space, up to ten million miles from Earth. But it was also a test of techniques for asteroid interception. It had been sent to close rendezvous with three asteroids and had been equipped to fire probes—yard-long cylindrical missiles—into the asteroids' surface. In the event, *Clementine* had failed after the first rendezvous, but that first mock-interception had gone well.

"*Clementine* was essentially target practice," Fahy said. "It was criticized by the science community for that reason—"

"Fuck the science," Hartle said. "Why the hell didn't we follow this up?"

Fahy felt even more nervous. "Sir, the scientists won the day, in the end. They argued that the money would be better spent on ground-based instruments that could detect an Earth-bound incoming. Better to survey the problem, rather than try flying spaceborne weaponry at this stage. Then there was opposition from the liberal lobby, who argued that the build-up of a deflection capability might be a simple cover for the continuation of weapons programs, in the wake of the end of the Cold War, by vested interests: the military labs, the defense suppliers. Carl Sagan at Cornell was vocal in—"

"Carl Sagan," Hartle growled. "Miss Fahy, for once in your goddamn life, get to the point. Listen up. Right now money is no object, for NASA. I'll give you what you want: Delta IVs to launch up as many nukes as you could wish for, all the ground-based resources you ask for. Now. *Tell me about 2002OA*. What options do we have for deflecting this goddamn incoming?"

She frowned. "I'm sorry, sir. I thought you knew. We don't have any options."

Hartle seemed baffled rather than angry. "There is always an option, damn it."

"Not in this case. We detected it too late. We're already in the terminal interception phase. Right now, 2002OA is only four times as far away as the Moon. The delta-vee we would have to apply is more than three hundred feet per second. It is impossible for us to achieve such a deflection, no matter what we threw at it. The best we could achieve would be to break the rock up. But then you'd have a multiple impact instead of one, along with an immense cloud of dust and debris hitting the upper atmosphere . . ."

Gareth Deeke said, "Like it or not, we no longer have the Delta IVs in the inventory anyhow, Al. We've run down too far. We just don't have the launch capability any more."

Hartle's nicotine-stained fingers drummed at the table. "You're telling me we can't shoot this thing down?"

"No, sir. Of course we don't know for sure if it's going to hit Earth anyhow."

"Let's start talking about what we do if it does. Gareth, are we prepared to strike at the Chinese? Should we launch before the impact? And what—"

An aide walked in, a girl. She walked towards Hartle. He watched her approach, impassive, his face like a piece of Mount Rushmore. Her gait was awkward, Fahy thought, her steps uneven, as if she were close to fainting.

"Sir," she said. "We heard from NORAD. They have a fix on the incoming's ground zero . . ." The girl officer started to cry, big salty drops rolling down her cheeks.

Everyone was standing now; orders were shouted back and forth.

The Atlantic, she heard. *The Atlantic.*

Two young officers had clustered around Al Hartle. "Come on, sir; we have to get you out of here, over to NORAD. There's a chopper waiting . . ."

Holy shit, Fahy thought. *They got confirmation. This isn't just some military wet-dream fantasy of Al Hartle's. It's real; it's going to happen.*

I'm going to die.

Holy shit.

Jake Hadamard parked at the foot of the Vehicle Assembly Building. His car was the only one in the lot.

When he looked up at the face of the VAB, it was like peering up at a cliff. In the flat morning sunlight he could see that the wall was heavily weathered, streaked with seagull guano, and there was even some lichen, he saw, busily burrowing into the face of the VAB, as if it was some immense tombstone. It was a little difficult to believe that modern humans, in some epochal moment of madness, had built such a monument.

He had a sudden, jarring sense that history was going to end, here, today.

He walked away from the VAB, towards the press stand.

The uncompromising old wooden bleacher was evidently abandoned now, its roof broken open to the daylight, dune grass colonizing the lower levels. He climbed a few steps and found a seat; he brushed it clear of dirt and sand and sat down, looking east.

He was looking towards the ocean, across the Banana River, and, beyond a treeline, towards Launch Complex 39. The sun, still early-morning low, was bright in his eyes. The press portakabins that had once stood here had long since been hauled away, and the other relics of human launches—the gigantic countdown clock, the flagpole—were gone, too. Nothing remained but obscure concrete podiums and platforms, already crumbling under the assault of sea and vegetation.

Beyond the treeline, on the other side of the river, he could see the two LC-39 launch complexes, side by side, blocky mechanical towers blue-misted by distance. Now 39-B was all but demolished; little had been left after the scrap teams had moved in but a shell of rusting iron set on a concrete platform.

An effort had been made to preserve 39-A, however; for the benefit of the tourist trade, Disney-Coke had erected a gigantic carbon fiber mockup of a Saturn V to stand alongside the launch gantry. It was easily visible now, a slim white tower, more than three hundred and sixty feet tall, tapering up from the flaring fins of the S-IC first stage, all the way to the pencil-thin escape rocket at the tip of the dummy Apollo spacecraft at the apex. But it was unpainted, many of the details missing, so that it looked like a child's unfinished model.

The sun was to his right and in his eyes, already hot. Hadamard was dressed in a suit, his tie loosely knotted. He adjusted his sunglasses for greater opacity.

He wondered if he ought to put on some sunblock.

He checked his watch. Well, if what he'd heard from his contacts inside NASA and NORAD was correct, he wouldn't have long to wait. He could risk doing without the sunblock.

Rosenberg and Benacerraf huddled together at the galley end of the hab module. The door to Bill Angel's quarters was closed; there was no sound from within.

Even so, Rosenberg and Benacerraf were talking in whispers.

"Sixty miles," Rosenberg said. "It's not so far. If we could manage ten miles a day, we could be there and back in a couple of weeks . . ."

Rosenberg was in a mood Benacerraf had learned to recognize, and mistrust: a mood of excitement, in which he would be carried away by some new idea.

The trouble was, around here it was only Rosenberg who came up with any ideas at all.

"Tell me again," she said. "You're sure this is a carbonaceous chondrite meteorite crater?"

"As sure as I can be." Rosenberg had spotted the crater, punched into the border of the big Cronos plateau, in *Cassini* orbital radar imaging. "The size is the thing. Look, Paula, the nature of the impacting bolide determines the cratering profile. The most common type out here, far from the inner System, will be weak, icy, cometary bodies. If an object is small and weak, it's going to break up in Titan's thick atmosphere. For a bolide of a given yield strength you have a minimum radius below which you shouldn't find any craters. For the ice bolides, that comes at around thirty miles. The stronger the material, the smaller the crater it can create."

"I get it. And the crater you've found on Cronos—"

"—is about twenty miles wide. Below the turndown limit for the icy bodies. Carbonaceous chondrite meteorites would have four or five times the density, and a hundred times the internal strength."

She tried to think it through. "So the crater you found can't have been caused by a cometary-ice impact."

"It's possible, but unlikely."

It was typical of Rosenberg to play the cautious scientist when he was asking her to make a decision that would put all their lives on the line.

"But it could be something else," she said doggedly. "A stony or iron meteorite."

"Yes, that's possible. But the flux rates for objects like that, out here so far from the sun, are small," he said. "Much smaller than at Earth. Really, Paula, a carbonaceous chondrite is the best explanation. And the crater I've found is the most likely chondrite crater for a few hundred miles. Paula, we're lucky to have found something so close."

She sighed. "So we have to go there."

"You know it. Paula, you've seen the figures. We just aren't able to achieve closure of the life support loops, particularly of the amino acids and some of the trace elements—sulphur, potassium, chlorine. Even Titan itself can't supply everything. So we have to look for manna from heaven, in the crater of a carbonaceous chondrite meteorite. We need that kerogen." He smiled, his thin face dreamy. "Before it fell out of the sky, the meteorite must have drifted around for five billion years, a fragment of the original circumsolar nebula. Food, cooked up in the interior of the first generation of stars . . ."

This kind of stuff was what worried her. This was Rosenberg's personal escape hatch, his way of retreating from the dull horrors of their life on Titan. Her worry was, what if there were other options for survival which he wasn't considering, because he was caught up with the idea of digging out the celestial stuff of life from some crater on Cronos?

"A hundred and twenty miles, across the surface of Titan. My God, Rosenberg. Do you really think it's feasible? The longest surface EVAs in NASA history were the last Moonwalks. Seven or eight hours outside the Lunar Module; a traverse of a few miles, every minute timelined, in those damn Lunar Rovers. All controlled from the ground, and all of it within a walk-back limit of the LM. Now, we're going to have to figure out how to survive independently of *Discovery* for two weeks or more."

He shrugged. "It will take some preparation. But I think it's possible, Paula. We'll need the sleds, of course, with food and water and stuff, and some kind of surface shelter. But remember we should be able to haul along a lot of mass, in the low gravity—"

"Rosenberg, we haven't reached a crisis yet. Maybe we should wait."

He looked confused. "What good would waiting do? We don't have any smarter options. It's better to attempt this now. While we're still reasonably healthy. Before the equipment starts to wear out. Before the life support loops start failing."

"You've worked this out, haven't you, Rosenberg?"

"Paula, I really don't think we have a choice," he said seriously.

He started talking about more expeditions they could mount later. For instance to the crater of an iron meteorite. Maybe they could find some way to refine the metal, and . . .

She listened with weary patience. He was off in his dreamworld of technology and science and achievement, that realm where all his schemes came to magical life, and where Tartarus became the hub of a spreading, glittering complex of science and technology.

None of it had anything to do with the real problem they faced about this EVA, she thought. Which was what to do with Bill Angel.

"El Dorado," he was saying now. "That's what we'll call the crater."

"Whatever you say, Rosenberg."

In the chaos, it wasn't difficult for Barbara Fahy to get out of the complex. She rode a steel elevator to the surface, and emerged into the early hours of a spring morning in Washington, D.C.

She checked her watch. It was nearly 6.00 A.M.; the briefings had gone on all night.

The streets were all but empty: there were a couple of street cleaners, a girl in a short skirt and inert image-tattoos making her way home, maybe from some club, one or two tense-looking office workers in suits, strutting anxiously towards their workplaces. The traffic lights were working, but randomly, it seemed to her.

She wondered where the President was this morning. Nowhere near here.

She walked.

She reached the Tidal Basin, and walked among the cherry trees near the Jefferson Memorial, around the reflecting pool walkway. The canopy of white blossoms filtered the morning light, so that it was like the glow of a skylight, shadowless, diffuse, warming.

She passed a small colony of homeless, huddled under paper and cardboard against the softscreen-coated wall of a bank. The softscreen shed flickers of light over clothes that had been reduced by rain and sunlight to shapeless, colorless pulp. But this morning there was no pattern to the softscreen's display, just formless gray static.

Maybe, she thought, she should warn someone. But what was the point? Let them enjoy the morning. Let them sleep, if they could.

Maclachlan had said he'd sweep the homeless from the streets. At the end of two terms—and as Maclachlan aimed to change the Constitution to allow him to run for a third—there were more of them than ever. And malnutrition in the Bronx, and cholera in Georgia . . .

But, she thought, all these problems would soon be swept away, more rapidly and effectively than even Xavier Maclachlan, in his wildest dreams, could have planned.

She felt she'd lived through an immense paradox. After that steel cavern, she could understand why people felt that science was a terrible thing. Maybe even an evil thing. But the fact was that one nuke, in the right place at the right time, could have deflected this incoming, the Chinese rock. There was the paradox. *What do we do when the dinosaur-killer comes? Accept it as inevitable? Throw philosophy books at it?*

But in the end it was science and technology which had delivered the evil on their heads. The paradox deepened.

She just hoped there would be people around to debate this tomorrow.

According to the projections prepared by her staff, everything depended on the geometry of the impact.

A hell of a lot of kinetic energy would be released downwards, into the crust, and upwards, into the atmosphere, first as a vapor plume and then as an airblast. If there was an ocean strike there would be earthquakes: Richter eight or nine. A lot of dust and salt water would be injected into the middle atmosphere; nobody cared to guess what that would do to the weather. And they were going to get global oscillations of the atmosphere and ionosphere. Upper atmosphere heating, high intensity atmospheric disturbances. Hydrogen-mixing would wreck the ozone layer, for good and all. A lot of nitrogen would be burned, into nitrogen dioxide, nitric acid. Acid rain. And the high-speed plasma plumes from the shock, reaching up to the geomagnetic field, were going to play hell with the radiation belts . . .

Funny weather. Storms. Auroras. Lousy communications. Stunning sunsets, from all that dust. The skies would be spectacular.

Even if the impact itself wasn't too severe, secondary effects could do a lot of damage. Nuclear waste repositories. Hydro-electric power stations and dams. Chemical plants. Nuclear power stations. She imagined a dozen Chernobyls, scattered along the eastern seaboard . . .

Still, it was possible humanity—even civilization—could survive the impact itself and its consequences. But then, everything would depend on the war that would surely follow, when the Chinese came over in their clumsy ships, and Al Hartle and his boys emerged from their bunkers in Cheyenne, and they started the work of finishing off whatever the asteroid left behind.

Even given enough survivors, she thought bleakly, it might be impossible to climb back. The post-impact world would not be a blank slate for a new civilization, now that they'd used up all the most accessible raw materials—ore, coal, oil. And besides the biosphere was already unstable. This might trigger the final plankton collapse, for instance . . .

It seemed incredible, here in the morning sunshine, on a day like all the other days, stretching back to her first bright memories. But today could be the last day of all. Maybe, she thought, in a couple of centuries, all that will be left of us will be a few relics on the Moon, whatever Paula builds on Titan, a handful of aging space probes heading out of the System.

She reached the Lincoln Memorial. She climbed the steps, and stared up at Lincoln's impassive face.

She sat on the step at the top of the Memorial. She was looking east, in the direction of the Atlantic. The sun was well above the horizon now, the sky a clear blue dome. Traffic was beginning to seep into the brightening streets, and its distant noise rose to an oceanic roar, suffusing the landscape.

Sitting here, with the warmth of the sun on her face, the solidity of marble beneath her, she tried to comprehend that by the end of this nondescript day, all this—the labor of centuries—could be lost.

She was hungry, she found.

Benacerraf lay cocooned in her sleeping bag, on an improvised mattress of insulation material and space clothing.

Every time she woke, she had two priorities: to keep warm, and not to open her mouth.

There were several layers of hull metal and insulation—the base of the hab module and the orbiter's cargo bay—lying between her and the hundred-and-eighty-below slush of Titan. Even so, the miles of ice below her sucked the heat out of her aging body during the night. She woke up in exactly the same position as when she'd fallen asleep, as if she'd trained herself not to move in her sleep, no matter how stiff she got. She'd found that if she lay still, on the patch of her sleeping bag that her body had warmed up, she could stay relatively comfortable. But if she moved, she would tip over onto a colder place, and the warm air she had gathered around herself would spill out, leaving her shivering.

So she lay, hanging on to the last fragments of the night's warmth, before she had to face the day.

She opened her eyes slowly.

Her reading light was turned off, but enough light leaked around the door to let her make out the lines of the little room: the aluminum mirror on the wall, the lashed-up shelf with her softscreen and her precious paper books, the toothbrush with the broken handle she'd had to tape together . . .

The realization of where she was pushed its way into her consciousness with all its usual, unwelcome force, and she felt black dread welling inside her.

She sat up. The sleeping bag fell away from her shoulders, and immediately she was shivering, despite the thick Beta-cloth clothing she wore as pajamas.

Still in the dark, she got to her feet. The sleeping bag made a cloth puddle at her feet. She could see her face, dimly, in the scuffed aluminum mirror. She saw an old woman, her face lined and patched with shallow frostbite scars, her hair a dirty cloud, crudely cut, her mouth a bloody mess.

She opened up her tube of lip salve. She smeared it over the lumpy scabs on her lips. Then she started to work the tip of her tongue gently against the lips, from the inside, until, slowly, they began to part, with little damage to the scabs that had welded together during the night.

Her lips had got damaged during an EVA, when her helmet seal had sprung a leak. She knew she had been lucky; she'd been just a few feet from the airlock. The cold, crowding into her helmet, had been intense. Startled, she had almost fallen, and her lips and chin had come into contact with the cooling glass of her visor. She had pulled her face back, leaving chunks of ripped flesh behind, and a violent burning sensation around her mouth.

She had clamped her eyes shut, and fumbled for *Discovery*'s airlock.

She got through with no serious frostbite damage. But her lips were a mess. Now, every time she ate, she got a salty mouthful of blood; and every spoonful of soup she lifted to her mouth was streaked with crimson. A couple of times, just after the injury, she'd opened her mouth during the night, or on waking, and had torn the night's new lip scabs right off.

Cautiously, she stretched her mouth a little wider. The clustered scabs ached, and she could see how some of the deeper crevices had opened again, so that they glistened bright red.

She thought ahead. She was due to spend most of today in the CELSS farm, cleaning out the nutrient pipes. And later she would have to find some time to work with Rosenberg on the details of the El Dorado EVA—

The door behind her opened quietly.

She turned, startled, and nearly fell; she banged her elbow against the shelf.

There was a figure in the doorway, silhouetted against the brightness of the hab module floods.

Anger welled up in her. This was her quarters, damn it, her one little island of privacy. "Rosenberg, I don't care what the emergency is. Get out of here."

"No," he said; and that single, gruff syllable told her everything she needed to know.

It wasn't Rosenberg. It was Bill Angel.

And, she realized with sudden horror, today his long decline was going to reach some kind of conclusion.

As the sun climbed and the mist burned off, the colors of Launch Complex 39 emerged more clearly. The snow-white of the toy Saturn was strongly contrasted with the battleship gray of the gantry which enfolded it.

After losing his NASA position to Al Hartle, Hadamard had entered semi-retirement. He couldn't have gotten another position in Maclachlan's Administration anyhow, and nor would he have wanted it. He had received a large payoff—that had been written into his contract when he was recruited from industry—and so he was financially comfortable. He had kept on his house in Clear Lake, but he hadn't spent much time in Houston.

He had no living family, no particular ties. He wasn't sure what he wanted to do with the rest of his life.

To Hadamard, looking back, his years at NASA had represented a kind of slow crisis for him, like a long breakdown.

He had gone into NASA to dismantle the Agency, much as he had dismantled and reassembled several corporations and Government departments before. By the time he emerged, he had spent years trying to defend it.

He toured the country, visiting relics of the space program: the rusting tracking station at Goldstone, the mothballed Shuttle launch facilities at Vandenberg, the old Saturn construction and test facilities around the country, abandoned or converted by Boeing and Rockwell. He gained a sense of the impermanence of it all; it was as if some insane occupying power had swept across the country, developed these immense facilities at enormous cost, and then abandoned their foothold.

Jake Hadamard, after years running NASA, still didn't understand the meaning of the space program, nor even his own shifting reaction to it.

Perhaps there was no single meaning, no single valid reaction; perhaps the event was simply too huge for that. But he'd come to suspect that it was only for space—human footprints on the Moon, and on a satellite of Saturn—that his nation would, in the longest of terms, be remembered.

Or even, he thought, his species.

When he'd heard leaked reports of the incoming rock, he'd decided there was only one place he wanted to be.

. . . There was a spark of light, high in the sky.

Hadamard shielded his eyes with his hands and looked up, searching for the source. It had been hot, yellow, liquid, like rocket light.

It came in at an angle, far to the east, a blindingly white line scrawled across the sky. It was a crack in the Aristotelian dome, Fahy thought, allowing in the monsters.

Asteroid 2002OA had arrived.

She had to turn away, it was so bright.

It was going to be an ocean strike, then. Just as NORAD predicted. A few hundred miles off the coast, she guessed.

The dazzling light had faded now.

So it was true. She thought she'd imagined, with some soft unscientific part of her, until this moment, that it might be just some fantastic hypothesis.

Well, Earth hadn't suffered a strike like this for millions of years. Human written culture went back maybe five thousand years. There was no institutional memory of such an event as this. No wonder it was hard to comprehend, even to plan for. It should be.

Clouds were boiling, scudding across the sky. The spectacle was playing out in an eerie silence. Even the traffic noises seemed to have stilled.

The atmosphere would have provided no effective shield against the strike; the asteroid must have reached the ocean with no significant loss of mass or velocity: a mountainous mass of rock, moving at orbital speeds, through the delicate atmosphere of Earth. There was essentially an immense cylindrical explosion going on right now, its effects scouring outward over the surface of the planet.

From orbit, she thought, it would be a hell of a sight: the crater still visible, a glowing red puncture miles across, keeping the sea at bay with its raw heat; an immense column of dust and pulverized rock and vapor rising up above it, its lip extending tens of miles into the atmosphere; the clouds bubbling outward in ranks, like the concentric rings around a bull's eye target.

A breeze, warm and heavy, pushed against her face, pressing from the east. There were flecks of moisture on the wind. She licked her lips. Salt: ocean water, scooped up and hurled across hundreds of miles.

Maybe there would be tsunamis. But the geometry was

dicey; it depended precisely where the impact was, the topography of the ocean bed. Gradual slopes could reflect the wave energy back to the Atlantic . . .

There was noise now, at last, a deep bass rumble like remote thunder. The light continued to fade.

The ground *shifted*, the solid marble of the Memorial's vast plinth shuddering like a live thing.

For the first time, she was scared. The ground wasn't supposed to move under you, damn it. It was as if some deep superstitious part of her had woken, an animal peering up at a violent sky in terror.

With her back against the wall of her quarters—the little room wasn't much bigger than a closet—Benacerraf held up her hands, palms out. "What is it, Bill? What do you need? Are you hungry?"

With sudden, brutal force, he pushed his way into the quarters. She squirmed back against the wall, but his chest and legs pressed against hers, and she could smell the milky sweetness of his breath.

She felt shocked, violated, her last secret place broken open.

He dragged the door shut behind him, and she was immersed in the near-dark once more. She tried not to scream. But her mouth twisted open, and the pain in her lips stabbed at her awareness. She turned her head and pulled her hands back from him, so reluctant was she to touch him.

Again he was still, a huge presence resting against her. He seemed to move in bursts between moments of stillness; it was like the motion of a lizard, rather than anything human.

With an effort she moved her hands forward, in the darkness, until she touched his shoulders. She could feel his chest rise and fall with his breath, raggedly. "Bill, you know you shouldn't be in here. This is my room. We all need privacy—"

"I'm not a fucking kid." He reached up and closed his hands over hers. His fingers were powerful, stronger than she would have imagined, and he bent her fingers back, making her cry out. "I'm sick of you talking down at me, Paula." Now he pushed her hands against her chest so that she was shoved back, painfully, against her shelf.

"I'm sorry," she said.

"I want respect," he said. "You can understand that, can't you?" He brought his face closer to hers. "Some things I can still do, eyes or no eyes."

"Of course you can, Bill. I always—"

He pushed his head forward. He shoved his lips against hers. The muscles of his face were strong, and he easily forced her lips open, and jammed his tongue into her mouth. His lips worked at hers, his teeth scraping hard over the wounds there. Her scabs broke and came loose, the crevice-like wounds opening. She could taste her own blood, the salty tang of saliva and sweat and snot.

The pain in her mouth forced her to cry out again.

He jerked his head back, as if startled, his movements precise and inhuman.

"You're hurting me, damn it." Her voice was slurred as she favored her damaged lips. She longed to wipe her mouth, to spit out his dirt.

He began to drag his right hand down over her body, still trapping her fist. His fingers clawed at her breast, through layers of Beta-cloth.

"Bill, for God's sake."

"Come on," he said, his voice a harsh whisper. "Haven't you heard the news? Don't you know what's about to hit Earth?"

"What are you talking about?"

"It's the end of the fucking world, Paula. There's just us now, alone here, a billion miles from home. It's a new world. Adam and Eve."

You're crazy, she thought. But if she said it, she sensed, it would make it so, now and forever.

Behind Angel, the door to her quarters was swinging open;

the glare of the hab module floods washed over her, outlining his face.

He forced her hand down to his crotch. She tried to keep her fist curled, but he squeezed and shook her hand until she was forced to open her fingers, and he clamped her open hand against himself. She could feel his erection, a hot cylinder pushing against the coarse Beta-cloth.

"Oh, God," she said. "No, Bill. Not that."

"Come on. We can do this. Adam and Eve."

In Seattle, Jackie Benacerraf was woken by a sound of thunder, miles away.

She lay there for a moment, thinking about her mother's descriptions of storms seen from orbit: *Over central Africa, I could see lightning sparking constantly, over cloud systems spanning thousands of miles. The lightning moves through the clouds like a living thing, growing and spreading. Its glow shines from beneath the layer of cloud, and you can see a three-dimensional structure within the cloud, edges and swirls of purple . . .*

Her mother was a long way away.

She sat up, alone in bed.

The lights didn't come on.

She got out of bed. In pitch darkness, she felt her way to the softscreen coating one wall. Maybe she could get a look at the weather channels, find some kind of satellite view . . .

The softscreen didn't work. She pressed at its surface, but it remained inert, a window into darkness.

She started to feel scared.

She went out into the hall. No lights turned themselves on there, either. There were flashes of lightning now, big gaudy bursts that turned the windows into illuminated panels—but no accompanying peals of thunder, just that continual rumble.

There was a smash outside, a clatter of breaking glass.

She ran to the door, opened it. The night was warm; from somewhere, from the east, a hot wind had sprung up, and it pulled at her nightdress and hair. Above, clouds streamed, thick and gaudy; she could see lightning crackle beyond the lowest clouds, in big gaudy sheets, flaring parallel to the ground.

The streetlights were out, she realized; the only light came from the intermittent bursts of lightning, a purplish glow from the streaming clouds.

Even the orange glow of Seattle was invisible.

In her bare feet, she walked down the drive towards the security barrier.

On the corner, two cars had run into each other; their fronts had crumpled, head-on, and steam was rising from a cracked radiator. The drivers had got out, and were slowly walking around the wreckage. The headlamps of the cars cast a pool of light in the middle of the darkness.

She looked around. As far as she could see, there wasn't a single softscreen working: street signs, house decorations, ad hoardings—all of it was dead, inert, black. It was bizarre, to be without the endless unraveling of colors and shapes all around her: there was an optical stillness she hadn't experienced in the city for years.

Something, she thought, is very wrong.

And yet, somehow, in some hidden chamber of her heart, she had always known it would come to this.

The boys, she thought. They are the main priority now. Thank God they are both home. Perhaps she should go and wake them.

. . . But what if the shit really was hitting the fan? How could they prepare? Perhaps they ought to go to the store. Buy canned and packet food, long-life milk. A butane stove. Blankets, torches, thick coats, an axe. Gas for the car.

A gun.

Somewhere, a siren started a mournful wailing. It seemed to puncture her.

They finally did it, she thought. Her plans broke up in her head, and she cried out.

It was over, she realized, with a deep, unwelcome stab of comprehension. The last vestige of control she could exert over her life was gone. She wouldn't even be able to save her children.

Rain began to fall: heavy, scummy droplets of it, breaking open on the sidewalk. She lifted her face into it; the rain was salty, and stung her eyes. She wondered where Saturn was, in the hidden sky.

Was it worth it, Mother? Was it worth all this, blowing everything apart, just so you could get to walk in the slush up there?

The rain fell harder, soaking her. She hurried up the path to her children.

Dark, thick storm clouds streamed over the sky above Fahy, obscuring the sun. Rain started to fall, big droplets, pelting against the marble surfaces, her clothes and hair, heavy and warm and salty.

She permitted herself a fragment of hope. After all she wasn't dead yet. The strike itself was over. The world was going to be a piece of shit after this, war or not; but maybe, just maybe, she might live through this to see it.

Maybe NORAD and the rest had miscalculated, she thought. Maybe 2002OA just wasn't a big enough punch to—

But there was something on the horizon, now: a gray wall, perhaps a bank of cloud.

Oh.

The secondary effects need not concern her any more, she thought.

The wall was water, a bank of it that had to be a mile high. Already it was marching inland. Even from this distance she could see debris embedded in its curving, steel-gray flank: rocks, fragments of ships, pieces of smashed-up buildings. It was the debris that would do the damage, she knew; with its help that wave could scour the ground clean of any sign this capital city had ever existed.

We don't deserve this, she thought. Although maybe it looks different if you sit in Beijing. And there are those who say something like this, some terrible conclusion, was inevitable, that the huge technological project we've been following was bound to end in grief and destruction.

But I know we don't deserve to have this done to us. Sure, we got things wrong. And we're guilty of being the only nation in history to have dropped an atomic weapon on an opponent. But didn't we beat back the Nazis and the Japs? Wasn't it a good thing that we won the Cold War, and not the other side? Was it really such a terrible thing, to aspire to walk on the moons of Saturn? . . .

I will, she thought, never see the sun again.

She felt a wrench, a deep sorrow.

The clouds thickened, and moist air buffeted her face, driven ahead of that horizon-spanning piston of water.

He looked oddly beautiful, she thought with a rogue part of her mind: his face blank and intent, ruined eyes closed, that WASP hair shining in the hab module floods. And he was so strong.

He pulled at the neck of her T-shirt, trying to rip it. The coarse hem burned into her neck. The tough fabric wouldn't rip, so he pushed his hand up inside her clothing instead. He reached her breast and grabbed it, squeezing hard. Then he shoved his hand downward over her belly, trying to get into her pants.

He pushed his face forward and began to gnaw at her lips once more.

Her left hand was free.

She grabbed the door frame and yanked backwards, as hard as she could.

On Earth, perhaps she couldn't have budged Angel. But here they were in one-seventh gravity. Locked together, they began to tip over.

Angel released the hand he'd held over his penis, and reached behind to brace his fall. She tried to keep from falling with him; she grabbed at the doorway. But his other hand was stuck inside her clothing; he dragged her down on top of him, helpless.

He landed heavily on his arm, and there was a snap, like the breaking of a thin branch. Angel screamed. He scrabbled against the floor, like a turned-over beetle, his ruined eyes turning back and forth.

She rolled away from him. It was the first moment since he'd burst into her quarters that she hadn't been in physical contact with him. He was stirring. Clutching his damaged arm against his chest, he was turning over, getting to his knees.

She tried to stand up, but she felt weak and off-balance. She crawled away, towards the galley.

He reached out and grabbed her ankle. The effort cost him the support of his good arm, and she could see him fall flat on his chest. But even so he was able to drag her back towards him.

She was rolled onto her back. For a moment she lay with her feet mere inches from his face. With one slam of her heel in his face, she thought, this could be over. She lifted up her free foot, trying to make herself do it.

Angel flopped towards her, so that his mass trapped her legs, his bad arm pinned between them. He didn't seem to notice the pain now. With his good hand he reached up and grabbed at the waist of her pants, trying to haul them off her.

Suddenly, Rosenberg stood over them. He held one of their improvised snow shovels, with its sharp blade of Apollo hull section. Holding the handle with two hands, he raised the blade over his head.

His bespectacled face was blank, thoughtful, as if he was considering some abstract problem.

"Rosenberg! Don't . . . we have to . . ."

He brought the blade swinging down through the air, as if he was chopping wood. The blade hit Angel's neck, with a moist, soft noise, like slicing cabbage.

Blood splashed. Angel stiffened, throwing his head back.

Then he slumped forward against her, his hand still locked in her waist band. The blade seemed to be stuck in his neck.

Rosenberg bent and grabbed Angel's long hair. He hauled, and just peeled Angel away from her. She saw blood—her blood?—dribbling from Angel's mouth.

Rosenberg dumped Angel aside. The blade came free of Angel's neck now, and tumbled to the floor with a clatter.

Benacerraf sat up. The neck of her T-shirt was stretched, but not torn. There was a smear over the front, of blood and saliva and snot. Angel had managed to pull her shorts down as far as her hips, and her bony pelvis was exposed, a dark rim of pubic hair. She tugged at a flap of cloth, covering her crotch.

"He's dead," Rosenberg said evenly.

"I think he broke his arm, when I fell on him."

Rosenberg shrugged. "Brittle bones. He had the skeleton of an old man. To hell with him."

"Are you all right, Rosenberg?"

He studied her, as if examining a specimen of gumbo. "I don't know. I've come a long way from JPL."

"Yeah."

She shuddered, and pulled her arms around her torso.

Hadamard was on his belly, on the ground. Immense chunks of debris, rusted and torn, clattered down around him.

An earthquake, in Florida.

His arms were splayed out, over the ground. His face was pressed into the sweet grass. The grass, he noticed, was a rich green, and still moist from the dew of the morning, and where his cheeks and chin had crushed the blades, there was a warm chlorophyll smell.

There was blood on the grass, though, a deep crimson, and a sharp stab of pain in his mouth. He probed gingerly with his tongue. The front of his mouth was a mess; it felt as if his lower teeth had been smashed, and his lip felt ripped open, as if his teeth had jammed themselves through the flesh.

He had difficulty moving his jaw. Perhaps it was broken.

Now he pulled his hands towards him, and he felt the moist grass rustling beneath his palms. With his hands beneath his shoulders, he pushed, as if attempting a press-up.

He couldn't lift his chest off the ground. And when he tried, a pain in his legs and knees, extraordinary in its intensity, came flooding over him.

He slumped back to the ground. As he did so, he felt something grind inside his chest, a new source of astounding pain.

Probably he was trapped under debris from the press stand. Maybe his legs were broken too. And it felt as if there was a busted rib or two in there . . .

His orderly catalogue broke down, as his thinking was overwhelmed by a new wave of agony.

He was thirsty.

He managed to turn his head to look across at the VAB. The big cube of a building had cracked, from the lip of one of the huge Saturn-V-size doorways all the way to the roof. Gigantic blocks and sheets of concrete were falling away from the walls of the building, exposing fresh, unweathered material beneath, which gleamed briefly in what was left of the sunlight; for a moment Hadamard had a brief vision of how this magnificent folly must have looked in the 1960s, when it was fresh and new and unweathered, the embodiment of a gigantic technocratic dream.

But then the cracks widened, and the interior of the structure, its skeletal framework within, was exposed.

At the foot of the crumbling building he saw a splash of red metal, splayed out beneath a fifty-foot slab of concrete. It was his car, crushed like a bug.

He twisted his neck and looked across the Banana River.

It looked as if 39-B had gone altogether. 39-A was tilted at a crazy angle. Next to that defiant, rusting skeleton, the Saturn mockup had been snapped in two. The first stage was still standing, like a stump of broken bone, but the upper stages and the fake Apollo spacecraft lay, indistinctly visible, scattered on the ground at the foot of the gantry.

No more Moon flights for a while, he thought.

At least the Moon rocks ought to be safe, those unopened samples in their vaults in JSC. Maybe archaeologists of the future would find that huge, twenty-billion-dollar cache, the unopened cores and sealed boxes, and wonder how so much of this alien rock had found its way to the planet Earth.

The water in the Banana River was draining, as if a plug had been drawn.

The shocks returned.

The overgrown meadow in front of him lifted up. He could actually see the pressure wave traversing the surface of the ground, as if the Earth itself had been shocked into some new fluid form.

There was an immense groan, a rumble deeper than the roar of any rocket engine.

And then the ground lifted up beneath him. He was thrown into the air, his limbs dangling like a doll's. The pain in his legs was excruciating.

But the experience was oddly exhilarating, as if he were a child, thrown up by his father, with safe, strong arms waiting to catch him.

He caught a last, wheeling glimpse of Florida sunlight.

She showered, scrubbing herself in as much hot water as *Discovery* could feed her. She was bruised, on her breast and her stomach, where Angel had grabbed at her. Her neck was burned from the Beta-cloth. Her lips were a mess, and she knew she would have to ask Rosenberg to treat them.

But not today. She couldn't stand the thought of being touched again. Not today.

When she was done she dumped her soiled clothes outside her quarters. She got back in and closed the door. She straightened out her sleeping bag, which had been kicked around during the struggle.

She got inside, and wrapped her arms around herself, trying to stop shivering, unable to sleep.

Outside she could hear Rosenberg moving around the hab module, hauling at heavy loads.

When she got too thirsty, she dressed, and pushed her way out of her quarters.

Her little pile of clothes had gone. And so had Angel's body. The place looked clean, as if nothing had happened.

She went to the galley and dug out the coffee. There were only a few ounces of freeze-dried grains left, and they were hoarding them for rainy days. But, she thought, her days weren't going to come much rainier than this.

She drank the coffee, thick and black. The hot liquid burned at her broken lips, but the pain was somehow welcome, cleansing. The Titan water in the tanks was as fresh as run-off from a Colorado mountain.

Rosenberg came in from the airlock.

"I saved you some coffee," she said.

His smile was thin. "Thanks."

"Where is he?"

"Buried in the gumbo. But he ain't going to stay there."

"You're going to feed him to the water oxidizer."

"Damn right. Now he's frozen out there, he will be easier to uh, dismantle. I'm no wet butcher, Paula."

"My God," she said. "Sometimes I think you're as crazy as he is."

"Was."

"Won't it give you any qualms, to feed off life support loops containing the corpse of a human?"

"Why should it? We've been eating each other's waste products for two billion miles anyhow. Look, if it bothers you, I'll just pass him through the SCWO and vent the products, discard the residue."

"The main thing is to get him burned, right?"

"Do you object?"

She pictured Bill Angel coming at her, and shuddered. "It was my fault," she said slowly. "I handled him wrong, from the beginning."

"What the hell could you have done?"

"He seemed so *competent*," she said.

"This helps us out with our life support equations. But the logic of our situation hasn't changed, Paula. In fact—"

"What?"

"We had news from home." He looked at her, searching her face. "They raised the stakes on us again, Paula. It's even more important we survive."

She felt chill. Bill had said something . . . She'd thought he was raving. "What do you mean?"

He smiled. "I ought to fix up that lip of yours," he said.

"Later, Rosenberg."

"Sure . . . You know, there's always work to be done in the farm."

The farm. That was what she was supposed to be doing today.

The thought of entering the tight walls of the old Apollo, with the racks of green, growing things under their sunlight lamps, was suddenly powerfully appealing to her.

"Yes," she said. "The farm." She sipped the coffee from Earth, trying to make it last.

Rosenberg went to the comms panel, and tried to find a signal from Houston.

Book Five
EXTRAVEHICULAR ACTIVITY
A.D. 2015–A.D. 2016

In 1990 its controllers had had *Voyager One* look back and take one last picture sequence before shutting down its camera.

Voyager swiveled its instrument platform and shot a panoramic view of sixty images, encompassing in a single sweep every planet from Neptune, past Jupiter, past Earth, in to the sun. It was already so far from home that it took more than five hours for each pixel, traveling at the speed of light, to reach Earth.

The sun was still striking, a brilliant point object millions of times brighter than the brightest star. But the planets, even the gas giants, were mere points of light.

Even so, had *Voyager* repeated the experiment now, it would have been able to observe the changes that swept over Earth, in the year 2015.

As the clouds rolled across the face of Earth's oceans, the planet became a brilliant point source of reflected sunlight, its color lightening from blue to white, a twin of scorched Venus.

Patiently, conserving its attitude fuel, the blocky spacecraft sailed further from the sun, pointing its antenna home, obeying its iterated software instructions, calling steadily to Earth.

As Titan's long night drew to a close, Benacerraf and Rosenberg prepared for their expedition to El Dorado, the crater on Cronos, in search of kerogen.

Working in the scuffed-up gumbo around the orbiter, they prepared to load their sleds. The sleds—six feet long, two wide—were improvised from Command Module hull sections, and had a covering of parachute canvas. Right now the sleds were configured to slide across gumbo; later, on Cronos, Rosenberg expected them to face a surface of raw ice, so they were carrying runners made from steel struts.

The equipment pile was dauntingly high.

Benacerraf bent and started to haul gear up onto her sled, the heaviest stuff at the bottom. The bulky items responded oddly in the low gravity; she had to haul to get them moving, but then inertia took over and she had to guide them, rather than lower them, into the right place on her sled. She checked each item off on the ring-bound checklist she had strapped to her wrist.

The first item was the S-band radio they would use to navigate, triangulating off *Cassini*. Next came a light, high-density power cell, cannibalized from the skimmer, and bottles of oxygen and hydrogen to feed it. Every time they stopped and made camp they would have to recharge the batteries in their EMUs; and the power cells would have to keep them warm during the "nights." There were spare lith canisters for scrubbing carbon dioxide from their suits' circulation: precious, irreplaceable. Benacerraf packed a tent, the flimsy hemispherical affair taken from the skimmer.

There were skis, improvised from pieces of *Jitterbug*'s frame. A length of rope. A small bag of tools. Spare parts for the gadgets that would have to keep them alive, Clancy clamps and silver bell wires. Their snow shovels. A medical kit, assembled by Rosenberg: cream for their hands and Benacerraf's lips, powder and gel and antiseptic cream for skin afflictions and wounds, plasters for blisters, cuts and rubbed raw patches of skin, drugs and painkillers, Lomotil for diarrhea. They had pethidine and morphine—opium derivatives—and various forceps, scalpels, hypodermics and stitching needles.

The rations were based heavily on what was left of the dehydrated stock they'd brought from Earth. Benacerraf hated to exhaust these final supplies, making them almost totally dependent on the CELSS farm thereafter, but Rosenberg insisted. Their diet, he said, was crucial. He had calculated they would each need five thousand calories per day. He showed her how the diet he planned would be high in fats—nearly sixty percent—whereas their normal diet was more than half carbohydrates.

When the load was assembled, Benacerraf had trouble closing her canvas over the top of it. She had to repack a couple of times, trying to balance the mass of the load and to give it all an even shape.

At last she had it tied up with rope. The sled, bound together, was the size and shape of a coffin. Benacerraf hoped that wasn't an omen. When she was done, she felt exhausted already: she was hot, her breath pumping, her limbs aching from fighting the suit's stiffness.

Rosenberg estimated that each of their sleds, on Earth, would weigh more than five hundred pounds: the best part of half a ton. Here, gravity reduced that to seventy pounds.

Five stone, to be hauled across a hundred and twenty miles, in full EVA suits.

She pulled her harness around her torso.

The sled harness was improvised from Apollo seat restraints and Shuttle orbiter foot loops. There was a bandolier set of straps she lifted over her shoulders and chest, and a belt around her waist. There was a buckle at the front of her chest, relatively easy for suited fingers to reach and manipulate, and adjustable straps on the shoulders. The most difficult thing about designing the harnesses had been ensuring they would not foul any of her suit's essential equipment, like the control panel on her chest, and the umbilicals carrying oxygen and water from her PLSS.

She leaned forward, and let the straps take her weight. She adjusted the shoulder straps until they felt comfortable through the layers of her suit.

She thought it was ominous that her sled didn't move at all in response to her body weight.

Benacerraf looked back, one last time, at Tartarus Base.

Discovery looked like a DC-10 that had come down in the ice. But her white upper surfaces were uniformly coated with tholin, obscuring what was left of the colorful Stars-and-Stripes and NASA logos. The big windows on the flight deck, streaked by tholin, showed no lights; the interior of the orbiter was black. All the nonessential systems in the orbiter had been shut down, so they could save every last erg from the Topaz reactors while they were away. And that meant almost everything, save the heating and the nutrient, lighting and air supply for the CELSS farm. She played her helmet lamp over the orbiter's flanks, which glistened with gumbo; it looked as if Titan was drawing *Discovery* gradually into its icy belly.

She stood beside Rosenberg.

"You remember to cancel the newspapers?"

"Yes," he said gently.

"Let's get out of here."

She turned her face resolutely away from the orbiter. Her helmet lamp cast a ghostly ellipse of white light on an anonymous patch of gumbo. The greater darkness beyond, which they must penetrate, was concealed.

She leaned into her traces, with her full body weight. Her snowshoes pawed at the gumbo. The harness rubbed at her shoulders and hips.

The sled, stuck to the gumbo, wouldn't move.

She straightened up and looked back. There was a hummock in the gumbo, just in front of her sled, to its right. She was catching on that.

She turned again, and leaned into the harness with her left shoulder. She jerked at the harness, throwing her weight into it, trying to keep her footing in the tholin.

She felt something give. She almost stumbled over.

She looked again. The sled had moved forward, a couple of feet.

Rosenberg whooped. "Way to go, Paula."

"Sure," she said. She'd covered two feet, out of a hundred miles.

She leaned into the harness again, and jerked. The sled moved forward, coming free of the sticky gumbo with a slurping noise.

She pawed at the slush, trying to keep a steady rhythm. It got easier once she'd started, as long as she maintained the momentum of the sled. Whenever she stopped, she could feel the sled sink back into the welcoming mud. Still, her movement was jerky and uneven, stop-start.

Soon it felt as if the canvas band around her stomach was crushing her insides against her backbone.

It would be a comfort to think the sleds would get lighter as they proceeded, as the two of them ate up the food. But Rosenberg was insisting that they retrieve every piece of waste they produced—every drop of piss, every dump—and haul it back to feed the hungry CELSS farm. It made sense. But the thought of hauling bags of her own shit for a hundred miles across the surface of Titan did not chime with her romantic dreams of what exploring an alien planet should be like.

A wind blew up. It came straight in her face, heavy and dense, and the gumbo rippled sluggishly before her. Her suit temperature dropped as a wind chill set in; she could feel the hot diamonds of her heaters trying to restore the balance.

Rosenberg called, "We have to expect a lot of this. That wind is a katabatic. A gravity-fed wind, blowing downhill, out of the heart of Cronos—"

"Shut up, Rosenberg."

She bent her head and pushed at the gumbo, the harness digging at her shoulders and hips, Rosenberg's katabatic wind shoving against her chest, driving onwards.

The light level rose slowly. A burnt orange glow seeped uniformly into the sky.

The gumbo glistened before her, like a plain of dried blood, unmarked and without frontier.

It wasn't like a dawn on Earth.

As the light came up, there was no sense of opening out, of liberation from the confines of the night. The horizon was so close by, just a couple of miles, and obscured anyhow by the murky mist and haze. And the sky overhead, even on a cloudless day, was a lid, complete and orange and seamless. It was like being in a box: orange haze above, purple-black slush below, bound in by a horizon as close as a fence. And as she walked, bringing nothing but more miles of tholin slush into view—no roads, no trees, no gas stations—she became oppressed, trapped by the lifeless murk.

Benacerraf started to develop sharp twinges in her shoulder muscles, and shooting pains in her shoulder blades. And besides, her right foot was beginning to feel cold and raw. Forward motion was only possible with sharp tugs at her load; she could feel the pressure points in her shoulders, waist, knees and feet.

She stopped, trying to work the stiffness out of her shoulders, but confined in her movements by the heavy suit. The pressure of the harness bands on her chest and gut receded, briefly; she could feel bruises gathering, and burns about her hips where the harness was too tight.

She dropped her head, and ploughed forward again, yanking the sled away from the cloying gumbo.

They spoke rarely.

Mostly, she was alone with the rasp of her breathing, the high-frequency whir of the fans in her backpack and the hiss of oxygen across her face.

She tried to dull out her thoughts, not to think about what lay ahead of her and behind her, how every step was taking her further from *Discovery*. She concentrated, for instance, on the familiar noises of her suit; she tried to imagine she was in space again, in low orbit above the glowing, beautiful Earth, and that the suit was a bubble of warmth and comfort around her.

But the pain broke through that too easily, from her sore foot, her hands, her shoulders.

She tried not to think about the silence on the comms links. *The extinction of mankind.* Rosenberg, figuring from what he knew of the parameters of the rock the Chinese had dropped, said there could be little possibility of human survival. It was the K-T boundary event over again, he said.

What proportion of "mankind" could she have met during her life? A few thousand? And how many did she care about?

Three people, she thought. Just three. And now she couldn't even find out if they were dead or alive.

Way to go, Paula.

Later, she got angry.

She got mad at her balky sled, every time it stuck in some particularly viscous patch of gumbo and dragged her backwards, yanking at all her sore points. She got mad at the dull Titan weather, at the winds that chilled her but failed to freeze the gumbo to a useful surface.

She got mad at Rosenberg. That wasn't hard.

She could sink inside herself and pick over some aspect of Rosenberg—the things he said, the body stink when he opened up his suit—and chew on it inside her head—for hours, she found, building up the irritation to a near-hatred. Even those CELSS farm baby carrots, too bitter for her to eat, which he religiously devoured, insisting they were good for oxygen deficiency.

She could plod like this, steadily hating Rosenberg, and then, when she looked at her astronaut's Rolex, she'd find—if she was lucky—that maybe an hour had passed, bringing her that much closer to the moment she could stop.

After a time, though, even the anger didn't work. There was too little stimulation for her mind, in the dull landscape of gumbo and haze; she was turned inward, her thoughts stale and repetitive, churning and festering, with no external distraction to relieve her.

Sometimes she wanted to howl, to raise her face to the

orange sky and just scream like a frustrated ape. But she knew she couldn't. If she did, it would let out the beast at last, the Bill Angel craziness she suspected lay deep within her. She would lose her ability to manage this, once and for all.

So she plodded on, muttering. *Stick it. Stick it. Stick it.* Until the urge to howl dissipated, and the blackness receded a little.

After five hours, they had completed six miles. Benacerraf was exhausted, the little water spigots in her helmet running dry, the air circulating in her suit stale.

Rosenberg pulled alongside her. He ran a gloved finger over her bandolier. "Look at this," he said, and he lifted up a harness joint with a fingertip. The stitching was torn, and Benacerraf's harness was twisted. "This joint is double-stitched, but these couch harnesses were never designed for the kind of stresses we're subjecting them to now. I guess you didn't notice. You've been dragging the sled with the harness out of alignment. Your torso must have been twisted. No wonder your shoulders hurt."

"Rosenberg, I'm done. Let's get the tent up."

"We haven't completed the schedule, Paula. Another three or four miles and—"

"I know about the schedule. I don't care about the damn schedule, Rosenberg. I'm telling you I need a break."

"It's just that right now we're in as good a position as we're going to be. We're still full of food, and our core body temperatures are high, and we've had plenty of reasonably natural sleep back in the hab module. Later, it's going to be harder to—"

"Help me raise the fucking tent, Rosenberg, or you're going to get a sled runner up your ass." She pulled the parachute fabric off her sled.

Still complaining, he helped her haul out the tent.

The skimmer tent was a ball eight feet across. The airtight skin was reinforced with parachute canvas, to give it additional strength. Rosenberg roughly inflated it with a feed from oxygen and nitrogen tanks. They anchored it to the gumbo with ropes and wide, flat, anchorlike spikes, driven deep into the slush. The tent sat on the slushy surface of Titan like a sad beachball, its muddy yellow surface drab and uninspiring, fat air and power lines snaking into it from the tanks in Rosenberg's sled.

Now the two of them worked with the snow shovels to cover the tent over with a thick layer of slush. This ought to retain some of their heat. It was slow work; the slush at first just slithered off the canvas, and it took long, hard minutes of labor before the tent was covered over.

Rosenberg led the way into the tent, crawling through the crude airlock. Benacerraf followed. In her bulky suit, she kept colliding with Rosenberg's limbs and helmet; she felt like some bug crawling around inside a cocoon.

Rosenberg hooked up a low-watt light and an electric heater. "Wait a few minutes until we warm up."

The elements of the heater started to glow crimson red, a sharp color very unlike Titan's dull orange. She sat close to the heater, watching the elements grow brighter, seeing their multiple reflections from the layered visors of her helmet. It was, she thought, heat brought to this ice moon from the remote center of the Solar System.

Rosenberg spent the time fiddling with the spare PLSS. This backpack— intended for Nicola Mott—had been rigged with a powerful vacuum pump and blower. They would use it to keep the tent air circulating through its lith hydroxide carbon dioxide scrubbers. If either of their packs failed during the march, this spare would serve as a backup.

At last, Rosenberg said the air and temperatures were okay.

Benacerraf cracked the seal of her helmet.

Chill air gushed into her helmet, at her neck and over her face. Her breath immediately misted before her face, and gathered as frost on the glass of her faceplate. She coughed, and took a deep breath. The air was so cold she could feel it burning at her lungs, and digging into the flesh of her face. The warmth of her suit seemed to gush out at her neck, and the cold seeped deeper into her.

"My God, Rosenberg."

"Can you breathe? What can you smell?"

She sniffed, but her nose seemed blocked. "It's so damn cold."

"I know. I'm sorry. It isn't going to get a lot better."

She tried again, dragging the air through her nostrils. The cold of it seemed to scour at her nasal passages, the back of her throat.

The air stank.

"Bad eggs," she said. "Farts."

Rosenberg cracked his own helmet now; she could see steam billow out around his face, as if his suit was a mobile sauna. He grimaced. "Methane," he said. "Other shit, too. Welcome to Titan, Paula."

"Let's get this over with."

Benacerraf took off her boots and gloves; her fingers immediately felt numb and the tips turned pasty-white, but despite the cold, it was a relief to get the boots off her sore feet.

She began digging around inside her suit, opening zips, trying to get at her urine bag. When she had it, she tipped it up into a larger plastic storage bag. She tried to keep the whole operation sealed up, but her cold hands were clumsy, and a few drops of the thick piss escaped and splashed on the gumbo-streaked fabric of her sleeves. She sealed up the bag and passed it to Rosenberg; he pushed it into a corner of the tent, far from the heater, where it would freeze quickly.

Mercifully, neither of them had taken a dump into their suit collectors during the walk. That was something to face another day.

She plugged her PLSS into the power feed, to charge up its batteries. She checked the status of her lith canisters and other consumables.

Rosenberg had brought a couple of bags of Mount Othrys water into the tent. These had refrozen, of course, during the haul; now he held them close to the heater and mashed them up with his boot.

There was enough water for seven or eight days, enough to be able to make it back to *Discovery* from the edge of the ice sheet without resupply. After that, they would be on the ice of Cronos, and ought to be able to collect local water.

When the ice was melted, they used the water to drink, and to resupply the spigots in their helmets, and to rehydrate a couple of packets of food.

Washing, they had decided, was a luxury for this trip.

The menu was soup, rice, biscuits and chocolate, with a handful of baby carrots. Benacerraf gulped down her food as rapidly as she could. The soup made a tiny warm place at the center of her body. The carrots still tasted bitter, but Rosenberg devoured his, and she passed him her portion.

Rosenberg measured the amount she drank. They had to watch out for dehydration. Cold air couldn't hold much moisture, and with every breath she took, her nose and mouth were trying to humidify the air. She could lose a gallon of water a day that way, through her nose and breathing passages. It was a vicious circle; the more she dried out the less thirsty she would feel.

She gulped down the last of her ration. "I'm done," she said, shivering. "I think I'll seal up again."

He checked the Rolex strapped to his wrist. "Not yet, Paula. Remember what we said. We have to leave the suits open a full hour before sealing up; we have to get the moisture out."

Benacerraf thought of arguing against that, but he'd already relented on the schedule today.

Anyhow he was right. If the dampness from her body seeped into the suit's layers, it would shortout their insulating effect. She could even freeze in there.

"Let me look at your foot," Rosenberg said now.

"It's just a friction injury."

"Then let's stop it getting any worse," Rosenberg said mildly. "Come on, Paula. Doctor's orders."

With great reluctance, Benacerraf removed the sock she was wearing on her right foot.

The side of her foot was rubbed raw, all the way back to the heel. Rosenberg rubbed cream into it, and stuck a plaster over the worst of her blisters. "If this keeps up we'll have to think about cutting a chunk out of that boot. I guess it wasn't designed for hiking."

"No. Thanks, Rosenberg."

When Benacerraf had sealed up her suit again, she lay down on her side, facing the soft plastic wall, away from Rosenberg. When she reached out to the wall and touched it with her gloved hand, she could feel how stiff it was, and a rime of frost gathered from their breath and the moisture emitted by the hot Earth-born bodies inside their suits scraped off on her fingertip.

She would be waking up to darkness again, she realized, to another day of tough hauling across the bleak, featureless gumbo.

It was impossible to settle her head inside her helmet. The damn thing wasn't designed to be a pillow, after all. Tomorrow night, she'd put some kind of cushion inside here, something from the sled. Anything soft, even a scrap of parachute canvas.

She closed her eyes and tried to ignore the stiffness of her shoulders, the way her hip dug into the ground, the soreness of her feet, the sucking cold of the icy slush below her.

The suit heater labored to warm her; gradually the cold of the tent was dispelled, and the fresh oxygen-nitrogen blowing across her face dispelled the stink of methane.

The news from home, they'd taken to calling it.

It was impossible to grasp the scale of it, and so she didn't even try. Maybe their isolation and abandonment had, in an offbeat way, actually helped. After so many years away from Earth she found it hard to remember that there were members of the human race beyond the handful who had left Earth orbit with her, in 2008. After so long in confinement, the hab modules and landing craft and pressure suits making up a series of high-tech prisons, stretching back years, it was difficult to imagine walking, unimpeded, in the open air. Even if by some miracle she could be transported home now, she suspected she would be some kind of agoraphobic, a recluse, shunning company and light.

Even her family, Jackie and the boys, seemed to be receding from her. After all, the boys had lived half their brief lives without Benacerraf. If she had been taken home, she wouldn't have recognized them, nor they her.

They'd been cut off up here, on this ice ball in the sky. They couldn't have gotten home anyhow. The fact that home may not even exist any more really didn't seem to make much difference. She still faced the same grinding numbness, the same lengthy list of chores to stay alive, every time she woke up, whether humanity lived or not.

It made no difference.

They didn't talk about it, much. Rosenberg never referred to people he had lost, places he would never see again.

But that was Rosenberg. He was probably happier up here on Titan anyhow; human society had never done many favors for smart, goofy kids like Rosenberg, no matter how much it needed their inventions.

As for herself, maybe she was working through some kind of post-shock syndrome. Christ knows, she thought, I'm entitled to. Here she was stranded with an unfit wacko on a moon of Saturn, and it looked as if the world had come to an end, and she appeared to be developing crotch rot. How was she supposed to react? *Now here's my plan . . .*

On the whole, she concluded, however, she was handling this pretty well. In a way, even the walking helped. Even the pain. Something to do, to occupy her mind during the long, slow-time Titan days.

Sleep times, however, were harder to handle.

On the fifth day, they reached the lip of the ice plateau Cronos.

Benacerraf stopped, and leaned against her harness.

The break in the landscape was surprisingly sharp. Maybe a half-mile ahead of her, the gumbo visibly thinned. Then a ridge of eroded gray-white water ice pushed its way up out of the tholin, like a beach rising from some sludgy polluted ocean. The slope was shallow at first, but Benacerraf could see how it continued on upwards, until it was lost in the thick band of horizon haze. The ice was worn with gullies and grooves, like old sandstone, and Benacerraf could make out stripes and stains of tholin down the gray buttresses.

As far as she could see the ridge continued, a band of dull gray like a wall across the world, merging at last with the horizon.

Rosenberg came up to her, breathing hard, leaning against his traces. "Magnificent, isn't it?" Rosenberg's voice was odd: light, fragile. And his stance seemed awkward; he seemed to be leaning too far into the traces. She tried to look into Rosenberg's helmet. But his visor was obscured by an orange reflection from the hazy sky, frost, a smear of tholin. Rosenberg was the doctor; Benacerraf had been focusing on her own minor ailments, and trusting Rosenberg to look after himself.

Maybe he wasn't.

She looked up dubiously at the slope they would have to climb. "Magnificent. Absolutely. Let's go on."

She led the way once more.

It got easier, despite the slope. It was like climbing Othrys. The gumbo got gradually thinner and less clinging though less supportive of the sled until at last her snowshoes were clattering on bone-hard ice, and the sled's base was scraping with an ominous grind across the slope.

She stopped again, and waited for Rosenberg to catch up. Even in such a short distance he seemed to have fallen a long way behind, and it took him some minutes to make up the ground.

"Time for the great changeover, Rosenberg," she said.

His breath was a noisy rasp, and he didn't attempt to speak; he just let himself out of his harness and began to unpick the knots on his sled cover.

They had to fix their aluminum runners to the bases of the sleds. Benacerraf found it difficult to handle the big wing nuts with her gloved hands. The first time she twisted too hard, and the thread of the bolt sheared right off, coming away in a spiral twist.

Rosenberg dug out a spare for her. "Take it easy," he said. "Steel is brittle at these temperatures, remember."

Next she fitted her skis to her feet. These were just slats of hull metal, with opened-out overshoes fixed to them for boots.

After stowing the snowshoes and lashing up the sleds, they resumed again.

It took her a few hundred yards to get used to the skis, and the half-sliding action they required. There was a lot of work for her knees and ankles, against the stiffness of her suit. Soon her joints were aching, and muscles on the back of her calves were announcing their existence with pulses of stiffness and pain.

But when she settled into a new rhythm, she seemed to make faster and easier progress than before. To haul the sled she was able to lean steadily into her traces, rather than having to yank at the sled as she'd had to over the gumbo, and that smoothed out the pains in the pressure points on her shoulders, hips and waist.

This haul was never going to be easy, but it was, she conceded, a relief to be free of the clinging of the gumbo.

For a while she felt almost exhilarated.

She reached the mouth of a wide, shallow gully.

In the white light of her helmet lamp, the gully walls were blue-gray, and there was a scattering of loose ice on the floor.

The slope further up was undulating—it was gathering itself into a series of huge, frozen waves—and the gully, although it got steeper and more narrow towards the end, seemed to offer the easiest route forward.

She looked back. A way below, Rosenberg's gumbo-streaked suit and the yellow-gray canvas on his sled were easily visible against the orange-gray ice.

She pushed up into the gully.

She could feel loose granules crunch beneath her weight. But it didn't get any easier to pull the sled; the friction actually increased, and she felt the granules grind beneath her skis.

She bent down, stiffly, and scooped up a handful of the ice granules. They were hard and round, nothing like the snow of Earth. On the surface they were loose, but a little deeper they stuck together—presumably thanks to a surface layer of organics—to form pebble-sized chunks that she could crush in her hand. What the geologists called duricrust, she thought.

She took a look at the runners on her sled. There were fine grooves scratched into the runners' base by the ice crystals. She knew that at normal human temperatures, sleds and skates worked by melting a fine layer of water at the top of the ice, and then sliding across, lubricated by the water, with almost no friction. Here, these small, hard crystals wouldn't melt under the pressure of her runners; they were like grains of sand, and what she was doing was more like dragging a sled across a desert.

She felt an unreasonable, crushing disappointment. They just got no breaks with the conditions here.

As her climb up the gully wore on, the gradient increased in severity. Soon she was free of the clinging granules, but now, to her irritation, the ice grew too slick. She just couldn't win. Sometimes her skis slipped backward at every step, and the only way she could proceed was to tack back and forth at forty-five degrees to the slope, which added a lot of extra distance to the whole.

Even so, soon she had risen so far that when she looked back the ground was hidden in the haze. And still the slope continued above her, eroded and ancient, up into the orange mists above. She got her head down and climbed on. She forced any thoughts of the future—even the pleasure of getting her boots off, or the distance they still had to cross—out of her head.

At last, she reached the top of the steepening gully. The landscape opened out before her. She seemed to have reached a plateau.

The ice at her feet was jumbled and cracked. And when she looked ahead, she saw a sprawling mass of ice, locked in suspended animation. Waves of ice, which must have been a hundred feet tall, reared up, caught in the instant of crashing against each other. Huge open chasms showed dark against the gray-white mass. There was noise here, too: deep groans resounded from the belly of the ice, pulsing back and forth across the broken landscape. Each ice wave was carved, sometimes into elaborate shapes, with fluted channels and sharp crests. The giant shapes marched to the close horizon, so big they were visible as they receded over the curve of the world, like ships sailing over a frozen sea.

A layer of methane cloud, dark and threatening, lay like a lid over the shattered icescape, obscuring the haze and merging with the ice at the close horizon into a complex band of gray, black and orange.

After some minutes, Rosenberg came staggering up the gully after her. He leaned against his sled, breath rattling, and stared out at the ice sea, which was reflected in his visor.

"Pressure ice," he said. "Paula, I think this whole continent is a giant magma extrusion, distorting one whole side of the moon. It's like the Tharsis Bulge on Mars. Maybe such features are common on small worlds like this . . . And all this ice is flowing slowly outward and downward from the magma extrusion, a huge, continent-sized viscous relaxation."

Benacerraf looked around with new understanding. The pressure ridges were ice waves, magnified by Titan's low gravity, frozen in time. She shivered, feeling dwarfed in space and time. If she could accelerate her perception—if she could live for a million years—she would see the ice flowing thickly away from Rosenberg's magma mound, like warm icing off a wedding cake.

After a couple more minutes they pushed on, Benacerraf leading again.

She tried to select a route which would take them threading between the worst of the pressure ridges.

The waves took a variety of forms. Some of them were sharply defined ridges, some of them rounded hummocks; some took still more exotic shapes—rounded boulders, even torpedo shapes, forms out of nightmares, mounted on eroded, fragile-looking pillars that looked unable to hold up all that mass, low gravity or not.

Ways through the ridges were winding and uneven. She tried at first to use her skis, but the paths were too narrow and twisting, and the skis just got in the way. She took them off and stowed them in her sled. The paths were covered besides by an uneven layer of loose granules, difficult to judge; sometimes the granules crunched beneath her boots, taking her weight before bottoming out, but sometimes she would find her heel thudding against ice as hard as rock, concealed by a quarter-inch of gritty granules. Her sores and blisters chafed. Her sled bumped and rattled over the surface, every step a jarring uncertainty, and her harness dragged over her shoulders and waist, burning her. She found herself growing nostalgic for the miles of compliant, sticky gumbo.

She was forced to scale some of the ridges.

They were exactly like frozen waves, a hundred feet tall or more. She tacked at a shallow angle to reach the top of each ridge. At the top she turned so that the sled went ahead of her as she slid down the slope on the far side. Then it was time to clamber painfully up to the top of the next ridge. She was like an insect, she thought, struggling over the meniscus of some giant pond.

She had no crampons or ski-sticks; she had to paw at the surface with her gloves and the sides of her skis to gain leverage. Soon her knees and elbows were bruised, and her fingers and toes ached. Sometimes her sled slid sideways and pulled her back down into a trough.

She paused at a crest. The ice was bare and blue-gray. Gritty granules lay in the hollows. The ice here was polished, and when she ran a gloved hand over it, it felt as smooth as glass, hard as concrete. The wave had been scoured out by gritty granules, and then polished to a sheen by fine aerosol dust.

When she looked back, she could see Rosenberg toiling through the valleys between the waves. The great ridges thrust upward all around him, dwarfing him, and his helmet lamp splashed little puddles of yellow light against the shimmering walls around him. Sometimes he would pass a clearer patch of blue ice, and his light would penetrate the bulk of the waves; Benacerraf would see the beam glimmering within the bulk of a wave, scattering and sparkling from complex fissure patterns within the ice, an arc of Earth light illuminating these giant, dead, silent fairy castles.

Rosenberg stopped, several times, and took samples, scrapings of the eroded surfaces. He photographed the wave shapes. He even measured the angles of the frozen crests. His voice was weak, but Benacerraf could hear his enthusiasm as he found the opportunity to do a little science. "So beautiful . . . Benacerraf, each of these waves might be a million years old. And as the wind wears away at them, it's exposing ice billions of years older than that—ice older than life on Earth . . . so beautiful . . ."

She found a new hazard.

She had to skirt huge crevasses; they looked to be hundreds of feet deep, with walls of a clean Earth-like blue where her helmet lamp shone on them. As the ice flowed out of the heart of Cronos, it was splitting along gigantic faults.

The crevasses parallel to the flow weren't difficult to handle, as they pointed the path she wanted to take, towards the heart of the continent. But in some places, where the ice was compressed as it flowed, the crevasses ran transverse to the flow. She had to take wide detours to reach a narrowing of each crevasse, so that she could straddle them with her skis.

In the most difficult country there was a mix of transverse and parallel crevasses, presumably because of some distortion of the flow. The crevasses intersected, cracking the ice into gigantic, parallel pillars, some of which had tumbled and shattered, so it was as if she was picking her way across the smashed sidewalk of some giant, ruined city.

She kept a weather eye on Rosenberg; his progress was slow, but he was plodding along in her wake, his head down.

After some hours of this, she found a place to camp. It was at the hollow between two giant pressure waves, a patch of regolith granules not much larger than the area of their two sleds. They had to anchor the tent to the sleds, because their metal pegs would not drive into the ice layer.

All around, as far as Benacerraf could see in the orange-brown light, there were pressure mounds and cracks. Their little encampment was like a small boat, she thought, lost in a giant sea.

Before they could crawl into the tent, a wind came up, blasting through the valley as if through a wind tunnel.

This was the seventh night, some fifty miles from Tartarus, and they were getting into a routine when they established camp.

Benacerraf hadn't managed to take a dump that day as she walked—which was the preferred way, because then at the end of the day they just had to dig the crap out of their diapers, and some semblance of privacy was maintained. But now she could feel pressure building inside her. She suspected she was coming down with some kind of diarrhea. It was probably the antibiotics she was taking.

"Sorry, Rosenberg," she said in advance.

He was piping water into today's ration bags. He looked at her, his eyes glassy, and shrugged.

She opened her suit as wide as she could. She stood up and bent over in the tent's cramped confines, with the open front of her suit close to the heater. She fumbled to get an old ration bag inside the suit. She found her butt. The skin of her buttocks felt flaccid, the flesh depleted of fat. It was, she thought, an old woman's ass. She clamped the bag as best she could over her butt, and let go.

The crap emerged as a hard, hot spray, accompanied by an explosive fart. She tried to catch it all in the bag, but it wasn't easy, and she could feel excrement splashing her hands, sleeves and legs.

The smell, erupting from the interior of her suit, was moist and pungent. *My own contribution to Titan's methane layer*, she thought.

She closed up the bag and pulled it out, and her first priority was to close up her suit, trying to trap whatever warmth was left. Then she swathed the bag of sludgy excrement in a couple of other bags, wiped her hands on the back of her legs—the stuff would freeze off there tomorrow anyhow—and lodged the bag in the corner of the tent, with her piss bag.

She huddled closer to Rosenberg and the fire, shivering, her arms wrapped around herself.

Rosenberg was working at the cooking, but slowly. His left hand had got frostbitten a few days before, when damp had gotten inside his glove, and the cold of the ice ridges to which he had to cling had found a route to his fingers. Now, three of his main finger blisters had burst, the dead skin falling away to reveal raw stumps, like uncooked meat.

"Rosenberg, that looks like agony. You want me to take over?"

"No," he said. His face was thin, the flesh disturbingly slack; his cheeks seemed to descend in folds over the corners of his mouth. "It's not so bad now the blisters have burst. Before, sometimes the fluid in them would freeze."

"Ouch."

"We both got problems. Here. Eat."

She took her food packets; the warmth, cupped in her hands, was welcome.

The meal passed in uncompanionable silence.

During the last couple of stops, the sour thoughts she'd previously been able to leave outside the tent's airlock had started to seep inside.

She'd come to loathe Rosenberg's personal habits. The yellow stink of his urine bags. The icicle-like dribbles of snot and saliva and tears that formed on his spindly beard. The way the wounds of his hands wept over her food.

And she started to become obsessed with the fairness, or otherwise, of the way Rosenberg handled the food.

The business with the carrots was one thing. Benacerraf had tried again to eat the things, but failed. So he got to eat all the damn carrots. And now Rosenberg had developed other little habits. Like he would take her discarded soup bags, turn them inside out, and lick the inner surface clean of any residue, before stowing them for use later. It drove her crazy. She started to insist on a turn making the soup, so she could get to lick the bags.

The NASA rations, in their bags and tins, were easy to split fairly. But the stuff from the CELSS farm—the carrots, their crude bread, wheat, rice—had to be divided. And if they had to choose between two portions, Benacerraf became obsessed by the need to stop Rosenberg getting the bigger portions, every damn day.

They came up with ways to deal with it. They took turns working the food. If something had to be split, one would make the break as fairly as possible, and the other got the chance to choose. They would alternate that, day by day.

Benacerraf got to look forward to the times when she could make the choice after Rosenberg's split. That way she was guaranteed to finish up with a few fractions of an ounce more than he did. She woke up remembering it was her turn, with a lighter mood.

She understood what was happening here. They were both in such foul and increasing discomfort that they needed someone to blame. The real candidates were too impersonal and remote to be hated, satisfyingly: Titan's ghastly conditions, the lousy equipment, the treachery of NASA and its political masters in abandoning them here, the Chinese and their hammer rock.

There was nobody else to blame. Only each other.

Understanding it, though, didn't make it any easier to contain.

After the meal, they went to work on each other's wounds.

Benacerraf had developed hemorrhoids, a consequence of the sweat and moisture trapped inside her suit. Rosenberg had brought a cream she could apply. Her back, shoulders and stomach were sore continually now, from their battering by the sled harness. It felt as if her pelvis was starting to protrude through the raw patches over her hips, as her body fat fell away. Her lips were still a problem; the scabs and crevices stubbornly refused to heal, and she still swallowed salty blood with every mouthful of food.

And she had indeed developed crotch rot; her inner thighs and the area around her pubic hair were rubbed raw by the inner layers of her suit, even though she treated the area with Canesten powder.

Rosenberg had a dose of crotch rot, too. With the innocence of a child, he showed her his genitals. His scrotum was a shrunken bag, red raw from the rot. And somehow his penis had gotten nipped by the frost. It had swollen up to a shapeless mass, and the end was blistered. He shrugged. "What you pay for being circumcised. One less layer of insulation. Add that to the list, Paula. *No Jews on Titan, without boxer shorts.*"

He took a look at Benacerraf's right foot. For days she had been favoring the foot as she marched, but that had just generated more problems. Now she had an abscess, swollen up on her Achilles tendon, where her heel was pressured by the rim of her boot. Rosenberg had been giving her antibiotics from their precious, dwindling supply, but they seemed to be doing little but give her the squits.

Today, Rosenberg said he would have to operate.

He gave her two deep injections of Xylocaine. For a couple of minutes he covered up her foot, protecting it from the cold while the anesthetic took hold. Then he took a scalpel blade— one he'd sterilized back in *Discovery*—and plunged it deep into the swelling. He made diagonally crossed incisions with brisk, confident strokes.

Yellow pus poured out of the wounds, and he collected it in an empty ration bag.

When he was done he cleaned the wound, coated it with antiseptic, and bound it up with bandage.

Benacerraf turned and began to pull on her sock.

When she sealed herself up again that night, Benacerraf found herself immersed in a deep animal stink. She knew that inside her high-tech suit she was becoming progressively more foul and filthy. She was an animal, stranded far from home and encased in this technological bubble, gradually fouling her own mobile nest.

The hell with it. For now, the dirt was another layer between her and the cold.

She turned her face to the tent wall. She pictured the way Rosenberg picked icicles of snot out of his nose-hairs. Warmed by irritation, she sought sleep.

At last the giant ice ridges began to diminish.

She came to a place where the waves, somehow sheltered from the wind, were smaller—no more than six or seven feet high, reduced almost to a human scale. Benacerraf decided to change her tactics, to attempt a frontal assault.

She waited to make sure Rosenberg was in view; then she

donned her skis again and set out directly east, cutting across the first wave, a characteristic frozen wave-shape.

Hauling her sled behind her, she made it to the narrow ridge at the top of the wave. Her sled was suspended halfway up the slope, and the harness hauled back at her, rubbing the chafed parts of her skin. The ridge of the next wave was only about four feet away, and she reached out towards it, hoping to bridge across the gap with her feet. But the sled fouled on a ridge of the ice, and jammed; she was hauled backwards, and almost lost her balance.

Irritated, she leaned forward and lunged, trying to clear the sled. It bounced into the air and came free suddenly; unbalanced again she tumbled forward, scrambling with her skis to avoid falling down on the steep far side of the second wave.

So she proceeded.

The waves gradually declined in size, until she found herself skiing almost unimpeded over a plain of ridged ice, scattered with gumbo and pockets of gritty granules.

Gradually, they penetrated the heart of Cronos.

On the ninth day she started to find the going harder. After a while she realized the ground was sloping up beneath her. She pushed on through the uniform haze, ignoring the pain in her knees and feet.

The slope became dramatically steeper.

The ground was pushed up into a wall as far as she could see, from north to south, like one giant wave, its termini disappearing into the misty horizon. The ice was uneven, scoured by ankle-snappers: narrow, gumbo-streaked gullies which plunged down the steepening contours.

She walked a zig-zag path, at an angle to the line of steepest slope, and that got easier on her feet, because the skis, sideways on, laid over all but the widest of the gullies. But the gullies snagged repeatedly at the runners of her sled, jerking her backward.

Beyond the miniature horizon created by the crest of the wall, a mountain was rising, its gray-white flanks streaked by gumbo, like a model of Othrys.

The crest of the ridge came up suddenly. The ground leveled out and she found herself on a narrow, eroded shelf, maybe fifty yards across, puddled with gumbo. With a final effort she hauled her sled up and over the edge. She unbuckled her harness, and dropped it gratefully to the ice.

She looked back the way she had come. Her runners and skis had left no visible trail on the bone-hard ice. She could see how this great wall swept up out of the plain in a smooth concave sweep. Much further down the slope she could see Rosenberg; he was a dark, toiling speck, dwarfed by the bulk of the sled he hauled.

She turned and walked forward to the far edge of the wall. The ice here was smooth and relatively free of gullies and crevasses, and she slid easily on her skis.

She reached the edge of the wall. She stepped carefully, avoiding the edge and any brittleness there.

The wall stretched to left and right, foreshortening and dimming out in the horizon mist. Its inward curve was just visible. That mountain peak, a neat cone, lay dead ahead of her, its base lost in the murky haze of distance.

She was clearly standing on the rim of a crater, a great walled plain which curved around that central peak. It looked too symmetrical to be natural, like a huge artifact.

She looked down into the crater plain. The wall here was steeper than on the other side; the crater was clearly a wound dug deep into the countryside. In a belt at the foot of the wall the ice surface was shattered into giant chunks which would make traveling difficult. But beyond that chaotic country, the land smoothed out, and was coated by a thickening layer of purple gumbo.

The sky was a dome of unbroken, twilight orange, empty of cloud save for a high, light scattering of nitrogen-ice cirrus.

Rosenberg came up to her. Like Benacerraf he'd discarded his harness; as he stood alongside her he leaned forward, letting the mass of his pack settle over his center of gravity, and his arms dangled, limp. His breathing was as noisy as ever.

"El Dorado," he said. "I guess we made it. It looks just like in the radar images."

She stared at the crater floor gumbo. She could see that it wasn't the uniform purple-black bruise color she'd become used to, back around Clear Lake. Purple predominated, but there were streaks of lighter reds—even a trace of scarlet—mixed in. The whole mess looked like a puddle of oil paints, the multiple colors mixed up and streaked together.

"Well, it's different," she said. "Do you think there's kerogen?"

"I can't tell," he said testily.

"Try your IR."

He reached up to switch on his night-vision visor. "I don't know if this tells me anything or not." Then he lifted his head, and in his visor she could see the reflection of the mountain, the orange sky.

". . . Oh, wow," he said. "Look up there, Paula. Use your infrared. Oh, wow."

She turned on her own visor, and looked up.

Through the milky-gold haze, beyond the feathering of cirrus cloud, was rising the huge, multicolored crescent of Saturn.

It was almost local noon here, so the sun was directly over her head. Saturn looked as if it was tipped on its side, a half-shadowed hemisphere with its bright round belly thrusting upwards. And jutting ahead of the globe of the planet, pointing vertically up towards the sun, she could see the brilliant rings, thin, striped ellipses.

It was the first time she had seen Saturn since they had dropped out of orbit.

Suddenly she realized where she was. It was a surge of perspective, as if the walls of the Universe opened out around her.

She had let this sunless bubble-world of ice and gumbo and haze and crotch rot eat into her imagination, until it was as if the gumbo extended on, beyond the visible, to infinity.

In fact, she was crawling over a ball of ice, a billion miles from the warmth of the sun.

I'm on Titan, she thought. Here I am—Paula Benacerraf, human, American, grandmother—gazing up at the rings of Saturn.

I made it.

They camped in the lee of the crater wall, on the edge of the chaotic terrain.

Rosenberg, a shapeless mass in the layers of his grimy suit, crawled over the tent floor and inspected Benacerraf's feet. That early injury to her right foot still hadn't healed up, and now she had frostbite in a couple of the toes of her left.

Rosenberg himself had developed some kind of tremor, rendering his own fingers too clumsy to apply the scalpel precisely. Benacerraf did most of the doctoring for both of them now.

Under Rosenberg's direction, she lanced the swollen lump on her right foot, and the worst frostbitten toe on the left. Multihued liquid matter pulsed out of the new wounds.

The throbbing pain ebbed slightly.

"I don't think that right foot of yours is good news, Paula," Rosenberg said. "I think you have a deep-seated infection in the bone itself."

"Terrific," she said.

"I'll increase your antibiotics. We still have some Metronidazole and Flucloxicillin. They're not the most effective, but—"

"It's all we have. I know."

She used the scalpel to slice off squares of paraglider fabric, and plastered them all around the wounds. She pulled her socks back over her feet, wincing when the fabric tore at her new incisions.

She helped Rosenberg pull open the layers of his own suit. She had to pull carefully at the fabric, she found, or she would tear away great transparent strips of flesh, like sheets of onion-skin. The flesh seemed loosely attached, but nevertheless caused a lot of pain to Rosenberg when they came loose.

It was scary. She had problems herself, but loose skin wasn't one of them.

Inside the suit she could feel Rosenberg's ribs, the bony ledges of his pelvis, the slack thinness of his legs. The bulk of the suit masked this degeneration; out on the surface all she could see was his clumsiness, his slumps and lousy posture. It was astonishing he could walk at all, let alone haul a heavy load across the surface of Titan.

She rubbed cream into his armpits and stomach, the raw regions of his crotch. She even worked the cream into his frost-nipped penis, which was still swollen and sore.

Hemorrhoid cream was all they had left. But it seemed to soothe.

She hated to do this, to be so close to another human. She'd make a lousy nurse, she thought. To get through, she made herself think of how she'd handled Jackie as a kid.

He lectured her about their Belsen-like boniness.

"It shouldn't be a surprise, Paula. We've been expending calories at a hell of a rate. More than we've been replacing them with food. We're slowly starving, in fact. We've already metabolized a lot of our body fat, shifting it as a fuel supply into the bloodstream. All this is part of our bodies' strategy to cope with what we're putting them through: heavy exercise, without enough fuel. Our bodies are eating themselves up, trying to keep going as we demand . . ."

"Eat your soup, Rosenberg."

With his hands swathed in lengths of parachute canvas, Rosenberg tried to raise his soup spoon to his lips. His hands shook too much, and the spoon clattered pitifully against his teeth, like a bird tapping on a window.

She put her arm round him to steady him, and guided his hand to his mouth. He sucked the soup gratefully.

Later they lay, back to back, in the confines of the tent. There was nothing before Benacerraf's eyes, through the window of her helmet, save a patch of plastic wall reflecting the dim low-energy bulb, and a couple of piss bags, slowly freezing.

"You know, Paula—"

"What?"

"Sometimes I want to give up. Just stop. Lie down on the ice, or in the granules or the gumbo or whatever damn stuff, and just stop. Go to sleep. You know?"

"We can't call in a rescue chopper."

"I know, Paula. It makes no damn difference."

She lay silently for a moment. "Then why do you go on?"

"Why do you?"

She thought that over.

"Because of Jackie."

"Your daughter."

"Yes. And her kids. In case they're watching me, the stills and video we transmit."

"Paula, we haven't heard from Houston since—"

"I know. I didn't say it was logical."

"So it's *the clan*. Right? You got the clan in your heart, even here, a billion miles away, on Titan. So far away you can never do anything to affect them again, for good or ill, or they you. Even though the world has ended."

"Yes," she said. "If you want to be anthropological about it. I'm doing it for them. Can't you understand that, Rosenberg?"

"Sure. It's just primate logic."

"So what about you? What stops you giving up?"

He slouched; it was a shrug, masked by the layers of his suit.

She turned over, to face his huddled back. She reached over his waist and put a gloved hand over his; his glove felt as if it was empty. "Listen, after eleven years I know you. You back off into generalities and theory whenever anyone gets too close. Tell me why you keep going, Rosenberg."

At length, reluctantly, he said: "Curiosity. I always wanted to know how it all worked, Paula. It drove me crazy to think that one day I would die, and I'd never see all the science and exploration and discovery that would follow me, all the things people would figure out. And now, here I am on Titan, for God's sake. A world nobody's visited before. Every hill we climb offers the prospect of something new, something nobody's seen. Right now I'm excited." He smiled at her weakly. "I mean it. I'm looking forward to getting this kerogen, or whatever it is, back to the hab module. Maybe it will keep us alive a little longer. And even if not, it's something nobody's seen before."

"At least you made it this far."

"Yeah. But—"

"But what?"

"If the Universe is just a puzzle box, it doesn't mean a damn thing, does it? It's not enough. Not any more; maybe it never was."

Rosenberg had reached a kind of ultimate logic, she thought. He must be spending *his* walking time addressing the final question science couldn't answer, in this godless age:

Why bother to live at all?

But that wasn't really his problem, of course. She'd never met anybody who knew themselves worse than Rosenberg. Except maybe Bill Angel.

Rosenberg's problem was that he was alone. He'd come all the way to Titan, because of that, and now he was here, and he was still alone.

"Rosenberg," she said.

"What?"

"If it's any consolation, I need you. I've never depended on anyone so much in my life. No human has been more dependent on another, than you and I."

"More primate logic, Paula?"

"We are primates, asshole."

"This is just *perlerorneq*, Paula."

"Huh?"

"The winter blues. An Inuit word. Good night, Paula."

"Good night."

They walked into the crater basin, and loaded the sleds with as much crater-bottom tholin as they could carry.

They turned for home.

The journey didn't get any easier. Her sled was even heavier than when they had set off from Tartarus, laden with bags of frozen urine and feces, and with canvas-wrapped bundles of kerogen-soaked gumbo—so they hoped—from El Dorado. And as Rosenberg had weakened, she had been forced, surreptitiously, to transfer some of his load to hers.

Once again Titan's slow rotation had taken this hemisphere into night. They would stay in darkness, in fact, until they reached *Discovery*. So she walked on, with only a splash of light from her helmet lamp ahead of her, and the faintest of diffuse orange glows from the haze above and around her.

The pain in her feet dominated her mind. It was as if she was trapped in some tunnel, walled in by pain, receding ahead and behind her to infinity.

She tried to objectify the pain itself.

She imagined the pain as outside her, even as a living thing, a malevolent creature. It was a red-hot poker embedded in her bone, a crucifixion nail driven into her foot, a gigantic invisible snake-head with its jaws clamped over her foot . . .

If only there was some way she could make it stop. If she was on some dumb stunt of a polar expedition, she'd call in the relief planes right now. If she was subject to some ghastly torture, she'd confess, give in, betray anybody or anything. Just to make this stop.

But through all this the pain was still there, lurking beneath the distracting superstructures she erected inside her head.

And every time she slipped or caught her boot on a ridge in the ice the pain would come bubbling up, overwhelming her conscious thought, raw and primeval.

She kept getting ahead of Rosenberg. Each time she stopped, it seemed an increasing wait before his circle of helmet lamp light came weaving across the ice towards her.

The journey just went on, without meaning save survival, day after day.

After fifteen days out, they got back to Tartarus Base.

In the light of her helmet lamp, the orbiter and Command Module, side by side, were just mounds in the gumbo, their surfaces streaked by bruised-purple tholin deposits. They were unrecognizable as man-made artifacts save for their symmetry of construction.

Somehow, Benacerraf was disappointed. She'd been building this place up in her mind as her home, like a cliché of a family-Christmas fireside, somewhere warm and safe that would shelter her. But it was no such thing, of course; all there was here was a couple of downed spacecraft, a tiny, shivering farm, a cooling nuclear pile.

She unbuckled her traces. She retraced her tracks, back towards Rosenberg. Her footsteps, in the dim yellow light of her helmet lamp, were shallow, infilling craters in the gumbo.

She got them both into the airlock. She cracked their suit seals and took off their helmets, boots and gloves. Rosenberg's helmet came away with strips of skin and tufts of hair and beard clinging to the lining.

She led him through into the interior of the hab module. The air here was hot, thick and moist, hard to breathe, and so sterile it almost smelled antiseptic. Bizarrely, she found herself missing the warm, almost cozy suit-stink she'd been immersed in for two weeks.

She helped Rosenberg to one of the Command Module couches. He sat there like a melting, gumbo-streaked snowman, his bony hands dumped in his lap, his head slumped forward.

Benacerraf made her way to the far end of the hab module, her ruined socks leaving trails of sticky blood on the clean metal surfaces.

She stripped off her own suit. She was stiff all over, particularly in her lower back, shoulders and hips; it was painful to put herself through the contortions required to shuck off the suit's layers. The inner layers clung to her damaged flesh; she had to tease the cloth and plastic away from her skin, trying not actually to break her epidermis or pull away scabs. The suit was worn and badly damaged in places. They'd been lucky the suits had worked to carry them so far—the EVA had been well beyond the suits' design limits.

At last the suit lay as a heap of soiled Beta-cloth at her feet. She stood naked, shivering despite the cloying warmth of the hab module.

She was skeletal, her ribs protruding under flat sacks she didn't recognize as her breasts, her buttocks lumpy and flaccid, her knees and elbows hard knobs of bone. Her feet were a mass of lumpy, pus-filled growths and open frostbite wounds and scars. Crotch rot spread from the dark triangle of pubic hair, out over her thighs and belly, angry red. There were pressure sores where the harness had dug into her, and where her suit had chafed, over her hips, under her armpits and around her chest and waist. Her personal hygiene during the EVA hadn't been too effective. Her upper legs and buttocks were flecked with yellow urine stains and smears of what looked like dried excrement, and there were patches of glaring red skin infections around her waist and legs, the parts of her body where she hadn't been able, or willing, to reach.

She allowed herself two minutes to shower. The hot, clean water felt like acid on her skin; it was actually painful to have the layers of filth lifted from her ghost-pale flesh.

She padded to her quarters. She pulled on underwear, and

an old Beta-cloth T-shirt and shorts. She tried to don her Beta-cloth slippers, but they wouldn't fit over her swollen sores; so she wrapped old T-shirts loosely over her feet and bound them up with duct tape.

She gave herself a moment to run her hands over her belongings, her books and photos, anchoring herself once more in these relics of her life, her personality.

As an afterthought, she put on a facemask and a pair of surgical gloves. Then she made her way to Rosenberg.

He was still in his suit. She stood him upright. He felt disturbingly light. His head was a mess, the hair matted with filth and patchily bald; there were cracks around his mouth, nose and eyes that had opened into fissures as deep as razor slices, dribbling thin blood.

Slowly, she got him stripped. His undergarments were even more matted with waste and filth and blood than hers had been. It looked as if he had suffered some kind of dysentery attack and fouled his pants; when she pulled off the suit, hot stinking liquid flowed out over the clean floor of the hab module.

Benacerraf got his longjohns away from his arms and lowered them around his legs. A shower of skin fragments and pubic hair fell onto the metal at Rosenberg's feet. His legs and groin seemed to have been stripped clean of skin, left raw and compressed into folds. His kneecaps were just ripples of flesh, his genitals rubbed raw. She could see deep wounds dug by the edges of the harness straps, and within the patterns of straps she found eruptions like small, festering boils.

The soles of Rosenberg's feet had split, each of them, down the middle: almost neatly, like the soles of cheap shoes. The casts of dead skin came away like plastic molds in her hands, leaving roughened, raw tissue, from which a watery fluid leaked.

"Dear God, Rosenberg."

He whispered, "It's not as bad as it looks."

"What the hell is wrong with you?"

His head lolled, and he sighed, his voice a rattle.

"You know, don't you?"

His head rolled around until he was facing her. "Yes, I know what it is. I think, anyhow. You need to take a few blood samples to—"

"Tell me."

"Vitamin A poisoning. Those damn baby carrots." He opened his mouth to laugh, and spittle looped between his lips. "Remember, Paula? They were too bitter for you. Well, you were right. More vitamin A than dog liver. Another failure of this toy ecosystem we're trying to maintain here. No buffering . . . the whole thing's too small . . . levels of toxin all over the place. We just couldn't control it well enough. We gave it a good try, but it was going to get us in the end . . ."

There was a flap of skin, loose, beneath his ear. Like a ring-tab, she thought. With a sense of dread, she touched it. It was dry. She pulled at it.

The epidermal covering of Rosenberg's ear came away intact, a complete cast. It drooped between her finger and thumb. "Oh, Jesus Christ." She shivered violently and flung the thing away.

He fell against her, clutching at her arm. "You have to get the samples in, Paula. Look for the kerogen. Do it while I can help you. Everything depends on that—everything—"

His head lolled again, and he went limp.

Gently, she tucked her arms under his body, and lifted him like a child.

There had been no signal from the ground, of any kind. Benacerraf checked every day, and bounced test signals off *Cassini*, to ensure there was no fault with the satellite. And she sent transmissions home, regular updates, with their results, and some personal messages.

In case anyone was listening.

The choice was not to send at all, and that would have felt like giving up. Or as if, by her own loss of faith, by not acting as if there was someone left down there, she might actually somehow bring down the catastrophe they both feared.

She could picture Seattle, almost as vividly as if she was there. She could picture the house where she'd grown up, the places she'd lived with Jackie as a child, her grandchildren . . . It was more real, to her, than this murky shit-hole.

How could it be gone, ruined? How could there be *nobody*, walking the dog, watching the news, mowing the lawn?

In the privacy of her room, though, she grieved, little by little, for her family. It was as if she was allowing herself to face the huge loss, piece by piece.

What she feared most was the thought that she and Rosenberg might be all that was left. She hated the idea that her actions, the rest of her trivial life, had suddenly become so significant.

She wished she had some way to climb up above the clouds, to lash up some kind of telescope and peer at the Earth, and *see*.

Rosenberg sat on a Command Module couch. He was wrapped up, pupa-like, in layers of clothing and thick blankets of Beta-cloth, but he still complained about feeling cold. He wore heavy sunglasses—they'd belonged to Bill Angel—to protect his eyes from the glare of the hab module floods. He'd lost most of his hair, and much of the skin from his scalp and face; swathes of raw tissue showed where his flesh was exposed, riddled by crimson crevasses.

Benacerraf made herself a meal: rice, boiled in Titan melt, with lettuce and some beef jerky from the stores. She sat opposite Rosenberg as she ate. She'd already fed him tonight, spooning the contents of one of their last soup sachets into his mouth, trying not to react to the blood and hunks of loose skin that followed the spoon back out of his lips.

Rosenberg had become the defining feature in her mental landscape now, as so much of her time was given over to caring for him: medical attention, tending to his basic needs—*wiping my ass*, as Rosenberg put it—and covering his work for him.

He told her what he'd found in the samples from El Dorado. His voice was a thin, robotic rasp.

"I found a lot of interesting products. Beyond the usual organic sediments that come from the stratospheric chemistry, there are traces of urea, organic acids, diacids, some amino acids. Products of tholin hydrolysis. Other amino acids resulting from cyanogen addition to nitriles. Results of cyanogen and nitrile polymerization, including imidazole, purines, pyrimidines. I got aldehydes, ketones, acetaldehyde—the results of alkyne hydrolysis. Some Strecker synthesis—aldehyde-nitrile condensation. Aldehyde polymers, including sugars, glycerol, some other species of—"

"Christ, Rosenberg. Did we find kerogen or not?"

". . . No," he said. "I'm sorry, Paula. I guess I was wrong; El Dorado can't have been a carbonaceous chondrite crater after all. My best guess now is that it was formed by a fragment, a calving of a much bigger bolide, which was probably water ice . . . There is a large water ice crater system a little further to the west." His head rolled back and forth. "And that's recent. Maybe the impact was in historic times. Maybe it could have been visible from Earth through a telescope, if anyone had been looking that way, a giant ice comet smashing into Titan . . . A hell of a thing."

"So we're fucked. The EVA was a wild goose chase."

"All the products I found were the result of reacting Titan materials with water from the bolide. I'm sorry, Paula."

She grunted. "It was a good shot. Anyhow, I didn't have any smarter ideas."

He seemed to be trying to lean forward; he struggled,

feebly, within his Beta-cloth layers. "Look, Paula. We have to face facts. We're beyond rescue from Earth. We're on our own here. We ought to look at the worst case."

"The worst case?" She laughed, around a mouthful of rice. "Look at us, Rosenberg. What could be worse than this?"

"We are the last humans."

He fell silent, his breathing a noisy rasp.

She felt the motion of her jaw slow, without conscious volition. Saliva pooled in her mouth, flooding the rice grains and lettuce there, swamping her sense of taste.

Rosenberg said, "The great unspoken truth, huh."

Deliberately she started to chew again; she swallowed a mouthful of saliva.

"But what difference does it make?" she said. "We're fucked anyhow."

"True. Without the kerogen supplement, our ecosystem isn't going to last long. A couple more system crashes and we won't be able to recover. We just aren't viable here. We tried hard to make it so, but in the long term we were always going to lose. And the whole thing will die with the two of us anyhow."

"Right," she said brutally. "So what does it matter? Rosenberg, Earth is a billion miles away. We could try to eke out our lives up here for years, or we could blow up the damn Topaz today. So what? It makes no difference, except to ourselves."

"You're wrong, Paula," he whispered, his ruined mouth gaping open. "I'll tell you what difference it makes. We're still part of Earth's biosphere, even if we are a little seed pod transplanted across a billion miles. Even here, we're still connected; in fact, we have a greater responsibility. *We might be all that's left.* You and I as individuals are going to die here. But what we do before then might determine the future of Earthlike life in the Solar System. We have a responsibility, Paula."

She stared at him. "You're crazy, Rosenberg," she said

bluntly. "You're such a pompous asshole. Everybody's dead, except us, and we have no resources at all, and here you are talking about the destiny of life."

His cracked lips spread in a grin. "I have a plan."

"You and your plans, Rosenberg."

"I think I know a place where we can find liquid water . . ."

The surfaces of all Saturn's moons had been shaped by impacts. Titan's surface had been shielded by its thick blanket of atmosphere, but its huge mass had acted to focus impacting objects onto itself.

Thus, there were impact craters all over Titan.

"Paula, think about a pool of impact melt at the bottom of a crater, dug into Titan ice, heated by the kinetic energy of the impact. It cools down to the freezing point, and stays there at constant temperature—zero degrees—as it freezes and shrinks. It can only lose heat by thermal conductivity. It's a slow process. The conduction equations are well understood. And water is good at retaining heat . . ."

"It will stay liquid."

"A crater a hundred miles across might have an impact melt pool ten miles wide. And it would take ten thousand years to freeze."

She frowned. "So if the crater beyond El Dorado, the primary that spawned the smaller crater we found, is only a few hundred years old——"

"It should contain a pool of liquid water. With a concentration of organics of a few parts in a thousand . . ."

"Holy shit, Rosenberg."

"Yeah. That's not all. What about impact ejecta?" Ejecta was material thrown out after an impact, through the explosive decompression of the shocked solid surface. "On the Moon, ejecta is thrown out into a near-vacuum, and it's a mixture of vapor and solid. But on Titan, with its thick atmosphere, you'll have something more like the cratering process on Venus.

Ejecta will flow in blankets over the surface, to three or four times the crater width, and maybe a hundred yards deep. And there will be a lot of organic-containing sediments mixed in with the surface ejecta flow. You can calculate the cooling life-time using heat conduction partial differential equations which—"

"Cut to the chase, Rosenberg."

"Yeah. There will be ponds of liquid water, maybe a hundred yards deep, scattered over the surface around the primary crater. Even they should last for centuries, maybe longer. They'll freeze over, of course; so will the impact melt pool at the heart. It will have a thin crust of ice, but will be liquid beneath. With time, as the layer of liquid water shrinks, it will become more concentrated in organics, and you'll get a whole spectrum of reactions: amino acids, aldehydes and ketones, nucleotide bases . . . In those pools, we should find an emula-tion of nearly all the prebiotic chemical pathways on the early Earth, except for the steps involving phosphates . . . Damn, damn."

"What?"

"If only we'd gone a little further. I might have found it all, just waiting under the surface, a thin crust of ice. Just waiting for a seed."

"Waiting for a . . . Oh." Suddenly, she saw his plan. "You're kidding."

"No." His sunglasses slipped down over his bony nose. His eyes were blue rocks in the crusty red mass of his face. "Paula, I'll show you what to do. I made notes in my softscreen. You have to go back to Cronos again. Go further than we did before. Find the primary crater beyond El Dorado, and the impact melt pool at its center. Or maybe you'll find ejecta ponds. Liquid water, Paula. I'll prepare a package—"

"What kind of package?"

"Earth-origin microbes that can metabolize tholin."

"We don't have the facilities for genetic engineering."

"We don't need to engineer them," he snapped. "Don't tell me my job, Paula."

"I'm sorry."

"I'm talking about common soil bacteria. Aerobic and anaerobic . . . *Clostridium, Pseudomonas, Bacillus, Micrococcus* . . . They are present in our nutrient solutions in the farm. They can extract their carbon and nitrogen requirements from tholin . . ." He started coughing, big spasms that racked his body inside its Beta-cloth shroud. "Drop them in that liquid-water soup of prebiotic organics and they'll thrive . . . Earth life, surviving on Titan . . ." He coughed again.

She stood before him. "Rosenberg, maybe you ought to rest. I'll clean you up."

"No." His eyes were still steady, despite the shuddering of his body. "I have to be sure you understand. The responsibility."

"I know." She knelt before him and put her hand on his bony arm. "Responsibility for the future of Earth's biosphere. All on your shoulders. I understand, Rosenberg," she said gently. "But—"

"But what?"

"I still don't get it. Even if I find the ponds, even if I seed them, they're just going to freeze over, in a few hundred or a thousand years."

"Sure."

"So what's the point?"

He shuddered. "Things will change. In time—billions of years, Paula—the sun will reach the end of its life. It will become a red giant . . . And then, for a time, Titan will be as warm as the Earth. Titan summer. Maybe our bacterial spores will give rise to a new evolutionary sequence. You see?"

She pulled back from him. Suddenly she felt chilled. "You think big, Rosenberg."

"Little packets of bacteria . . . Seed the planets, the comets. If you're serious about spreading life to other worlds, that's how you'd do it. Cheap, too. It's absurd to carry humans around . . . all that plumbing . . ." His eyes closed, the big broken lids sweeping down like curtains.

She picked him up, and carried him to the hygiene station.

Sitting on the floor of the hab module, a Beta-cloth blanket thrown over them both, she cradled him. His head felt huge in her lap, the massive skull with its paper-thin covering of flesh and skin, but his body was feather-light.

He whispered: "How can I die? How can the world keep turning without me? I'm unique, Paula. The center of the universe. The one true sentient individual in an ocean of shapes and noises and faces. How can I die? It's a cruel joke."

Dear Rosenberg. Analytical to the end.

"They'll remember you for coming to Titan. A member of the first expedition. That's one hell of a memorial."

"If there is anyone left to remember. Anyhow, even so, I'll just be a freak in a circus show."

She said gently, "No god waiting for you, Rosenberg?"

He tried to laugh. He whispered, "What do you think? God died in 1609, when Galileo raised his telescope to the Moon, and saw seas and mountains. We flew to Titan. But with that one act Galileo discovered the Universe. God can't share the same cosmos as a Moon like that."

"No," Benacerraf said sadly. "No, I don't suppose He can. But where does that leave us, Rosenberg?"

"Fucked," he said brutally. "Science is a system of knowledge, Paula. Not a comfort."

"I know," she said. She stroked his forehead, and crooned her words, as if to a sick child. "I know."

He gripped her arm with a clawlike hand. "Paula. You have to put me through the SCWO."

"Sure, Rosenberg."

"I mean it. You can't afford to waste the biomass. But freeze yourself, Paula. Go out on the ice, when . . . It's important . . ."

He coughed, but even that had lost its vigor. The color seemed to be draining from his face, even from the exposed tissue there, as if his blood was drawing back to the core of his body.

His head rolled on its spindle of neck across her lap. "You know, I'm not afraid. I thought I would be. I'm not."

She squeezed his hand; it felt as if his bones were grinding together. "You don't need to be afraid, Rosenberg. I'm here."

He said, with a spark of sour energy, "It isn't that. The human stuff, monkeys holding hands against the dark. I never thought that would make any difference. And I was right. But you and I—"

He coughed, and shuddered; his ruined eyes fluttered closed.

She leaned over, closer to his bleeding mouth.

"You and I, with what we're doing here, are the most important humans who ever lived. We will cast a shadow across five billion years. And that's a hell of a thing," he whispered. "A hell of a thing."

He relaxed, with a rattling sigh, and lay still, collapsing into her arms with a slow-motion, low-gravity calmness. "You know, I learned a lot," he whispered. "More than I expected."

"You did good, Rosenberg."

"But you know, I never figured out why . . ."

"What?"

"Why did it *feel* like this?"

She could feel his body settle, the internal organs relaxing and losing their tension; the last gases escaped from his stomach in a long, low fart.

She got him into the frigid ground only an hour later.

The grave was just a shallow ditch, scraped out of the

gumbo, already infilling. His naked body lay at its base, thin, skeletal, glistening with the frozen water ice of his body.

Once again she had to find words to say over a corpse.

She checked her transmission link to *Cassini*. She wanted this moment to be sent to Earth. Maybe there was somebody there to listen; maybe not. If there was, maybe this would somehow help them.

"I'm sorry I didn't have a flag to wrap you in, Rosenberg," she said. "Anyhow, I know this was what you wanted, in spite of what you said. And if you think I was going to have your sorry ass circulating around *my* ecosystem, you got another think coming.

"*Casting a shadow across five eons.* Maybe you will at that. You did good, Rosenberg."

I guess that will do, she thought.

She threw a handful of Othrys ice crystals into the grave, and began to drag her snowshovel over the gumbo, filling in the shallow pit.

In the last days she spent a lot of time in the CELSS farm, trying to stabilize it as much as she could. She kept power supplied to the farm, and left it seeded with a new crop, of wheat, barley and lettuce.

She felt a great responsibility for the drawn, etiolated little plants here. They were, after all, the only living things other than herself on this whole moon, and she felt loyal to them, and regretted she was abandoning them to die.

But there wasn't much she could do for them. She figured the CELSS farm might last without human intervention a few weeks, before a pump broke down, or a nutrient pipe clogged, or a short burned out half the lamps, or some runaway feed-back biocycle caused the miniature ecology to crash.

Even if by some miracle that didn't happen, eventually the power from the Topaz reactors in *Discovery*'s cargo bay would fail. The lights would dim, and the last, spindly plants would finally die, as Titan's cold broke in.

She took spare seeds and wrapped them in airtight bags. She buried them, under a marker, in the gumbo outside *Bifrost*. That way, perhaps they would survive, deep-frozen, until *Discovery*'s next visitors came this way, whatever became of her.

She spent a last night in the hab module. She took a long, hot, luxurious shower, extravagantly spending the reactors' reserves of energy.

She tried to read a book on her softscreen, but could barely concentrate. She kept on thinking that this would likely be the last book she ever read. The words seemed just a foolish dancing, against dark emptiness.

She put the softscreen aside.

She looked at her images of Jackie and her grandchildren. She stared into the sunny photos, trying to will herself into the pictures with her family.

She slept well, in her quarters, with the lights off and the door closed, shut in against the shells of emptiness around her: the deserted hab module, the empty moon, the billion miles separating her from Earth.

When she woke she ate a gigantic breakfast, using up a lot of stores: dried apricots, an irradiated breakfast roll, rehydrated granola with blueberries, ground beef with pickle sauce, noodles and chicken, stewed tomato, pears, almonds, drinks of grapefruit and strawberry.

She went to the hygiene station and took a long, slow, luxurious dump. She cleaned herself with antiseptic wet-wipes.

She stripped naked. She folded up her Beta-cloth clothes neatly and put them away in a drawer. She washed one last time, then put plasters and bandages over the places where she knew to expect problems from cold and pressure sores: her toes and ankles and the sides of her feet, her hips, stomach, chest and shoulders. She put cream—all that was left was the hemorrhoid ointment—over her groin, in anticipation of crotch rot.

She pulled on her suit. She took great care over each layer; she wouldn't get another chance to fix it, and she would hate to go to her destiny with a fold in her underwear rucked up her ass.

Inside the suit layers, duct-taped to the fabric, she stored Rosenberg's canister of bacteria samples—protected there against the cold—and a little packet of photographs, old-fashioned hard-copy images, of Jackie and the kids.

She sealed up her helmet, gloves and boots, and ran methodically through the suit checklist fixed in its ring binder to her arm. She went through the list twice. In a way her biggest dread, now she was alone, was that without anyone to check her she would miss out some crucial step, kill herself through carelessness.

She looked around the hab module one last time before leaving it. It was clean, tidy, everything stowed away, as if ready for reoccupation. She felt obscurely proud; she'd remained civilized to the end.

Just like Captain Scott.

She slipped on her Apollo hull-metal snowshoes and stepped out into the gumbo. The tholin slush sucked at her feet with its familiar stickiness, and she felt Titan cold immediately seeping through the layers of her suit.

She looked over Tartarus Base.

She could make out the delta shape of the grounded orbiter, with the cone of the Command Module alongside. The cover they had erected over the open cargo bay of the orbiter was still in place, the parachute fabric stiff and streaked with gumbo. In a final extravagant gesture she'd left the flood lights of *Discovery*'s flight deck burning; the yellow Earth-like light now glared out through tholin-streaked windows, shining over glimmering slush.

There was little geologic activity here; the ground was stable. Even the tholin deposition rate was slow. It might take a billion years, Benacerraf thought. But at last Titan would claim Tartarus, its patient tholin drizzle ultimately covering over the pyramidal peak of Apollo, *Discovery*'s big boattail. The spacecraft hulls would ultimately crumple and shatter, until nothing remained of this, the first human outpost on another planet, save a thin, isolated layer of metallic crystals, and a few anomalous deposits of organic residue.

She looked up, towards the marginally lighter horizon. She cut in her IR visor and made out the spark of light, pixel-blurred, that was the sun. From here, the entire orbit of Earth was a circle the size of a small plate held at arm's length, with the planet itself—with all its freight of humanity, and hope and love and war and history—a dull-glowing bead on the rim of that circle, impossible to make out. She could hold up her bulky gloved hand and obscure the entirety of the orbit, the whole span of human experience before the *Discovery* expedition.

She buckled the Command Module couch harness around her. She dug her snowshoes into the gumbo and shoved. Immediately she felt twinges from the sites of the pressure sores she'd suffered last time, at her hips and chest and shoulders.

The sled came free of the clinging gumbo with a sucking noise. She staggered forward.

The sled was heavier, this time, than when she'd set out for her previous extended EVA with Rosenberg. This time, all the essentials—the tent, the recharged skimmer power cells, all her food and water—were stacked high on this one sled.

On the other hand, her food load was lessened. Just enough for a one way trip.

Soon, she managed to settle into a steady rhythm, with each step jerking the sled free of the gumbo which clutched at it.

Every instinct told her that Rosenberg's billion-year scheme couldn't work.

It was, of course, a typically arrogant technocratic fantasy—

in a way an extension of the gigantic, ludicrous journey they had undertaken to come here—to suppose that it would be possible, with a handful of micro-organisms thrown into a lake of ejecta melt, to reach out across billions of years and shape the evolution of a world.

For instance, Rosenberg had made a lot of assumptions about the viability of bacterial spores over such huge deserts of time. And who could really say what the future evolution of the sun would be like? Nobody had actually *watched* a star follow through its ten-billion-year evolutionary cycle, from birth to death; every theory was inferred from humankind's mayfly-like snapshot perception of the stars that happened to be scattered through the universe today. Maybe the red giant sun would grow so huge it overwhelmed Titan, boiling away its atmosphere in moments. Or maybe the sun would just go nova, blasting Saturn and its ancient moons to fragments . . .

It was, she thought, a pretty dumb plan.

But, in the end, it gave her a goal.

Thus her life would end, she thought: struggling to fulfill another project, one more technological dream, because she had nothing better to do.

After a few paces she looked back. Tartarus Base was already lost in the thickening orange haze, the deepening gloom of Titan twilight.

After forty-eight hours, the last light had leaked out of the orange haze layers.

Benacerraf walked through the dark, fighting the resistance of the invisible gumbo as it sucked at her sled and snowshoes. All she could see was the splash of lamp-light on the glistening gumbo hide ahead of her, its diffuse reflection from her own nose and eye ridges, the ancient bone structure of her own human face.

Titan was a world of enclosure.

She lost track of time, of the day-night cycle of the distant

Earth. She would check her Rolex in the light of her lamp, and find that ten, or twelve, or fourteen hours had worn away, as she had driven on through her tunnel of blindness, dark save for the splash of light from her helmet lamp, silent save for the scratch of her breathing, the whir of fans and pumps in her backpack, the muttering of her own voice.

. . . She brooded. What if Rosenberg had been right, in his worst-case projections?

What if the clouds had rolled over the face of Earth—what if she was, truly, the last spark of awareness in the Solar System?

There were theories that consciousness was a quantum process. That reality—the Universe itself—was called into existence by conscious minds, as, by observation, they collapsed the infinite possibilities of each quantum wave function into a single, definite event, embedded in history.

The Universe, it was said, needed consciousess to create itself.

Then what if she *was* the last?

Here she was in this bubble of darkness, the limits of her personal cosmos reaching no more than five or six feet in any direction. Was there anything beyond the intangible walls of the hazy dark? Did she call into existence new stretches of the gumbo as she walked over them?

If she did not look at the Earth, did Earth any longer exist?

And when she died, as the last bit of consciousness departed, would the world—Titan and ringed Saturn and the remote sun and Earth and the stars—would all of it fold away and dissolve, with the cold gray light underlying creation breaking through, like a projector's lamp through a trapped and burning film frame?

At times she felt more frightened than she'd ever been in her life.

She welcomed the familiar pain of the harness pressure points and in her feet. The pain gave her something to think about, outside her own sterile thoughts.

She made camp, proceeding slowly and carefully, double-checking every step before she trusted herself to crack the seal of her suit.

She cleaned herself out. She felt free to dump her bags of frozen urine and feces rather than haul them with her. She tended clumsily to her various wounds and injuries.

She developed another big, ugly abscess, this time on her right foot around the ankle, where a flaw in her boot had rubbed and caused her skin to blister. She decided she had to lance it. She took a sterilized scalpel, closed her eyes and stabbed at the abscess, letting the momentum of her bunched fist ram the blade into her flesh. The pain was extraordinary, sharp, and penetrating, much worse than when Rosenberg had operated on the same kind of injury.

When she looked down, pale, watery pus was leaking from the wound. She squeezed out as much matter as she could, and wiped the incision with a scrap of parachute fabric. Then she dosed it with antiseptic fluid and dressed it.

She ate from a packet of reheated soup, and drank melted Othrys water. Then she sealed up her suit and lay down against the plastic tent wall, layers of parachute fabric beneath her.

She propped her photographs in front of her helmet. She stared into those fragments of bright Seattle daylight, trying to believe she wasn't alone, as she waited for sleep to claim her.

She made rapid progress.

She reached Cronos, and crossed its rim of pressure ridges. She skirted the walls of the crater they'd called El Dorado.

She walked into Titan's murky daylight once more.

Beyond El Dorado, high on the gumbo-stained ice plateau of Cronos, she came to a ridge of broken, jumbled ice, maybe twenty feet tall. She had trouble hauling her sled over this; several times she had to go back and grab the lip of the sled, dragging it bodily up and over.

When she reached the crest of the ridge, she was facing a

plain that looked as if it had been crudely assembled from jammed-together blocks of ice. Pressure ridges criss-crossed it.

The persistent, bone-deep cold seemed to recede. It was warmer here.

She descended the ridge, and began to make her way over the plain. The blocks and upthrust ribs in the ice were a foot or more high, and frequently snagged the runners of her sled. The ice creaked and shuddered; evidently great plates of it were sliding over each other in vast tectonic evolutions. She had the sense of riding the scaly hide of some huge, sluggish animal. But that elusive warmth seemed to gather.

She stopped. With the edge of her ski she scraped away the thin layer of gumbo and loose ice crystals from the surface.

The ice seemed thin: perhaps a foot thick, or even less. She thought she could see a dark liquid beneath the complex flaws of the ice, and bubbles of some gas trapped there.

At last she came to a dark break in the ice surface. It was a lead, a stretch of open water, within a crack in the ice maybe six inches deep. The water was dark and scummy, polluted with tholin and hydrocarbons.

"Hot damn," she said. "You were right, Rosenberg. I wish you could have gotten to see this."

She loosed her traces and leaned clumsily over the lip of the crack. She dipped one gloved hand in the water. Immediately the cold penetrated the layers of her glove, and the heater diamonds stung her flesh. Close to its freezing point, the water was a hundred and seventy degrees above the ambient temperature.

Water was molten rock here. It was as if some suited monster had come to Earth, and dipped its hand into the scalding red-hot lava stream of a volcano. But she was the alien, here on Titan.

She lifted out her hand. Away from the water surface the air temperature dropped quickly, and the droplets of oily water that clung to the fabric of her glove spread and froze, turning to frost patterns. When she closed her fist the frost crackled and broke away, hard ice fragments falling back to the water's dark surface.

She stepped over the crack in the ice and hauled the sled across.

She came to more leads of open water, slick with hydrocarbons, opening and refreezing. Some of them were too wide to risk crossing, and she had to detour, tracing up and down between the leads. In some places the ice was so thin it was spongy and creaking, and if she stepped too close to an edge it would crumble away into the open water. She found a lead that was closing, its edges grinding noisily together. Where the two plates met, the ice was cracking, its sharp sounds ricocheting out across the emptiness, echoing from the iron-hard ice.

The ice field stretched on; ridges and plates pushed out of the plain like pieces of gigantic, abandoned furniture. From all around her rang out the aching, grinding noise of moving ice, crackling like the shock waves from a Shuttle launch. The noises came together in great waves, punctuated by godlike silences.

As she penetrated the field of frozen-over ejecta, the visibility opened out, the pervading gloom of Titan's orange sky lifting a little. Thin methane clouds, dark and tangled, blew ahead of her, obscuring the tall orange sky. Perhaps the relative warmth of the water was clearing the air of some of the organic haze.

At last she came to a place where the broken layer of methane clouds, ahead of her, grew still darker. The darkness—near to black—seemed to begin in a sharp discontinuity, almost a straight line, scraped across the sky.

She smiled. Rosenberg had warned her to expect this.

It was a water sky.

There must be a wide stretch of open water, no more than a few miles away, reflecting darkly from the low methane clouds of Titan.

She pitched her camp on a large plate of ice, hundreds of yards from any open leads. The air was so warm that she was able to strip off the outer layers of her suit. It felt like a great luxury, as she rubbed handfuls of half-melted ice over her bruised skin to clean herself.

She drank her fill of cool comet water.

That night, as she lay huddled against the tent's plastic wall, she listened to the muffled groaning of the thin ice beneath her. She imagined the slow swell of the comet water, the big underground waves traveling back and forth across the ejecta sheet.

At any moment this plate could crack, pitching her into the cold water, suit and all. But somehow that wasn't a frightening prospect. She was, after all, made of water. Water was home.

She slept, without dreaming, as well as she had done since Rosenberg's death.

She went through her waking ritual for the last time.

She breakfasted on dried strawberries, crackers, and tiny, sweet lettuce leaves from the CELSS farm. She took a final dump, into an empty plastic food bag, and cleaned herself thoroughly.

She blew her nose on a fragment of parachute fabric. It was the last time she'd be able to do that, even.

There was a last time for everything, she thought: not just the grand actions, but the small, human things. It all counted.

She pulled on her suit. She tucked her little packet of photos inside her suit, over her heart. She sealed her helmet and gloves, and turned the switch that powered up her PLSS. She heard the familiar high-pitched whine of the pumps and fans, the cool hiss of the oxygen blowing over her face.

She packed away what she could: her food and waste bags, the power cell. Soon, the tent was as neat as she'd left *Discovery*.

She pushed her way out of the tent's cramped little airlock. Outside, standing on the thin, grinding ice, she tucked Rosenberg's canister of spores under her arm, to keep it as warm as possible.

She looked around her little outpost. The half-empty sled stood on the ice, its parachute-fabric cover loosely knotted over it. The tent, closed up, was compact and neat.

She fixed her Hasselblad to the S-band antenna stand, and lined it up so it framed the tent and sled. She checked that the antenna was still aligned correctly on *Cassini*; it was possible the drifting of the pack ice during her sleep had pushed it off its line.

Feeling self-conscious, she went to stand in the camera's field of view. Standing there before her little camp, in her grimy, battered, much-repaired EVA suit, she held up her canister of spores, while the camera fired image after image up to *Cassini*.

She hated these Armstrong poses. But maybe, she thought, this one was justified. After all, if Rosenberg was right, with this one act she might be shaping the future of a new biosphere.

These might be the most important photographs ever taken.

She wondered whether to smile or not.

Her residual sense of orderliness made her walk around the camp once more, checking everything was intact and stowed away.

Then she turned and strode off, across the ice, towards the water sky.

A wind began to pick up, blowing off the broken ground in front of her, hard and piercing; she found she relished its resistance.

She could feel her packet of photographs, a hard rectangle pressed against her chest by the suit.

She felt as if she was discarding her life, in huge layers: first Earth itself, shrunken to a pinprick of light by the huge distance she'd traveled; then Tartarus Base, with its painfully assembled and repaired life-sustaining gadgets; and at last even the trappings of her own little encampment out here on the water ice. Now, she was left with nothing but her body, and the battered suit that was its last protection.

The leads began to widen and interconnect.

Soon the ice was broken up into isolated islands, some only a few feet across, separated by channels of gray, scummy water. Ahead, fragmented ice stretched in a loose mosaic. She could see the open water ahead of her, a dark band encroaching from the horizon, flecked with loose ice floes.

She pressed on, climbing over the narrower channels, taking care to stick to the larger ice floes. But the ice was fragmenting rapidly. Soon, even the biggest floes were unstable beneath her feet.

She couldn't go any further. This would have to do.

She kicked off her skis, and stacked them neatly to one side. She wouldn't be needing them any more. She took a last sip of orange juice, from the worn plastic nipple inside her helmet.

She walked to the edge of the ice. She took Rosenberg's canister of spores, and dipped both her gloved hands in the water. The cold of the water was a thrilling shock, easily penetrating the feeble resistance of the gloves' heating elements.

Under the water, she opened Rosenberg's canister, and shook out the spores, scattering them as widely as she could.

When the canister packet was empty she withdrew it, shook it clear of ice, and tucked it neatly into a sample pocket, buttoning closed the flap.

Then she stood straight. She looked around at the haze-drenched world around her: the cramped, close horizon, the scattered darkness of the methane clouds above, the shattered ice landscape, with that band of free water, just out of reach.

She reached up and snapped the switch on her chest that shut down her PLSS.

The sound of pumps and fans died immediately. The air stopped washing over her face, and felt thicker, more stale. The cold of Titan dug into her flesh through the pattern of heating elements. And she could hear the moan of the wind, a remote bass tone, and the deep crackling of the ice sea, emerging from all over the landscape.

It was the first time she'd heard the music of Titan, unmasked by the man-made noises of her equipment.

She walked forward, across this icy beach.

Before she could reach the edge of the floe, the ice crumbled under her weight.

There was a moment of falling—extended by Titan's low gravity—long enough for a small stab of terror to dig into her consciousness. But then her feet and legs hit the thick, oily surface of the water. The meniscus rushed up her body, its cold mass enclosing, and joined over her head.

Her suit made her more dense than the water, and so she sank into darkness.

She fell slowly. She let her arms and legs relax, and she felt them drift away from her torso, separated by the flow of water.

She turned slowly onto her back.

Above her she could see the surface of the water, the dim orange glow of the sky above, huge oily ripples creasing the meniscus. But the surface receded, its detail lost, and soon the sky was invisible, save for the faintest of orange glows.

The water felt comfortable as she fell deeper into it, as if she was returning to a kind of home.

Now, at last, it was all gone. The Universe had collapsed down to the layer of water that pressed against the surface of her suit, the bubble of air in her helmet. There were no more choices, no decisions, no plans.

Maybe this was mankind's last moment, she thought, here on this remote beach, the furthest projection of human exploration. Maybe, in fact, the sole purpose of the human story, fifty thousand years of crying and living and loving and dying and building, had been to deliver her here, now, to this alien beach, the furthest extension of mankind, with her little canister of seeds.

The cold dug deeper. For a while she found herself shivering, and she wrapped her arms around her torso. But that seemed to pass, and she felt comfortable again.

She knew what was happening. This was hypothermia, her core body temperature falling, as her body heat leaked out through the suit's unresisting layers into the giant welcoming mass of fluid beyond.

It didn't really matter.

She thought she was unconscious for a time.

It was hard to be sure.

Then she thought she could see *Columbia*, far below, rising towards her.

She smiled.

The orbiter's leading edges glowed, a faint orange. The floodlights in the payload bay glowed like a captive constellation. And beyond *Columbia* there were stars: thousands of them, easily visible to her dark-adapted eyes, like the blackest desert night on Earth. She could even see the great sweep of the Galaxy, the ragged edge of the dust-clouds at the core.

The EVA was over. She reached up her hands, and started to take off her helmet.

Book Six

TITAN SUMMER

Voyager One **reached the** boundary of the Solar System.

This was the heliopause, the sheet in space where the wind of ionized particles from the sun grew so feeble it was overwhelmed by the broader stream of interstellar ions. Already *Voyager* was a hundred times Earth's distance to the sun, ten times Saturn's distance.

When gushes of solar plasma hit the heliopause, immense radio blasts—a hundred trillion watts—were generated. *Voyager*'s instruments, almost overwhelmed, recorded this, and faithfully attempted to download the data back to Earth.

Still there was no reply, no reassuring command stream.

Even beyond the heliopause, the sun's gravity held sway; there were clouds of objects out here—ice moons, a trillion comets, never observed by humans—circling the central star. *Voyager* soared through this new realm, its radioisotope power slowly fading.

Voyager tried to contact Earth until its reaction gas failed, and it could no longer point its antenna. And by 2020 there was no longer sufficient power to drive the radio transmitter. Still the software cycled through its reacquisition algorithm, sending commands to inert attitude thrusters and radio transmitters, until the last trickle of power died.

It took twenty thousand years for *Voyager* to cross the Oort Cloud, the sun's immense swarm of comets. At last it was free of the Solar System, its final gravitational bonds broken.

Its power and radio transmitter long dead, *Voyager* embarked on a new journey through the silent calm of interstellar space: an endless circling of the heart of the Milky Way galaxy.

There was almost nothing here to damage the derelict craft. The stars were so sparsely scattered that *Voyager* would never encounter another stellar system . . .

☆   ☆   ☆

As time eroded, the logic of physics unfolded implacably.

The sun was no longer young.

Its core became denser and hotter, as it clogged with the accumulated helium ash of billions of years' hydrogen fusion. The sun got brighter, at the rate of eight percent per billion years.

But for a long time Earth's surface temperature remained the same. Earth was protected by matter and energy feedback cycles maintained by living and geological processes. And as the temperature rose silicate rocks weathered more easily, absorbing carbon dioxide from the atmosphere.

But it couldn't last forever.

Eventually the carbon dioxide concentration in the atmosphere fell so low that the plants and trees could no longer photosynthesize. That put an end to the biosphere's carbon supply. The rocks continued to weather, and the carbon dioxide concentration fell still more rapidly, and Earth heated quickly.

Maybe humans could have prevented this, with some huge feat of planetary engineering. There were no humans around to try.

On the parched planet, one species after another faced what human biologists had called thermal barriers to their survival. The more complex plant and animal species diminished first, as Earth shed the biological complexity painfully gained over billions of years.

After a billion and a half years the surface temperature averaged fifty degrees Centigrade, above which no animal, fish, crustacean or insect could survive. Most vascular plants and mosses succumbed as well, leaving the land and oceans empty save for microorganisms: multicelled animals like algae and fungi.

But above sixty or seventy degrees the structural characteristics of even the simplest multicelled creatures—like membrane systems—could not be sustained. The survivors now were one-celled creatures, like cyanobacteria and some photosynthetic bacteria.

Above seventy degrees photosynthesis ceased at last.

The last survivor of Earth's once-rich biosphere was a hardy bacterium, swimming through the sulfur-rich waters surrounding a black smoker ocean-floor vent. The story of life on Earth had come full circle, for the heat-loving archaebacteria were among the oldest life forms: they had arisen on a younger, hotter Earth, and become the progenitors of all subsequent life.

After another hundred million years the oceans began to boil.

Huge clouds of vapor were suspended in the atmosphere. A new greenhouse factor came into play, driving temperatures higher still, ever faster.

The end came at two hundred and fifty degrees Centigrade, above which the very stuff of life—the giant molecules, nucleic acids and amino acids—was broken down.

The water clouds did not last long. The water vapor was broken up by energetic sunlight and its hydrogen was driven off into space, leaving a planet baked permanently free of water.

And the loss of all water stopped the weathering of silicate rock, the process which drew carbon dioxide out of the atmosphere. Volcanic carbon dioxide began to accumulate in the atmosphere. New clouds rose, and the planet began to bake . . .

At that remote time, Venus and Earth became at last what humans had dreamed in ancient times: twin planets, alike in every significant detail—scorched dry, their surfaces cracked and flattened under a dense, sluggish atmosphere, utterly lifeless.

It was different, for Titan.

The heating of the sun ruined the old surface of Titan, the gumbo-streaked, icy landscape humans had explored. The ethane of Clear Lake boiled, evaporated. The gases dissolved there—nitrogen, methane, hydrogen—thickened the atmosphere still further, adding to a greenhouse effect that accelerated the warming of the atmosphere.

Eventually the comparatively thin shells of ice over the magma—the ancient ammonia oceans—melted, exposing the primal seas once more. Ammonia and water vapor enriched the air and boosted the greenhouse effect still further.

It got warm.

The remnants of ancient biologies stirred. A story of life, interrupted billions of years earlier, was able to resume.

For a while. But it was a life which would not have long to flourish.

Soon, the sun neared the end of its stable Main Sequence lifetime; it began its final, deadly bloom.

When the sun's core hydrogen was exhausted, the fusion fire there dimmed. For ten million years the core contracted. Then a shell of hydrogen outside the core started to burn. That started the expansion of the outer layers.

The sun grew gigantic, its surface billowing towards what was left of the inner planets. Confronted by the huge face of the sun, Earth's surface temperature reached three thousand degrees, only a little less than the surface of the expanding sun.

Life on Titan shriveled, baked, as even the water ice bedrock began to melt.

. . . Like a desiccated dragonfly corpse adrift on a breeze, *Voyager One* circled the heart of the Galaxy.

At last the slow sublimation of metal caused the aluminum structure to weaken to the point where its ten-sided framework collapsed. The fragments of the spacecraft—instrument booms and power generator, pitted and tarnished, metal walls reduced to a paper thickness—drifted away from each other. The directional antenna, as thin as a dried autumn leaf, crumbled away from the curving spars that supported it, so that the ruin of the spacecraft was surrounded by a cloud of glittering aluminum dust.

Voyager was a fragment of American technology, a thing of metal dug from the vanished Earth, some twenty thousand light years from the sun. It was the last human artifact in existence.

. . . **Rosenberg was lying** on his back.

His eyes were closed. He was warm, comfortable. He was aware of his body—his face, arms, legs were a tangible, solid, massy physical presence—but there was no EVA suit around him, no sleeping bag.

He seemed to be rising. As if he was in some huge elevator.

He opened his eyes.

He was in darkness. He could see only the fuzzy patterns, starbursts and whorls, generated by the hard-wiring of his own nervous system.

He could *hear* nothing.

Maybe he was in some kind of sensory deprivation tank.

He tried to remember how he'd got here. He remembered Titan—the Cronos EVA, those damn carrots, Benacerraf nursing him back in *Discovery* . . .

I ought to be dead, he thought.

Was this some kind of hallucination? Was he still propped up in that lumpy Apollo couch in the hab module, wrapped in Beta-cloth, his senses failing as his body slowly fell apart?

He felt a stab of panic.

He reached up to his face. He felt his cheeks, the pressure of his hands, the bones of his nose.

His cheeks were smooth. Free of stubble. And when he ran his palms up over his face, there wasn't a hair on his head: no eyebrows, no eyelashes.

He reached down to his groin. He was naked. His hands cupped his genitals, warm lumps of flesh. No pubic hair.

He jammed a finger up his left nostril. No hairs there, either.

Puzzling.

And, he thought, you're moving pretty well for a guy in the last stages of Vitamin A poisoning, Rosenberg.

Anyhow, this was no hallucination. *I can feel my balls, therefore I am.*

He dropped his hands to his sides. His hands hit something. It was a soft, pliable floor of what felt like plastic. It seemed to have no temperature, neither hot nor cold.

He felt to left and right. The floor stretched under him. He could push his fingers an inch or so into the material before he reached the limits of pliability, where it became tough and hard.

Maybe he was in some kind of bubble.

He didn't have enough data to work on. He ought to wait. Maybe he could sleep.

Sleep, right.

He tried to control his fear.

Be logical, Rosenberg. Whoever has brought you here, wherever *here* is, can't mean you any harm.

He ought to separate the world into pieces he could understand. Dismiss the problems he could do nothing about.

Like, the air. Where was it coming from? How was it replenished? Was it poisoned?

Here's my plan: *don't breathe, until we know more . . .*

He had to accept the air. He had to accept the temperature, the living conditions.

Later, he would be hungry, thirsty. He would have to deal with those problems when he could.

Great logic.

He found he'd cupped his hands over his genitals again. A primate reflex, he thought. I'm just a scared monkey, alone in the dark.

On impulse, he spoke. "Hey."

He could hear his voice.

"Testing, one, two. How about that." He clapped his hands. He heard no echo, just the dead sound of the clap itself. So, a little more data. This bubble, or rubber room, whatever, was anechoic . . .

Something changed.

There was a light above him, deep crimson, barely visible. The intensity varied as he moved his head from left to right.

Work it out, Rosenberg. That means the light is external to you. There's something above, which is differentiated from what is below.

The light seemed to spread, as if across a flat surface. He thought he could see ripples, scattering oily highlights. Maybe he was rising up through some fluid, towards a meniscus.

He looked down at himself. He could see his body, emerging in the gathering light, chest and legs stretching away before him, his nipples dark against a hairless chest, a faint landscape of flesh.

He was bald, but healthy. No sign of the Vitamin A crap that had killed him.

. . . The light brightened. Suddenly he was approaching the surface. It was indeed a meniscus, the surface of some body of fluid, and he could see slow, fat ripples, streaks of some scummy deposit—

The surface broke, in a pulsing circle, directly above him. The fluid spilled down over the hull of his protective bubble.

He saw a sky. It was high and tall, and scattered with thin, ice-white cirrus clouds. There was a fat red sun—*too big*—near the zenith, bright enough to dazzle him, surrounded by a fine halo. Contrails criss-crossed the sky.

That sun really was too damn big, and the sky was a rich blue-green.

The fluid fell away. The chamber was dimly visible around him, like a soap bubble, in glimmerings of refracted light.

Rosenberg sat up.

All around him, beyond his bubble, a solid mass was breaking the liquid.

The surface was corrugated, and it glistened, deep green. And as it rose, he could see how the platform bulged upwards, a dome perhaps fifty yards across. His filmy bubble perched, squat, on the top of the corrugated dome, as if on the back of some immense turtle.

Rosenberg got to his knees. He pressed his face and hands flat against the warm surface of his bubble, and stared out.

The dome, still rising from the liquid, was an island in an

oily sea that stretched to the horizon. The fluid wasn't clear; it was overlaid by a purplish scum, frothing in places. There were a couple of pink-white ice floes, clustering amid the scum islands.

The air was clear, if green-tinged, and he could see thick, fat ripples proceeding in concentric circles away from the rising mass he rode. Further out there were waves—they looked gigantic, mounds of liquid maybe a hundred feet tall—and they drifted across the sea, driven by the prevailing winds.

He could see land.

Perhaps a mile from him, there was a shallow beach; and beyond that, a cliff, steep, gray-green and heavily eroded.

It could be Cronos, he thought.

He wanted to try something.

The bubble was too small to allow him to stand up, but by squatting on all fours he was able to thrust himself up into the air, by a foot or so.

It took him maybe a half-second to sink back to the floor.

He tried it a couple more times, before he was satisfied. The gravity here was low, surely no more than a seventh or eighth of a G.

Right. He was still on Titan. But a Titan that was changed, out of all recognition.

. . . *And the sun was too big.*

It was the central fact he didn't want to face.

It was so big it outsized the fat yellow sun of Earth, let alone the shrunken disc he'd observed at Saturn. And it was a deep, angry red. He thought he could see spots, gigantic black flaws, sprawled across its disc.

He could only think of one way the sun could have gotten so big, so red.

By getting *old*.

Oh, shit, he thought. I am a long way from home.

It was all too big, too much. He was a scared, naked primate, stranded in an alien future . . . He could do a Bill Angel, retreat into some dark primitive recess he'd brought with him, all the way from the past . . .

The hell with that. Think, Rosenberg. Categorize.

He thought about the gravity. The waves.

All that proved the laws of physics were still working. And he could still figure things out. Even run experiments, test hypotheses. Hang onto that, Rosenberg. Whatever the hell is going on here, science still works. I can figure it out.

Anyhow, isn't this what I wanted? To cheat death—to see how it all came out in the end?

. . . But, deep down, he had expected some kind of team from Earth to retrieve them, human faces peering over some kind of hospital bed.

Not this.

He wanted to curl into a ball, retreat into sleep and incomprehension. But if he did, he might never come back out.

His shadow, blurred by its passage through the bubble wall, fell over the corrugations, shortened by the high angle of sunlight.

He tried to feel the corrugations through the bubble material, but the stuff wasn't flexible enough to give him any real sense of touch. He thought he could see something of a cellular structure, though: there was a crude graininess to the corrugations, lumps maybe the size of rice grains. Cells, maybe. The surface looked almost porous, where he could see it closely. There were beads of some liquid gathered there, and a crusty, solid deposit . . .

I bet that solid's cyanogen. His mind raced. This is some kind of *animal.*

Ammonia life?

Come on, Rosenberg, you know the theory. His huge steed must drink ammonia, respire by burning methane in nitrogen. But cyanogen, the carbon dioxide analogue, was a solid at these temperatures. And so the hide of this creature was dripping with ammonia, and crusted with cyanogen waste.

In that case, he thought with growing excitement, he had to be rising out of an ammonia ocean, polluted with complex, melted hydrocarbons. There must be some form of photosynthesis going on here: ammono plants, using solar energy to turn respiration products—ammonia and cyanogen—back to methane and nitrogen, closing the matter loops. But cyanogen could only circulate in solution, not as readily as gaseous carbon dioxide in the air of Earth. That must mean the photosynthesis-analogue was going on in the oceans—some kind of plankton equivalent there. Perhaps there were no land-colonizing plants here . . .

Perhaps the creature whose back he rode was the flowering of the ammono-based life forms whose prebiotic chemicals he had glimpsed near Tartarus Base.

It was as he'd predicted to Benacerraf. It was Titan summer.

How about that. A hell of a lot to deduce from a few grains of cyanogen, Rosenberg. But it was comforting, hugely so, to be able to figure stuff out. And—

And the surface under him lurched. His bubble rolled. He tried to grab at the yielding wall but could get no grip. He slid down the wall, his chest rubbing against the soft, warm material, and finished on his front at the base of the bubble.

The bubble stabilized again. He climbed back up to his knees.

Beyond the rim of the corrugated surface, the ocean was receding from him rapidly, its oily ripples diminishing, and he could see the reflection of the swollen sun as a disc on the sluggish surface. His bubble sat on the back of a mass of flesh, maybe a hundred yards wide, a big flattened sphere. Those complex bruised-purple corrugations spread all the way to the rim. Maybe the creature needed a lot of surface area, for its bulk.

He could see a shadow sailing over the ocean surface. It was the shadow of his huge steed. There were ropy objects trailing beneath, maybe tentacles, waving passively in reaction to the breeze of the flight . . .

The shadow was under him. The damn thing was *flying*, now, like some immense chewed-up balloon. He was riding a jellyfish the size of a football field, as it flew through the green air of a new Titan . . .

Wonder battled with fear, threatening to overwhelm him. He longed to be enclosed: he longed for the cozy warmth of his EMU, the tight metal walls of the hab module.

. . . So how was it flying? He couldn't see any wings, jets, propellers.

Anti-gravity?

Think, Rosenberg. Look for the simple explanation.

The thing was probably buoyant. Simple gas-bags, somewhere within this fat structure, would be sufficient to lift the jellyfish from the ocean, and up into Titan's thick air.

There was something else riding the back of the jellyfish, about twenty yards from him.

It was another bubble, resting like a drop of water on the back of the ammono creature.

He threw himself at the wall of his translucent cage and stared across. It was like trying to see inside a droplet of scummy pond water.

He thought he saw something in there, an inert white form.

He shouted, banging on the wall of his bubble. He even tried to roll forward, within the bubble, to make the whole thing roll across the jellyfish, like a hamster in a plastic ball. But the bubble resisted his efforts.

His mind seemed to dissolve. To hell with the red giant sun, the new biosphere. All he wanted was to reach that other human being.

He was soon panting, his hairless flesh coated with a sheen of sweat.

He gave up.

Even if he'd gotten over to the other bubble there wasn't anything he could have done to reach its occupant. If he could somehow breach this bubble—even if the temperatures outside were tolerable—the air of this new Titan was surely toxic, laced with hydrogen cyanide and ammonia.

But it was sure as hell worth a try.

He was finding it harder to breathe.

He felt an uncomfortable pressure in his bladder. He needed to take a piss.

He looked around. There just wasn't anywhere to piss into, inside this sheer-walled, seamless bubble.

He tried not to think about it. But of course that didn't help.

In the end, he just stood up in the center of the bubble, grabbed his dick, and let go. What else could he do? Warm urine splashed up over his feet. A puddle gathered at the lowest point of the bubble floor, green and frothy, and he stepped back quickly, trying to keep his bare feet out of it.

When he was done he retreated to the wall of the bubble, watching the urine lake. It spread slowly over the bubble floor, quivering as the jellyfish surged smoothly.

A shadow, wide and long, swept over the bubble.

Rosenberg flinched, raising his hands over his head, cowering naked against the floor of the bubble.

It was as if a roof had spread over the jellyfish, a ceiling of translucent, leathery skin, green-tinged; where the sun shone through, Rosenberg could see a coarse graininess, a sketchy skeletal structure.

The skin ceiling moved away, and sunlight, suddenly bright again, shone down into the bubble.

Rosenberg kneeled up and stared after the departing platform. It was like a kite, roughly diamond-shaped, the size of a 747. It glided, one pointed corner first, through the thick air. That papery flesh stretched over a frame-like skeleton. The anatomy seemed sketchy. There looked to be a spine along the axis, bulging in places; maybe there were organs—a digestive tract—in there.

It was like the pterodactyls of antique Earth. Or a Wright brothers fever dream, he thought.

This was Titan, Rosenberg reminded himself; the living things here could only be built from the raw materials to hand. And so, the bones of the kite-thing were probably made of water ice.

All along the leading edges of the diamond wings there were gaping cavities, like jet inlets. Maybe they were mouths; perhaps the creature fed on smaller airborne life forms, cruising like a shark. Like the jellyfish he was riding, the kite seemed passive, inert, as if saving its energy; he could see no sign of motion, anywhere across the kite's huge frame. And that immense mass of skin showed another similarity with the jellyfish: a lot of exposed surface area for the kite's mass.

He couldn't see any legs, any means of landing.

Perhaps it never landed at all; perhaps it spent its life in the air, feeding on the airborne particles, even breeding there.

The pterodactyl receded, slowly, its sharp rectangular profile diminishing.

Rosenberg kneeled against the wall. The urine, cooling, lapped against his feet.

And now a dark form cruised over the surface of the ocean, far below him.

It was shaped something like a terrestrial ray, but it was immense. Those hundred-foot Titan waves broke like ripples in a bathtub over its oily, corrugated back; it had to be a mile across at least. Rosenberg could see vent-like mouths all along the ray-thing's leading edges, and its back. It was turned to face the waves, but it didn't appear to be moving; he could see no sign of a wake, no frothing or disturbance from any kind of impellers. He was reminded of a big basking shark, cruising through beds of krill and plankton, its huge jaw gaping. But this basker did not trouble to seek out its feed; it just sat in the prevailing current, waiting for plankton-analogue or whatever other organic goodies were suspended in the ammonia ocean to drift into its multiple mouths.

So, Titan life. There were common characteristics, he thought dully. Huge size. Large surface area. Passivity.

The jellyfish continued to rise. Now he was far above the surface of the ocean, and he had risen above the lip of the Cronos cliffs. The land on the plateau was a plain of gray-green ice, pocked with craters. Most of the craters were just sketches, palimpsests, their walls diminished by relaxation. The old craters were empty of their ethane lakes now, although he thought he could make out a purplish, filmy crust in the crater basins.

The world was split in two: an ocean hemisphere to his right, the flat gray-green ice of Cronos to his left. The horizon was blurred by mist and vapor, but curved sharply; the world was small and compact, a ball suspended in space, visibly smaller than the Earth.

He thought he caught glimpses of more baskers. Their delta shapes were arrayed across the surface of the ocean, like huge factory ships slowly processing the plankton-analogue.

Tiring, his lungs aching, he sat with his back resting against the pliant wall, his legs outstretched.

His thinking was feverish, getting fragmented, as if he was lacking sleep.

In fact he started to feel bored.

Now, that was just ridiculous. Here he was, somehow restored from death by Vitamin A poisoning, preserved across—oh, God—preserved across billions of years, maybe, and revived in an ammono-life ecosphere . . .

But he had nothing to do but sit here and sightsee. He wanted to get out there and *do* something. He wanted to take samples, run them through his lab in the hab module.

And he craved mundane things: to take a shower, read a book.

He wanted someone to talk to.

The sky, stained bottle-green by methane, was getting perceptibly darker. He must be rising out of the troposphere, the thick bottom layer of the air.

He looked up at the sun. Its bloated disc seemed a little

clearer, though it was still surrounded by a faint halo.

He wondered if it was possible to see Earth from here. If Earth still existed, it must be lifeless: no more than a cinder, skimming the surface of the sun's swollen photosphere.

No help for me there, he thought.

His chest was dragging at the air.

He tried to suppress panic, to keep his breathing even and steady.

Something was wrong.

He was going to suffocate in here, in this bubble suspended over the bizarre surface of a transformed Titan, here at the end of time. He would drown in his own exhalations, awash in urine—

A pillar thrust out of the surface of the jellyfish, ten feet from the wall of the bubble.

Rosenberg screamed. He scuttled backwards, over the yielding surface, getting as far as he could from the pillar.

To his shame, more urine dribbled out of his shriveled penis and leaked over his legs.

The pillar was six or seven feet tall, maybe two wide. It was made of glistening crimson flesh. Its surface was like the jellyfish carapace: the same purple-black coloration, that complex ridging pattern. But the ridging was on a smaller scale, the gouges and bars separated by a couple of inches. It was topped by a cluster of large, complex-looking cell groups. Perhaps they were some form of sensor; perhaps he was being inspected.

Maybe it was here to give him more air, to feed and water him.

The pillar was utterly still.

The way it had moved was eerie. It had been reptilian: a burst of motion, followed by stonelike stillness. Perhaps it was that quality which made him feel so nervous and suspicious.

What did it want?

Take me to your leader. His ragged thoughts ran on in uncoordinated hypotheses, as his fear bubbled in his hind brain.

He coughed, and the pain in his lungs sharpened; black spots swam in his vision, clustering at the edge of his field of view.

He crawled forward, through the puddle of urine, to the wall facing the pillar. He slapped the bubble's surface with the flat of his hand. "Can't you see I'm dying in here? Why don't you do something about it? Hey! . . ."

The pain in his lungs started to spread outward, up through his throat and out across his chest.

He slumped, resting his face and chest against the yielding wall. He slid down, onto his back. He could feel the cooling piss lap against his feet and lower legs.

"You weren't expecting me to be conscious. You don't know how to handle this, do you?"

Black flecks gathered at the periphery of his vision. Through the filmy upper surface of the bubble, the sky deepened to a rich emerald green. He was lying here in his own urine, gasping for air like a beached fish. What an end for mankind, he thought; what an epilogue.

There seemed to be something descending from the sky towards him: a broad, purple-black disc, a glimmering bubble, softly distorted . . .

He could see through it. It was a reflection, of his rising jellyfish, in some kind of translucent sheet above him.

They've roofed over the world, he thought.

He thought he saw more of those pillars, thrusting out of the carapace around him like fingers.

He tried to grip the plastic surface under him, struggling to stay conscious, to make this interval last as long as he could, before another unimaginable period of nonexistence overwhelmed him.

But the cold green darkness was washing over him. He cried out as it pushed into his eyes, his brain; but he could no longer hear his own voice.

Paula Benacerraf had no memory of waking.

Suddenly, she was aware of herself again. It was as simple, and as brutal, as that.

She was standing. Everything seemed to be red. Her feet were cold.

She tried to look down, to see what she was standing on. When she moved her head, her eyes didn't track properly, as if they were badly controlled automatic cameras, and her head seemed to slosh, a bag full of fluid.

The redness turned abruptly to gray, and there was a clamoring of bells in her ears.

The world tipped up around her. She saw a huge sky wheeling past, a sun like a dish of red light.

But it was taking so long, as if in a dream.

She collapsed gently against the ground, on her back. The landing was soft, but she could feel the spiky hardness of the ground, and where it pressed against her flesh, in a hundred places along the length of her body, it was ice cold.

Her heart's hammering slowed, and some of the color leached back into the world.

That sun, straight above her, was immense. Much bigger in the sky than Earth's sun, it was huge and red and dim. The disc was mottled with spots, complex black pits surrounded by crimson-gray penumbrae. She held up her arms, and moved out her hands, to accommodate the sun's disc. Her hands finished up a yard apart.

She remembered her last walk to Cronos. The water. The seed packet. Her choice to die.

Oh, shit, she thought. *I'm alive.*

She felt—disappointed. Life would go on. She was going to have to eat, and drink, and sleep, and maybe figure out what was happening to her.

She'd have to make choices. She'd thought that was all over, for her. She felt cheated.

She closed her eyes. But the world wouldn't go away, the gritty reality of it in her lungs, under her back.

So where was she? A hospital?

In the open air?

She opened her eyes, and lifted her arms. She was clothed.

Her hands were bare, but her arms were encased in long sleeves of some translucent material, like golden-brown polythene. She pulled at the material; it gave a little, but would not stretch, and when she pinched at her cuff it was impossible to tear.

She reached up to her face. There was no covering: no helmet, no visor, no face mask.

. . . She was in the open air, unprotected.

The shock reached her. She felt a moment of panic; she felt her lungs constrict, as if she was drowning.

She forced herself to relax. She took away her hands, opened her mouth, and deliberately sucked air into her lungs.

She wasn't in an EMU. But wherever the hell she was, there was evidently an oxygen-nitrogen atmosphere.

She put her arms flat against the chill ground and tried to push herself up. As soon as she got her head upright, the ringing and grayness returned.

"Take it easy."

The voice startled her.

"Lie back for a while." A head moved into her field of view above her, silhouetted against the broad face of the sun. It seemed hairless, and the neck and shoulders supporting it were swathed in some transparent substance that caught the light. "I don't think they got your fluid balance quite right. Orthostatic intolerance. It took me a couple of minutes to adjust, but it passes."

"Rosenberg. I should have expected you."

"Yeah." He knelt down beside her. "Yeah, it's me—I think." He was wearing some translucent all-in-one coverall, which left only his hands and head free. And he looked younger.

"Good grief, Rosenberg. What happened to your hair?"

He laughed. "The same as happened to my eyebrows, and nasal hair, and chest hair, and pubic hair . . . I guess they forgot to put it back."

"They? Who are they?"

"One step at a time, Paula."

"You don't have your glasses."

He touched his face, looking surprised. "So I don't. I don't seem to need them. They grew back my foreskin, too."

"*They?*"

"How are you feeling? Do you think you can sit up?"

"I'd rather stand up. This ground is freezing my ass off."

Rosenberg laughed. It was a brittle, icy sound. He got an arm under her armpit and lifted; with his help she scrambled to her feet. She still felt dizzy, and her heart pumped a lot harder than she'd been used to, but she wasn't going to faint again.

She and Rosenberg were out in the open. No hospital. No buildings at all, in fact. They were standing on some kind of plain. It was coated with sparse, low vegetation—stunted dark green bushes, a little grass—but there were no people, no cars or houses. The air was clear and her vision was sharp; the horizon seemed close by.

Off to her right was a long, straight, gray-white cliff which slid towards each horizon.

That big balloon of a sun still hung directly overhead. The sky and land were drenched in a dull dried-blood red. There were high icy-looking cirrus clouds, draped over the roof of the sky; some of them cut across the face of the sun and glowed crimson, as if on fire.

The only sound was the soft hiss of a breeze over the spiky grass.

This ain't Seattle, she thought, with gathering dismay.

And Rosenberg—

Under his golden-brown translucent coverall, Rosenberg was naked.

He clamped his hands over his private parts. "Will you stop staring at my dick?"

She touched her scalp. It was bald and smooth, the skin cold to her touch. She glanced down. Under a translucent suit, past the low swell of her breasts, she could see her pubic mound, as bare as Rosenberg's.

"Shit," she said. She covered her breasts and groin with her arm and hands, while Rosenberg kept his hands clamped over his balls.

They stared at each other. "This is ridiculous," she said at last.

"I agree. I won't stare if you don't."

"It's a deal."

Deliberately, she lowered her arms; she looked him resolutely in the eye.

He laughed again. "A hell of a thing. We cross billions of years, and we bring all our dumb primate taboos with us." His voice was brittle. Almost hysterical. And—

And he'd said, billions of years. "How long? Where the hell are we, Rosenberg? How did we get here, from there?"

"One step at a time, Paula. Come on."

He turned away, and began walking slowly across the plain. His footsteps lifted him up in the air, so that he bounded forward in a series of short half-hops, Moonwalk style.

Oh, she thought.

This wasn't even Earth, then.

She started to feel scared.

"Where are we going?"

"Damned if I know."

She felt an absurd reluctance to move away from here, the place she'd come awake. As if she ought to wait here, on this anonymous patch of a uniform plain, until somebody came by to tell her what to do.

She sat down, ignoring the cold.

She didn't want any of this. Choices, a structured world to

figure out, even a relationship to manage. The hell with it. I did all this once.

She lay down and curled up, burying her head in her arms.

I want to go home, she thought. To Seattle. And if I can't go home, I don't want to be here.

But the world wouldn't go away. She couldn't even go to sleep, the ground was too hard and cold.

She opened her eyes.

The plain, the big red sun, Rosenberg waiting patiently, squatting on his haunches, a few yards away.

She got angry. She kicked at the ground, dug out great handfuls and threw the dirt around, rubbed it over her bare scalp. "Why couldn't you leave me alone, damn it . . . ?"

She got tired quickly. She stood there, panting, hot inside the suit, dripping bits of dirt.

Rosenberg just waited. He didn't even watch her.

Reluctantly, she walked up to him. He got up, and walked on, and she followed.

Sensory impressions crowded in on her, unwelcome, forcing her to think, to analyze.

She found she was wearing some kind of booties, welded onto the suit, as clear as the rest of the coverall. When she lifted up her foot she could see there was no grip on the sole, no ridging, but she seemed to be able to keep her footing nevertheless.

The ground was a sandy, crusty, rust-brown soil; it crunched when her weight settled on it. There were stunted trees—they looked like willow, or birch—scattered over the plain; none of them came much higher than her shoulder. Between the trees, grass grew. Near her feet there was a splash of flowers, almost white despite the ruddy light, the petals as big as her palm. She knelt down and pulled up a handful of grass. She rubbed the blades between her thumb and forefinger; there was a sharp herbal aroma.

Rosenberg lifted up what looked like a mushroom, a huge puff-ball a foot across. "Mosses, lichens. It's hard to see in this red light, but I'll bet these things are livid green."

"Chlorophyll?"

"Of course these aren't true plants. They're just organisms descended from some root stock, which have radiated to fill the various ecological niches . . ."

She dug up a little of her anger. "Radiated from what? What are you talking about? You're so full of shit, Rosenberg."

He said irritably, "Radiated from whatever terrestrial-biosphere samples the ammonos managed to retrieve from our bodies, or the ruins of our base, or the seeds you planted."

"Ammonos?"

"I told you we had to take this one step at a time."

She looked at Rosenberg. "You know," she said, "I'm hungry. And thirsty. Shit. They had no *right*."

"What?"

"To bring me back."

"Yeah. Well, they did it. And I'm hungry, too." He shrugged. "Try anything. We've no way of knowing what's toxic, even lethal . . . We have to trust the design."

"You mean you don't *know*?"

"Just try something, Paula."

Near her legs grew a couple of the mushroom-like puffballs, some sparse grass, and a scratchy growth like bruised-purple heather. At random, she dug her hand into a puffball. It imploded, like a meringue, and a cloud of some kind of spores blew up around her arm, clinging to her flesh and the suit. She came away with a handful of the mushroom's meat. It was white, soft, cold, slightly moist. She suppressed a shudder; the feel of it was repellent.

She lifted it to her mouth, bit off a chunk, and chewed deliberately.

It crumbled, collapsing to a hard residue, like bad sponge

cake. It was still cold, and there was the faintest of flavors, an aftertaste of decay.

She swallowed the residue.

Rosenberg watched her intently. "Well, you haven't choked, thrown up or keeled over."

"But I'm even more thirsty."

"Come on," he said. "I think the ground dips down a little over that way; maybe we'll find some fresh water."

They began to walk, parallel to the looming gray-white cliffs.

They came to a stream.

It ran sluggishly through a shallow gully, eroded into the ground. The water was running away from the direction of the gray cliffs, Benacerraf noticed. It looked a little muddy, and dirty gray ice clung to its banks.

Rosenberg squatted and dipped a hand into the steam. He pulled it back quickly, but he brought up a little water cupped in his hands. "Ouch. Cold as all hell. I guess it's glacier melt, running off those cliffs." He stared dubiously into the little puddle he cradled.

"Drink it, Rosenberg."

He sighed. He lifted up his hand to his mouth, and sucked in the water noisily. He grimaced. "A little salty. It's okay. So cold, though."

She knelt down beside him, and began scooping up water. It splashed over her face, the cold stinging; and she could feel its icy passage down her neck and into her stomach.

Rosenberg said, "These suits seem to keep us warm enough. But drinking this stuff will bring our core temperatures down. We need to find a way to build a fire."

"Those trees look as if they will burn."

"We don't have any way of lighting the fire."

"Didn't you ever go camping, Rosenberg? . . . No, I guess you wouldn't. You take a couple of sharpened sticks, and——"

He held up his hands. "I believe you. Show me later. Just don't lecture me about it." He plucked at the chest-cover of his

transparent suit. "I got a more urgent problem. I need to pee."
He clawed at the plasticlike sheet over his genitals, comically.

She realized that the cold water had run straight through
her, too; soon she would face the same urgency as Rosenberg.

What were they supposed to do? Just let go, and walk
around sloshing? Suddenly her suit seemed constricting, even
claustrophobic.

She stood with Rosenberg, and experimented with his suit,
pulling the clear material this way and that. At last, she found
that if she pinched both sides of the suit's neck, a seam opened
up. Once the split began, it ran quickly along the lines of
Rosenberg's body, over his arms, down his hips and the sides of
his legs.

Gently, Benacerraf pulled at the neck, and the front of the
suit just peeled away from Rosenberg, like a parting chrysalis.

When the suit lay in a clear puddle at Rosenberg's feet, he
clutched his arms over his chest. "Christ, that's cold."

"Don't be a baby, Rosenberg."

He walked away, hopping gingerly over the icy ground on
the balls of his feet. He moved behind one of the trees, and in
a couple of seconds Benacerraf heard the heavy splash of urine
drops against the soil, and saw wisps of steam rising around
Rosenberg's legs.

To get Rosenberg back into the suit, they found the easiest
way was to lie him down, inside the back section. Benacerraf
lifted the front over him and ran her pinched thumb and forefinger up over the opened seal; the material melded together
seamlessly.

After that, she took her turn. Oddly, she felt naked out of
the suit, even though it had been all but transparent. The
ground was hard and icy under her bare feet as she squatted.

So here she was, eating and drinking and pissing and talking,
life going on, just as if nothing had happened, as if the world
hadn't ended, as if she hadn't died and been dug out of the ice
and . . . hell, all of it.

It had never struck her before how much of her time, her conscious attention, was taken up just with the business of being *human*.

She rejoined Rosenberg, who stood by the stream. They looked at each other.

"Where are we, Rosenberg? Is this Mars?"

He looked confused. "No. Not Mars. Of course not. Mars is gone. *This is Titan.* Don't you get it? You're still on Titan, Paula." He glanced up at the wide, flawed face of the sun, which filled the dome of heaven above.

Something connected in her mind. Cosmology lectures. Carl Sagan. "If this is Titan—" Oh, shit. "A red giant," she said. "The sun's become a red giant."

He laughed brutally. "You figured it out. Just like I had to. Sorry there aren't any comforting answers. We might be ten billion years from home, Paula."

The ruined sun seemed to hang over her head, huge and heavy, as if it might crush her; she wanted to escape from it, run under a tree, hide her head with her hands. "Tell me what's happened to us, Rosenberg."

His face hardened further. "You want the short version? You died. So did I. We all died. We were frozen into the gumbo. Later—a lot later—aboriginal life forms dug us out and restored us. Quite a feat." His voice was thin, trembling.

"We're stranded here. Is that what you're saying, Rosenberg?"

Again he looked confused. "Stranded? Of course we're stranded. Who do you think I am, H.G. Wells?"

She felt a snap of irritation. "Lighten up, Rosenberg. I'm just finding all this a little hard to handle."

"What the hell do you expect me to say? I woke up ahead of you, that's all. This is as hard for me as for you. And I'm stuck here, too."

"No way home, huh."

He frowned. "Paula, Titan is our home now. For the rest of our lives."

She lifted up her face to the distorted sun.

She thought of home: of Houston's sticky heat, the corroding sea air of the Cape, the fresh green of Seattle. It was impossible to believe that all of that wasn't still up there somewhere: that huge, sunlit Earth, infinite and eternal, full of problems and dreams, the disregarded backdrop to her own life.

How could it all be gone?

"Come on," Rosenberg said. "Let's follow this brook downstream."

She shrugged. She didn't have any better plans.

As they walked, he told her about the first time he'd woken, the glimpse he'd gotten of ammonia life.

They walked for a couple of miles, away from the cliffs. The ground started to slope downwards, as if they were walking down a long beach, and the stream became broader, its eroded banks more ragged.

At last, the covering of topsoil wore thin, and bare ice bedrock pushed through the surface like bone, pale red-gray in the light of the sun. Only a handful of plants grew here, clumps of the grass-analogue struggling to survive in the scrapings of topsoil. The exposed ice was sharply cold under Benacerraf's feet.

They topped a shallow crest.

Before them an ocean stretched to the horizon, blood-red and murky, huge waves moving sluggishly across it. The liquid lapped at the edge of the shore, and flecks of ice crusted its surface.

Rosenberg grunted. "We're on Titan for sure. Look at the size of those damn waves. And no tides to speak of."

"What do you think the fluid is? Ammonia?"

He looked at her quizzically. "Of course not. The temperature's wrong. It's water. What else?"

She wrapped her arm around his. "You're going to have to give me a little time, Rosenberg. I'm not so smart as you."

"Then you're lucky."

"Come on. Let's go find somewhere we can sleep."

Maybe a mile inland from the water's edge, they found a thicket of trees, with a thick blanket of topsoil and fat white flowers beneath. When they crawled under the layers of low branches, Benacerraf had a feeling of shelter; the shade shut out the unchanging, ruddy sky.

They ate and drank a little more. They tried to build a fire, Benacerraf rubbing sticks back and forth earnestly, but without any success. Maybe the wood needed to dry out.

They huddled together to sleep. They lay on the ground, back to back, then face to face. They couldn't get comfortable, and Benacerraf was cold, even with her face tucked down into her suit.

She had an idea.

They stripped off their suits, and pressed their four halves together, pinching the magical seams. It took a little experimentation, but eventually they had made a kind of shapeless sleeping bag large enough to take the two of them.

They crawled into it, face to face. Rosenberg's flesh, where it touched her at knees and hips, was hot. Soon the bag started to grow warmer.

Benacerraf felt something pressing against her stomach.

"Rosenberg . . ."

"I'm sorry," he said miserably. "A primate reflex, here at the end of time. I can't help it."

"You're so pompous, Rosenberg."

She touched his face. It was wet.

She said, "What's wrong?"

"Do you want a list? I want to go home. I don't want to be stuck out here, like this, in the open air, trying to sleep in the daylight."

"Have you lost your curiosity, Rosenberg?"

"No. But I hate not knowing what tomorrow will be like."

"Rosenberg—"

"What?"

She reached out and ran her hand over his chest. Rosenberg's body, shorn of hair, was soft, almost girlish.

She climbed on top of him, keeping the suit bag huddled over her. She bent down and kissed him gently on the mouth. "Let's get warm, Rosenberg."

"Yeah."

He took hold of her hips, and pulled her down towards him.

There was a scratching sound, from a few yards away. Maybe it was a cat, she thought sleepily.

She had one arm stuck under Rosenberg. He had his thin back to her, and was snoring softly. Carefully she pulled the arm out from under him; it tingled as the blood supply was restored to it.

She rolled on her back. That huge, swollen sun still hung above her; maybe it had dipped down from the zenith a little way.

Morning on Titan: no birds were singing, no traffic noise, no radios or TVs blaring, no softscreen billboards shining.

Shit, she thought. It's real. I'm still here. I'm stranded billions of years into the future. Earth is gone, and I'm on Titan, transformed by person or persons unknown.

Yesterday had been—unreal. Overwhelming. But waking up today, with a pain in her back and a gritty taste in her mouth, the reality of her situation seemed mundane. Even irritating.

And there wasn't a cup of coffee on the whole fucking moon.

Away from Rosenberg's warmth she could feel the hard coldness of the ground under her, and the chill air seeped into the improvised sleeping bag at her neck.

She had the feeling that Rosenberg was awake, but was lying there with his eyes closed, hoping the day would go away, or maybe that she would take some kind of responsibility for it all. She could understand that. Hell, how were they supposed to cope with this? Surely they both had some kind of post-traumatic stress to work through. And—

. . . *What cat?*

She rolled over and pushed up to her knees, resisted by the cramped, linked suits.

The creature was six feet away from them. It was the size and shape of a dinner table, and it picked its way across the ground on eight spindly, insectile legs, each maybe four feet long. The legs terminated in points, and didn't leave footmarks. The main body, the table-top, was a corrugated, purple-black carapace; there were clusters of what looked like blackberries all around the table rim. The whole table-shape was swathed in a translucent golden-brown blanket, evidently the same material as Benacerraf's suit.

Arms—six or seven of them—reached down from the underside of the table-top, and poked at the ground. The arms were skeletal bars of a glassy, semi-transparent crimson-gray substance, and Benacerraf couldn't see how they moved; there was no evidence of anything like muscles or cables. The arms terminated in spiky claws with opposable thumblike extensions. The claws dug gently at the surface, delicately picking up fragments and lifting them up to some kind of stowage under the table-top.

Rosenberg woke up with a start, his eyes puffy with sleep. "What the . . ."

"Shut up," Benacerraf hissed. "Look."

He rolled onto his belly, his bony hip bumping against hers. "Holy shit," he said.

The creature, or artifact, was all but still. Only its arm-extensions worked, methodically picking over the soil. Occasionally a leg would rise, folding up delicately, and set down again. The motions were slow, deliberate, almost reptilian.

She had no sense of threat. The thing was so slow it was impossible to imagine that it could outrun humans, if it came to a chase. And besides, those limbs looked pretty fragile. Maybe they were made of water ice.

There were some heavy chunks of wood-analogue left over from the abortive fire from yesterday, within Benacerraf's reach. If she had to she could reach out and find a club. It wouldn't be hard to shatter those icicle legs.

The creature was standing over the patch of ground she had used as an improvised john yesterday, and it was taking salami slices off half-frozen lumps of feces.

"U.S. Cummings, I presume," said Rosenberg.

"What?"

"Science fiction. Philip Dick. Never mind."

"Rosenberg, I think it's picking up one of my turds."

"I don't think you need to whisper," Rosenberg said—but he was whispering, too. The two of them were propped up on their elbows, inside their sleeping bag, like two kids watching TV in bed. "It must be aware we're here. But I'm sure it's not going to bother us."

"You think it's some kind of machine?"

"No. I think it's alive. It's an ammono creature. The coloration, the ridging on its back: all of that's characteristic of the aboriginal life forms here."

"How do you know?"

"I saw them, remember. Anyhow, you can see for yourself. Look at that blanket over the main body."

"What is that, some kind of insulation?"

"No. Look at the frost; the temperatures in there must be low enough to allow ammonia to be liquid. Don't you get it, Paula? It's a spacesuit. The warming sun has brought the end of the world to Titan as much as to Earth. Now, this ammono animal is forced to take an EVA on the surface of its own planet."

"So what's it doing with my turds?"

"Sampling. Come on." He struggled up to a kneeling position, and the last of their night's warmth and musk dissipated. "Let's get out of here."

They shucked off the bag. Rosenberg pulled the suits apart, and Benacerraf hopped over the chill ground to a clump of trees, where she took a leak.

When she got back to Rosenberg, shivering, she found herself covering up her breasts and crotch until he'd helped her into her reassembled suit. It was odd, but she felt more embarrassed about her nudity in front of the thing Rosenberg had called an ammono than she had before Rosenberg.

The suit sealed up neatly around her, and warmed rapidly.

The two of them walked out of the little copse, and onto the plain. The ammono stayed behind, still sawing industriously at Benacerraf's crap.

On the open plain, little had changed since the day before. The plain was just a gently sloping tundra, studded by the clusters of low bushes and scratchy grass, bordered at one side by the white cliffs of ice, and on the other by the black, oily, placid sea.

But now, there was movement—delicate, precise—everywhere.

The ammonos were scattered over the plain, from cliff to ocean's edge. There had to be hundreds of them. And they all looked identical to the table-shaped creature which had disturbed them: the swathe of translucent blanket over the rectangular, ridged carapace, the spindly legs, the arms industriously scratching at the soil.

"They can't all be taking samples of our dung."

"Of course not," he said, faintly irritated. "It isn't us alone they're interested in. It's the whole of this biosphere."

"Why? What's the point?"

He pointed east towards the cliffs. "Come on. That way."

"Why?"

"For one thing, that's where the ammonos are coming from."

She looked more carefully. Rosenberg was right. There was a greater density of the ammonos in the direction of the base of the cliffs.

"And for another—" He pointed upwards.

There was a contrail in the sky, white and sharp and unmistakable, scratched across the orange sky. It was rising up out of the east, from the land beyond the ice cliffs.

They walked.

She looked down on the ammonos as she passed them. It was like walking through a field of huge beetles. She could hear the soft clattering of the ammonos' claws as they worked, a gentle sound like the click of cutlery on plates at some quiet restaurant. The ammonos dug blades of grass, complete little plants, out of the ground. They took black buds from the trees, pulling them gently away from their branches, and plucked seed packets from flowers. They seemed to be trying to avoid damaging the life forms.

When an ammono walked, its limbs would straighten out. Then icicle legs would ripple around the rim, flashing pink highlights, their motion too complex to follow. The table-top body of the ammono would glide evenly over the surface, through seven or eight yards, until it found another place to sample.

Actually, the ammonos hardly ever moved.

Only one in a hundred would be in motion at any time, save for the delicate clatter of limbs; this scattered herd of them together was almost stationary, eerily so, their Zenlike stillness quite unlike the chaotic jostling of terrestrial creatures.

She remarked on this to Rosenberg.

He grunted. "Paula, chemical reactions are dependent on temperature. By the time you get to the region where ammonia is a liquid—under thirty degrees below zero—you're looking at a relative rate of maybe a hundred to a thousand times as slow as at room temperature for us—"

"You're saying these creatures have a slower metabolic rate."

"Much slower, yeah. You can see it in the way they move:

those long periods of gathering energy, then a quick burst of motion. But it's not going to be as simple as that, of course . . . reactions with the right activation energies won't chill out, so they would be selected preferentially. And all that ammonia will have a complex effect, helping or hindering reactions. The only way to know for sure would be to take one of those critters apart, and see what's sloshing about inside its carapace."

That suggestion offended her.

She bent to pick a flower. "Maybe we shouldn't be asking questions."

"Huh?"

"Here we are at the end of time. Everybody we knew—everything we understood—is long gone. What does science, figuring things out, matter now? These ammonos seem to have given us a place we can live. Maybe we ought to be content with that."

He laughed. "If my forebrain had an off-switch, I'd agree with you."

She dropped the flower and walked on.

When she looked back, after a few paces, an ammono had crawled laboriously over to the flower and was picking it apart with its scalpel-sharp claw.

They took breakfast on the hoof. Benacerraf tore off handfuls of mushroom flesh and washed it down with water from an ice-flecked brook they found. She splashed water mixed with snow over her face and scalp; the cold was sharp and refreshing. One good thing about being hairless, she thought: at least it was going to be easier to keep clean.

As she walked on, her breath steaming ahead of her, she started to warm up. Soon she had to pull open the seams at her shoulders to keep cool. But the suit must be porous; it wasn't trapping excessive amounts of heat and sweat.

"Somebody remade Titan, Rosenberg. Engineered it so we could live here. Breathe the air, eat the fruit. Who? People?"

"No. I think it was the ammonos, after the sun got too hot for them, and they had to retreat. Titan ice is primordial stuff, Paula. It probably contains dissolved carbon dioxide, ammonia, methane, organic molecules, sulphur, salts. When it melted it must have outgassed volatiles. Good for building a new atmosphere."

"Volatiles I can understand. But this is an ice moon. Where did the topsoil come from?"

"Any particulate matter in the ice would settle out, as dirt on the sea beds. Maybe the ammonos dredged that up. Hell, I don't know."

"*Why,* Rosenberg? Why did they do all this? Why are we here, for Christ's sake?"

He had no answer.

As they neared the base of the horizon-spanning cliffs, the ground began to slope upward and grew harder and colder underfoot. The topsoil was sparser than on the lowland plain, the vegetation struggling to get a foothold, although there were still clumps of tough dunelike grass struggling out of cracks in the ice bedrock.

Soon it became more of an effort for Benacerraf to continue her steady Moonwalk bound over the surface.

There were fewer ammonos here; in their shining transparent suits they trooped, in their reptilian spurts, back and forth, evidently shuttling between the plain and some kind of base on the Cronos plateau.

A wind blew up, pushing parallel to the cliff face and across their path. Clouds shouldered across the sky: fat cumulus clouds of water vapor, just like Earth's. And then a rain began to fall, big fat heavy drops that descended with a snowlike slowness, and splashed noisily against her golden-brown suit.

The horizon disappeared, and an orange-gray mist closed in around her, obscuring the cliffs.

Rosenberg came up to Benacerraf. He had slipped his hands inside his sleeves, and wrapped his arms around his body; rivulets of water ran down from the dome of his head. "If this cliff is the edge of Cronos," he said, "we're heading due east, roughly."

"Or maybe west," she said. "We don't know which side of the continent we're on."

He shook his head, and water sprayed off around him. "No. This has to be the western periphery."

"How do you know?"

He pointed upwards, then tucked his hand back under his armpit. "We can't see Saturn. I figure we've been returned to the region of Tartarus Base. Anyhow, the winds are blowing out of the north. Which is what I expected."

"How come?"

"Titan is still a small world, Paula. The weather system is going to be simple. Like on Earth, the sun's heat at the equator pushes up piles of moist clouds. The clouds flow north and south, dumping their rain on the way. But here, the gravity is so low and the distance to the poles so short that I'd expect the hot air to make it all the way to the poles. When it descends, that's where you'll find the deserts . . ."

Mercifully, he stopped talking.

Benacerraf looked up. The huge sun was visible as a brighter disc above the gray-white clouds. Raindrops, fat and slow, fell towards and around her, like a hail of bullets falling from infinity. Some of them had turned to snow, now, and they swirled languidly in the updraughts.

She was shivering; the rain on her bare scalp was cold and actually painful. The few ammonos here had their arms tucked under their carapaces, and rain puddled on the clear coatings over their backs. And now the rain actually seemed to be getting harder, turning to sleet.

"Shit, Rosenberg. Understanding the mechanics of the weather wouldn't help me half so much as a hat."

He nodded, his motions jerky, shivering. "Let's keep moving. At least that will keep us warm. This can't last forever. Maybe we'll climb above it." He set off.

She tucked her head into her shoulders, folded her arms across her body, and walked after Rosenberg, who was already receding into the misty haze.

The walking didn't require much attention, and, like her walks on Titan before, she tried to lose herself in daydreams, fantasies, to escape the dull reality of the world.

But the dreams wouldn't come.

Maybe the ammonos had rebuilt her, but they didn't seem to have put back her imagination. Or maybe there was some part of her which knew there was nothing much for her to dream about.

By the time they reached the foot of the cliffs, the rain had stopped, but there was still a thick layer of laden cloud which obscured the upper reaches of the cliffs. The cliffs here were steep and forbidding, thrusting out of the ground like a wall, their base littered with some kind of loose scree.

Rosenberg went forward and tried to clamber over the scree, but it was slick with half-frozen rain, and the fine plates slid over each other easily. Despite the buoyancy of low gravity, Rosenberg slipped, repeatedly, and stumbled.

After he bloodied his nose he gave up.

The chaotic clusters of ammonos had reduced to a couple of files here, like columns of ants. They were going head-on at the cliffs, without hesitation; their legs seemed able to clamp onto the slick ice surface, and they hauled themselves straight up even the steepest sections of the cliff. Looking up, she could see the trail of ammonos dwindling into the mist and low cloud above, their carapaces dark stains against the dull gray-red surface of the ice cliffs.

"I wish I had their legs," Rosenberg said, rubbing his mouth. "Come on. We'll follow the cliffs a ways. It can't all be as tough as this."

They stood, shivering, each waiting for the other to lead. Neither of them wanted to do this, she realized. The truth was, they both just wanted to go home.

She said, "Which way? North, or south?"

"You choose, Paula. What difference does it make?"

"North, then." She turned to her left and began to walk. "And if we walk all the way to the pole and find a desert there, I'll know for sure you're a smart ass, Rosenberg."

"That's my job," he said, wiping blood from his lip.

After a couple of hours of steady walking over the slick ground, they came to a narrow gully. As far as Benacerraf could see it was incised all the way up the ice face, and into the clouds above. It looked as if it had been cut by a stream, which was now vanished.

At the foot of the gully there was a short section of the treacherous scree. She stepped carefully over this, watching her feet.

Then she came to the gully itself. Its mouth, at the base of the cliff, was broad, and there was a litter of topsoil, evidently washed down from the gully sides or from the Cronos plateau above.

She walked forward. For a hundred yards the going was easy; the ground sloped up steadily, but the gully was broad and paved with gritty, rough topsoil. But soon the walls narrowed around her, and the base of it narrowed to a thin V. She had to walk—climb, in fact—with her feet splayed outward, braced against the gully's two sides.

As she climbed, the grip of her soles became less reliable, and her feet slipped from under her. The clutch of gravity was feeble, but the pain was great as she banged her knees and hips against bone-hard ice. Her bare hands soon started to turn white and numb from the cold of their contact with the ice. She pulled her sleeves down over her hands and gripped the cuffs in her clenched fists. But that wasn't satisfactory, because the stretched material rubbed painfully at her shoulders and the back of her neck. And besides, it was almost impossible to get any grip without opening out her fists.

Her world closed down to the aches of her body, the few

feet of ice gully around her, the eroded surface in front of her face, the focused search for the next handhold. She couldn't even move fast enough to work up a decent sweat, and she grew steadily colder. She was a billion miles from home, eons in the future, but as her discomfort closed in she might have been anywhere, she thought.

Her irritation turned to misery.

She climbed into a layer of billowing mist. The droplets of water vapor were hovering balls the size of her thumbnail, and they caught the diffused crimson light of the sun. They looked too big to be suspended in the air, but here they were, the swirling updraughts easily counterbalancing Titan's feeble gravity. Walking through them was something like entering a zero-G shower. When the droplets hit her translucent suit they splashed but didn't stick, and secondary droplets spun away, shimmering. But the drops that hit her face and hands and bald scalp spread out rapidly and soaked into her. Water started to seep inside the suit, at her neck and cuffs.

She tried to wipe the excess liquid off her face with the edge of her hands, or her cuff. The mist as it dried was leaving a fine residue on her flesh, a sticky organic scum.

She ached all over. The hell with this. She started to get angry.

If she couldn't lose herself in daydreams of past or future, then maybe she ought to concentrate on the present, the obstacles she was facing, how she could make things easier.

Crampons, for instance.

Maybe she could improvise something from those scrubby trees on the plain. A flexible branch, maybe a rope woven from some kind of creeper.

She needed gloves, of course. And a hat. Maybe they could sew together some kind of fabric of leaves.

She thought about knocking over one of those ammonos. That might solve all their raw materials problems. But if Rosenberg was right, the ammonos, inside their chill space-suits, were breathing out ammonia and cyanogen. Slicing open one of those suits would not only kill the ammono, it would do the two of them a lot of damage too.

Anyhow, such violence *felt* wrong. This wasn't her world, after all.

So: hats of leaves, or bark. Maybe they could stuff their suits with grass and lichen to improve insulation. They would have to do some kind of inventory of the vegetation here: investigate what they could eat, what they could use for other purposes, like construction and even medicine . . .

Thinking, planning, wiping the waxy organic sheen from her face, Benacerraf continued her climb.

At last the gully grew narrower. Looking up, Benacerraf could see she faced maybe ten or fifteen feet of sheer ice, beyond which the land flattened out. She could see tufts of grass-analogue bristling out from the lip of the plateau above her, black and wiry.

It wouldn't be a difficult climb, she thought. Just a little scary.

She looked down. She'd risen almost all the way out of the mist layer now, she realized. The mist was a lumpy gray-white ocean beneath her, from which thrust this ice cliff. She could make out Rosenberg, as a toiling pink-brown speck in the mist layer, perhaps a hundred feet below her.

She turned again, lodged her fingertips in crevices in the ice, and hauled herself upwards. The low gravity worked in her favor, and the climbing here was actually easier than the slog up the gully.

She reached the top in a few minutes, and dragged herself up over the edge.

The land flattened out here to form a plateau, sharp-edged by this ice cliff. Further off, she could see no sign of further uplands, although a shallow wavelike ridge in the ice hid much of the landscape from her. There was grass growing close to the cliff lip, and some of the swollen mushroomlike things. A layer of thin cirrus cloud coated the eastern sky, stained red by the light of the aged sun.

She peeled open a couple of seams to cool down. She sat at the edge of the cliff, her legs dangling over.

Rosenberg took a further half-hour to reach her. He hauled himself clumsily up over the last lip of rock and threw himself flat against the ice, his arms outspread. His face was coated with a thin frost rime.

"I never thought," he said, "I'd be so pleased just to be somewhere flat."

She scraped the frost off his skin with her fingernails. "You're not a physical kind of guy, are you, Rosenberg?"

"Oh, I'm learning to be. Boy, am I learning."

She collected some food, mostly mushroom flesh. They drank ice-cold water from a small rivulet nearby, that fed the bigger system that had carved out the gully they'd climbed.

When his breathing had gotten back to normal, Rosenberg pushed himself to his feet. His hands and mouth full of mushroom flesh, he did a slow scan of the world from this new vantage point. He gazed down over the gray, lumpy clouds that covered the lowlands, then turned and looked inland.

He stopped. Even his jaw ceased its chomping.

"Rosenberg? Are you okay?"

He was staring inland, a green light reflecting from his face. "Stand up," he said. "Stand up and look at this. My God."

She got to her feet, her legs still aching, and stood alongside him.

The sky to the east, over the interior of this ice continent, had cleared; the cloud layer was breaking up. The sun was a huge blood-red ball, battered and pocked, dominating the orange sky above.

There was a layer of green light at the horizon.

At first she thought it was a smog belt. But it was flat and sharply distinguished, at its upper edge.

It was a roof.

There were tall trees—no, *towers*—evenly spaced within the green. And the towers were tall, she realized now; they were poking above the horizon, their bases hidden by the curve of the moon.

Some huge form, diamond-shaped, moved between the towers, within the roofed enclosure.

"My God," said Rosenberg. "I was starting to think I dreamt it. That's where I was, the first time."

The first time? "Where?"

"In there. That's a worldhouse. The last refuge of the old ammonia-based life system. It's like a greenhouse. Except, colder within than without. In there, the conditions must be as they were when the ammono life was at its peak, when it covered Titan. That's where they retreated when the sun got too hot, when the ammonia oceans started to boil and the bedrock melted. It must be where these ammono beetles are coming from now."

"It's like our CELSS farm."

"On a gigantic scale . . . *Oh.*"

The mist in the air was lifting. And in the east—beyond a horizon obscured by that immense artifact—Saturn was rising.

Saturn was autumn brown, against the green sky. Perhaps a quarter hemisphere showed. Time seemed to have been kind to the huge planet: Benacerraf could make out the familiar bands of cloud, tipped up almost vertically towards the ruined sun, and the splashes of white that marked interior-driven storms . . .

"The rings," she said. "Rosenberg, what the hell happened to the rings?"

The planet's huge face looked denuded, without that narrow, tilted-up ellipse of banded light, the matching, complex shadows in the cloud tops.

Rosenberg said, "They were only chunks of ice, Paula. I guess it just got too hot." He threw down what was left of his mushroom and dusted off his hands. "Let's go see what's over the next ridge."

He stalked off, eastward. He bounded away, taking big bunny-hops, and was soon fifty yards ahead of her.

His mood had swung to its manic, energetic pole, she thought gloomily.

She followed more sedately, trying not to pine for Saturn's rings.

The ridge, maybe fifty feet tall, was a pressure wave frozen in the ice, and easy to climb. Rosenberg waited at its crest for her.

From the crest, the landscape seemed to open up, as the horizon receded to the east. The land beyond the ridge was pretty flat, though in places cracked and compressed.

At the foot of the ridge there were beetle ammonos, the first she had seen since leaving the plain. They toiled in complex patterns across the barren ice fields here. They made their way in roughly radial patterns to what looked like a jumble of low hillocks at the center of the plateau, neatly sliding over or around the worst crevasses. That cluster of hills was perhaps five miles from them and a half-mile across, or less. The hills thrust irregularly out of the plain, their contours rounded, as if melted, their facets glimmering in the light of Sol and Saturn.

Glimmering.

Actually, it looked like a downtown.

"Oh, my," Rosenberg was saying. "Oh, my."

"That's artificial," she breathed. "Isn't it, Rosenberg? Holy shit. Those aren't hillocks. They're *buildings*. That's a city."

"Oh, my."

They both moved at once, as if some spell had broken. They hurried forward, hopping carelessly down the side of the ridge. Rosenberg led the way, and the pace he set was more a half-run than a fast walk. The ice here was flat and not too badly broken up, and it made for fast progress. Even so, Rosenberg tripped a couple of times.

A part of Benacerraf would have liked to take this a little slower. One bad fall, one twisted ankle—or, worse, a break—could be a catastrophe for both of them.

Part of her felt like that.

The greater part of her soul was with Rosenberg in his desperation, running ahead of the constraints of the ice, running ahead of caution, to the city on the plain.

They ran more frequently into files and clusters of ammonos, as they picked their way earnestly across the ice. Benacerraf, with her residual caution, tried to avoid the ammonos. Not Rosenberg, though: his head was up, and he simply ploughed through the ammonos' orderly ranks. But they reacted smoothly to him, their files breaking and reforming as he stomped through. It was like, she thought, seeing a column of gigantic ants skirting a boot placed in their path.

Even Rosenberg slowed, though, as they reached the edge of the city.

It was, she thought again, like walking into a downtown.

The structures here were grotesque spires of ice: some, she guessed, were more than a half-mile tall. The nearest was an octagonal pillar, tipped away from her, Pisa-like. The ground around its base was littered with irregular blocks of ice, some feet high. The surface beneath was smooth ice, as flat as a freeway. And slick, with a thin layer of surface water. Like an ice rink.

Machined.

She clambered past the worst of the ice blocks and walked forward, across a free stretch of floor, until she reached the wall of the structure. She looked up at it. The wall, one of the eight comprising this octagonal cylinder, narrowed as she peered up, merging at infinity with its neighbors into a crimson-gray line.

Suddenly, staring up at the pillar, she felt giddy, as if with reversed vertigo; some primitive primate fear, as Rosenberg would say, that the thing might tumble down and crush her seemed to be about to overwhelm her.

She put out her hand. She touched a cold, hard surface.

The ice was like rock, but there was a slickness to it. When she pulled away her palm, her skin was wet. And now she looked more closely she could see the edges of the building, between the huge facets, were smoothed over.

The building was melting.

She heard Rosenberg's footsteps receding, so she hurried around the octagonal pillar and followed him, proceeding deeper into the city.

It was like walking through an ice-sculpture caricature of Manhattan. The buildings—spires and pillars, even some narrow, inverted cones—towered over her, their washed-out crimson-gray lines obscuring the sky. In some places she could see lacy bridges connecting the peaks of the structures, but there were a lot more stumps and broken arches than complete spans. The narrow, regular streets between the buildings were cluttered up with rubble, smashed-up ice fragments, some of them huge.

About all of this there was a sense of smoothing out: of rounded corners and edges, of melting. There were even icicles dangling down from the stumps of bridges. Most of the buildings seemed open, with immense archlike doorways like cathedral entrances. When she peered inside she found nothing but scattered rubble.

The ammono beetles toiled in thin files towards and away from the dense center of the city. With what seemed an inexhaustible patience they worked their way around the innumerable ice-fall obstacles that cluttered up the orderly streets; if she watched for a while, Benacerraf observed that the ammonos always followed the same path around each obstacle, like ants following a biochemical trail.

She met Rosenberg at the center of a small square, bounded on all sides by elephantine ice walls. He was peering up at the huge buildings. There was water on his cheeks; it shone in the pink-gray light of the ice walls.

"All the damage is at ground level. See? That's where the walls are smashed up and cracked . . ."

She looked at the building with new eyes. "You're right, Rosenberg. So how did they get this way?"

"Isn't it obvious? They *fell*, Paula." His eyes were a red-rimmed mess, she noticed. Evidently his mood had crashed again. "Suppose you were building, here on Titan, in this one-seventh gravity and all this thick air . . . Wouldn't you build up as high as your materials could go, huge Gothic structures, stilts and spires and bridges miles high? Why, you could pump your walls full of air and use buoyancy to get even more of a lift . . . But then the sun blew up, and the damn stuff just started melting."

She walked up to him and took his hand. "Shit, Rosenberg. You're crying again."

He looked down at her. "Don't you get it? Look around you: the ancient, ruined crystal city . . . This is Xi City. Maybe the houses turn to follow the sun—"

"What?"

"Didn't you read Bradbury? *This is the way the Solar System was supposed to be,* Paula. This is why we went to the Moon, why we sent out the probes to Mars." He walked a few paces ahead, and turned around, his arms outstretched to the huge, sculpted ice walls. "This was what we were looking for all the time. This! It's just come billions of years too late, is all. Damn, damn . . ." He ran a hand over his face, smearing tears and snot. "I'm sorry."

"I know. Come on, Rosenberg."

Hand in hand, they walked on, deeper into the heart of the crystal city.

A few hundred yards further in, the buildings thinned out, and the crimson light grew brighter; it was like entering a clearing at the heart of a forest thicket.

Benacerraf led the way through the clutter at the base of the last of the buildings. When they stood at the edge of the clear area beyond, she could see across it to the buildings at the far side, maybe a quarter-mile away.

The floor here was clear of the debris of falling rubble. And there was a single structure, as far as she could see: a slim spire maybe twenty feet tall, at the geometric center of the clearing, dwarfed by its skyscraper cousins.

Ammonos moved in complex, interlacing files across the surface. The clearing was roughly circular, and the blank faces of structures walled it in on all sides, as if fencing off the now cloudless crimson sky.

The spirelike object stood at the center of an inner disc of ice, which was clear of even the smallest loose debris; in fact, she thought, it looked as if it had been repeatedly melted and refrozen.

She noticed that the ammono beetles studiously avoided the melt crater, even if they had to take a long detour to do so.

The spire was actually slimmer at the base than at its tip, and now she looked more closely she thought she could see some kind of opening at the top there, pointing up at the face of the sun.

Like an air-scoop mouth, she thought.

And at the base of the spire—

"Fins," Rosenberg said beside her, pointing. "The thing has fins, Paula. Will you look at that."

"It's some kind of rocket, Rosenberg."

He frowned up at the scoop. "Methane. That's the propellant. Methane, scooped out of the atmosphere and burned in oxygen, mined from the water-ice." Now he scratched his bald head. "God damn, Alan Nourse had it right after all."

"Who?"

"Never mind . . . I think we'd better get out of here."

"Huh? Why?"

"Look around."

The ammono beetles had gone.

Rosenberg said, "The ammonos have built Cape Canaveral in the middle of Xi City. I guess I don't want to be around when the ship goes up."

He reached for her hand. Together they walked away from the methane rocket.

They found a valley, maybe a mile from Xi City. It was just a rough gouge in the ice, but it afforded some shelter from the wind. And on its floor there was a shallow, running stream, and clumps of grass-analogue, and some of the mushroom plants.

They zipped together their suits and huddled close beside each other. They sat facing Xi City, and munched mushroom flesh.

"So how long do you think we have, Rosenberg?"

"How long?"

She waved a hand. "Before we lose all this. For instance, it's too hot for Titan to retain an atmosphere now. How come the air doesn't evaporate?"

"Oh, it is evaporating," he said. "But it will take a while. The oxygen atoms at the top of the atmosphere must be bleeding steadily into space. But the mass is big . . . Paula, it will take tens of millions of years for all this air to leak away. It's like melting the bedrock ice. It will take a million years or more to melt even a few miles of ice, and there are hundreds of miles under us. You have to think in terms of planetary masses, Paula. Nothing happens suddenly. Anyway, it makes no difference. The sun won't keep still that long. I think it has some growing to go before it's done with its red giant phase."

"How do you know?"

"Because this place is so damn cold. The black-body temperature here will be closer to nine hundred degrees, when the giant phase reaches its climax . . ."

"Shit."

"Yeah. The atmosphere will evaporate first. Then the ice mantle will melt, and boil away. Nothing left but the rocky core."

"How long?"

He shrugged. "I'd say we have a hundred thousand years."

"A hundred thousand years. Not much."

He grunted around a mouthful of mushroom. "Only twice as long as the human species existed before we were born. You just don't think big enough, Paula."

"No. Hell, I guess I never did. So," she said. "What are we supposed to do now?"

"I guess that's up to us. We could try to talk to the ammonos. You know, I've been thinking about why we're here."

"You have?"

"Yeah. Think about it. They terraformed their own planet. They rebuilt our biosphere, or a copy of it, from what we left behind, as best they could. And they found us in the ice, and managed to . . . repair us. But I don't think they understand what we are. They don't react to us, except as some kind of animal, and they've made no attempt to communicate with us. Paula, they might not even know we're intelligent. Yes, talking to the ammonos would be a hell of a challenge." He looked up. "Maybe they could tell us what happened to Earth, to mankind. Maybe I could make a telescope. Grind some ice into lenses. It would be interesting to see what else is out there."

"What else?"

"We could *fly* here."

"We could?"

"The light gravity, the thick air . . . Da Vinci flying machines would work." He frowned. "Maybe some kind of winged bicycle would be the best solution. Hell, it would be easy. You could glide most of the way. I've seen it done. And then we could think about making our own methane rockets. Maybe we could even borrow some of the ammonos' technology. Paula, this is a moon, but a big damn moon. We can explore it from pole to pole . . ."

After a time, Benacerraf sat back. "Plans and schemes. Busy, busy, busy. But what's it for?"

"Huh?"

"Rosenberg, this isn't some dumb camping trip. It's not even an EVA. We're the last survivors of the human race, stuck here in the far future. Are we supposed to repopulate the planet?"

He coughed, spraying out mushroom. "Sorry," he said, wiping fragments off their joined suits. "I wasn't expecting that. I sure as hell am no Adam."

"And I ain't no Eve," she said firmly.

Anyhow, the phrase reminded her uncomfortably of Bill Angel.

"I don't think we need to," Rosenberg said. "I think I know what that rocket ship is for."

"It's pretty damn small," she said.

"Huh? The rocket?" He looked puzzled. "Small for what?"

"For an evacuation. Titan is doomed, right? But you wouldn't get a single ammono beetle in that thing."

He laughed. "You're thinking like a human, Paula."

"What do you expect?"

"That's not a human artifact. And what lies behind it isn't a human motivation. You have to learn to think like an ammono. We're dealing here with a race who, when confronted with the destruction of their world, retreated into their worldhouse, and rebuilt their moon to accommodate *us.* Terrestrial life. Can you imagine humans doing the same?"

"What are you saying?"

"I'm saying these guys think big. Bigger than we ever did. But in a different way. I think they are trying to save their biosphere. And ours. But they're doing it the way we should have done it. And could have, if anybody had provided the funding." He looked up at the sun's diseased face. "But we weren't smart enough, Paula. We blew it. We dropped a fucking rock on ourselves. We lost ten billion years. We might have covered the Galaxy by now. But we blew it."

"I think we did okay, Rosenberg," she said gently. "We're here, aren't we? We came to Saturn, and in the end, we found something wonderful. And if you're right, because of us, Earth life is going to live on, to survive even the death of the sun . . . Do you think this is what it was all about? All those millennia of struggling, the whole bloody human story, just to deliver the two of us, here, to the end of time? . . ."

The light around her changed. She looked up, to the east.

The sun, a broad, ruddy disc, was descending towards Saturn's limb. The grand, slow eclipse had started, she saw, with a perfectly circular arc of darkness bitten out of the sun's swollen face, and red sunlight glimmering around the rim of Saturn, the layers of atmosphere there. She thought she could see the shadow of Saturn sweeping like a wing across the plains of Cronos towards her, and the air grew dark and subdued. She thought she could see a fine, glittering line stretching up towards the zenith: perhaps the remnants of the rings.

. . . Hey, Paula. Scuttlebutt from home. Some double-dome from JPL is saying he's found life on Titan . . .

Benacerraf could feel the elemental human warmth of Rosenberg's bare skin, all along her flank, from shoulder through hip to ankle.

They planned further.

Today they should try again to build a fire, she said. With a fire they could warm themselves, heat up some water, maybe try cooking some of the vegetable life and see if that improved its flavor.

And beyond that they ought to think about a shelter. Maybe they could construct some kind of log cabin from the wood-analogue of the trees here. But it might prove difficult to cut the wood. Ripping off small branches for a fire was one thing; carpentry for a serious construction would be something else, without metals to work into tools.

Rosenberg started talking longer term. There might be metals to be extracted, from meteorites embedded in craters in the ice . . .

To the east, over the shadowed ruins of Xi City, white rocket light flared.

Epilogue

*T*he mirror array drifted through the rubble of what had been Saturn's ring system, the ruddy light of bloated Sol casting sharp highlights from its structure. The array was a hundred yards long. Six cup-shaped mirrors, each a yard across, were spaced along a spider-web boom.

The mirrors were pointed away from Sol. The array was looking for planets, of other stars.

For three months now, it had maintained its focus on a young blue-white star, as bright as any in the sky: twenty-seven light years from Sol, fifty times as luminous as Sol in its remote heyday. The six mirrors gathered the star's scattered photons and focused them on a single collector.

The design was subtle. The collector operated in the infrared part of the spectrum, where planets shone most brightly. Even so, the star was still millions of times brighter than any planet; but light waves arrived at the six mirrors slightly out of phase and canceled each other out, allowing planetary light to shine through.

The images formed were ghostly, faint, building up layer by layer.

There proved to be twelve major planets in the new system: three gas giants, the rest rocky or icy worlds. Of the smaller worlds, two lay in the habitable zone for Earth-like life—seven times as far as Earth from Sol—and one lay further out, in a region which might support ammono-like life.

The subtle collectors, slow and persistent and patient, detected spectroscopic traces of atmospheric gases: carbon dioxide, oxygen, water, ammonia, methane.

These worlds, it was decided, were valid targets.

The sail spread like a flower, its silvered surface capturing blood-red pools of sunlight.

It was five hundred yards across. The payload at its heart, a mere two hundred pounds, was a small, black pod.

The probe would not carry much on-board intelligence. The only passengers were microscopic life forms, engineered either for Earth-like conditions, or for Titan summer.

Slowly, slowly, the sail billowed out, driven by the energy-thin drizzle of photons from the fat, faded sun. The probe, still orbiting Saturn, began to spiral outward, fine lines hauling at the sail so that it tacked in the unwavering breeze of light.

It took a thousand years to achieve solar escape velocity.

The journey took twenty thousand years.

The cruise was uneventful. The minuscule acceleration reduced as the light pressure from Sol dwindled with distance, and the interstellar medium—hydrogen atoms and ions— exerted a tiny but constant drag at the sail.

Each capsule contained diverse species. Many were extremophiles, able to adapt to extremes of temperature, pressure, acidity. Those landing on the Earth-like worlds contained organisms similar to blue-green algae. Most of the species were single-celled, but some were multicellular eukaryotes. Eukaryotes were more fragile. But there was evidence that on both Titan and Earth the progression to multicellular forms had formed an evolutionary bottleneck, of such low probability that on many worlds it might never happen. If eukaryotes could be protected and prosper, billions of years of evolution could be shortcut.

But the microorganisms traveled through a deeply hostile environment.

They had to be shielded against ionizing particles and ultraviolet radiation. And the organisms were engineered to withstand heavy radiation fluxes; what was carried amounted to spores: biologically inert, free of water or ammonia.

At the midpoint of the twenty-seven light year journey there was a shift in polarization, so that the sail's silvered surface was now directed towards the new star, the darkened side towards the diminished red blur that was Sol.

With the mirrored sail reversed, a long deceleration began.

☆   ☆   ☆

There was a variety of designs, of strategies.

Some of the probes from Titan headed for clouds where new stars were being formed. Some of them were designed to colonize comets; at closest approach to a parent star the comet would spew spores into interplanetary space, for later capture by planets.

And so on.

This was panspermia: the delivery of life forms to other worlds, other star systems.

There were some on Titan who hypothesized that the worlds of Sol had themselves been seeded, in the remote past, by an early starfaring race. If that were true, the resulting life forms were morally obliged to continue, to spread life further, as far as possible.

On the other hand, if it were not true, if Sol life was the first, then the moral imperative to spread, to propagate, was all the greater.

So a cloud of solar sails drifted outward from Titan, like thistledown on the light of dying Sol, fleeing the doomed world. A wind of life, blowing between the stars.

The star was the heart of a young, vigorous system. A disc of protoplanetary debris still encircled it, through which its planets swam.

On arrival, the sail was ejected.

The probe entered a neat elliptical orbit around the brilliant central star. The outer edge of the ellipse touched the orbits of the Titan-like planets, the inner edge the orbits of the Earth-like worlds. At the inner and outer points of its orbit, the probe ejected a multitude of tiny parcels: hundreds of thousands of them, shielded against ultraviolet radiation, each containing thousands of organisms.

Over twenty years, the parcels distributed themselves into sparse rings around the central star. The parcels were coated with a substance whose reflectivity varied with the intensity of the light falling on it. Thus, each parcel oscillated between the limits of its habitable zone, maximizing the probability of capture.

The target planets moved through the rings, sweeping up capsules. Many of the capsules, entering at unfavorable geometries, were burned up in the thick atmospheres of their target worlds. But some survived, and drifted down through cloud layers of water vapor or ammonia to settle like silvered snowflakes on land, or oceans.

The thin metal coating of the capsules corroded. The parcels in which the microorganisms arrived were egglike, containing a small amount of prepackaged nutrients. This helped the organisms survive as they adapted to local conditions.

The awakening microorganisms, released, began to disperse and evolve. They were adapted to rapid and efficient mutation.

Biological processes began.

The surfaces of these worlds bore the scars of recent, and continuing, planetesimal bombardment. This would not be an easy place in which to survive. But on each planet, a handful of organisms survived. And began to breed.

Together, the children of Sol began to remake the worlds of a new star.

AFTERWORD

The untimely death of Carl Sagan (1934–1996), who has a cameo role in Book Two of this novel, was a sad footnote to a year full of scientific wonders.

Sagan was an astronomer and planetary scientist, and author of accessible and uplifting nonfiction and science fiction. As a scientist, Sagan played an active role on spaceprobes such as *Mariner 9* to Mars—Sagan ensured the probe was positioned to photograph Mars's moons—and *Pioneer 10* to Jupiter and beyond, on which Sagan was responsible for placing a message to alien life. Sagan's speculations on terraforming Venus—the first serious scientific speculation on the subject—on the possibility of permafrost on Mars, and on conditions on Titan, helped influence the thinking of subsequent workers and writers—including myself.

Like H.G. Wells, Sagan seems to have believed that the future of mankind would be a race between education and catastrophe. In 1984 he co-authored the concept of nuclear winter which may, perhaps, have helped avert that very catastrophe from befalling us. As we near the end of a millennium still largely gripped by the madnesses which dominated its opening, we cannot afford to lose Sagan's brand of clear-thinking, cheerful, communicative rationality.

Carl Sagan's death was announced after I had drafted his appearance in *Titan*. So, sadly, this book is already alternate history. But I decided Sagan should stay in.

—Stephen Baxter
Great Missenden
January 1997